Kit Reed

@expectations

By Kit Reed

NOVELS

@expectations
J. Eden
Little Sisters of the Apocalypse
Catholic Girls
Fort Privilege
Magic Time
The Ballad of T. Rantula
Captain Grownup
Tiger Rag
Cry of the Daughter
Armed Camps
The Better Part
At War As Children
Mother Isn't Dead She's Only Sleeping

COLLECTIONS

Seven for the Apocalypse
Weird Women, Wired Women
The Revenge of the Senior Citizens**Plus
   Other Stories and The Attack of the Giant Baby
The Killer Mice
Mr. Da V and Other Stories

AS KIT CRAIG

Short Fuse
Some Safe Place
Closer
Strait
Twice Burned
Gone

Kit Reed

@expectations

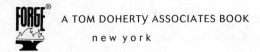

FORGE® A TOM DOHERTY ASSOCIATES BOOK

new york

@expectations

Copyright © 2000 by Kit Reed

A Forge Book
Published by Tom Doherty Associates, LLC
175 Fifth Avenue
New York, NY 10010

www.tor.com

Forge® is a registered trademark of Tom Doherty Associates, LLC.

Library of Congress Cataloging-in-Publications Data

Reed, Kit.
    @expectations / Kit Reed. — 1st ed.
        p. cm.
    Title begins with the "at" sign, i.e., an a within a circle.
    ISBN 0-312-87486-3 (acid-free paper)
    1. Married women—Fiction. 2. Suburban life—Fiction. 3. Online chat groups—Fiction. I. Title: At expectations. II. Title.

PS3568.E367 A613 2000
813'.54—dc21

                                                                00-033852

First Edition: September 2000

Printed in the United States of America

0 9 8 7 6 5 4 3 2 1

For Paul Mercer

—Virgil, is that you?

"Love is always blind. A screen just makes it easier."
—Sam

Kit Reed

@expectations

one

JENNY

Can you guess what it's like to love two men at the same time or how hard it is, shuttling between two worlds when you don't know where your heart belongs? The tension is tremendous. It's all you think about. I love Charlie Wilder, I love him to the bone but when he kisses me and leaves me behind in sleepy Brevert, the best part of me goes running out to StElene because Reverdy is waiting in the GrandHotel StElene, at the center of the neverending party. I am deep in the life of the offshore island, where everything is slightly different.

Sometimes I zone out while Charlie's talking, replaying the last thing my secret lover said to me. Sometimes when I'm with Reverdy, my heart and body go running back to Charlie, and these alignments change without warning. This is how in love we are: Reverdy knows all about Charlie, and Charlie? I can't tell him. How do you handle this kind of tension? Smile, and dissemble.

I'm not this kind of person, really. It just happened. I can't figure it out, so how can I explain it? I fell in love with Lieutenant Colonel Charlie Wilder on sight, I fell in love with his sweet, steady manner and that deceptively easy grin. I married him for life, and ended up in this dismal town. Marooned. Then I met Reverdy, and now ... Who knows how these things happen? They happen.

In my office today, sixteen-year-old Amanda Yerkes drones on. I nod in the right places, but I don't hear her. I hear Reverdy and me:

"Reverdy, this is intense."

"Of course. There's an expression for this kind of love," my lover says. "Imagine we are living out Goedel's Theorem. Do you know about Goedel's Theorem?

I'm dying of it. When are we going to ...

But Reverdy says, "Oh, love! The more we have to be apart the better it gets—think about it. Everything we care about is *right here*. Shimmering. Because it's waiting to be realized. Beautiful!"

"Beautiful, but it's so hard!" I want to understand. *Goedel's Theorem of Incompleteness: can I find a book that completely explains it? Will it explain Reverdy?* I press. "Explain."

"Nobody can," Reverdy says, "that's the whole thing. Everything you care about, suspended. Anticipation. It's the tension! Proofs are dead objects. Closed cases. Finished." This is how he overturns me. "Our future is forever."

It is profound. More powerful than sex. My lips move but no sound comes out. "The future is forever."

It's all I think about. It keeps me going, and slow, humid little Brevert, South Carolina is hard going. If I'd grown up down here it might be different. But I am the outsider, no more entitled here than the off-duty Marines who wander up and down Front Street, bored blind and homesick for some big city. I am homesick for my loft on lower Broadway, busy day and night, filled with people, where Brevert is dead empty. It's like being dropped on a dead star by a ship from an overpopulated planet. The houses along the bay look like bit players out of *Gone With the Wind.* Overhead, Spanish moss hangs off the live oaks like The Mummy's wrappings. They say a privateer went down out there in the channel and I half expect the bones of the dead to come to the surface and reassemble.

It's not my fault I grew up in big brown-shingled house in the deep North instead. It's not my fault I was an only child. *Come straight home after school and don't let anybody in until I get back from work.* I kept running to the window. Right, I had an only mother, but that wasn't her fault. It's nobody's fault that my father's nuclear sub went down and never surfaced, it just didn't. We get stuck with our lives. Back when I still told Charlie everything he said, "Stop beating yourself up. I love you and I promise to make you happy."

So I married him. Now he's never here and I keep running to the window. I didn't know I was marrying the Corps. "Look," he said after we'd set the date, "bad news. I'm being transferred."

"How long have you known?"

He got red and wouldn't answer. So that was one deception. But he handed his heart to me, saying, "If you want me to leave the Marines . . ." The idea was so terrible to him that he couldn't finish. He blurted, "Can you handle it?"

I love him!

I packed everything I cared about in boxes and came with him. I tried. I did! "Pretty," I said when we rolled down Front Street that first afternoon, but I was thinking, *Oh, my God.*

His hand closed on mine and I felt that familiar shock of love and desire. He is so *warm.* "I know, I know," Charlie said;

he's trying too. "It's OK, baby, it's only for a little while."

It's not his fault that every time he calls me baby I get smaller. "Don't worry, Charlie, I'll be fine."

"Oh, Jenny, I love you so *much.*" I was getting used to my new name. Jenny Wilder. "Jenny, I need you."

"Me too." *Whither thou goest, I will go.* I guess, but he should have warned me that he was being transferred.

That's not the only thing he kept from me. There's not much room for me in the new house. It's filled with leftovers from Charlie's first marriage.

And my friends and my loft aren't the only things I left behind. I left my practice. Right, some of the most messed-up people are therapists. As if, solving other people's problems, we can get a grip on our own. I'm *trying.* So I told my funny, articulate urban neurotics goodbye; it was a stretch but I told them they'd do fine.

Now I deal with neurotic Southerners, which is why I am sitting here listening to Amanda Wetherall. Sweet old Martha Henderson saw my references and brought me into her practice. We work in this antebellum house on Front Street—Tara with strip lighting.

Patients sing their old, sad songs for me while I murmur creatively and stare out the window. My Southerners are all sad because they have problems but they're proud, too, because whatever's eating them dates back to the War Between the States, losing it was the last big thing that happened in this small town. Some of these family pathologies have been festering since the first settlers waded in through the marsh grass. I listen, but my heart goes out the window.

When Amanda winds down I crank her up with another question and I fix my eyes on the point where the marsh grass verges into the bay and flows into the inland waterway. If I squint I can almost see StElene.

I can hear everything Reverdy said last night and everything that's waiting to be said, I'm on fire with it. Then the querulous little hook in my patient's voice tells me she's done for now.

"Yes Amanda," I say. "I think you're onto something."

She knots her knobby little hands in her skirts and blushes. I smile and dissemble.

I'm doing OK, too, dissembling, until Martha sticks her head in. My nice partner is like a mom, good-natured and a little worn, and she's the closest thing I have to a friend here. She sees that we're summing up but she and Amanda are old friends. "Sweetie, you're looking better. Jenny, when you have a minute? Amanda, don't look at me that way. You really are filling out a bit!"

Amanda turns white and protects her concave belly. Poor anorectic kid. She wants not to eat; her parents want her plump and pretty for her debut at the St. Cecilia's Ball. Brevert is one of the last places in the world where things like debuts matter. Amanda and I both know where the eating disorder comes from, but knowing a thing and doing something about it are different matters. Martha gives her a pat and waits until she's halfway downstairs and out the door.

My heart is halfway down the stairs and out the door too, but I smile nicely. "So. Martha. Sit down?"

"Sometimes I think parents ought to be tried for war crimes."

"Or force-fed, like geese," I say. "Poor kid."

"But we can't let her starve herself to death." Now that she has me off guard Martha pounces. "Jenny, are you all right?"

"Who, me? I'm fine. Why?"

"This is me you're talking to. What's going on?"

I keep it light. "Nothing, Martha, there's nothing going on."

"Yes there is. You've gotten so . . ."

I don't want to hear her say, *distracted.* "I'm fine, it's a little tired out today, OK?"

She grimaces. "How are you with the words, *strung out?*"

I face the window so she won't see the expressions chasing each other across my face. *Strung out.* Everything boils up. Should I tell her? Not tell her? "I'm fine. Really."

You can't fool another shrink. "Don't give me that, Jenny. You were one person when you came here. Now you're some-body else."

Bingo. "I love you, Martha, but I can't talk now, I've gotta go. The kids are expecting me."

"Jenny, if you ever want to . . ."

"No. Don't. Just later, OK?" *Even if I explained you wouldn't understand it.* I hug her and run home.

The kids. The hell of going home is that it isn't my home. It's Charlie's house, complete with Charlie's children. That's the other thing Charlie forgot to tell me until we were almost married.

Coming home to Charlie's house is like walking into a se-quel to *Friday the Thirteenth.* The camera tilts. Either the enemy is lurking or it isn't. I unlock the door and wait on the sill. I listen. For the shish of fabric rubbing round, fat bodies, the giveaway giggle, or harsh, wet breathing. Are they lying in wait again? Did they mean it when Charlie made them swear there would never be another ambush? Thirty-four years old, and Charlie's kids make me feel like a fifth grader. Ten years old, when I didn't know anything and everything could hurt me.

I stick my head in. The house smells of mildew and cam-phorwood and damp rugs but not of Pop-Tarts or macaroni in the microwave. Cheer up, you could be alone here. "Anybody home?"

Nobody answers.

"Patsy? Rusty? If you're in here, say so. Enough, OK?"

Time passes.

Fine, I think, and shut the door behind me. Tracking shot through the empty house: living room, nothing; nobody in the hall closet, no one in the kitchen. I relax a little. I make tea, and all the time I am listening hard. Still no sign. I'm alone! Maybe I can sneak off to StElene for just long enough to calm my heart and maybe, oh maybe, touch base with Reverdy. I start upstairs; everything in me goes soft with anticipation, my blood quickens . . .

Wham. "Hahahahaaaaaaaa!"

I ought to be used to it by now but my heart hits fast-forward and I shriek. "Dammit, Rusty. Patsy!"

Patsy lunges, too late to scare anybody. It's silly but she does it anyway, with her pudgy arms rigid in that movie monster lurch. "Heeeee!"

I shriek again, so she doesn't feel slighted. Any mom would do the same, even an unwilling one. Kids who've just lost a parent deserve all the kindness you can manage.

("It's so great to see you getting along," Charlie says with such joy that I can't bear to tell him they hate me. "After all, they're your children now." *No they aren't.*)

So this is the worst thing that Charlie kept from me. That his ex-wife Nelda settled the custody matter for once and all by getting herself killed in a car wreck. When we went to the Carlyle to meet his family the day before the wedding Charlie tried to make it look like a wedding gift! At the door to the family suite he said:

"Jenny, I have a wonderful surprise for you."

When the door opened I was looking higher, expecting adult faces—his parents. Somebody gave the children a little shove; their father ordered them to smile, but they didn't.

"Mine." Blindly, he beamed at me. "I knew you'd love them."

When we'd done lunch and the Radio City Music Hall with his kids, when we'd bought them presents at Schwarz and ice cream at the Plaza and we'd sponged the chocolate off their fronts and delivered them back to their aunt; when we were finally alone I said, "God, Charlie! Why didn't you tell me?"

Then *my Charlie* put his heart in his hands and gave it to me. His eyes filled up and his face crumpled in apology. "Oh Jenny, I love you so much. I was scared you wouldn't marry me!"

Grinning, he spread his arms. I walked straight into them.

Now wonderful Charlie is safe in his bright, neat office on the base and we are here. Rusty is giving that high, false mean-little-boy laugh. Patsy sulks, glowering. I keep trying but they really don't like me. If somebody said, "Kids, this is your new mom," would you like me? *No it isn't.*

"Look. Guys." I've been there! Orphaned is where alone starts. I offer hugs but they struggle free. They won't let me love them; they won't even let me like them. I can buy a smile with forbidden food. I would do anything. "Tell you what. Dad's going to be late, let's get pizza."

So the kids are muttering on the rug in front of the TV when Charlie comes in. Let them wallow in pizza cartons and Moon Pie wrappers for God's sake, if it makes them happy. I am beached on the sofa, pretending we are a family while they hide in their own little world. Charlie sweeps me into a hug but over my shoulder he sees the rubble. "Oh, baby, if you feed them junk food they'll never shape up."

That his kids are unhappy bothers him, but Charlie can't say that. Instead he picks on something he thinks he can change. Their body images are in direct collision with his sense of order. Rangy, fit Charlie and his schlumpy children don't match. With that military carriage, my man looks like a Marine officer even when he's naked—a living reproach to the butterballs clinging to his legs.

"Shhh Charlie, they're trying."

"Look at them!"

They suck in their cheeks and tighten their bellies.

"Jen, really." He doesn't say it but I know it by heart. *My father trained me to run a taut ship.* "They're . . ."

I whisper into his neck, "Don't say *fat*," and he doesn't.

For my sake, he makes his voice bright. "Tell you what, kids. Let's go out for a walk!"

Somehow I get left behind in the shuffle. If the kids could make me disappear, they would. In these family encounters, Charlie feels their loss even more strongly than I do. He indulges them and I love him for it. But I need him too! I try, "Charlie, when there's time I need to . . ." *Talk to you.*

"Mmm?"

"Aren't we supposed to tell each other everything?" What can I say? Not clear. I can't let this drag on, loving Reverdy and not telling Charlie.

"Sure, honey, sure." He kisses me. "Later, yes?"

"Yes." *I love you, Charlie, I just . . .*

Gently, Charlie runs his knuckles down my cheek—a promise of things to come, but when we finally get the kids to bed we are at cross purposes. We both want the same thing but there's something I have to do.

"Where are you going?"

"The computers. I forgot to store these records." If Reverdy left a note for me at StElene, it will turn up in my email.

"Yeah, records. You're an email junkie, admit it."

"It'll only take a minute."

He's sleepy, he wants me, he reaches out. "What's the point? It'll only be Martha dumping more work on you. Computers. Pieces of junk."

"Necessary pieces of junk." I slip away. "Right back, I promise."

"Let it go, babe. You won't die."

That's what you think.

Thank God he doesn't come after me. It doesn't take long. Reverdy's note has been forwarded. *Two a.m.* I am on fire with it.

Back in our safe, warm bed, Charlie and I make better love than ever. I really do love him and I know if loving Reverdy makes loving Charlie even better than it is, it can't be such a bad thing. Besides, by the time we're done it's too late to start anything and if I tell him, it will only hurt him. Another minute and Charlie will go crashing into sleep. In my heart I've already left the room and when he turns to kiss me good night I murmur into his neck because what I have to say evaporates just like everything else I've ever tried to tell him.

Confusing, this. And wonderful.

Waiting for Reverdy is sweet but lying here is sweet. Our breath synchronized, our flanks touching. But my mind does the same dance it does every night, seesawing between guilt and anticipation.

I don't have to go tonight. I don't ever have to go back, I think, if Charlie turns out to want the other thing I want, the thing I haven't named because I'm only now coming to terms with it. Which is: I am sick of being outnumbered here. I can wake him up and open the question, but if I do, I'll never get away in time. If we talk, it will make me late!

Two a.m.

Reverdy will leave because he thinks I'm not coming.

But this is the man I'm married to for life, there is something we both want that he doesn't know I want, and if I can only . . . I touch his arm. "Oh, Charlie." It's crazy. *Let's have a baby.* He sighs in his sleep. I shiver and slide closer to the edge of the bed.

I can't just come out and *say* that.

So sometime soon after, I run my hand over Charlie's profile—when I'm leaving the bed this way I never touch, I just bring my fingers close. I don't want to wake him up, but I want him to feel the air—the grace of the gesture—and know that he is loved. I let my fingers outline his strong neck, the line of his shoulder and then I ease off the bed like a sailor jumping ship, blow him a kiss and slip out. When I look back the bed is bobbing in deep shadow like a small craft in the bay. Charlie likes a taut ship, but to me right now the bed looks like a raft with Charlie on it, floating away.

I'm not hurting anybody. I'm not!

@two

ZAN

In the deep, still night while Charlie sleeps and his cranky children sleep and the town of Brevert sleeps, Jenny slips away to the offshore island of StElene.

She could find her way in the dark. Torchères light the path from the dock to the GrandHotel StElene with its generous porches; lights twinkle in outbuildings. The sprawling resort is an odd, psychic frontier where Jenny can shed her problems and walk free.

A thousand lights burn in the Victorian heap and inside, the regulars meet and talk and fall in love and keep coming back because everything they want is just ahead, if they can only find it. The air buzzes with promise. Some nights it's like coming into a costume party on the eve of the apocalypse—festive, crazy. In this hothouse everything runs close to the surface—love and loss, loneliness, desire. Identities are protected here, and with their faces obscured, people can be anybody. Do anything. Boundaries flex and change, and a married woman like Jenny Wilder, boxed in the deep South with two hostile kids that don't belong to her can forget the hard parts for a few hours, and play.

Home, she thinks, passing through the paneled lobby with its Bokhara runners and graceful damask settees. After the house on Church Street, it's a welcome change. Almost everybody here is glad to see her and even this is a change. *Definitely home.* Here on StElene talk flows and transformations are easy. The transition transforms Jenny, too. Here, she goes by a different name.

"Zan!" Her friend Jazzy greets her with a hug; he was her first friend here. They are both grinning. "What's new in Magnolia country?"

"Sameold sameold," she says. "I've got to wonder, are my patients boring because Southerners are slower than New Yorkers, or because they're less neurotic?"

"Probably they have more boring neuroses," Jazzy says. "That's the great thing about surgery. Your patients *don't talk.*"

"Talk." Zan laughs. "If only I got paid by the word . . ."

Cahuenga cuts in, "Yeah, but head cases never code on you. Hey, if you want neurotic, I'm available."

"Hey, if I want neurotic, *I'm* neurotic," Zan says, but she is skimming the faces in the room—Reverdy—not here yet, where is he, where is he.

Fearsome mutters, "You say you want *necrotic?*"

As Zan, Jenny can shed the shrink's professional gravity; she can even afford to be flip. "Oh Fearsome, give up. I know corpses cuter than you."

"Corpse?" Del says evilly. "Did someone call my name?"

If her patients talked half as well as her friends here—OK, if she could laugh in Brevert the way she does on StElene, maybe it would be OK. No wonder she loves coming here. "Neurotic, necrotic, narcotic, there's not a dime's worth of difference," Zan says.

"Say what? Necrophiliac?" Jazzy says and he and Fearsome and Del start free-associating, doing a riff while Zan looks for a fresh conversation. Nobody minds; people are easy here.

"Oh Zan, I finally did it," Harrald whispers. Zan has heard her friend's confessions over time and in an odd, sweet way, he depends on her. What's more, unlike Amanda, this is a patient she can help. "I told Faye it's over. Really over. And I got a place!"

"That's wonderful." It's funny, she thinks. We are who we want to be here, but we're still very much ourselves. Over the months Zan has helped several friends in crisis. They start playfully, safe behind their party masks, but sooner or later their true selves emerge. She's heard Harrald's particulars—bad marriage, worse job, no money, image problems; he's working on his weight, amazing what people tell you in this oddly confessional space.

Harrald beams. "Moved yesterday. I feel like a new person."

"Fantastic." On StElene, Zan is more friend than therapist; she can even have opinions. Where Jenny has to be cautious and professional, Zan can be blunt. "Faye was bad for you."

In the ballroom, chilly old StOnge waves to her; he's a long-timer here, a Director! Flattered, she's still smiling when she bumps into her friend Articular. She'll needle him, but with a grin because they spend hours talking about how much time they waste on StElene. "If you've kicked your habit, A., what are you doing here?"

"Just passing through." Articular winks. He spares Zan his daylight troubles and she doesn't tell him hers. "What's your excuse? OK, if you must know the truth I've started a grape arbor by the swimming pool. Bamboo chairs. A dance floor."

She guesses, "With vines that drop down and strangle people."

He grins. "Only people who aren't smart enough to know you can pick the grapes and make wine out of them."

"And how many hours would that be? Of your time, I mean."

"Oh, time, what's time for, unless you can waste it?"

Everything Articular does spells itself out in elaborate metaphor. "Sweetie." They are both laughing. Unlike people she's met in Brevert, her friends here on StElene are smart and playful. Converging in the night, they try on lives and experiment with things they'd never dream of doing anywhere else. "You spend too much time here."

"You should talk."

"So I'm a conversation junkie." This is only part of it.

Delphine joins them with a warning. "Red alert. PMS. I'm ready to explode and hurt somebody. Shrapnel everywhere."

Zan feeds her friend the straight line. "Does it hurt much?"

Disarmed, Delphine grins. "Only when I laugh."

"Reverdy's tied up," nineteen-year-old Lark reports breathlessly. A sudden, gawky presence, he hugs Zan. "Big meeting with the Directors."

"The Directors?" She hugs too. "But I just saw StOnge."

"That's another story. Rev sent me to explain."

"He could have left a note." Zan is in love with Reverdy and Reverdy's in love with politics. "I wish he didn't have such a big stake in the way things are run here."

Lark shrugs. "You know him. He won't do anything halfway."

It's exactly what she loves him for. "I know."

Lark coughs. "Ah. Could we talk? Look, I hate to bother you but. Oh Zan, listen. If a guy keeps having dreams about . . .

I don't know if I should tell you what I dream."

"Sweetie, people can't help their dreams."

"This one is kind of ugly."

Zan is closer to this kid than anybody here, with the one exception. She knows how hard it is for Lark just to get through the days. "Lark, if you can't tell me, who can you tell?"

After an awkward pause, he whispers, "It's a variation on the old dream, you know, but this time it . . . I'm kind of scared."

It will take her almost an hour to talk the kid down, lead him through the maze of doubt and self-hatred to the point where he's mostly OK. "You're stronger than you think, Lark. Hang in."

Leaving, he gives her a hasty hug. "Mail me? You know where."

Her heart goes after him. "You're in my address list. Take care." She and Lark have been in touch by daylight, not just here. Yes she remembers Jazzy's early warning: *Be careful here. Don't get in too deep.* "And if you need to talk, you have my number."

Of course Lark isn't his real name. Half the excitement on StElene comes with anonymity. The rest comes from trusting somebody enough to tell them who you are. And where you live when you're not here. In life away from StElene, Reverdy goes under the name his parents gave him, not the one he chose. Solemnizing their relationship, Reverdy and Zan exchanged real names like marriage vows. And started sharing their daylight lives. Reverdy has told her about his work, told his secrets, about things he wants and things he's afraid of. He's told her all about the worst parts of his bad marriage. He's told her everything, in fact, except his home phone number and where to find him off StElene.

It's killing her. So is waiting.

She came to meet Reverdy, and Reverdy's with the Directors. If she stays too long Charlie will find out, but she needs him!

Impulsively, she goes to Reverdy's place. In a dazzling synchronicity, they arrive in the Dak Bungalow at the same time. Her heart makes that familiar lurch. "Oh, Reverdy."

"Zan!" Reverdy hugs her in that wonderfully doomed way he has. Everything in her lover rides close to the surface: aspiration, love, pain. Immediately funny, quick and articulate, Reverdy is in fact a pageant of inner states. She loves him for the vulnerability. It's as if, stripping his soul naked, he's declaring that their love is the only place in the world that makes him happy.

Yes he needs her, OK, she needs him needing her. "Reverdy, I missed you! Look, this thing with the Directors . . ."

"Let's don't talk about that now. I missed you too! It was close tonight," he says. "I wasn't sure I could get away in time."

She knows this isn't about the Directors. "Trouble at home?"

"There's always trouble at home."

She and Reverdy tell each other everything; they always do. They can talk for hours and never run out of things to say. Sometimes they talk about nothing—movies, food, confessions out of childhood. Sometimes they don't talk at all. It's just a pleasure to be together, dreaming, smiling, just being together.

Reverdy's first gift of trust was describing the historical project he is attached to. He's coding for a group of academic blockheads. Zan explained what it's like to have patients she can't help. They went deeper. In a breathtaking demonstration of trust Reverdy walked her through what he calls the Stations of the Cross, the stages of his terrible marriage to Louise. They exchanged confidences like gifts. Zan told about falling in love with Charlie and finding out later that he had ulterior motives— the kids!

Reverdy said, "I know just how you feel." They talked, they talked! She hoards scraps of their conversations as if she can glue them together and build a whole person she can keep. When she's alone she rehearses all the things he's told her, from what favorite foods and which music to terrible scenes with Louise. Her treasure is the bizarre, intense vision of Reverdy at fifteen. Onstage in the high school play he'd written—overturned like Saul struck from his horse. When he came to himself he was shuddering with discovery. *No matter what you do in this world, it's never enough.*

But tonight they are too starved by separation to talk about anything but love. Zan says, "I'm so glad we're here!"

Reverdy says, "Forget the world. We're here. That's all that matters."

It is but it isn't, you know? "If only we could . . ."

"Shh."

What if she told him how close she came to telling Charlie about their affair, a step toward leaving him? She knows what Reverdy will say. *It's too soon.* They've talked about it often enough. Reverdy temporizes. *We have to wait for the right time. It would hurt too many people.* She's so glad to see him that she can't stop herself. "I wish . . ."

"Sshshh. Not yet, love." Reverdy keeps her close with promises. "It isn't time." *When the time is right they'll know everything and we can be together. When it's time.* It keeps her going.

Sometimes she tries to rush it, begin a timetable. *We'll tell them after . . .* She does not spell out the *after*, she can't. Jenny spends her life solving other people's problems and she can't figure out her own life. Off StElene she is married to Charlie Wilder and she loves him so much that she's determined to work it out, but when she's here . . . "When, lover?"

"Oh," he says, "in good time."

When Zan is with Reverdy, she believes only in their future together. In the myth they are writing here, both marriages are beyond redemption, which in Zan's case is not exactly true. No. It's true when Charlie's gone. Rather: when she and Reverdy are alone together on StElene, he is the most exciting man she's ever known. But he is holding something back, and until he stops holding back, she can't let Charlie go. In a way, she's holding back too. When Reverdy tells her he's leaving Louise . . . Then she'll decide what to do. She needs him to tell her where he lives. Where she can phone him and send email instead of leaving notes on StElene. After all, she knows where Charlie is. Charlie's in bed waiting for her, but when they aren't together Reverdy's whereabouts are a mystery. When he tells Zan which house on what street in which town or city, she'll choose. In a way, she wants them both! *Now, that is not good for me.* It makes her weird. "Rev, what if Charlie finds out about us?"

He hugs her close. "You're here now. There is no Charlie."

Like *that*, Charlie vanishes. "Oh my love, I do love you!"

"And I love you."

"And we have time."

"Yes, my darling. Time."

Zan is trembling. "If only we could be together."

"Love. Lover, we are." This makes her eyes sting and her belly soften. "You and I are closer than you and Charlie could ever be."

Quickly she adds, "Or you and Louise."

He doesn't affirm; he just continues. "Closer than anyone."

"If only we could meet . . ."

"We have met! Are meeting."

"You know what I mean."

"What are bodies, when our souls are fused?"

"I just need you so *much.*"

Reverdy knows where this is heading. Married as she is, Zan would leave Charlie in a flash if she could be with Reverdy on StElene and off it too, not just on these nights, but always. And married as her lover is . . . she doesn't know where Reverdy is with this, married as he is. He never says. Would he leave Louise? Could she leave Charlie? She doesn't know. "Shh," he says. "I want to run my lips across your hair. Here, in the soft place by your ear."

Zan shivers. All the fine hairs at the nape lift and tremble. "And you will." Exquisite. Everything between them is expectation.

"And you want me to."

"I do."

"Then I am." Reverdy calls this miracle *performative utterance*; it's magical. He is the master of performative utterance. Scientists limit the meaning but for dreamers like Reverdy, words have tremendous power. Find words for what you want, he says. Say it and it becomes true.

Mesmerized, Zan murmurs, "And you are."

"And then you will touch me *here* . . ."

Which is how it begins. Making love. What they say and do to each other in these sealed spaces is intense and intensely private.

And so, like a sleight of hand artist distracting with a flourish while he steals the family silver, Zan's lover begins the first movement of the beautiful, extended sequence they slide into when they are alone together with the time and the leisure to make long love. What passes between Reverdy and Zan in these private times is specific to them and constructed to please them—nothing here to remind Jenny Wilder of her lovemaking with Charlie, who is strong, loving and relentlessly physical. Brilliant, gifted in love, Reverdy knows how to make love to her soul.

What Zan and Reverdy do together begins with individual arias that match and fuse, gesture on gesture, phrase on phrase. They create a duct that leaves her shaking with passion as, in the space they occupy—in their minds and hearts, at least, if not in physical fact—they become one. Their joined words stand taller in her imagination than anything she and Charlie can ever do. Love here on StElene, with Reverdy, is a little masterpiece of creation, with certain passages repeated for effect and others improvised, cadenzas building to climax, so that what they do together is always fresh and it is always different. Approaching the moment, Zan and Reverdy move as one, pure thought distilled into pure love. But at the end Zan cries aloud. "If only I could hear your voice!"

"You do, Zan. You do."

She does and she doesn't, you know?

As if he knows what she is thinking, Reverdy waits until they have had their fill of each other and are breathing hard and then, to remind Zan that he loves her even though they can't be together past sunrise, he lets her into his life in the outside world. "I'd have been here sooner but the project chairman won't green-light my time line!"

"That's terrible." It isn't so much what he tells her in these interludes that makes her love him, it's what she puts into the interstices. Every new detail is like a little gift. Don't they know how smart he is? "Why not!"

"They claim I'm trying to rewrite history, when I'm only trying to organize it. All my projections focus on the ideal. How things *ought to be*. Do you know how important that is?"

"Historians! Of course I do."

He gives her a hug. "You're the only one who does."

"You're light-years ahead and they just don't get it."

"Like Galileo." In his field, Reverdy is a self-styled maverick. Erratic. Intuitive. Quick. "If you can't organize history, how are you going to learn from it? Flexibility!"

"They're just slow, lover. They'll catch up."

"I wish. You know as well as I do that you can code anything. I know how to subdue and order history and they're too stupid to see. They don't want to see and until they do, my hands are tied."

This daytime confidence is to make clear that on StElene Reverdy loves Zan, and in life away from here, he loves her too.

She says, "If you could only meet with them. Sit down in the same room."

Then he surprises her. "That's what I love about the project, I never have to see the bastards. It's one of the great things about working online."

She catches the tune. "And you make your own hours."

It is an old litany. "And I'm my own person."

"And you can wear anything you want."

He laughs. "T-shirts. Bunny slippers. Underwear."

"One of those rubber bowties that lights up," she says fondly, but she is thinking about Reverdy in his underwear.

"No ties. Definitely no ties."

"But it must get lonely, working alone."

"I'm never lonely." This is what Zan has been waiting for. This is the pledge. Reverdy finishes, "I have you."

Everything in her warms. "And I have you."

"Yes, you do."

"We're pathetic, both of us." Zan is fishing and he knows it. He grins. "Terrible. We're a matched set. A pair."

"Yes." Satisfied, she moves on. "But this history committee chairman or whatever he calls himself says he doesn't trust your findings?"

"Only because the data I'm collecting will prove that there is no such thing as history. Everything's subject to revision."

Zan of all people should know this. On StElene, entire lives are subject to revision. The physical present. The past. "True, but *dates* stay the same. Hiroshima, Pearl Harbor."

"But opinions on what happened differ. You see it, don't you? Facts change from day to day; even the past is in flux."

"Of course," Zan says. "Like this place." Life on StElene has taught her that existence is fluid. Relieved of the exigencies, lives flex and change. Even the present is subject to revision. "That's what I love about you. You make me think!"

He says quickly, "Do we have time?"

They don't have to discuss it. "Even if we don't."

They are in the middle, then, Zan and Reverdy; Zan is trembling and a flush cloaks her throat when there's a noise in the room. A noise, right in this room where she and Reverdy are making love! Her lover senses the distraction even as she jerks to attention with a little gasp. His words stand as if written on the air in front of her. "What, my darling. What?"

"N   There isn't time to type anything more.

Somebody's in the room! Wild with interrupted passion, shaken, Zan can't even tell Rev goodbye. Pushing her hair back and pulling her robe around her neck to hide the flush spreading at her throat and along the collarbone, Jenny Wilder switches off the computer and stands, knocking over her chair. "What. What?"

As Reverdy blinks out of existence. In this rushed atmosphere of daytime desires and clandestine nights, people drop out of sight in a flash. Virtual love is subject to interruptions and crashes. It's like loving in a blackout, with no time for explanations or apologies. The difference is that all communication stops, love stops, the connection stops precisely when the power goes off.

She has disconnected the man she loves most. With a flip of the switch, Jenny Wilder has extinguished Reverdy and deleted the evidence. She turns to the small, plump figure fidgeting in droopy pajamas. "Rusty! What are you doing up?"

In spite of the heat Rusty is shivering, *aren't you cold?* How long has he been standing there? "I couldn't sleep!"

"Sweetie, it's the middle of the night! Go back to bed."

He's craning at the darkened screen. "Are you playing Doom?"

Cooling, she sighs. "It isn't Doom. Now go back to sleep!"

"I can't."

"Why?"

Rusty's wise look makes her squirm. "Because you're making so much noise up here."

Guilty, Jenny says, "I wasn't making any noise."

The little boy says, for Charlie, for all betrayed husbands everywhere, "Well, you're up here *typing*."

"All right." Love shatters and falls at Zan's feet in shreds, like a ruined globe. Standing, she trails her fingers across the screen. *Goodbye.*

He nudges like a reproachful sheepdog. "Tuck me in?"

Poor kid, Jenny thinks. But she's been shut up in the box alone with her lover. *Poor me.* She can't smile for the child but she makes her voice soft. "Sure."

Because she's standing here grieving and hasn't exactly moved, Rusty presses. "Could we go to bed now?"

"Oh hell, Rusty." She means, *why do you want me to put you to bed when you don't even like me?*

He squints at her screen, as if trying to read the afterimages burned into it. "If it wasn't Doom, what was it?"

"Nothing."

"Tetris? Nope, it sure wasn't Tetris. I mean when I came in it was all words."

Words. "Don't be silly, I was..."

You were kind of..." late night makes Rusty confidential, *"weird."*

"Working! I was working. I'm..." Jenny looks at the screen but she can peer into it until the sun comes up and Reverdy will be just as gone. "I'm sorry I kept you up, OK?" she says, taking his hand. "But next time, promise you'll knock?"

When she puts Rusty to bed in that tight little room cluttered with Star Wars models and monster models and comics and clandestine candy wrappers and Entemann's cartons that Charlie so deplores, Jenny takes advantage of the moment and, in spite of the fact that Rusty's teetering on the brink of eleven, kisses the top of his musty red hair. Then she goes out and closes the door.

Most lovers shower before they get back in bed with the injured party, but like so much that Jenny is invested in, this love is ephemeral. Nothing. In material terms, she and Reverdy have done nothing. And yet.

The flush at her throat, the aura are too pervasive to be erased by scrubbing. Physical love you finish and forget, but what Jenny has with Reverdy grows in the imagination. It fills rooms. No. The words that they exchange faster than thought—

what they say and do, the expectation of what they will say and do next time and the anticipation—are lyric. Their love is tremendous.

Paddling back to the raft where the sleeping Charlie waits, she thinks, *Oh, Charlie, I really am sorry.* Then she steps back from the marriage and studies the size and the shape of it, and thinks maybe Charlie brought this on himself. She says, almost loud enough to wake him, "If only you'd trusted me. You should have told me about the kids."

He stirs but does not wake. If he did wake up maybe they could talk about it. Sort this out. Sighing, she pulls back the covers and slips back into bed, only slightly assuaged by the warmth, the nice, clean, familiar Charlie smell. Charlie sighs and rolls over, throwing his arm wide; in the moonlight she sees into his curled hand, touches the cords in his upturned wrist. He doesn't stir. She jostles him slightly; if she can rouse him maybe he'll turn to her, half-awake; they can embrace and make love and change or at least finish what Reverdy started, but Charlie sleeps on.

Never mind, she tells herself, and with the grace of complete recall, starts at the beginning and replays her tapes—everything she and Reverdy said and did tonight, thinking that tomorrow night can't come soon enough, and they can do wonderful things to each other in depth and at length. While Charlie sleeps.

"We're not hurting anybody," she murmurs with a twinge of disloyalty. "It's only words."

three

JENNY

The hardest thing I've ever had to do is making love to Charlie without letting him guess even for a second that my concentration is torn in two; it could be a sex-linked thing. If you're a woman, maybe you always are distracted at first. It is his job to get your attention and it works best when you go into it knowing that he always will. In the meantime he has to share your consciousness with worries and fragmented images and old memories and bits of remembered dialog, comprehending your split concentration until everything else disappears in that instant when what you are doing and what he is doing become the same thing.

By the end Charlie and I are practically the same person; for a second there he's erased everything from my mind, even Reverdy, but the minute I am lucid, Reverdy comes stealing in. *Don't.* I tell him. *Stay back. I'm won't be on StElene tonight, don't wait for me.* I won't, I think, I can't do this to Charlie any more.

He and I lie there watching the morning light on the ceiling. It's sweet the way he can't let go of my fingers; it's Saturday and we're lying close with our hands linked. I hear the kids thudding down to the kitchen. I hear the TV and the low snarl that means they are fighting. In a minute we're going to have to get up and go downstairs and deal, but ever since Reverdy fell into my life and shattered my concentration I've been pressed. I have to cram too many things into not enough space: Charlie, Reverdy; Brevert, StElene, long work days and the needs of those miserable kids—too much to think about on not enough sleep. Life in overdrive. I try to stay cool, I want us to be happy but I have to start.

"Charlie, there are things we have to say."

Next to me, Charlie stirs dreamily. "Mmmm?"

I am trying to figure out how to tell him what's happening. I have to figure out how to do it without hurting him. It won't be a confession. If only it could be like the talks I used to have with my father when I still had my father. If something was wrong I could fix it by telling Daddy. Just saying the words made it all right. If I can only tell Charlie about this weird other life of mine, maybe he'll say the right things and I won't need StElene. I'll just walk out on Reverdy and come back to him for good. The trouble is, I can't figure out how to sum it up. I don't know where to start or how to start. I choke. "Important things."

"Shh." He tightens his fingers in mine. "I'm afraid we'll end up saying the wrong things."

"It's . . ." I can pretty much hear Reverdy's cynical laugh. *He wants to hang on to his baby sitter, that's all.* It stops me cold.

"Babe, what's the matter?" Charlie rolls closer; his warm breath fills my ear. Even though the nickname diminishes me I don't move away. I lie close but Charlie knows something's wrong; he always knows. I can hear his heart breaking. "Is it something I did?"

Yes. No. I don't know! I can feel Reverdy pushing me. He wants me to tell Charlie that I don't love him and it's over between us, but neither of these things is true. If I did tell him would Reverdy come for me?

I do love Charlie and it can't be over, we're just getting started. Yes I love two men but I'm only sleeping with one of them, is that so terrible?

"Jen?"

I love two men and I need them both. Charlie's warmth, Reverdy's soul.

When I first told Reverdy what Charlie did to me, he got furious. I'd been telling myself it was a loving deception, but . . . you know? On our first long night together on StElene I let it all out—how Charlie snared me, heart and body, without ever telling me what I was getting into. How he waited until the last minute to spring the kids. In a way, when I told Reverdy, I was testing the information the way abuse victims do, thinking maybe I had misread something and men lied to their women this way all the time. The poor guy! ("I was afraid you wouldn't marry me!") Protecting me. It felt good to get it all out and the whole time I was telling Reverdy I was secretly thinking, *maybe it isn't as bad as I thought.*

Reverdy blew up. His passion told me it was even worse than I thought. *I could kill him for what he did to you.*

I still can't be sure if I'm more angry at Charlie than I am hurt. I love him too much to reproach him with the lie. As injured party, who happens to be a little bit ambivalent herself, as in—not technically unfaithful, but—I don't look so good. I love Charlie and I want to tell him everything, but I can't. I say what I can say. "I just wish you didn't have to be gone all the time."

Charlie's laugh bubbles with relief. "Oh, babe, is that all it is! I was afraid you were pissed at me about the kids."

And so we end up at cross purposes. I hear a thud downstairs and Patsy starts mizzling, one of those long kid whines that curls up the stairwell like smoke. "It isn't that, I wish. I just *wish*."

There is the sound of a smack. Now Rusty is screaming too. As I get up to go deal, Charlie gets out of his side of the bed to go deal. We exchange looks. His voice overflows with love. "I do too!"

@four

REVERDY

What does it take to move into a conceptual space like StElene and comprehend it so fully that you become part of it? What skills do you need to control the new world so completely that it becomes your element? To find lovers and close friends and make enemies bent on destroying you?

It's a rhetorical question, Reverdy thinks, grinning in the triumph of the survivor. It's all rhetoric. Lingering in the Dak Bungalow with Zan gone and Lark away and the Directors conspiring against him, he frames answers.

It takes time. The willingness to tinker with code and trust strangers you can't see or hear but come to *know* better than any of the people you live with. It takes equal measures of persistence, intelligence and folly, because only idealists or fools would spend their nights colonizing territories they can't plunder or profit from. StElene is not of the physical world. It is beyond it. And in this new world—the world according to Reverdy, he can transcend everyday life with its pain and terrible exigencies.

Cyber—no, what Reverdy prefers to think of simply of *space* is his element. He is master here. This universe of electronic connections spreads like infinity, apparently boundless. Wonderful and daunting. At first. *We are the pioneers of the millennium*, Reverdy thinks, *setting out without benefit of maps or compass.*

Awesome! Striking imaginary trails across the noosphere like an armature for dreams, technocrats and hackers colonized. Now player-programmers have thrown a net around this bit of the unseeable and brought it down to human scale. In their way, they're like the early settlers, who laid out grids of streets as if mapping would tame the endless prairie, putting up shelters to keep out night terrors and protect them against the prodigious unknown.

No. We're like Adam, naming names to bring things into being.

Claiming the territory, StElene's pioneers created an island, lovingly coding every detail down to the functions of carnivorous plants and the fish that dart in the uncharted waters. They built the vast hotel, with its lavishly furnished public rooms and crypts and cul de sacs. Describing, they shaped the unknown. Start putting names to things you've never seen before in a strange, unfamiliar place and immediately you're less afraid. You have begun to subdue it.

StElene beggars any spa or resort in the physical world.

It would overflow the physical world. Mathematicians say you can add an infinite number of rooms to a hotel registry— new numbers fit between the extant numbers. On the same principle, colonists have designed so many rooms here, so many intricate settings that no blueprint or map could contain them. From here Reverdy sees the beach curving to embrace the bay— his work. Bungalows sit like glittering satellites in the encroaching jungle and at the perimeter, the rest waits. Everything is potential, text opening on text with no images to direct or limit the imagination.

Clumsier designers would have put up graphics, using pictures for backgrounds, scanning in paintings or landscape drawings, even scanning in crude "avatars" to represent players, not caring that the mind usually stops short at the image. If pictures limit the imagination, words expand it. Meanings get huge in the mind. A world made out of words is whatever you want to make of it.

Welcome to the world of performative utterance, where *you are what you type.* The potential makes Reverdy shiver with excitement.

He is surrounded by restless souls. Typing from outposts at the four points of the earth, thousands meet here, in the territory of the imagination. In a miracle of synchronicity, disparate souls collide and in the emotional compression that marks life in such places, fall into instant friendship. Or love.

Zan. Or out of love. "Like Mireya," he murmurs. He has one ex-lover who will never forgive him.

Or into hate. Mireya has turned her tough new man into his worst enemy. "Fuck you, Azeath."

If somebody in the hall outside the room where he is typing calls, "Are you all right?" Reverdy won't hear her.

Mireya and Azeath aren't their real names. Pretending anonymity here, where they are already unseeable, players take new names to seal the difference. On StElene, names don't define or limit. They enable. Off StElene Reverdy is shackled to his given name with its built-in expectations; he is like a wild animal dragging a trap. He can't gnaw his leg off, so he escapes this way. Here, he can be whatever he wants. Gorgeous, if he chooses. Powerful.

The naming of names creates control, or the illusion of control. This is control through rhetoric. Unless it's control through illusion.

But there is a flip side to life here. Even though Reverdy burned himself out campaigning against it, Suntum International, the corporation that put up StElene, has appointed a board of directors. Thirteen of them. The thirteen have been in control for the last three years, meddling here, punishing there, trying to regulate life in what should be free space.

Reverdy hates any limitation of freedom. He also knows better than anybody: whoever controls the rhetoric has the power. *It's their sandbox,* he thinks angrily, *they can do anything they want here. Until I find a way to change things.*

When he talks about control through rhetoric, Reverdy points to the Memory Palace. In a way, StElene has a lot in common with the famous mnemonic device put in place by a long-ago Jesuit with a mission to China. This priest with a passion for organization went to enlighten the imperial court in fifteen something-or-other. Burning to teach, Matteo Ricci designed the Memory Palace—a system for organizing all knowledge, or everything the Jesuit knew. If Father Ricci understood that providing the rhetoric put him in control, he did not record it. He thought if he could only get everything of importance under the one roof, he could teach it better. How beautiful his scheme is, how orderly. Guiding his students into this palace in the mind, he would lead them to the light!

Like StElene, Reverdy thinks, *it is conceptual.*

The priest tried to organize all knowledge within the floor plan of an imaginary palace. His Memory Palace is vast and richly appointed, with treasures in its lavishly furnished rooms. Everything inside stands for something: the arts, theology, areas of knowledge, facts, dates. He put historic events in these chambers here, theological fine points over here, the arts in one wing and science in another. Within these imagined walls every major date, fact, happening, every concept has its signifier. Every object—each vase and tapestry and every porcelain stands for something. This intricate jade screen may represent the Punic Wars, that geometric Persian rug, *The Gilgamesh*. Memorize the layout and the location of objects, see them in the rooms where Father Ricci left them centuries ago, and you can know everything Father Ricci knew.

There is a problem. With the Jesuit's device, you can only see things his way. Results are built in. Creating the rhetoric for the exercise, the priest set the tone and the parameters—the way users move through his palace and what they will take away from it. Perfect, yes? Ricci's scheme. His rules. Go through his rooms at his pace and you will make not your, but his discoveries.

As with StElene, even though Reverdy fights it. Suntum Corporation put it up and their rhetoric defines it. Island, slightly romantic, with threatening bits for the gamers. Big hotel, it's social. There are parameters: the code. Access, which can be denied. Thirteen Directors to enforce it. And if the Directors are out to get him? Well . . .

But, he thinks, grinning, rhetoric can't accommodate accidents and surprises. Maybe some of Matteo Ricci's followers were so entranced by the beauty of the palace, so beguiled by its gorgeous furnishings that they forgot where they were going. Rapt, they marveled at surfaces without ever once seeing what the master was trying so hard to teach them.

Now Reverdy is looking for the wild card. Some contingency Suntum's system can't cope with. If there is one, he is damn well going to find it and hack into it and play it. And if there isn't one, he will, by God, invent one.

Even the Memory Palace comes out of chaos. Look at the paradigm. The model that inspired the priest. In imperial days, courtiers were seated in the banqueting hall according to family, rank and station. Then during the emperor's banquet God played a wild card. An earthquake leveled the palace, killing all the courtiers. Entering the ruins, survivors identified the dead revelers *according to where they had been sitting.*

Location is everything.

Sitting in the Dak Bungalow, he types, for no particular reason: "*Welcome to StElene.*" On the screen the program gives back,

    You say, "Welcome to StElene."

Say it, and it *becomes.* Welcome to the world of performative utterance, where what you say, *is.* Although all the world he cares about is on the screen in front of him, Reverdy hears his own voice. "Wonderful." *The way you look and what you do and what you own outside count for nothing. The only thing that counts here is intelligence. You are who you want because you say you are, and there's nobody in the place who can disprove it.*

The potential is tremendous. *Oh, God I love this place,* he thinks. All this life, stored in a machine located at the headquarters of Suntum International. All this life, inside of what is, essentially, a box!

Grinning, he checks to see where his new enemy is playing today. Time to stir up trouble. He is famous for testing the limits, to the point where StOnge has delivered the Directors' last warning. One more offense and he's erased. Barred forever.

What's life without a little risk? *@join Azeath,* he types. It is the excitement that keeps Reverdy here long after Zan is gone, while everybody he cares about sleeps. *If you can't make sense of life, you can at least make story.*

Never mind what's going on outside the room where Reverdy sits typing; never mind what the physical world makes of him. His life inside the box is intense. It's all that matters.

five

JENNY

I'm on StElene almost all the time now, I even log on from the office; if a patient cancels, it's like a gift of time. When Martha goes out to lunch I log on, dropping crumbs in the keyboard like bread crumbs in the forest so I can find my way back. Even when Reverdy's not around I feel close to him, just hanging there. Right now my life with Reverdy on StElene means more to me than a week in Myrtle Beach with Charlie or a month in Marrakech, for that matter, or St. Tropez, but that's because of what happened last night. And if more and more I leave Charlie behind and sneak away to StElene, it will serve him right. Put it down to what happened last night.

It wasn't exactly a fight. Charlie probably thinks it wasn't anything.

Whatever it was, it kept me awake for hours and then woke me up again at 4 a.m.; I lay there jangling for as long as I could stand it. At five I sneaked upstairs and logged on. Thank God Lark was there; trouble with his folks, he couldn't sleep either.

We've been talking ever since. Charlie just woke up, I can hear him rattling around. I hate to leave Lark but I have to go downstairs and cope. My friend Lark, a.k.a. Hubert Pinckney, is only nineteen, college dropout, claims he's a mess in real life but when we talk I forget which of us is the kid.

Downstairs Charlie calls: "Jen?" With a twinge of guilt, I ask Lark, "Do you think we're running away from something here?"

He grins. "More like running toward something."

"Real communication?"

"Realer. Where else can people get inside each other's souls?"

It is a kind of vindication. "That's it!" I hug him and disconnect.

Downstairs, it's time to take charge—find Rusty's hightops, slosh milk over Lucky Charms and strawberries for Patsy, start buttering toast in the aggressively yellow kitchen while my Charlie sits at the maple table with his wet-combed hair shining, smiling as if nothing between us has changed.

In a minute he'll melt into me: "I love you *so much!*"

And when he holds me like that, no matter how hurt I am, no matter how angry, my body can't refuse and I melt back. And I kiss him goodbye and send him off to the base as if nothing is wrong here and I'm not homesick for the loft where my old life still sits like a favorite coat that accidentally got left behind in the rush.

It is a relief to go in to the office and deal with my patients, who are hard to like and almost impossible to help. You bet StElene is an escape.

But that's only part of my love affair with the place. And Reverdy is only part of it. I can explain the rest for the rest of my life and if you haven't been there, you'll never understand.

Have you ever gotten lost in a book? So deep in the story that it's the only thing that matters and the world outside seems like the dream? Did you ever hear the people talking, so deep into what happens that you see what they see and feel what they feel?

I have. I used to run home after school and hide inside a book. I went in so deep that I rolled with every punch. I was desperate to find out what comes next. It was the one place I always felt safe. Books taught me how to talk, what was funny and what was dangerous, I learned how to treat snakebite and how to find my way out of the forest if I got lost. And I learned about love.

My mother hated it. Me, reading, while she toiled. "Why do you always have your head in a book?"

The truth would only make her cry. I loved her, but I liked the people I met in books a lot better. They had better lives! I fed on them. I could share what they felt and walk into their countries and be more at home than I ever was in the big old brown-shingled house in New London where everything was boring and my mother yelled at me, and if I'd known how to write books I would have done it, moved into the book and never, ever come out, it's one of the best ways I know to get into a prettier world and make your story come out just the way you want.

StElene is like going to live in a book.

It's the one place where I'm in complete control of my life. I can be in love and make my own story and write any ending I want!

Stupid to think Charlie and I could do that IRL. *In real life.*

I met him at Kath Cleary's beach house. He stood at the screen door and called. "Hello?" The sun was at his back so I couldn't see his face at first because the light dazzled me. For a second, Lieutenant Colonel Charles Wilder USMC, coming in the door, looked like my father, going out. Who knew

Daddy would never come back? Who knew this handsome young officer would walk into my life? I dug my nails into my arm and drew blood. To mark one fact and remember it forever. *This is not your father. He was killed, and you'll never get him back.*

Then Charlie walked into the cottage and took off his cap. He smiled and I was lost. "I'm Charlie Wilder, who are you?"

"Jenny. You're a friend of Kath's?"

"Yes. No. I'm a friend of her brother's. What are you reading?" Damn you, Charlie, I told you and you told me what you liked about the damn book!

I took it as a sign. "A Marine, and you read?"

"I do." He laughed. "And without moving my lips."

"Ooop. I'm sorry. My. Uh. Father was a Naval officer."

"Then you know."

Our two lives added up. I heard the tumblers click. "I do."

"Then you also know I can do a lot of other cool things."

Talking to Charlie was so easy! "I bet you do."

We started seeing each other. We fell in love and told each other everything, or what passed for everything. I didn't know what *everything* was until I met Reverdy. Going to the Carlyle to meet Charlie's family that last afternoon, I was nervous and excited. "What if your mother doesn't like me?"

"Um, ah," he said, "we're not going to meet my mother. It's. Ah." He coughed. He stopped the elevator between floors and took my hands. This is how he set the terms of his betrayal. "Oh honey, something's happened. I love you and I need you to be OK with it."

"Oh, sweetie, of course!" And I am, I try!

About last night. It's easier to deal with other people's problems than to face your own, so I'm at the office. I let poor little Amanda Wetherall do her instant replay of last night's dream while I brood over last night's fight. By the time I see Reverdy again, I'll have it by heart. Who else can I tell? He's the only one who understands.

The trouble is, reconsidered in broad daylight, it isn't exactly a fight. It's just another of those sweet, sad misunderstandings, where Charlie and I love each other so much that we run toward each other head-on, and then forget and miss the connection.

Cross purposes.

I want this *so much!* I was sure it would bring us together. Now I'm scared to death it's going to blow us apart.

It's been on my mind, and after what Rusty said to me last night, it bubbled to the top. Charlie was late and we were more or less alone—the last two people in the world and Rusty was rigid with dislike. I don't know what I thought I was doing but I slipped down onto the floor and tried to give the kid a hug.

"Rus, I know how you feel about your mother, but it's going to get better."

"No you don't." He turned away.

"I do, Rusty. You want to know how?"

"Not really." He wouldn't look at me.

"Because it happened to me." OK, I brought it on myself. "Like, when I was your age? My. Ah. Father got killed. In. Um. His submarine." It still hurts but I had to try. "First I pretended it wasn't true and then I felt awful and then..." for Rusty's sake, I lied. "I kind of got over it. What it took was. Um. Time, and one other thing? Do you want to know what the other thing is?"

"No."

"Keeping busy." His ears were turning red but I couldn't

stop. "It didn't make things any better, but it took my mind off it. OK?"

He wheeled with a snarl, ready to bite. "Could we please not talk about this right now, please?"

"Sorry! Let me give you a hug?"

"Fuck you!" He lunged to his feet and blundered out, and I thought: *I want at least one kid in my life that won't push me away.* And it came in on me. *I want this so much!* The idea snagged, it hooked me deep and I could feel my insides spasm. Crazy, this fit of neediness. I actually swore, *I'll leave Reverdy, I'll never go back to StElene if Charlie will only give me this.*

It seemed like the answer to everything—the kids, the loneliness, the sense of loss that's been walking on my shadow ever since I hit Brevert. I waited until Charlie got home, I waited while he ate. Then I waited until we were in bed and even though I know better than anybody that this kind of suggestion is contraindicated this early in any marriage, I put my face in his neck and I said, "Oh Charlie, what if we had a baby?"

"A baby?" This is how little my Charlie thought of it and how far back his betrayal went, and how deep. Yawning, the man I married kissed me and turned, mumbling, "Why would I want a baby?"

My mouth filled with water; I reached over and pulled him back so we were facing in the dark. "Charlie! What if I do?"

"Shhshh, babe, shsshh." And my blind, loving, sleepy, thoughtless Charlie kissed me on the nose and cut me loose forever. "We don't need a baby, Jenny. I already have my family."

So that's what I carried through the day, all day, and that's what chased at my heels tonight when Charlie called from the base to say he wouldn't be home because he had to fly to Cherry Point. And that's why my heart did a joyful, guilty little flip when he said he wouldn't be back until tomorrow.

After I get the kids to bed I can go to StElene and if I want to, I can stay all night.

six

ZAN

@*find reverdy.*

I t's always the first thing she types.

    Reverdy   The Dak Bungalow   Disconnected for 12 hours.

Reverdy is not logged on.

Am I in too deep? Jenny wonders, going to the grand ballroom instead. It is like coming home, *at least here people are glad to see me.*

Wonderful Jazzy spots her immediately. "Zan." They hug.

"Zan!" Articular greets her with that grin and a hug.

"Hey guys, it's me." Zan beams. For the first time today she's among friends. And, waiting for Reverdy, she will cheer herself with the talk. The talk, the talk!

StElene isn't a substitute for life, she thinks; *it's a new kind of life.*

The speed and ease of connections, the anonymity intensifies life on StElene. Unseen, people can and will say anything they want, and if they don't like the way things are going, they can just disconnect. They can joke or play with ideas, float theories or troll for sex or take out their aggressions, reducing unseen victims to tears. There are a few dynamic personalities—people like magnets, who know how to make others fall in love with them or fear them or want to murder them. Sometimes Zan suspects that they spend so much time here because IRL—*in real life*, they are quite different. StElene may be the one place in their lives where they have affect. Passing through the physical world without making a ripple, they come here to make waves. Like the ones who shout insults or secrets in the public rooms and then leave, feeling purged. Confession comes easy when you're casting words into the dark.

So does sympathy. There are a few blowhards who come to brag or preen or posture, but most people come to the grand ballroom to talk. And talk, because the species loves to talk about itself. For lonely people like Zan, it is a Godsend. After a bad day in quiet Brevert it's a delight to be surrounded by smart people with plenty to say. Skimming, she's cheered because StElene may be supported by Suntum's database, but the soul of the community is talk.

"It isn't the heartbreak that kills you," someone says, "it's answering the farewell note."

A dozen threads are overlapping in the grand ballroom, multiple conversations scrolling up Zan's screen so fast that she forgets the frustrations of the day and starts to laugh.

"Oh, Nietzsche, Nietzsche, Nietzsche's just a club she uses to bash people over the head with."

"Art movie. Awful movie. Boring. Imagine *Waiting for Godot* in SlowMo."

"It's a great cookbook but she's a bitch about spices. 'Don't even dream that the spices from your supermarket are any good.

By the time they reach your country from India, they are too old.' "

"Amy? Amy! Is Amy here?"

"Still driving a 486. Metallica T-shirt. You know the type."

"I do *not* want to be in one more fight about Mac versus DOS."

"What goes around comes around; in the next election, liberal backlash is bound to sweep the government clean."

The conversation becomes general. "Somebody ought to sweep the government of this place clean. The Directors. Really. Dictators!"

"That's what Reverdy says."

"Do you really think StElene is controlled by thought police?"

"What do you think, hmm? As in, who do you think put up the database?"

"What do you mean?"

"If the nature of the questions determines the results of a quiz, Reverdy's right. It's all programmatic; what the program permits and doesn't permit. We think we're free agents, but the Suntum Corporation's calling the shots."

"Careful, they're probably listening."

"What are they going to do to us, pull the plug? If the corporation channels everything anyway, what's the point?"

"A little regulation never hurt anybody."

"That's what you think. They're cutting us off at the knees."

Playing on group paranoia, someone says cleverly, "Unless they're running us like rats."

Who's out here talking? *People like us,* Zan thinks, letting the talk scroll by as she reflects. *People nothing like us.*

Then Jazzy says, "It's not the pudding you have to prove, it's the chef."

She types, *If this is the pudding, are we the chefs or the plums?*

Five people respond. Look at them all! Strangers like packages, waiting to be unwrapped. Zan trusts her personal radar; some of the people she meets here are keepers; others, she's let slip away. Jazzy's a keeper. "Think of this as the oven," he says, making her laugh.

"And Suntum's the kitchen. And if we can't stand the heat . . ."

Several people laugh. Then hostility smashes into her like an incoming wave. "If this is a kitchen, bitch," Azeath says to her, "why don't you give us all a break and jump in the fire?"

Jazzy says, "Watch it!"

But this enemy Zan has never met tells the room, "Watch out for that one; she may look sweet, but she's Reverdy's puppet; everything she types, he writes."

She types: look at Azeath. **The description is daunting.**
Azeath is God's demon in a platinum tunic: tall, blond, imposing. His naked biceps and his huge thighs tell you that he is an expert love machine. And a killing machine. He knows the law to the letter and is ready to die defending it. Behold him. Be afraid. Be more than afraid. He is a terrible enemy.

His girlfriend Mireya jumps in, no surprise. "Oh, Reverdy." Everybody knows she and Reverdy used to be lovers and Mireya snarls at Zan as if she still owns the man, studding her insults with asterisks. "We know all about Reverdy's *tool*s. Correction. Reverdy's *fool.* Lady, can't you tell when you're being used?"

When Zan doesn't rise to the bait, Mireya says, "Only a fool would come in here talking Reverdy's line without ever wondering. If he's not using you, prove it. What do you have to say for yourself?"

"Sorry, I don't do catfights." Not caring what Mireya says behind her back or that both Mireya and Azeath will page her relentlessly, sniping at long distance, Zan goes home.

Safe in Zan's Tower at the top of the hotel, she considers. This is life, all right, but it's life in a pressure cooker. Here in the dark we are all equal, the attached or unattached, carefree or careworn, the large and the unwieldy, the halt and the ugly, the lovelorn . . .

No. Lorn. Lorn, she thinks, strung out it. And what about Reverdy? Is he lorn? Maybe we are all lorn, she thinks, lorn being the condition of missing something terribly without knowing what it is.

Shaking off sadness, she opens a post from Lark.

```
Last night after they went to sleep I sneaked up to
the kitchen and made those white chocolate chunk
brownies I told you about, and I put them in a beau-
tiful box I had and took them over to my girl-
friend's house? You know, Daisy? Well, she was
almost my girlfriend before I got sick so I
thought, when she comes to the door I'll just give
them to her and she'll know, I put my phone number
in so she can call? But oh shit Zan, I got there OK,
and they were still up and all, but I never saw her
because I couldn't get up the guts to ring the bell.
It made me so sick that on the way home I threw them
off the bridge. I'll log back on as soon as they let
```

> me, I have to talk to you; right now my dad has to
> use the phone.

If she and poor Lark could talk it would be better, but if synchronicity is one of the wonders of life in space, it is by no means guaranteed. Things happen in the world outside that keep people from logging on. Exigencies separate friends when they most need to meet—power outage, computer crash, the server's down or someone is disconnected in mid-conversation because downstairs his wife just picked up the phone. Zan mails Lark instead, not knowing whether she'll still be here when he reconnects. StElene is built on talk, but it's held together by mail. She writes:

> Oh, Lark, I'm proud of you for making the gesture
> and I'm sure if Daisy knew what you'd done for her,
> she'd be proud of you too. I wish you'd stayed long
> enough to see if she came to the door. I knew if she
> could just talk to you, she'd know how special you
> are. Have you thought of sending her a note?

Zan wants to keep writing, to tell him about Charlie and the baby she can't have because it hurts so much that she has to tell somebody, but her sense of privacy is too strong. Let other people spill their stories incessantly in public rooms and on StElene's dozens of mailing lists. She doesn't complain.

She'll wait for Reverdy.

And he is here. "Zan!"

They hug. "Love, I'm so glad!" Of course Zan tells him everything she said last night, what Charlie said before he fled into sleep. Tears glaze her cheeks here in the third-floor room in the physical world as on StElene she tells Reverdy, "I feel so lost."

He says, "You're like Gauguin painting for a blind man. He can't see it. He can't see you at all." This is why she loves Reverdy.

"We're in love."

What he says next warms her. "Not the way you and I are."

"Charlie does love me, it's just. The kids. They're like military orders that he has to follow, damn the torpedoes."

"You deserve better, Zan. You deserve everything you want."

She's tempted to ask whether he would let her have a baby but the territory's brand new and she knows better. "Oh, Rev."

"Let me be here for you." He quotes the poet she loves best. "In this and the other kingdom."

Reverdy is so quick to understand that Zan tells him things she's never told anybody else in the world. They know each other so well that they talk in shorthand; almost every point of reference is shared. Her lover knows she is crying RL and he says all the right things to her, every one; weeping with gratitude, she says, "I've never known anybody this way."

"You mean all the way through to the soul."

Softly, she repeats, "All the way through to the soul."

After a pause he builds on it, leading her. "As if we're the same person. I know we're not, but we are."

Deep inside Jenny in the night in the quiet third-floor room, love twists like a leaping fish. Yes it's sexual, but she has to elevate what she feels or she can't be here. Swiftly, she transforms it. "Or the same soul."

"That's the beauty of meeting you here."

"Meeting you anywhere." She knows where she'd like this

to go; what they have here is beautiful but it's conceptual. She imagines meeting Reverdy in some real place where they can really touch.

"Oh Zan, who would I be if I'd never met you?"

"You'd be you. Oh, I'm so glad you're you!" She is casting for something she may not be able to name. "I love you and I trust you with my life. And you . . ."

Reverdy does not exactly address this. In fact, she tells him everything and there are a number of things he's never told. He offers this, to make it better. "I tell you things I never told Louise. Things I could never tell Louise."

"She doesn't understand."

"Exactly. She can't! But you . . . It's as if I know what it's like to be inside your skin. And I love what I see." He lets a little of his daily life show through, delicately hinting at the pain: "Being with you is so *different*. Louise . . ."

"I know." She does; they've talked about it for hours.

"Yes, you know." Smiling, he touches her hair. "And I couldn't live without you knowing."

It's strange and wonderful that Zan is deep inside Reverdy's consciousness, when her true knowledge of Charlie stops at the sweet smile on his blunt, loving, uncomprehending face. "Charlie is a good man, but he doesn't . . ."

"Love you?"

"Understand. I wish you and I could be forever."

And this is the joy and the danger: his love! Reverdy seals it. "We are."

seven

HUBERT PINKNEY, A.K.A. LARK

Everybody has to disconnect sometime. Either you have to sleep or everybody you care about has gone to sleep. Nobody you know is logged on. You don't have the psychic energy to start up with strangers, fishing for something to talk about with players you don't know. Life's too short to waste on the hundreds of anonymous guests who drop in with their unformed expectations, discover they can't handle it and go. You've read all the posts on your favorite mailing lists on StElene, starting with *complaints. You've even posted a few sassy notes on *politics in hopes somebody will post a response or mail you privately. You've @*investigated* every room in the GrandHotel and nothing's going on.

Your ideal world is as good as dead. For now.

You're sick of waiting for your friends. Your bladder calls. *BRB*, you type, for "Be right back," but there's nobody around who cares. You might as well disconnect. Push back your rolling chair and turn your back on the vacant screen. Type @*exit* and your brilliant, colorful, crowded world goes out like a light. It is like a little death. Lark, a.k.a. Hubert Pinkney, is brought down.

Bad things happen to you in the interstices. Lark knows. You have to take care. "Take care," Zan said to him right before she disconnected, when was it, 2 a.m? Just now Reverdy said, "Take care" and typed @*exit*. It's even night in Alaska, which Lark happens to know is where Reverdy lives IRL. In, as they say, Real Life. Lark looks around the cluttered basement at 553 Poplar Avenue, where he grew up. This isn't life. It isn't safe!

Off StElene the world is fucking fraught with peril. People are hard to take and shitty to you. Alone is the only safe way to be. And the only safe place to be is: LOGGED ON.

Lark is . . . No. Sadass Hubert Pinkney is on the floor in farthest corner with his feet sticking out in front of him, gleaming in Nikes that the mother bought in hopes they'd inspire him to go out and run a mile. Yeah, right.

He looks about the way Zan thinks he does—skinny and anxious, triangular face with lemur eyes; the accuracy of her imagination would make her smile. Until Jenny Wilder stepped in and took a look at him, assessing with a professional sigh: *He is not a whole human being.*

Yeah right, I'm not. Lark is pretty messed up. Yeah, they can call him Hubert but he's Lark even here, the 'rents are just too stupid to see it. And he knows they can't stand him.

Howard and Marjorie Pinkney's son the computer junkie stays out of sight but he lurks in the mind. No, he looms in the mind, which is why they are determined to get him out of here. Like kicking him out will make him all better. The mom thinks he'll, like, hang out drinking coffee in some nice, healthy student union far, far away from Poplar Avenue instead of crouching like a raptor at his keyboard in their very cellar, which is usually lighted only by the eerie cathode glow from his computer screen. Eviction will be good for him! Their little Hubert can make friends, get some color in his face. Build some muscle, out in the fresh air.

Look, he can't keep going on the way he is.

"You can't keep going on the way you are. Right, son?" Marjorie, looking at him with those swimmy eyes. That's the problem with moms, even when they don't like you. They hope.

Howard, he just wants the kid unshelled—un. fucking. shelled. He was a freak accident. They thought they were done having kids. Two grown sons, both gone. And now ... this! Freak accident, as Howard never ceases to remind him. They are too old!

When the 'rents sent him off to college they thought the inconvenience was finally done with. Threw a private block party and redecorated his room. Not their fault that like a bad check, he bounced. And landed here. Last thing he wanted, and look at me. Not his fault. Not theirs.

Marjorie keeps holding these sad little conversations from the top of the basement stairs. "Son, why don't you go out and play?"

"I'm too old to play."

"You're not too old to have fun."

"I'm nineteen."

"You know what I mean. You've got to come out sometime. Son?"

"No I don't." If she knew he went out at night she might lock the house and not let him back in. "I'm cool right here."

She acts friendly, but Lark knows. The father sends her to ask when is he going to get a job. Howard even writes her damn lines: be warned, they are done paying these phone bills from you always being on that terrible internet what are you doing out there where we can't keep an eye on you. It's time to kick the habit or else get a damn job or think of something you can sell to pay for your keep here. That useless comic book collection? Your CDs? Why don't you sell that damn computer, it brings nothing but grief, look what happened to you in college. Sell sperm or something, help with this huge phone bill. Sell your blood. But that's Howard talking.

The mother never says anything straight out. She just starts in that lala voice of hers, "Your friends Ed and Ben called."

"I don't want to see Edward and Benjamin right now."

"They're only home for two weeks. Spring break. Harvard!" He can hear the tears in her voice. "UCLA. You could have a party."

"I don't go there."

"Son, why won't you look at me?"

Because I can't look at people. Not straight on. "I am."

"If you'd only go out! Or let your friends come in."

"I don't go there, Mom. Go away."

"You never go out!"

"Is that a problem for you?" *But I do. Just not that you know about,* he thinks and can't know if he means the deep hours when he slips out the back and goes running or the daily escape to StElene.

"Oh Hubert, you're going to lose all your *friends.*"

"I don't have any friends." His heart turns over. *I have closer friends than anybody. Just not here.* A phrase bounds across the screen of his imagination: *not of this world.*

This Tuesday, my God, she came down. Crept up behind him and touched him on the shoulder. "For God's sake, son. At least tell us how you *are!*"

"I'm fine, Mother. I'm fine." *You're in my space.* Stand. Stare at her feet. Wait for her to go.

Tuesday she craned to read what was scrolling up his screen.

"At least let me see. Are you writing a book down here? Tell me you're writing a book."

"No Mother, I'm not writing a book."

She swelled, filling his space. "Then what is it? Let me see!"

"No!" He threw his body over the screen to keep her from seeing the scrolling text.

Reverdy just said: Your mother is some bitch! Zan was saying: If only I could arrange ten minutes with them. They don't even know who you are!

Marjorie was pushing so Lark had to shove. Hard. "Go away!"

"You hit me!" Wounded, Marjorie regrouped. "I thought you might be writing something. You know. To get back into school."

"Fuck school." *I'm sorry about the fucking nervous breakdown, Mother. If that's what it was.* "I can't talk now. I'm busy."

"I just don't understand you, Hubert. In the dark all the time. Wasting your life down here in the dark."

"All right, I'll show you. I'll fucking show you." Desperate, he types *BRB* and then *home*. And on StElene, Lark disappears from the Dak Bungalow and returns to Lark's Mandala. Let the mother read what he has wrought. If she asks, he'll open some of the puzzles for her, *@unpack* the coding that supports his elegant schemes.

"For God's sake, Hubert. Stop typing. The sun's out!"

Why do I need to see the sun when I can build a world? What Lark does is too huge to explain to outsiders. On StElene he has built a bungalow; the text presents a neo-Victorian place with a little cupola, an exterior in keeping with the island theme, but he has customized the interior. Enter Lark's place and you're inside an Oriental contrivance, text describing spheres within spheres. The first solution to the problems set by the mandala admits you to an inner sphere. The mathematical scheme is based on those intricately carved sets of ivory balls within balls with a beautiful kernel at the center. Each sphere in Lark's place contains a series of games, puzzles. Solve each set and eventually you find your way to the center of the inmost sphere and the lotus throne. Lark sits here. Solve all the puzzles and you'll get to the center of Lark. Some day the perfect woman will find him waiting here. Until then, Lark is content to wait. The thing took months to devise. Hours spent coding followed by hours in the hotel talking to his friends, how much more life does a person need? What could Hubert Pinkney tell his mother about this? What could he really, really say to her? "OK, Mother," he said at last. "You want a look? Then look!" And stepped aside, trembling, so she could read his screen.

Reading, Marjorie blinked. And blinked and blinked. He still doesn't know why it made her so angry. Screaming, "This is it? This is all?"

"Yes this is it. This is fucking it!"

Furious, she pushed him. "Don't speak that way to me. Don't you dare speak that way to me."

And he pushed back! "Oh, go to hell. Just fucking go to fucking hell. *Mother, do you have any idea who I am?*

"Is that all you can do, hit me? You hit me twice!"

"I'm sorry, I was upset."

"That's twice. That does it! I'm telling your father. Then we'll see."

OK, the fire in the kitchen wasn't only logical. It was inevitable. And yesterday Howard came downstairs and read him out. Hubert this, Hubert that. Then he yanked all the plugs.

So the 'rents are pissed about the fire. Lark and his computer, his things. That he sneaks upstairs in the night and steals food. That they never see him go out. Now they're in the kitchen talking about him. He guesses the sun's up. He hasn't slept, so what else is new? Day, night. It's all the same to him. But the 'rents are regular. It's their breakfast time again. He hears them shambling around up there on muffled feet, padding around in their matching slipper socks like worried bears, circling the kitchen on a loop. Trapped inside those thick, sagging bodies, wedged into narrow minds while on StElene, Lark soars.

It's sad. No. It's terrible. Here, IRL, he's like one of those big bugs that when you turn them over on their back, they're powerless. And they're fixing to drive in the pin. What words the senior Pinkneys exchange will be not so much overheard by Lark as *known.*

If life on StElene is pure thought, Lark is the genius of extrapolation. He doesn't have to see the spit bubbling on Marjorie's sad bear muzzle or inadvertent tears running down the round bear nose. He knows what she's saying.—Howard, did you speak to him?

Father bear exposing broken fangs.—I spoke to him good.

Mother: choke-sniffle, hesitate. She doesn't want to feel guilty, but she does because she is, after all, a mother. Still a mother, like it or not.—Well, when is he going?

Sighing, Lark slinks to the foot of the basement stairs.

The father says,—As soon as he's packed.

Lark creeps to the top step so he can hear better.

—Oh God, Howard, packed!

Lark leans his forehead against the door. *What'll I do?*

—It's past time. Father bear with the belly and the loose, wet mouth. Glasses too tight on his fat nose. Howard condescends. Makes a fucking point of being bigger, like Lark is a damn bird with a broken wing that he can stomp on. *Well, fuck him. He doesn't know that I can fucking fly.* Howard says,— He's got to go.

Lark groans. *Where?* Can he get through the glass screen of his terminal and disappear into the ether? Climb inside the box and move to StElene for good? He may be crazy, but he's not that crazy.

—But Howard, what will he do?

—That fool computer I bought for him. He can damn well make a living with that high-end electronic crap of his. Five thousand dollars, and look! He can damn well run figures for some finance company. A bank. They use those things in banks. But I tell you this. That boy won't lift a finger as long as he can get a free ride here.

The mother cries,—How can he make a living when he can't even make his bed?

Yeah, how?

—That's his problem. He'll thank us for it later, I promise. After he goes.

After he goes. Something deep inside Lark founders. *How will I connect? Where will I keep all my things?*

He hates them so much! He hates himself for not being able to go up there and tell them to fuck themselves. He wishes he could just stomp up these stairs and walk out, slam the door and leave them all behind, along with his junk that he has to have just to keep going, cartons that he can't live without. Things he needs. Collection of comics. Baseball hats. Character mugs and rock group T-shirts. Books he bought and can't let go because they're still unread. He isn't free! Worse, he is financially dependent here. Lark has zero income, he has only debts.

And he's about to lose it all. Once the father yanks the plugs and jerks the surge protector out of the wall for good, once Howard jams the computer components back in the labeled cartons he's so thoughtfully provided, he'll lug them upstairs and set them out on the curb and Hubert with them. Lark will be disconnected! Cut off from his friends and everything that matters. It's too horrible to think about. He'll have to turn tricks or panhandle just to connect from some crowded, terrifying internet cafe. Strangers looking over your shoulder. Reading the intimate things you type. He'd die.

He hears the mother hum-humming. Hey, if she's wavering . . . —Oh Howard, maybe we shouldn't.

Steely dad:—We have no choice.

—But he's so young!

—Your safety, Marjorie.

—Safety! Howard, he's my *son*.

The father says,—The fire in the kitchen, Marjorie.

—It was an accident.

—He set it. Who knows what he was trying to burn away?

Below stairs, Lark dies. *The fire in the kitchen is nothing. You keep this up and you'll see what Lark can do.*

It isn't really the fire anyway. It isn't even the hours he keeps. They are just sick of him. Sick of him bopping around nights until he crashes and crawls into bed after dawn, coughing and shivering until he thinks he's slept and it's OK to get up and connect to StElene because being away is like being dead. Sick of him screaming when one of them tries to make a phone call and he gets disconnected. Sick of the extra wash because Lark has to scrub himself raw twice a day and change all his clothes and the sheets too. He just has to, OK? Plus that he won't eat with them because he can't stand being watched. Like he would explain? He just sneaks upstairs when they're sleeping and steals food. Plus, OK, the discomfort of having a third person not exactly *there* but always present. They fret: *What is he* doing *down there?* Make a midnight food run and accidentally run into one of them: *Oh, are you still here?* Plus the bills. The bottom line is financial. With Howard, it always is. He's pissed about the phone bill because Lark is always online. It's his connection. The best one is his account at the college he dropped out of. Trouble is, it's in Colorado. His computer has to phone up Colorado every time he logs on and so he stays logged on. Hundreds of dollars.

Unless the bottom line is that they grit their teeth and look away because they can't bear the sight of him. It's like he's something wrong they did, that they can't bear to face.

Upstairs:—Do you want to speak to him or shall I?

Oh yes I am afraid.

If Howard comes down here and finds out Hubert has unpacked his stuff and reconnected, God knows what he'll do. Sinking to the bottom step, curling around his misery, Lark begins to rock. But he's not a stupid person, he's a smart one, and wacked as he is, he knows he can't just sit here, waiting for Reverdy to come rescue him. Slowly, he unfolds. When his feet stop feeling like dead sponges, he tiptoes over pins and needles to his desk.

Sobbing, he types:

`stelene.moo.mud.org 8888`

The minute he does, he feels better. Then he types:

`co` **(you don't have to type the whole word to connect)**

`lark` **(the program is not case sensitive)**

and last, he types his password, which he guards with his life. Nobody is going to sneak into Lark's place pretending to be Lark; the Directors on StElene have made it clear to all players. NEVER GIVE YOUR PASSWORD TO ANYONE. They'll never guess his:

`bfltzpyk`

The StElene display comes up but Lark knows it by heart. Sometimes it scrolls up the screen in his dreams. He goes to the hot plate and makes instant coffee. When he comes back to the terminal he is sitting in:

Lark's Place. Where he can be safe.

You are in a light, bright library, the outer
chamber of the sphere where Lark lives and works.
It is his alone. He is writing his novel here. On
the curved walls are Lark's art collection, Lark's
Morocco and gold-bound books. Light comes from an
unknown source and the sphere is lined with gray
velvet sofas that invite you to sit but note this.
There is more to Lark's Place than is immediately
evident. The scroll: READ ME; the smaller sphere
glowing in the center of the room suggest that
there is more here, even as there is more to Lark.
Much, much more. Find your way into the next sphere
and discover. Look on his works and admire.

His face relaxes into a smile. Home at last. Then he types:
    @find reverdy, thinking: be here, please be here.
The display comes up:

Reverdy last disconnect 5 a.m. PST The Dak Bungalow

Oh hell, Reverdy isn't here. Neither is Zan, but he knows how to reach Zan, a.k.a Genna Wilder, she's a psychologist RL, she'll know what to do.

We have to talk, we have to talk! Everything hurts. We have to talk. And Reverdy? No matter when he comes in we'll talk and I can tell him everything.

eight

JENNY

Bad feelings gnaw at you from the inside out, whatever's eating you feeds until it's so big that there's no getting rid of it. Pain has a way of scrambling your synapses. You start to say one thing and something else comes out.

I've got to tell somebody.

Nice Martha is sitting in my big chair with late sunlight striking her gray frizz. She's relaxed and wide open; this would be a good time to run the baby thing past her—am I over-reacting here, or was that a mortal hurt? Charlie and Reverdy and Charlie revolve in my mind like tigers biting each other's tails and all I can talk about is StElene. "Martha, I've gotten into this new place, this virtual community? It's a whole new world."

"You're in a . . . what?"

I can't tell her about Reverdy but I'm desperate to tell her something. Sure it's crazy. In a way StElene is like good sex. If the person you're telling hasn't been there, there's no way you can explain. The more I tell Martha, the more she doesn't get it, and even when her eyes glaze over, I have to explain. "Martha, I have these amazing *friends* there!"

This gets her attention. "My God, you don't give these weirdos your name!"

Another of those things I'd better not tell. "Relax, we all take character names. Besides, you can tell a lot of things about people from their descriptions."

"Descriptions?"

"What they write about themselves." I keep mine simple.

```
ZAN stands for considerably more than what you read
  here.
Carrying:
Ring from Reverdy          Official Lark Friend Badge
```

Oh God this is hopeless; I grin. "I guess you had to be there." When I disconnect from StElene the program adds: Zan (sleeping) is here. My description stays behind to stand for me. If Reverdy comes in while I am asleep he can still trace my outlines, like a man in love with a ghost.

But Martha's freaking. "My God, you're in a chat room!"

"Is that all you think of me? That I'd do something that little and stupid and cheap?" Yes I am shouting. "Think of a gigantic virtual building, with hundreds of rooms. Imagine thousands of people all living together in a really big small town . . ."

"Just tell me you're not in a chat room. Foxy Lady. Sexy Man. Please. Jenny, it's so not you!"

"Don't condescend to something you don't understand!" I don't really want her following me onto StElene but she looks so hurt that I say, to make up for yelling, "If you knew them. If you could only meet my *friends.*"

"You mean if *you* could meet them," she says; her look says, *this is for your own good.*

"They aren't just anybody, Mart, they're logging on from universities and corporations, not just . . ." I start over. "Professionals, most of them. Lawyers, writers," I leave out the randy teenagers and a couple of other categories she doesn't need to know about. "I met this great doctor from Australia . . ."

"Doctor, yeah right." Martha gives me that look. "He says."

"He *is* a doctor!"

"How do you know?"

"Believe me, I know." How can I explain how you learn to identify people you can't see or hear or touch, or how you in your bones know which ones you can trust. It's like swimming or riding a bicycle; once you know, you know. Martha's so skeptical that I keep numbering them: philosopher-politician in Canada. Artist in Oakland, friend doing social semiotics in London, anthropologist, physical therapist. Programmers, students, scientists, I tell her it takes brains to hang out in ephemeral space, OK I spare her the crazier ones, like Harrald, and Lark . . .

But now Martha's worried. She grabs my hands. "Jen. Jenny. Tell me you don't give these people your real name or say where you live. Swear."

No. It would be lying. I say, "Only my closest . . ."

"You're out there in this made-up computer thingy with a bunch of creeps and weirdos that you can't see and you don't know about, and you've told them your real name?"

I've told them a hell of a lot more than that. "Only the ones I trust."

"For God's sake Jenny, be careful! You hear terrible things about stuff that happens on the Internet. Terrible things." This from Martha, who can't open her email without help. "Women get murdered because they trust some guy they've never seen,

they go to meet some guy they picked up in some sleazy, anonymous . . ."

"Martha . . ."

To her credit, she doesn't say, *chat room.* She sighs. "You
don't know who these people are, Jenny, or what they really
want from you!"

"I know what I want, Mart. Something a little bit bigger
than Brevert."

Her eyes are crossing slightly with incomprehension. "This
is sick, Jenny. How did you get so tied up in something you
can't see? You think you're in a movie or something? Or is it
more like a game? Are we talking imaginary playmates, or
what?"

"It's as real as you and me sitting here."

She shakes her head. "It's all typing in the dark to me."

"We type, and things *exist.*"

Bang, she's all over me; she snaps, "Performative utterance."

Reverdy's exact words drop into my heart like a stone in a
well. "Yes."

"Like, say it and it's so?" Martha is leading me.

I am too upset to care. "Yes!"

"Well, it isn't. It isn't so. There's a thin line between that
and wish fulfillment."

"Do you really think I'm that stupid? Do you have any idea
what it's like to get to the level of pure thought? StElene is like
that; people getting past the superficial, meeting on the plane of
pure thought." I am not about to tell her there is a hell of a lot
more to life on StElene than that. I say, "Look at us. You. Me,
here in this room. Eight thousand distractions. Interruptions.
Physical static. The fax, the phone. Broken fan on the AC. Dust
in the room. Visual cues—what we're wearing, who's thinner

and how that makes us feel and am I boring you, and did you just stifle a yawn? How can we possibly get to the truth? Think of the freedom!"

"You mean freedom from responsibility."

"Freedom from *all this crap*."

It's all wasted. My friend. My friend Martha, *Martha* finishes me off with that sweet, uncomprehending smile. "And this chat room. Is it a hobby with you?"

"It's not a chat room!" I smack my hand down on the desk. "It's a world."

"No. This." And Martha smacks her hand down on the desk. Harder. "This is the world."

"Stuff in this room, in Brevert, it's extraneous, Mart. I'm talking about getting to the center."

And my only friend in Brevert asks carefully, "What do you think is the center?"

My life in the South backs up in me like the contents of a faulty drain and I can hear my voice beginning to crack. "Whatever it is, it isn't here and it probably isn't now."

"Oh, I get it. Escapism."

"No," I say hopelessly. If I can't make even Martha understand, maybe my time on StElene really is wasted. "I. Agh. Imagine a society where everybody can know everything. And all at once."

"Isn't that what the devil promised Adam?"

"It was Eve." Oh shit, is she going to make me cry?

Then—just like that—my good friend comes down on me out of nowhere like a SCUD missile. WHAM. "Are you and Charlie all right?"

There is this terrible pause; I see my whole life flash before my eyes and it is over. *Oh Charlie, we started so well, how did we end up here?*

My friend Martha just smiles and waits.

"All right?" I want to tell her and I can't tell her; if I start crying, I'm fucked; instead, I flee. Even though it is my office, not Martha's, I grab my shoulder bag and go, stopping just long enough to reassure her, unless she's a bomb I am trying to defuse. "We're fine! Why wouldn't we be all right?"

Then on Front Street, I hear somebody hurrying to catch up with me—Martha, I think, but it isn't, it's my obsessive-compulsive patient Rick Berringer, a local lawyer who is keeping things together with my help. In the chair in my office, Rick Berringer is one thing. Out here in the street, he is another. As tall as Charlie, dark-haired and slightly driven, like Reverdy. Now that we are out in the open, he has an off-center smile that I like. Something is flickering at the periphery of my imagination; I turn and wait.

"I saw you walking and I wondered if you'd like a ride."

"Thanks, but I need the time to unwind."

"OK if I walk along with you?" Nice-looking guy, I probably know too much about Rick for us to be friends but if it doesn't bother him it shouldn't bother me, and it doesn't seem to be bothering him. He says easily, "I'm done for the day and I need to stretch out."

Sometimes going along Front Street I see other officers' wives eying me from late model cars with base tags. They all hang together and turn out for official gatherings; I don't and Charlie tells me I am missed by which he means, he is judged. I think it wouldn't hurt to have Charlie find out that I've been seen walking along the bay road with some nice guy he doesn't know about. "Sure, I have to go home and get supper for the kids."

"No problem." Rick's quick, rumpled grin lets me know that he is something waiting to happen. "It's cool."

"You know I'm married, right?"

Then my patient astounds me. "I know you're unhappy, right?"

Reverdy? Don't be ridiculous, he . . . "Rick, I don't know if we should . . ."

"It's just a walk, Ms. Wilder. Just a walk."

And not for the last time today my synapses tangle; I am so on the verge of asking Rick if he's ever heard of StElene that I manage to stop. In my present confused state it would be too much like trolling for sex. Still, I can't stop suspicion jumping inside me like a silver fish—unless it's an attack of wish fulfillment, Jenny, cut it out, lay back. I say quickly, "I'm sorry, I forgot something and I have to go back to the office, but next time, OK?"

Near dawn I am caught short in my sleep, rigid with terror; my breath stops. It may be a dream but I can't be sure. If it's a dream, then I am submerged in it, I am drowning somewhere off StElene, swimming against an undertow to a place I'll never reach, and it is as real as StElene has ever been real—I'm swimming through letters that bob like phosphorescents in a black ocean, microorganisms glittering in the night, the water I am inhaling is line after line of scrolling text; the island and the offshore currents and this undertow are made of text; I try to grab a string of words like a lifeline to pull myself out but the words have fragmented into hundreds of sparkling letters and the letters themselves implode like dying stars. I am sobbing, halfway between terror and delight when the surface shatters and I reel with shock; like God or some huge child reaching into a dollhouse or maybe a lifeguard rescuing a drowning swimmer, strong hands break the surface and take hold of me, relentlessly pulling me out.

It's Charlie, calling, "What's the matter, what's the *matter?*"

I am sobbing, incoherent. "Oh, oh Charlie, it hurts so much!"

"Shh, don't, it's OK. You were crying."

"Oh." I am shivering with loss. Broken glass, I think, that's what hurt because rescuing me, pulling me out of StElene or the dream of StElene, Charlie shattered my computer screen! After Daddy got killed I used to dream about being happy in Oz and never having to come back to our empty house, "Oh," I can't stop sobbing. "Oh!"

"Don't." Warm and close in the night, Charlie is rocking me. Something about my desperation rattles him; he is crying too. "Please don't."

"I can't help it."

"Shh, Jen. Another dream about your father?"

"I don't have those anymore."

"You're sure?"

"Not since I met you. It's not about my father, OK?"

"Then shh, just shh, babe, I'll take care of you, I'll always take care of you."

This makes me wail with guilt. "Oh, Charlie. Oh!" Now I know why I couldn't walk home with Rick, I love Charlie and I would never . . . near occasion of . . . Rick is a near occasion, whereas Reverdy, Reverdy and I have never touched. I'm not unfaithful; I am.

"Shh shh, whatever it is, it can't be so terrible. What is it, Jenny, what's so terrible?"

I am thinking about the baby. *I already have my family.*

I'm thinking about the baby and I can't tell him that either. "Nothing."

"If you love me, you'll tell me."

"I love you and I . . . I don't know." And a deep, disloyal part of me is thinking, *I do know, and Reverdy, Reverdy knows.*

"Jenny," Charlie says into my hair, "I don't know what's going on with you but I love you, if there's anything, anything at all that I can do . . ."

And this is the hell of it. I love Charlie and I can't ever tell him. "It's OK, Charlie. Really. It's just a bad dream and I'm fine."

@nine

ZAN

I spent the afternoon at Brevert Hospital, sitting with the Yerkes while the people in the ER pumped their daughter's stomach. That poor kid let herself get so skinny that it didn't matter what I said or did, she couldn't pull out of the spiral. The mother found her. The Yerkes parents blamed themselves, they blamed Amanda, they blamed me. Why not? I do. What is it with me and these Southerners, that I can't get through to them? Is it something with me? I don't know, I only know the failure made me feel rotten, as if it was somehow my fault. We hung in together, I did my best to talk the family through but we were only spinning our wheels, which we kept doing until the doctor came out and said Amanda was going to be fine. She asked for me. Mom and dad got up too but the doctor waved them off. So I went in to talk to her; I brushed her cheek. "Amanda, I'm not going to ask you why."

She raised her chin like a cat being stroked. "Tell them if they force me to eat I'm going to do it again."

"Oh, Amanda."

"Promise."

I didn't promise. I did what I could. When I was done the family hugged all around, but the mother had that look. The thing is, I can give this case everything I've got—no, more than I have to give—and that mother will still be that mother with those social expectations, and as long as she has that mother, Amanda will starve. I'm lobbying for boarding school in the North, but helping Amanda is a little bit like sweeping the beach—every day the same debris washes back in. I came all the way down here with Charlie thinking at least I could start over with new patients, but these people have problems that I can't touch.

I did what I do to decompress. I shopped for shrimp and snow peas and sesame oil and soy sauce, dried mushrooms and tree ears and ginger root and went home to cook. I threw in chicken and peanuts and made spring rolls, in hopes. Usually when Charlie and I sit down together these meals are like little celebrations, and we both need a celebration about now.

But Charlie comes in late and he's in no mood to celebrate. He's trying to smile but his face sags; even his khakis have wilted in the humidity. He's trying to be nice about it but his voice is heavy with disappointment. "All the other wives were there."

The commandant's party. "Oh Charlie, I forgot!"

He sighs; our lives in Brevert are not what either of us expected. "You're so great-looking, I wanted the commandant to *meet* you."

"I was coming, I was, but then . . ."

"Everybody was asking for you. Swede, Rebel, Jay."

"I had to go to the hospital, emergency."

"You look all right to me."

"Suicide attempt." I'm trying hard to tell him more than just what happened, but it isn't getting through. "By the time I got done with the family I was too wrecked to remember any-thing."

Charlie is trying to keep it light, but he can't. "You were missed. The brass are starting to think I hallucinated you."

"I'm sorry, I couldn't leave the family."

I bring on the food; it is depressing, he eats without noticing what he's putting into his mouth.

It's more depressing, scraping the kids' plates into the sink. Three dishes and they wouldn't touch even one of them; I even gave them forks. They just pushed back their chairs and went outside to wait for the ice cream truck. Charlie follows me into the kitchen. "Is there a problem?"

"Do you think I'll ever make anything that these kids like?"

"Kids?" Charlie sounds faintly surprised. *What kids?*

"Your kids." ... *All the family I want ... oh, Charlie.* I don't tell him that tonight they ambushed me again. I didn't flinch so Rusty tried something new. I'm going to have to cut the bubble gum out of my hair. "Kids, you know. Patricia? Russell? Look like you, sleep in those cute bunk beds?"

"Oh, the kids," he says absently. "Don't sweat it, they'll get used to you."

"Great." He never asks if I can get used to them.

Then he surprises me. "Babe, you look like you could use a break. I'll find a woman to take care of the kids. Go to New York and go shopping. See your crazy friends."

"My friends?" So much has happened on StElene that I have a hard time remembering who those people were. I am staring into Dispos-al. "Why would I want to go without you?"

"You seem so ..." Charlie can't find the word. He scrubs his hair with his knuckles. "If only you and I could get some *time.* The thing is, things at the base are tight right now, I have to be on deck so many nights that I just thought . . . Look. Go have fun in the big city. Have drinks at Windows on the World, get a makeover, buy some pretty shoes. Take in a Broadway show," sweet, heedless Charlie says.

My God, don't you know me? Don't you know me at all? "Makeover? Take in a *show?*"

"Whatever. I know you miss New York."

Homesickness rattles through me like a summer storm and in seconds, clears out. I have StElene to go to, I have Reverdy hanging on my arrival; my old life means nothing to me now. "I can't."

"Come on, babe. It's on me." Charlie puts his arms around me from behind, looking over my shoulder into the sink; I can hear his words vibrating in my skull. "Put everything on my plastic." Generously, blindly, he blows it by adding. "OK, Mom?"

"Don't, Charlie." I am trying hard to tell him something.

"What?"

Funny how you don't necessarily want a thing until somebody tells you that you can't have it. Part of me is crumpling like tinfoil and I bark to counteract the pain. "Don't call me Mom."

He hugs me anyway. "Now I know you need to get out of here."

Anxiety flickers in my belly. And leave Reverdy behind? Spend hours at airport email kiosks trying to connect just so we could talk? Could I connect? What would Reverdy do if he came into my room on StElene and found me gone? What would he think? Something terrible could happen to our love. I am suddenly so panicky that I surprise myself. "I can't!"

Charlie frowns. "Jen, are you OK?"

"I'm fine, it's." I have a hard time getting it out. "It's just.

I can't leave right now. I have people depending on me."

"Oh," he says, "your patients."

"Right." Let Charlie think I mean my patients. I mean Reverdy and Lark; our lives are so tightly tied up that there's no undoing the knots; cut the skein and one of us will die.

"You'll remember that I offered," Charlie says. Then, just as I'm starting to feel guilty all over again, he moves on to the next thing on the list in his head. "So, if you're going to be here . . ."

"I am, Charlie. I'm going to be here."

And this is how this wonderful, inattentive guy my husband releases me. "Do you think you could get Rusty a date with an orthodontist? He needs braces but Nelda never got around to it."

It's finally deep night in the thirties stucco on Church Street, which Jenny thinks of as Charlie's house. There's nothing of her here. For her, it's just a staging area. Charlie's living room is dominated by his Chinese rug, his mother's jade chrysanthemums, the chow bench he bought in Honolulu. Pots and pans from his first marriage fill the kitchen. The closets are crowded with Charlie's things and his kids are in every room. Wherever Jenny goes, they are. Big-boned, unconscious Charlie takes up more than his share of the king-sized bed, turning that well-muscled back to her, sleeping in absolute peace. He's kicked all his unwanted covers into a heap on Jenny's side, crowding her out. Across the hall, Charlie's resentful children are snuffling into their pillows. Even in sleep they occupy a tremendous psychic space.

This house contains nothing of her, but when Jenny Wilder tiptoes upstairs and closes herself into the third-floor room and turns on the computer, her perspective changes. She changes. She is going to her place. Silent. Secure. Hers alone.

In seconds she's connected to StElene. She sees: StElene is . . . She doesn't need to read the opening statement of purpose; she has it by heart. . . . philosophical experiment in international communication.

Is that really why I'm here? Is it why any of us is really here? She loves the incantatory tone, she loves the sense that she is one of the elite—smart and tough and funny and flexible enough to make her way on a plane far above the one where ordinary people spin out their ordinary lives.

Most people stay trapped inside bodies and behind faces, rooted in what Reverdy calls "physical life." Who wouldn't rather be here? What Jenny can't understand is how this got to be more real than the patient in the hospital, the kids downstairs, the husband in his car, driving away to the base. With her palms hot and her mouth tight she types:

co for CONNECT *zan* and then she types in her password: *lalation*

And is in her room on StElene. *Zan's Tower.* Her place, where no one comes uninvited. She built it herself. In a way, it is the only place she has.

```
Zan's Tower is a bright, airy space at the top of
the GrandHotel StElene. Moonlight streams in
through long windows and soft Caribbean breezes
lift gauzy mauve curtains in this lovely plant-
filled room with its silken pillows and Aubusson
rug. In this peaceful place where souls can fuse
and become one life is sweet and peaceful. Outside,
the moon's reflection strikes the water in glit-
tering points. Sapphire is here.
```

Sapphire. The sleek leopard Zan programmed to do a few tricks and then set aside, one more decorative object in this lovely room. The room description comes up like a mantra, soothing and expected.

But there is extra text on her screen. An intrusion.

`Mireya is here.`

Violated, she shudders. Reverdy's ex-lover. Here. "Mireya!"

"I have to talk to you."

"No."

"You have to listen," Mireya says.

"Why, when I know you hate me?" Reverdy laid it out for Zan when they became lovers. "You'd better know, I have enemies here. Grave enemies." Mireya and Reverdy hate each other with the ferocity peculiar to ex-lovers. Reverdy hints at a bitter betrayal, but betrayals in this compressed space are tricky, and even though Zan has tried to get to the truth of it, truth in this new dimension is elusive too. She knows it was ugly and that at the end, they fought like tigers. Still do. And even though Mireya's with macho Azeath now, she harangues and posts poisonous attacks to a dozen lists because she wants more than anything to bring Reverdy down. She won't quit until she has him erased from StElene. And Reverdy? He still isn't over it. It bothers Zan, that he knows each injury by name; he doesn't just number them, he dwells. "It's all lies."

"What makes you so damn sure?"

"How did you get in?"

"What do you care? I have ways." She does. An adept programmer, she's been on StElene four years, rallying people against Reverdy. She can thwart any security system. Except Reverdy's.

God, Zan thinks, *I should leave now, before she has a chance to poison the well.*

page Reverdy Where are you?

"I know you're trying to page him," Mireya says. "And you know as well as I do that he isn't here."

"He'd do anything to avoid you." If only she could phone him! It's Mireya's fault that Reverdy won't tell her how to get in touch with him offline. This is grave: *Understand, I am protecting both of us.* He has Jenny Wilder's phone number and street address but she doesn't even know where in the West he lives. She dreams of opening her queue one morning and finding an email from Reverdy or picking up the phone and hearing his voice, but it's impossible, he won't do anything to give away his location, not even to her. He refuses even to take a numbered post office box and it's all Mireya's fault. "You know how he feels about you."

Mireya scowls. "My point. Now, are you going to listen or what?"

"Leave or I'll disconnect." Time and again, Reverdy has rehearsed it—how with one careless, loving gesture, he let trouble out of the box and into the house where he lives. It almost ruined his life. The bitch almost wrecked him IRL. His fault: he thought it was real love. He and Mireya exchanged real names. She wanted more. Just tokens, she said. Tokens of love. Little things. His phone number, a gift in earnest. His address. Reverdy's fatal error was giving them. She started calling the house.

The words pop onto her screen like bullets. "Are you that scared of what I'm going to say?"

"I'm not afraid of anything. Now, go." Their breakup was uglier than divorce. Mireya took revenge out of StElene and into Reverdy's daytime life. She got on the phone. She called day and night with her sordid accusations. If Reverdy answered, she clicked off. The most disgusting bits, she saved for his children.

The sexiest, she told his wife. The most damaging, she gave to his employers—he damn near lost his job! He unlisted the phone, too late. The damage was done. Letters came. Packages. A bloody skirt. Muddy bikini underpants. Mireya poisoned his wife with lies. ("Zan, she had Louise so crazy with suspicion that I almost lost my kids! Mireya's insane," he warns. "She'd do anything to hurt me. Anything.") *My poor dear!* If only they could talk! It's killing her. She'd give anything to see him, to run her hands over that craggy face and make him smile. She just knows he's handsome, in that dark, brooding way, even though he swears he has the kind of face that stops trucks. She doesn't know why his pain is such an overwhelming aphrodisiac, but it is. All she thinks about is meeting him RL. What they have is fated. Unlike Charlie, he understands her. He knows her straight through to the center; he knows she's the only person alive who can make him happy. If only they could meet! And she can't even phone!

"I won't go until you hear me out." Mireya is bulging with secrets, hot to tell Zan all the things a new lover doesn't necessarily want to hear but is dying to know.

"I don't have to be here." But she does. Perhaps because from childhood she's been taught to believe everything she reads, Zan is a little intimidated by Mireya's terrible beauty, the authoritative way she raps out speeches that insist on being read.

The description alone is commanding:

`Beautiful Mireya is slender and elegant but strong . . .`

It goes on from there. Now, life in electronic space is not fixed, it's fluid. Accounts and interpretations vary, which means that Zan has no way of knowing whether what Mireya types about herself is truth or wish fulfillment. What she does know is that in this society built on compression, emotions get huge.

There's a command Zan can type to get her angry rival out of her quarters. She enters it. Nothing happens. She is reduced to shouting. "GO!"

Mireya sneers. "I won't move and you can't move me. You might as well shut up and listen. You'll thank me for this later, they always do, you know we're not the only women who . . . Your sweet, sacred Reverdy . . ."

"Lies!"

Mireya says craftily, "What makes you so sure I'm lying?"

"I know what you're like, Mireya. He's told me all about you."

"I bet he has," Mireya says sourly. "What makes you think he's telling the truth?" Then, surprise, she adds conversationally, "You know, if it hadn't been for you, Reverdy and I would still be together. I bet you didn't know he and I were meeting RL."

"In real life!" *So she* is *crazy,* Zan thinks. Relieved, she says what Reverdy would want her to say. "After what you did to him? No way!"

Then these words come up on her screen: Mireya [to Zan] "I dropped the bastard because he was two-timing me with you."

"That isn't true."

"You think." Mireya laughs. "Do you really believe what he says? Poor bitch!"

"Shut up." If Zan flees, Mireya will follow. If she disconnects, she'll lose Reverdy for the night. She types: *page Reverdy Help!* The display comes up: Reverdy is not connected.

"He's done terrible things here, that you don't even know about. Sedition. Harassment. Baiting these poor people who . . ." Mireya doesn't finish. "I'm getting up a bill of particulars. Pretty soon all thirteen Directors will have it in their queues. Want to know what your lover does when you're not around?"

"Don't even try. Reverdy's warned me about you."

"And you believe him?" The woman won't quit. "Do you really think you're the only girl in his life right now? Ever?"

"Enough!"*Reverdy?* Hopelessly, Zan types:

@find reverdy

The display comes up just as she knew it would:

```
Reverdy The Dak Bungalow last disconnect 4/18
                3:36 a.m.PST
```

"Go away!"

"No," Mireya says. "We're not done. Want to hear the truth about this lover of yours?"

"No!"

"Then you're a fool. A double fool. Refusing my pages. Returning my posts. I have *things* to tell you. Important things."

Then just as Mireya's about to overwhelm her, Lark comes. Like a superhero, he glides in on silver boots. "STOP THAT!"

```
Lark stands before you clothed in silver. Look
closely and you may see wings at his heels. He is
swifter than lightning and impervious, as if he is
made of something more precious than platinum, but
try and touch him and he will vanish because his
powers make him lighter than air. The costume is a
little silly, but it covers a noble heart. He is
laughing.
```

Hug Lark. It is a relief to see him. "Lark!"

"Get out," Mireya growls. "This is private."

"Not any more. You're leaving," Lark says. He types a string that moves Mireya out of the room.

Cool, Jenny thinks, sitting at her computer laughing in relief. Bizarre, how real this is. She gives herself a little shake, caught for the moment between two worlds. *If only I could move people around like that* RL. Get the kids out of the living room when they start fighting. Move Charlie back from Pendleton or Cherry Point or wherever the Marine Corps takes him when I need him most. Takes him in spite of the fact that we got married so we could be together. In Zan's airy tower on StElene, Lark is grinning too.

Hug Lark. "Thanks!"

Lark hugs Zan. "My pleasure."

"How did you do that?" She laughs. "You vanished her!"

"Little trick I know," Lark says. "When I logged on and saw she was here I knew she was getting in your face. My pleasure."

"I couldn't budge her." It is a programmatic trick Zan hasn't mastered. "Show me how?"

"Happy to. Just copy this verb from me. Then you can type @*qmove . . .* " He walks her through the simple formula.

Cut and paste. She downloads the information and stores it for later. "Mireya. Where'd you put her?"

"Volcano bowl," Lark says with the delight of a committed programmer. "My friend LavaKing's coded a crypt. The Directors liked it, so they jiggered it, which means it's extra diabolical. It'll take her hours to get out and before she does . . ." Lark grins. "I'll beef up your security."

There is a lapse in communication that tells her Lark is typing in extra strings of code to enhance security in her room. Imagine being able to type in a predictable sunrise and moonfall, in your so-called real world, a string that will admit your friends and exclude your enemies. The kid is adding messages that will make it clear to intruders that this is Zan's private space. *My*

God, Jenny thinks, unless it is Zan thinking. *It really is a game.* "Brilliant," Zan says.

"It's nothing." Lark beams. Swashbuckling in the silver superhero costume he's written for himself, Lark bristles with technical competence. The archetypal, volatile programmer, living out fantasies in a world where he has complete mastery and control. His skill takes him a long way on StElene but does nothing for his life outside the box. He's nineteen! When he disconnects, Lark has told her in confidence, he's barely functional. Living people terrify him. He can't look at them! After the breakdown that put him in the hospital his folks insulated a room in their basement, remote enough to let them ignore his weird habits and crazy hours, close enough so they can keep the lid on him. Then there's his life here. Gawky and pathologically shy at home, he's a charming swashbuckler here.

In the game. Which is so *not* a game. "Where's Reverdy?"

"He's been delayed. That's what he sent me to tell you. To beg you to wait." Then, right here in Zan's place, Lark loses it. He blurts, "Oh look, Zan. I'm in awful trouble, RL." In real life.

"The parents, I bet." *It's interesting,* she thinks. *We are who we want to be here, but we're ourselves, too.* She and Lark are close. He opens up to her, dropping the mask so she can see into his misery. It may be because she listens and tries to say the right things. And because he trusts her, because on StElene people love to talk about themselves, Lark tells her everything. Not the first time here that Zan/Jenny has done a little vigilante therapy and watched him bloom. And that's a rush: *working with somebody I can actually help.* They pick up in mid-conversation. "You tried my trick for getting used to people but it didn't work?"

"It worked, but only for a while. I'm so afraid they'll yell! I'm scared all the time now, and this. This is *so bad.*"

"Oh, Lark. What is it?"

"It's nothing. It's . . ." He can't quite tell her. "I'm cool."

"Is it the parents?"

"Again. Geez, Zan, they are so awful. If it wasn't for you and Rev . . ." He's cool, but he isn't. He blurts: "Dad said that he's sorry they ever had me."

Hug Lark. "That's terrible."

He responds with extraordinary sweetness, "It's my life."

That isn't a life. In fact, Lark's real life is here. Zan has never seen him RL but has a picture in her mind: tentative Dickensian waif in a baggy sweater, sleeves hanging to the fingertips and turtleneck pulled up to his chin. "Oh Lark," she says and because she will do anything to support him she rushes on; unlike Amanda Yerkes, this is somebody she can help. The therapist in her knows not to make promises, but this is Zan, too, and impulsively, she says, "Reverdy and I can't change your life but you know we love you, Lark, and I promise, we'll take care of you."

@ten

MIREYA

In miserably cold Boston, where the lonely typist who calls herself Mireya connects to StElene, snowy drizzle has turned into sleet. The night air is damp and soft in Brevert, South Carolina, where Jenny Wilder lies next to Charlie, feeling too guilty and frustrated and wired to sleep. More than a thousand miles separate the two women, but their lives are about to intersect.

If Zan should type look at Mireya, this is what she'd see:
Mireya is slender and elegant but strong, with waist-length blonde hair and a tan that doesn't stop at the bikini line. Her warm, sexy laugh makes you love her and when she talks the talk, you will follow her anywhere. Color her gorgeous. Your dream woman is here in the room with you, and if you treat her right, you can share the dream. She is capable of great pleasure and amazing insight. Share your hopes with her and she'll take you places you've never been before, but be warned. The pikes

on the walls of the fortress are lined with the
skulls of Mireya's enemies. Details? Feel free to
ask.

    Carrying:

    Love song from Azeath

    Magic wand

    Mireya's cantos

    Locket of revenge: you know who you are

In real life this typist, who spends too much of her conscious time on StElene, holds none of these things. In her life outside the box, people don't give this woman a lot of presents. In the movie of her life this person is the homely girlfriend whose function is to make a fuss over the presents men give her gorgeous best friend—except she doesn't have a best friend, IRL.

Nor is she any kind of beautiful in spite of the description she has so carefully crafted. In real life she is five foot two if she stands tall and, admit it, she carries a few more pounds than she should, she's relentlessly *plain,* no matter how pleasantly she smiles at you. Look closer and you'll see rage boiling behind the mask. It's not Mireya's fault that she got trapped inside this stupid body. Her soul is a lot thinner. The hell of it is, the outside's the first thing men notice. It takes a special kind of guy to get past the externals and love a woman for herself.

Mireya isn't her real name either. Her name is Florence Vito Watson. She got Watson from ex-husband Harry. She's thinking of getting it changed legally, no firsts, no lasts, just Mireya, the glam. As if that would make the difference. She's still trapped. Rather: she was trapped, until StElene. StElene has turned the ex-Florence into an escape artist, witty and clever. Glamorous.

On StElene you see what Mireya wants you to. She can break your heart or rip your head off, whichever is her pleasure.

Stuck with a one-year contract teaching English in a suburban junior college, Florence is too good for what she does. On StElene her skill with words takes her a lot farther. In a society built at lightspeed, the fastest typist wins the game. See Florence on the street and pass her without noticing. On StElene, Mireya turns heads.

This is the power of life in imaginary space. Even Reverdy, who knows Mireya all too well—even Reverdy thinks she's beautiful. No wonder logging off is like a little death.

The minutes Florence has to spend offline—eating, sleeping, dealing with students, at the fucking Laundromat—stretch like lifetimes. Off StElene her life is marginal at best. She is miserably in transition. Out of her marriage. About to be out of a job. She is freshly divorced from Harry, who is a full professor at the state university and never lets her forget it. Midterms are in—a million papers to grade—and a sticky wet snow is falling.

No wonder she's glued to her computer, shaking with anticipation. Zan's gone from StElene by this time. If she can be alone with Reverdy . . . Florence/Mireya is logging on from a city miles away from the house where Jenny Wilder sleeps, but their lives have overlapped. In real life, Florence Vito Watson seems soft-spoken and accommodating, but she is a passive-aggressive, so watch out for her. Jenny doesn't know it yet, but Zan is in danger.

Mireya has just connected when the office phone bleats. Frustrated, Florence barks: "What!!!" As on StElene, her lover Azeath greets her with a passionate hug. "What do you want Harry," she shouts. "Why are you calling me in the middle of the night?"

"Don't bite my head off," her ex-husband growls.

On her screen, Azeath's words dance. *"I died waiting for you."*

She types: "*Darling.*"

She also types: @*find Reverdy*

Harry says, "Cynthia wants to know when you're coming to pick up the rest of your stuff."

So her heart breaks all over again. Poor Florence tries to sound angry instead of shocked and hurt, which is what she is. And vulnerable. "My stuff! Your new popsy wants to get rid of my stuff?" She hears Cynthia flapping in the background, feeding Harry his lines.

"Wait a damn minute," Harry says.

Azeath senses the trouble RL. "*Are you all right?*"

She yells, "Isn't it enough that she made you get rid of me?"

As she types to Az, "*Thank you for caring. I can handle it.*"

Harry's voice, when he figures out how to respond, is surprisingly gentle. "Cynnie just wanted to be sure she was out when you came to get it, is all. Spare you the encounter."

"*It's that bastard Harry.*" Azeath types. "*Right?*"

Simmering, she types, "*It's that bastard Harry.*"

"Spare me. Yeah right," Florence says bitterly. "And you called me to tell me this in the middle of the night?"

Harry says, "Cynnie was worried. She cares about you."

"She what?" Furious, she glances at the screen.

Azeath is saying, "*Dearest. Be cool. At least I'm getting rid of Reverdy. I'd do anything for you.*"

Getting rid of Reverdy! Her heart lurches. "*No. Wait!*" Juggling both conversations, she types as she roars into the phone: "Fuck you, Harry, don't you know I'm loved?"

Azeath types, "*Bastard. I can hurt him bad. I'll make him pay.*" Does he mean Reverdy or Harry?

Wounded, Harry whines, "Cynnie is a caring person, OK? She just thinks having your things here isn't so good for the ..." There is a pause; he says suspiciously, "Are you keyboarding?"

Unexpected anger flashes. "Well, fuck Cynthia. I'll get my stuff when I fucking well feel like it. She can wait until she rots." Florence slams down the phone.

Azeath has typed: "*And Harry. I'll take care of Harry* RL."

She types: "*I can take care of myself, thanks, Az.*" And Mireya disappears deep in life on StElene. Dissembling, she asks Azeath to wait while she does a little electronic housekeeping. He has to quit at eleven. Mysteriously, her handsome lover logs off at eleven every night. Eleven p.m. on the button, sometimes in midsentence. She could write the Directors later, but in the lexicon of revenge, sooner is better. She gets off four quick mails to the Directors accusing Reverdy of things even Reverdy would never do. There is the harassment issue, for one. She's developing grounds. She posts toxic stories about him on public lists. This is designed to push Reverdy to rage, which is where she wants him.

Outside, the wet snow splats against her office window in the thickening night. Hundreds of uncorrected exams pile up on her desk and spill onto the floor. The cubicle where Florence sits is filled with the stale residue of student farts and tears and sighs and complaints that have piled up in here for decades and will not dissipate. It's like being pressed to the bottom of the ocean; escape, Florence, before you're crushed under the weight of other people's miseries. *Hurry!* "Az," she types. "It's time. Let's make love."

"Yes," he says. "Yes my darling! I touch you *there*."

She says, "Aaaahhh . . ." And the whole time, she is thinking about Reverdy. She'll never forgive him for dropping her, but Mireya gets hers. Here's Azeath typing clumsy, passionate words of love that sort of work plus she has something going with the mysterious player Chaplin, who Azeath doesn't know about, and there's the arousing pleasure of being in hate with

Reverdy. *Anybody who hates me that much is still secretly in love with me.*

Reverdy was Mireya's first love on StElene, and in the way of first things, the wildest and best. In the same week that she caught Harry with a raunchy little *student* (Cynthia's just the latest in a series of skinny college girls), she found StElene. She'd fight with Harry and then log on and take out her aggressions on some unwitting guest. Quick as a wasp and more poisonous, Mireya loves to lay waste and pillage on StElene, typing barbed insults; she knows how to wreck people and make them cry. Pissed at Harry, she could get her rocks off by roaring through the GrandHotel, hunting down the vulnerable. She can take a person apart, word by word. OK, she gets off on it.

In their final face-to-face, the fight that ended the marriage, Harry said, "I'm sick of living with a hobbit. If you can't lose weight, at least shave your damn legs." She wanted to tear Harry apart but she was sobbing too hard. Instead she locked herself in her office and logged on: *take it out on somebody here.*

Instead she met Reverdy. Shot a barb at him and discovered she'd met her match. StElene was brand new in those days; they were both new to it. She tried to make him angry; he managed to make her laugh. It was his description that seduced her in the long run, forget Schwarzenegger biceps and action-hero capes. It was beautifully simple: *Reverdy is not what he seems.* Yes!

Her mind filled in the blanks. It was love! Understand, the man in your mind is always a better lover than the man in your bed.

Their first night together she repeated, "Reverdy is not what he seems?"

"Exactly." Even his smile was mysterious.

"So you are who I think you are." She corrected herself. Mireya is not stupid. "I mean, you are whoever I think?"

"You're very quick." He laughed. Then he delivered the clincher. "I admire that. But remember. *Reverdy is not what he seems.*"

"I don't care!" Flirting with danger, Mireya almost told the truth. "Neither am I."

But Reverdy had already found her deepest place. "Do you know what drew me to you?"

"No, what?"

"Your intelligence."

Bingo. It was glorious. Breaking up with Harry had turned her days into shit. Her nights were something else.

Their love was perfect for her at the time. "I don't care what you look like," Reverdy told her, "you'll always be beautiful to me. And besides—" this is how close they were. He admitted, "You wouldn't want to meet me in a dark alley. I'm a little scary looking myself."

Mireya imagined him as the Beast, magnificently craggy— what was it the French called a massively ugly person—*beau laid*. She confessed, "OK, I'm kind of short, truth to tell. And my eyes are ..." She couldn't bring herself to admit her eyes are too small in this fat face.

"But you're beautiful inside." He left her smiling, smiling! "We are both beautiful inside."

They began by quoting poetry and ended exploring the nature of love. *It's philosophical,* Florence—no, Mireya—told herself. *Simply philosophical. We aren't even touching.* Except the talk slid into talk of sex that somehow mysteriously turned into sex of an odd but powerful kind, and in the strange intimacy of a space where they are unseen she and Reverdy grew ravenous and devoured each other, word by word.

Understand how this happens. At some point in their early conversations, after they have learned all they care to tell each other about themselves, he says, "I set my fingertip in the hollow just below your ear."

Miles away, she shivers, imagining his delicate touch. It is more immediate than anything in the room where she types. She responds, "I lean into your hand and press my face into your palm." Framing a wish, she makes it come true.

They are both breathing faster.

Anticipation. This love is perfect because it's all about anticipation. The lovers vibrate, shimmering at the brink of things to come. Everything is in the future. This powerful love affair built out of words.

He says, "Every one of us is an island, yes, but with you, I feel less isolated. If only we could . . ."

She says, "We see the best parts of each other."

"The essence. Work with me and we can make it fuse."

"If only I could be with you."

"You are."

Reverdy and Mireya are both extremely good writers. Lesser lovers type pornography at each other. It is cheap and heavy-handed. But experts can make words stand for much, much more than face value. When the lovers are finished for the time being, tremulous and shaky, she asks him the most intimate question of all. "What does the room look like that you're typing from?"

Her lover says, "I can't tell you that. I don't know you well enough to tell you that."

"You know me better than anyone."

"You only think so. Darling. And because you are my darling I'm going to remind you. Look at me." Reverdy used to tell Mireya this. When they finished he would leave her with the reminder, *Reverdy is not what he seems.*

It was wonderful. They were wonderful. Until.

Until he betrayed her, just like fucking Harry with his fucking size-four post-teen popsy. She caught Reverdy with Velvet. All right, she spied. If she'd only logged off and trusted the man, she'd never have found out. Instead she logged back on after saying good night and caught the two of them together. Another woman! Her exclusive love! So it was Velvet, not Zan, who took Reverdy away from her, although Velvet tried to poison the well by implicating Zan. Mireya stuck it to him. Reverdy accused her of spying. She gave him hell for being unfaithful. He said, "You sound like my wife." Livid, she attacked: "I AM YOUR LOVER, AND DON'T YOU FORGET IT! I'M NOT ANYBODY'S WIFE!" Once they began to fight they couldn't quit. Mireya logged on day and night in a frenzy of jealousy, typing, *@find Reverdy, @find Reverdy*, and even though she never again caught him with Velvet, they fought. They fought.

Poor Florence pinned everything on him. Everything. Exposed herself in all her weakness. He knew all her soft spots and he hit them every time, hitting until she was ragged and weeping at the keyboard and in real life, but they were still in love. They were! Then she made her big mistake. OK, she phoned his house. She spoke to the wife. She moved into the man's physical world and he'll never forgive her. They made love one last time and then fought to the finish and kept on fighting; they can't get enough!

Now Mireya is with Azeath. Azeath walked in on one of their bitterest fights, saw the words burning themselves into the screen and did the right thing. He leapt to her defense. Az is a hunk, he's handsome, she loves having a defender. Awkward with words, but what isn't to love? Still. Az says he hates Reverdy for the way he treated her, but there's more.

He hates Reverdy for being smarter. Quicker. For writing better and making fun of him. And Azeath has a temper. Reverdy kited a post into his online enemy's everyday offline world and it is this that Azeath will never forgive him. "I'll kill him," Az says, without explaining to Mireya where his physcial life spins itself out or how Reverdy's post has affected it. "Even if he doesn't tell you where I am."

She can't ask her ex-lover. He'll only torture her by not telling. Mireya prompts, "You are . . ."

"In trouble with some people," Azeath says significantly. He's feeding on her interest. "If you love me, don't ask."

OK, she has a weakness for men who aren't necessarily good.

And Reverdy? Reverdy's been with a dozen women since their colossal breakup, nobody important, Mireya knows. Until Zan.

Until Zan came along, Mireya had hopes. Zan ruined everything. Mireya thought Reverdy would get tired of his cyberbimbos, he'd see how superficial they were, how brittle and stupid, and he'd come back to her. No more. It's over. All because of Zan.

Her one great love has gone sour.

Well, Mireya has soured too. She tried to warn Zan about the bastard and what did she get? Insulted. Thrown out. *If Reverdy wants me to know, he'll tell me.* Doesn't the bitch want the truth?

I'll show her, Florence thinks, furious. *I'll get her out of my life.*

Zan doesn't know it, but she has a mortal enemy. And she'll know it soon enough. Mireya won't just finish her on StElene. She's going to step out of the box and do something conclusive to the bitch in her actual space. Learn her name. Find out where she lives. Go there.

Ruin her life.

eleven/@eleven

JENNY/ZAN

How do you fall in love with a man in a place you know by heart but that exists in what is, essentially, ether? Fast, because you think you'll never see him. It happens in an instant. Snap. Like that. Sex is one thing; true love is another. He lives halfway across the world; there are a million electronic seekers out there and yet you find each other.

As if it is fated.

You can't see him so there's nothing to make you hesitate, or reconsider. You fall into each other's minds. It's like plunging into a volcano, brilliant.

You think you'll never meet him. The miracle is that you don't need to see him, what you have together is perfect. Then you understand you'll die if you don't see him, so go figure.

How do you fall in love with a man you've never met? Like this.

The first thing Reverdy said to me was, "Are you all right?"

I was sitting in Brevert, South Carolina, with my mouth filling up with tears, he was typing from God knows where and we were *so close;* it was astounding. He knew me! I said, "Does it show?"

"It's OK." He was astonishingly sweet with me. "There are a lot of unhappy people here."

It was the week after we moved to Brevert. I married Charlie so we could stay close and he was already leaving. I'd made lamb vindaloo, but his promises were like air kisses, empty gestures. He was just back from Cherry Point. He sauntered in whistling, after we hugged he said in that absentminded way of his, "I thought you'd have me packed."

I covered the lamb he wouldn't have time to eat. "Packed? For what?"

"For Washington. Oh honey, didn't I tell you? I know I just got back but I have to go to DC." He put his arms around me and I let him move me upstairs; I touched his cheek. When our bodies moved together like that I could convince myself that the kids were no problem really, Charlie and I fit so well that we can make it through anything, but his mind was somewhere else. He pulled out a bag; it was not the weekender. "Something's come up. My aide was supposed to phone and give you the word."

"Your aide!"

"I have to do some stuff at the Pentagon. It's important."

Just when I thought we were . . . "Oh, Charlie! How long?"

"Three weeks. You'll be fine."

"Three weeks!" I grabbed some things and threw them in on top of his. Clothes. Jewelry. Underwear.

"What's that about?"

"I can't do without you for three weeks, Charlie." I was thinking, if I could only get this man alone in some hotel, I mean really alone, if we could have just a few hours to ourselves without those needy kids of his . . . "I'm coming."

"Oh, babe, you can't." He was already unpacking my things—regretful, maybe, but firm. *No way.* This is how the man I thought I knew put me in my place for good and all. He ran his hands down my arms with a sad, sweet smile. "What would we do with the kids?"

"The kids? A sitter?" I was too hurt to see what was coming.

"It's too soon." He was already shaking his head. "If you could just hold the fort for me?"

There are things you never say because you know they'll undo a marriage. I did not say: *Is that why you married me?* I said, "Oh Charlie, I miss you already."

The kids behaved right up until Charlie's plane took off. Then they grew fangs. Rusty set his action figures on fire and jammed all of Patsy's Barbies into the flowerbed head down. Patsy threw a book at him but it hit me and she bawled. I thought about how they must be missing their mother and I said, "It's OK, he'll be back."

Rusty snarled, "What do you care?" It was embarrassing, they were about to see me cry, poor kids, lost their mom and now this, we should be bonding and we can't. Try. He was sweaty and struggling but I grabbed him, in the striped T-shirt he was like a fat, cranky bug.

"I know just how you feel." I reached for Patsy, thinking we'd all feel better if we hugged. I meant, I would feel better if I could only get a hug.

"What are you *doing*?" Rusty squawked. "Cut it out!"

"I just."

Patsy knuckled me in the breast. "Let *go!*"

"So, what." *Never let them see you cry.* "Is this war?" It took a while to talk them down. Did I really hear, "Wicked stepmother"? It took hours to get them to bed. By that time I was too wired to sleep. I went upstairs to Charlie's computer. I did what you do when you're miserable, I loaded Netscape and started clicking around on the World Wide Web. The funny thing about netsurfing is, it gives you the illusion that something is just about to happen. I wasn't looking for sex sites, I wasn't looking for anything in particular, I just wanted to take my mind off hurting for a while.

OK, I sent the search engine after entries under "excitement." You can imagine. Ads for services you don't want to know about, home pages where a person could download porn or order leather underwear, hot spots for interactive sex sites, piercing, you name it, sites for people who liked being tied up. It was like a tour of the velvet underground, stuff you read about in abnormal psych. Sniffling, I clicked around until I hit the Suntum web page: this corporation was sponsoring an experimental community, it sounded pretentious but clean— "gathering place for high-level professionals and intellectuals from all over the world." Why not?

Text, it was just text. A change from the jumpy, bizarro graphics on the web. StElene was so *quiet.* It was like opening a book.

```
The name Guest is taken, so you will be Tourmaline_
Guest. You are blundering around in a dark vestibule.
It is littered with the luggage of transients and new
players checking into the GrandHotel StElene; you
are isolated here, alone in pitch darkness, al-
though you can hear others talking. This is where
you'll stay until you learn how to live in our so-
ciety. To learn more about how to get around, type
"House Rules." Just outside you hear a party going
on, but you have to learn before you can join it.
```

You are aware that there are others waiting here in
the dark. The island of StElene is unknown to you.
You won't know who you're talking to until you've
been here a while, so be careful what you say to
strangers. StElene is a party, but it's only as
good as what you bring to it.

My imagination did the rest.

The vestibule was jammed with people jabbering; dialog
scrolled up my screen so fast that I couldn't catch the tune. I
should have typed: *house rules* to find out what was going on
but I couldn't quit reading the conversation! It was like magic,
strangers I couldn't see were typing—no. *Talking* to each other;
I followed, speed-reading until I hit Mach 4 and began to hear
their voices. Instead of being alone in the room I was surrounded by talks—funny talk, stupid talk, snappy one-liners,
off-the-wall come-ons and cries for help.

I saw at least five separate conversations going on. I tuned
in on one that I liked—somebody named Jazzy (*Jazzy is ter-
minally frivolous. He looks so festive that you know you've gotta
dance*) said, "... shrinks have a name for people like that. Put a
fortune up their noses."

Wait a minute, I thought but did not say. I am a shrink.

LavaKing said, "Snow angels."

Stone_Guest said, "Or snow cones."

Brilliant said, "Snow business of mine."

Fearsome said, "Snow good. Here's who snows you,
shrinks!"

Hey, I'm a shrink. Words, that's all they were doing, playing
with words; it made me grin, even though I was home alone
typing and nobody could see. *Should I say I've met the enemy
and she is me?* Funny—I was completely protected, anonymous

—Nobody even noticed Tourmaline_Guest and I was still afraid of looking like a jerk. I was the new kid on the block—hot to play and scared to death of looking dumb.

"Do snow angels go to snow heaven?"

"You want heaven?" Jazzy laughs. "Azeath thinks heaven is life without Reverdy. Azeath even got him barred from here."

Fearsome said, "Barred from the vestibule?"

"Az said he was a bad influence. Said he was poisoning minds."

"The vestibule." Fearsome snorted. "Who the hell wants to be in the vestibule?"

Jazzy said to Fearsome, "You're here." <NUDGE>

"That's different."

"Yeah, right," Del said. "What are you, our resident internet stalker? <<grinnnn>> Fearsome, get a life!"

Granite_Guest said, per instructions, "Hello, I'm new here."

LavaKing *bubbles ominously.* "The thing is, when Reverdy gets his mind around people, he can make them do anything he wants. No wonder the Directors hate him."

Fearsome said, "Careful. Reverdy hears everything."

LavaKing said anyway, "He wants to overturn the government."

Wait a minute, I thought. This place has a government?

Granite_Guest said, "Isn't anybody going to talk to me?"

"Reverdy knows everything, too," Jazzy said. "If you're his friend, terrific, but if you're *not* . . . The man forgives, but he *never forgets.*"

"If you hate him, Jaz, why don't we just get him erased?"

"I don't hate him, I like the guy. It's Azeath who wants him erased."

I wanted to ask what Reverdy had done that was so bad, but I was afraid to speak.

Fearsome said, "Because he's a manipulative bastard?"

"Simpler than that. Azeath wants him off because Mireya told him that's what he wants. The guy is a dim bulb. Mireya's tool."

Granite_Guest said, "Can anybody hear me?"

"And what Mireya says, Az does. Leads him around by his . . ."

". . . Dick."

For the first time since Charlie left, I laughed. This mysterious setting, the rapid-fire talk were exciting. And there was this—what. Hint of intrigue. Just lurking there in the vestibule, I felt furtive, like a thief grabbing bits of other people's lives. Then I thought, *Why? I'm not hurting anything. I'm not even doing anything.* All this life! It was unfolding almost too fast for me, you bet I was excited, never saw anything like it, walk into the world's longest-running soap opera and *become* someone!

Del said, "Oh, Mireya, Mireya. Talk about your woman scorned. She's pissed because Reverdy dumped her. It's all about sex."

"Isn't everything?"

"Face it, StElene is about sex."

Jazzy was quick. "Depends on who you are."

"And what you come for."

"And Reverdy, what do you think Reverdy comes for?"

Fearsome said to Granite_Guest, "Too much spam in here. We can't hear ourselves think. Want to go someplace quiet?"

I thought *that* was interesting. Electronic singles bar?

Jazzy said, "Reverdy comes here for power. It's that simple. That's why they want him out."

"Because he tangles with the Directors? He's a damn hero."

"Or a spoiler. You choose."

Fearsome said to Granite_Guest, "I know a private place."
Granite_Guest disconnected.

The chorus went on. "The Directors move fast." "Forget Reverdy, Reverdy's over." "One more black mark and he's out on his ass."

Pebble_Guest said, "Anybody here from Australia?"

Anybody here from South Carolina? What if one of these people was really my patient, Rick Berringer? What would go on between us here? I was alone at Charlie's computer and at the same time I was surrounded. Connected. It was so immediate and so vital that all I wanted was to belong. Lives sprang up in front of me like figures in a pop-up book. *I'm not a voyeur, I'm a psychologist!* My inner watchdog bared its teeth in a sardonic grin. *Yeah, right.*

OK, I stayed because I couldn't *not* stay. One hour on StElene and I was deep in the neverending story. Hooked. This place I couldn't see but *could not stop reading* was huge, and it was real. I had walked into unfolding history, with its heroes and villains. This Reverdy. Who was he? Listening, I leaned in so close that I almost fell into the screen. I was like Alice with my nose pressed so tight to the looking glass that it fogged up, wondering what came next. Reverdy, I eavesdropped until a noise in the outside world distracted me and I looked up and it was dawn.

What was it exactly, that excited me? I wasn't sure. I slept badly and woke up wired. That morning I didn't hear what my patients said, I was too busy replaying dialog from StElene— funky, erratic and truer than anything that got said in Brevert that day. The second night Charlie was gone I logged on and typed "House Rules." I couldn't bear to miss the party in the vestibule so I printed the instructions to study at the office. Between patients, I learned what to type to get around on

StElene. Commands for "walking." Teleporting. Directing speech. Strings that would bring up information on other players—their descriptions, where they were on the island at a given time. How to build a room of my own—*no need, I'm just passing through.*

Still. Charlie was gone, I was only the sitter, what better did I have to do? Why not give his kids Happy Meals and park them in front of the TV, which is where they've made clear they'd rather be? I was starved for company. Maybe I missed my neurotic New Yorkers, maybe I missed adult conversation, maybe I just felt trapped. I went upstairs and logged on to StElene. It wasn't like walking into a movie, it was like going to live in one. Being unseen was liberating. Strangers typed in real time; their words took flight. I saw close friends, enemies and lovers gossiping and politicking. They made me laugh. Something big was happening.

I was damn well going to learn how to make it happen to me.

And if Charlie came home and found me typing? Too bad. "Can't talk," I'd say, "I'm busy." *Fair's fair,* I thought, *Charlie hasn't been straight with me. I deserve to have a secret or two.*

The fourth night Charlie was gone I dropped the kids at a movie and went home to StElene. I set a kitchen timer to remind me to log off in time to pick them up. Then I rushed them to bed, not caring that they shook off my hugs. I had to get back to the vestibule. I cranked up the nerve to speak. "Hello."

Somebody typed, "NEWBIE ALERT!"

Fearsome zoomed in on me like a singles bar smoothie. "We can't hear ourselves think i cn here. Want to go someplace quiet?"

Knowing the scam made me feel like an insider. "No thanks."

Jazzy said, "Smart guest." He smiled. "But if you're that smart, you won't stay a guest. You'll want to get a character and be one of us. Type @*commit*. And when you choose a name, get back in touch and I'll show you how to build a room." He was so nice that it made my mouth water. "I think we're going to be friends."

On the fifth day Charlie was gone, Suntum International mailed my registration number and password, I thanked them and promised to make them proud of me. I got the name I'd asked for. The Directors knew who Jenny Wilder was, but to the rest of the community I was a brand new person. Forget Jenny, who is easily hurt. Meet Zan.

ZAN

So on the fifth night Charlie was gone, Zan turned her back on Church Street and moved bag and baggage onto StElene. It was intense. What if she messed up and they laughed? What if the regulars found out how little she knew? Fat chance. They ignored her. Even after she found her way out into the elegant foyer, regular players came and went, oblivious. She might as well not be there at all.

W, she typed, to go *west,* into the grand ballroom. The beautifully described parquet, the crystal chandelier and vaulted ceiling dropped into her mind like a Japanese flower that blooms in water. The ballroom she built in her head was magnificent. And the company! Brilliant. It was like walking into a cocktail party in full cry, everybody talking at once. Speeches unfurled so fast that she couldn't follow. Threads overlapped at such a dazzling speed that she got high on the conversation: *In the grand ballroom there is always a party going on.*

Old friends took their brains out for a walk like pet show dogs: ("You really think you can establish the exact location of God with Zero Knowledge Proof?"

"You don't have to go through the city to prove you've been there, Devo. All you have to do is name an intersecting point.")

Three hackers with funky names were trashing Luddites everywhere ("If language and math are the two great logical systems, face it, code is the third,") while two builders swapped intricate Chinese recipes ("only a clod would use five spice powder in a red-cook because she was too cheap to go out for anise stars"); another group haggled over, what—the possibility of freedom within a society that needs rules to survive. ("Set the rules and you control the game. Yes hell the Director-proggers are holding the reins.") Jazzy was nowhere around.

The players were smart, they were funny and in the dizzying freedom of anonymity, they sounded like the most interesting people she'd never see.

Reverdy! His name kept coming up.

"Hello?" She typed the line suggested in House Rules. "I'm new here. Who's Reverdy?" Heedless, the regulars talked on.

"Oh," someone said coldly. "You are *sooo* new!"

People repeated the comic airline riff ("welcome to StElene. Your tray tables should be closed and your seat backs returned to an upright position . . .") while in a quiet corner, a flirtation went on—Fearsome and Basalt_Guest. House Rules said to type *look at Basalt_Guest* to see what people had written about themselves. This one read like a singles ad.

```
Basalt_Guest is long and lean and round in all the
right places. Her robe slips just a little, expos-
ing one shoulder and the pink tip of one breast. Are
```

you the right one for her? Page her if you want to
know her better.

Creepy. Jenny—no, Zan—felt maybe a little soiled, reading
it. But she couldn't stop watching as Fearsome asked questions
[Fearsome is tall, 6'2", dark, 26. Sinister, until
you get to know him]
and Basalt_Guest replied until in perfect concert, the couple disappeared. Zan was too new to know that she could type *find
Fearsome* to see where they'd gone. Voyeurism? You bet. The
combination of sex and politics was confusing. And who were
the bunch in the corner, arguing DOS versus Mac?

Reverdy's name surfaced in the text like a silver fish. Factions formed: pro Mireya. Pro Reverdy. Thunder said every experiment needed its gadfly. Without people like Reverdy to test
its motives, Suntum could turn StElene into a dictatorship.

Dictatorship? In an imaginary place? The idea was either
silly or exciting. Zan tried, "Dictatorship?"

They ignored her. Life just kept happening, multiple conversations running like parallel trains, that she wasn't on. It was
as if the new player Zan didn't exist for them. *Am I doing something wrong? Do I smell bad?* She might as well be stuck by the
front door on Front Street, waiting for Charlie to come back.
She tried: "*HELLO?*"

Mireya said crossly, "Don't yell."

Azeath: "If you don't know how to act here, don't be here."

It was humiliating. But she couldn't quit. Sitting with one
foot in Brevert, South Carolina and the other in StElene, Jenny
Wilder was lonely and isolated. *Not Jenny,* she reminded herself.
*Zan. New name so none of these internet stalkers I read about
will know who I am or how to find me and hurt me.*

Hurt me, they won't even talk to me!

Funny, how much you need to know to be at home in these electronic spaces. She'd forgotten what to type to quit. She was tempted to turn off the computer and walk away, but what if that was so wrong that they'd never let her come back? *This place is silly*, she told herself miserably, typing one thing after another to no effect. *Just a bunch of misfits playing games.*

Then Reverdy spoke. She saw:

"Reverdy says to you, 'I said, are you all right?' "

Startled, Zan mistyped. OK, it was a little creepy being noticed after all this being ignored; what if this player so many people loved to hate was a . . . She didn't know what if. She typed:

look at Reverdy The description he'd written for himself read,

Reverdy is not what he seems.

An odd description. Cerebral. *Is this all we are,* she wondered. *Descriptions popping up on a screen?*

"Oh my," Reverdy said after a couple of minutes in which Zan failed to speak and he learned everything there was to know about her within the game. "You really are new."

Moved by this fact that a player had spoken to her at all, flattered that it was he, she typed, "I'm so new that I don't know what I'm doing here." After a pause she typed, "What am I doing here?"

Reverdy laughed. "Exactly. It's existential. We're here to find out what we're doing here. It's the object of the game."

They were setting a rhythm. "And where is here?"

"Exactly where you think it is." He grinned. "It's all in your mind."

"You don't really believe that."

He said, "Another of those things I'm here to find out."

"Then you're not . . ."

"Like Fearsome? No. If you have a few minutes, let Dr. Frankenstein explain this place to you."

Nice. Fine, Zan thought. The life of the mind. It was like coming into the territory. Yes. Still, she hesitated.

He reassured her. "Remember, if you don't like what's happening, you can always disconnect." They went to the end of the dock to talk—a public area, nothing like Fearsome's lair. The turrets of the great hotel were at their backs. Reverdy indicated the gazebo where he'd brought her. "Like it?"

"It's beautiful."

"I built it. The dock and the gazebo are all mine."

"It's wonderful."

"Now let me show you a few things. How to have a private conversation, for one." Reverdy taught her what to type to say things only he could read. *page Reverdy* He warned, "Be careful what you say and do here. It's the first rule of the game."

Her heartbeat quickened; she felt altered, daring. "And we're here to find out the object of the game."

"You really are smart." He laughed. "Not too many people here understand that it's the central question. Everybody has a different answer. It's an analog, right? Yeah, we're put here to find out."

IRL. Jenny Wilder shivered. Zan said, "Kind of like life."

"Exactly like life. Think microcosm. It's what we are. The question is, *why* we are. What Suntum International is doing with us here. Thousands of us living inside a clever corporate design."

She said, "People say the corporation is out to get you."

His grin warmed her. "And you're quick, too. The Directors

know I'm closing on it. Whatever is the truth. Suntum's objective for StElene. It's clear they're manipulating us for profit. If it kills me I'm going to find out how."

"You mean they're using us?"

"I think so. I think they're designing an application they can use for . . . I don't know yet. Profit, certainly. That's another thing." Reverdy whispered, "They're manipulating us."

"That's ugly."

"I knew there was something special about you. It's the intelligence. Now listen. I'm about to tell you something important."

"Yes," Jenny said, unaccountably committed. No. Zan said. Brand new here, attentive and grave. "I'm listening."

"It's this. When you set the parameters of a society, you control what people are able to do within it." The resonance made Zan shiver. "See how everything's spelled out in House Rules. How to move, what you're allowed to build, what's done, what is *not* done. It's like sociologists who determine their results by the way they frame their quiz."

"Or psychologists, by which questions they ask."

He laughed. "Yes! Did you notice how much you had to tell Suntum to get a character? Your name and age and sex, your home address? That's only the beginning. It's a hop, skip and a jump for them to your credit ratings, medical history, what you buy at the store, which drugs. The Directors say StElene is a democracy, but it isn't. The corporation's running us like lab rats."

"Then why do you keep coming back?"

Reverdy grinned. "To see how far I can push the envelope."

"Why not just walk away?"

"Can't live without it."

Oh my God, what if he's crazy?

"Forget I said that. Look. If we let industry set the parameters for any society, even an electronic one, then pretty soon industry controls society. Somebody has to fight. And from within." Then he dropped in the phrase that reverberates, filling her thoughts. "Performative utterance. What we say—is. We, not Suntum, should be the ones who *say*."

"And the object of the game?"

"If it is a game. Too soon to tell. We can't just play without question."

She was falling in love with his mind. "Explain."

Which Reverdy did, spinning out his theory about Suntum, about the nature of electronic space and the art of manipulation, and when he had Zan riveted he said unexpectedly, "You're not very happy, are you?"

Sitting at a keyboard who knew how far away from this intelligent, wonderful friend she'd never met, Jenny Wilder was blindsided by tears of gratitude. "Does it show?"

"It takes one to know one," Reverdy said. Astonishingly, he offered a confidence in return. "My bed is pretty cold."

She jumped. "You too?" Amazing how close you get and how fast when there are no surfaces to stop you: expressions to deceive, tone of voice to distract. This flexible space is more personal than any secret place, more private than the confessional. Secrets shared in the dark are privileged, as if exchanged on a remote star. *Yes,* she thought, *it's safe. Let the feelings out.* "Oh Reverdy, you too?"

In the crashing intimacy of space, people will tell you amazing things. The stranger Zan suddenly knew to the bone confided, "If I leave Louise, I'll lose my children. I love them too much . . ."

"Oh Reverdy, I'm sorry."

"It's." He thought the better of it. Too soon to exchange

names, but too late for both of them, they'd fallen in love with each other's minds.

In the end they logged off because one of his children was crying in his sleep wherever Reverdy lived RL and Jenny had to feed Charlie's children and dress for work. Without the exigencies they would type forever, separated but mysteriously and forever linked. The day that followed that first night without sleep found Jenny jangling with excitement. She knew the object of the game! It was Reverdy. This wonderful new man who saw straight into her heart. She loved the intelligence, the trust that let him confess all his needs and the way he anticipated hers.

What the eyes can't see, the heart supplies. She fell in love with his mind. The rest followed. In time they exchanged real names to prove that Reverdy loves Zan on StElene but in his life, wherever he is living it, Tom Dearden loves Jenny Wilder too.

In the physical world, love is love. It feeds on itself until it runs out of fuel. Love in this invisible but very real space is love idealized. Perfect. In ideal love, there are no bad times and no misunderstandings. There is only expectation.

It's gotten so Zan prays for Jenny's days to end so she can be with Reverdy. When life disconnects them, she dies every minute that falls in between.

@twelve

ZAN

Jenny knows when Lark sends an e-mail to her IRL that it's an emergency. *hpinkney@udenver.edu* subject: *Showtime* If it was less than drastic, he'd wait for her to show up on StElene or as he puts it, snailmail her at home. This couldn't wait. He's kited his cry for help into what other people think of as the only *real life*.

Urgent. Big trouble. Have to talk. 10 p.m.?

She emails back:

StElene. My place, at 10.

When Zan and Reverdy first fell in love, Lark was a jealous third party. He and Reverdy bonded on his first day on StElene. Unlike Lark's rigid father Howard Pinkney the pragmatic businessman, Reverdy was playful and kind. Lark fixed on him like a navigator following a star.

Then Zan came and the configuration changed. Before she knew Lark she knew he was upset, lurking at the fringes of all their encounters, saying without having to say it, *Reverdy, look at me, look at me!* The first night she followed Reverdy into the

Dak Bungalow and he locked the door behind them, Lark grieved as if all his stars had gone out.

Zan could hear him outside calling, "Are you guys OK in there? Are you OK?" when what he meant was, *What are you doing in there?*

"Shh," Reverdy whispered, "ignore him and he'll go away."

"But he's your friend!"

"And you're more important than any friend."

"He needs you, Rev."

His next words made her go weak. "And I need you."

Even though she wanted nothing more than to be alone with Reverdy she said, "We can't just lock him out like this."

For the first time I touch you—here! He murmured into her neck, "It's just for now. I love you, and all that matters is now."

Zan trembled. She couldn't know why she felt so disturbed. She disengaged, saying, "Please. He's really upset. He needs you to go out and tell him it's OK." She meant, *I need you to tell us that what you and I are doing is OK.* And because Jenny Wilder has never been sure of this, Zan added, "It is, isn't it? OK?" How odd that she should let herself fall in love this way!

"OK?" Reverdy said gravely, "of course it's OK. What we say and do here belongs to us here. It's ours alone." Seeing how uncertain his new lover was in this new place in their online relationship, how deeply she needed to be reassured, Reverdy crooned to her, "We aren't hurting anybody. We aren't even being unfaithful."

"But we're . . ." It was so new, so strange, so strikingly sexual that she thought of Charlie and felt guilty. "What is this?"

"This is ours," Reverdy whispered, "ours alone. Nobody knows."

"But we're . . ." Zan was still waiting for some kind of benediction, which Reverdy freely gave.

"Not hurting anybody. In the perfect marriage of the minds, nobody gets hurt." He called to Lark. "Friend, five minutes. Trust us."

Zan thought, *five minutes?* She didn't know that when she replayed the dialog in her heart it would stretch like hours.

"I just wanted to make sure you were OK." Later, when Zan began to hear Lark's troubles like confessions and say just what he needed to feel better, Lark fell in love with them as a pair.

If a couple is really in love and completely happy it should be enough, but it never is. It's like furnishing a beautiful room. What you have is only beautiful to you for a time. You need to see it reflected in somebody else's eyes. A third person has to come in and envy you a little, and admire.

Every couple in love needs a mirror to prove its happiness. Lark is theirs.

Jenny excuses herself from the dinner table and goes to *Zan's Tower* to meet Lark at ten, as agreed. Charlie didn't come home until 9:45, kissed her absently and sat down at the place she had left for him. Her mind was on StElene and his was on his work. He tried to explain what had kept him at the base and she tried to understand, but she couldn't concentrate; she has Lark to take care of now. She put the warmed over casserole on a TV table for him and started upstairs. On the landing she looked back at Charlie with his sandy head bent under the light and thought: *Got to do something about that soon* and had no idea what she meant. She had promises to keep. She's needed here.

How long has she been here? In *Zan's Tower* the lacy curtains blow in the ocean breeze while Lark talks and talks without saying much. He wants Reverdy in place so he can tell them both at the same time. Waiting has left them strung taut. Because they've been hanging in space for several seconds with nothing new on the screen between them, Zan says, "OK, Lark, I don't know what's holding him up but I have to go soon. What's the matter?"

"OK," Lark says finally. "The 'rents have set a deadline. If I don't get out they're throwing me out."

"Are you OK?"

"Not really. It was the father. I have till Friday. He . . ."

"What set him off?"

"You don't want to know. If a person doesn't have anyplace to go, where does a person go?"

"I'm not sure. I'm exploring options." Jenny wants to say, *you could come and live with us,* but she's unsure. Lark's passions are more manageable at a distance. What's he really like? Abstracted, he's easy to see into and in the abstract, his problems seem soluble, but she can't guess how much physical space he occupies because they've never met in physical life. What would he be like living in her house, in 3-D and living color and carrying whatever baggage his parents have freighted him with? What would happen if she presented Charlie with this troubled, needy souvenir of her secret love, and how could she explain? *Patient of mine. I could tell Charlie he's a patient of mine, staying with us until he gets on his feet. Or say I hired him to babysit . . .* It'll never wash. Lark is Lark and Zan knows him through to the soul but he's part of a life so remote from Brevert and Charlie that she can't begin to build a bridge from Lark's offline life into hers. She does what she can. "I can send you startup money. First week's rent?"

"Nobody's going to rent a room to me. Not RL. People don't like me." This is not what he means. He can't say the rest.

"I'll write recommendations. Find you a job."

"I can't get a job because of the thing with the hospital."

"Ex–mental patient. Right. And your folks won't help . . ."

"Forget it, that's over."

"Oh, Lark! What about your big brothers?"

"They're twenty years older than me. They've got their own problems. Shit, I might as well go back to the ward."

"Don't even think that!"

Lark admits, "Look. It was about the fire in the kitchen."

"Fire!"

"Pretty much."

"God, what did you do?"

"It's kind of embarrassing."

He's just about to tell her when Reverdy comes. On StElene everybody multitasks. It is possible to hold a secret conversation with another person in the middle of a crowd. Because it's programmatically possible to do this while carrying on a public conversation, Reverdy is both talking to Lark and whispering to Zan. His speeches will show up on both Zan's and Lark's screens—the rest is directed to her alone. "Zan. Love . . . Hey, Lark!" At the same time he whispers, just to her, [Dearest! I can't stay!]

[Reverdy, oh my darling hello do you know how much I've missed you?]

Lark says, "Rev, terrible troubles at home."

[You know I love you and I can't stay and it's killing me!] Reverdy turns to Lark, "Problems?" even as he says privately [Trouble I can't talk about right now]. He is rushed, intent on other business. He tells them both, "I can't stay. Something's come up."

Zan flinches. [Lover, are you all right? What's happened? The project? Something with Louise? God, tell me it isn't Louise!]

Lark says, "Is it the Directors?"

Reverdy doesn't answer. "I have to go." [I can't tell you now. I'll explain when we're alone.]

[But when are we going to be alone?]

Lark may guess there is a private conversation going on, but he can't know. He says, "Look, Reverdy, I've got big troubles RL. Man, my folks are . . ."

"Lark's folks are kicking him . . ." Zan whispers, [Five minutes!]

[I don't even have five minutes.] Reverdy says to Lark, "Hang in, guy. We won't let it happen." He is quick and loving and distracted. He doesn't tell Zan what's come up that makes it so impossible to stay or which sector it's in—whether it's his unloving wife or one of the kids or trouble on his research project or a dispute with the Directors here. "Remember what I told you," he says to Lark. "What they say can hurt you but it won't kill you." He warms Zan with a secret caress. [I love you. Tomorrow.]

Lark cries, "Where am I going to go?"

[Tomorrow! I could die before then.]

[But you won't. You never do.] "Lark, I'll do what I said on the phone. I'll call the dean at your ex-college. Denver, right? I can pretend to be your dad, whatever. Make them promise you a room in the dorm. Can you handle living in a dorm again?"

Jealousy clenches a fist in Zan's belly. "You and Lark have talked on the phone?" If they have, they won't tell her. It's eating Jenny up, that she doesn't even know where Tom lives and Lark has spoken to him on the phone.

On StElene Lark brightens. "I could try. Would you? Call them?"

Zan puts it to him. [You've talked, RL? Lark has your home number and I don't?] She already knows this is a question

Reverdy will let pass. In the erratic world of telnet connections, Zan is never sure if tough questions get lost in space or overlooked or consciously ignored.

Her lover tells Lark, "If I say the right things, maybe we can get you reenrolled." It is Reverdy's pleasure to do favors. It's how Tom and Jenny met in the first place [Oh my God, Zan, I do love you!] "Then all we have to do is line up financial aid for you."

Jealously, she tries, [Maybe you and I should both go to see the poor kid. Work with him.]

[You know I can't.]

She can't let this stand. [From the Dak Bungalow Zan strokes your throat. "Some day . . ."]

[And some day my darling we'll have time . . .] He leaves her hanging on the promise.

This. This is what keeps her coming back. Things you can't say, but that you whisper. [Oh God, Tom. I wish we could be . . .]

While Lark describes the scene with his father, Zan and Reverdy make what they can of the moment, communicating in a privacy that is charged with romance.

[Together? But we are.]

[Forever. For real.]

[We're more together than Charlie and you or Louise and me. We're together in eternity!]

Interesting how a few words can make up for everything.

[And for eternity.]

[Exactly.] Everything.

Lark is saying, "You don't get it. The 'rents have set a hard deadline. The father wants me out of the house by Friday night."

Reverdy says, "Friday! Are you sure it isn't just a threat?"

"From what Lark says, they really mean it this time." Being

so close to the man she loves and not being able to get closer is the worst thing; the separations kill her. [You really can't stay?]

[I love you, but no.]

[Then I'm going to type @exit now because I can't do this. I can't be here and not be able to be alone with you; I love you too much and I can't.] It's late here in Zan's tower and it's getting late downstairs in Charlie's bed. She imagines she hears Charlie stirring, his breath filling the hallway and curling up the stairs. Soon it will be light. [I can't keep losing you. I hate goodbye.]

And as he and Lark talk, Reverdy invades all Zan's secret places, with his touch reaching all the way to Jenny, as soft and pervasive as smoke. [Neither can I. Dearest, I touch you here.] But he has responsibilities. On StElene her lover is everything to a lot of people. "Remember what I said last night. You'll be all right," he tells Lark. "Try doing what I said."

[Last night?]

"But what if it doesn't work?"

[You never told me you and Lark were here without me,] she whispers, betrayed.

"I'll make the call." Reverdy begs the question. [Tomorrow night, my dearest. And longer. Better! Same time.] "Lark, I've got stuff going on on RL but trust me, it's going to be OK."

[Tomorrow.] Because Lark is upset and depends on her, because Reverdy expects it, Zan says, "Lark if you need it, I can write a bangup letter to your college about what a terrific student you are. They have to believe me, I'm a shrink." [ReverdyReverdy. I could die before then.]

[Darling, don't die! I can't live without you!] Reverdy promises because promises here are easy, "Be cool, Lark.

Some day Zan and I will get a place. You can come live with us." [You are my life.]

She fixes not on the declaration but on the possibility. *"A place."* Not Zan's fault her heart leaps. Her heart leaps even though she doesn't know if he means a place RL or here. Love makes her generous. "With us," she says to Lark. This isn't true, but the three of them thrive on fantasy. It's one of the attractions of this place. And in Lark's imagined life in an ideal world he has real parents—Reverdy. Zan, who whispers to Reverdy, [Love!]

[Love.]

Lark brightens. "Really?"

"Count on it, Lark." Sometimes Zan thinks this with Reverdy is even sweeter because they are always caught like this, suspended at the brink of departure. If they could be together forever, would they get enough of each other, and get tired?

"You guys are great." Lark beams.

"You're pretty cool yourself." Reverdy whispers, [It's trouble with her.]

[Who? Mireya? Louise?]

[. . . trying to destroy me, the hateful, vindictive . . .]

Zan can't be sure which woman is ruining his life. She can't be sure if he means life here or life back in the house where he and Louise circle, hissing like scorpions. [If only I could . . .]

[But you can't. I love you but I have heavy things to deal with. You see?]

[Of course I see; I love you and I always see.] She doesn't. "Oh, Reverdy!" Zan's heart is running out of control. [Tomorrow.]

[Tomorrow we can be together.]

Zan presses. [Promise.]

Lark says, "Sometimes I just want to die . . ."

[Oh my love oh Zan, I do.]

"No you don't, Lark. Really." Zan spins her life out on these tomorrows. "Sleep on it. I promise, tomorrow will be better."

Lark slouches miserably. "It had better be."

[Now, disconnect so I can disconnect, just to prove that you love me.]

"It has to be," Jenny says to Lark, to Reverdy, to herself as she quits the place. "It has to be."

She types *@exit*. It's like turning out all the lights in the world.

@thirteen

REVERDY

"Love is to a man a thing apart. 'Tis woman's whole existence."
—George Gordon, Lord Byron

Zan, if you have to ask me what that means, there's no way I can explain it.

If there is a tension between VR: *virtual reality* and RL: *real life,* nobody relishes it more than Tom Dearden. With Zan logging on from the east coast and the Dearden house located so far north and west that Tom's room gleams with refracted light from a midnight sun, their clocks are perpetually out of synch. The minute his lover disconnects, sorrow slips off Reverdy like a velvet cloak and he disappears into the game. Perfect, it waits for him.

These are some of the ways you guard yourself against incursions. First, travel light and always live alone. Too late for Tom Dearden. First there was Louise, so pretty at first! Then the pregnancy. Marriage. Another kid. No money. Life circumscribed by this house, when Tom grew up thinking he would go out and roam the world. In retreat from a daily life that's less than tolerable, he needs the power that he has on StElene. In the physical world, he supposes, he is no more or better than any other person. His superiors on the project fob him off with half-answers; Louise often forgets what he is saying before he's finished; even his kids don't always listen.

Here, he has *effect.* In the kingdom of the blind the one-eyed man is king. An intelligent, sophisticated programmer is de facto a member of the ruling class. If StElene is the new Memory Palace, then Reverdy is its prince. Live the life of the mind and you are master of a world you are creating. It's a little like being God.

Never mind what the room looks like where Tom Dearden sits typing. It's only a launching pad. StElene is the world to him. The one place where he's happy and safe. Everything he cares about is here. He is deeply invested in the way things *work.* His ego is tied up in it.

He will do anything to protect his position here.

For Reverdy, heaven is not a theological location. Relentlessly agnostic, he thinks of heaven as an area of the spirit where truth floats. He actually believes there is a best world, and that he can help make it. A place where truths are told on a new, higher plane, where all things are equal and nothing is held back. Where promises are kept and people bring the best of themselves to the unending feast of ideas. And everyone can know everything at once.

If there is indeed an existential plane on which everybody comprehends everything at once, Reverdy thinks, there is the outside possibility of convergence. Minds and spirits together forever in a state of elevated consciousness that another kind of thinker would call the mind of God. People on StElene either love Reverdy or they hate him. And the truth he hides? He is an idealist.

He does what he can.

Today he begins by sending posts both here and IRL on behalf of Hubert Pinkney, a.k.a. Lark, who has major problems in his life outside the box. Can the shy, wildly intelligent kid make it outside his basement room? Should he go back to college, where he self-destructed in the first place, or does he belong in the state hospital? At this distance, it's hard to know. Feeling a little like a storefront psychoanalyst, Reverdy posts a note to *problems*, in hopes of getting feedback from players who've survived something similar. He'll email RL from the university account set up for him through the history project. The profs Tom works for may be able to do Lark some academic favors. Unless they're so pissed off by Tom's views on the project that they delete his mails unread.

Lark isn't the only person Reverdy is helping, here or in physical life. Life in a community like StElene is built on support, friends reaching out in the night to others who are also connected, like minds caught like stars in an invisible net; when someone is in pain, the entire web jangles. Hear that person out, say the right thing and make them feel better—what a rush! Do something about it and—that's power. He loves networking. He loves doing favors and being thanked. It's easy to do favors here, and Reverdy knows how these things are done. He can hack his way into any system, and has. Now, that's real power.

On StElene Reverdy is a hero, in his own way.

It's easy to be a hero here. Therefore when he goes out among the people here Reverdy is loved as well as hated. Even the ones who hate him—certain Directors, Mireya, Azeath— treat him with respect.

When he's taken care of Lark he runs @*find*, to see who's on StElene today, and where. With whom. If they're friends, he knows it. If they are politicking against him, he knows it. If they're badgering the Directors with petitions to erase him, he knows and, grinning with delight, he will take them on in the ballroom or in savagely articulate posts to *sex* and *pol* (for politics), the two hottest mailing lists. His sardonic posts are famous. Nobody knows that he keeps them all! In addition to pirating crucial bits of the operating system, Reverdy has down-loaded the stored-up acrimony of two dozen disputes—his with Mireya! In case.

He has more friends than enemies connected today. Some of the brightest are logged on, along with known flakes and assholes that Reverdy loves to bring down.

It's time to go out and show himself to the people.

He starts with arrogant, pretentious Mink, who Reverdy happens to know is a graduate student RL. "If you've solved Fermat's Last Theorem, show me. Paste in the proof." Some days he reduces Mink to tears; fair's fair, he thinks, imagining smug, supercilious Mink sobbing at his keyboard in some university office. "Just MOOmail me the answer," he says, letting Mink off the hook for today.

Then he pulls Nebraska's chain: "So, you really believe in capital punishment? Don't you know that in civilized countries, governments brand their criminals on the forehead and set them free?" Hit her PC button with an un-PC thought and watch her rant; it's all part of the game. Grinning, he moves on.

Sometimes he hangs out in the music room, flirting. But only when Zan is gone. He learned a hard lesson from Mireya. But he gets off on dancing on the edge of discovery. Part of the fun of StElene is making people angry and staying out of trouble and the other part is getting in trouble and talking his way out of it.

Today he visits Articular, his friend the blocked painter who stays logged on for hours, designing new environments for role-playing games, for the Dungeons and Dragons types who come to StElene to try their skills. Articular xknows the world loves games but a game is only a game. The pleasure is in creation.

Sometimes he and Reverdy lose hours tinkering, while outside the locked bedroom door RL, Tom hears Louise yelling at their children; if he stays logged on and doesn't intervene, she won't hit them—or so he tells Zan.

He and Articular have built a topiary maze inhabited by a monster; find the lantern, the sword and the mantle of invisibility, plot your moves like a chess player and you can slay the thing. They've coded a man-eating Barcalounger and a following settee. Stare deep into the mosaic Articular has coded in *The Roman Forum* and you disappear into caverns that would impress Tolkien. Test your wits and skill in the process of escaping. Here there's no problem that can't be solved and there's a way out of every trap.

It's what Tom loves about electronic life. There is an absolute quality to it, a purity that is elegant and endlessly seductive. There is nothing in programming that can't be solved through trial and error. In time. Try this, try that, beat your head against the wall because no matter how complex the question, there is an answer. Solutions are complete and absolute. Rewarding. Solve it once and you can always solve it.

Gadfly, intellectual batterer, power freak, practical joker: Reverdy is all these things. On StElene, he signifies. He can be anything he wants. This is his home. Here, he is secure. And outside this world? Chaos waits; it makes him afraid.

To survive your life in the world, first you must secure your world.

If you can't live alone, you must have at least one room in the place where you live that you can be alone in, no incursions, nothing to threaten your arrangements or jeopardize your perfect design. It is important to secure it against intruders. Cover all the exits. Leave nothing unprovided for and no next steps unplanned. Position yourself in the corner so your adversaries will always have to face you. This way no one can whisper into your ear unseen and nobody can ever, ever come up on you from behind. In the world, a dead end waits at every turning.

Listen. On StElene, there is no entrance without its exit. In the exquisitely precise world of computer programming, there is no problem without its solution. If only he could disappear into it and never come out again.

Here, he has options. Options: he loves the game!

By the same token, he hates spoilers. He particularly hates clumsy, flat-footed newcomers who log on to StElene like Huns swooping down on a palace, *bring on the maidens*. For them, Reverdy's devised a second, secret identity. He becomes Precious, a glamour pot who looks like a good prospect for a hasty virtual roll in the hay. Slinky Precious comes on strong in fishnet stockings and a lowcut black dress, and when she intercepts a heavy-handed sex troller she preens and flirts, the works. She targets sex-trollers, those horny, anonymous male Guests who log on with sweaty hands because they've mistaken StElene for a virtual bordello. They think they can do anything here because they've invisible. Assuming that every woman in the place is panting for it, they're heavy-handed as horny eighth graders, bent on typing sticky-fingered porn to some like-minded woman who will be equally thrilled. Disguised as Precious, Reverdy targets intruders who hit on the regulars. Their pickup lines range from clumsy to disgusting and Reverdy hates them for it because, in an odd way, it cheapens his own romances.

When he spots a mark he has to move fast, or Velvet will snag the sex-starved typist and lure him into her quarters, the *Velvet Underground*, before sultry Precious can ask, "Do you come here often?"

It's illegal to run two characters on StElene, but Reverdy does it. Defying corporation guidelines is half the thrill, and the rest is vigilante justice. Unless the rest is getting away with it.

As Precious, he talks the talk, drawing the predator away from his intended prey, who usually grins and pages, "Thanks." Laughing at his keyboard, Tom Dearden has Precious lead this Casanova wannabe down to the *Lovers' Glen*. And when the fool is deep into what he's convinced is ultimate virtual passion, gasping and vulnerable, Precious turns into Benjy, a huge hairy lumberjack with tattooed biceps, cauliflower face, the works. Snagged in midair, the ersatz Casanova is horrified to read:

```
CRACK! Just when you least expect it, Precious
turns into BENJY. Benjy is a lumberjack in combat
boots with CURLY BLACK HAIR growing down his arms
and he is about to beat the crap out of you. Before
he tells the FBI you're a pedophile corrupting kids
by posting porno on the net.
```

Benjy growls, "So, you think you can come in here and say 'Hi, you don't know me but let's fuck. And our women will be thrilled.' " His voice gets huge. "Well, YOU MADE A BIG MISTAKE." Then Benjy adds, to put the fear of God into his mark, "I happen to be the onsite man for the FBI." And muscle-bound Benjy at *The Lovers' Glen* and Reverdy at his keyboard in rural Alaska cackle happily because whoever he is, the fool who dropped into StElene expecting cheap sex is humiliated and terrified. The would-be virtual Casanova disconnects fast. He won't try that again.

Yes, Reverdy is courting trouble and he knows it. The problem with Edens, of course, is that they are filled with people, and by nature, people have a way of messing up. Even Reverdy, who knows every Eden has its rules. Precious is only one of the secrets he is sitting on.

He has a secret plan. He dreams of pirating StElene out of the clutches of Suntum International and making it perfect. In fact, without the Directors' knowing it, he's downloaded the database and stored it on his own machine. He would like to demolish StElene and move everybody into one of the high-speed multi-gigabyte machines that he builds and maintains in his home office the way a rich man fills his stables with glossy, top of the line sports cars. Freed from fascist corporate constraints, which demand that everything march in order, his version of StElene can indeed become the ideal society. He's sure of it.

But if Reverdy leaves StElene, can he take enough players with him to make it fly? Like a retreating army, he wants to scorch and burn what he leaves behind so nobody at Suntum can use it ever again. Can he hack into the database and write a bit of code that will take the Directors and their system down for good? He's halfway done. Before he finishes, he has to make sure his friends are in place and except for Zan and Lark, he's not certain of his friends. If word leaks out before he's done he'll be @*erased* from StElene. He could end up alone in space— and here and in the other kingdom, Tom Dearden is terrified of dying alone.

He has to figure it out! He has things to do, he thinks, putting Precious to bed and logging back on as Reverdy, people to see. *Azeath*, he thinks for no real reason except that even in Eden, a man is tempted to shoot himself in the foot. @*find az* he types. Grins. Bingo.

@fourteen

AZEATH A.K.A. VINNIE FULLER

The librarian in the state penitentiary at Wardville looks like he's working—easy enough to do when your job is staring at a terminal. But IVR (in virtual reality, where his life is located) Azeath sits in *Azeath's Little Hell* brooding. His login watcher, which notifies him of significant arrivals, tells him Reverdy's just logged on to StElene. Handsome, smart, thought-we-could-be-friends. IVR, in virtual reality, Azeath is studying ways to destroy his nemesis in both places.

Azeath hates Reverdy more than he loves Mireya, but Mireya doesn't know it. True. It's why he hooked up with her in the first place, he thought Reverdy would feel the insult every time Azeath and Mireya got it on IVR, well he was wrong.

He and Reverdy can't meet without sparring. Azeath comes out of these debates with blood in his palms RL, where he's clenched his fists so hard that his nails cut crescents in the flesh.

Could have been friends! They're the two best programmers here, Az thought they would be powerful allies but the supercilious bastard thought he was too good for him. They clashed from the first over how things on StElene were supposed to be.

The Directors want the power to end disputes. Azeath said they should have it.

Reverdy said, "In an ideal society, everybody is equal."

Well take it from Azeath, he knows better. "Face facts. Nobody's perfect. Somebody has to be in charge, might as well be us."

So much for his hopes; Reverdy snapped, "In a new democracy?"

Well, every democracy needs its cops, just ask Azeath.

Freedom. Equality. The sugar-coated liberal wouldn't quit! Fucking Reverdy could argue God into a hole. Over time he stuck the goad in so deep that at his keyboard, Vinnie fell into a frothing rage RL and IVR, Azeath shouted: "What is it about me that you can't stand, that I'm a better programmer?"

Mr. just-don't-I'm-above-it-all just laughed and came back, all holy and superior: "Call it a difference in personal style."

What Azeath hates most about Reverdy is, Reverdy honestly does believe he's above it all. Comes on spouting thousand dollar words like a storefront intellectual, *well I'll show him.* And he will. *When I get out, I will.*

What Azeath wants before he gets out is to have Suntum make him a Director. It is his aim. He's a good programmer. He's smart, even if he can't talk the talk like Reverdy does. He'd be a Director right now if it wasn't for that smooth, swift-mouthed shit.

Everybody's supposed to be equal on StElene, but these Suntum Directors, they get special powers: to eavesdrop on even the most private transactions in supposedly secured spaces; to pass or strike down people's building plans. To destroy objects—including characters, like, they can take out entire people!—when it serves the corporate aim. Thirteen Directors, distinguished by the "St" attached to the character name: StOnge for one. StBrêve for another. StPaulo and StPhil. Two are women, but they're pretty much sexless, the way a good Director should be. Like saints.

Azeath wants it. He wants it bad. In fact in the prison library where he works eighteen-hour days to the delight of his supervisor, he keeps a placard he made in shop. He'll put it on his desk when the time is right: *StAz*. Hell, when he becomes a Director on StElene he can throw Reverdy out himself. WHAM.

He had a nice thing going, sucking up to StOnge and aiming for StBrêve, who he happens to know is a little bit higher up the food chain than the others. StBrêve is an actual company man paid by Suntum to keep the society on StElene doing like it should.

In Wardville, Az has learned a couple of things. *If you want to get ahead, volunteer.*

So he started by offering to sort data for StPhil, maintain mailing lists, that kind of thing. Moved up to Reaper, going into the database and eliminating players who still had character names but had stopped logging on. He's good at computers. Always has been, likes it because, unlike fucking humans, computers do what you tell them and they *don't talk.*

Az got StOnge and StPhil's confidence; they were working the other Directors, getting support for him. They were going to introduce him at a party in the grand ballroom, like he was going up for membership in some kind of flossy rich man's private club. He was waiting for the Saints to come marching in when Reverdy arrived.

Already he knew this was going to be bad. "Go away."

Reverdy just grinned. "Not until you hear what I have to say."

Az tried to move him *@blitz!* but he would not be moved.

Rev said, "I know you don't like me, but you deserve to be warned. You're being co-opted. Don't let Suntum eat your soul."

"What?" OK, he didn't know what co-opted meant. "Say what?"

"Watch out." Damn Reverdy's superior, I'm-hipper-than-you-are way. "The corporate sharks will chew you up and spit you out."

"Go to hell." Partly he was pissed because he was confused, he yelled, "You just go to hell and fuck yourself to death."

"You don't get that they're using you?"

"Shut up. Shut the fuck up!"

Reverdy didn't shut up, he just kept on. Taunting. Warning.

Vinnie shouted, "What do you know? You don't know anything."

"I'm smart enough to know when I'm being used."

This heated Vinnie to boiling. "Like I'm not?" When Reverdy didn't answer, he yelled, "YOU THINK I'M NOT SMART?" OK it was a dumb thing to do: Azeath pasted in his best image: a devil—fangs, claws, the works, along with these words, spelled out in massed Xes and Os, UP YOURS.

At the exact moment that StOnge and StPhil and the other ten teleported in. To see their protégé looking like an asshole. Az wanted to blame Reverdy but it was too late. Just as he launched his stupid display, he read: Reverdy disconnects.

So that's one.

To get back in good with the Saints, he had to turn into a goddamn workhorse. It took him fucking years to get back into their confidence, and to add StAndrew to his FRIENDS list. Years.

StOnge and StBrêve, they mostly like him now. He runs tables and searches logs for possibly subversive talk from players

and sets up surveillance bugs to track how far these conversations go. He can do projections and crunch numbers with the
best. Director material. Definitely Director material, and he secretly happens to know that when Suntum gets its shit together
and puts this StElene application on the market, the regular
programmers will get nothing because hell, it's a game they just
happened to be playing, but the Directors. The Directors are
going to score.

By that time he'll be out. Directors run Suntum too, he's
pretty sure.

It was so close that Az could almost smell the money, until.

OK, him and StOnge and StBrêve were hanging out in the
grand ballroom *just like friends* last March. StOnge had brought
StBrêve around to prove Az was a new person and Azeath was
trotting out his best devices to show them how far he'd come:
the puppet programmed to log every conversation where the
name Suntum comes up, the bugs players inadvertently attach
to themselves; if he wants, he can record everything they say
and do. He showed them the *propriety* mailing list he'd started,
where people file anonymous complaints naming players who
get out of line; "We've got to weed out the riffraff," he said,
and the saints nodded their heads.

He was beginning to figure out how to use their jargon,
play on their fears. "Kick out anybody that's bad for the enterprise."

"Yes," StOnge said soberly. "The enterprise." So they were
all, yeah, yeah, they were like, Good Work, and then fucking
Reverdy dropped in. Dropped in out of nowhere, did some kind
of pirouette right there in the grand ballroom and said TO EV-
ERYONE:

"Kissing ass again, are you Azeath? Brown-nosing like a
good little boy?"

And right there in front of StOnge and StBrêve that Azeath had spent all this fucking time on, this holy, vicious Reverdy, revolutionary and known enemy of the corporation, tarred Azeath with the same brush. What he did was throw his arms around Azeath and give him a big sloppy kiss on the mouth.

"Ghah!"

Reverdy grinned. "Good man. Infiltrating the Directors, just like I said. You get in there and do like I told you, right? Destroy from the inside." He finished with a hearty slap on the back. "Good going. Good man, I'm proud of you. That's my boy!"

Tarred, right. With the same brush. And Reverdy was laughing at him. Laughing! It was too much. IRL and IVR Vinnie Fuller lost it. Azeath just fucking lost it. He started throwing things around: Reverdy, the furniture. Ooops. StBrêve and StOnge.

Hell, if he didn't have this rotten temper he would of laughed it off and the Directors would still be cool with him. Instead they saw him lose it in front of everybody, *in front of them* and StOnge typed to StBrêve: "Too bad. Not our type after all."

And StBrêve typed back: "Definitely not our type."

And thirteen Directors teleported out.

But Azeath's going to get his. He's going to get it back and he's going to get it soon. He spends all his days these days cataloging, both on StElene and off. On StElene he's been logging evidence, compiling things Reverdy's said against the corporation. Criminal! Doesn't he understand they are all beholden? If it wasn't for Suntum International, they wouldn't have this place! Az wouldn't be rehabilitated like he is, in line for a job in data entry at Suntum just as soon as he gets out, as a Director, he can rise.

So every time this Reverdy starts in, wherever he is, Azeath adds it to his log where all the damaging evidence festers. Now his collection is approaching critical mass. He's making a bill of particulars. You might not be able to send a person to jail for the things Reverdy's called Suntum: thieves, fascists, dictators, but you sure can get him kicked out. *Or send him to hell,* he thinks.

Next week Vinnie's going to call an online meeting of all thirteen Directors and if they come, if it goes right, they'll attach "St" to Azeath's name and make him Director number fourteen.

He's not a slick talker like his enemy so he's been writing his lines ahead of time.

"You've got a snake in your belly. He's out to ruin this place." That's one. Maybe he'll say Reverdy is a terrorist and he's using StElene as an online launching pad for terrorists planning to bomb Israel. Or blow up Palestine. Or explode the headquarters of Suntum International. Whatever, either way. Trouble here is, Azeath is still working out the details and he can't move on it until he figures out a story that will fly.

OK, there's always Plan B. Plan B is convince the Directors that Reverdy's trying to bring down Suntum International by introducing *industrial spies.* People from Apple and Microsoft. They're already here! Zan for one, Lark. "They're going to steal your application right out from under you and make a zillion bucks on it."

Sounds good, but who really thinks outsiders could steal StElene? OK, Plan C. Better go with Plan C. Azeath spends his time working various Directors, not sucking up, exactly, just kind of building character. Credibility, he guesses, that thing

Reverdy says he so lacks. The guy is so fucking insulting! "Azeath! You know what your problem is, my friend? Your problem is, you lack credibility."

And I thought we could be friends.

Never mind. Azeath is back in good. He thinks. This means he knows what kinds of things bother the Directors, at least he knows firsthand what's bothering StOnge. He has a list. StOnge doesn't know it but every time StOnge mentions a problem, Azarael writes it down in ballpoint on paper in real life. Directors can tell if you're logging them so Vinnie wrote in this notebook, that he keeps RL. Right here at his desk in the library where he sits at his terminal from 9 A.M. when the place opens until 11 at night. But this is a bonus day. Inventory. The library is open all night.

He's printed a list of things the Suntum Directors are afraid of. He writes better than he talks, as they will see. This is it:

The Things Suntum Directors are afraid of are:

1. Anything that brings bad publicity to the corporation. That means players on StElene getting into trouble that leaks off the island: a stalking that bleeds over into RL; sexual harassment; virtual rape. If a guy went to jail for "raping" a woman in text on a couple of bulletin boards, it can happen in StElene.

2. Any bad publicity that might bring down the feds. Suntum doesn't want feds snooping around StElene disguised as characters; players are warned to be careful of what they say and naturally everybody tries to be careful what they say in whose presence, but in text, those dark glasses and raincoats are harder to spot.

3. Anything that brings down federal regulation. Obscenity charges, kiddie porn. Supreme Court decisions at stake. StElene is a free society, within the parameters set by Suntum, and federal regulation would end the experiment. Proud of the big word!

To this last, Azeath has appended a note:

Question. WHAT EXPERIMENT?

He's put it to StOnge, who mutters about a brilliant application, but it isn't exactly an answer. Whatever Suntum International's up to, it's going to make money. And when it starts making money, Azeath's damn well going to be in on it.

He'd be in on it now, if it wasn't for Reverdy. Well listen, he's shat on Reverdy some himself. Like when he moved in on Mireya and made her fall in love with him, dumb bitch. She loves Azeath and like Azeath she hates Reverdy and they have a pact. It's only a matter of time before they bring him down.

And if you can't fuck somebody over right now, well at least you can fuck. She's so beautiful. *Mireya, babe.* It's almost closing time in the library. He's alone. She's about to log on. It's their private time. He'll wait for her here in *Azeath's Little Hell.*

Then his login watcher show that StAndrew, StOnge and StBrêve have just logged on. He types: @*find stonge.* The three Directors are in the grand ballroom with a group of other players. Can't let this one go by. Azeath swaggers into the grand ballroom and smiles broadly, waiting to be recognized. In case the Saints haven't noticed, he says, "Been reading up on arbitration systems in other communities." That always pricks up their ears. StAndrew smiles. StOnge smiles. StBrêve smiles, but it's no big deal. They go on saying whatever they were saying. Still, he's been noticed. Azeath will wait for an opening and say something really smart.

When Mireya arrives they'll hug in front of everybody—and if the Directors ignore them they can split for *Azeath's Little Hell* to raise a little virtual hell and have some passionate sex. Meanwhile, he can belly up to his friends here and build a little character. He's just getting in tight when Reverdy drops in like the death's head looking for the feast. He doesn't say anything; he doesn't do anything; he just grins.

Then before Azeath even guesses what's coming Reverdy says right in front of everyone—shit, StOnge! "Oh, Azzy dearest! Thank you for last night." And smears him with an outrageously detailed sloppy kiss. Too fucking much! Azeath's rage flames.

Boiling, Vinnie is shaking so hard that he can't get out his rejoinder. "Dxhm."

Laughing, Reverdy drives in the knife. "Chill, sweetheart, you're losing it. Get real."

And with three Directors and a crowd watching, Azeath lunges for him. "Real? Real?" He is trembling with rage. "THIS IS REAL."

"This." Reverdy sidesteps, still laughing. "This isn't real."

Azeath's fingers slide on the keyboard as he types, "THE HELL IT ISN'T." Somewhere between here and there someone is roaring, not speech, just pure sound.

"What's the matter, sweetie, can't you take it?"

In the library in the penitentiary at Wardville, Vinnie yanks out the plug, but not before Reverdy's last barb burns into his screen:

"Don't you know this is only a game?" IRL Azeath yanks the plug so hard that his computer sizzles. It is like a little murder. On StElene the room sees:

                    Azeath disconnects

In real life somebody grabs a pencil, roaring, "Only a game, only a *game!*" In real life, somebody screams with pain.

In the library in the state penitentiary at Wardville, Azeath a.k.a. Vinnie Fuller (manslaughter) doesn't just slam the pencil down hard enough to break it in two, which it does. He slams it down so violently that the point penetrates the back of his left hand.

fifteen

JENNY

OK, I'm not altogether sure that my secret love is good for me, but I can't live without it. Things are happening so fast that the compression is killing me. I have to let it out somehow! If I expect to keep going through this hard summer, I have to find some way to tell my secrets without telling anything.

I've started talking to Martha about things that happen on StElene without mentioning that StElene is where they're happening. It helps. "Martha, my friend the phobic is in trouble."

She knows all about Hubert Pinkney, a.k.a. Lark. Everything except the one thing. She looks up. "Anything I can do?"

"Let me run this past you, OK?"

If I told Martha these people who fill my life are my best friends I've never met, she'd turn me off with that clinical glare: *You know it isn't real.* But it *is* real. Real people who really need me. I know, if you haven't been there, there's no explaining it. So I never tell her where these people *are,* just how important they are to me. I say, "Remember the kid I told you about, my friend Hubert? He's in trouble."

She gives me that clinical look anyway. "Friend, or patient?"

"Both. I love the kid, he opens up to me. This boy is brilliant, but he's so *shy!* Can't go out in the daytime because he thinks everybody's staring at him. Lives at home. Now for no reason, his parents are getting cranked up to throw him out of the house."

"Patients' versions of what happened don't always jibe with reality," Martha says.

"He tells me they're fed up because he doesn't talk to them, don't they know he *can't* talk to them?"

"Apparently not." Martha sounds maybe a little too dry.

"But he's their son!" I am getting upset. "How could they live with him all this time and not know?"

Martha says the logical thing. "Sounds like you need a family conference. Why don't you pull him into the office for an evaluation? Start the dialog?"

"Can't," I tell her, without giving anything away.

"If you're too close to it, maybe I can help. Bring him on in."

It costs me to say, "He lives in Pennsylvania."

"Pennsylvania!" Martha gives me a look. "How did you get onto the case?"

"Private referral." Does she see me blush?

"And there are no relatives to intervene?"

"None that I know of. I'm afraid if the parents kick him out, he'll fly into a million pieces. He's only nineteen, he's put together with toothpicks and baling wire and I'm scared to think what will happen if they cut him off!"

Martha warns, "Professional distance, Jen. If you're too involved, how can you stand back far enough to help?"

"Martha, I'm the only person who cares!"

"Sometimes I think you get too close to your patients," Martha says. "Rick Berringer, for one."

I shake my head. "No."

"You're young, I know Charlie's away a lot, I'm sure there are temptations." Martha's trying to lead me into a confession I don't need to make because there's nothing to confess. "Jen, is there anything you want to tell me?"

"I told you, I'm worried to death about Lark!"

"Lark? Who's Lark?"

I cover quickly. "I mean Hubert, the Pinkney case."

Martha lowers the glasses and squints, as if it will help her see me better. "I've seen the way Rick Berringer looks at you. Be careful, Jen, this is a very small town."

I groan. "Life is a very small town."

"Any conversation we have here is privileged."

"Believe me, if I were going to get in trouble, and I'm not about to get in trouble, I would *not* pick one of my patients, and certainly not this close to home."

"About the Pinkney boy. Can you speak to the parents?"

"Not if I want him to trust me."

Martha nods. "Try to buy him some time. Tell him he needs to negotiate, you know, see if they'll extend the deadline. In exchange for certain things. An hour a day upstairs with them. Dinner, maybe. You've got to get the kid out of that basement."

"I'll try."

Martha is very good at this. I've told her everything about Hubert Pinkney except the fact that I know him better than any of my patients and I've told him things I'd never tell her. Martha says, "Get him upstairs and maybe they can sort it out."

"Makes sense." I can't stop pacing. Reverdy crowds into my

mind, he fills it up and I can't afford to let him into the room. "Hubert's extremely bright, but he's volatile. And the parents hate him too much to talk to him, much less help him sort it out."

"Reality check. Hate's a pretty strong word."

"Resent. They want him out of there. I'm afraid for him."

"Listen," Martha says maternally, "a therapist can't get too personally invested and still do her job. There are patients you can help and patients you can't help, and we can't always know the difference ahead of time."

"You mean like Amanda Yerkes."

In spite of the air conditioning, Martha's face is damp with earnestness; sweat snaps her hair into tight curls. "Keep your distance or your patient will pull you into the problem. And know when to cut your losses and move on to help somebody else."

"I know. I know!"

Then out of God knows where Martha comes at me: "You're not all strung out because of this stupid StHelen thing, are you?"

I grunt like a shafted antelope. "Who, me? Of course not. No!"

"Well, *something's* the matter," Martha says.

"It's StElene, Mart. And I'm cool." I am grinning uncontrollably. "I'm cool." And am profoundly homesick for StElene and my real friends, who really care. I back out grinning and go home early. I need to check on Lark so I can talk him through, I pray that Reverdy's around in the daytime for once, listen, if nothing else, at least I can check my mail. Maybe I can find Jazzy because . . . OK, I am becoming aware that StElene is a physical addiction; I need the reassurance of the same old text coming up on my screen, as predictable as sunrise, and I need the unpredictable rhythm of the talk, I need the sense that there is a world out there where I matter, and I need more than anything to be in touch with it. I need to log on. I need *thereness.* More than anything, I need Reverdy.

sixteen

REVERDY

Deep in the game, Tom Dearden has started writing. He will use history to get what he wants. Once he has it right, he thinks without being exactly certain what he means, he can mount the revolution.

stelene.moo.mud.org 8888

If you are already here, you may think you know why you're here and how to be here, but you don't. The program is not case sensitive; from the telnet prompt a player can type in the address in lower case; type *connect [your name] [your password]* and you're on the MOO. StElene brings you the world not in a grain of sand but in an island, but it's still a MOO.

It stands for *Multiple Object Oriented* or *Multiple Owner Operated.*

MULTIPLE. More than one mind put StElene in place and multiple minds keep the MOO operating, beginning with the thirteen programmers Suntum calls *Directors*. Ask yourself, are they Directors because they're better than us or is it a company scam? Their names all begin with St, as if to make you think saints are in charge. It's the Directors' job to maintain, not-so-subtly supervise. In case we get out of hand. They debug when necessary and keep objects from getting so big that they overload the database and take the operating system down with them in the crash.

OBJECT. This particular kind of invention—creation by definition—begins when you log on and choose a name. It advances when you write a description, beginning *@describe me as . . .*

Objects, including characters—in the database, players like Zan and Lark—me! are objects too. Customized by the thousands who request characters and, entered in the database by a registrar delegated by Suntum International, log on.

You have moved into our town. If you're any good, you get invested here. You care about the environment. Inspired to put part of yourself into the new society, you build.

Pioneers tamed the frontier by naming names. You understand, this is the new frontier? Move into this large town or small city and you add to it as soon as you build a room and begin to describe it. If you need a model, look at the Dak Bungalow, but do not try to come here. Go to the dock, which I also built. Note the sunrise, listen to the gulls. I built them. "Reality" is in the details. Places where visitors can sit, objects they can examine, pick up and use.

OBJECT-ORIENTED. Yes our egos are tied up in it. The best of us code for hours on StElene, expanding the territory. If you're new and don't already code for a living, it may seem hard at first. Then it gets hypnotic: try it this way, try it that way, keep dinking until you get it right. Get it right and feel the rush. Code is like poetry.

But there are limitations, no matter how good you are. Everything has to get past the Directors' review board. Stop and think. Is it a personal triumph or just flattery that gets a space you've built approved, and linked to the environment? Ask any Director. You won't get a straight answer.

MUD. MUD originally stood for *Multiple User Dungeon*, OK we're descended from Dungeons and Dragons, but we prefer the new definition. *Multiple User Domain.* The original MUD attracted the people who started with D&D offline and moved on into imaginary spaces with interactive computer games like Zork, the granddaddy of them all.

Pretty soon they figured out how to meet online to play roleplaying games. MUD opened new worlds. Players could forget the body stuck at the keyboard and move out. You could enter the MUD as if moving into a new landscape, assume the mantle of priest, wizard, monk or warrior. Buckle on that sword and swagger. Become that character as you never could before because you were deep in the territory of the imagination. It was big enough to contain vast caverns and palaces, mountains, plains—this new space that opened up turned out to be labyrinthine, unlimited. And because it was conceptual space, it was easy to get around. Players could cover great distances in nanoseconds, fight dragons, elude the thief, and, wait. More. There were other *people* there.

It wasn't long before they stepped outside the game and talked. About the game, at first. Then anything they wanted. About themselves. Together. In real time. Imagine!

People like presents waiting to be opened and explored. What strikes you first, divorced from the prison of your body and the room where your computer sits and transported into the life of the mind, is the mobility. The freedom! But there's more. With the illusion of freedom comes power, or the illusion of power. If you don't like the party you can leave. If you don't like a person you can have that person removed. You can spy. Teleport at will. Be everywhere at once. Communicate as if by ESP. If you don't like your name you can change it, and if you can change your name you can change anything. You are free in space. Who would ever want to live anywhere else?

The freedom!

More. Synchronicity. No matter where they were in the world the MUDders could meet in real time. Nobody has to be alone. Speak and be spoken to. Act and see others react. Better than email, more social than the conference call, and in the breathtaking freedom of anonymity, more intimate.

Imagine. Us. Together here. Now.

It was like landing on Mars.

Who wouldn't get drunk on the possibilities? Because even on StElene which is not, repeat, *not* about roleplaying games, people take roles. Free of the physical world, you can try anything. Put on new selves like teenyboppers trying on dresses in a mall. Things happen. People change. Are they pure, naked souls or is this another kind of roleplaying game?

The object of the game changed so fast that not even nethistorians can mark the exact moment. Who wants to win the game when you can win lives? Who wants to explore imaginary caverns when you can explore real souls? We don't MUD but we do play to win.

StElene is a game and yet it is so *not* a game.

It is so not a game and yet it *is* a game. Assuming new names, do we really reinvent ourselves?

With a sense that he isn't finished, Reverdy types, *You are what you type*. And instead of sending, stores.

He is torn between two wants. Part of him wants to separate and take everybody with him. Trash the database and bring down Suntum as he goes. The other part wants to expose them so they will go and he can stay. The corporation. What is Suntum really up to? What is it doing anyway? Things run too smoothly here on StElene. The surface is lovely—relentlessly bland, with the hint of menace that lets people shiver in the delicious certainty that no matter how wild it gets it's only pretend and they're really safe. Nothing threatens their lives outside the box. It's like being on a fun ride, excited and scared with no real danger because nothing is real and nobody gets hurt. The Directors provide calculated distractions: parties every night, to keep people too busy to ask questions. To keep them from confronting each other—unless it's to keep them from confronting the truth. Troublemakers are *@erased*, whisked away like streakers at Disney World. Weird things go on in darkened party rooms and individual chambers like Velvet's *Velvet Underground* and Fearsome's *Wishing Well*, but the surface is so lovely, so aggressively squeaky-clean that Reverdy wonders.

If he can only find out what's going on and expose them, he can change StElene and make it his. He is planting questions.

What if we're psychological lab rats? he asks Articular. Paging because he's still in the Dak Bungalow, figuring out his moves.

He pages Jazzy. *Or some kind of sexual exhibition?*

He arrives at his best question. *What if they're lying when they say what happens in the private spaces is really private? If the Directors can spy, who else is spying on us here?*

It has crossed his mind that Suntum sells high end customers tickets to their secret lives. His problem is hacking into the Suntum server and getting deep enough into the peculiar Suntum operating system to find out. Without leaving any tracks.

Idealist, lover, Reverdy is also relentlessly political. Zan is right about one thing: he lives under unimaginable pressure. StElene is his psychic anchor, and at the moment his position is precarious. If they catch him, he's fried.

And Mireya has filed charges. Harassment. That he's come to her house RL and threatened her life. Azeath has been out to get him ever since Reverdy mailed the warden from behind his firewall. The bastard is collecting evidence like a diamond prospector. If Az and Mireya find out that he's hacking into the Suntum system and prove it, they'll get him erased. The Directors are already debating whether to have the Dak Bungalow recycled because he is a gadfly here. If they take a vote and it's positive, the character Tom has so passionately designed and so lovingly maintains will be eliminated. If the ballot passes, Reverdy will be @erased.

The best part of Tom Dearden will cease to exist. And he is torn. He doesn't have enough support to take StElene with him. Or enough inside information to bring Suntum down. Yet.

He will do anything to maintain his position here.

It's time to go to the grand ballroom. Through the electronic miracle that everybody here takes for granted, he'll teleport in to work the crowd. He has his constituents but he needs more. If Suntum really find grounds to erase him before he's done hacking, the @erasure will come to a vote. He needs his support in place.

But first he uses the second electronic trick they all take for granted—spying—he surveys the cast of characters already in the ballroom. He sees Mireya's there. So is Azeath. It's disturbing, knowing that he and Mireya are pledged to hate each other forever, when they used to be in love. It's a puzzle, not knowing why they can't put it behind them. Turn the page. Move on.

He types: *page Mireya, "I warned you to stop phoning Louise."*

In the ballroom, Mireya will keep talking to Azeath as she secretly pages back: *"As if you never told Harry about us. Are you going to keep paging or are you going to join me and have this out?"*

"You were already getting a damn divorce," Reverdy pages, knowing as he does so that Mireya's smooching her new lover, but never too busy to haul over the bad old ground. Why can't they forget it and move on? At long distance, he taunts. *"Harry? I did you a favor, I made him jealous, but Louise . . ."*

"Louise, Louise, she stopped fucking you long before I ever fell in love with you."

"In love?" This is a low blow, tugging at parts of him that still hurt. OK, Mireya loves to duke it out in the ballroom, in front of an audience. So does he! This abiding anger carries its own erotic power. He'll go when he's damn well ready. He pages, *"Love. Love! What do you mean, love? I never even liked you!"*

Mireya taunts, *"Rev-baby, come on down and say that where the people can hear you."* He knows what she wants. She wants to get him there and then scream that he's attacking her. Another false charge.

"And bring the Directors down on me?"

Her response comes up on his screen almost before he's done typing. *"What. You're too chicken to come?"*

To maintain his position here, he has to keep his head down and stay out of public brawls. Ah, but he loves baiting her. *page Mireya "How's Harry's cute new wife?"*

Mireya pages, *"What's the matter, Rev. Can't face me? Could you be . . . afraid???"*

Fine, Reverdy thinks. Full audience. Fine, even though he knows the Directors' witnesses hover like shrikes, poised to pounce at his first false move. Log it. Post it for the world to see. There's nothing the matter with a little danger; Reverdy gets off on personal risk. And he types, *@be ballroom.* And is there.

A crowd is collecting to watch. Including Azeath. Including StOnge, the righteous Director who sits up nights thinking of ways to *@erase* him for good.

"Fine," Reverdy says to Mireya so the whole room can hear. "What is it this time? Pistols or daggers? Invective? Your lies?"

"Acrimony," Mireya snaps. "Oh right. And evidence of treason."

"Wonderful." *Does she know anything?* "How did I guess?"

Psychodrama, another of the staples on StElene. Reverdy scopes the room. The population seems to be fifty-fifty—friends, enemies. Azeath, the masked avenger, is already pissed, watch out. And Reverdy's resentful ex-lover—a *woman scorned.* Mireya was the first. She may have been the best.

"Idiot," Reverdy says to her, more fondly than he's ready to admit, "a happy fuck you!" And so Reverdy and Mireya move into the old dance like accustomed lovers sliding into the act. Blood will be shed before they quit. Accusations. Ugly disclosures about real lives. He and his old lover will fight to a draw, which each will claim is a win. They'll taunt and rage until they're both exhausted and Tom Dearden is shaking with anger here at his keyboard. They always do. Ugly old laundry hung out to dry and ironed to knife-point folds that cut like Ninja throwing blades.

His life here is sharply focused. Intense. Where by daylight Tom Dearden's life in the quiet house in the snowy stillness is circumscribed, Reverdy feeds on adventure. Enemies. Threats to his survival. StElene is like a hothouse. Loves blaze. So does hate. Excitement: on StElene the future shimmers in the vestibule of the uncreated. Life here isn't only about power, it's about passion. Sometimes fury is better than sex.

They begin.

At which point the bedroom door Tom thought he'd locked against intrusions swings open. His daughter Susie pads in, soft in her flannel nighties, and crawls onto his lap. He snuggles his child the way he always does even at heated moments like these, and with his chin resting in her sweet hair, keeps typing.

"What are you doing, Daddy?"

Absently, he says into her hair, "Working, honey."

"Daddy, it's breakfast time!" She turns in his arms so she can see the screen. "What's all that, Daddy?"

"Words," he says. "Just words."

Good thing the child hasn't learned to read.

Just as well, too, that Tom doesn't know that in the fury of the interrupted argument, which is in its own way like an act of love cut short, Mireya has turned away from her terminal IRL and picked up the telephone. Zan may know she has a grave enemy in Mireya, but she does not know that in real life, in physical life outside the idealized world in the box where they spend so much time, Florence Vito Watson has cracked Zan's site information and is on the way to getting the Wilders' home phone number.

seventeen

JENNY

G o on, Rick."

Rick goes on.

Daytime, my office. I am only Jenny Wilder, who loves her husband Charlie, hard at work. I know that Charlie loves me too, but not enough. Today I hurt a lot, whereas at night Zan is, I don't know exactly—unassailable. Perfect. Loved.

My patient says, "I can't go out without wiping the knob a dozen times."

"I know," I say, "I know." I didn't do a hugely elaborate job of describing Zan, but on StElene she can be with our lover in an eyeblink, even though he is thousands of miles away. Get into his soul. Can you even guess what that's like? Reverdy tells Zan that she's perfect. What a rush! Potentially perfect, I think, which is closer to the truth.

Parts of us are out there waiting to be completed, me and Reverdy, Reverdy and me.

"But I'm getting better about scrubbing my nails."

"I see your fingers have stopped bleeding, that's a very good sign." In Brevert I have Charlie, but up close, Charlie is just

Charlie, with his rumpled hair and nice smile, and he is diminished by his cranky kids and distracted by his work while everything I want is glitters in the future like an electric dream. Oh God, how can I love Charlie and still be so wrecked in love?

Did I groan out loud? My darkly appealing obsessive-compulsive patient says, "Um, Miz Doc, did you say something?"

We are close to the end of his hour. "No, Rick," I say. "I just got snagged on something." I'm hung up on love, I know, but can not say.

"Something I said?" Rick's been talking about the fact that every time he gets too close to a woman he finds a way to shoot himself in the foot.

Look, the man is my patient, I owe him something. I say, "Related to something you said."

"Ma'am?"

"The part about how you always get in trouble with a woman when you get too close." I am thinking there is one arena where people see into each other's souls without touching and somehow Rick and StElene get mixed up in my mind. As if he lives there too. The air in the room is soft and sweet and I am teetering on the brink of something, I don't know what. I ask my patient, "Your compulsiveness. Is it a mechanism for keeping you from getting close?"

"I never said that!"

I'm not sure why my voice is shaking. "People find ways of putting obstacles between them and what they really want."

Rick's my patient, I'm supposed to be helping him, but here he is saying in that gentle Southern voice, "If there's a problem you'll tell me, right, Miz Doc?"

"Of course," I say. "Now, if you'll just let me help you pull those patterns out so we can have a look at them . . ." The poor guy can't do anything or go anywhere without a dozen compulsive rituals. He's already numbered the repetitive acts he has to complete before he can leave his home office just to come here. Rick talks on, but I don't hear. I am fixed on my own secret, impossible love. I guard it like treasure, a present so tightly wrapped that only I can open it. What Reverdy and I have together is the creation of both our souls. It's bigger than any love in physical life.

Rick puts this in the room between us. "Could we talk about something else?"

I say out of nowhere, "I'm thinking, you say that at least when you're at your computer you have control."

"Exactly! Nothing I can't handle, you know?"

I don't know what's driving me. "And do you ever. Um. Go online?"

"It's a way of going out without having to go out." He has a really nice smile.

"Exactly," I say. "And you. Um. Talk to people, you know, on the internet?"

"Sometimes."

"What kind of people?"

"Miz Doc, it's not sex rooms!" Suddenly uncomfortable, Rick clears his throat. "So, Miz Doc, the clock says we're done." He does not get up. Instead he studies me, good-looking guy.

"I guess we are." I see that he wants to move this along from doctor-patient. If he tries, I'll have to turn him over to Martha.

Still, his voice is gentle. "But I was wondering. One more thing?"

Like a teacher, I am responsible to the people I treat, it is my job to keep the relationship professional. I try to sound cool. "Yes?"

"You look so sort of . . . Miz Doc, is there something going on with you?"

I can't help it, I turn color. "This isn't about me, Rick. This is about you. I'm just thinking if your computer is one arena where you have control, we may be able to figure out a way for you to expand your area of control."

"We could make it about you." He makes me think of Reverdy, but Reverdy is safe in the box, and Rick is here.

"This is your hour, Rick, not mine." This is an extremely attractive guy, my patient, and he cares enough about what I'm feeling to keep me talking.

"Let's don't stop at an hour," he says, smoldering the way he did when he offered the ride I didn't take.

Charlie's distractions and repeated departures have left me in a weakened condition. I say, "No, Rick. If it stops being about you, I have to hand you over to another therapist."

"If you fired me, would you go out with me?"

I shake my head, but I make no move to dismiss him. "Your areas of control. Beyond the techniques I've taught you, is there any place in your life where you feel safe?"

"Tell me the truth, Miz Doc. What are my chances?"

I say automatically, "If you want to get better, you will."

"You know that's not what I'm talking about." In this light he is surprisingly good-looking.

We are teetering on the brink of something. "Your computer. Do you ever go online?"

Rick grins. "Online? Who, me? How do you think I get through the nights?"

"Um," I say; I can feel my belly tremble. Something may be happening. I think it's one thing, and he . . . "What. Um, what kind of thing do you do on the net?"

He thinks it's another. Laughing, he shrugs. "You know,

chat rooms. Singlz-R-Us, opera chat, I'm in one about scuba diving, forget I'm scared of water . . ."

"Oh. Chat rooms." I see the sprawl of StElene, with its mystery and complexity. I see Reverdy, and the knowledge that he's out there, not here, leaves me weak with relief.

On guard, Rick challenges. "Do you have a problem with chat rooms?"

"Only if you're using them to put off for solving your problems RL."

"*Real life?*" His head lifts. "Miz Doc, are you out there?"

"Not like you."

"If you want me to give up chat rooms, I'll give up chat rooms." Rick's look tells me he'll do anything for me. "I'd much rather be here talking to you, or out somewhere, talking with you."

"We already are talking, Rick."

"Not like we could." He says, "You don't always look happy, Miz Doc, I just thought."

"No," I say to him, to any kind of extramarital encounter. The life of the mind is one thing; getting down with this good-looking patient of mine, going out into the soft air where Charlie might see us together is another—the embarrassment of unfamiliar bodies, the difficulties of finding the right place, the awkward business of taking off clothes. "No, Rick. Let's keep this on a professional basis. If we can't . . ."

"I know, I know." Reluctantly, he gets up. "You'll have to fire me."

"Nothing that drastic, it's just."

"Next week, same time?" He won't leave until I promise.

"Next week, same time." Relieved, I show him out.

When I get to StElene tonight Reverdy will be there and everything will be perfect. Do you understand how that is?

@eighteen

ZAN

In its own way, StElene is like Manhattan, wonderful on some days, good on most, and on some days, like the city, it can be a hard place. From the minute you arrive things start going wrong. Lark is nowhere around; Reverdy hasn't been here since early morning and—new. He didn't leave a note. Before she's had a chance to read her other mail Zan gets a page from Harrald, who has big news. She joins him in one of the elaborate sitting rooms off the grand ballroom; it's a *trompe l'oeil* room painted like a birdcage:

> Designed years before you were born, the room is painted like the inside of a cage. Around you, vines twine in and out of the bars, which protect even as they keep you in. The bars support several brilliantly painted birds. Stay here long enough and you will figure out how to make them sing. Stay too long and you will be forced to sing.

"I'm getting married," Harrald says breathlessly.
Zan nods, unless it's Jenny, chalking up one more patient

she's actually helped. "That's wonderful! Where? When?"

He says, "Here!"

Zan can't let him know how uncomfortable this makes her. "You're getting MOOmarried?"

"Oh yes. You think I'd do anything this stupid *real life?*"

"MOOmarried," she says. "Um. Who?"

Harrald grins. "Velvet. Thursday week. She's wearing red."

"Oh." She doesn't have to remind him that Velvet spends her nights on StElene seining the population for new men to take into the sex chambers. Love is supposed to be forever and Velvet's a known slut. Odd, how Zan saws back and forth between two lives, responding, but not with the congratulations Harrald expects. Instead she asks the professional question. "How realistic is that?"

"Oh, it's real all right. We're in love."

"As in, real love, here and off StElene too?" She is thinking of Reverdy. "As in, will you ever meet?"

"You think I'm crazy? We're meeting in Dallas RL at the end of the month. If we like each other, we may even . . ." He doesn't finish.

He doesn't have to finish. "Um, be together."

Harrald shrugs. "Or not. You never know about these things." Then he beams. "But however it works out, we're getting MOOmarried and we're staying MOOmarried no matter what her husband says RL . . ."

Zan stirs uncomfortably. "She has a husband RL?"

"Doesn't everybody?"

"That's different."

She can't see his face so she won't know whether he is thinking, *oh, sure it is.* Harrald says, "Oh yes, but that doesn't keep us from being married here."

"I'm not sure that's such a good thing, Harrald. Being married only here."

"Take it from me, it's the best. No recriminations. No morning breath."

"It depends on who you think you are." With Reverdy, she thinks, it's going to be either or. But she loves Charlie so much that she can't know which either she means, or which or. *In the mind*, she thinks, *I love Charlie with my whole heart and body but Reverdy and I love each other in the kingdom of the soul. Oh God I am confused.*

Then Harrald confides, "Don't worry about me, I've been MOOmarried before."

"You have?"

"Eletheria," he says.

Zan can't stop herself. "That tramp?"

"It was just a passing thing," he says brightly. "I don't want you to think for one minute that's what broke my wife and me up."

"Your wife here?"

"No, my wife RL." Harrald goes on, pulling Zan into unwelcome complicity. "Faye, you remember Faye."

"I remember you telling me about Faye."

"And you helped me get the guts to dump Faye. Anyway, Faye found out about Kismine when she and I were meeting in Vegas and . . ."

You were meeting Kismine in Vegas? "Oop," Zan says. *This place is* not *good for me.* "Somebody's here RL. I've got to go."

She disconnects. Disturbed, Jenny waits until the display tells her that Harrald's logged off for the day before she reconnects. He's a data entry clerk, she knows, and his internet access ends promptly at five. Only a few more hours and Reverdy will be along and in the meantime, there is the business of Lark. Zan does not expect to run into Mireya which is like running headlong into a buzzsaw, nor does she expect Mireya to call her a slut for loving Reverdy.

My God, she thinks, *does she think I'm like Velvet? Kismine? I am nothing like Velvet or Kismine.* She types @shutup so she won't have to listen to Mireya any more. Still, the two exchanges have shaken her, and when Reverdy finally logs on she flies into the Dak Bungalow and starts talking before they even hug. "Oh," she says, "I'm so glad you're here!"

Tom homes in on her distress as surely as if he's been tracking her state of mind. "Maybe you'd better tell me," he says. "I know you're upset, and you know you can tell me anything."

Uncertainty makes her inarticulate. *MOOmarried*, she thinks, *is that all I can hope for?* She wants to ask; she's afraid to ask. "I wish," she says. "I just *wish*."

He hugs, rubbing his chin in her hair; even sitting at her keyboard thousands of miles away she feels the outline of his jaw, the loving pressure. "Life is wishing," Reverdy says.

Afraid to go on because she's afraid of what she'll hear she asks, "Have you seen Lark?"

"Not today. But I think it's OK. Last night he said he'd bought some time. But that's enough about Lark," he says. The words come up like grace notes aimed at her heart. "I really only want to know about you."

She can't stop herself, she says, "I just wonder when we're going to meet."

He temporizes. "If we need to, we'll meet when we need to."

"What if I need it now?"

Reverdy doesn't answer. "Would meeting keep *us* from being perfect?"

"Oh, Rev!"

"Now, if you'll let me touch you *here* . . ."

Needs it, needs him, needs not to be here right now because the implications make her tremble; she loves Tom so much and he will only come part of the way. Stay and she'll start to cry; instead she says, "I love you, Tom, but I can't be here right now." She won't type: *I'll come back when you're ready to commit.* Right now she's so confused she can't be sure she'll ever come back.

nineteen

REVERDY

Context, Reverdy thinks as Zan disconnects. Everything is context. He loves her, she'll be back. In a world you make up as you go along, you always get what you want.

On StElene, *you are what you type*. The hitch is, that in the realm of performative utterance, words define you and they also limit you. Reverdy can't be any better than the text he writes. It is a puzzle. He wants to flow out of the box and into his lover's bedroom RL but as long as he keeps her at a distance, their love is safe. No accidents, no surprises, just a miracle of control. He can no longer identify the parts of himself he has invented here, and which are real. Nor can he know how much of the real truth remains. Is Reverdy a pencil sketch faintly perceived by others or does his lover, for instance, really know him to the soul? Is what he presents here on StElene the real truth of Tom Dearden or only something he made up?

In this ideal life on a plane far above the daily exigencies, he's cast himself as ideal lover: articulate, witty, a hero perhaps . . .

This is also Tom Dearden, typing with a cigarette clenched

between his teeth and ashes dribbling into the keyboard. *God,* he thinks, *what part am I really writing for myself?* Doomed hero? Not sure. Committed lover? Jury's still out. Reckless, he thinks. Laughing, rakehell, because at heart at bottom, inside and in spite of the outer, physical shell that people in the drab polar landscape he inhabits RL will see if they care enough to look, what he types is who Tom Dearden really is. He thinks.

Reverdy is not what he seems. What does it mean?

When Zan pressed him, he responded with a question. "What do you want it to mean?" It may be that he doesn't know himself.

But if there is a snake in every Eden and the snake is us, there will always be some part of earthbound Tom Dearden that needs to keep shooting itself in the foot.

page Mireya Do you really think I care that you are fucking that thug?

page Azeath You only think Mireya loves you. She's using you to get me back.

page StOnge Tell the others. I'm on to your game.

For reasons he doesn't necessarily understand, all the elements: his scheme to expose Suntum and pirate StElene, the public push-and-shove with Mireya and her pigheaded, most righteous Azeath—his plan to post his completed history— suggest that Tom Dearden a.k.a. Reverdy isn't just flirting with disaster. He's coming on to it. And he's coming on strong.

twenty/@twenty

JENNY/ZAN

The minute I typed *@exit* I was sorry. I wanted to go back. I need Reverdy, but Charlie's here! He walks in with an armful of presents and apologies for being gone overnight. What was it this time, the duty, or a visiting bigwig from the State Department with round-the-clock meetings, or just some party at the club? He's gone so much now that I forget. Correction. I look forward to it because I can put the kids to bed early and log on. I can play all night if I want to, or I could. But now I see Charlie's sweet face and I know this has to change, I love him and he's right here! Standing *this close,* while Tom is locked away from me, safe inside the box.

OK, I just decided to leave him there. It's time to quit StElene.

Am I trying to detox? Unclear. If it isn't an addiction, I'm showing signs. I've been hanging online half the night, living on StElene even when Reverdy's not around. I read the posts on endless, stupid mailing lists or look for friends and in the absence of friends I find new players to talk to, anything to fill the void until Charlie comes home. I port into the grand ballroom laughing like a schoolgirl at a party, hugging here, waving there, you bet I'm wasting time. I'm short on sleep and testy with my patients. And if Martha looks at me with growing— not concern, exactly, but with that professional eye ... I crash in front of the TV and sleep until it's time to put the kids to bed; I nap between patients and sometimes I drift off while they're talking, coming to only when I hear that ominous silence that lets you know your client's waiting. Most useful phrase at this point? "And what do *you* think?" I've been short-shrifting my life!

I'm done obsessing over it. Take today. He'd promised we'd meet, we were supposed to make up for everything we failed to say and do to each other last time. He came on weird, evasive. What kept him, anyway? What does he do when we're apart?

Being on StElene is getting to be like working a second job—too many friends counting on me, too much gossip to deflect, Reverdy's political posts, supporting letters he wants me to post. Last week StElene was down overnight, all connections refused. If I couldn't be there, nobody could. Not Mireya, not Azeath, not Reverdy or his enemies the Directors. In a way, it was a relief.

So it's time to quit. Turn my back and walk away. Except, of course, from Lark. Unlike Tom, who doesn't trust me enough to tell me how to reach him off StElene, Lark and I are in touch RL. When he's feeling stronger, we're going to talk on the phone. Quitting's easy, I know. Just go to the end of Reverdy's dock in front of the GrandHotel and jump.

How can I not? Charlie's standing here with that big Charlie grin; it should be easy to forget the hotel, all that *happening* in the night. "I missed you so *much*." We hug, later we make love; he thinks it's great sex but I am squirming with guilt. How can this nice guy still love me when the best part of my life goes on in a place he doesn't know about? Where I'm unfaithful with a man I've never met? I'm no better than Harrald or Velvet. But I am.

Ridiculous, I think, burying my nose in the sweet Charlie smell that made me fall in love with him in the first place. *I don't need all that. This is Charlie, that I've promised to spend my life with. And we're going to spend it here.* Safe with Charlie, I tell myself, *This. This is what matters. This is real.* I'll end it tonight. And in spite of my best intentions I groan.

Charlie tightens his arms. "What's the matter?"

StElene is only a trap. A beautiful, seductive trap. Grief overturns me. *I just won't go back.*

Charlie touches my face. "You're crying! What is it?"

"Nothing, I just."

"This isn't about wanting a baby, is it? I mean if it is, we could . . ."

For a minute, I can't take his meaning. That hurt has gotten old. It's so old that I have a hard time remembering who that person was. And I am crying for real. Sobbing, I roll closer. "Charlie, it's nothing, I just!"

But I am gasping with fresh knowledge.

Over. StElene was a temporary aberration, now I'm over it. Zan and the man she loves best have no future in this world and in that one, the more I see Tom, no, Reverdy, the more I want to see him and the harder it gets to be anywhere else. *Our marriage isn't suffering.* I feel Charlie moving under my hands and I feel sorry for him. And extremely powerful. *Yet. But it will,* I think, and as Charlie and I embrace I begin the countdown until I can connect. Which I will do later, flushed and still shaky from making thunderous love RL. And I will do it because of what I now know.

I can't leave StElene without saying goodbye.

ZAN

Fine, she thinks resolutely as Charlie slips away from her, submerging in sleep. *It's over. I just won't do this any more.* But she has to tell Reverdy goodbye. She can't just quit StElene without telling them; Lark will worry. Tom could die. She'll just log on one last time and explain. She'll just leave Reverdy a goodbye note—she can slip in without paging him, and if he happens to see she's logged on and wants to join . . . well. Look, she has to tell Lark. They'll definitely stay in touch RL—phone, visit, whatever it takes to help him get strong enough to keep going. She is, after all, a therapist. She needs to plan with Lark, send farewell posts to Jazzy and Harrald, oh, and drop in on Articular; she can't just vanish from her friends' lives without explaining. She slips out of bed, leaving Charlie behind. If she wants to kick the habit, it has to be a clean break.

She has people to see, things to say, so much to do.

Shaking, she types: *stelene.moo.mud.org 8888.* By the time she connects she is in tears. And without being able to stop herself she types *page Reverdy I've come to say goodbye*

And in seconds, Reverdy is in her beautiful, beautiful room, rushing to his grieving lover in the serenity of *Zan's Tower.*

"I thought you'd *never* come back!"

"Oh, my dear!" She begins to cry.

"My God, my darling, what is it?"

"Nothing." She is weeping in both worlds. "I just."

"Is it Charlie? Is it something about the baby? Love, tell me what's the matter? I love you so much!"

She wants to tell Rev and she can't tell him; Zan, who can say anything to her lover on StElene, who has said anything, can't find any way to tell Reverdy, no, Tom Dearden, she can't tell Tom Dearden that she'll never see him again, it would break their hearts. She can't find the right words for goodbye. At least not yet. "It's Lark," she says. "I'm worried to death about Lark."

"Don't be, we'll take care of him. He's safe here. The three of us, together."

"Here?" She can't stop crying. "For God's sake, Rev. Which *here*?"

He knows what she means. In their long, loving talks about everything, Zan and Reverdy have sawed back and forth over distinctions. They measure the differences between this ideal world they have created and the world outside the box; it is more real to them than the sheer ugliness, the constraints and crude exigencies of the physical world. They talk about how little that world matters, the one they can't control.

"Here, of course," he says. "The only here that matters. *Our* here. We love each other in eternity, Zan. We can take care of Lark here."

"How, if we can't help him in real life?"

Then Reverdy says the most beautiful thing. "We give each other the strength!"

"The strength?"

"Everything. Through love."

"But." She begins the old argument. "What if it isn't real?"

"You know it is. We've found a way into each other's souls. I know you better than anybody I've ever known, Jenny Wilder, and I love you better than anybody I could ever love."

"Oh, Reverdy. Oh, Tom!" She is crying again. "Oh! I came to tell you I . . ."

"Shhshh. Don't. Don't say anything. I know what you're going through, both here and RL. I know how hard it is for you. Don't you think we're both being torn apart? It's hard for me too."

"Being apart?"

"Being together!" Reverdy tries to smile. "Wanting so much. And being apart and wanting you more. And more." He hesitates. "But maybe wanting is the best part of us? Sparks flying upward."

The tears stop. "And everything that rises?"

Reverdy completes the loving formula. As if they are making a pact. "Will converge. We'll all be together some day, I promise."

It takes her breath. "You promise?"

"I do." In a few words Reverdy sketches a beautiful island where he and Zan can be together forever—happy forever, generous in their ideal love. "I'm working on it now."

She needs to break the news but it's getting harder; her will falters and fails. "With a place for Lark?"

"Yes." He seals it. "With a place for Lark."

"If only," Zan says. "If only! And you and Lark and I will . . ."

"We'll all be together in a great new place some day, I promise."

"A new place?"

"I promise. If you promise to stay with me."

"Oh, God. Oh, Reverdy. How could I not!" And, comprehending the impossibility, Zan is ripped from top to bottom by grief; then she's in her lover's arms, he who sees straight into her heart, sobbing because of course she can never leave him and Reverdy, Reverdy is saying all the right things, no of course she can't leave him not ever, he'd die and she says she would die and he says once again for both their sakes that they aren't hurting anybody.

She sobs, "If only we could be together RL."

"But we are my darling, we are."

But are they really?

She doesn't care! In a few graceful phrases she and Reverdy slip into the dance, so unlike what people in the physical world perceive as "real," that their love incandesces, more powerful, more moving than anything Charlie can do to her in physical life because this kind of love knows no limits. Free of all constraints, it expands in the mind, blindingly bright. Thoughts planted in the imagination blossom in explosions of light and this best of all possible loves shimmers precisely because it is incomplete and all the best parts are just ahead. As they make love Zan loses all sense of time passing until she hears Charlie's kids stirring downstairs. He'll be getting up! It's time to leave.

The goodbyes are hard to say, but they are sweet. Shuddering, Zan hugs her lover, shaken by how close she came to losing him. Then she sits for a moment in front of the blank screen with the tears running down. It's several minutes before Jenny starts downstairs to dress and make breakfast; it's time to take care of them because in her part of the world, at least, it's dawn.

twenty-one

JENNY

It's breakfast time. Coffee brewed, orange juice poured, crumbs on the table, newspaper folded, everything in our yellow kitchen just the way it ought to be with the one exception.

We are in the kitchen, or Charlie is. I'm somewhere else. The most important part of me is lost somewhere between the night on StElene and here. I hurt all over, I came *this close* to losing Reverdy! I logged off too late to crawl back into bed. I can hardly bear to begin another day. I am hung up on the problem: I can't bear to leave but I know I shouldn't stay, I'm spread so thin that I yip when Charlie speaks to me. "What, Charlie? What!"

"I said, your eyes look like two cigarette holes burned in a sheet. Is there something you want to tell me?"

I love him too much to say. "Nothing, Charlie. I don't know."

"Honey, what is it?" He strokes my arm. He doesn't want to worry me, he says, but he's been getting anonymous phone calls, some strange woman, doesn't give her name, she keeps trying to tell him something in this harsh voice . . . I go stiff in his arms. "Babe?"

"Just tired. So. Somebody phoned and they said. What?"

"She was trying to tell me . . . Agh. I don't know what the hell she was trying to tell me. It was ugly, I don't need that."

Mireya? If it is Mireya, he couldn't begin to understand what she's trying to tell him. Unless. What if it's somebody calling about me and Rick. Did I accidentally let Rick get too close? "Some local crackpot?"

"Whoever this woman is, she's crazy. The voice is halfway between obscene phone caller and Nazi schoolteacher, as soon as I find out it's her, I hang up."

"What makes you think it's a her?"

I feel his knuckles in my hair. "Jenny, is something going on that I should know about?"

This brings me back to earth so fast that my neck snaps. "Nothing!" *Does he know? What if he knows?*

"Honey, you're strung so tight that I can't reach you."

Has Mireya come offline and messed up my life? "If it's the calls, forget about the calls."

"You know it isn't the calls, Jen. What's going on with you?"

What gave me away? I dissemble. "Bad day at work, I guess."

"Like, your weird patient." He is fishing.

"What?"

"That compulsive guy you told me about, dark hair, came to the base looking for me?" Charlie's squinting, as if he sees Rick Berringer loping out of the middle distance, closing on us.

"He . . . what?"

"I blew him off, I could see he's crazy."

Relieved, I laugh. "Right, and he's been phoning you." Just

as long as it isn't Mireya, I think. *He knows. He doesn't know.*

"Not unless he's had a sex change."

"Or disguised his voice. It's just a crank call, Charlie."

But he doesn't back off. "Or not. I'm worried about you, babe. What are you doing up there all night, locked in with the computer?

If he does know, what am I going to do? "Is there a problem?"

"I think so."

So he does know. "Then I guess we'd better talk about it."

He says blindly, "You're working too hard and it's starting to show."

Thank God. He doesn't have a clue. I touch his cheek. "It's just work, Charlie. I'm fine, Really."

"No you're not. You're wired all the time now. I worry."

"Well, don't. The office, I can handle. Rick, I'll hand off, OK? And I've been jamming on a . . . project." Inspiration grabs me by the throat and drags me through. "A special project. Don't worry, I get like this when I'm in a work crunch. It'll be over soon."

"If you can't get it done in the daytime, it can't be good for you. Babe, you work too hard!" Charlie's eyes are warm in the sunlight. His tanned face spreads in a morning smile; fit and energetic and smelling of real life in the Carolina sunshine, my real-life mate Charlie Wilder looks so sweet and normal that I am ashamed. It's like meeting a citizen from another world.

"I promise, I'll be fine."

"All that time on the computer. Running on no sleep. It's eating you up. Can't you keep it inside office hours?"

So I let him have it. "It's not as if you're home in front of the TV every night."

"That's different," Charlie says.

I am on shaky ground here. "How?" And the secret, selfish part of me stands back and laughs because he can't even guess the answer.

Then he blindsides me. "Look at your hands, they're jerking like grasshoppers on a griddle."

I look down; the veins are blue, as if the blood is running so close to the surface that the skeins of my central nervous system are starting to show. And. Surprise. My hands really are twitching. It takes a conscious effort to hold them still. "I'm fine."

"No you're not. You need to take a few nights off and chill."

"I can't!" Wait. Way too sharp. Temporize. "I can't do this job in the daytime." I am thinking fast. "It's a communications project."

"Communications?"

"Yes. A communications project that depends on my subjects, and my subjects are only available at night. It's just research, Charlie." Bingo, I have the right story to tell him. Justification. I am *not* wasting my time. "I'm doing this, like, online survey?"

"A survey."

"For *The American Review of Psychology*," I tell Charlie and as I do, like yang meeting yin after a long separation, the two parts of my life meet and snap together with a satisfying click. In a way, it justifies all those hours I've spent at the keyboard, languishing until Reverdy logs on. I don't understand my obsession with Tom Dearden and I certainly don't want to try to explain it to Charlie, but I have just hit on a way to talk about my life on StElene to outsiders and make it sound like a rational thing.

"You're writing something?"

"Yes. I'm interviewing people in a great big online community. I'm going to write about it and publish, Charlie." A survey. Yes! I'm not hooked on StElene and crazy in love with Reverdy, I'm doing research. "After all, I'm a professional."

"You are, you're a real pro, you can work anywhere." Charlie really is wonderful; he will go to any lengths to be happy. My loving, workaholic husband says, "That's what I love best about you." If he's about to say anything more, or different, he swallows it.

"Then you're OK with it?"

"Can't wait to read it," he says nicely, but I can see that he is studying me. If what's going on behind my face is too intricate for him to read, that doesn't keep him from squinting hard; yes he suspects but can't prove that there is something going on.

I say, "And it keeps me out of trouble while you're gone."

"If you're getting in trouble while I'm gone." His voice is uneven. He's off to Cherry Point for the weekend, which puts him in an ambiguous position here. "I know this computer thing is worthwhile, but I really do worry about you. Oh honey, if you want me to cancel this one, I can try."

Yes, he definitely suspects there is something going on and it doesn't make me feel any better to know that he'll never understand what. Best not to talk about it. If we don't, it can't hurt us. I smile. "Don't worry, I have my project to keep me busy."

"And the kids."

"And the kids." I look at my watch. "Charlie, you're going to be late."

He knows; he doesn't know. He says, "This is more important."

Willfully, I misunderstand. "I'm so glad you think so! I'm asking some pretty hard questions. About what these people think they're doing spending half their lives online. So all this, ah. Typing. Long nights at the computer that you're worried about. It's research." I am making sense of it for both of us. *Research, of course.* What a relief! The minute I say it, it becomes true.

twenty-two

LARK

Boy, safe at the top of another week thank God. One more week guaranteed. It's Monday and in spite of Reverdy's splitting just when he most needed him, no apologies, no excuses, Lark has survived. He is still safe in the basement of the Pinkney house. In spite of hardhearted Howard's efforts, Lark, who will never let anybody call him Hubert ever again, Lark is connecting from the Pinkney manor, basement level, the elevator DOWN stops here.

1. Monday, by God, and he's still here. He's hanging on by his toenails but he's here. Friday was Howard's big deadline. Friday came and went and he's still here. They had a fight.

2. Instead of marking the End of Life as we know it, with his computer disassembled and him out on the curb, the fight with Howard went Lark's way. Without hitting anybody, he kind of won.

What he can't figure out is where Reverdy's gone, he just took off at the top of the weekend! Hasn't been back even though Lark posted him.

```
Date:        Thursday, May 3, 11:30.02 199-PDT
From:        Lark (#053042)
To:          Reverdy (#010024)
Subject:     Emergency
```

Pal, I'm really going to need you Fri. If you don't
help, the 'rents are going to kick me out at six.

But I'm still here, Lark thinks, trembling with excitement.

It's a very big deal for him. Keeping his connection. It means
he can still get to StElene. If he got cut off from there, he'd die.
Everything he cares about is there. No matter how bad things
get RL you can make it if you know you have friends out there
that care about you, that you can tell what's ailing you. On
StElene even people that are terribly busy will stop what they're
doing to help you with your troubles. You tell and they say,
and it always makes you feel better—not worse, like the college
shrink and the hospital shrinks told the 'rents, who are always
blaming him. Real friends always know the right thing to say.
Having somebody there to talk to helps, and StElene is the one
place where Lark doesn't get all strangled when he tries to speak.
On StElene, he can talk!

StElene is the biggest thing in his life. Without it, he would
die. Talking with people *F2F*—face-to-face—RL has always been
hard for him, his blood clots around his tonsils and his throat
seizes up, but on StElene he can pour out his soul. Support
comes streaming in. It's the one place where he knows he's
loved. Being loved is what makes you strong. When he's half
crazy with worry and ready to die all he has to do is tell his
friends on StElene and they're all *there there*. He can even laugh.

He's terribly lucky, knowing them. Like now. Incredible
things have happened in just three days. The mails are pouring

in. Since Friday he's had MOOmails from Jazzy and Eva and Katherone and Rosie and practically everybody else he cares about, even crusty Domnita gets out of the leather mode when he's around, she's very sweet with him. When he checks in on the grand ballroom, which he does regularly although he's actually logged on waiting for Reverdy, sympathy comes pouring out to him even from players he hardly knows. All StElene is on his case, and that's on his case in a good way. Everybody who matters, that is, which makes him feel kind of important. It makes him feel good.

Everybody knows. It's the brand new mailing list. * *lark.*

It's what got him through. His friends gave him courage when he needed it most. It was Zan's idea. She said he needed support to get through this and put up a new list: *lark.* It's growing by leaps and bounds! Zan started it Friday morning, because Reverdy was still missing. Lark was grieving and he has to face it, Zan is grieving too. She did it to cheer them up.

Reverdy just split. God, is he all right?

About Howard's deadline. Bingo-bango, disconnect Hubert and get him out of the house. Lark sneaked upstairs in the night and found Howard's Things To Do list on the month-at-a-glance calendar: *Friday, 6 p.m. Move Hubert out.* At six p.m. Howard expected to drag Lark's stuff upstairs and kick him out of the Pinkney house. He thought Lark had found a place to move his stuff to. How? How's he supposed to go renting a room when he's broke plus he has trouble talking to people RL plus, he's so busy on StElene that he can't disconnect long enough to start?

Well, he's hanging in here in the basement, he's made it safely into Monday, no thanks to Reverdy. Still no sign of him. He doesn't log on. Lark keeps typing *@find Reverdy @find Reverdy page Reverdy Where are you anyway?* He's even phoned

Tom Dearden's house a couple of dozen times RL, but the machine's off and nobody picks up the phone. Should he be angry or scared?

Thank God for the list. Friday morning Lark was all bent about his deadline and Zan was all bent about Reverdy vanishing, they got talking and out of nowhere the list *lark* was born. "Rev would want it," she said, like it would bring him back.

"Yeah," Lark said. He sat with her while she took a nonspecific *list* object from the object catalog. Then he showed her how to make a dedicated list, and she created *lark*. She crossposted the announcement to all the other lists so everybody on StElene knows. Except Reverdy. Maybe he'll find out about the list and come back!

lark is a mailing list where Lark writes about his problems and people who care about him can post what they think. Turns out they all do. Everybody cares. The regulars are having a little forum, mailing back and forth pro and con about whether Lark's dad should back off kicking him out altogether or just pay him a year's support in a place of his choosing if he agrees to move out.

And the mail, the mail! Lark's had offers of startup money, places to stay, a friend in Seattle even offered him a job in their office if he can make it out there, and a divorced mom he's never met posted an offer to front for his ticket, people have been flat out knocking themselves out day and night all weekend, just being nice. Lark's been up nights and half the days just keeping track of the posts, posting responses to the list plus sending individual mails to everybody who writes. He's kind of a celebrity, it's weird. People are like, *We know you can make it through this, terrific guy and good player like you, so please hang in there and stay cool.* This is the best thing about life on StElene. Knowing all these great people, real friends who are always there for you.

But he misses Reverdy terribly. He has so much to tell! Truth is, Lark isn't in all that good shape after all, with the pressure piling up, and in the lacuna while he waits for Reverdy to show up on his screen, he tries to sort it out.

Here's how it came down. Friday Howard shouted into the basement before dawn. "You have twelve hours." Lark pretended he didn't hear and kept typing. He was posting his survival log on *lark*.

```
Message      1 on *Lark
Date:        Fri. May 4 03:57:04 199-PDT
From:        Lark (#053042)
To:          *Lark (#4030)
Subject:     Today's the day.
```

First I want to thank Zan for creating this mailing list especially for me so I can keep you guys up on my situation without spamming too many lists.

OK, are you with me? Something awful's coming down in my life.
Here's the deal.
Today's the day. You see, while you guys thought I was all happy and everything, some bad things were coming down in my life. I have a deadline! And it's today!

Unless I can think of something amazing, today's the day the father kicks me out. I know hardhearted Howard thinks it's going to make a man of me or some damn thing, but the truth is, he's killing me. Does anybody really believe that throwing me out into

```
the world is going to make me talk to people, when
except for him and the mother and of course here with
you guys, where I get to talk my fkn head off and you
love me for it, I can't talk to people at all?
```

The post got lots longer, of course. He owes it to anybody who @*subscribed* to *lark to give the chronology. He let it all hang out. *1 on* *lark was followed by others he posted on the half-hour, because once you start a crisis thread on a mailing list, you owe it to people to keep them up to date. There were players staying logged on just to see how the story came out. No. Better! They were staying logged on to talk him through. He was getting dozens of posts by that time, with more to come. Dozens of them! Friends and people he hardly knew were filling the list with messages of love and support. When this is over and he's living in some really nice apartment somewhere with his workstation and his stereo and a squashy sofa and lots of light coming in the windows, Lark is going to download the list and print it out for his grandchildren, but right now he's too frantic keeping up with them.

It went like this. Every hour on the hour Howard yelled down the basement stairs like a gorilla roaring into the tight end of a tunnel, "Six p.m., do you hear? You get done packing and get your crap up here by six or I come down and get you myself. I don't know where you're going but the truck's coming at six p.m. I've hired a damn van to move your stuff."

Of course Lark didn't answer because Hubert's not his name. He was thinking: *shut up. Shut up and let me type.*

But Howard never lets anything go by. "Hubert? HUBERT! Son!"

I'm not your son.

```
Message      25 on *Lark
Date:        Fri. May 4 16:57:09 PDT
```

From: Lark (#053042)

To: *Lark (#4030)

I hate my father. I hate his voice. He's still at it
up there. It's killing my ears. He sounds like he
wants to come down here and kill me. No. He sounds
like the truth. That he wants me dead.

Even when Lark screamed in pain, the yelling never let up.
Somewhere upstairs the mother was bawling. Lark had just finished posting this information when the whole house shook.
Howard was thumping down the basement stairs on those fat
feet. Lark ran @*time* on StElene. My God, it was half-past six!
The U-Haul truck was out front. Howard must have figured it
out that Lark wasn't coming up, at least not on his own, so he
came down. Howard came tramping down into the cellar, yelling. Lark did what you do when that happens: you turn around
and try to stare him down.

Howard was shaking all over, hugely pissed. "You keep
making that face and I'll sock it."

Lark just stared. Hard. How could he keep up with his posts
when he was in this staring match with his father that he can't
stand the sight of? He couldn't see to type! He could almost
hear the mail piling up on *lark, fresh posts dropping in. But
he was locked onto Howard, and he couldn't let down until
Howard's eyes wavered and this thing was settled and done.

"I said wipe off that face!" Finally Howard had to sock
Lark, just to make him stop staring. Knocked him off his chair.

Lark stood. He and Howard faced off. The asshole is bigger
than his brilliant but erratic (Lark read that somewhere and he
likes it, "brilliant but erratic," he's added it to his description
on StElene) son. Howard got him in an armlock and grappled
him up the cellar stairs, no problem, the man is big as a cow.

Howard got him upstairs into the kitchen OK, Father Triumphant, but then the battle went the other way.

```
Message      26 on *Lark
Date:        Fri. May 4 17:02:44 199-PDT
From:        Finster (#07930)
To:          *Lark (#4030)
Subject:     Been there, had that.


Gad, man, your post brought back so much bad shit I
hadda log off and take a three-mile run to cool down
so I could write this because I've been where you
are and I know where it's heading. Let him hit you
and get away with it and it's only the beginning.
So this is going to sound crazy but since I've been
where you are and come out the other side, I want to
tell you where to be at with this. You have to log
everything he does to you and take it to the law. No
stuff, you might even get him put away for this. I
did.
```

Desperation may not make you strong, but it makes you smart. In Marjorie's kitchen Lark went limp like a war protester, he was, like: *I'm not doing this, you are. Kill me and it's on your soul.*

Do you know how hard it is to drag a dead weight?

So instead of shoving this, like, embarrassment to him, this perpetual inconvenience, out of his life and onto the street, Howard Pinkney got wedged in his own front doorway, frustrated and puffing hard. He couldn't even get the door open because Lark slumped against it until Howard gave him a kick in the soft part under his ribs and he slid to one side and fell over. Lark grunted in pain because he could hear the mother sniffling and he had the sense that this was right. "Ez-*eff!*"

Behind them, Marjorie gave a little shriek.

"Marjorie, you stay out of this!"

Howard got the door open.

Outside loomed.

It was terrifying.

Lark froze.

They were in stasis.

```
Message     30 on *Lark
Date:       Fri. May 4 17: 05:01 199-PDT
From:       Jazzy (#08930)
To:         *Lark (#4030)
Subject:    Patience and Fortitude
```

We all love you, Lark baby. Hang in!

Lark flattened like a postage stamp while Howard banged on his own chest, trying to get his breath and in the background, Marjorie failed to muffle a sob. Moving with great caution Lark shifted until he was composed with feet crossed and arms folded and his hair streaming, just like the statue of a drowned knight. When he caught Marjorie looking, he did the last thing. Cleverly, he smiled.

When your son smiles at you like that, for the first time since he left for college, what are you going to do? How can you let a third party throw him into the street?

Lark has never really been sure if Marjorie likes him much, but she is a mother. Typing to his friends on StElene, some of whom are mothers, Lark's learned how to use the mother thing, use it for all it's worth. He murmured what Domnita told him to say, "If anything bad happens, it's on you."

This shook her.

The father made a terrible tactical mistake. He barked, "Get up." He gave Lark another little kick. "I said, get *up*."

"Eh-z!"

Marjorie snatched the father's arm. "No, Howard. We can't."

"But we agreed!"

"Not like this."

"He's had his deadline, Marjorie. He's past it."

"Look at the poor kid, he's shivering."

He was; it was true. Howard had wrestled the door open wider. Outside, the truck was waiting. Too many people out there! Lark wanted to roll onto his belly and wriggle back toward the kitchen. All he wanted in the world was to snake back down to the basement, but he couldn't. Not yet. He had to stay in place and hold his breath and wait for this to play itself out, praying hard for the grace to hold perfectly still with his arms crossed over his chest.

Marjorie said, "Please. Just give him a little more time."

"Time for what?" The father was furious and breathing hard; Lark's frail but he's tough and the struggle took it out of Howard, dragging him up the stairs. He glowered. "Time for what?"

That's one fucking hard question. Lark squinched up his eyes. *I don't know.*

The mother said it for him; she showed her husband empty palms but her voice was sliding around in entreaty. "I don't know."

"We can't just let the little . . ."

"Howard, look at him!"

"It's disgusting."

You think Lark's been wasting time MOOing? No way. Lark lay still and let this happen just like his friends told him to; clever Lark.

```
Message      39 on *Lark
Date:        Fri. May 4 17:32:30 199-PDT
From:        FloridaMae (#109030)
```

```
To:          *Lark (#4030)
Subject:     Mothers Unite
```

Oh, sweetie, if you were mine I'd bake pies for you
all day every day and let you stay logged on forever, if you'd promise to spend it talking to me,
you are the best and the funniest! I totally feel
for you and what I have to say right now is, look to
the mother. She's probably the source of all your
troubles, mothers are the enemy and they can not be
trusted, I should know. Moms have their hearts in
the right places OK and they probably want to be
strong but they're really very week.***oh, my typing and no backspace*** WEAK. When I was nine my
stepfather tried to have sex with me. When I told
her she just said I had a dirty mouth, so you just
hang in there sweetie, OK? Hang in and trust no one
and takecaretakecaretakecare.

"Howard, there's no point throwing him out in the street if
he's just going to lie there," the mother said reasonably. "The
police will only bring him back inside."

"Nobody's going to just lie out in the street like a goddamn
refugee. Not even Hubert. He'll move."

"Don't be so sure. Remember what he was like when we
got him back from college."

Lark opened one eye: *I wasn't* that *bad. Or was I?* OK, he
wasn't exactly fine. He hated college, his soul naked and quivering out where everybody could see it was too much; all those
strangers, it was like being peeled and dropped onto a griddle,
the heat was killing him! Then he crawled into his computer one
night and it was OK. He went netsurfing and lucked into St-
Elene. Fell into this life. Who wouldn't want to stay here, con-

nected to a place where he could value and be valued, where he could talk his head off when real-life encounters make his lungs so tight he can't breathe and he dies a dozen times and his head explodes with unspoken words. On StElene even at the beginning he was eloquent, witty. They think he's debonair. He stayed up nights and into the days ignoring entreaties from his roommates; when they kept bothering him he locked the door and left them hammering in the hall outside . . .

```
Message     43 on *Lark
Date:       Fri. May 4 17:50:30 199-PDT
From:       Jimbo (#302036)
To:         *Lark (#4030)
Subject:    Asking For It
```

FloridaMae, don't blame your mom for what happened. Us guys know you are one succulent, come-hither babe. Ha ha.

Like a passive resister, Lark lay still, but unlike a passive resister, he would not cover his head. Crazy as he was to get back to the computer and report on this outrage, he kept his arms folded across his breast and let his eyes follow the mother as she paced, trilling in entreaty.

"Consider, Howard, you thought people would be good for him. Just look. Look what college did to him!"

```
Message     50 on *Lark
Date:       Fri. May 4 17:54:10 199-PDT
From:       Cheribelle (#025033)
To:         *Lark (#4030)
Subject:    Jimbo's egregious post
```

This may be a laughing matter to some of you fools out there, but Jimbo should be ashamed of himself.

```
This is serious business and we need to pull to-
gether to help Lark through.
Well, FloridaMae, you think you're right about
mothers, but I'm a mother and I'm here to tell you
that you're wrong. Lark's mom has a perfectly good
right to be trusted because there are more good moms
in the barrel than bad ones. I think Lark's lucky to
have a mom at all. Just think. What would happen if
you woke up one day and your mother was dead?
```

Howard snapped, "I can't help it if he's an emotional cripple. Besides, that was before the hospital. It was before the drugs. I put out a fortune for those drugs."

OK, so what if he really was disconnected and raving when they broke down the door to his dorm room and paramedics dragged him out? That was a long time ago. Last year; hell, he was only a kid. Eighteen, and if he had to do some time in the hospital and they wouldn't let him out until he promised to take the drugs, so what?

About the drugs. Howard doesn't know it, folks, but Lark has definitely left off taking stupid drugs. Goofballs and la la pills may mellow you out but they also slow your reflexes beyond dreadful, and there's no place for slow players on StElene.

"He'll get himself together," Marjorie said, like she really believed it. "He'll get going on his own."

On his own. The words chilled Lark's bones.

"No he won't."

"Just a week," Marjorie said and to Lark it seemed like the eternity he needed. "Just one more tiny little week." She looked down. "You promise you'll get it together, don't you, dear? If those are the terms?"

And Lark opened both eyes for the mother and he smiled his best baby brother smile.

"See, Howard, he's promising."

```
Message      92 on *Lark
Date:        Fri. May 4 19:30:02 199-PDT
From:        Baggins
To:          *Lark
Subject:     Patience and Fortitude
```

Lark, baby. Are you OK? You haven't posted in more
than an hour. Do you need the StElene Raiders to
come and rescue you?

"OK," Howard said finally. "OK."

So here he is, and he has another week. A week. And such
outpourings of love! Never mind that the mail's piled up eight
ways to Sunday, Lark will answer every single post if it takes
the rest of his life. It's easier than jump-starting a life outside
the house.

Hey, anything can happen in a week. Reverdy could come
back and fix everything. Howard could drop dead, or change
his mind. The world could turn over for Lark and open up like
an Easter egg. He could turn over and open up like an Easter
egg. He could make it upstairs for dinner tomorrow and sit at
the table talking to the mother and dad and the next day he
could go out and get a job . . . and meanwhile there's the list.
He has to keep up with the list.

Look, in a week Reverdy could come home to StElene.
Apologize. Get him back into college because Reverdy's so
slick. Plus Reverdy is well-connected; he could sort it out with
Lark's dean or whatever, and if he can't, his friend Zan is working on a plan. Lark has called her office in South Carolina and
they've talked on the phone RL. She'll think of something or
Lark will, but meanwhile the sky is blue and the birds are singing on StElene and posts are piling up on *lark* so he's got that.

They are his public and he owes it to them to give back as good as he got. At this very moment people are crowding the grand Ballroom waiting to talk to him, Lark is this week's MOOcelebrity so he might as well get up and smell the flowers while they're still growing in his life.

@twenty-three

ZAN

In her months on StElene, Zan has run into dozens of social scientists and communications researchers examining players like so many specimens on a lab table. Exploring motives. Dissecting relationships. Unless they're driven to quantify something Zan perceives as easy to analyze but impossible to explain, or to study the phenomenon precisely because they don't understand it. Some are longtime players who launch projects so they'll feel less guilty about being here all the time. Others came in from the outside and they come in cold, complete with preconceptions. Or to generate confessions they can sell for profit: *My Life as a Virtual Sex Symbol.* More scholarly researchers drop surveys into players' queues or approach them in the grand ballroom, solemnly asking questions. To nobody's surprise they get answers, because there is a central fact about life in this space created out of the unknown and mediated by text: people love to talk about themselves.

Zan used to think researchers had to be condescending academics or, worse, closet voyeurs who got off on passing the magnifying glass: "Behold the natives. Aren't they *quaint.*"

Now she is deep in a survey of her own. Lost without Reverdy, who simply *has not logged on* since she tried so hard to say goodbye forever, she's like an astronaut in free fall. It's late and, as good as her word to Charlie, she's compiling interviews. Adrift without Reverdy, she has only the project to anchor her.

A survey. Zan isn't crazy in love. Look, she isn't even crazy. She's doing a survey. *My God, he's only been gone three days! What's the matter with me?*

This morning Martha said, "Charlie's only been gone three days. What's the matter with you? Or did you spend the whole weekend inside that computer?"

"So what if I did? I have to be there."

"That's what I was afraid of. Jenny, look at yourself!"

"There's nothing the matter with me."

"You look terrible, all woolly and distracted. It's that St. Helen thing."

"It's not St. Helen, Mart, it's StElene!"

"Whatever."

"I'm interviewing people for a paper. The place is a microcosm, OK?" She thinks she sounded clinical, maybe even competent and in control. "It's time somebody analyzed what makes these people tick. I'm there on a research project."

"Well," Martha said in a dead level tone. "Are you."

She can handle Martha's sarcasm. If Charlie catches her logged on in the middle of the night she has a ready answer now, one that makes sense even to her. Product, she tells herself. *I'm going to come out of this with product.* She is wasting nobody's time.

Maybe we all have to do something to dignify our efforts here.

Zan's survey is considerably less organized than the others, consisting as it does of conversations conducted over the interminable weekend with Reverdy gone and Charlie out of town. It's helped her get through. She's made it safely through to Monday in one piece. She's retreated to *Zan's Tower* to reread the logs. First she has to edit out repetitions the StElene program dishes up. She saves the interviews under Phase One. Next, the questionnaire.

She scrolls through the logs with her head tilted, half-listening for Reverdy. Because she can't help herself she types, *@find reverdy*

And again and again, gets the time of his last disconnect.

```
Reverdy      Thursday 23:50 PST    The Dak Bungalow
```

Never mind. Having a project consolidates her. Zan isn't hanging in space in a lovelorn fog, she has work to do. She tried to frame a question that wouldn't influence the answers, but rereading, she sees that she slipped and let herself show. Still, it's a start.

```
Zan asks, "What do you think we're doing here?"
```

The answers tell her everything. Or they don't tell her anything. She started with Jazzy, her first friend on StElene. She had him meet her at the Gazebo Reverdy built, and the log begins with Reverdy's words. Reading the description he wrote is like taking out a snapshot of him. It warms her every time.

```
The Gazebo is a Victorian fantasy built to match
the architecture of the hotel. It is the seat of
emotions for some. For others, it is the site of
dreams. To the north the bay spreads like a glit-
tering net cast by a magician to catch starts. At
your back the hotel is ablaze with lights. The long
dock leading back to the shore stretches like a
link between solitude and the joy and confusion of
```

```
life.
Zan and Jazzy are here.
hug jazzy
You hug Jazzy
Jazzy hugs you
Zan [to Jazzy] So Jazz, we all have so much invested
in StElene.
What do you think we're doing here?
Jazzy [to Zan] I can only talk a minute; I'm on call.
Zan [to Jazzy] I'm trying to find out whether people
think the MOO is a great enterprise that we're all
in together or a terrible addiction. I guess my
question is, is there something wonderfully right
about StElene that we keep coming back to it? Or
is it because there's something terribly wrong
with us?
```

OK, if she really is writing a paper on the psychology of the population in virtual communities, she already knows her approach is questionable. As interviewer, Zan is in too deep to be impartial. Martha would point out that pouring yourself into the questions this way pollutes the answers, but then Martha's never been here; she's never done this. There's no way she can understand. Besides, Martha's never ached as much as Zan does tonight.

```
Jazzy [to Zan] Wrong, as in . . . ?
Zan [to Jazzy] As in lacking. StElene. Is it a good
thing or a bad thing?
Jazzy [to Zan] Both. It's existential. Why can't
you let go and let that be enough?
```

```
:scratches her head.

Zan scratches her head.

Zan [to Jazzy] I'm *thinking.* Maybe that's it.

<Sigh> Maybe nothing's ever enough.

Jazzy hugs you.

hug jazzy

You hug Jazzy

Jazzy [to Zan] OK, put me down as saying it's a good
thing. How else could you and I meet and be friends?
```

In a funny, colleaguely way, she and Jazzy are close even though she's in South Carolina and he is typing from Australia. Jazzy is smart; he asks questions and he thinks; the marvel is that he has time for StElene because he's a neurologist RL.

```
Botero [to Zan] What's all this with the stupid
questions? Have you got head problems or some-
thing? Get out of my face.
```

OK, Botero. Botero's a flake, brilliant programmer, she's told, just eighteen, weighs close to four hundred pounds. But the others? Everybody on StElene has thought about it. They think about it all the time. *If the object of the game is to determine what is the object of the game, what's the object of the game?* Everybody asks the question. Everybody comes up with a different answer.

Zan picked up Saturday night's interviews in the grand ballroom; the floor was filled with players who didn't have a Saturday night date RL, or a mate to take them away from all this.

Rosemary_Thyme [to Zan] StElene? It's the best party anywhere!

LavaKing [to Zan] If you have to ask, you'll never know.

Merce [to Zan] StElene to me, anyway, is about having interesting conversations with people from anywhere. If you make a friend so much the better.

Draco [to Zan] Interesting question. I've been wondering myself!

Zan [to Draco] That isn't an answer.

Draco [to Zan] Could I get back to you on that?

Melamanana [to Zan] At work I keep StElene in a window? Boss thinks I'm busy even when I'm not.

Zan [To Melamanana] But it's Saturday night.

Melamanana [to Zan] <grin> You got it! Cute guys!

Freebaser [to Zan] Takes my mind off heavy things, OK?

If Bruno Bettelheim was right and we all have to tell ourselves stories about our lives just so we can make it through our lives, the stories players on StElene tell about themselves are as varied and complicated as the people telling them.

Furioso [to Zan] I may be alone but I never have to be lonely.

Lark [to Zan] Fun. Fun and games! There's always a party going on.

page Lark Sweetie, what about your dad?

Lark has received your page.

You sense that Lark is looking for you in the grand ballroom.

```
Lark pages you "Dad? What dad? Don't worry. I'm
cool."
Earthworm [to Zan] You've got to know as well as
anybody that the MOO is very interesting ground po-
litically. I think the two most interesting things
in the world are sex and politics, don't you?
Zan [to Earthworm] <blush> I'm just asking the
questions today.
Earthworm [to Zan] Studying democracy in the MOO.
It's the future!
```

Zan goes through the logs, deleting extra lines. Regular players are so used to the duplications that they hardly notice, but an outsider reading the logs would be confused. To direct her response to Earthworm, she typed:

:looks only slightly skeptical
—earthworm Are you sure that's all you're doing here?

On her screen those lines show up immediately followed by what Earthworm sees:

```
Zan looks only slightly skeptical.
Zan [to Earthworm] Are you sure that's all you're
doing here?
Earthworm laughs. "Like, you think I'm really here
for the sex?"
Imelda [to Zan] Anonymity = freedom. We can do
*anything we want.*
```

Implied: *act without consequences.* If this is action. She doesn't know. This fact, or belief about life on StElene has so many ramifications that she can't begin to analyze it until she has a big enough sample to determine the norm—if there is a norm.

At the edge of a chasm. In the room at the top of Charlie's house Jenny says aloud, "What are norms?" With a pang she remembers Reverdy in one of their early conversations—at the beginning, before she let herself fall into love.

"No guilt," Reverdy said; she could tell by what he said that he had a dazzling smile. "That's the great thing about here. We can do anything we want. What are we anyway? Minds meeting in a void."

She said uncertainly, "Real people."

"Committing text, not sins. Whatever we do, we're not hurting anybody." This is the path Reverdy laid down for Zan to follow into their consuming love: "Think of the power. Here, we can do anything!"

"Power," she said, and did not add, and this is what bothers her: *without responsibility.*

Is that why Reverdy spends his life on StElene? To do whatever he wants and not be held accountable? What about Zan? She doesn't know. She thought it was the company. Unending conversation about everything—smart, dumb, witty, banal. On good days, she sits down to a feast of ideas because people smart enough to function in a big, complicated virtual space like this one are more intuitive than the average, more adventuresome. More exciting. On bad days, she thinks it's all about Reverdy. No. It's only about Reverdy.

With Charlie perpetually on duty, she thinks she's here to save her life. And if the compression is killing her? Fine. Pushed to the limit, forlorn and exhausted, Jenny is ready to admit that a part of her is starving, helpless in love.

The more she knows Reverdy, all she wants to know is

Reverdy, and the mad, compelled part of her wants to log off and get in the car and fan out over the country in growing arcs, looking for him.

She'll just keep driving until she finds his home town wherever it is and locates Reverdy's house and knocks on his front door. If he doesn't answer she'll just go in. She will find the room where Tom is typing and stand there until he turns and sees her and for the first time ever she and her lover will be together in physical space. She doesn't know what they'll do then, but she does know she can't go on like this. She wants to damn well find Tom and see him and feel him and touch him, because the partial, unseen Reverdy that Zan knows so well loves her more powerfully and persuasively than the whole of handsome, physical Charlie Wilder. For the first time ever she understands what true love is, and if her inner sentinel warns that what Zan and her lover have together on StElene is perfect precisely because it sits firmly in the vestibule of the uncreated, never mind. She's beaten that reserved, judgmental self to death and shoved the remains into the garbage and closed the lid.

And with Reverdy nowhere around she does what you do. Keep busy. Keep busy, whatever you do. Posting to *lark*. Editing her logs. Keeping watch like the wife of a sea captain lying awake in the night, waiting for the floor to shift under the weight of his first step.

```
Winston [to Zan] You know what life is for me now,
like how they told me the operation would work and
it didn't, or how much it hurts. On StElene I can
walk again. It's the one place where I'm as free as
I was before I got hurt. Thank God I can still type.
```

So there's that.

```
Fearsome [to Zan] <<<grinnnn!>>> Sex. It's the
sex.
```

At least Fearsome is funny about it. Others—Domnita, Sadissimus, for instance—are dead earnest. Enhanced experience. Unbelievable sex. And the sex, whatever sex means to this group of players that Zan treats so gingerly, covers the spectrum. Player descriptions range from *Playboy* and *Cosmo* fantasies to heavy leather to BDSM regalia complete with cock rings and nipple clamps. Fastidious Zan avoids them all as if they're carrying impetigo. She is resolutely above all that. *What we have is different.*

```
Articular [to Zan] You know where I'm coming from.
It's the roleplaying games. There's no roleplaying
game I can't eventually dope out, so. I have fun
writing bigger, stronger games.
Zan [to Articular] So <grin> your role here is game
master?
Articular [to Zan]:) Sure. But how about you?
What's your role?
Zan [to Articular] Role? I'm not playing any role.
I'm me!
Articular [to Zan] Yeah, right you are. You're like
me, describing the dragon. You're choosing which
parts of yourself to show.
Zan [to Articular] You mean, like not telling you
that I have greasy hair and weigh eight hundred
pounds? Articular [to Zan] OK, you got me. I'm
laughing RL, but I'm not. You know what I mean. See,
I think we're all in costume here.
Zan [to Articular] Embarrassing, isn't it. We are!
```

```
Articular [to Zan] So I admit it, this is one place
in my life where I can totally be in charge. That's
my reason. What's yours?
Zan [to Articular] Good thing he couldn't see her
face clench or her hands tremble. That's what I'm
trying to figure out!
```

Smart man, Articular, running away from life so fast that all he sees is the game. But he's put his finger on the question. If they are all playing roles—is Jenny really only typing in the character of Zan the beloved? Is this ache that possesses her real, or is it something she and Reverdy have confected to pass the nights?

```
Zan [to Solomon] You've been here since the begin-
ning. What do you think we're doing here? Is St-
Elene life or is it only a simulacrum of life?
Solomon laughs.
```

Solomon is too famous here to direct speech to you. He knows he has your attention no matter who else is in the room.

```
"My, you really *are* young in the game, aren't
you? This isn't life, it's an act of creation."
Zan [to Solomon] For the log, if you'll please just
clarify.
"It's a collaborative effort. Creative."
Zan [to Solomon] For the log. By creative, you mean
the programming, designing all these new spaces
for players? Objects they can use? Features so they
can express themselves?
```

"That? That's nothing. Beyond the database, the programming that goes on here is mostly baby steps."

Zan [to Solomon] Then what are we doing?

"My dear, we're writing a collective novel about ourselves."

Zan [to Solomon] This is nothing like a novel. It's . . .

"Text. We're creating text."

"No." *Why is this so disturbing?* "This isn't text, it's life!"

"It's just typing, everything we do is considered. A literary act."

"Solomon, we're talking! We're all together here."

She doesn't know why this is so important to her, but it is. "And we're really here."

"In the greatest collaboration since Greek drama."

"Thank you, Sol. I'm so grateful for your time."

Funny how chronological age is eclipsed by age in the game. Solomon's been around so long that he is one of StElene's famous wise men, but age on StElene is never physical. @*about* reveals that Solomon just turned twenty; he first logged on in the dawn of the community, when he was fifteen. This is another oddity: unlike life in the real world, in this virtual life, age equals wisdom . . . It's—

Oh hell why can't she stop typing @*find reverdy*

And then suddenly, unaccountably, he's back.

    Reverdy   Connected   The Dak Bungalow

In the next second, he is in her room. And, God, she's so relieved! In Brevert, Jenny hears her own voice. "My love.

You're here!" It may be relief, it may be compression of three days of waiting for Reverdy, maybe it's a premonition that this is the beginning of the end. Whatever it is that prompts her, emotion blows up in Zan like a line storm and sweeps through her, cleaning her out and leaving her flattened in its wake like a desert ghost town.

But Reverdy can't know what Jenny Wilder is thinking because Zan hasn't entered a response. "Zan?"

My God, what to say? Even though Zan knows she is tempting fate or the devil or threatening Tom Dearden's profound solitude IRL she does not stop to ask her best love, "Where were you?" or, "What happened?"

She doesn't even ask, "Are you all right?"

Instead Zan, who has never really been anybody but Jenny Wilder, really, stays silent, wide open and temporarily exhausted; she is just burned out.

"Zan?"

And, crazy with love and loss, foolish Jenny leapfrogs into the next dimension, inadvertently sending this message. She drives it like an arrow directly into Tom Dearden's secret, unknowable heart. She types:

"DEAREST I HAVE TO MEET YOU. REAL LIFE. NOW!"

It is Reverdy who falls silent now.

When her lover does not respond, Jenny types, "Oh my God, Tom, I love you so much please don't let's us ever be separated again."

He does not respond.

"I'll find you. We have to be together. We do!"

Still nothing.

Her hands are trembling. Her breath hangs in front of her like a tropical mist. Jenny knows she is pushing where she ought to hang back but she can't stop herself. No. She can, but she won't. She's been torn apart for too long and she has to solve this. She has to solve her life!

"I love you, Tom. It's time. I want us to find a place we can meet so we'll always be together. We have to really be together and really touch each other and never, ever have to come apart!"

And if Reverdy hangs there without responding, Jenny won't know it. If he groans aloud and disconnects she won't know that, either. She'll be spared the embarrassment if he disconnects and the misery if he stays logged on long enough to refuse her. She won't have to face the fact that she has just stripped naked without knowing whether Tom wants that, because if Reverdy is back home at last on StElene—

—God. Charlie is back home too, RL!

She may have heard the front door open, maybe she heard him speak to the kids but deep in love, Zan is deep in denial. She heard Charlie on the stairs but she has Reverdy here, he's finally *here*. She's typing blindly, thinking *not yet not yet*. She hates the intrusion. Now. Just when she and Reverdy are . . .

Words pop up. On the screen she sees, "Zan!"

Behind her in the room, Charlie says, "Babe?"

"No!" Shattered, Jenny switches off the computer so Charlie won't see the afterburn of her infidelity. So he can't see the desperate, incriminating demands she typed, her crazy love for Tom Dearden a.k.a. Reverdy etched on her screen.

Zan disconnects before she can see or begin to grasp what this loving threat has done to Reverdy. Torn between this and Charlie, she cries, "How did it get so real?"

twenty-four

REVERDY

Zan, what are you *doing? I WANT TO BE WITH YOU. RL. NOW.*

In both kingdoms, Tom Dearden shudders. Too many threats, he thinks, shaken. First the corporation. Now this. For too many reasons, his days here are numbered now.

Never let the people know what you're thinking.

To survive your life, you have to barricade the city. Close your gates. Let nothing show. If your enemies even guessed what was inside you they would crack you wide open. They could ride into you like The Wild Bunch and lay you waste, blasting away until nothing is left standing, not even the shell.

Nobody knows what's going on inside the self that Reverdy protects. Not Zan, not Suntum International, not the Directors with their Saint-names. To a man who keeps himself locked tighter than the Forbidden City, privacy is everything. Containment is essential, Reverdy thinks, and is surprised to find Tom Dearden's jaw clenched like a bear trap as his spirit hangs in space, cut loose from its moorings. In her mad rush to broach the perimeter, Zan overturned his expectations. Arm the battlements!

When he first found rich, fluid StElene, where souls come together in the dark and everything you do is secret, he was joyful. Excited. The new Eden! Alone on StElene last Thursday night he found bugs everywhere. In Zan's Place. In the Dak Bungalow. On the Suntum server, which he has cracked. They've been listening!

When your world is threatened on all sides you do what you have to. You keep busy. Reverdy knew Suntum was ripping off the players and now he can prove it, so there's that. The bastards have been pirating applications developed here and selling to the highest bidder. That, he could handle. In the freemasonry of life online, the best things are shared.

But that isn't the worst. StElene is a voyeurs' paradise. After he found the bugs he prowled through the corporation server until he unearthed proof. High-end customers have been paying Suntum untold amounts to log on and spy on the intimacies unfolding here. His intimacies! So everything Reverdy has said and done here is readable, for a price. Suntum's customers tap into private lives here as cynically as they turn on the TV. But not for long. He's sent them mails from behind his powerful firewall. More. He's inserted a few strings of code that'll make Suntum rue the day the corporation tangled with him. Tom Dearden is very good at what he does. They'll never trace it to him.

Listen, at some level he always knew. The "expectations" Suntum laid out without calling them *laws* came with a warning from the Saints. Death to any player who says or does anything to attract the attention of the Feds. Do what you want as long as you don't bring scandal on StElene and the Corporation, or enable a Federal Indecency Act. But people are people. *We fall in love,* he thinks. *We say and do things the physical world wants to make us sorry for.*

Things that they can only do here.

Reverdy thinks about it every time he and Zan make love, but he's more in love with her than he's ever been with anyone, and StElene is the only place where they can meet. Their imaginations join and fuse in love in this rich, perpetual night, and Reverdy knows the best, the only eternal love is the kind that blooms in the imagination like a jungle flower.

Spies? All right, he can live with it.

He was going to tell her some of it tonight, but she didn't give him a chance. Instead she knocked him off his foundation with one line. "I HAVE TO MEET YOU." It is like a violation. And disconnected before they could straighten it out.

It has thrown him into a transport of reflection.

If Reverdy is alone in

`Zan's Place    Zan (sleeping) is here,`

if an infernal machine at the back of his mind was dislodged by his lover's shocking threat to step out of the box and into his arms, it is rolling downhill fast. It gathers speed as it careens into the forefront of his consciousness like an engine of destruction. Nobody outside the fortress can know. Lover and beloved, adventurer and enemy, typist and avatar, man and ideal, with real and virtual characters and lives so inextricably mingled that he can no longer separate them, Tom Dearden a.k.a. Reverdy is profoundly disturbed.

I can't!

Stay here.

Can't leave.

It would kill me.

Distress makes him reckless. Movement may not be action but if you keep moving fast enough you don't have to think.

Reverdy types @*join azeath*

It is a bizarrely self-destructive act.

```
Azeath's Little Hell is wallpapered with the
scalps of his enemies. You are standing ankle deep
in their bones. If you come here, you can be de-
stroyed here, but hell is never secured. Hell is
wide open to all comers. Make one wrong move and
you'll never get out alive. Azeath is here.
```

"What the fuck!"

Reverdy grins. "It's time."

"Time for me to tear you apart IVR?"

"Reality isn't virtual. It's real."

"I thought you said it was only a game."

"Oh, me." Reverdy grins. "I'll say anything."

"Smartass with your smart mouth. What the fuck are you talking about?"

"There are a couple of things you should know. Real things."

"What kind of things?"

So deep in the game that he's almost happy, Reverdy grins. "Things about here."

"I thought you said this wasn't real."

"No, I said it *was* real." He has confused Azeath and this is a delight and a pleasure. Now it's time to drive in the stake. "At least it's *for* real. So."

"So what, asshole?" Azeath is a blunt instrument. Azeath's a fool.

"Asshole? Is that the best you can do?"

"Go ahead. Start with me. Just fucking start and I'll show you what I can fucking do. What the fuck did you come here to tell me?"

"Funny you should ask." Reverdy is grinning not just here but at Tom Dearden's keyboard in physical life. He's nimble and funny and intelligent enough to orchestrate these exchanges before he enters them. He has studied his enemy over time like a scientist peering into an ant farm; he does not know the real typist but he does know exactly which buttons to push to drive Azeath into a murderous rage. He'll play the guy like a synthesizer, wring organ music out of these keys. The dance to come is going to be so exquisite that he's almost reluctant to begin it. He's been designing it ever since he met Azeath and they fell into hate at first sight. With a sigh that vibrates in the room where he is typing, he takes the first step. "So. You think Mireya really loves you."

"I fucking know she does. I give her something you could never . . ."

"Yeah, right." Reverdy quotes. " '*I swell up inside you so big that you bust in pieces, screaming.*' You call that good sex?"

Azeath scowls threateningly. "How did you . . ."

He throws his grenade and leaves before Azeath has time to think, much less respond. "Like, you think Mireya hasn't been downloading your sex scenes and mailing me the logs? '*Mireya, you make me holler like a wild bear, you are my MATE forever.*' " And before Reverdy's speech, complete with direct quotation straight out of the logs, shows up on Azeath's screen, he types @*join Lark.*

By the time Azeath assimilates what Reverdy's just revealed, by the time he begins raging, typing detailed threats, Reverdy is long gone. By the time he gets the death threat Azeath sends after him like a heat-seeking missile, programmed to follow wherever he goes, he'll be deep in *Lark's Mandela*, where Azeath can not follow.

Reverdy finds Lark at the center of his intricately designed quarters, mailing. He's the only player allowed in this particular private space. He feels only a little guilty because he hasn't read post one on *lark and as the kid's champion, he has an obligation to keep track. Lark's so thrilled to see him that he overloads the database with a bunch of questions and conflicting commands and accidentally disconnects.

Grinning, Reverdy reads: *a flame from hell! Azeath pages you. He pages, "You're going to die for this."*

page Azeath, Yeah, right. You're going to get me kicked off StElene.

Azeath pages, "I'm going to kill you in real life."

Is Reverdy entering a new phase in the game or is he burning bridges? He would tell Lark that he's baiting Azeath to smoke out the Directors, who will do anything to keep StElene out of the news. The last thing the Saint-guys want is a murder attempt launched on StElene. If he can pull Azeath into some violent act that makes the newspapers, TV, online news services, he's accomplished two things at once.

Humiliating his enemy is not enough. Bringing scandal down on StElene is gravy. And if the typist who calls himself Azeath shows up on the RL doorstep in the frozen north where Tom Dearden makes mortgage payments? Well, the bastard has to find him first.

Funny how it hypes your sense of power, reducing an enemy to incoherent rage. Azeath's bound to squawk. Reverdy will hear from the Directors soon enough and that, too, brings a sense of power. The officers on his historical research project RL may ignore Tom Dearden's suggestions and blow off his contributions to the time line he is coding for them, but nobody ignores him here. Here he can make women fall in love with him; he can make people cry. He can drive them to rage. He can make men do things they will be ashamed of. He can piss off the Saintly Directors any time he wants to. They'll never see it his way. They dignify him by fighting him.

Right now Azeath's escalating threats are boring Tom and so he moves on to something completely different. That nobody who cares about him knows about, and that nobody on StElene suspects.

By the time Lark pulls himself together RL and reconnects, Reverdy's reduced his window on StElene to a slot at the bottom of his screen and moved on. This means that the character named Reverdy is idling in *Lark's Mandala* while the physical Tom Dearden moves on to another phase in his odd dance of the intellect. Therefore, although Reverdy is still in Lark's inner sanctum (Reverdy [distracted] is here), the typist who moves Reverdy and breathes life into him has vacated, leaving Reverdy to idle. He is active, but on a different screen.

Active. Very active, and on StElene. The first commandment in this particular electronic community forbids duplication. The Directors are like God standing at the gates of creation, handing out souls, decreeing that every human passing through the starting gate will be issued exactly one (1) soul, and only one. Unless it's that souls are entitled to only one (1) body each. On StElene, a registered player is allowed exactly one character. The Directors monitor the site information to be sure each player runs only one character. No more.

When Reverdy does what he does, then, Tom Dearden knows he is committing a serious breach.

For reasons he is not entirely clear on, Tom Dearden chooses this particular moment, when Azeath is furious and vigilant, filled with hate and loaded for bear, to do the illegal so he can do the wonderfully silly thing.

Tom telnets to a secret account and logs on to StElene as Precious, the illegal second character he designed for this part of the game. As described by Reverdy, Precious is pink and voluptuous in her leather shift and stiletto heels. Precious likes to parade in public rooms waiting for one of those dirty old men who treats StElene like a 900 number or, to be precise, a sleazy strip where only hookers stroll. When Precious finds a slavering sex-troller, she goes into her act. Lascivious intruders always respond. Precious latches on and won't quit until Guest has followed Precious into a secured room Reverdy designed for just these little confrontations. He sweeps it regularly for surveillance devices. If he gets caught, he'll be *@erased* from StElene, and he knows it.

It gives Tom an edgy pleasure to lead these horny bastards on and bring them down. So when the moment's right he'll morph into Benjy and. He loves the rest. It makes him laugh. He really needs to laugh. Especially now.

@be the grand ballroom

```
Rejoice! Precious is here. Your fondest dream.
```

Perpetual midnight on StElene, and it's business as usual. Everybody's here. Solomon, who seldom comes out of the game masters' conference room—he's tempted to page and say hi but it would blow his cover; Jazzy and Articular, Merce and RedWriter, old friends and assorted guests, even a couple of the Saints. Reverdy notes only peripherally that Azeath is here. He could not say why he's chosen this high-risk activity at this exact time; disrupted as he is by desires in collision, he may not know what he's doing. Correction. Reverdy knows exactly what he's doing; he just can't say why he's doing it now. Maybe if Zan came back she could deflect this, but she's gone and right now, he is afraid of Zan. Crazily, he doesn't wait for the dance to begin, he brings it on.

twenty-five

JENNY

You may wonder why I am replaying the material I collected on StElene inside my head, instead of sitting at my computer editing the logs. The truth is, I can't get to StElene right now. OK, when you can't have what you want, you need to get in touch with what little you have. I'm so afraid!

It is extremely strange, riding along in the car with the soft coastal breeze blowing through my hair while all the important parts of me are stranded on StElene. This is the last place I want to be, but here I am. Just when I most need to see Reverdy, to find out *how we are* together, Charlie is taking me away.

```
Zan [to Heraclitus]. Do you really think players
come here in character? I mean, are we ourselves or
do we turn into somebody else?
Heraclitus [to Zan]. That's obvious. It doesn't
matter what you want to pretend, there are things
you can't hide. The more we try to escape ourselves
here, the more we become who we are.
```

"Babe, did you say something?"

"No."

Tanned, wonderful Charlie makes a half turn in his seat to look at me. "Are you OK?"

I need to sort through my material. I have to make sense of it. I am fending off conversation so I can think. "I'm fine." Too late. The log evaporates. Everything evaporates except the fear. I don't know who I am afraid for, myself or Reverdy, but I am shuddering with bad vibes.

The car's air conditioned but Charlie is driving along with the windows open, what did he say when he scooped me up and bundled me inside? "It's a nice day. Let's get in touch with reality."

Does he think this is real, him and me crossing the long causeway with nothing to talk about but how I am, and nothing to see but blue sky and gulls rising, marsh and sawgrass whipping along on either side with water beyond?

Charlie's voice is warm, but he sounds a little like a lost boy. "I just want you to be OK," he says.

"I am." I am lying. "Really, Charlie, I'm fine."

He says this is for my own good. How could Charlie know what's good for me? It's like being ripped limb from limb. I need to be on StElene right now, I have to see Reverdy, no big thing, I just have to find out if my life is still in place, and now, God!

Charlie thinks he's staging a rescue—romantic getaway, just us, wonderful week at the beach. I guess he caught the vibes— distress signals, S.O.S., unless I was sending up flares without knowing it. He didn't ask what I needed, he just walked into the exact moment when my heart was in terrible danger and took charge. I can't find Reverdy! Charlie came upstairs to the computer room, all brusque and loving and take-charge, very

Charlie, very Marine, and barged into my consciousness. "I stashed the kids with their kid friends. I've got reservations in Myrtle Beach. I don't know what's the matter with you Jenny, but you . . ."

"In a minute, Charlie, I'm busy."

"Now. Come on, Jen, what's the matter with you?"

The hell of it is, I can't begin to say. I love him for knowing something's wrong and I love him for wanting to make it right but I've come a long way since he told me *I already have my family* and there's no coming back. "Nothing, really." I was willing him to go away.

Instead, he kept talking, talking, talking me offline like a mentor in a twelve-step program frog-marching an addict back to life. ". . . and now, just shut that thing off and we can . . ."

I can't! "I can't go anywhere now, I'm . . ."

"Your patients? No prob. I talked to Martha. She's covering."

"But it's the middle of the night!" Or not. To my surprise, it had gotten to be daylight. I was waiting for Reverdy, and Reverdy? There is one thing about Tom Dearden's physical location and one thing only that I can verify, and that's the time zone where he logs on. Tom lives so far west that where he is, the night goes on and on. But Reverdy wasn't anywhere!

Charlie tugged at me, RL. "No it isn't. If you bothered to look out the window you'd see it's morning again. I love you, Jen, and I'm worried about you . . ."

"I'm fine, I just."

"And we're going away."

"Away! We can't!" *Oh Charlie, don't smile like that!* "Wait, I just need to do a couple of." God, I had to tell Lark. I had to leave Reverdy a note!

But Charlie had me by the hands. "No you don't. We're going away and nothing else matters."

I tried to smile for him. "At least let me log off."

Charlie turned me so we were both facing the blank screen. It was like looking into the face of a dead friend. "Jenny, you're not logged on. Come on, let's go."

"My clothes!"

"I packed you. We're leaving." I don't know what I said or did to give it away but he tilted his head, assessing. "Something's wrong."

"Wrong?" *Love, goodbye. Love!* "What could possibly be wrong?"

This is how Charlie Wilder dragged me out of the box and back into the room at the top of the house on Church Street and pulled me out of the upstairs room like a princess out of her tower and this is how it happens that we are leaving home for a whole week, just seven days, but a lifetime for Zan in the world of compressed emotion on StElene.

Like a ghost, poor Zan [sleeping] hangs in limbo, an empty vessel abandoned in electronic space. And Reverdy? I don't know, I don't *know!*

Meanwhile Charlie and I are bombing along in the sweet sunlight, tasting salt in the air. In a way, it is a relief. If I can't get to Reverdy, maybe I don't have to. Maybe it's OK to crane out the window at two-bit motels and cement pelicans in a world filled with sunburned sailors and their girlfriends and bright, nonbiodegradable beach toys. Love my husband. Have fun.

As we roll into Myrtle Beach, Charlie says, "I got another phone call."

"Phone call!"

"That woman. She won't stop calling. About you." His voice drops. "I listened this time."

Mireya! "What does she want?"

"She says . . ." This is hard for Charlie. "She says you're . . ."

"The woman is crazy. Whatever she says, it's a lie."

Pain shreds his voice. "She says you're seeing somebody else."

He's been in charge; oddly, now I am in charge, the consoling lover, unless it's therapist, making him feel better with the truth, which is only partly the truth. "Charlie, you know I would never do that to you. You also know from the kids that I don't go out when you're away and nobody comes to the house."

He says softly, "I know you get lonely, babe."

"And you know nobody comes." Dissembling, I take his hand. "Charlie, she's just an ex-patient. Psychotic. You know those people, they'll say anything. She wants to hurt me any way she can!"

Jenny's first love brightens so quickly and predictably that it makes Zan terribly sad. "So you haven't!"

Not in this life, at least. "Oh Charlie, no." Ripped in half, I am grieving for both loves. "I promise you, never!"

"I knew it wasn't true!" He is giddy with relief. "Oh honey, here's our motel. Let's have a hell of a week!"

This is how, ripped out of context so fast that I am scattered and gasping, I end up marooned in the physical world. No. Stuck at the beach. Charlie and I are at the beach, prone on striped towels with the Atlantic crashing a few yards away and our hands spread like starfish on hard-packed white sand. The sand rims my mouth and gets under my fingernails which, in some attempt to turn this into a real vacation, I have painted abalone white. Lying on my belly in the bikini Charlie bought and threw in the bag for me, I can feel the cool, damp conforming to the weight of my body; I can feel the sun on my back and the residual dampness wicking up through the towel. For the first time in a while I am in touch with the flat, unequivocal quality of the physical, but inside my head?

I am elsewhere. Our last scene replays endlessly, me, Reverdy, Reverdy, me. I can't quit trying to interpret it and predict outcomes. All I have to go on is our last words to each other, scrolling up the screen behind my eyes. When Charlie shakes me gently and says, "We've had enough sun for the day," Zan rises like a waking dreamer and follows him up the beach to the motel where Charlie and I will make love, of course, and it may be the result of compressed anxiety or of interrupted passion with Reverdy or it may really be that Charlie and I are well married and a perfect physical fit; whatever it is, I am left shuddering and sobbing with delight and relief.

"We are good together," Charlie says.

"We've always been good together. That's why I'm here."

Later we get up and go out to dinner, Charlie with his beautiful skull and neat haircut and that rigid back, looking military even in the T-shirt and jeans, and Zan in a full-skirted dress Charlie bought me in the motel boutique this very afternoon, a resort item straight out of a tropical fantasy with white hibiscus silhouetted on a red ground; it leaves my shoulders bare and the full, heavy skirt swings against my shaved, shining legs. At my neck the shells Charlie bought to garland me glisten white against the pink-brown beginning tan. I lean into Charlie as we walk out to eat fried chicken with our fingers in a crowded seafront restaurant where waiters in white starched mess jackets pass buttered biscuits and we grin at each other with grease and crumbs spreading across our faces. After weeks of living inside the box I am in sensory overload. The combination of tastes and colors and sound is too much! I miss the purity and conceptual space, where I am safe.

One minute I'm grinning at Charlie and the next, I'm gone. Have I lost Reverdy forever or is he there now, waiting for me? Is he through with me or has he gone the distance I wanted to take him? What if he's hanging on StElene, waiting to set a time and place so we can meet in physical life? What if while I'm eating fried chicken in Myrtle Beach, I miss my big chance? Does Reverdy miss me, is he worried, does he care? Does he think I've left him? Is he afraid I've died? Or is he out looking for somebody new? What if he's come looking for me RL? Will Charlie and I go home to Church Street and find Reverdy waiting? Will he come out of the oleanders by the front door and walk into my arms and take me away?

"Hello?" Charlie passes a hand in front of my eyes, snapping his fingers and then spreading them. "Jenny. You there?"

"What. Oh!" Blinking, I remember to smile at him. "Of course I'm here."

"You look tired."

"I am." I see Charlie but I don't see him, I can't stop seeing Reverdy—gaunt, not handsome but magnetic in an irregularly craggy way, dark hair, deep-set eyes blazing with intelligence, *we will know each other at once. We will.* He's tall, I think, lean and yes he slouches under the weight of the forced marriage to Louise, but he keeps it all in . . . And disturbed as he is by our last encounter, he is grinning. *@find reverdy*

"Are you all right, babe?"

Oh, Charlie, with your nice, uncomplicated Charlie smile, how can you possibly know? "I'm fine." I look up. My ice cream has melted. The place has emptied out.

Charlie covers my hands with his. "I know it's been hard

for you, but we're going to figure this out, OK? I want us to keep working with it until we've solved it."

"Solved?"

"How to be together." He sighs. "It's all so new! You know I love you."

Guilty, because I've lost all track of where I belong and with whom, I smile. "I do."

Then Charlie's patience snaps. "Let's go."

Days on the beach, nights on the strip, followed by that loving tangle I know so well. I feel very close to Charlie even when part of me is very far away. At night we walk for blocks, I lead Charlie without his knowing it; I take him through bars and flossy hotel lobbies, through every garish theme park sideshow place that beckons, following a trail lined by neon and flashing lights. Charlie thinks he's in charge, but I know. We walk on the beach some nights but I don't like it. No possibilities here. The sand hides sharp objects and you can put your foot down in the wrong place because you can't see, you can get hurt by sharp things you aren't expecting. Yet we go along and the whole time I'm looking for something, never mind what Charlie . . . never mind.

I don't want to lose Charlie but I can't let go of StElene. Is that so hard to understand?

When we come in from the beach on the next to the last night Charlie takes me by the shoulders. "You there?"

My heart turns inside out. God I hurt. God, I am confused. "Oh Charlie, I'm here!"

@twenty-six

Precious holds up a big sign:
NEW HERE? PRECIOUS GIVES GOOD HELP.

In seconds Molybdenum_Guest pages, *"Can you help me? Really?"*

Hiding deep inside raunchy, Barbie-perfect Precious, Reverdy snickers and pages back: *"What kind of help are you looking for?"* Unless it's Tom!

Usually Precious likes to finger intrusively obvious sextrollers before she engages in this act. The worst people deserve the worst treatment, right? Usually Precious works the vestibule, where the clueless lurk, but tonight he's picked the busiest room in the hotel. His worst enemies are here. Azeath looks at Precious and doesn't have a clue. Mireya glances; if she knew that her ex-lover is hiding inside Precious, she'd turn him in to the Directors and have done with him for good. But Reverdy's enemies are too busy building character with StBrêve and StOnge to notice a woman player they don't know. It's tempting, but he can't stir up his old adversaries without blowing his cover. The minute the room knows Reverdy's typist has logged on in a new body, his time on StElene is done. The Saints will swarm all over him and they won't quit until he's done.

From the grand ballroom Molybdenum_Guest licks his
finger and touches you, you know where. He says,
"Baby, you know what I'm looking for. The good
stuff. And I'm the best. Wanna go somewhere?"

Yeah, a live one. Description including length and girth of schlong: just crude enough and detailed enough to tell Reverdy that he deserves what he gets. Precious pages, *"Depends."* But at the same time, Tom is distracted by a heated debate—some of the smartest players are arguing rights of privacy here, and whether copyright pertains. Reverdy thinks everything he and the others do and say here is private property. This is why he hates Suntum, well, one of the reasons. For all he knows Suntum International isn't only admitting paid voyeurs, which he's proved. Suntum could also be selling the logs to God knows who—the media, other corporations, anybody who wants to dissect StElene's private lives, using their findings to develop God knows what.

Privacy. Copyright. It's an old argument; like so much in this place, ideas cycle and recycle, players assume stances and take each other's brains apart and in the heat of talking and mailing, reconfigure and start all over again. Precious goes back to the chase. *page molybdenum Hello, big guy.*

Molybdenum_Guest has received your page.
Molybdenum_Guest pages you. "So do you wanna?"

Privacy. The ability to keep the best parts of yourself secret. It's what draws Reverdy. Fuck incursions, these clumsy, vulgar guests . . .

Jazzy says, "Copyright doesn't ensure privacy."

It's a good argument on a touchy issue. LavaKing asks whether privacy is a constitutional right. Reverdy is torn. Come back as himself and join the debate?

He has plenty to say but he's wearing stalky Precious tonight. He put her on like a Halloween costume and if he wants to maintain his position on StElene, nobody can know. His best lines have to stay unsaid. Precious types *look molybdenum* and discovers—no surprise—that Molybdenum_Guest has @*described* and elaborated on his description—studmuffin with piercings, You Know Where. Yeah, this guy is asking for it. Lascivious asshole, he thinks that in the virtual world all you need to do is talk dirty and you'll have women who don't know you and could care less in your arms, quivering in virtual lust. *Plus ça change,* Reverdy thinks, the more it's the same fucking thing. And the Directors? Instead of niggling over regulations, they should deal with this kind of crap.

Molybdenum_Guest pages you. "Depends on what? WINK."

Reverdy thinks but does not type, Clear off and die somewhere else, you dirty old man. The routine is stale and predictable.

"On what you're interested in." Even typing this is stale.

Still the party goes on.

Molybdenum_Guest pages, "Do you know a place where it's quiet?"

It's odd, the way Tom feels tonight, Tom Dearden, who had such great hopes for life here. The talk goes on and it's good talk about ideas, about the object of the game, gossip about people he knows and speculations about the corporation, but like too many other conversations here it is on a loop; everything is patterned. The copyright argument rages but he watches it scroll past with the growing sense that the ideas are nothing new and there may be nothing new in the world for him. StElene may be the great society Reverdy envisioned, but it is diminished by the players jabbering in this elegant room. The ideal place he loved has become less than it should have been. They bring it down! Instead of distilling the contents of pure minds, StElene has become a soapbox for towering egos and, God, can the depressed people who hang out here be a little less depressed and can the lonely women who linger in space find anything better to talk about than how lonely they are? Tom's jaw is so tight that his temples ache.

Deep in argument, his friends posture while Azeath swaggers and Mireya preens and in their own little sanctimonious cluster the Directors watch, and judge. It is this as much as anything else that troubles Reverdy—*I had so many hopes. Now look at us.* He could pirate StElene to his grand new place and all he'd have is this. A divine scheme populated by—not disembodied gods, just people. That's the problem with all divine schemes. They all boil down to people, just people, yammering in a room.

Then, pressed and shaken, pushed to the limit by Zan's loving threat, Tom Dearden crashes through the membrane into the moment when it all goes bad. Suddenly and almost inadvertently pulls the ripcord on everything he has invested here, Reverdy does a fatal thing. As Precious, Tom pages Azeath, making it perfectly clear to the enemy who's out to get him exactly who the typist moving Precious is, RL:

"Here's a little message from Reverdy. Reverdy says, fuck you."

Then, unaccountably weary and eager to get it over with, Reverdy stops paging and speaks out loud. Precious speaks directly to Molybdenum_Guest. Without knowing why, he wants the entire room to read and know what his invention, this Precious, is about to do.

Exposure? Fine. So be it.

Reverdy speaks aloud. The Directors see it, Azeath sees it, and when the inquiry to follow follows, it is Azeath who will tell the Directors who Precious really is. Once they know, Reverdy's time here is done. So, fine. It's time! Jazzy and Volcano see it, along with all the other players and guests; Merce is there and sees it and so do Bartlebooth and Tower; RedWriter sees it too:

```
Precious [to Molybdenum] So, you think you want to
fuck me? OK baby, let's do it right here. You're in
for a big surprise.
```

twenty-seven

JENNY

So much to say, so much to unsay and no way to do any of it because I don't know where my lover lives or how to get in touch with him. I think about him so much that, like a watercolor in sunlight, he begins to fade. Then on our last night in Myrtle Beach I find what I've been looking for. My voice is bright and false.

"OK if I check my email?" It's an internet cafe.

"Email? Honey, you're twenty-four hours from home!"

"Martha was going to mail me a progress report on the Wetherall kid. It's crucial to the outcome, OK?"

And because it's our last night, Charlie says, "OK."

I'm so frantic that it takes me three tries to connect to StElene. I am typing several things at once, paging Reverdy and, before he has a chance to answer, anxiously typing.

@find reverdy

Oh my darling where are you why don't you come are you here can I . . . Oh! At worst the display will tell me when he logged on last, but! Terrified, I let it come out. "Oh!"

Charlie comes to my side. "What's the matter?"

I lunge with my arms spread because I have to cover the screen. "Thing about this patient. I'm sorry, Charlie, it's privileged."

"Sorry." He backs away.

It is like reading about a death.

@find reverdy

```
"reverdy" is not the name of any player
No players to display.
```

Reverdy has dropped from the face of StElene.

It's as if he was never there. While careless Zan was lost in Myrtle Beach getting drunk on fresh air and sprawling in strong sunlight, flattened by love and picking up a tan, something terrible came into StElene and erased the person she cares most about. God! Cares most about. Yes. Reverdy has vanished. Suicided? Erased? I can't know, I can't know! Gone. As if he had never been.

And here in the internet cafe Charlie is lingering, half-turned and trying to see over my shoulder without looking like he's looking. I should be vigilant. But I can't. This has to be a mistake. I can't stop typing *@find reverdy* again. Again. My God!

Desperate, I type, *@find lark* Thank God Lark's still a player but Lark last logged off yesterday; Lark is nowhere around.

I keep trying. I stop caring whether Charlie sees.

Then, God, what was I thinking? What if Reverdy's left StElene to come looking for me in real life and this is his way of letting me know? What if he's left Louise to come and be with me? *Poor Charlie.* The lover you don't know is always more compelling than the lover you can see. When Charlie and I get home tomorrow I'll find him, dark-eyed with love and brooding, Reverdy. No, Tom Dearden will be slouched by the front door of Charlie's house. He will step out of the shadows of the oleanders that overhang the steps and we will know each other at once. *He loves me,* I think. I think, *Poor Charlie! Reverdy loves me well enough to blow his cover, blow off real life as he knows it, he loves me well enough to step out of the box* . . . I come to with a start. I've told my lover more than once where I live, but what makes me think he kept the address?

My mouth dries out. What if he gets to my house and I'm not there?

At my back, Charlie is shifting like a cluster of stormclouds racing across the night. With Reverdy gone, I type a quick MOOmail to Lark, repeating my RL name, the phone number, the address. I end the mail *Forward to Reverdy. And of course this is for you! Use it if you need it. Promise?* Because Lark is my last link; because Lark may know what's happened, I add, *call me. We have to talk.*

And like a terminal patient saying goodbye to everything I care about, I type, *@exit.*

Better not to look inside Zan in the next twenty-four hours as I go through the motions in the role of good wife on romantic vacation, better not to see the turmoil. It's enough that I can still speak when spoken to, although I'm edgy and my stomach is sour and my hands are shaking from a staggering shortage of sleep. At least my God we are heading back to the house, and I can lose watchdog Charlie and log on.

As we roll into Brevert, I go through all the right motions. "I'll make us a late supper while you pick up the kids."

"Can't, babe," Charlie says apologetically. "The commandant's expecting me."

"He what?"

He shakes his head. "Sorry, I stretched this vacation as long as I could, no, I stretched it too long, so I'm afraid the end will be short. I didn't tell you, but I have to drop you and run out to the base. OK?"

Sameold, sameold. I don't answer.

"Late meeting, are you OK with me staying at the BOQ?"

"Whatever you want." Look, before Charlie's car clears the driveway I'll be running upstairs. I can connect to StElene! Maybe it will turn out that a system crash caused the anomaly. The database backup will be in place and my lover back where he belongs! Reverdy isn't gone, he was just missing for a night.

Charlie's tone is full of all the things we never managed to say to each other. "I'm sorry, babe, I love you, and it's been great."

"Me too. It's been really nice." I can't wait to connect.

Then as we round the corner and pull up in front of the house I see a shadow unfurling in the darker shadows of the oleanders that overhang Charlie's front steps, somebody getting to his feet. Accidentally, I say his name. Charlie looks bewildered but he can't linger long enough to ask. Instead he lets me out of the car and heads off to the base.

"Reverdy!"

But it isn't. It is Lark.

twenty-eight

AZEATH A.K.A. VINNIE FULLER

Everything is perfect. Reverdy is whacked. He's done for. Wiped off the face of StElene like an ugly grin, and since Azeath's the one that fingered him, Azeath is in solid with the Directors now, especially StBrêve. He'll be a Director himself in another week or so, StOnge has promised, "gesture of gratitude." He'll be a Director, and then you motherfuckers watch my dust.

He should be on cloud ten, miles above cloud nine. But.

On top of which, he's getting out of Wardville. What with time off for good behavior, his sentence for the thing he did is up. He has his exit interview with the warden today at 4 p.m. and he's out the main gate by five, personal effects restored, walking around money from the state, new suit for interviews which he doesn't need because StBrêve fixed him up with Suntum and he's got a startup job, data input won't need to meet people which is a damn good thing given his looks and his short fuse. All these years of living his life by the numbers and Vinnie Fuller is bellying up to free!

Good. He should be feeling really, really good. But!

Plus, the real Mireya is coming to real Wardville and they are going to fall into each other's arms IRL for the first time. The frosting on the cake. Mireya, I mean Florence, is coming to town. Florence. OK, it's a kind of a comedown of a name, but she'll always be Mireya to him. God, how many times has he pictured Mireya in his mind, pictured her in his arms doing all those great things they do to each other on StElene. Listen, if they both kind of hinted that IRL they didn't look exactly like their descriptions, the sex was so good that their minds forgave, or forgot. Never mind what Mireya says, Vinny knows what Mireya really looks like, she's got to look amazing. Pretty, and she loves him. Florence. Got to get her to lose the corny name.

Mireya's going to drive him back up to Boston. It's arranged. Vinnie's going to stay at her place and they are going to mash faces and all their other private parts like they keep typing about and have never done, but tonight they're going to do it for real, real bodies in a real bed in a motel.

Weird, he has Reverdy to thank for this. The plan blew up like a whirlwind the night he and Mireya got rid of Reverdy for good. When Reverdy was still fighting Mireya tooth and nail she was too gnarly to talk about meeting face-to-face, Vinnie doesn't know how he knows this, but he knows. So he owes Reverdy a big one after all. It was bringing Reverdy down that brought about this meeting. It left Azeath way high!

Cocky bastard, you'd think he'd of been more careful. The bust came down like a ripe fruit, just fell right into Azeath's lap. You go nuts plotting and at the last minute it falls into your hands. It came down perfect.

It came down strong, too. What happened was, Az and Mireya dropped into the ballroom. Right after he and she had the fight.

The fight. The other night when he tangled with Reverdy

and the bastard started spewing Azeath's secret, sacred love songs, Vinnie went up like a torch. Reverdy, the enemy of his life, claimed he got what they said to each other from Mireya, word for word. Azeath went flaming out of there and into her velvet bed screaming. "You. You..." He couldn't find the word. His fingers were slick. "You told Reverdy about us. About *us?*" He was so mad that he almost... Well, it was a good thing Mireya was typing from wherever she sat typing and Vinnie was in Wardville or he would have snapped her neck like a wooden kitchen match. Her denials made him madder. "He says you showed him our sex. Our sex!"

"That's a fucking lie! A LIE!" Mireya was screaming at Azeath as if it was him she was mad at, and not Reverdy. Crazy.

"Then how the fuck did he get it?"

"He spied, the son of a bitching bastard spied!"

"That's not what he says."

"DON'T YOU KNOW HE HATES ME SO MUCH THAT HE'D SAY ANYTHING?"

Listen, it's a goddamn good thing they weren't in the same bed just then. No. Good thing they weren't on the same planet. He would have rammed his fist down Mireya's throat just to stop her mouth. Instead Azeath gave her chapter and verse. "He quoted stuff. Intimate stuff. What we do together. You and me." And quoted back.

A terrible minute passed. "He said I did that? I would never." Another minute. Then she got cold and still. "This is the end. I hate him. I hate the son of a bitch."

"You hate him?" Vinnie still doesn't know what makes him so mad, that she hates Reverdy more than she loves him? "OK, prove it!"

"You bet I'll prove it. I'm going to kill him." *Yes!* Then Mireya said something that didn't exactly register in the frenzy, except it did. It's stored on Azeath's hard disk, for retrieval later. "No. I'll call him up! Hell no! I'm going to his house!"

Reverdy. She knows the bastard's phone number!

Of course she hurried to patch it up. She was so wild she let a detail slip. "Oh, you think I told him those things and you're hurting. Oh Azeath, my best beloved, I would never let Tom . . ."

"Tom?" *Tom. The motherfucker's name is Tom. Well on StElene, the motherfucker is dead.*

"I mean Reverdy—Reverdy is a programmer. Don't you think he knows how to sneak into our places and plant listening bugs?"

OK! Sitting here in Wardville, Vinnie got a great big hardon. Nobody ever called him "beloved" anything ever before.

They celebrated by going to the ballroom, that was when Precious a.k.a. Reverdy blew his cover and Azeath was right on top of it. He followed the bastard, he was loaded for bear. Nailed Reverdy in the middle of, like, you would never believe. Shame coming down on StElene, this thing could wreck Suntum if it got in the papers, it could land Reverdy in jail. And Azeath was there. He followed Precious into Reverdy's private place and secretly logged everything that came down. What Reverdy a.k.a. Precious said to the mark, what the mark said.

Gotcha! Perfect. Azeath logged the evidence and queued it to every one of the Saints. They had a secret conclave about it. Reverdy was toast.

So after he trashed Reverdy on StElene, Azeath and his best beloved—shit, he has a best beloved now!—he and Mireya had a little victory party in *Mireya's Boudoir* and after they quit congratulating each other and having MOOsex they got to talking and Azeath focused: *she knows where Reverdy is* RL. So that is eating at him, but you don't tell them that. Instead he hugged

Mireya and danced this dance of triumph which at the end of it, and who knows what causes these things, Azeath said, "We have to meet. RL."

"Meet!" Like that. Some women, you make love to them in the dark and they go, "Oh let's don't spoil it," but not Mireya. Mireya rushed into it, typing so fast that it scared both of them, "When?"

"I don't know exactly. Soon." What Vinny meant was, *I'm getting out soon,* but he couldn't say that because Mireya knows what he does at work, but he's never said where he does it. He never fucking told her where he logs on from. It never came up. They exchanged vows. "I, Vincent Fuller, promise to meet you . . ."

"Florence." Mireya smiled. "Florence Vito Watson."

Florence! "That's a pretty name." Trouble is, it's not.

"And we are going to be together, Vincent . . ."

Typing, he formed the word with his mouth. "Vinnie."

"Dearest Vinnie!"

"And we are going to do it. Do it. Do it!" Typing with this neverending hardon. "We are going to do everything. And soon."

So that was that night. And ever since then, he and Mireya have made incredible, triumphant love IVR and now he and his lover Florence are closer than he's been to anybody RL ever.

They slipped into it, and he knew: *I'm getting out soon. Soon I am getting out.* Thoughts running through his head, Mireya all loose and excited, *wham,* it sort of escalated, love and craziness boiling up, he could pull this love out of the box and set it on real fire, real bodies in a real bed in a real place.

Then last night on StElene they were making love online, so easy, so often, so sexy, so safe, and when Azeath least expected it everything kind of came in on him, how he didn't know where he was going to log on after tomorrow afternoon at four o'clock, and he could feel fear like fingers crawling through his scalp: *what if Reverdy gets back onto StElene in spite of what he did and I can't connect and fight him? What if? What if?*

Getting Reverdy bounced off StElene isn't enough.

He wants him dead. And on his hard disk: *she knows where he is.* Which is not *really* why he proposed. Look, Vinnie Fuller really has never been anybody's beloved before in any life and he needs somebody to call him "beloved" while they fuck. He needs to fuck! It all piled up, he got filled up to choking with imperatives, have to this, have that, Mireya called him "my best beloved" one more time and it spilled over and came out of him. "We're getting married." The words fell out on the screen and it was as good as done.

"Married!"

"And we'll find other, better things that I can do to you."

"That I can do to you," she said. "And soon."

So fast! "Tomorrow," he typed, and told her where to come.

She's meeting him in Wardville tonight! But he's got a double agenda with this beautiful girlfriend that he's never met, so he's going to have to take it easy, play it cool. Other guys, their squeezes write regular, they come on visiting days. Their women will be waiting outside the gates with the motor running, take 'em home and love them to death knowing where they've been all this time, whereas Azeath. Vinnie will tell her who he, Vinnie/Azeath, is RL, OK, but he's got to soften her up first, like, make amazing love to her before he breaks the news. And maybe find out what he needs to know so he can move on to what's next. At the back of his mind Reverdy sits like a god that has to be destroyed: *Tom. His name is Tom. Tom something. She knows what. She knows where the bastard is.*

They're meeting in front of the Burger Chef on Central in downtown Wardville at six p.m., which gives him time to take the bus to town and walk over, pretending that he has a car but he just parked it somewhere else. A friend in the laundry got him this nice shirt to go with the state's suit and he's been growing his hair so play your cards right Vinnie, and your woman not only will never know what you were in for, she'll never guess you're an ex-con.

You bet it should be the happiest day of his life. In a funny way, he never expected it, even though he knew it was today. You spend 10 to 15 in the can on a 24-hour basis and see if you still believe there's life outside. He's getting out! He's going to meet his lover soon. They'll go someplace together and do everything for real for once, tumbling in a great big bed.

Then why isn't this the happiest day of his life?

It is and it isn't, Azeath thinks, taking one last look around at *Azeath's Little Hell*. Reverdy, he thinks. I wanted him to squirm, I wanted him gutted and twisting in the wind and the Directors just. It happened too fast.

In another ten he has to go and see the warden. Before that, he has to disconnect. He types @*find reverdy* but he knows what he'll see. Reverdy is no more. If the Directors are right, he's @*erased*. Gone for good. He's gone but he isn't gone, you know? It went too fast. There are things Azeath has to say to him. Things Vinnie Fuller wants to do to him. It isn't finished, it is not . . . He's getting out today. He's meeting his lover at six. But before he can do any of this he has to disconnect.

His hands freeze on the keyboard. He watches the ballroom convo go scrolling by. StOnge has just asked him a question. If he logs off, how can he answer? It makes him writhe. *I can't!* But the screw is standing over him. Yo, Fuller. "You're not getting weird, are you?"

"Who, me? Fuck you!"

The screw says mildly, "Some of them do."

"Well not me."

"Some of the hardtimers do." Fuck, right. Ten years. He stares at Vinnie until Vinnie types @*exit* and turns off the machine.

So like a man overboard, Azeath flounders. He has to be led down to the warden's office and led outside. He paddles into the ambiguous light of five o'clock. After ten to fifteen with time off for good behavior, Vinnie Fuller is loose in the world.

It is bigger than he thought. The bus driver waits while he stares down at the coins in his hand and then, like a vendor in a foreign country helping a tourist with the currency, reaches over and fishes five quarters out. Then he stares until Vinnie lurches down the aisle to a back seat and sits down.

By the time he reaches the Burger Chef excitement has outrun fear and he has the old Mireya hardon. It stays with him for the better part of an hour which is just as well because he ends up waiting for the better part of an hour. Jangling, he paces up and down. It takes him too long to realize that a small, squat woman in a raincoat has been pacing on the same loop for quite some time now, going along with her collar turned up and her hatbrim pulled down. Customers go in and out and every time a good-looking woman goes by, he jumps. Odd, every time a good-looking guy goes by, the woman jumps. Finally they both turn and face facts. She says,

"Vinnie?"

Shit! "Um. Florence?"

Her voice is up but her face falls. "Vinnie. I didn't know you."

"Yeah right," he says drily. "Me too."

Falsehood in advertising. Right. You'd think the woman

would rush to hug him. He ought to hug her, but he won't. He's been inside too long. He's too far outside of these social situations for too long to be able to say the right things in them. Instead he opens his fucking mouth and these words fall out. "You don't look anything like her."

It's a relief to see that she is more angry than hurt. "Well," she says. "You don't look anything like him."

Vinnie thinks. *I'm going to fucking kill him.* He says, "You'll get used to it. I love you. We're getting married. I got a motel room. Let's go."

twenty-nine

I

"Don't be scared, Lark. I promise not to hug you."

It's just as well Charlie let me out in front of the house and drove away; it's just as well that his kids are still at the sitter's, because it's all I can do to handle Lark right now. No. It's all poor Lark can do to handle me. He is jittering like a space module waiting for liftoff. Personal contact! In spite of all the confidences we've exchanged online, this prematurely old kid or very young man is so shy that after the first agonized flash in which his eyes stab mine, blazing with pain at the intimacy of recognition, he won't look at me.

"Oh, Lark." I'm gentle but he keeps flailing, all spit and embarrassment. "Lark, I know it's you, but will you please do something to confirm that it's you so we can go inside now?"

He shakes his head. He can't. Oddly, except for the fact that he's in a *Dr. Who* T-shirt instead of the baggy sweater, Lark looks just the way I thought he would: skinny, pinched and highly intelligent, like an overtrained chess prodigy. Anxious.

"You look so cold. It's summer, Lark, why are you so cold?"

The silence is killing me, not knowing what's happened to my love is killing me. Here is the only known witness and he can't talk! I need to hear every line Reverdy said so I can scour the text for clues, but I can't press Lark. I know better than to touch him or try to renew eye contact. One word and I'll flush him like a wild bird and lose them both. Instead I sit down on the steps and wait for Lark to sit down next to me which he does, finally, but only after an agonized interlude in which he strangles on unspoken words and I sit, resolutely staring straight ahead. When finally he sits, staring at the exact spot I'm fixed on, I say with a doomed feeling, "It's about Reverdy."

All the air rushes out of him. "Yes."

"But you. Are you OK? It's OK, you don't have to tell me. I just care, is all." Then I hold my breath because this is a delicate bird and the least disturbance will panic him.

"Oh fuck," he says finally.

I bite my lip. *Don't ask, wait. Don't say anything.*

"My week is up and I'm out on my butt," Lark says finally. He's managing not to cry. "I don't have anyplace to go." His shoulders are rattling like coat hangers in a windstorm. "Oh, Zan. They kept my stuff, they kept my stuff!"

"I'm so sorry."

"They fucking disowned me and kicked me out."

"That's terrible." I want to touch him but he won't let me. I can't even tell him what I want to say, *I'll take care of you.* He'd fly apart. I decide on, "How did you get here?"

He can't find the answer. "You're the first person I thought of to tell."

"I love you, Lark."

"I love you too, Zan." He still can't bring himself to look at me and I'm still afraid to touch him; he might self-destruct.

"I thought if anybody knew what to do, you would."

"Come in. I'll get you a sweater."

Lark is buzzing with passion but he can't start. He fans crumpled papers. My letterhead. A receipt for his bus ticket— on Howard's plastic, what did the poor kid do to make his way here, pretend to be mute and pass notes? He's shivering like a bluebird in an arctic chill. I feed him soup, I feed him a six-pack of English muffins, I feed him leftover Indian takeout nuked in the microwave. Wondering at how cold he seems here in the soft Carolina night, I wrap him in Charlie's sweater and after the first bit in which I ask if he wants more of this, some of that, after I pour him a little wine, he takes a deep breath and expands.

It's as if his soul has just come back. "I'm so scared. I don't know what to do!"

"You'll be all right." I want so much to hug him and can't. His grip here is tenuous. "I'm trying."

"I'm glad you came. Maybe I can help." I'm rummaging in my head for resource people, placement possibilities, best money says work with a college and then sort out the rest; I know he has more than this to tell me. My mind is drumming: *@find reverdy, @find reverdy, @find reverdy* "Get you back in school."

"I don't know." Lark assimilates this offer; I see the *click* as he stores it for processing later. He blurts, "Without Reverdy, what's the point?"

So it's OK to start the conversation. "What do you mean, without Reverdy! I came back to StElene and oh Lark, he was gone. It's as if he never lived there. As if he'd never been." My heart falls out. "Where did he go?"

Lark hugs his skinny shoulders. "He isn't anywhere."

"What happened?"

"I can only partly tell you."

"Lark, look at me!"

"I trust you, but I still can't look at you. Is that OK?"

"It's OK," I say. "Of course it is."

His eyes flick here, there. "Is this where you log on?"

"Here? Home instead of the office, yeah. Third floor."

Like a hopeful child, Lark asks, "Should we go up and give it one more try?" It is a measure of our lives in the imagined kingdom that we're both straining toward the stairs as if we can solve all our problems or at least stave them off by logging on.

"We could." Two addicted players confecting reasons to connect, as if the familiar will ease the pain that gnaws our hearts. I brighten. "Maybe he's not gone after all."

"Forget it. He's gone as hell," Lark says. "Big tribunal, they tried to keep it a secret but I know. They purged him."

"Tribunal!"

"The Directors. The Suntum site man. They had to act fast. The corporation was scared shit it would get into the papers."

"The papers! What would get into the papers? What do they say he did?"

"That's the problem, he really did it."

"Did what?" I'm trying to sound professional, but I've lost it. "They can't just purge him. Whatever happened to freedom of speech?"

"It's their sandbox," Lark says sensibly, "they can do anything they want. One guy against the corporation? Sure they axed him. They can't allow anything that makes them look bad."

"Execution with no trial. No proof of guilt. It's illegal! We'll go to court to get him back online if we have to," I say irrationally. "Publish the logs."

"The logs are gone. Wiped off the database, along with all

the angry posts everybody sent." Lark has the smooth, untroubled look of a person who knows he's tried everything. "You don't think I checked while you were, like, totally gone just when everybody most needed you?"

"I couldn't help it!" Don't cry! "Charlie took me. He took me away!" Inside me, something changes. Charlie. How can I forgive him for this? "Oh God, if I'd been there maybe I could have . . ."

"No way. When it came down, nobody could help him. Not me, not you."

"Oh, Reverdy!" Loss tears through me like a forest fire. I miss him. I miss him! "What got him?"

"He kind of got himself," Lark says heavily. "But who really nailed him was fucking Azeath. Azeath followed him and logged the whole deal and got the Directors involved and they nailed him. It was so fast!"

"Nailed him? You make it sound like he was . . ." I don't finish.

"Well, he was. They got him for just cause. I'm only a geek dropout, but I know stupid when I see it. Rev was, like, doing his Precious thing? And Az . . ."

"Oh, Azeath. Azeath's a . . ." Yes I am angry. "He was doing his *what*? What Precious thing?"

Accidentally, Lark looks straight at me. His eyes are blue! "You mean he never told you about Precious?"

"No." I feel—not betrayed, exactly, just different. It is as if I've lost him twice. "I thought he told me everything. He does!"

"Nobody does. On StElene, nobody tells everything. It's OK," Lark adds hurriedly, to make me feel better. "It's no big thing. Just this, like, game Reverdy used to play?"

He lays it out for me then, the illegal second character Reverdy used to humiliate outsiders who mistook StElene for a sexual smorgasbord. "So that's one thing they got him for, the illegal second, but that isn't the only thing they got him for. He was . . ."

I'm quick. "Playing a game." Reverdy, with his saturnine grin, his darkly beautiful declarations of love, Tom and I have lived inside each other's heads for so long that the vacancy is killing me.

"Reverdy, he got this player in the *Precious Den*, he hadn't bothered to sweep the place, you know, to be sure nobody saw what he was up to and nobody came in? So he didn't know Azeath had sneaked in there, much less that he was logging the whole fucking scene. Used it to kill him, chapter and verse. He's *@erased*. Look," Lark says. "I called his house. I can't get him on the phone."

"No!" As if to drown out the news I replay our last moments, Reverdy's and mine—Reverdy, who knows me better than Charlie ever could and, yes, loves me more!

"Yup."

Loves me and phones Lark RL instead of me. It's like discovering an infidelity. My lover doesn't give me a clue where he goes when he leaves StElene. He lets himself be *@erased* without even trying to warn me it was coming, or explain. Erased. I say defensively, "So what if he plays a few games? What's StElene about if it isn't about games? How many other people play jokes on guests and newbies and, OK, on us?"

"Yeah well," Lark says. "That's the problem. Like, who he was playing it *on*. You know, the, like, victim, that filed the complaint and got Reverdy whacked?"

"Some idiot complained?"

"Bigtime. Az put him up to it."

"Azeath. Azeath would."

"Rev always said he could tell a dirty old man when he met one? Well this time he made a huge mistake. Turns out his Precious was pretend doing the nasty with . . ."

"What, Lark. What?"

Lark coughs. "OK, he scared the crap out of some stupid twelve-year-old kid whose folks let him stay up too late. And the dad is a lawyer. One flame and the dad is on the phone with the corporation. Threatening to sue."

"But. Precious. Nobody knew Precious was Reverdy." I give him a sharp look. "Except you."

"Yeah right," Lark says bitterly. "Do you really think I would . . . Face it. The people who find out about these things, that would only be the people that, like, Reverdy wants them to know." His tone makes it clear that he too feels betrayed. "Reverdy knew Azeath was out to get him, no question."

"He should have been careful!"

"No." Lark shakes his head. "It's like, you want to commit suicide but you want somebody else to come in and do the job."

"Suicide!" I groan. "Oh!" Reverdy is gone. Vanished from my life. We are in my kitchen discussing a virtual loss, and it turns out to be more profound than any I've felt RL since Daddy. Intolerable.

"He knew what he was doing," Lark says. "He blew his cover with Azeath right before Precious led the Guest off to her lair."

I dodge this point. I am studying Lark, who's spoken to my virtual lover IRL, who knows where he lives. Does he really know where Reverdy lives? "He wouldn't throw it all *away*."

"But he did. Like he was asking for it."

"Lark." I am swallowing hard. My throat is so dry that I can hear my lungs squeak. "You've talked to him since it happened?"

"No." We move into the next phase. "He's not taking calls."

"Email. We could mail him! He's mailed you!"

"Forget it. No. I'm worried as hell about him."

"Me too." I am moving carefully, constructing something I can work with. The next thing I say is equally true; Lark's color is bad, he's like a complex mechanism chattering toward implosion. "And I'm worried about you."

"I'll be OK," Lark says, but he's gulping air. "Just as soon as I . . . As soon as Rev helps me figure out what to . . . Oh Zan. If I could only talk to him!"

"Yes! If only I . . ." So I'm not enough for Lark, the poor kid needs Reverdy as much as I do. Part of me is drifting out the door, as if I can fly into the ether as swiftly as I do on StElene, @*finding* him and @*being* in the physical space where Tom lives, RL. But the faculties I have on StElene don't travel. We're earthbound, stuck in the realm of planes, trains and automobiles. This is how quickly a plan forms, how fast a professional woman in her right mind can construct a farewell note in her head, and how this woman, who is married IRL, can make plans with her gawky visitor, who is her best friend in the world next to Reverdy. This is how a person can make a life-changing decision in less time than it takes to log on in the realm of the imagination. "If only *we* could talk to him."

What I'm planning is wrong but when I see Lark's face brighten as he divines where this is going, I think we are doing the right thing after all. *This feels so good it can't be bad.* After all these months of subterfuge I'll come clean with Charlie and be done with this. What I really mean is that I love Tom Dearden now more than I love my life and I can not make the leap in reason from there. I can't know what Tom will say or what we'll do the first time we see each other, I only know that I have to find out. I am proceeding on hope. Unless it's on faith.

Of course we try to phone. It shakes me when the voice on the answering machine—"We can't take your call right now but leave your number . . ."—turns out to be a woman's voice. Reverdy's married, yeah, but I know all about cold, vindictive Louise. And if the voice on the machine sounds light, almost sweet, well, I know better. Tom's told me what it's really like. At the beep I hand the phone to Lark, mouthing: "Message?"

He shakes his head.

My heart shudders. I enter Phase Two. I mouth the words, "Surprise him?"

"Yes! Let's go."

"OK." Gently, I disconnect. "Where does he live?"

Lark still won't look at me but his voice is steady. "It's pretty far. Zan, I can't use Dad's plastic again, I almost got busted charging the ticket to get here, and I—I'm pretty broke." The face-to-face encounter is too much. He's shaking like a badly made model in a windstorm.

"Lark, shhshh. Don't. You came all this way to tell me what happened, it's the least I can do. I'll put both plane tickets on my card. I'll go anywhere to help Tom but oh Lark, I don't know where he is!"

Then Lark pulls out a third piece of paper—folded and re-folded and re-refolded, fingered to a high gloss like a pious old woman's holy card. This is a snailmail from Tom Dearden—an old fashioned letter in an envelope with a first-class stamp. It is typed. No letterhead, no pen changes, but it is signed. "I got a letter."

For the first time I see Tom's handwriting—bold strokes in a black pen. The first outward and physical sign that the man I am in love with really exists outside my mind. I am liquid with excitement. *Tom.* Everything fuses and becomes real. "Let's go to him."

"When?"

This is terrifying. Love comes true. No. It's been true. It's becoming real. I proceed cautiously. "You know where?"

He is fishing in his back pocket. "It's on the envelope. I had it right. Oh never mind, I memorized it."

It's important to be matter-of-fact. "Charlie has the car. We'll have to cab to the airport." After all these days of being strung out, I am finally on the move. Testing, I ask Lark, "Are you OK with planes?"

Sweet. Lark's smile, now that it comes, is delirious, as careless as a baby's. He looks improved. Stronger. Better. *I have a plan.* "I got here, didn't I?"

"You're not just saying that, right? You're sure?"

My gosh he is almost looking at me. His head comes up and he is fixed on something I can't see. He says, too loud, "I always wanted to see Alaska."

"Alaska!"

"Alaska. Didn't you know?"

No, I didn't. I didn't know, and he told Lark and that hurts. It's hard.

Writing the note is even harder.

CHARLIE, I LOVE YOU. I LOVE HIM BETTER. FORGIVE ME.

How can I leave Charlie a note like that? He doesn't even know there is a Reverdy in my life. How can I tell the man she's married to that Tom Dearden, whom I've never seen RL, Tom Dearden and I are desperately in love?

I tear up the note and start over.

CHARLIE, SOMETHING IMPORTANT I HAVE TO DO. I'LL BE BACK.

Covering my bets, I add, even as I go out looking for Tom Dearden—no, Reverdy—no, Tom. I add because I really do still care about Charlie,

PLEASE UNDERSTAND.

thirty

FLORENCE AND VINNIE

Motel room, looking about the way you think it would, Florence Vito Watson in the shower, washing Vinnie Fuller out of the folds and creases in her—only an English teacher would say it, her too, too solid flesh, and thinking *at least the sex is good*; clearly they both needed it but this is nothing like the love Mireya and Azeath make on StElene; it's nothing like the love Mireya made with Reverdy in the palmy days, and in the lexicon of push and shove Mireya/Florence wishes she had kept this one in her gauzy boudoir on StElene because sex is sex and it looks different when you get too close. On StElene it is sex in the abstract and bizarrely exalted, but this! This is definitely not anything you'd ever want to take home or come home to, but now to her surprise this guy Vinnie Fuller is in the shower with her and that's OK except he sinks sharp teeth into her shoulder and she digs an elbow into his ribs and when they both crackle with the pain that he mistakes for ecstasy he shouts, "We did it! Fucking Reverdy is wiped off the face of StElene."

"He's gone," she says with her heart breaking. "And we did

it." She can't believe she will never see Reverdy again.

"We did," Vinnie says, soaping his hairy belly, white and round where his legs are white and scrawny, whereas Azeath's description was so perfect, so burnished, big, buff body with every muscle outlined; Vinnie is gurgling . . . "You and me."

"You," she sobs. "And me." Even the Dak Bungalow is gone.

Vinnie says cleverly, "So if we did it, how come I don't feel better?"

Automatically Florence says what she would have typed, "You want me to make you feel better? Just wait till I wash my hair," but her heart hurts. *If we did it, how come I feel so bad?* A part of her life is over; her marriage to Harry Watson is over, so is her long love affair with Reverdy. She has to go back to StElene—loves/hates him, can't live without it—but as soon as she gets out of here she's done with Azeath, breaking up in the fluidity of conceptual space is hard to have over and done with, but she will manage it. Still she and this Vinnie person have to get through the rest of this encounter so she can proceed. Afterward she'll lie on the bed and wait for him to fall asleep. Then she can get dressed and go.

He says, "But when we fuck it's gotta be perfect."

She's not too good at dissembling; all she can manage is "Mmm."

As it turns out, Vinnie is in the grip of a bright idea. "It's OK, I know how to make it perfect. I know what we'll do."

Uneasy, Florence says, "It's already perfect. Look at us! We're here." Disappointment drives her voice into the cellar. "Irl."

"Hell no it isn't perfect. We have to find the bastard." He lathers Florence roughly and rinses her and steps out of the shower, waiting for her to follow. Clearly he's ready for another round, when all she wants is to get this over with. He goes on talking in that reedy, nasal voice so unlike anything she imagined for him. "You know how to find him and you're going to help me find him," Vinnie says.

She stiffens. Rigid, she lets the water beat down on her head.

"And then, oh boy count your blessings baby, it's going to be perfect." The voice is reedy but the tone is pure Azeath, all bluster and bile. "It'll be pretty near perfect when the bastard sees it's us that came to get him, and better than perfect when he figures out what we are doing."

Alarmed, she tries, "We don't need anything more. We're perfect now."

"Bullshit." Vinnie's voice hardens. "You've got this guy's site information, you already told me, so don't try and claim you didn't because I know. And I know that isn't all you know, *Florence,* so after we get to where he is we'll just." A mass of tangled synapses, he regroups, wheedling. "I don't have to tell you what I want baby because I know you want it too . . ."

Her face opens under the steaming shower in a suppressed scream. She wants to turn off the water but her hands won't obey her. "Vinnie, I."

"Us together forever baby, right? And perfect." His next words freeze her solid. "It'll be perfect when we fuck on his grave."

thirty-one

JENNY

I t's as if Lark and I have spun through several lifetimes just
getting where we are going.

As soon as the airport taxi cleared town and headed into
the low marsh country that lies south of Brevert, I said goodbye
to all that. And was not sorry; I am leaving my old life behind.
Riding along under the arches of liveoaks, with Spanish moss
hanging down like mummies' wrappings, I knew it was time.
When we hit the last long causeway into Savannah the marsh
started slipping past at great speeds, spooling past the windows
like a background process shot in a movie about Jenny, going
away. Then the cab driver let us out at the airport, Lark came
alive and we began to talk. We sat together eating frozen yogurt
in the Savannah airport, so focused on talking that I lost time
and boarded the plane without noticing. We sat together eating
airport nacho plates and Buffalo wings in Atlanta and Chicago
and Minneapolis, dry-mouthed and short on sleep because air
travel in America may be as fast as any once the planes take off,
but the hours between connections are weighted with delays.
This is nothing like travel on StElene.

Now Lark and I are in Seattle, waiting for our last plane. We are in the departure lounge, planted like rocks in a stream of travelers. We've been together for so long now that we're like near relations, spiritually joined at the hip. In the hours we've been on the road we've told each other everything and now we are bonded by all that talk and by what we think we're doing. *The right thing. We're doing the right thing.*

We're going to Reverdy. Everything in me is rushing ahead to the moment. *He needs me.* This isn't only in the kingdom of imagination. I don't just imagine he needs me. I know!

Like all committed players who meet outside the game, Lark and I talk about everything in the world, knowing that in the end we will talk about the game. The locations and characters are as real to Lark and me as we are to each other sitting here, welded to molded plastic seats under this unremitting fluorescent glare. We make our own private space in spite of heavy sighs and footsteps pounding along the concourse behind us, in spite of CNN on the ubiquitous area TVs and the blue tweed industrial carpeting that spreads at our feet like what passes for grass in some ugly future we don't want to think about. I say to Lark, "You seem to be OK with people after all."

"These aren't real people," he says.

I grin. "It's as real as it gets."

"RL." Lark says mildly, "This is the most people I've been around since I got sick."

"You're not sick any more." I reach for his hand, but it's too soon. Keep him strong *so we can help Reverdy,* I think, not knowing what that means. I say, "Look. You made it this far."

"It cost me."

"Yeah, but you made it. I know a lot of sick people, Lark. You're not give-up-and-let-it-wash-over-you sick."

"Yeah I am," he says almost easily, "but I'm getting used to it. It's like when you get trapped in the hospital and they keep sticking things in you and turning you upside down and stuff? After a while, you stop caring who looks."

I laugh. "That sounds like better." I can work with this. Get him back into college, fix his life. It's nice, in a time when I'm sick with worry and crazy in love, to see my friend Lark hand himself over to me. He follows my lead with a sweet, bland look of undiscriminating approval. It is as if for the purposes of this trip, at least, he has relaxed into trust.

"You wish."

"Not to worry. I'll take care of you." Better. I know I *can* take care of him. All the best parts of me are running after Reverdy, but IRL I can still cope. I'm even good at it; he's in better shape than he was when we started out. I can tell from the easy way he sits in the plastic seat, mainlining chocolate. I can tell from the way he eats without worrying about what eating looks like to the people he's usually convinced are watching him. The way he lifts his head and looks around. For now, he's become my child. Closer, at least, than Charlie's kids, and as for any of my own? I can't go there right now. I can't afford to go there. My heart stops at Lark.

Then he reminds me who we really are. "When was the last time you connected?"

"Myrtle Beach, just five minutes. My God, it's been two days."

"Some airports have these post-thingys where you can connect?"

"Email kiosks." I don't mean to sigh. "Not this airport. I looked."

Lark shrugs. "I guess we're in StElene detox."

"You could call it that." No surprise. We are both twitchy because we haven't connected in days. Maybe it really is a physical addiction, but there's more. My friend Lark says he's more at home in electronic space than he is inside the trap of his body, in this life. Wait. So am I.

He nudges. "Think we'll get used to it?"

"Too soon to tell."

Then Lark says, "I talked to StBrêve right before I left for your house. I told him how pissed I was over what they did to Reverdy. They erased him without a public hearing!" He is in mourning. "They gave the gazebo to Azeath."

"That's terrible!" I say irrationally, "They ought to be in jail. And Azeath. He ought to be in jail."

"Oh, Azeath. Azeath's a fuck."

"He does what Mireya tells him to."

"Or not. StBrêve wouldn't even come down to the lobby to tell me what they did to Rev. He made me come up to the top of the hotel, into the boardroom, like I was on trial or something, when they're the ones that did wrong."

"Mireya." I am bitter for more than one reason—those phone calls to Charlie, that made him take me on the road. "Mireya started it."

"Whoever," Lark says. "Anyway, StBrêve sat me down in the big mahogany chair at the far end of the big mahogany table with the lions' feet? And do you know what he said? He said they @erased my best friend for the good of the fucking community."

"To keep their name out of the papers, you mean."

"Not exactly. Maybe. Partly, but there was more. He said they had to do it."

"They didn't have to do it."

"He made them do it."

"Azeath?"

"No, Azeath didn't make them do it." Lark sighs. "Reverdy did."

I am shaking my head like a fresh war widow. "But they didn't have to do it."

"StBrêve said Reverdy was a negative presence. Divisive."

"No. This is about their image. Reverdy was onto them and they were afraid."

"He said Reverdy was poisoning the community."

"That's a lie!" Pain makes me extraordinarily bitter. "They knew he was onto their game."

"You want to know something wild?" Lark gives me a sweet, bemused look. "I'm not sure they have a game. Like, this whole weird, complicated thing you do and I do, that thousands of us do and care so much about? This island of ours, all of us with our own special places, plus enough room for the stuff underground and in the volcano and on the grounds? This whole wild society takes up less than a gig in a computer in some back room in the Suntum home office. We're all in a box stuck under a desk somewhere!"

"It's much, much bigger than that," I say.

Then he says, "Like, are any outsiders really accessing us?"

But I'm intent on my own track. No. I'm speeding along Reverdy's track, on rails waxed with paranoia. "If they aren't using us, they will. It's only a matter of time."

"Like, does anybody really care what we do?"

"You bet they care! There's profit in it and Reverdy knew it, so they had to erase him before he could blow the whistle. He was onto their game. . . . Whatever it was."

"Is. If there is a game."

"Lark!"

He sees where I need us to be going. "StBrêve did say they'd do anything to protect it."

"The game?"

"The corporation."

"So they did set him up. Murdered him!"

"If you want to call it that." Licking chocolate off his fingers, Lark says pensively, "Unless it's suicide."

"Don't even joke. It's an ugly word."

Lark is looking at me now, here in the middle of the airport lounge with the physical world flowing by on either side, my rickety, pathologically shy friend is looking straight at me. His eyes drop into my consciousness like perfect stones. Anchoring me. "If you want to know the truth, Zan, it's got me scared. Reverdy bails without a fight. Doesn't tell me. Won't mail. Doesn't return calls. What's happening to him?"

"Nothing. He's fine and he'll be back!"

Lark groans. "It's like he's over. Done."

"No! As soon as we find him, he'll..." The rest of the sentence eludes me. Our flight has been called. "And we'll be fine."

Lark stands. He touches my arm! His expression tells me he's not so sure. For the first time he doesn't flinch when I move toward him; we lock for a minute in a hug. Grimacing, he mouths but does not say: *I hope so.*

"We will. We'll be OK." And with my eyes gritty from lack of sleep and my hands sticky from travel, paddling through this industrial wasteland, I am stricken quite unexpectedly right here at the gate to our last departure lounge. What I feel is sudden joy. When we get off this plane we will be in Alaska. We can rent a car and drive to the city where Tom Dearden lives. We'll go to the address Lark has committed to memory and I will see

Tom, and if I wonder why, when he loves me so much, he hasn't tried to come for me, I can't afford to consider the implications. For the first time since we fell in love, Reverdy and I—no, Tom Dearden and I are going to meet. Blood and bone. Flesh and flesh. Him, me.

What he said that keeps me going: "We'll be together soon!"

thirty-two

FLORENCE/VINNIE

I *don't feel good.* It's been two hours. After ten years in the penitentiary at Wardville Vinnie Fuller may know how to beat a secret out of anybody but he won't get this secret out of her. He won't get anything out of this squat, stubborn, embattled woman in this squalid roadside motel on this particular night in her miserable physical life. What Vinnie doesn't know about Florence Vito Watson is how strong she is, deep down. Or how much in love.

If Vinnie has other ways of finding Tom Dearden, whose right name he does not yet know; if he is going to devote the rest of his life to hunting his enemy down, Florence will die without knowing it. She is in the act of defending Reverdy to the death.

There is blood in the room. She hears ugly noises—threats and a guttural song of pain. *Is that coming out of me?* Other things are happening. Vinnie is yelling and she . . . Mireya goes back inside her head, where it's safe. She won't see or hear the ugly, struggling physical avatars for the ideal Mireya or Azeath in the ugly sounds they make RL.

On StElene, Mireya is protecting her lover, and whatever Florence Vito Watson is outside the box, in her heart, the Amazon princess Mireya is strong. Florence is wearing Mireya now, she has put on her idealized and powerful virtual persona and locked it around her like armor. Nothing can hurt her now.

"Tell me, *bitch!*" Thwack.

Never mind what this violent man she *thought she knew* tries to do to her. Never mind how much her pathetic, baggy old body hurts; Florence is safe now, girded in Mireya, and Tom Dearden's secrets are safe. Her real lover's particulars IRL are written nowhere. They are locked inside her mind; she would never go into an encounter with Tom's address IVR or IRL written on a piece of paper that just anybody could find. Not even Azeath, whom she thought she loved. Nobody's going to locate her dearest Tom and go there. Nobody can hurt him as long as she's alive. And if Florence dreamed that Reverdy would hear about this RL meeting with Azeath/Vinnie and be jealous and come for her, that hope has gone by. But if she's done nothing else on this day she has done one thing, is doing it now, and in spite of the questions and the hammering, is doing it extremely well.

And if there is eternal love and there is justice, Mireya thinks as Vinnie's fists come down and keep lifting and coming down again, the man she loves most in any world, this or the other, will know how much she loved him. She wants Reverdy—*love!*—she wants Reverdy and Tom Dearden both to know that Florence Vito Watson loved him so much that she protected his site information and his home phone number and his location in a cul de sac in a suburb of Fairbanks, Alaska, forever. Is protecting them with her life.

Before StElene they were nothing—sour, frumpy school-teacher. Two-bit convict in the pen for not much. Changed, el-

*evated by the story they have been weaving, two ordinary people are transformed. In a feat of performative utterance they have become the roles they wrote for themselves. Valiant lover. Powerful villain, fixed on revenge. They are different from what they were: someone **more**.*

The last thing she hears is Vinnie screaming, "Wake up and fucking talk to me, you bitch. Wake *up!*"

But she won't.

Maddened by frustration, Vinnie keeps beating on her until even he understands there is no point. Then he turns Florence over and starts rooting through her pockets for a scrawled phone number, list, address book, scrawled note, anything that yields what she refused to give; later he will gut the car before he remembers that he has her key-ring and that one of the keys must open the apartment in Boston where Florence Vito Watson lived in what used to be her real life. Vinnie will scour the place; he'll turn it upside down. If he has to, he'll turn what remains of her intelligence upside down too, shaking until the truth falls out. He'll sweep her computer's hard disk until he finds it. The motherfucker's legal name! His address! After all, Vinnie has nothing but time, and now that Florence is dead, he has a place to stay. He has nothing but time.

Hatred has fast-forwarded this recently unshelled convict into a new identity. He has stopped being Azeath; he is no longer Vinnie. He is an engine of vengeance steaming toward a collision that will be realized sooner or later, he vows, even if it takes the rest of his life.

Time is not important to Vinnie Fuller. It doesn't matter how long it takes him to finish this. He's got as long as it takes. If he has to pursue his enemy through the archives at Suntum International he will pursue him. If he has to threaten or bribe the Directors RL he'll find a way. He is going to find fucking

Reverdy. He'll hire detectives if that's what it takes. He is going to crack Reverdy's site information and find out where the bastard sits when he logs on. Vinnie is going to hunt him down; he will go wherever the pursuit takes him.

Like the Frankensteins, baron and creation, master and monster, they will finally collide. Vinnie Fuller and Reverdy are going to fight if it takes the rest of Vinnie's life to bring him down. He will engage the bastard and grapple him up and over the last horizon if he has to, Godzilla and Rodan, enemies to the end of the earth.

thirty-three

ALASKA

y love is everything I think he is. Then why am I so scared? Partly, it's being this close to something I never knew I always wanted, and the rest? Too soon to tell.

We are flying into Fairbanks, Alaska. Making it this far has cost Lark and me. He's twitching in and out of sleep while I drift in limbo, stretched taut between Charlie's house on Church Street and here, and the *Dak Bungalow* on StElene. I can't see it or touch it but the lost *Dak Bungalow* is more real to me right now than anything on Church Street or in this plane. When I logged on and found the bungalow and all the things Reverdy and I built together and cared so much about had vanished, @*erased* by the Directors, I was torn in two. Part of my life had ceased to exist. Imagine walking into the ruins of a burned-out city where everybody you care about has died.

Now I am flying into Fairbanks, Alaska, to put myself together again, but oh. What's going to happen next? What if he's nothing like I think? Impossible. I know what he's like. Typing to each other over months, Tom Dearden and I have stripped each other to the soul. He let me see right into him, and he saw me. We know and love each other to the bone.

But what if, I can't stop thinking, what if? What if he isn't what I think? What if I find not Reverdy but one of those unseen typists we used to make private jokes about, some twisted soul typing from an institution, what if he turns out to be hideous or bizarrely transgendered, a woman waiting, where I thought I was in love with a man. Worse, what if my glorious partner is only the archetypical fat geek in a shrunken T-shirt, the post-millennial flip on Cyrano? Oh God, what if he's only a randy teenager who's duped me over time?

Impossible. In the intimacy of space, love is intuitive. Quick. And sure. We know things about each other without having to be told.

He needs me now. I know this without having to be told.

I am flying in to rescue my lover from his life. Tom wants me but he's held in place by decency, won't walk out on Louise, won't take another man's wife . . . All I have to do is tell him that I've left Charlie for good. When he sees me come in that door . . . Grief rolls into me. *For good!* What I did when I left Brevert without telling Charlie was burn my bridges. I'm burning them now. So what if I'm a little scared?

We'll be together soon enough. I see us blazing into eternity, like matched stars.

Imagine our first meeting. I can't! Zan hasn't even seen a photo; there are no sense memories between us, nothing to go on but the word portraits we've typed—who we are to each other on StElene. This is crazy! No. It's wonderful.

Linked souls. We will know each other at once.

As the plane circles for the descent, I scour the grid of dismal streets and Monopoly-board houses that crosshatch the map of Fairbanks. It looks so bleak! If I stare hard enough, I think, I can home in on Tom Dearden's house. *page reverdy I'm here!* He'll hear. No, he'll divine—the man will *know* without being told that I'm circling overhead. I'll look down and because it is fated, Tom's front door will smash open and he'll come running out. I'll see him standing in the street below me with his arms spread and his mouth wide. "A miracle," I say recklessly, wondering whether this is what Tom means when he talks about convergence. *We'll know each other on sight.*

In the seat next to me, Lark stirs but does not wake.

It helps to say his name. "Tom? Tom." But even though we come in low over a housing development, coasting *this close* to the ground, no front doors pop open. Nobody comes out. I can't even be sure that this distorted checkerboard is part of the right development or even the right neighborhood. And there is no sign of Tom.

Anxiety rolls in like a medieval war machine. *What if something's happened to him? What if he was in an accident, or worse. What if he's trapped inside the house?* The first fear is crazy; the second is logical. My Tom has angered the Directors of a major corporation here. They've betrayed him and the only way he can get back at them is to go public. Suntum's a big corporation, oh God, they're bound to have a security arm. What if the officers at Suntum have put him under house arrest? He could be locked in there, angry and trapped. Like Achilles, sulking in his tent. Reverdy loves StElene so much, he had such dreams!

"Oh, Tom!" I'm flying in to see a man who pinned his hopes on an ideal society, and now look. Forget democracy, my love. Come away with me. But he won't. He'll want me to stay and fight. I'll get him a lawyer. Then we'll show them all right, I know a few things about using the press. American Civil Liberties Union. Electronic Frontier Foundation. TV news. Louise will see how much we love each other and she'll go. We can stand back to back, fighting the Suntum Corporation to the Supreme Court.

The plane touches down, bounces and rackets to a stop. Lark jerks to attention. "Well," he says in a thin voice. "This is it."

"Yes!"

Then we're on the ground, half-sick and unsteady from sitting too long. I totter out to rent a car. "Well," I say.

We aren't ready; we are. Being this close has silenced Lark; it's as if God saw him smiling and filled his mouth with cement.

Never mind. It's hard enough here, just doing the right things to get us moving. I don't have the energy to respond. I wonder what exactly we're doing in this unfamiliar landscape, what we're going to do when we get to the house. "Should we phone ahead?"

Lark grimaces.

"Yes? No?"

He mouths, but no sound comes out. "I'm not supposed to give out the number."

A question hangs between us. *What if we call and he tells us not to come?* I nod. "Maybe better not."

Lark looks relieved.

I am not exactly praying, but I am: *Oh please, let me get this right.*

Lark pulls the area map supplied by Avis out of the dashboard. He's turning it this way, that way, as if by squinting he can match coordinates with the printed email Tom sent. "Oh God," he says at last. He sounds like the Tin Woodman, unrusting. "Alaska! We're really here."

"Yeah. We're here."

Lark is staring out at the tarmac with a wild, disconnected look. The poor kid is trying; he's *trying* to be cool but it's clear that the pressure is getting to him. His—OK, his idol, Reverdy, in this city, so near. No wonder his voice quavers. "Too bad we don't have one of those cool programs with the area map and a blip to track the car."

"Too bad we don't have the laptop to run it on."

"Or the modem." He wants to joke, but we both know it isn't funny. "We could log on."

"Just one more hit before I go cold turkey." My voice shakes. We are so close. Resolution plows into me and I blurt, "I'm through with logging on."

"As *if!*" We try to laugh.

Lark falls silent. It's as if a boulder has dropped out of the sky and smashed him flat. I want him to keep talking while I drive, I want him to say something, anything, to take my mind off what we're about to do. I need background music for this progress to the connector that takes us into a city I never dreamed I'd need to know.

I try, "It's cold!"

Spring hasn't found this place. It looks like upper New York State in November. Bare and cold. Blinking like an astronaut walking out on a new planet, I wind along the road out of the airport and find my way into the raw landscape. It's beautiful but blasted looking, as if a firestorm came through, taking everything that might soften the outlines, and then moved out. Unhospitable. No wonder Tom wanted to move to StElene. This place is stranger than Mars. Next to me on the front seat, Lark is gnawing his knuckles.

Oh God, what am I doing here?

Please tell me what to do, make something happen. At least make Lark talk to me.

But he doesn't. Unless he can't. When Lark finally does get his speech back it's to ask, "D'you think he'll be glad to see us?"

"Of course he will!"

"I hope."

"He has to be. After all, we came to help." My mind won't stop fast-forwarding to our meeting, never mind that I can't see us, I don't need to. I am fueled by everything Tom ever said to me and everything I hope to say to him. Reverdy and Zan. "He's waiting for us. Right, Lark?"

"Right." Lark lapses into expectations of his own.

He knows. He knows! I catch a sudden, wild glimpse of us together. Tom will see me from the upstairs window. Zan! He'll rush downstairs and come running out and we'll know each other at once. We'll hug right there in the street in front of Lark and Louise and everybody, we will fuse like two parts of the same person, blood and bone. When he and I bury ourselves in each other we won't care who sees, I'll feel his bulk, I can absorb his distinctive smell, and then . . .

My imagination stops short. I've never seen or felt or touched Tom Dearden RL. What fills my senses now is the familiar Charlie smell, his heartbeat, the sweet drone of our lost all-night conversations. The rush of sensation leaves my throat tight. Every cord in my body is twanging. It's as though I've been brought down in midflight by a tripwire, or smashed into an electrified fence.

Lark's voice filters in: "Are you all right?"

"Who, me? I'm fine." I catch a glimpse in the rearview mirror. No I'm not fine. I look like a wraith in a windstorm, and Lark? Lark is looking a little glassy himself.

Lark strangles. "We're here."

It's too soon. "My God."

I've found the house. We are in front of his house. Tom's house. It looks so ordinary! Split level development ranch model with aluminum siding in a depressing gray, beyond ordinary, with a mean little second-floor window, how little, how squalid, how not Tom! There are crumpled paper plates and napkins strewn on the bare, muddy front lawn and drooping balloons still tied to the mailbox—must have been a party here—and inside somewhere, Reverdy, no. Tom.

The trouble is, my lover is bold, reckless and expansive, he moves through space like a man from a much bigger . . .

Lark's voice goes flat. "This can't be it."

"But it is." Tom never told me what the room looked like where he was typing. In the absence of information my mind supplied the details. I imagined it as. Well. *More.*

"It's kind of small."

We could be talking in the thin air at the top of Independence Pass, eleven thousand feet above the world. Our voices are that strained. We are gasping for breath. "Yeah." My hands on the wheel look like they belong to somebody else. The house looks like it belongs to somebody else. The front door does not smash open. Nobody comes out. Too much time goes by.

The thin stream of air coming out of Lark finally turns into speech. "What are we going to do?"

"Go in."

This is so terrifying that neither of us moves.

After a while I say, "Do you want to or should I?" Is there somebody in the upstairs front room, moving behind the curtains? I don't know. My heart's been running ahead of me for all these hours and now it threatens to stop. Everything is still. Especially Lark.

I wait. Lark and I sit for a very long time. It's hard to know what day it is but it's near dusk, at least in this continuum. The congested suburban block the house sits on is ugly, banal, flat, but from here I can see mountains; beyond the ridge, the sky is wonderfully soft. In the street ahead there are children playing. Somebody else's? Tom's? I'm afraid to get out of the car; I want to get out of the car and hug them all. I want Tom's children to come running to me and pull me into the house, *pretty, not like our mother, you know about our mother, she's . . .* But I don't know about Louise, I only know what Tom says about Louise. I want Tom Dearden to come out of his goddamn house and end this; I want him to come rushing out of the house with Louise hard behind, begging him to stop. I want him to come straight to me, I want him to wrench open the car door and pull me out of the car and hug me and never stop. I want him to hug me so tight that Louise knows and the children know and the world knows. I want him to do it right here in front of them all.

On StElene, I could teleport. I could be with him instantly. *@join reverdy.* Here I am fixed in time, rooted in physical space. I want to begin. I'm afraid to begin. "Lark?"

Lark whispers, "You go. I can't."

"Oh, sweetie." We are riveted by a thud. A child's ball has hit the roof of the rented Hyundai. Helplessly, I watch it roll down the windshield and dribble off the side of the hood. Then because there is no help for it, I unbuckle and get out. I feel naked, standing out here on the walk in suburban Fairbanks, Alaska. *Gone;* I shudder. *What if we've come all this way and he's gone?* But I know better. The balloons on the mailbox bob brightly; they're today's. I can see movement in-side the house. A figure passes the standard plate glass win-dow, headed for the front door. I hear my own bootheels. *Click. Click. Click.*

I don't even have to knock. A woman opens it and comes out, easy in jeans and a denim shirt open at the throat. This must be Louise. Where is my voice?

Louise Dearden's voice is low, pleasant, modulated. "Excuse me. I couldn't help seeing the car. Are you in trouble? Is there something I can do for you?"

Oh, God, she doesn't look anything like he said.

"Mrs. Dearden?" A part of me goes scurrying after the hope that *this lovely woman* is somebody else. It can't be Louise Dearden, it has to be Reverdy's sister, his daughter from a first marriage. Anybody but his wife. There is no way that this good-looking woman with the pleasantly expectant smile can be the terrible Louise. Tom's unlovable wife is plain and spiteful. He's told me so. This can't be Louise, the real Louise has got to be lurking somewhere behind that front door, crouched to spring.

Unless that part is a lie.

"Yes, I'm Louise Dearden."

Oh God, please don't smile, Louise. Please don't smile at me.

"I. Ah. I'm. I came to see Tom."

"Oh!" Oddly, this pretty woman is blushing. I've caught her unprepared. "I'm afraid he isn't . . . we were just."

She doesn't have to explain; it's clear from the glow in Lou-ise Dearden's face, in the flush that begins in the neck of her open shirt and spreads up her throat that she and the man inside the house have just left off making love. Later, when there's time, I'll wonder just exactly what was wrong with me that I don't turn and go right then. What flaw keeps me standing there at Tom's front door like a bull at the knacker's waiting for the mallet, weaving with my head bowed because I know I'm beaten but I'm too weak to lie down?

I cough apologetically. "I've come a long way. I need to see him."

"See him?" Louise looks surprised. "Are you from the history project? If you're from the history project, you already know . . ."

God, this is so humbling. "I'm sorry? Mrs. Dearden, I think he'll see me, we're both part of this . . . I . . ."

"If you're from the project, you already know he doesn't see people."

"I just need to know if he's all right!" I'm like a beggar with my hat in my hands, craning to see past Louise as if all I have to do is see Tom, or *let him see me,* and we can get through this. Our lives together will begin. "I've come a long way."

"I'm sorry," Louise says again. Like a nurse calming a patient, she puts a hand on my arm. "He isn't seeing people."

It crosses my mind that he can't. But no. It would kill me. "I can come back." *Please let me come back.*

"You don't understand. He isn't seeing people," Louise says.

"But this is different. I've come so far!" I guess it's exhaustion; I don't falter exactly, I just go off balance, all of a sudden, and Louise's face softens.

"I'm sorry." Whatever Tom Dearden is, she is protecting him.

"Please!"

"If you know Tom at all you ought to know. . . ." It's as if she's breaking the news of a recent death. "He just doesn't."

"Why not, why *not?*" This is not the worst thing. Nor is Louise Dearden's invitation to come in for tea the worst thing, even though I know I can't bear to be in the same house with

Tom and not touch him. Nor will having to sit in that pleasant, banal living room trying too hard not to cry be the worst thing. The worst thing will come later.

His wife is waiting with that nice smile. "Please."

I follow her into his house.

thirty-four

'm in his house, *This can't be his house,* I think as Louise goes for a tray. *Too ordinary, too small.* There are no traces of my lover in this room: off-white Kmart curtains, green sectional, white birch coffee table, painted tole lamp, plastic flowers, plaque. *Wrong.* These can't be his things.

"If you're not from Tom's history project," Louise says, returning with the tea, "is it about that silly game of his?"

He can't be here. If he's here he'll hear me. He'll come down. I raise my voice, in case. "I'm sorry, Mrs. Dearden, there isn't any game. My name is Jenny. Jenny Wilder."

"That game." She shakes her head. "Oh look, I'm so sorry!"

"What?"

She says sadly, "And you came all this way."

There is a chance he doesn't know I'm here or he knows somebody's here but can't guess it's me. "Jenny," I say louder. "Jenny Wilder." And I think I hear movement overhead; a stir as if someone big has come out into the hall and is waiting just out of sight, leaning over the rail at the head of the stairs. *Rev-*

erdy? Tom? In a second our spirits will fly out of our bodies and meet midway and as if it is fated, fuse.

"You don't have to shout. Really. Tom knows you're here."

Nothing happens.

She reaches for my hands and as Zan jerks them away she sighs. "Oh dear, it really is about that game."

"This isn't a game!"

"I understand," Louise says understandingly (Tom: *she doesn't understand me, she never understood me*) when it's clear she can't possibly understand. "I just wonder if you understand Tom."

"Oh, Tom." Pain drives me to my feet. *Tom.* If I can only see him, and explain. "Tom! It isn't a game!" Am I shouting, does he hear? Will the sound of my voice bring him or is he waiting for me to shoulder Louise aside and run upstairs to him? "It's everything," I say, making a lunge for the stairs. My head fills up with the sound of her voice. "Everything."

"Oh my dear, I am so sorry." Louise is on her feet, blocking the little hallway, prepared to protect her husband with her life.

"Get out of my way."

"Please don't," she says with a sweet, sad look. She adds in his words, Reverdy's words! "Please don't. It isn't real."

But I am wild. I shove her out of the way and push on, shouting, "Well, real people get hurt!"

And I charge the stairs. At the top I hesitate, breathing hard. The air in the small, dark upstairs hallway ripples as if stirred by a recent disturbance, its texture changed by a residual whir, as if somebody has just turned and fled. Someone—Tom?—just darted into the room at the far end of the hall. The door swings shut. I throw myself against it. "Tom." Trembling, I knock.

Wild, I keep my voice light and clear so that there will be no mistaking it. "Tom, it's Jenny. Reverdy, it's Zan!"

Nobody answers. I hear the *click* as the door shuts and the distinctive final crash of the dead bolt slipping into place.

I won't call again. I won't put my ear to the door or shout and I certainly won't hammer. Instead I stand in the empty hall with my breath shuddering and make myself count to a hundred before I turn to go down to confront Louise, who stands waiting discreetly at the bottom of the stairs.

Louise says, "I'm sorry."

I say, "So am I."

The next to worst thing comes in the seconds after I've thanked Louise and excused myself and blindly headed down the front walk, hoping I can figure out how to explain this to Lark. The worst thing doesn't even come when I knuckle the tears out of my eyes and look back at the dim little second story window and see a man's figure behind the curtains. I see a tall shape lounging against the frame. And knows he sees me, although the curtain hides his features, masking his expression. It is, of course, Reverdy-who-was. I am looking at Tom Dearden looking at me.

There is a rustle at my back. Lark has come up the walk to meet me and he stands, staring up at the house. "Oh shit," he says. "It's him."

"Yes."

He understands everything. "Oh, shit."

So the worst thing in this *passage* that I'm going to play and replay for the rest of my life, replaying it for as long as I'm physically able to get up in the morning and dress myself and go out into the world and greet my grown children and their grandchildren and go through all the motions of being a three dimensional person IRL.

The worst thing is the moment when Tom Dearden—who in spite of all my passion and all my hopes has never been anything more or better than this fugitive figure at the window—when Tom acknowledges everything that has passed between us.

And waves goodbye.

thirty-five

stumble back to the car. When I slide into the driver's seat I turn to face Lark. For the rest of my life, I'll owe my friend here for not asking, "What happened?" Or, worse, "What are we going to do?" And I owe him for not responding with the easy, automatic and previously coded StElene *warm hug*.

What we do from here on out has not been coded. It needs to be considered. We can't log on and expect somebody else to take our minds off it or help us solve our problems; we won't go back until we've confronted them. We have to solve them ourselves. Lark and I have been through a lot together; by this time we're so close that it's OK for Lark to keep his distance, not hug, not say the expected *there-there*. He is too rocky himself for *there-there*. He lets me know how he feels by letting me see into his eyes.

I love him for not asking, "Are you all right?"

What he does instead is say with a wry grin, "Guess we'd better activate Plan B."

My hands are jittering on the steering wheel. "As soon as we get a Plan B."

"I can't go home."

"I don't know if I can." I'm trying to figure out what's best for us. I'm too wasted right now to know.

Lark and I get each other home. Better. We face what's ahead together and get each other through. At Lark's suggestion I book motel rooms at the airport so we can get unwrecked before we go back to our lives. It's important. We have to put our lives back together before we can even think about what's next. At the motel, we crash and burn. We sleep until we can't sleep any more. Then we eat. Then we begin the long progress back to Brevert.

We don't talk about what has just happened—we can't. And we don't talk about StElene. No way. And Tom Dearden? It hurts too much to talk about that now. Maybe never, I think. He's as important to Lark as he is to me. Correction. Was to me. Stuck in Brevert, South Carolina, where I never belonged, I went into an imaginary world and rode out to what felt like happiness on a dream. *Wait a minute, lady. You knew what you were doing. That wasn't any dream.* I went into a conceptual world and rode out into the wild blue on nothing more than my expectations. So what if I did? I understand now that it was never about StElene, Reverdy's world of performative utterance where what you type *is*. It was about me.

But Lark and I are mending. It hurts to think about where we've been or what we have discovered; there's no way we can talk about it now. Instead we start cobbling a plan. If I can get Lark back into college, at least I will have done something to make his life better, and mine? Too soon to tell.

Boarding lounge to boarding lounge, Buffalo wings to nachos to frozen yogurts, Lark and I decompress in stages. It's like coming up from the Mindanao Deep. We have to surface

slowly, to keep from getting the bends. So we talk. About everything in the world, except Topic A. We talk about the world,
and about futures. About exigencies in our physical lives. About
all the personal stuff I've left behind in Brevert. About what's
next for him.

Because there's one thing left to do and I know it needs
doing, I find the email kiosk at O'Hare and log on to collect
my mail. I think I can shake off StElene but tendrils keep clinging; they trail behind me like shreds in the aftermath of a long
dream. Never mind. I have a piece of unfinished business.

If I know Tom Dearden, we aren't finished yet.

"How did I guess?" There it is. A mail for *jwilder* from
Tom Dearden. He must have posted it seconds after he saw me
run away from his house without giving me the dignity of a
last-minute *wait!* My unseeable lover is mailing me from behind
a firewall. To make his loving plea, he has chosen a protected
account that delivers mail with no hint as to the location of the
sender. My throat goes sour. I can axe this message unread. I
can drop kick Tom Dearden into oblivion without finding out
what he has to say. It's what he deserves! But I have to finish
this. In the realm of last things, I think, this is the last thing.

DEAREST ZAN, he writes in all capital letters, *what's the
matter Tom, why are you shouting?*

WE HAVE TO TALK. I HAVE FOUND A NEW
PLACE FOR US! MEET ME THERE TOMORROW
NIGHT AT TEN, YOUR TIME. I LOVE YOU, I WILL EX-
PLAIN.

And as if he's secure in my love and supremely sure of his
authority—as if he knows I'll follow wherever he leads me, Tom
supplies the telnet address I am supposed to type in so we can
be together. Sort of.

DAKBUNGALOW.MOO.MUD.ORG 8888

LOVE ALWAYS IN ALL TIME AND ALL SPACE

REVERDY

This is what you do when it's over. Control D. Delete. Empty your trash so you will never see it again.

How could I have gambled everything I have for this?

By the time the cab from the Savannah airport glides along the bay and turns off Front Street and into Church Street, it's night again. Lark and I are back in the world that looked so drab compared to my life on StElene. The cab's headlights flicker in and out of the Spanish moss and light up bits of architectural detail on the town's big houses. I can smell the salt air coming in over the water; I can almost hear the beetles moving in the marsh.

What makes me feel both touched by grace and guilty at the same time is the certainty that Charlie will be glad to see me! I tore up the note that ended our marriage. He doesn't know! He'll let me in without guessing that an entire world has ignited and gone out like a torch in the short time I've been gone. He can't know that I've survived a wild, compressed emotional lifetime since he last saw me or that it began right here, after he brought me down Front Street, only half-kidding, *this is your new life.*

The cab spills us on the sidewalk. I am rehearsing my first line. "Oh Charlie, I'm so glad."

Lark and I have a tentative plan. We've built a story. I tell Charlie that Lark is one of my patients; he cracked up in New Orleans and I had to fly out there to help, emergency, no time to call. I stayed to talk my patient through his admissions interview at Tulane because thanks to me, he's going back to school. At least that's true. He is.

"I'll help you get started, OK? Don't worry, you'll be fine."
Lark says, "Cool."

"I'll tell Charlie you're only living with us until we finish the paperwork and get your parents to agree to pay? I'll say, 'I'm writing a piece on computer mediated therapy.' "

Lark's shaky but game. "Then I'll say, 'And I'm Exhibit A.' "

"You'll be fine," I repeat and he nods. I try to sound strong and confident. "And I'll be fine."

In time. But right now, we have *this* to get through. At my elbow Lark spins like a fugitive, ready to break and run for cover under the oleanders. I grab his arm to steady him. I pull him to one side of Charlie's front walk and over the grass. We crouch in the flowerbed under the lighted front window. I put up my hand. "Wait."

Side by side, we stand on tiptoe and look in. I feel bit like the lost sea captain who comes back from the dead to find out that the world has gone on without him. His marriage died while he was gone; there is a whole new family sitting in the room he used to dominate. I am like a survivor fresh from my desert island, dumped in a world so changed that there's no place for me.

No. Everything looks the same. It's me that's changed. My husband Charlie and his children are snuggling on the sofa. Their backs are to the window. Some shift in the atmosphere makes Charlie turn and look out at the night. The light is in his eyes. He can't see me looking in.

Lark whispers, "I can't do this."

"I can't do this without you," I hiss.

Then my amazingly smart kid friend says, "Are you sure you want to do it at all?"

"No time for that now, we've got to get you back on track."

I pull Lark away from the window as if rushing him out of a movie before the final credits roll. I start toward the front door. "Come on. They're nice people, you'll like them."

"You hope."

"And they'll like you." I say for both of us, "It's only for a little while."

"I know."

"You can do anything, for a little while."

He says again, "Are you sure you want to do this?"

I think but do not say, *I'm doing it for you.* "I have to do *something.*"

We go up the front steps. It is a measure of my uncertainty that I don't use my key. Instead, I am poised to tap on the door. My first line? I haven't written it. Then I look at my friend. I can't do this to him.

No. I can't do it to me.

The part of me that was just about to walk in that door is already grieving for whatever Charlie and I had for such a little while, but! I've come this far from my immersion in StElene and I'm not about to go back to being what I was. I grab Lark's arm.

Lark says, "What. What?"

"You want to do something scary?"

"This," Lark says. "This is scary." He is looking at Charlie's house.

I have nothing on me but the clothes I'm wearing and the contents of my shoulder bag—a few dollars in cash but a few thousand in plastic. "Come on," I say. "It's only a five-minute walk to the bus station. We're going to New York."

Introduction

"The Angel Would Like to Stay, Awaken the Dead, and Make Whole What Has Been Smashed"

AWAKING TO HISTORY ON MANHATTAN ISLAND

Present-day New York City is one of several command posts of the global economy, a vital relay point in the current capitalist world system in which digitalized telecommunications technologies enable the geographic dispersal of economic activity and, increasingly, the disarticulation of finance from material production.[1] Although today's global economy has no fixed nucleus, globalization has given rise to relatively stable clusters of concentration, agglomeration, and integration that convene in the central business districts of a few cities—for example, London, Tokyo, and New York City.[2] Despite the dramatic structural shifts of the late twentieth century, much of New York City's business district and the headquarters of major transnational firms are still located in lower Manhattan and thus stand, quite literally, on the multilayered foundation of the city's colonial past and sedimented legacy of social and racial inequality. With the exception of a few historic landmarks, the visible traces of the city's colonial history of violent conquest, appropriation of Native American lands, and black slavery were buried beneath the city's infrastructure during the rapid conurbation and construction booms of the Industrial Revolution and subsequent economic transformations. Of course, an abundance of well-preserved written records document New York City's early sociocultural development. But on the whole, the dominant U.S. liberal nationalist historiography slights the city's colonial entailments.

A contribution to the fields of colonial studies, urban studies, immigration history, and historical studies on race and racism, this book excavates New York City's colonial past. Specifically, this study offers a historical analysis of the project of colony building on Manhattan Island from 1624 to 1783 and, in doing so, maps points of articulation between the ideal and material relations of colonial domination that together overdetermined racial formation in the port town erected at the island's southernmost extreme. For the purposes of this study, the project of colony building designates the early modern phase of colonial expansionism in which European colonizers transported enslaved Africans and European immigrants to overseas territories, where the transplanted populations gradually displaced the native populations and built permanent settler colonies that served European maritime nations as launch sites for military operations, suppliers of raw materials, markets for European exports, and asylums for Europe's surplus population.[3] In this study, racial formation (or racialization) not only refers to the discursive construction of race, but also to the identificatory process by which an individual (1) assumes (or occupies) a racial subject-position in relation to other racialized subjects and in articulation with other constituents of social subjectivity—for example, language, religion, birthplace, sexuality, gender, and class—(2) contests the hierarchical ranking of humankind into inferior and superior races in the context of a racist culture, calls into question the value ascribed to race, and even redefines the prevailing conception of race.[4]

By the early sixteenth century, the French word *race* had been adopted by or had a cognate in each of the other major European languages.[5] At that time Western European elites regarded Christianity as the kernel of civilization and assimilated the emergent conception of race to their ideal of civilization. In this respect they forged race into a culturalist concept that asserted the hierarchical ranking of civilizations and the superiority of Western European culture, especially its Christian religion. Although Christendom promoted the notion of a single creation and the unity of humankind, early modern European elites grouped and then ranked people on the basis of their closeness to and remoteness from an idealized Christian norm: Christians were assigned to the rank of the superior civilized race while non-Christians (so-called heathens) were relegated to the rank of inferior uncivilized races.[6] The latter groups included precisely those peoples whom, according to biblical authority as they saw it, Christians could legitimately dispossess of their lands and enslave. However, the binarism Christian/heathen proved to be an unreliable schema for imposing order on the wide range of human diversity that Europeans encountered during the early modern era of territorial conquest and colonial expansionism. Over time, the movement of populations to foreign lands, sustained contact between previously isolated peoples, the permeability of cultural boundaries, and the malleability of culture itself rendered culturalist conceptions of race, along with the categories of Christian and heathen, unstable and open to amendment. Beset with the contingencies of uncertainty and change, the project of colony building required ever more fixed identificatory boundaries, including increasingly rigid constructions of race.

The era of European colonial expansion demarcates a historic juncture in the process of racial formation—namely, the commencement of a shift in the conception of race from an ascribed identity defined by the nonbiological criteria of religion and other alterable cultural traits to one defined by the biological criteria of seemingly immutable heritable traits.[7] Although the biological conception of race did not congeal into a coherent construct until the late nineteenth century, the inauguration of this conceptual shift is evident in the early modern discourse of natural history, wherein "race" became a term denoting a major division of the human species whose members share certain stable, if not unchanging, heritable traits that they do not share with members of the other major divisions of the human species. For naturalists of the early modern era, taxonomies of race, along with other categories of classification, rendered the mounting and polysemous corpus of information on the plant and animal kingdoms less perplexing. "In the midst of extreme confusion," the Swedish naturalist Carolus Linnaeus (1707–78) asserted, "there is revealed the sovereign order of nature."[8] Linnaeus is best known as the inventor of the binomial system of nomenclature by which categories of plants and animals are given a unique name, consisting of a generic and a specific component. While the Swedish naturalist did not use the term *race* in his writings, he did subdivide the human species into seven varieties,[9] which the German naturalist Johann Friedrich Blumenbach (1752–1840) and the German philosopher Immanuel Kant (1724–1804) would use as a template for subdivisions of humankind called "races." Whereas Linnaeus used the criteria "culture" and "situation" for establishing distinct divisions of the human species, Blumenbach and Kant used more stable traits of human physiognomy, along with changeable cultural traits and environmental factors, as the criteria for dividing humankind into separate categories. In this way, Blumenbach and Kant contributed to the construction of ever more fixed categories of race, whose discursive construction discloses the desire to establish a ruling natural order for humankind firmly grounded in the surface, bodily appearance of human physiognomy and later, by the late nineteenth century, in the interior, biological mechanisms of the human organism.

Of paramount importance to the discursive construction of increasingly rigid taxonomies of race is the binary logic of natural history's procedure of classification. According to the protocol of natural history, the naturalist discerns the governing natural order of things by filtering out the confusing complexity of nature and selecting a few privileged traits of the objects under observation as the basis of comparisons that yield distinct categories of beings. Focusing on a narrow range of preselected traits and, within that delimited scope of investigation, the similarities that appear among individual specimens, the naturalist establishes a principle of inclusion and exclusion for constructing a category of classification that ultimately coheres as a group of individuals that share common traits that they do not share with others. A binary logic of identity and difference thus structures this procedure of classification. Importantly, the protocol of natural history abstracts things (i.e. plants and animals) from the semantic thicket of sedimented meanings that supposedly veils their essential, eternal being. The naturalist is thereby liberated from the encumbrance of the baffling multiplicity of sensory data—for example, the infinite array of colors, smells, tastes, and textures that emanates from nature—and, finally, is empowered to observe only the surface, contour, line, and angle of things that leave a pure impression on the mind and reveal intrinsic, timeless truths to human understanding. Human physiognomy—for example, facial angle, the contour of the nose, the shape of the lips, and other surface features of the human body—supplied the naturalist with such relatively stable, visual data for grouping humankind into distinct racial categories. Hence, the discourse of natural history increasingly shunned the manifold, constantly changing phenomena of culture and habitat, preferring instead to focus on the seemingly purer, less complex and changeable, bodily surface of people to establish the categories called races.[10] More generally, the discourse of natural history applied this procedure of classification to all living beings that came within its scope and constructed, as the historian Michel Foucault has put it, "a flat world of animals and plants, engraved in black and white."[11] Writing about natural history's "observing gaze," Foucault notes: "Natural history did not become possible because men looked harder and more closely. One might say, strictly speaking, that the Classical age used its ingenuity, if not to see as little as possible, at least to restrict deliberately the area of its experience. . . . To observe, then, is to be content with seeing—with seeing a few things systematically. . . . With seeing what, in the rather confused wealth of representation, can be analyzed, recognized by all, and thus given a name that everyone will be able to understand."[12] In this way Foucault aptly summarizes the episteme of natural history and its goal of reducing complexity to simple, manageable taxonomies. Remarking on the merit of his racial classification schema, Blumenbach stated that "it will be found serviceable to the memory to have constituted certain classes into which the men of our planet may be divided."[13] Likewise, Kant found the grouping of humankind into distinct categories called "races" useful as an aid to "memorization," "understanding," "bringing creatures under headings," and "bringing them under laws."[14] Whereas earlier naturalists obtained information about human variation from classical texts, Kant, Blumenbach, and other naturalists of their generation increasingly relied on contemporary European travel and exploration literature for their primary source of data on human diversity. Hence, the history of the construction of racial taxonomies in the early modern discourse of natural history was an elaboration of the knowledge-producing activity of European expansion. As Europeans from various maritime nations left the shores of their homelands and colonized overseas territories, they required a system of representation—a schema of naming, classifying, cataloguing, and enumerating—that would render newly encountered varieties of humankind intelligible to European colonizers and thus subject to colonial domination. Forged under the colonialist imperative to systematize and rule, *race* became a name invested with a seemingly stable, universally recognizable meaning, an expression of the "sovereign order of nature."

Although shifting historical and political contexts have altered the meaning and valence imputed to the discursive category "race"[15] and the present-day science of biogenetics has demonstrated that, as an objective category, "race" has no biological validity,[16] the concept "race" remains a powerful commonsensical way of giving meaning to, naturalizing, and legitimating ways of acting in the world.[17] Whether as an abstract concept of scientific discourse or as an element of vernacular, "race" has seldom, if ever, been deployed apart from the diffusion of power and the individual's subjection to the disciplinary mechanisms that

regulate everyday life. This book demonstrates that racialized subjects are formations that arise out of historically specific projects and strategic relations of
power—in this case study, the early modern project of colony building on Manhattan Island and its relations of colonial domination.[18]

During the early modern era of European expansion and the emergence of the capitalist world system, Manhattan Island became a crossroads for
the articulation of the ideal and material relations of colonial domination that
produced relationally constituted and differentially valued racialized subjects—
for example, civilized and savage, colonizer and colonized, enslaver and enslaved, black and white. Charged with the task of implementing Holland's plan
of colonial expansion in the Western Hemisphere, the quasi-military trading
monopoly known as the Dutch West India Company built the first colonial outpost on Manhattan Island. For the jacket and frontispiece of this book, I have
chosen a black-and-white engraving, circa 1643, in which two allegorical figures
personify the ideal relation between Holland and its colonies in the Western
Hemisphere—or, as the caption announces, *Cum Privilegio Ordinum Hollandie
et West-Indiæ*. In the foreground of that engraving, a domineering burgher
clutches a parcel of fur pelts in one hand and, with the other empty, out-
stretched hand, commands a demure maiden to surrender a basket of colonial
produce. Though the maiden peers at the burgher with a reluctant gaze, she
seems, nonetheless, willing to obey his directive; both the angle of her posture
and the flow of her skirt indicate she is in the midst of performing a pirouette of
compliance. Moreover, the packed cargo of colonial produce at the burgher's
feet suggests that this is not the first time the maiden has relinquished her
bounty to him. In any case, this scene aptly allegorizes the colonialist project of
a European power in the act of subjugating a foreign land. Here, the ideal relation between nation and colony finds its paradigm in the gendered relation of
male domination and female submission. Importantly, the engraving's oblique
reference to Adam and Eve in the prelapsarian state of nature slyly naturalizes
that asymmetrical relation of power and thereby places the colonialist project
outside the space of history and its material relations of domination.

Whereas the engraving's foregrounded allegorical scene offers an idealized vision of the relation between nation and colony, the figures and scenery in its
background provide a literal depiction of the material exploitation of enslaved
black laborers, which enabled the extraction of wealth from overseas colonies
and made Holland, leading carrier of colonial produce in world trade during the
seventeenth century,[19] the envy of other European maritime powers. In the
background of the engraving, directly behind the allegorical figures of the well-
clad burgher and maiden, half-naked black laborers haul raw produce across a
crude landscape. An *object in the midst of other objects*[20] in the engraving's background, the partially exposed, muscular body of the black laborer bears the burden of extracting material wealth from a miserly colonial frontier. Farther in the
background Dutch sailing vessels, laden with the fruits of exploited black labor,

engage in the transatlantic carrying trade. Finally, on the horizon, just before the engraving's vanishing point, appears New Amsterdam, a booming colonial seaport at the tip of Manhattan Island. At this point the engraving's depiction of New Amsterdam reverts to fantasy and becomes a phantasmatic projection of Holland's colonialist aspiration to build on the North American frontier a permanent settler colony that obediently serves the emerging nation-state's imperial interests. However, in 1643, New Amsterdam was hardly the bustling seaport depicted in the engraving. Having, in reality, not yet recovered from a destructive Indian war, New Amsterdam was on the brink of collapse and faced an uncertain future. The absence of Native Americans in the engraving is both a symptom of the colonialist disavowal of the damages that the frontier outpost had sustained from desperate Indian reprisals and a reflection of the near extermination of the island's native population by 1643.

Within scarcely more than two decades, Holland's rival, England, would conquer New Amsterdam and rename that colonial outpost in honor of the Duke of York, later King James II. Following the Conquest of 1664, the English colonizers, like the supplanted Dutch colonizers, transported European settlers and enslaved Africans to Manhattan Island and enlisted them in the project of colony building. On that island-peninsula, the settler population established numerical, cultural, and institutional dominance over the sparse native population and the increasingly numerous enslaved African population. Over time, the English colonizers, along with the transplanted settlers and slaves, transformed the fledgling colonial outpost named New York City into a flourishing entrepôt or transshipment site for regional and international commerce, the seat of the colonial government, a garrison town, and the locus of cultural institutions.[21] The personnel of colony building also gradually developed the adjacent countryside into a prosperous hinterland of commercial farming that raised livestock and produced mixed crops of grain, fruit, and other foodstuffs.

While the plans of early modern colony builders anticipate the role Manhattan Island would play as a staging ground for merchant capitalism in the Western Hemisphere and as a strategic military stronghold for the European powers that claimed that corner of the globe, they offer few hints that the project of colony building, together with the relations of colonial domination that enabled the destruction of the island's indigenous population and the exploitation of enslaved African laborers, was laying the foundation for a city that during the late modern era would become a citadel of global capitalism. Buried beneath the subterranean basements of the formidable skyscrapers that grace present-day lower Manhattan's skyline, nearly all material manifestations of that formative stage in New York City's history were consigned to oblivion until one day in June 1991, when an archeological team, working in the midst of the construction of the Federal office building at 290 Broadway, unearthed an assemblage of slave burials dating back to colonial times. Except for a handful of highly specialized scholars, the public was amazed to discover that in the shadow of the twin towers of New York City's World Trade Center the skeletal remains of an estimated 20,000 enslaved laborers were buried under nearly 25 feet of landfill, stretching across roughly six acres of prime Manhattan real estate.

Greeted with amazement, as an unrecognizable image of New York City's past, the discovery of the colonial slave burial ground in lower Manhattan calls into question the pervasive myth of American exceptionalism—namely, the liberal nationalist narrative that ascribes the unique attributes of the U.S. national character to the averred democratic culture and widespread material prosperity of the settler colonies that eventually comprised the northeastern United States.[22] Even though scholars from a broad range of academic disciplines have contested this myth,[23] the academic field of early American history has, for the most part, persistently represented its object of study in ways that perpetuate the ideal of an exceptional American cultural identity and elide hemispheric and global perspectives on the centrality of racial domination and other legacies of colonialism to the formation of U.S. national culture. The historian Jack P. Greene writes, "No less than other arbiters of American culture, American historians seem to have found it difficult to come to terms with its slave origins. As long as they could continue to believe that New England, the region of colonial British America in which black slavery was least well entrenched, was indeed the most direct and important source of later American sociocultural patterns, historians could continue to perpetuate the comforting illusion that slavery, that blatant anomaly in republican and egalitarian America, had never been central to American culture but had always been only a marginal institution confined to the cultural peripheries of the colonial British American world."[24] In his perspicacious rebuttal to the marginalization of racial slavery and the colonial South in some of the most influential historiography on British North America, Greene demonstrates that prior to 1800 the southern colonies and the institution of racial slavery epitomized U.S. social and cultural development, while colonial New England and the marginality of racial slavery in that region deviated from the mainstream. According to Greene, New England did not remain an aberrant cultural zone within British North America. Rather, his developmental model posits the "emergence of a common cultural core as a result of a steady process of social amalgamation" that culminated in an "astonishing similarity" between the British North American colonies. This shared culture, Greene argues, consisted of the modern ideal of possessive individualism and formed the marrow of the U.S. national character.[25]

Although the northern and southern colonies in British North America underwent a common developmental process of modernization, the northeastern seaboard, especially New York City, is the privileged signifier of modernity, representing, within the U.S. national imaginary, the twin triumphs of capitalism and freedom.[26] A celebrated fixture of present-day New York City's iconography perpetuates this image: With gigantic torch in hand, the Statue of Liberty watches over the citadel of global capitalism and illumines the progress of freedom across the nation and the world. Substituting the euphemism "early American history" for the term *colonialism*, liberal nationalist historiography reinforces this idealized representation of U.S. sociocultural development and constructs a useable past largely disarticulated from the history of colonialism and the relations of domination that subtended the founding of the United States. Although scholars working in the academic fields of colonial and post-colonial studies have focused attention on the structures of inequality that traverse and transcend national borders,[27] the evolution of democracy within the geopolitical boundaries of the United States, rather than colonialism and slavery in hemispheric and global perspectives, remains the defining telos of the regnant historiography on the antecedents of U.S. society and culture. The myth of American exceptionalism has proved to be an effective strategy of narration for dissociating national history from the colonial past. Yet, as Etienne Balibar points out, "In a sense, every modern nation is a product of colonization: it has always been to some degree colonized or colonizing, and sometimes both at the same time."[28] Inhabited by the descendants of both the colonizers and the colonized, the United States is inextricably linked to the history of colonialism. While the liberal nationalist historiographical tradition largely disavows the integrality of colonialism, the displacement of Native American populations, and the institution of black slavery to the creation of the U.S. national character, the history of New York City during the early modern era confirms their formative role in the social and cultural development of the northeastern United States and hence in the evolution of the United States as a modern nation-state.

Nearly four centuries ago, European colony builders dislodged Manhattan Island's indigenous population and assembled a multicultural, polyglot immigrant population of settlers and slaves at the island's tip. On that site freedom and material prosperity coexisted with black slavery and other colonial relations of domination. As the enslaved population grew and fear of slave insurrection mounted, the slaves were subjected to increasingly coercive measures of racial subordination, and by 1712 social equilibrium in New York City and the adjacent hinterland was predicated on the suppression of the entire black population, enslaved and free. In colonial New York City, black slavery and antiblack racism served the political interests of the ruling elite by fostering a bond of racial solidarity between the colonial rulers and the majority settler population—the large and small merchants, shopkeepers, and artisans of diverse birthplaces, languages, and religious confessions—and by minimizing the antagonisms that, for example, divided rich from poor, English from Dutch, and Anglicans from Calvinists and other dissenting congregations. Although the solidarities of racial whiteness proved to be an imperfect solvent for the antagonisms that divided the city's diverse and factious settler population, the biracial division of society offered the ruling elite a seemingly less volatile field of conflict than a social terrain fractured along the fault lines of class, religious, and linguistic differences. "Race" thus assumed a crucial political dimension in colonial New York City, where a large free settler population, if not given sufficient incentive to accept the rulership of the governing elite, might one day rise in insurrection.

In the early modern colonial port town on Manhattan Island, as in the ancient Greco-Roman city-states,[29] the enslavement of alien others proved to be politically serviceable to the ruling elite. In exchange for the settler population's loyalty to the colonial government, New York City's ruling elite granted Protestant settlers of European descent liberties and privileges that exempted them from enslavement. English rights became the exclusive property of the white Anglo-

Saxon Protestants, who were a majority of the settler population, while the social death of perpetual bondage became the sole inheritance of most black Africans and their descendants. Even impoverished white indentured servants held a firm claim to the rights of British subjecthood, whereas free blacks, even those who owned land, were so severely circumscribed that they were prevented from enjoying the basic privileges of freedom. For colonial New York City's ruling elite, antiblack racism became a vital disciplinary mechanism, a means of governing the whites as well as the blacks. And, as was the case for the Athenian demos and the Roman citizens, the institution of slavery nourished the settlers' esteem for freedom. Except for the poorest immigrants among them, the settlers, in town and in the surrounding countryside, not only exercised the rights of British subjects but also acquired land, established independent households, and became prosperous merchants, shopkeepers, artisans, or farmers who held black Africans in lifelong, heritable bondage. In this way the complementarity of freedom and slavery, which first arose in ancient Western civilization, gained renewed vigor.

Moreover, in colonial New York City and the farming districts within the city's orbit, the importation and exploitation of slave labor became an expedient solution to the shortage of indentured servants and free laborers that resulted from unmanageable contingencies, such as the sudden curtailment of immigration flows from Europe during outbreaks of international war between rival European powers.[30] In contrast to the staple-crop colonies, slave labor never became indispensable to that northern port town's maritime commerce and the adjacent hinterland's economy of mixed agricultural production. Nevertheless, "slaveholders in such societies," the historian Ira Berlin has pointed out, "could act with extraordinary brutality precisely because their slaves were extraneous to their main business. They could limit their slaves' access to freedom expressly because they desired to set themselves apart from their slaves."[31] In colonial New York City, the ruling elite constructed a biracial social order in which the legal institution of racial slavery and the disciplinary mechanism of antiblack racism separated, as far as possible, the black population from the white population. A shared interest in the violent subjugation of blacks, enslaved and free, became the glue that cemented a politically efficacious though precarious solidarity between the ruling elite and the city's diverse and factious settler population. In this respect, colonial New York City resembled colonial Virginia, where black slavery and antiblack racism became a political solution to the threat that the intermediate stratum of restive settlers posed to that southern colony's ruling elite.[32] The historian Edmund S. Morgan writes, "Virginia's small farmers could perceive a common identity with the large because . . . neither was a slave. And both were equal in not being slaves."[33] To be sure, other commonalities—for example, a shared material culture based on the cultivation of the staple crop tobacco—also served to foster a solidarity of interest among planters in colonial Virginia.[34] Nonetheless, it was the institution of black slavery and antiblack racism that most effectively dampened the social antagonisms dividing colonial Virginia's ruling elite from its numerous free settler population. Unlike the English gentry, the large planters of tidewater Virginia, Morgan notes, no longer needed to base their prosperity primarily on the exploitation of poor Englishmen, since they derived their wealth less from collecting rents from tenants, or taxes from freemen, than from exploiting enslaved black laborers.[35] In a similar way, colonial New York City's governing elite minimized cultural differences and subordinated social antagonisms within the city's settler community by enslaving black Africans and their offspring while reserving the status and privileges of freedom for the white Anglo-Saxon Protestant settlers and their descendants. Although rarely acknowledged in the historiography on British North America, black slavery and antiblack racism were perhaps nowhere more serviceable to the ruling elite than in colonial New York City. In that northern seaport, they not only served as instruments for regulating the black population but also offered the ruling elite a means of rendering more manageable—that is, less complex—the problem of governing the diverse and factious majority settler population. Thus in colonial New York City, racial formation, black slavery, and antiblack racism had an enormous impact on the individual settler's experience and the broader settler community.

While an ample number of community studies examine the communal life of the northern settlers[36] and several more recent studies investigate the northern slave experience during colonial times,[37] the available historiography on the colonial North, taken as a whole, does not fully appreciate the momentous effects colonial relations of racial domination had on both settlers and slaves.[38] Instead, much of the scholarship on the colonial North accepts two largely untenable suppositions: First, black slavery in the northern colonies was a benign institution; second, black slavery was marginal to the northern settler experience. A few basic considerations relating to colonial New York City cast doubt on these assumptions. To begin with, the laws of slavery and the municipal ordinances for the regulation of the city's black urban population were as restrictive as the black codes in the colonial South and, for that matter, any slave society.[39] Moreover, the custom of granting informal privileges to slaves was in no way unique to colonial New York City and other northern settler colonies. Everywhere in the Americas, slaveowners endeavored to cloak, whenever possible, the fundamental relation of domination inherent to chattel slavery through acts of benevolence that served to counteract slave discontent.[40] Equally important, the labor conditions for slaves in colonial New York City were scarcely less harsh than the work settings for the enslaved labor force on the staple-crop plantations in the colonial South. At the port of New York, slaves performed backbreaking labor in an intemperate climate of extreme cold and heat. Though the urban setting afforded the city's enslaved workforce with a degree of mobility unavailable to rural slaves in the southern colonies,[41] the northern urban slaves of colonial New York City generally lived in their masters' houses and in this respect led more confined, closely monitored lives than their counterparts in the rural South, who more often lived in separate slave quarters. By 1703, approximately 41 percent of New York City householders owned at least one slave, whereas 6.6 percent of householders in colonial Philadelphia and only 2 percent in colonial Boston kept one or more slaves.[42] Overlooking this significant difference between these port towns, historical studies on slavery in British North America tend to lump the northern seaports together and to draw an overly simplistic contrast between the colonial North and the colonial South. Yet during the colonial era, slaveholdings in Philadelphia and Boston closely resembled the pattern of slave ownership in the market towns of the Chesapeake region— for example, Port Tobacco and Benedict in Maryland, where, as Jean Butenhoff Lee has shown, a small proportion of townspeople owned slaves, usually in small lots.[43] Furthermore, the wide dispersal of slaves among the townspeople in colonial New York City set that port town apart from other towns in both the northern and southern colonies of British North America, except Charleston, South Carolina, which resembled New York City with regard to the broad distribution of slaves among the townspeople.[44] Last, the pattern of widespread slave ownership among colonial New York City's settler population had a direct and immediate impact on the settler's individual and collective experiences there. In that densely populated northern port town, the lives of the settlers and the slaves were tightly intertwined, so much so that it is impossible to comprehend the life-world of one group in isolation from the other. The historian Joyce Goodfriend notes that "social life and cultural forms reflected African as well as European influences." Goodfriend adds, "No one has yet examined the city's sizable black community in counterpoint to the European subcommunities that comprised the city's white society. Only by doing so can the nature of colonial New York City's pluralism be appreciated."[45]

Of course, an appreciation of the sociocultural complexities that characterized colonial New York City requires more than merely enlarging the frame of reference to include multiple experiences and simply studying interactions between the settlers and the slaves. It also crucially involves interrogating the history of racial formation in that northern port town and its connection to colonial relations of domination. Yet the available historiography on the colonial North rarely considers the historic processes that installed the inhabitants of the northern colonies in racial subject-positions. Even studies that provide an analysis of the symbiosis between black slavery and freedom in British North America tend to reinscribe rather than problematize binary racial categories. For example, the eminent historian Edmund S. Morgan writes: "In Virginia neither badges nor philosophers were needed. It was not necessary to pretend or to prove that the enslaved were a different race, because they were. Anyone could tell black from white, even if black was actually brown and red."[46] This study interrogates the commonsensical assumptions that made such confidence possible. Hence, it departs from much of the historiography on British North America not only by calling into question the apartheid narrative of U.S. sociocultural development, which separates the history of the white settlers from the history of the enslaved blacks, but also by providing a historical account of the identificatory process of racialization, which, during the early modern era, emerged out of the project of colony building and its ideal and material relations of domination.

Divided into two chapters, part I of this study investigates the project of colony building on Manhattan Island. According to mercantilist theory of the early modern era, overseas colonies were supposed to strengthen the colonizing nation by diminishing its costly economic reliance on other nations and thus enabling the accumulation of national wealth, which could be counted on to finance the buildup of large, well-armed military forces in an epoch of increasingly frequent domestic conflict and international war. These and other motives propelled European maritime nations to explore foreign lands and build overseas colonies.[47] It was in the context of an escalating international rivalry that England and Holland founded overseas colonies in North America. The colonization of Manhattan Island was, then, primarily a power maneuver in the scramble for empire between the two European rivals.[48] Asserting the doctrine of right to possession by exploration, these maritime nations claimed title to overlapping North American territories that encompassed Manhattan Island: England claimed all the land in North America between 34° and 48° north latitude by virtue of Henry Hudson's English-sponsored explorations in 1607 and 1608, and Holland claimed the entire region north of the Chesapeake Bay between 40° and 44° north latitude in view of Hudson's Dutch-sponsored exploration in 1610. These claims were tenuous at best. Any colonizing nation hoping to secure its title to such a massive territory would not only have to repel encroaching European rivals but also conquer and permanently occupy a remote frontier already inhabited by an indigenous population whose villages were dispersed across a rugged terrain.

Part I of this study shows that the colonization of that North American territory involved the relocation of populations from one place to another and from one task to another. This population movement coincided with the extraction of diverse peoples from the traditional relations of feudal society and their installation in the nascent social relations of capitalist production, a repositioning that announced the advent of modernity, the ascendancy of the bourgeoisie, and the early modern formation of race. Performing the role of key articulators in the emerging capitalist world economy, merchants and ship captains orchestrated the transportation of commodities and laborers from transshipment centers along the Atlantic littoral to Manhattan Island.[49] Over time, the transplanted personnel of colony building—settlers, servants, and slaves—displaced the island's native population, transformed the colonial frontier outpost at the island's tip into a thriving entrepôt, and converted the largely fallow hinterland into a prosperous region of commercial agricultural production. In addition to these features of colonization, part I of this study highlights several variables that affected the project of colony building on Manhattan Island: Amerindian-European relations during the early phase of colonization, the availability of preferred workers from Holland and the British Isles, the impact of international war on the flow of laborers across the Atlantic Ocean, the advantages and

disadvantages of free versus slave labor, and colonial policies for the encouragement of European immigration and the slave trade.

Chapter 1 tracks the Dutch colonization project on Manhattan Island from
1624 to 1664 and shows that following the Dutch invasion Manhattan Island became a dynamic zone of cross-cultural contact and polyvalent relations of
power between WIC officials, natives, settlers, and slaves. Chapter 2 tracks the
project of colony building on Manhattan Island following the English takeover
of the North American territory previously called New Netherland and renamed New York.[50] The chapter shows that the labor imperatives of colony
building produced a pattern of widespread slave ownership. Moreover, the colonization project on Manhattan Island, in town and in the surrounding countryside, resulted in a mixed system of labor that combined slavery, indentured
servitude, and wage labor and brought a diverse population from various birthplaces, religions, and languages to the island-peninsula. Chapters 1 and 2 thus reveal that colonial New York City's pluralism—its demographic and sociocultural diversity—was a direct product of the project of colony building.

Just as the colonizing nations' initial claim to the land was tenuous, so too was
the colonial rulers' claim to the loyalty and obedience of the newly transplanted
and heterogeneous peoples who wrested the land from the native inhabitants.
Part II of this study is divided into three chapters that highlight the problem of
governance in colonial New York City; the efforts of the English rulers to cultivate a shared sense of belonging to the English nation among the city's mostly
foreign-born settler population; the articulation of whiteness, Anglo-Saxon ancestry, and adherence to the doctrines of Protestantism in the construction of
Englishness; and the role that antiblack racism played in uniting the English
rulers and the settlers, who increasingly perceived the city's black population as
an alien and dangerous race. In this way, part II provides a historical account of
the political stakes involved in the racialization of the northern port town's constituent peoples, showing that the transplantation of uprooted peoples in a
strange land and the task of colony building on Manhattan Island required the
imposition of disciplinary mechanisms for the effective governance of a majority settler population that was largely disconnected from the sources of authority in England.

Chapter 3 points out that the English Crown relied on surrogates to project its
sovereignty to the English overseas colonies. Colonial administrators, clergymen, missionaries, and schoolmasters undertook the assignment of transplanting English institutions of governance and English-derived cultural institutions
and systems of representation in the colonial frontier. Yet neither the English
colonial administration nor the Anglican missionary organizations proved to be
capable of securely extending the reach of the English territorial monarchy and
its legitimating religious and cultural institutions to the growing multitude of
foreigners dispersed throughout the first British Empire. This was especially
true for colonial New York City, where competing loyalties divided the heterogeneous, mostly foreign-born settler population. Chapter 4 demonstrates that
the disciplinary mechanism of antiblack racism became a key instrument of
governance in colonial New York City. Drawn from various localities on the

West African coast, the Congo-Angola region of Africa, Madagascar, and the Caribbean basin, the city's black population was a diverse yet markedly alien presence in the midst of the northern settler colony and thus became the constitutive outside border that delimited the city's majority settler population. Chapter 4 shows that New York City's Slave Revolt of 1712 was the act of unacculturated native Africans and other slaves who, from their own distinctive worldviews, regarded colonial New York's institution of slavery as an unjust social relation. In colonial New York City, the moral economy of slaveowner paternalism failed to secure absolute obedience from the slaves. Although the well-armed settler majority quickly suppressed the slave uprising, the environment of the colonial port town—for example, the city's docks, markets, and taverns—afforded restive slaves with daily opportunities to spread the contagion of rebellion. In response to the Slave Revolt of 1712, the ruling elite and the broader settler population united to affirm their shared interest in the violent subjugation of the city's black population, enslaved and free. With the enactment of the Black Code of 1712, enslaved blacks were forced to submit to an institution of bondage as harsh as any slave regime in the English overseas colonies, and free blacks were denied fundamental English liberties, such as the right to bequeath land to their heirs. Drawn from various linguistic, religious, and clan groups in the Atlantic world, colonial New York City's black population now shared a common experience of subjection to colonial relations of racial domination in the guise of antiblack racism. Correspondingly, antiblack racism temporarily united white settlers of every rank, who now regarded the alien black presence in their midst as a dangerous domestic enemy against which the settler colony must be defended. Finally, chapter 4 shows that the specter of interracial sexual desire, especially in households where slaveowners and their families lived under the same roof with black Africans, imperiled the ideal of a racially pure settler community. Within the domain of sociosexual relations of power, an internalized taboo against miscegenation, rather than an antimiscegenation law, functioned as a prophylaxis against racial contamination. In this respect, colonial New York City began to resemble a normative society, in which self-disciplined individuals govern themselves without overt intervention on the part of the state. Whereas the English rulers used the threat of violence to regulate the city's black population, nonviolent mechanisms of hegemonic domination governed the city's settler population of propertied white Anglo-Saxon Protestants. Chapter 5 reveals that, by the 1740s, interracial socializing among colonial New York City's subaltern population of enslaved blacks, propertyless white servants, and transients troubled the ruling elite and its binary racial division of society. With the additional threat of an impending Spanish invasion, the aggravation of an unsolved crime wave, and the outbreak of a mysterious rash of fires during the winter of 1741–42, fear of the city's dangerous classes crystallized in the discovery of the "plot of 1741–42," an alleged conspiracy among enslaved blacks and several white outsiders accused of plotting together in secret to overthrow English rule, murder the city's white male settler population, enslave white females in harems, and establish a "Negro regime" under the protection of Catholic Spain. By discovering this conspiracy, the English colonial rulers foreclosed, for a brief time, the challenge that a hostile political faction posed to its government. However, antiblack racism, even when supplemented by the fear of an interracial conspiracy from below, could not permanently eradicate the antagonisms that divided the colonial elite and the broader settler population. Thus chapters 3, 4, and 5 disclose the political stakes involved in the binary formation of race in colonial New York City and the complex ways in which racial formation impacted both the settlers and the slaves as they assumed racial subject-positions.

Part III of this study consists of two chapters that spotlight subaltern insurgency and the collapse of colonial governance. Importantly, part III credits the lower stratum of colonial New York City's social hierarchy—propertyless slaves, servants, and outsiders—with engaging in sustained resistance to colonial relations of domination, but shows that during colonial times subaltern insurgency in New York City generally took the guise of individual acts of insubordination, rarely involved collective action, and never coalesced into a coherent social movement. With its victory over the British military forces, the colony-wide white settler revolt known as the American War for Independence brought about the demise of English colonial rule in New York State and the other revolutionary North American republics. Undertaken to protect the white settlers' liberty, which essentially consisted of the capacity to exercise rights, including the right to property in black slaves, the white settler revolt opened a split between the American patriots and the English colonial rulers through which tens of thousands of enslaved blacks escaped from bondage. This unpredictable reality of the Anglo-American War lent new gravity to the partial, finite, and fluid emancipatory practices of black subaltern insurgency, which were beginning to dilate the exclusionary boundaries that limited "the happiness of liberty" to propertied white males.

Chapter 6 investigates examples of insubordination, ranging from the unruly behavior of the city's laboring class in the streets, marketplaces, dock areas, and taverns to the remarkable bids for freedom on the part of runaway servants and slaves. Chapter 6 points out that the largely unregulated population flows moving in and out of the port of New York compounded the problem of policing the city's servile population. Strangers entered the colonial port town, often without notifying the authorities of their arrival, while runaway servants and slaves left the seaport, largely undetected by official surveillance. Importantly, newspaper advertisements for fugitive servants and slaves encouraged the captains of sailing vessels embarking from the port of New York to keep on the lookout for runaways. These ads usually provided a detailed description of the peculiar bodily marks and other visible indexes to the servile condition of each fugitive. By using this tactic of individualizing description, the newspaper ads for runaways not only enlisted mariners in the task of surveilling the city's servile population. These ads also aspired to produce an all-pervasive, captivating vigilance on the part of the broader settler population by educating the gaze of ordinary settlers and training it away from the reductive black-and-white regime of visuality that allowed far too many servants and slaves to escape. In this regard, eighteenth-century print culture offered masters and colonial officials a means of enlisting the public in the task of apprehending fugitives. An unintended consequence of the production of a vigilant public was the upward rotation of the settlers' vigilance toward the Crown-appointed authorities who, following the French and Indian War (1756–63), implemented unpopular colonial policies that in the eyes of many settlers amounted to a dangerous conspiracy to deprive them of liberty. During the seventh and eighth decades of the eighteenth century, a broad segment of the settler population became ever more discontented with English colonial rule. By 1775, disaffected settlers of every rank perceived a conspiracy from above and commenced an armed rebellion against English colonial rule, which ended with the American patriots' victory over the British military forces sent to subdue them and the founding of independent republics in New York and other former British North American colonies. Facing the collapse of colonial governance and the impending loss of England's most valuable colonial possessions in North America, British military commanders enlisted the black population in the British war effort and granted enslaved blacks freedom as a reward for their loyal service to the British cause. This British war policy marked the abandonment of the long-standing disciplinary mechanism of governing the majority settler population by cultivating a shared interest between the rulers and the ruled in the subjugation of the black population. Chapter 7 shows that the final split between the English colonial rulers and the settlers in British North America provided passports to freedom for runaway slaves, who during the white American War for Independence deserted their patriot masters, joined the British side in exchange for freedom, and eventually removed to the British military headquarters at New York City. Whereas for nearly a century the English colonial rulers had promoted the institution of black slavery and the disciplinary mechanism of antiblack racism as a means of securing settler consent to their government, during the white settler revolt against English colonial rule, British military commanders endeavored to subdue that rebellion by threatening to emancipate as many of the patriots' slaves as were capable of escaping to the British side. During the white American War for Independence, New York City became an asylum for thousands of runaway slaves from throughout British America. Responding to the several British wartime proclamations addressed to the enslaved population, fugitive slaves relocated to British-occupied New York City, where they labored in a variety of tasks associated with the British war effort, earned wages, formed new family units, reconstituted old ones, and received certificates of freedom from British military officers. At the conclusion of the war, 3,000 recently emancipated blacks embarked from the port of New York with the evacuating British military forces on sailing vessels headed for maritime Canada. The exodus of these ex-slaves from the shores of Manhattan Island marked a rarely noted denouement to the breakdown of colonial governance in New York City.

Many of the free black exodustors left behind family and friends who remained in bondage in the infant republics that initially comprised the United States. The epilogue of this study comments on the legacy of colonialism and its relations of racial domination—namely, black slavery and antiblack racism—that constituted a foundation of U.S. national culture and would become the object of protracted contestation between the racialized subjects who inhabited the nation. Importantly, the entailments of the nation's history of colonialism were not confined to the southern states but were also sedimented features of society and culture in the northern states. The legendary Mason-Dixon line, which so neatly divides north from south, freedom from slavery, modernity from feudalism, and the history of nation from the history of colonialism, is therefore more a phantasm of the U.S. political imaginary, a symptom of the disavowal of the deeply engraved social and racial divisions that traverse and transcend the geopolitical borders of nation, than a real geographical boundary. Yet, as Edward Said has pointed out, "No one can escape dealing with, if not the East/West division, then the North/South one, the have/have-not one, the imperialist/anti-imperialist one, the white/colored one. We cannot get around them all by pretending they do not exist; on the contrary, contemporary orientalism teaches us a great deal about the intellectual dishonesty of dissembling on that score, the result of which is to intensify the divisions and make them both vicious and permanent."[51] This book offers a historical analysis of the formation of the binary racial division that arose out of the project of colony building on Manhattan Island during the early modern era and took shape in articulation with divisions of class, religion, birthplace, gender, sexuality, and language. Last, the title of this book, *Black and White Manhattan*, announces its overarching goal—namely, to place the nostalgia for a simplified, clearly delimited past under erasure by mapping the binary logic that disavows the irreducible complexities of history and confines the past to the somnolent realm of timeless myth located outside the temporality of a living and open history. This book rummages through the pile of debris left behind by the violent storm of progress that elevated New York City to the status of global city. Souvenirs from that debris disclose the city's foundational history of colonialism, black slavery, and antiblack racism.

PART I

From Frontier Outpost to Settler Colony

The Project of Colony Building on Manhattan Island

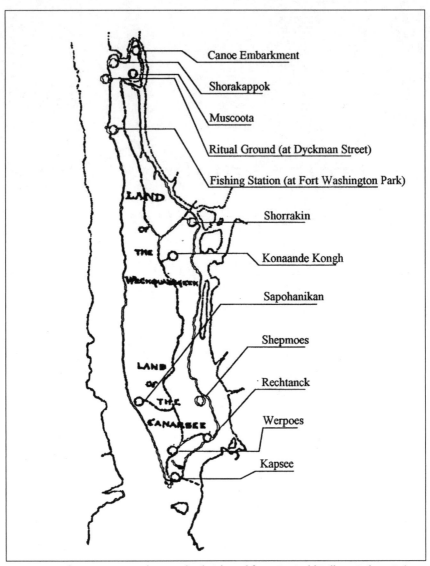

Figure 1.1. Indian Sites on Manhattan Island. Adapted from Reginald Pelham Bolton, *Indian Life of Long Ago in New York City* (New York: Schoen Press, 1934), 132–34.

"To Better People Their Land, and to Bring the Country to Produce More Abundantly"

TERRITORY, TRADE, CONQUEST, AND THE PROJECT
OF COLONY BUILDING ON MANHATTAN ISLAND
UNDER DUTCH RULE, 1624–1664

Approximately two miles wide and fifteen miles long, Manhattan is an island-peninsula located at the confluence of two rivers that pour into an ample bay; its southernmost tip, overlooking the narrows of that sheltered harbor, is within a few miles of the open Atlantic Ocean. Of course, islands connote isolation. Yet during the early modern era, Manhattan Island became the scene of intense contact between previously unacquainted peoples— Amerindian, European, and African. By the time European explorers reached Manhattan, that island-peninsula had supported the self-sufficient life of the Wappinger for at least 500 years. A subdivision of the Algonquian-speaking Lenape (or Delaware) who roamed the river valley that extends through present-day New Jersey, Delaware, eastern Pennsylvania, and southeastern New York, the Wappinger migrated to Manhattan each summer, assembled seasonal camps in the northern area of the island, cultivated maize on communal land, and fished in the waters nearby. In addition to its abundant food supplies, the island attracted these nomadic people because they maintained ancestral burial grounds there.[1] The Wappinger's Manhattan was, therefore, hardly a *terra nullius* of the sort that the maps and the papal bulls of the late fifteenth and early sixteenth centuries described. When the European explorer Henry Hudson first laid eyes on Manhattan, he did not discover a vacant land but instead observed a wooded landscape, interrupted by Wappinger housing compounds, burnt clearings, cornfields, canoe embarkments, and ancient burial sites.

In the reconnaissance report on his expedition to Manhattan and other parts of North America, Hudson described that territory as a "pleasant and fruitful country," certainly no paradise yet rich enough in natural resources to whet the appetite of his sponsors. Measuring everything he encountered against Western European standards, Hudson surveyed the inhabitants of what for him was a strange new world and concluded that the natives lacked the basic cultural traits and moral disposition of a "civilized" people. "They have no religion, whatever, nor any divine worship," Hudson reported. "They are revengeful and very suspicious, but with mild and proper treatment, and especially by intercourse with Christians, this people might be civilized and brought under better regulation; particularly if a sober and discreet population were brought over and good order preserved."[2] Hudson thus conjectured that European colonization of North America would benefit the natives by bringing Christian government and true religion to an untamed and godless people. Deploying a culturalist conception of superior and inferior races as a conceptual tool in the activity of cognitive mapping, of rendering the New World of difference on Manhattan Island not only meaningful but also manageable for the purposes of colony building, Hudson's report not only reflected the gaps in his knowledge about the indigenous population but also preemptively denigrated the natives' culture in preparation for the European invasion and occupation of their land. Only slightly less fanciful than the *mappamundi* that emanated from the imagination of European cartographers who never traveled abroad, Hudson's eyewitness travel account performed a procedure of erasure and inscription that transfigured Manhattan Island into a tabula rasa on which covetous European maritime nations projected their desire to render foreign lands available for conquest, the extraction of natural wealth, and colonization.

Hudson's Dutch sponsors coveted the island-peninsula for its strategic military value and advantages for trade. Situated midway between the major seaports in Europe and the burgeoning staple-producing colonies in the Caribbean basin, and downriver from an ample source of fur pelts in the North American interior, the Wappinger's Manhattan presented an ideal launch site for the military operations of the United Provinces of the Free Netherlands (also referred to as the Dutch Republic and Holland) in the Western Hemisphere and a promising opportunity for the expansion of trade under the management of that maritime nation's rising bourgeoisie.[3] With the termination of the truce with Spain in 1609, the United Provinces commenced another war against its Catholic enemy. The Dutch Republic's Estates General performed the executive functions of government, including foreign policy making, and that governmental body entrusted Holland's oceanic carrying trade, depredations against enemy sailing vessels, and colonization schemes to an oligarchy of Dutch merchants, who were not only shrewd businessmen but also zealous Calvinists and inveterate foes of Catholic Spain. To be sure, the lure of profit attracted these merchants and other wealthy Netherlanders to investment opportunities in overseas commerce. With state support in the guise of monopoly trading privileges, Dutch investors combined their financial resources and established joint-stock companies for undertaking business ventures in distant territories. This corporate structure became the primary vehicle for Dutch colonial expansion in North America.[4]

A few Dutch trading vessels visited the Hudson River between 1611 and 1614.

But Dutch entrepreneurs made no attempt to occupy the North American territory they named New Netherland until 1613, when, on behalf of the New Netherland Company (1613–18), Adrian Block built Fort Nassau (later Fort Orange) on Castle Island, a spot of land on the Hudson River only a few miles south of present-day Albany. Nearly eight years later, the Dutch sailing vessel *Jonge Tobias* arrived at Manhattan Island and deposited Jan (Juan) Rodrigues, a seafarer of African descent from Hispaniola. Though his shipmates had abandoned him on a remote island, he hardly lived an isolated life there. Rodrigues soon established a trade relation with the natives, married an Indian woman from Rockaway, and eventually produced several children with her. One of the first middlemen in the early Amerindian-European trade, Rodrigues negotiated exchanges with the natives for any European mariner who was willing to pay his commission fee.[5]

Following the expiration of the New Netherland Company's charter in 1618, the Estates General awarded the Dutch West India Company (WIC, 1621–1815) a monopoly on the trade in the territories of the Americas and West Africa that the United Provinces claimed by right of exploration. The Estates General also granted the WIC nearly unlimited authority over the development and governance of colonial outposts in these lands. An ad hoc, opportunistic, and quasi-military joint-stock company, the WIC at first engaged in privateering assaults against Spanish and Portuguese ships that sailed in the Caribbean Sea. In this way, the WIC contributed to the Dutch Republic's war effort against its Catholic rivals. Beginning in 1624, the WIC turned its attention to establishing trade relations with Native Americans and erected widely dispersed outposts of a dozen or so traders along the Hudson River—at Fort Orange in 1624, at New Amsterdam in 1624, at Beverwyck (later Albany) in 1652, and at Wiltwyck (later Esopus) in 1661.[6] Except for New Amsterdam, where 30 Walloon farming families cultivated the land just outside the Dutch fort, these outposts served as storehouses for trade goods and little else. Navigable for a 120-mile distance between New Amsterdam and Beverwyck, the Hudson River offered a superb natural travel route. When news about the arrival of newcomers spread to the North American Indian communities, Indian traders journeyed along the Hudson, contacted European traders who occupied crude outposts on the riverbank, and exchanged fur pelts and other native produce from the North American interior for hatchets, axes, knives, kettles, firearms, gunpowder, and other European manufactured goods.[7]

Besides metal utensils, guns, and ammunition, the European traders introduced the indigenes to strong liquor.[8] During his 1610 expedition to North America, Henry Hudson distributed free samples of wine and aqua vitae to the natives. Hudson's gift to the Indians was no altruistic gesture of good will but a means of discerning their inner moral disposition, of discovering, as Robert Juet explained, "whether [the natives] had any treacherie in them."[9] Much like a present-day scientist might conduct a laboratory experiment on the effects of alcohol on human subjects, Hudson contrived to intoxicate the natives with strong liquor, lower their inhibitions, and thereby come to know the worst in their character. In a short time the ritual of giving gifts of strong liquor to the natives became a custom at treaty-signing ceremonies and official negotiations that involved the transfer of Indian lands to European newcomers, who perhaps gained an advantage in these deals by impairing the judgment of Indian sachems with the aid of intoxicating drinks. Not all Amerindian-European encounters involving alcohol were laden with ulterior motives. European traders sold strong liquor to the natives in the frank pursuit of profit, and alcohol quickly became an important trade good in North America.[10]

The Indians' desire for the addictive liquor grew as they discovered that the new libation induced vivid dreams, which, the natives believed, offered spiritual guidance. The natives drank the strong spirits not to forget, as the European newcomers sometimes did, but to remember and to take counsel from the omens that appeared in their dreams.[11] The assimilation of this new sacramental libation into the Indians' ritual practices was largely unintelligible to Europeans, who, for the most part, remained unaware of the complexities of the indigenous culture. Alcohol had to be imbibed in large quantities to induce the revelatory (or hallucinogenic) effect that the natives desired. Some European outsiders regarded the Indians' drinking habits as excessive, as a mark of lawlessness and confirmation of the lack of civility that they attributed to the indigenous culture as a whole.[12]

Even though they complained that drunken Indians sometimes made troublesome neighbors, the European settlers, whom the WIC transplanted to the jurisdiction of New Netherland during the early years of colony building, were eager to trade with the natives and sold strong liquor to the indigenes in violation of the WIC's monopoly on trade. Insisting that the natives would find alternative suppliers, if they did not sell alcohol to them, these settlers were ready with an alibi that absolved them of any responsibility for the Indians' growing addiction to strong liquor. The Dutch traveler Jasper Danckaerts blamed the epidemic of alcoholism among the natives on the settlers who sold them addictive liquor. Castigating the settlers for their reckless behavior, Danckaerts wrote: "They brought forward the excuse, that if they did not do it, others would, and then they would have the trouble and others the profit; but if they must have the trouble, they ought to have the profits, and so they all said, and for the most part falsely, for they all solicit the Indians as much as they can."[13] In Danckaerts's view, the single-minded pursuit of profit led the settlers to deny the imprudence of providing the natives with limitless quantities of alcohol, not to mention as many firearms and as much gunpowder as the Indians could carry. Other WIC officials warned that under the influence of strong liquor the indigenous population posed a grave security threat to the vulnerable Dutch outposts along the Hudson River. Although the WIC authorities predicted that in the event of war the Indians would be better outfitted with guns and ammunition than the settlers, they were unable to defuse this potentially explosive situation.

In addition to the exchange of alcohol, firearms, gunpowder, fur peltries, and other commodities, the European invasion inaugurated an era of sexual commerce between male Europeans and female natives. The WIC officials and the Dutch Calvinist clergy in New Netherland associated this sexual mingling between formerly separate peoples with the erosion of Christian morality in the colony's European population. No longer conducting themselves in a manner befitting a civilized people, the European newcomers were, the colonial authorities warned, losing their mooring in Christian identity and degenerating to a savage condition. In an effort to reinscribe the boundary that ostensibly divided the Europeans from the natives, the "civilized" from the "savage," the WIC enacted a law that prohibited natives from visiting its outposts after sunset, a common occurrence prior to the promulgation of that prohibition in 1638. The same law also criminalized sexual contact between male Europeans and female natives.[14]

Living on the colonial frontier without the companionship of European women, some male settlers and WIC soldiers ignored the prohibition against sexual relations with female natives and under the cover of darkness smuggled illicit sex partners into the WIC's outposts. An official document reports that on numerous occasions Sergeant Nicolaes Coorn, a WIC soldier, had female natives "sleep entire nights with him in his bed, in the presence of the other soldiers."[15] Because the WIC military commanders could not afford to estrange this valuable soldier, whose service was crucial to the security of the Dutch North American territory, they verbally reprimanded Sergeant Coorn for behaving in a manner unbecoming a Dutch soldier and Christian, instead of imposing a more severe punishment on him. Pointing to the example of the WIC's secretary Cornelius van Tienhoven, who was rumored to have been frolicking about "the same as an Indian, with a little covering and a small patch in front from lust"[16] after the female natives, the WIC officials acknowledged that self-mastery of sexual passion was a test of manliness and civility that some European males failed while living on the North American frontier. Adriaen van der Donck confessed that he and other male Netherlanders found Indian women to be "well favored and fascinating." Commenting on the enduring bonds between male Netherlanders and female natives, he reported in 1655: "Several of our Netherlanders were connected with them before our women came over, and remain firm in their attachments."[17] These Dutch-speaking male foreigners no doubt benefited from matrimonial ties to Algonquian-speaking female natives. Admitted to native kinship networks through marriage to Indian women, they gained access to insider information and obtained assistance in dressing furs, translation, and negotiating exchanges, all of which proved to be indispensable to their success in the fur trade. Doubtless, these and other advantages encouraged male settlers to remain faithful to their Indian wives.

Whereas some male settlers maintained lifelong conjugal unions with female natives, others believed that Indian women were unsuitable for anything more than furtive sexual encounters. A male settler alleged: "Indian women are very much given to promiscuous intercourse."[18] Using this misrepresentation of female natives as an alibi, some male settlers and WIC soldiers sexually exploited Indian women, as if they were merely another natural resource. In this respect, the sexual conquest of female natives became a corollary to the masculinized project of European domination over feminized foreign lands and integral to the colonialist fantasy of unobstructed territorial expansion. Dominie Johannes Megapolensis denied that female natives could be sexually exploited, explaining that Indian women prostituted themselves for trifles and easily seduced male settlers. "These women," the Dutch Calvinist clergyman alleged, "are exceedingly addicted to whoring; they will lie with a man for the value of one, two, or three *schillings*, and our Dutchmen run after them very much."[19] Megapolensis and other European newcomers had slender knowledge of Native American communities, which regulated gender roles and sexual practices according to rules that were not readily legible to Western Europeans.[20] Following the European invasion, North America became an eroticized danger zone, filled with temptation and peril for Indian women. Female natives sometimes bore the burden of harsh communal chastisement for transgressive sexual behavior, even though European males had enticed or perhaps coerced these women to engage in unauthorized sexual acts with them. A WIC document reports that an Indian woman who had slept with a male settler after he had seduced her with the promise of a gift for sexual favors was left to wander the countryside with her hair cut off, denounced and exiled from her husband's support and protection.[21] Few European males fully comprehended the risk of natal alienation to which female natives were exposed when they engaged in unsanctioned sexual relations with strangers.

Despite the WIC's efforts to curb contact between the settlers and the natives, both parties continued to trade, drink, and even sleep together. Yet in many crucial respects, the natives and the settlers remained strangers to one another. The Amerindian-European trade involved exchanges between newly acquainted people who entered into negotiations without a common language and often under the haze of intoxicating drinks, which lowered inhibitions on both sides. From the beginning, Amerindian-European encounters were precarious affairs; the potential for violence was as great as the potential for profitable trade and amicable cross-cultural exchange. Over time, the semblance of intimacy between the European newcomers and the natives proved to be a dangerous illusion. This circumstance led a contemporary observer to warn that the greedy settler too often "withdrew himself from his comrades, sought communication with the Indians from where it appeared his profit would be derived, . . . produced altogether too much familiarity with the Indians which in short time brought forth contempt, usually the father of hate."[22] It was precisely this scenario that propelled the natives and the European invaders along the path to war.

Before his death at the hands of a young male native, Claes Smits, a Dutch settler, wheelwright, and occasional fur trader, befriended the neighboring Indians, who from time to time brought beaver pelts to his isolated camp on the shore of Turtle Bay, a strand of land along a small creek that ran into the East River. In the autumn of 1641, Smits entertained an Indian guest, a young man from Konaande Konch, the island's principal Wappinger village. On the surface there was nothing unusual about this encounter. Then suddenly, the Indian youth struck Smits on the neck with an ax, inflicting a mortal wound. It was later reported that the assailant had committed the homicide in revenge for the murder of his uncle, whom a party of European traders had killed some time earlier.[23] The bloody episode at Turtle Bay demonstrated how seemingly peaceful interactions between the European newcomers and the natives could, in a flash, become deadly affairs. Neither the settlers nor the indigenes fully appreciated the volatility of the early Amerindian-European encounters; few practical lessons of caution were drawn from the misadventure at Turtle Bay. Instead, leaders on both sides brought their people closer to the brink of war.

Incommensurable ideals of justice prevented the Wappinger sachems and the WIC officials from negotiating a peaceful resolution to their dispute over the homicide at Turtle Bay. Director-General Willem Kieft, commander of the WIC's enterprise in New Netherland from 1637 to 1647, demanded that the Wappinger sachems remand the accused murderer to the custody of the WIC authorities at New Amsterdam. After explaining that the killer had run away, the sachems offered to compensate Smits's widow with a payment of wampum. They also excused their kinsman's action, stating that their young people were unaccustomed to strong liquor, which the European newcomers sold them, and that, once intoxicated, Indian youths often flew into passions, a pattern of behavior that was unknown before the Europeans arrived. The European outsiders, they added, were addicted to alcohol and, when intoxicated, fought among themselves with knives.[24] According to the Wappinger sachems, the European invaders were neither a sober nor discreet people, and their appearance in the region hardly augured an era of good order. Director-General Kieft could not accept the Wappinger's offer to compensate Smits's widow for the loss of her husband's life with a payment of wampum, nor could he agree with their unflattering description of his people. Convinced of the moral superiority of Christians and the righteousness of the WIC's mission in North America, Kieft became inflexible in his resolve to punish the young male native who had assassinated Smits. For their part, the Wappinger sachems regarded the homicide at Turtle Bay as a legitimate act of retributive justice. Like other Native American communities, the Wappinger required the men of their community to avenge the murder of a kinsman, an obligation that could be satisfied by taking the life of an adult male from the offender's community, even if he had no direct role in the commission of the murder.[25] This Wappinger custom and ideal of justice reinforced the WIC authorities' perception that the natives were a vengeful, lawless, and therefore "uncivilized" race. Although they needed only to refer to medieval European codes of honor and manliness for a familiar analogue to the young male native's act of revenge, the WIC authorities regarded the murder of Smits as a savage crime, as incontrovertible evidence that the native population must be subdued under the civilizing yoke of Christians.

Hoping to build a consensus on Indian policy among the settlers, Kieft convened a public meeting at New Amsterdam on August 28, 1641, and directed the settlers to elect a dozen representatives who would counsel him during the present emergency. Following their deliberations, the "Twelve Select Men" advised Kieft to make one last effort to avoid open warfare and, if persuasion failed, then exterminate the natives. Pressuring the Wappinger leaders with the threat of annihilation, Kieft again demanded that the individual responsible for the bloodshed at Turtle Bay be brought before the WIC officials, who, he insisted, were competent to judge the accused by civilized standards of justice. The sachems never complied with the WIC leader's demand, however.[26]

Kieft's directive fell on deaf ears because he and his interpreters were perhaps incapable of translating early modern Western European ideals of justice into words the Algonquian-speaking natives could comprehend. The Dutch Calvinist cleric Dominie Megapolensis wrote a report on his missionary work among the natives that exposed the European invaders' inaptitude with the Algonquian language. The natives have a "very difficult language," Megapolensis admitted, "and it costs me great pains to learn it, so as to be able to speak and preach in it fluently. There is no Christian here who understands the language thoroughly; those who have lived here long can use a kind of jargon just sufficient to carry on trade with it, but they do not understand the fundamentals of the language. I am making a vocabulary of the [Indians'] language, and when I am among them I ask them how things are called; but as they are very stupid, I sometimes cannot make them understand what I want."[27] Owing in part to their infelicities in speaking the Algonquian language, the WIC officials and the Calvinist clergymen were powerless to translate Dutch commands into Wappinger obedience.

In addition to miscommunication involving the concept "justice," incommensurable notions of the value and use of land and the care of livestock became sites of conflict between the European invaders and the natives. Whereas the Wappinger prized land principally as a means of meeting their subsistence needs and as communal property of tremendous symbolic value for cementing the bond of tribal identity over the generations, the WIC officials regarded land primarily as a commodity, whose worth lay not only in its unique use-value but also in its relation to other commodities in their system of exchange. Regarding Manhattan Island as a commodity, Director-General Willem Verhulst (1625–26) offered the Wappinger goods worth 60 florins, the equivalent of 11 fur pelts, in exchange for the entire island-peninsula. Although the Wappinger sachems accepted the WIC's offer, they had no concept akin to the capitalist notion of private ownership of land and probably never imagined that the WIC officials considered the transaction to be a permanent transfer of exclusive ownership of the island.[28] The Dutch settler Van der Donck summarized the natives' ideal respecting the disposal of land and other natural resources, or notion of the "right of nature," stating: "They take this to include the wind, rivers, woods, plains, sea, beaches, and banks. All these are open and freely accessible to every individual of all the nations with which they are not publicly engaged in quarrels. They may use these freely and enjoy these in as much freedom as though they were born there."[29] It is, then, unlikely that the Wappinger sachems intended to convey sole right to the use and ownership of Manhattan Island to the Dutch newcomers. More likely, the Wappinger agreed to share the island, viewing the tendered European manufactured goods as a tribute (or veneration present) to their ancestors, whom the Wappinger regarded as the original occupants of the island.

Having, in their view, purchased exclusive title to Manhattan Island and thereby obtained the right to extract a profit from that land, the WIC officials, in early 1640, demanded a payment of rent from the Wappinger who occupied the northern part of the island. Also, these military officers perhaps regarded the compensation of rent from the Wappinger in the same way that medieval Europe's warlords looked on the extraction of tribute from European peasants, as an obligation of the weak to pay the powerful for military protection against foes and other safeguards.[30] However, the Wappinger sachems had their own system of clientage, now perceived the WIC and the settler population as a potential enemy, and refused to pay the Dutch-speaking invaders for the right to reside on ancestral land and to make use of it in accordance with their ancient customs. Ignoring the sachems' refusal or perhaps misinterpreting their answer, Director-General Kieft sent Captain Cornelius Pietersen to the northeastern shore of Manhattan Island to collect the demanded rent (or tribute) from the Wappinger. Mistaking a pile of Indian corn on the riverbank for the expected payment, Pietersen and his crew began loading the corn into their sailing vessel but were thwarted by an armed Indian assault and barely escaped death.[31]

The arming of the natives with firearms not only imperiled the lives of the European invaders but also endangered the region's wildlife. By 1639, the Indian hunters' use of firearms had led to the depletion of beaver, otter, and other fur-bearing animals in the lower Hudson River Valley. No longer the principal suppliers of fur pelts to the European traders, the Algonquian-speaking natives who inhabited that region and the coastal plain were now merely an obstacle to the permanent European occupation of these lands. At that time the WIC was enticing Europeans to migrate to the North American region called New Netherland with the promise that newcomers would receive substantial acres of land in that overseas territory.[32] In an effort to avoid misunderstandings that might lead to violent altercations with the indigenous population, the WIC officials supervised all land transactions between the natives and the land-hungry Europeans who settled in New Netherland. But conflicting values regarding the use of land proved to be impossible to suppress. The natives and European settlers soon clashed over land usage practices.[33]

Measured by the standards of the settlers, the natives were an unambitious, even lazy people who, neither improving nor making gainful use of the soil, lived a nomadic, seemingly indigent life, which disqualified them from being counted as rightful possessors of the land. The settler Johannes de Laet wrote: "Indians desire no riches."[34] Of course, the Wappinger were hardly an impoverished people and, for centuries, had managed to sustain a self-sufficient existence, free from scarcity, except in times of natural disaster and war. Complementing the European invaders' low estimation of the Native American moral character was their own high self-regard. The Christian settlers liked to think of themselves as a chosen people who now lived in a New Canaan in accordance with a renewed covenant with God, which required them to "be fruitful, and multiply, and replenish the earth, and subdue it: and have dominion over the fish of the sea, and over the fowl of the air, and over every living thing that moveth upon the earth."[35] However, New Netherland's early settler population neither enjoyed great success as tillers of the soil and fishers of the sea nor applied most of their energy to cultivating the earth and harvesting the fruits of their own labor but, instead, devoted themselves to the trade in furs, firearms, ammunition, and liquor. Insofar as the settlers made use of the land, they did so in ways that the natives did not readily comprehend. For example, the settlers enclosed land in fences and persisted in their habit of allowing livestock to roam about the countryside, even though their grazing animals sometimes trampled the natives' unfenced cornfields. The natives found this mode of land usage and care of livestock to be an unfamiliar and destructive practice. In 1639, some natives on Staten Island burned a Dutch flag and killed a hog in protest against the foreigners who continued to permit their livestock to destroy their unprotected cornfields. Director-General Kieft retaliated by dispatching a military expedition to punish the Staten Island natives.[36]

As a consequence of conflicting practices of land usage and care of livestock, incompatible notions of the value of land, and, above all, incommensurable ideals of justice, Amerindian-European relations deteriorated to open warfare. Any meaningful cross-cultural understanding between the European newcomers and the natives required a shared system of representation, mutually intelligible symbols, beliefs, and values of far greater sophistication than the trade jargon that served as a superficial mode of communication between the European traders and their Indian counterparts. Convinced that his people and the natives would never overcome the obstacles to mutual understanding, Director-General Kieft concluded that only a definitive show of force could achieve the goal of native submission to Dutch authority.[37] Henry Hudson's earlier prescription of "mild and proper treatment" thus gave way to brutal measures of military conquest.

In February 1643, Director-General Kieft sent soldiers to exterminate the natives at Konaande Konch, the main Wappinger village on Manhattan Island. Although this military expedition discovered that the Wappinger had evacuated that site, another WIC sortie, under the command of Captain John Underhill, slaughtered more than 80 natives at Pavonia (present-day Jersey City) and massacred another 50 natives at Rechtanch, near Corlears Hook in the lower East Side of Manhattan.[38] The settler David de Vries described the Massacre of Pavonia:

Infants were torn from their mothers' breasts, and hacked to pieces in the presence of the parents, and the pieces thrown into the fire and in the water, and other sucklings, being bound to small boards, were cut, stuck, and pierced, and miserably massacred in a manner to move a heart of stone. Some were thrown into the river, and when the fathers and mothers endeavored to save them, the soldiers would not let them come on land but made both parents and children drown—children from five to six years of age, and also some old and decrepit persons. Those who fled from this onslaught, and concealed themselves in a neighboring sedge, and when it was morning, came out to beg a piece of bread, and to be permitted to warm themselves, were murdered in cold blood and tossed into the fire or the water. Some came to our people in the country with their hands, some with their legs cut off, and some holding their entrails in their arms, and others had such horrible cuts and gashes, that worse than they were could never happen.[39]

The natives responded to this vicious execution of women, children, and other noncombatants by committing atrocities of their own against defenseless settlers in the countryside. Some terrified settlers reproached Kieft for jeopardizing their lives and property by conducting war against the natives, while he, they pointed out, was "protected in a good fort, out of which he had not slept a single night."[40] At that time the Narragansett sachem Miantonimo rallied the coastal and lower river Indians in northeastern North America to fight a war against all European invaders. Although the settlers in southern New England suffered hardships and fatalities, the Indian war had a more destructive impact on New Netherland, taking more European lives and severely demoralizing the surviving settlers in that Dutch North American colony. By 1644, only 200 European men and 250 family members and other dependents remained in New Netherland.[41] During the war, European traders evacuated the outposts along the Hudson River and, together with the settlers who were once dispersed throughout the countryside, consolidated themselves at New Amsterdam at the tip of Manhattan Island, where they lived under the protection of the WIC's soldiers and slaves. After several years of seemingly interminable warfare, some desperate settlers wrote to the WIC authorities in Holland: "Our fields lie fallow and waste; our dwellings and other buildings are burnt; not a handful can be planted or sown this fall on the deserted places; the crops which God the Lord permitted to come forth during the past summer, remain on the field standing and rotting in diverse places, in the same way as the hay, for the preservation of which we, poor people, cannot obtain one man. We are burdened with heavy families; we have no means to provide necessaries for wife and children; and we sit here amidst thousands of Indians and barbarians, from whom we find neither peace nor mercy."[42] Expansion into North America had at first appeared to be a sure path to riches for the European invaders, but the violent struggle with the natives served notice that wealth was not the certain outcome of their errand on the North American frontier. Also, while the war did not create an unbridgeable chasm between the natives and the settlers, the bloody conflict had lasting consequences for Amerindian-European relations. With the cessation of hostilities, the natives and the settlers returned to the traffic in furs, alcohol, firearms, and ammunition, but they now approached each other through a nimbus of disillusionment and distrust. War had shattered the phantasm of friendship between the natives and the European newcomers.

Even though the WIC's outposts along the Hudson River had been reduced to a single fort on Manhattan Island, the company could take solace in the fact that its show of force had nearly rid the coveted island of its indigenous population. Combined with the *nova pestis* smallpox, the devastation of war destroyed nearly half of the coastal Indian population. The remnants of that people witnessed significant alterations in their traditional life of self-sufficiency, as they became trapped, like a modern Tantalus, above the capricious waters of monetized market exchanges and struggled to obtain things that they once considered to be freely accessible to all by the "right of nature." The nomadic Wappinger gradually abandoned the seasonal migrations and mode of subsistence that they had known before the European invasion and increasingly focused on sedentary activities, such as the production of wampum, now principally esteemed as a medium of exchange in the fur trade and as a means of making rent payments to the Dutch colonizers for the privilege of residing on parcels of Manhattan real estate that were once their communal lands.[43] As elsewhere along the eastern coast of North America, the shift from Native American to European dominance on Manhattan Island gave rise to historic changes in the land. If a sailor who had traveled to the island-peninsula with Henry Hudson in 1610 returned there in the middle of the seventeenth century, he would have noticed striking alterations in the island's landscape. As a consequence of the European occupation, the forested island, whose lower and upper shores were once dotted with Indian seasonal camps, burnt clearings, maize fields, canoe embarkments, and ancient burial grounds, had, by the late 1650s, been transformed into a colonized region of modest farms and a fledgling colonial port town with a stone fort and storehouse, streets and canals, a windmill, barracks for the WIC's soldiers and slaves, other dwellings, and gardens enclosed by fences.

From the start, the WIC planned to develop the North American territory known as New Netherland into a permanent settler colony, which served the United Provinces' mercantilist agenda of national self-sufficiency by supplying that commerce-oriented maritime nation's rapidly expanding home market with agricultural produce that Hollanders previously imported from European rivals. To that end, the WIC hoped to transplant numerous Dutch farming families to New Netherland and employ them in the cultivation of crops that were largely unavailable through domestic producers and could be sold at a profit in Holland. But the project of colonization proved to be costly. As a consequence, the WIC revised its plan by shifting the expense of transporting settlers to New Netherland and cultivating the land to individual investors. Beginning in 1628, the WIC offered petty fiefdoms called *patroonschappen* (or patroonships) to its wealthiest shareholders on the condition that they transport at least 30 Dutch farmers to Manhattan Island or 60 Dutch farmers to other parts of New Netherland within three years. The patroonship proposal combined seignorial institutions and capitalist values. Like a modern capitalist, the patroon was entitled to the profits from his financial investment in colony building and, like a feudal lord, was endowed with the prerogative to establish his own court of law on his North American estate.[44] The WIC shareholder Kilaen Van Rensselaer accepted an enormous land grant of 1 million acres and just before the outbreak of the Indian war founded a patroonship called Rensselaerswyck, an 18-mile stretch of land along the Hudson River and adjacent to Fort Orange. Van Rensselaer was unable to convince Dutch farming families to settle on his North American estate but transported 216 settlers from England, Norway, and the Rhine to Rensselaerswyck. Other WIC shareholders founded patroonships in New Netherland, but they could not recruit adequate numbers of farmers from the United Provinces and other parts of Europe to cultivate their North

American estates. Failing to realize a profit from their investments, these share-holders aborted their colonization projects.[45]

The difficulty of attracting adequate numbers of obedient European farm laborers became a chief impediment against New Netherland's development into a profitable overseas colony. The WIC's monopoly on trade and its strict regulation of land transactions made New Netherland an unattractive final destination for Netherlanders and other Europeans who desired unencumbered title to land and the freedom to engage in trade. New Netherland's early settlers pursued quick profits in the trade with the natives. Except for a few dozen poor Walloon farming families, which the WIC transported to Manhattan between 1624 and 1626, European newcomers rarely cultivated the land. The WIC at first guarded its monopoly trading privileges by enacting laws that restricted the traffic in peltries to its own salaried employees and confined the retail business in vital provisions to its own storehouses.[46] Complaining that the WIC's monopoly on trade violated their liberties and that the company's employees engaged in profiteering at the expense of their survival, scores of disgruntled settlers, to the WIC's dismay, left New Netherland. In an effort to attract more settlers and retain them, the WIC in 1640 revised its policy and offered liberalized "freedoms and exempts" to Netherlanders who were willing to migrate to Dutch North America. That list of privileges rewarded settlers with generous land grants, opened riverfront land previously reserved for patroons to ordinary settlers, promised settlers a supply of slaves at a 10 percent discount, abolished the WIC's monopoly on the fur trade, and repealed other restrictions on the settlers' liberties.[47] The WIC's land grant program resembled the Virginia Company's headright system in the Chesapeake region. According to the latter plan, English farming families received land in tidewater Virginia at no cost as a reward for migrating to that English overseas territory and cultivating the soil. Similarly, the WIC's plan awarded a bounty of 200 acres of land to Dutch settlers, with the stipulation that each settler must pay for his own transportation and the passage of five additional settlers to New Netherland. Netherlanders were, however, little disposed to leave their prosperous and tolerant homeland, and those who were willing to uproot themselves mostly migrated to Brazil and Curaçao or else trekked to the Cape of Good Hope at the tip of Africa and to Dutch colonial outposts in southeast Asia. Since adventurous Netherlanders preferred these Dutch overseas colonies to New Netherland, the WIC extended its offer to potential settlers from parts of Europe outside the United Provinces and, as a further enticement, provided free ocean passage, making migration to New Netherland one of the cheapest travel packages to the New World.[48] Nevertheless, few European farming families migrated to Dutch North America prior to the 1650s.

In 1628, the Dutch colony's total population numbered only 500 inhabitants.[49] Settler outmigration, along with the WIC's failure to recruit replacements, meant that New Netherland's settler population grew slowly. A contemporary observer concluded: "The land, being extensive and in many places full of weeds and wild growth could not be properly cultivated in consequence of the scantiness of the population, the Dutch West India Company needed to better people their land, and bring the country to produce more abundantly."[50] The Dutch Calvinist clergyman Dominie Jonas Michaëlius added: "the ground is fertile enough to reward labor, but they must clear it well and till it just as our lands require."[51] Writing from New Netherland to the WIC officials in Holland, some farmers pleaded: "Were their High Mightinesses please to equip some ships for a few years, for the free conveyance and transportation of people principally Boors and farm servants with their poverty hither, together with some necessary maintenance until the poor people had obtained something *in ease*, their High Mightinesses would not only relieve many encumbered men, but also expect from God, through their intercession, luck, blessing, and prosperity."[52] The WIC was unable to satisfy this and other requests for farm servants, because even impoverished European peasants shunned New Netherland.

Finding that Netherlanders and other Europeans were unlikely to migrate to New Netherland in sufficient numbers to secure, permanently occupy, and cultivate its vast North American territory, the WIC acquired enslaved laborers from various parts of the Atlantic world as substitutes for European farm servants. Director-General Kieft endorsed this strategy, stating: "Negroes would accomplish more work for their masters and at less expense, than farm servants, who must be bribed to go thither by a great deal of money and promises."[53] The leading carrier in the transatlantic slave trade during most of the seventeenth century,[54] the WIC ordered the diversion of some of its human cargo from slave markets in the Caribbean basin to New Netherland. Because Curaçao was the main transshipment center for the WIC's African slave trade in the Western Hemisphere,[55] enslaved Africans were likely transported to that Dutch Caribbean entrepôt before being shipped to Manhattan Island.[56] Small cargoes and also a few relatively large shipments of enslaved Africans were added to Manhattan's population during the Dutch colonial era (Table 1.1). In addition, Dutch privateers occasionally captured enemy sailing vessels, seized free black and mulatto sailors, and sold these captives (or human prize goods) into slavery at New Amsterdam.[57] Enslaving the indigenous population was never a viable solution to the colony's labor shortage, though prior to and during the Indian war the WIC and some settlers enslaved a few natives.[58] The imperative of maintaining harmonious trade relations with the indigenous communities, the difficulty of preventing enslaved natives from making successful escapes into the interior, and finally the dwindling coastal Indian population meant that the European invaders could keep only a small number of natives in bondage.[59] The WIC thus relied on imported sources of slave labor.

Although the exact number is unknown, at least 467 slaves were brought to New Amsterdam between 1626 and 1664.[60] The first documented cargo of slaves arrived at Manhattan Island in 1626, two years after the founding of New Amsterdam. There were approximately 11 men in this inaugural shipment, and the WIC kept these slaves for its own use in New Amsterdam. In 1628, a Dutch trading vessel brought three enslaved women to Manhattan. The WIC records state that these female slaves had been purchased for the "comfort of the Company's Negro men" and that the WIC's slaves produced offspring.[61] Male slaves out-

TABLE 1.1 Documented Slave Imports to New
Amsterdam, 1626–1664

Date	Ship Name	
1626	Unknown	11
1628	Unknown	3
1642	La Grace	Unknown
1646	Tamandere	Unknown
1652	St. Anthoni	44
1655	Wittepaert	Unknown
1659	Speramundi	5
1660	Speramundi	3
1660	Eyekenboom	20
1660	New Netherland Indian	10
1661	New Netherland Indian	40
1664	Sparrow	40
1664	Gideon	291

Source: Compiled from Donnan, *Documents Illustrative*, 3:444.

numbered female slaves in New Netherland,[62] and the relative dearth of enslaved adult females retarded the natural increase of the colony's enslaved population, limiting the number of slaves born in the Dutch North American outposts to a small number. The majority of New Netherland's enslaved population were probably natives from the Gold Coast of Africa, the Congo, and Angola. By 1637, the WIC had captured the slave trading fort called El Mina from the Portuguese and, along with that commanding fortress, control over the transatlantic slave trade between the West African coast and the Americas.[63] In 1641, the WIC seized Luanda and Benguela, displaced the Portuguese slave traders in Angola and the Congo, and took over the transatlantic traffic in Angolan and Congolese slaves.[64] Brazil absorbed the lion's share of the enslaved native Africans that WIC sailing vessels transported to the Americas, whereas New Netherland received only a tiny fraction of this human cargo.[65] Independent slave traders and privateers carried enslaved laborers from the Gold Coast, the Kongo-Angola region, and other parts of the Atlantic world to the Dutch colonial outpost on Manhattan Island.[66] As the place-names of the first involuntary immigrants indicate, São Tomé and Portugal, as well as Angola and the Congo, supplied slaves to New Amsterdam.[67] Dutch slave traders also brought a few slaves from Brazil to that colonial seaport.[68] Of the slaves acquired from Portugal, São Tomé, and other conquered Portuguese territories in the Western Hemisphere, most were probably somewhat acculturated native Africans and American-born (or creole) blacks who, unlike recent native African captives, had already undergone the process of adaptation to the conditions of enslavement in the Americas. Some slaves among the enslaved human cargo brought to New Amsterdam perhaps spoke Portuguese, if only imperfectly, while a few perhaps comprehended a small number of Dutch words well enough to execute the orders of Dutch-speaking masters.[69]

The WIC relied on enslaved laborers to occupy, protect, improve, and cultivate the Dutch North American territory. Utilized as both a labor and military force, slaves became a vital stratum of New Netherland's population. For its operations in New Netherland, the WIC required an enslaved population of robust men. "In regard to negroes," a WIC officer explained, "they ought to be stout and strong fellows, fit for immediate employment on this fortress and other works; also, if required, in war against the savage natives, either to pursue them when retreating, or else to carry some of the soldiers' baggage."[70] The WIC enlisted its male slaves in military campaigns against the natives during the Indian war. These slaves did not bear firearms but instead wielded small axes and half-pikes.[71] Making the North American frontier safe for trade and colonization was foremost on the minds of the Dutch colony builders. Hence slaves also labored on the construction of a palisade, built on Manhattan Island along present-day Wall Street for protection against Indian attacks, and on other fortifications that enhanced the security of the frontier outposts along the Hudson River.[72] On Manhattan Island the WIC's slaves were shackled together and forced to work in gangs under the supervision of the WIC "Overseer of Negroes" Jacob Stoffelson and his successor, Paulus Heymans.[73] The WIC at first housed its male slaves in a separate same-sex barrack, located on present-day Fleet Street in lower Manhattan. By 1639, the WIC had moved the slave barrack northward to the vicinity of present-day Seventy-second Street and the East River.[74] With the removal of its male slaves to that northern area of the island, the WIC established a buffer zone against Indian invasion.

In addition to laboring on fortifications and serving as praetorian-like protectors of the vulnerable Dutch colonial outpost on Manhattan Island, slaves cultivated the WIC's six *bouweries* (or farms) on the island during the early Dutch colonial period. At that pivotal stage, the agricultural produce from these farms fed New Amsterdam's population and allowed that Dutch outpost to avoid the starving times that had plagued the first English outposts in North America. Except for the largest company farm, which encompassed an area of 100 acres, the WIC's *bouweries*, along with the slaves on the land, were eventually leased to European farmers.[75] The WIC lent slaves to its employees and sometimes transferred ownership of slaves to them as in-kind salary payments for service. Throughout the Dutch colonial period, slaves tended the farms of WIC employees.[76] Because the WIC's "freedoms and exemptions of 1640" granted European settlers a monopoly on lucrative trades, such as bricklayer and carpenter, few slaves were trained and employed in the skilled occupations.[77]

Even though the WIC extended some attractive liberties to European settlers and kept Africans in bondage, the joint-stock company did not establish a rigid racial hierarchy of rights-bearing white settlers and enslaved blacks with no rights. In New Netherland enslaved blacks enjoyed the right to testify in court, including cases involving white settlers.[78] Also, the WIC remitted wages to at least five slaves who, in 1635, petitioned the metropolitan authorities in Holland to order the WIC to pay them for their labor.[79] Although several laws and other official papers implicitly recognized chattel slavery in New Netherland, the Dutch colonial authorities never created, the historian Joyce Goodfriend has noted, a "legally and ideologically consistent slave system."[80] According to the historian Leon Higginbotham, slavery in Dutch North America was more a matter of custom than a mandate of law.[81] Importantly, no statute prevented the WIC from elevating slaves to the status of free men and women when circumstances dictated such action.

The Indian war presented a set of contingencies that required the WIC to upgrade the status of some slaves. During that war, the Dutch outposts in North America were under the constant threat of Indian attack. Yet at that time the WIC employed fewer than 40 soldiers.[82] Moreover, that costly war nearly depleted the company's resources, and food supplies ran dangerously low. At that moment of crisis, 11 WIC slaves, some of the same enslaved males brought to New Amsterdam in 1626, demanded freedom for themselves and their families. The WIC could not dismiss this petition as an unreasonable request, for the slaves' services were now more crucial than ever. The WIC had already enlisted its male slaves in military campaigns against the natives.[83] WIC officers knew that these slaves would be needed in the near future and therefore offered "half-freedom" to the slaves who were astute enough to take advantage of the escalating Indian war by petitioning for freedom. A written agreement stated that the black petitioners were "free and at liberty on the same footing as other free people here in New Netherland." But according to the "half-freedom" bargain, the WIC manumitted the 11 enslaved male petitioners and their wives on the condition that they were obligated to labor for the WIC when called on to serve and that their offspring were the WIC's property. This arrangement also stipulated that the WIC must pay the half-free blacks wages for their labor and that, during periods when the WIC did not require their services, these blacks were at liberty to provide for their own subsistence, as long as they paid the WIC an annual tribute of one hog, 23 bushels of corn, wampum, or fur pelts worth 20 guilders.[84] Following the Indian war, the WIC granted half-freedom to another two dozen or so slaves as a reward for their allegiance during the conflict with the Indians and for loyal service during peacetime.[85]

The liminal status of half-freedom proved to be a bridge to full freedom. Shortly before the WIC surrendered Manhattan Island to English invaders in August 1664, the company was forced to consider a petition from some half-free blacks who now demanded the removal of the remaining restrictions on their liberty and the emancipation of their offspring. Eager to secure their allegiance, the WIC acceded to the petitioners' request.[86] In addition to obtaining full freedom for themselves and their children, the petitioners acquired land on Manhattan Island. These black landowners cultivated the so-called free Negro lots, approximately 15 small parcels of farmland that the WIC subtracted from its *bouwerie* east of Hudson Street.[87] Like the *colonus* of the late Roman Empire, Dutch colonial Manhattan's black landowners tended their own farmland on the condition that they pay a yearly tribute of produce to the colonial rulers.[88]

Besides some WIC slaves, a few slaves of individual slaveowners managed to attain freedom. For example, in 1649, Manuel de Spanje purchased his freedom from Phillip Jansz Ringo for 300 guilders, to be paid over three years, and in 1654, Captain Pieter Jacobsz and Jan de Graue manumitted Bastiaen d'Angola, whom they had captured during a privateering venture in the Caribbean Sea but freed as a reward for faithful service.[89] During the decade and a half prior to the English conquest, most slaves brought to New Netherland were sold to individual settlers rather than to the WIC.[90] Even though slaves found it more difficult to obtain freedom from individual owners than from the company, the rise of individual slave ownership did not completely foreclose the possibility of manumission.[91] While a few free blacks in New Amsterdam entered into indentureship and apprenticeship agreements with settlers to avoid privation, most managed to maintain their independence and obtain a modest subsistence from their farmland during the Dutch colonial era.[92] The free blacks of New Amsterdam were never a pariah class. They strived to integrate themselves into the settler community, joining the Dutch Reformed Church,[93] having Dutch Calvinist ministers consecrate their marriages and baptize their children,[94] and organizing a weekly market and an annual fair.[95]

In 1664, New Amsterdam's population included approximately 75 free blacks and 300 enslaved blacks.[96] Even though slaves accounted for a majority of New Amsterdam's African-descended population, the WIC officials in that Dutch colonial port town were less concerned with establishing a rigid biracial social order than with securing the loyalty of the entire colonial population. The Indians (or *wilden*) posed a grave threat to the Dutch colony's survival. In New Netherland anti-Amerindian racism was far more pronounced than antiblack racism. However, losses to the settler population, due to the devastation of war and outmigration, meant that black slavery became more crucial than ever to the Dutch project of colony building in North America. A vital source of labor and military manpower, enslaved laborers were so valuable that on one occasion the WIC authorities commuted the death penalty on several enslaved black men who had committed a capital crime.[97] For the WIC officials in New Amsterdam, the imperatives of colony building outweighed any ethical considerations respecting slaves. Grasping for an expedient solution to the Dutch colony's labor shortage, they imported supplies of enslaved African laborers and kept most Africans and their descendants in lifelong bondage. By 1664, enslaved people of African descent were approximately 20 percent of New Amsterdam's total population of 1,500 inhabitants. This demographic factor gave New Amsterdam the distinction of having the largest proportion of slaves of any North American colony at that time.[98] Like other European colony builders in the Americas, the Dutch colonizers in New Netherland imported involuntary African immigrants without fully appreciating the social and political implications of introducing enslaved Africans into the embryonic colony. The Dutch colony builders were only dimly aware, if at all, that they were laying the foundations for an enduring social order predicated on the subordination of Africans and their descendants.

More evident to the Dutch colonial authorities was the heterogeneity of New Netherland's settler population. Multicultural, polyglot populations were, in fact, spawned everywhere the United Provinces planted colonies. Over time, a diverse assortment of settlers from various societies and cultures trickled into the Dutch colonial outpost on Manhattan Island. During the early phase of colony building, the WIC officials welcomed fellow Calvinists, including Walloons (or French-speaking Calvinists from southern Netherlands), to New Netherland, but banished Lutherans, Quakers, and other religious outsiders from the Dutch colony. Other than a small number of Walloon families, most Calvinists were, however, unwilling to migrate to the WIC's outposts along the Hudson River. Faced with this unforeseen contingency, the WIC rescinded its exclusionary immigration policy, by which the joint-stock company intended to prevent all but adherents to Calvinism from migrating to New Netherland. Gradually, Lutherans, Quakers, Baptists, Mennonites, Anabaptists, and other lesser-known sects were added to the Dutch overseas colony's settler population.[99] As early as 1636, the Dutch Calvinist clergyman Dominie Megapolensis complained that New Amsterdam was becoming a "Babel of Confusion."[100] In 1644, the Catholic priest Father Isaac Jogues reported that in New Netherland "there may well be four or five hundred men of different sects and nations; the Director-General told me that there were persons there of eighteen different languages."[101] George Baxter, the WIC's English translator, later noted that New Netherland's population was "made up of various nations from divers quarters of the globe."[102] New Amsterdam's diverse population doubtless included some peoples of mixed ancestry. Historical records indicate that a free person of Dutch and Moroccan ancestry named Anthony Jansen Van Salee settled in New Amsterdam in 1633 and eventually moved to Breuckelen (later Brooklyn), where he leased 200 acres of land from the WIC. As his place-name suggests, Van Salee was born in Salee, Morocco. His father, Jan Janse, was a Dutch pirate who, for a time, lived in Salee and, during his stay there, had a child with a Moroccan woman. Born of a Dutch father, Van Salee held a claim to natal belonging among the Dutch people, but his dark skin color and adherence to the Islamic faith distinguished him from New Netherland's predominantly Protestant, light-skinned settler population. Settling in New Netherland during the early stage of colonization, when that Dutch colony's labor shortage was most acute, Van Salee was allowed to cultivate his land. The official records, however, note Van Salee's presence in the Dutch North American outpost, referring to him as the "black Mohammedan."[103]

During his tenure as commander of the WIC operations in the Western Hemisphere, Director-General Petrus Stuyvesant (1647–64) bemoaned the WIC's failure to people New Netherland with numerous loyal Dutch settlers and complained to the Estates General that the Dutch overseas colony's diverse settler population hindered the WIC's project of colony building in North

America: "the *English* and *French* colonies are continued and populated by their own nation and countrymen and consequently bound together firmly and united, while your Honors' colonies in New-Netherland are only gradually and slowly peopled by the scrapings of all sorts of nationalities (few excepted) who consequently have the least interest in the welfare and maintenance of the commonwealth."[104] In 1647, at the time Stuyvesant arrived in New Netherland, that Dutch overseas colony's population included few settlers from the affluent region of northern Holland. Nearly 30 percent of the European settlers who migrated to New Netherland between 1630 and 1644 were from the Province of Utrecht, a region ailing from the decline in the linen industry, but the majority of the settlers in Dutch North America were Protestant refugees from the southern Netherlands, Sweden, Denmark, England, and the northern Germanic principalities and the Hansa cities to the east, such as Danzig and Königsberg. During the upheaval of the Thirty Years War (1618–48), these Protestants fled their homelands and with their families traveled first to Holland and then to the Dutch North American outposts.[105] The heterogeneity of New Netherland's settler population was, in large part, a consequence of the fact that the United Provinces and its overseas colonies had become havens for victims of religious persecution and refugees of war from outside Holland.

Holland had long been an asylum for Jewish exiles. With the aid of northern Holland's well-established Jewish community, 25 Jews from Pernambuco, Brazil, migrated to New Amsterdam in 1654.[106] At that time, Dutch Calvinist clergymen in New Amsterdam called for the deportation of these Jewish immigrants, complaining that too many heretics already resided in New Netherland. Dominie Megapolensis reported to the ecclesiastical authorities in Holland: "We have here Papists, Mennonites and Lutherans among the Dutch; also many Puritans or Independents, and many atheists and various other servants of Baal among the English under this Government, who conceal themselves under the name of Christians; it would create a still greater confusion, if the obstinate and immovable Jews came to settle here."[107] The imperious Director-General Stuyvesant despised Jews, who, he believed, would "infect and trouble" New Netherland with "their customary usury and deceitful trading with Christians."[108] Despite the WIC's official policy of extending religious tolerance to settlers, Stuyvesant attempted to expel the Jewish newcomers from New Amsterdam. But a group of Jewish stockholders in Amsterdam used their influence with the WIC officials in Holland to defeat Stuyvesant's deportation plan, reminding the WIC of the Jews' loyalty to the Dutch Republic, the enmity against Catholics that both the Jews and the Dutch Calvinists shared, and the service that the Jews rendered to the United Provinces following the Dutch conquest of the Portuguese overseas colony called Brazil. They argued that Jews ought to be allowed to settle in New Amsterdam and other parts of New Netherland in peace because "yonder land is extensive and spacious. The more of loyal people that go to live there, the better it is in regard to the population of the country." Recounting the Jews' history of alliance with the Dutch Calvinists, they insisted that the Jewish presence in the Dutch overseas colonies strengthened rather than weakened the Dutch Empire. WIC officials in Amsterdam recognized the merit of these arguments and, in 1655, granted the Jewish newcomers in New Amsterdam permission to permanently settle and trade in New Netherland.[109] Nevertheless, Stuyvesant remained hostile to the Jewish settlers and attached numerous restrictions to their privileges: The New Amsterdam Jews were prohibited from owning land, exercising the vote, holding public office, worshiping in public, and possessing firearms.[110] Even so, the Jewish newcomers managed to establish themselves in finance, overseas trade, and modest retail businesses.

When, in 1663, the zealous Calvinist Director-General Stuyvesant renewed his campaign against religious outsiders, such as the Quaker John Browne, and ordered all inhabitants in New Netherland to attend the worship services of the Dutch Reformed Church or else leave the Dutch Calvinist colony, the Estates General reminded him that the WIC must pursue a policy of religious tolerance in order to attract as many settlers as possible to the underpopulated Dutch colonial outposts in North America. The Estates General informed Stuyvesant: "We doubt very much whether we can proceed against [religious heretics] rigourously without diminishing the population and stopping immigration, which must be favoured at a so tender stage of the country's existence. You may therefore shut your eyes, at least not force people's consciences, but allow every one to have his own belief, as long as he behaves quietly and legally, gives no offense to his neighbors and does not oppose the government."[111] With this reaffirmation of the Dutch colonial policy of granting liberty of conscience to the settlers, sundry Protestant denominations and other religious sects found asylum in New Netherland and amplified the heterogeneity of that colony's settler population.

Viewing the linguistic and religious diversity of the settler population as a liability rather than an asset, the WIC officials and the Dutch Calvinist clergy determined to unite New Netherland's diverse settler population around the shared Christian duty of converting the natives and other so-called heathens to Christianity. Hence the Christian "civilizing" mission in North America not only offered the WIC a means of legitimating the project of colony building in an alien land but also provided the trading company with a disciplinary mechanism that could anchor the settlers' collective identity in the common Christian calling of service to God. In this respect, the missionary feature of the WIC's colonization project was principally designed for the promotion of communal cohesion among the settlers and only secondarily for the salvation of the Native Americans and the enslaved Africans. With the goal of encouraging settler solidarity foremost in mind, the WIC commanded the settlers to provide the natives and the slaves with examples of Christian virtue or, as Article Two of the Provisional Conditions of 1624 stated, "by their Christian life and conduct seek to draw Indians and other blind people to the knowledge of God and His Word."[112] Also, the Dutch Reformed Church insisted that the Dutch Calvinist slaveowners in New Netherland should be "responsible for instructing their Negroes in the Christian Religion and that time should be provided for all Negroes to assemble in a suitable place in order to receive instruction from a catechist."[113] For its part, the WIC pledged to take "effectuall care of the propagacon of the Gospel in the several Foreign Plantacons, by providing that there be good encouragement settled for the invitacon and maintenance of learned and orthodox ministers, and . . . to consider how such of the natives or such as are purchased from other parts to be servants and slaves may be best invited to the Christian Faith, and be made capable of being baptised thereunto; it being the honor of our . . . Protestant Religion that all persons in any of our Dominions should be taught the knowledge of God."[114] More interested in making profits than saving souls, the joint-stock company never fulfilled this pledge.

Distracted by border disputes, Indian wars, and other emergencies, the WIC all but abandoned its missionary agenda. As a consequence, the primary responsibility for carrying out the work of converting so-called heathens to Christianity fell to the Classis of Amsterdam, the chief governing body of the Dutch Reformed Church. Writing from New Amsterdam, Dominie Evardus Bogardus begged the Classis to send more ministers to New Netherland, but that ecclesiastical organization dispatched few clergymen to North America. Furthermore, the ministers who migrated to New Netherland rarely traveled beyond New Amsterdam, and those clergymen who did so made only a slight impression on the indigenous people. The records for the entire Dutch colonial period document only one Indian convert to Christianity in New Netherland. According to an extant report, that proselyte could recite the Ten Commandments, read and write Dutch, and give a public testimony of his conversion to Christianity. After two years of captivity, the Indian convert returned to his village, where he was supposed to proselytize among his people. But instead of leading an exemplary Christian life, the Indian soon pawned his Bible for some brandy, the imported liquor for which he had acquired a taste while living among the Christian settlers. This unexpected twist of events prompted Dominie Megapolensis to remark that his protégé had "turned into a regular beast, doing more harm than good among the Indians."[115] Overall, Christianity made only narrow inroads into New Netherland's Indian communities. As late as 1656, Megapolensis wrote: "We can say but little of the conversion of the heathens here, . . . and see no way to accomplish it, until they are subdued by the numbers and powers of our people, and reduced to some sort of civilization."[116] Megapolensis saw no contradiction in linking Christendom's "civilizing" mission to the military conquest of the natives and the occupation of their lands.

Even though the natives experienced devastating military defeats and sweeping transformations in their material culture,[117] they persisted in following their own religious beliefs and practices. In 1655, Adriaen Van der Donck reported that Indian women continued to mourn the dead in accordance with their ancient custom, entering Indian burial grounds with "dreadful and wonderful wailing, naming the dead, smiting upon their breasts, scratching and disfiguring their faces, and showing all possible signs of grief."[118] Van der Donck interpreted these "signs of grief" as the mark of a savage people, whom Christians could legitimately subjugate and dispossess of their lands "on account of their religion, of which," he concluded, "they have very little, and that is very strange."[119] Although Van der Donck admitted that the "savages are not at all excessive, wasteful, wanton, or affluent in their eating and drinking—even during their feast days,"[120] he nevertheless likened the natives, whom the Dutch-speaking invaders called *wilden* after the Latin cognate "savage," to Western Christendom's age-old models of wild men—for example, the Turks, Mamelukes, Tartars, Scythians, and barbarians.[121]

Van der Donck also noted that the Native Americans' skin color resembled that of the ancient Tartars and Scythians.[122] Unaware of the biogenetic mechanism of heredity and its relation to environmental conditions, early modern Europeans relied on available sources of knowledge about the effects of climate and cultural practices on the appearance of human beings to invent explanations for the variation of skin color in humankind. Climatic theories attributed the Native Americans' "olive'" or "tawnie" skin complexion and the sub-Saharan Africans' "black" skin color to overexposure to the sun, whereas anthropological theories attributed such deviations from the presumed epidermal norm of "white" skin pigment to particularistic cultural practices, like the Picts of Scotland's custom of painting their skin blue and the sub-Saharan Africans' alleged habit of putting turbid oil on their skin. In their encounters with Native Americans, early Dutch newcomers to North America, like Megapolensis and Van der Donck, were struck by the differences both of the indigenes' bodily appearance and customs. Importantly, they, like other early modern Europeans, applied a combination of cultural and physiognomic traits as the criteria for assigning individuals to distinct racial categories. In this respect, individuals and groups were "multiply racialized,"[123] as the criteria for defining racial typologies were drawn from multiple fields of perception and cognition.

The era of European colonial expansionism was a formative yet transitional moment in the history of the construction of "race." That concept remained polyvalent for much longer than many scholars have recognized. The historian Colin Kidd reminds us that as late as the eighteenth century "racial discourse remained transitional, a hodgepodge of biological, climatic, and stadialist interpretations of racial and cultural differences."[124] The cultural studies scholar Robert Young writes, "Racial theory was never simply scientific or biologistic."[125] The historian and anthropologist Anne Stoler adds: "There is good evidence that discourses of race did not have to wait mid-nineteenth-century science for their verification. Distinctions of color joined with those of religion and culture to distinguish the rulers from the ruled, invoked in varied measures in the governing strategies of colonial states."[126] The imperatives of European colonial expansionism—the subjugation of the natives, the arrogation of their lands for European occupation, the enslavement of sub-Saharan Africans, and the extension of colonial rule over foreign territories—involved the construction of legitimating discourses of race, grounded in the various knowledge bases available to early modern Europeans, including interpretations of the Bible.

While most Christians of the early modern period accepted the idea of a single act of creation and the notion of the original unity of humankind, by the late sixteenth century influential interpretations of the Bible traced the division of humankind to the postdiluvian migration of the tribes of Shem, Ham, and Japheth to different parts of the world, where they each achieved a distinct level of civilization, ranging from a wanton, lawless existence to an organized mode of life, characterized by language, religion, laws, and political institutions. These readings of the Bible encouraged Christians to regard themselves as the members of a superior subdivision of humankind, which lived and prospered in a renewed covenant with God, and to view the Native Americans and the sub-Saharan Africans as inferior categories of humanity, which Christians could lawfully enslave and divest of their lands. Early modern biblical exegesis also encouraged Christians to believe that Native Americans, sub-Saharan Africans, and other so-called heathens would dwell in spiritual darkness forever, unless they renounced false idols and worshiped the one true God. Confident in their own moral superiority yet acting on the belief that all human beings had souls worthy of saving, the European colonizers embarked on a "civilizing" mission of converting the "heathens" in foreign lands to Christianity.

A supplement to the WIC's project of colony building in North America, missionary colonialism involved the transplantation of Christianity in the hearts and minds of the natives. But few natives embraced the Calvinist version of Christianity. Here, the lack of a common yet sophisticated spoken language obstructed the Dutch Calvinist proselytizing mission among the natives. The Dutch Calvinist clergyman Dominie Jonas Michaëlius pointed out that he and other Christian missionaries communicated with the indigenes "as much by signs with the thumb and finger as by speaking, and this cannot be done in religious matters."[127] Frustrated by the apparent futility of his missionary work, Michaëlius concluded that the natives were incapable of comprehending the basic tenets of the Christian belief system. "If we speak to them of God," he reported, "it appears to them as a dream."[128] Like the early European explorer Henry Hudson, Dominie Michaëlius perceived the indigenous population through an ethnocentric lens, which rendered him unable to recognize Native American culture as a civilized mode of life, with its own laws and legitimate religious institutions, beliefs, and practices. The Dutch Calvinist minister stated:

> As to the natives of this country, I find them entirely savage and wild, strangers to all decency, yea, uncivil and stupid as garden poles, proficient in all wickedness and godlessness; devilish men, who serve nobody but the Devil, that is, the spirit which in their language they call Menetto; under which title they comprehend everything that is subtle and crafty and beyond human will and power. They have so much witchcraft, divination, sorcery, and wicked arts, that they can hardly be held in by bands and locks. They are as thievish and treacherous as they are tall; and in cruelty they are altogether inhuman more than barbarous, far exceeding the Africans.[129]

For the most part, Michaëlius's commentary on Native Americans focused on descriptions of their religion and culture. But he also mentioned the natives' surface bodily appearance when he thought it served as an index to their inner moral disposition. For instance, the Dutch Calvinist cleric drew a correlation between the natives' "tall" stature and their "thievish and treacherous" character. Here, the imputed indexicality of a visible bodily trait to an invisible moral disposition calls attention to the integrality of the regime of visuality to the history of racial formation and to the multiple registers in which the process of racialization takes place. As Michaëlius saw it, the natives' tallness, a visible physiognomic trait, in combination with their untrustworthiness, an invisible moral trait, made it possible to assign the indigenes to a classification of human beings whose members shared that unique ensemble of traits. Perhaps Michaëlius drew a correlation between the Indians' "tallness" and their putative "thievish and treacherous" behavior because the two traits are deviations from the classical Western European aesthetic values of balance, symmetry, virtue, and moderation. Ultimately, Michaëlius perceived Native American culture as a site of excess and the entire indigenous population as monstrous savages whose cruelty was "altogether inhuman" and "more than barbarous, far exceeding the Africans." With this assessment, he exiled the natives to the remote frontier of abject inhumanity. In this respect, Michaëlius's views on Native Americans already express the logical extreme of racism, not some neutral commentary on cultural alterity or a benign classification schema. This same pattern of perception and cognition structured and enabled the Dutch colonialist war of extermination against the coastal Indian population during the 1640s.

At the precise moment Amerindian-European relations in New Netherland deteriorated into bloody warfare, the Dutch Calvinist clergymen quit their proselytizing activities among the natives and turned their attention to the enslaved Africans, who, because of their enslavement, were considered to be less incorrigible than the indigenes.[130] These clergymen agreed with a Calvinist church elder when, in 1641, he wrote: "The Americans (Indians) come not yet to the right knowledge of God; but the Negroes, living among the settlers, come nearer thereto, and give better hope."[131] Believing that enslaved Africans possessed souls worthy of saving, Dominie Hendrick Selijns baptized several slaves during the early phase of his career in New Netherland.[132] Upon finding that Selijns had christened adult slaves without first providing them with instruction in Christian doctrine and obtaining a testimony of faith from each candidate, the Classis of Amsterdam began to worry that the Dutch Calvinist "civilizing" mission in New Netherland would result in the erosion of the hard-won distinction between Reformed Protestants and Papists. Importantly, Christendom of the post-Reformation era included several Reformed churches, each grounded in the emphasis placed on a laity that could comprehend the word of God.[133] In sharp contrast to the Roman Catholic practice of performing indiscriminate mass baptisms of adult slaves, the Dutch Reformed Church required all adult candidates to submit a profession of faith that demonstrated a correct understanding of the basic tenets of Protestantism before they were admitted to the sacrament of baptism.[134] With the objective of preserving the strict doctrines of Calvinism, outlined in the Heidelberg Confession (1562) and reaffirmed in the Canons of Dort (1619), firmly in mind, the Classis of Amsterdam informed Selijns that its rules pertained to enslaved Africans and other so-called heathens also: "The Classis deems it necessary that you observe the good rule of the church here in this land, where no one, who is an adult, is admitted to baptism without previous confession of faith. Accordingly, the adult Negroes and Indians must also be previously instructed and make a confession of their faith before Holy Baptism may be administered to them. As to their children, the Classis answers, that as long as the parents are actually heathens, although they were baptised in the gross (by wholesale, by Papists), the children may not be baptised, unless the parents pass over to Christianity, and abandon heathenism."[135] As a consequence of these restrictions, few adults of African descent were baptized and admitted to membership in New Amsterdam's Dutch Reformed Church. Between 1639 and 1655, the Dutch Calvinist ministers baptized only 57 converts of African descent; of that number, 49 converts were children. Conspicuously, they baptized no African-descended people between 1656 and 1664.[136] A visibly distinctive and culturally alien presence, the enslaved black African population served as a counterpoint for the settlers' self-identification as Christians and, more specifically, as post-Reformation Protestants.

Though largely a fruitless endeavor, the Dutch Calvinist "civilizing" mission of converting slaves to Christianity, combined with the Dutch Republic's avowed commitment to the principle of liberty, rendered the binarism of free Christian/enslaved heathen open to contestation. Since the thirteenth century, wage labor and various forms of temporary servitude had, in most parts of Western Europe including the Netherlands, gradually replaced the condition of bondage known as serfdom.[137] Early modern Hollanders took enormous pride in their liberty, zealously guarded it, and even refused to condone the enslavement of black Africans in the Dutch Republic.[138] Although Dutch privateers had been seizing African-descended people from enemy sailing vessels and selling them in the Americas since around 1609, the directors of the WIC, known as the Heeren XIX, were for a time divided over the question of the legitimacy of enslaving black Africans and their descendants. It was not until the WIC captured Recife, Brazil, in 1635 and gradually expanded into much of Pernambuco that the imperatives of developing that valuable overseas territory and the profits from the lucrative Brazilian slave market became an irresistible argument for the formulation of an unequivocal company policy sanctioning the transatlantic slave trade. At that time the Heeren XIX decided that, if the WIC were going to benefit from its enterprises in the Western Hemisphere, it must not only actively engage in the slave traffic but also exploit enslaved laborers in its own colony-building projects. At about the same time the Dutch jurist Hugo Grotius, citing Roman and Hebrew laws, endorsed the institution of slavery. Other pundits at the University of Leiden offered specific justification for the enslavement of sub-Saharan Africans, citing Genesis, Leviticus, and other biblical texts.[139] By the end of the 1630s, the authorities in Holland had sanctioned black slavery in the Dutch overseas colonies but not in the Dutch Republic. This elite consensus did not end all controversy over the enslavement of black Africans and their descendants, however.

The status of several slave children became the object of controversy, when, in 1649, some Protestant settlers in New Netherland sent a remonstrance to Holland, calling on the Estates General to ban the WIC from enslaving the offspring of the free black Christians who inhabited the Dutch outposts in North America. The WIC enslaved these children, the petitioners asserted, "though it is contrary to the laws of every Christian people that anyone born of a free

Christian mother should be a slave and be compelled to remain in servitude."[140] In defense of its actions, the WIC replied that there were only three such slave children in New Netherland and that all lived in Christian households and received humane treatment from their masters. Black Africans benefited from their enslavement, the WIC argued, because it placed them under the civilizing influence of Christians.[141] The Dutch Calvinist clergy's dismal slave conversion record belied the WIC's claims, however. Dominie Selijns explained that the Classis of Amsterdam required him to follow its restrictive rules of admission to the sacrament of baptism and that he now refused to baptize adult slaves, "partly on account of their lack of knowledge and of faith, and partly because of the worldly and perverse aims on the part of said negroes." "They wanted nothing else," he added, "than to deliver their children from bodily slavery, without striving for piety and christian virtues."[142] By excluding these adult slaves from the baptismal rite, Dominie Selijns obeyed the "good rule" of the Dutch Reformed Church. But the Estates General never issued a clear statement on the WIC's practice of enslaving the offspring of free black Christians. Compounding that ambiguity, neither the Estates General nor the WIC ever promulgated a civil law that explicitly sanctioned the institution of slavery in New Netherland. For this and other reasons, the status of black Africans and their offspring remained open to contestation, as the 1649 remonstrance and the successful petitions of the free blacks of New Amsterdam demonstrate.

In 1657, some Protestant settlers in Flushing, Queens, sent a remonstrance to the Estates General, accusing the WIC of violating the Dutch Republic's avowed principle of extending liberty and Christian brotherhood to all people. That complaint raised fundamental objections against the enslavement of black Africans and their descendants in the Dutch overseas colonies. "The law of love, peace and liberty in the States [United Provinces]," the settlers wrote, "extends to the Jews, Turks, and Egyptians, as they are considered the sons of Adam, which is the glory of the outward state of Holland."[143] With this reference to the "sons of Adam," the Flushing settlers dismissed proslavery arguments that defended the enslavement of black Africans on the grounds that these dark-skinned people bore the Noachidian curse on the sons of Ham and were therefore lawfully enslaved. Asserting the notion of the essential unity and single origin of humankind, the settlers tacitly countered that, while sub-Saharan Africans could not be definitively traced to Ham and his descendants, they were irrefutably the sons of Adam, as were all human beings, and therefore ought to be treated like the rest of Adam's lineage. In its defense, the WIC offered no elaborate justification for its enslavement of black Africans and merely noted that the joint-stock company followed the well-known example of other European colony builders in New Spain, Brazil, and the Caribbean.[144]

As a result of the Dutch colonization projects in the Western Hemisphere and engagement in the transatlantic slave trade, enslaved Africans could be found laboring at Dutch outposts throughout the Atlantic world, in military regiments that protected Dutch colonial possessions in that part of the globe, and on Dutch ships that sailed the oceans. Importantly, the slave trade and the exploitation of slave labor in the overseas colonies underwrote the high standard of living that made seventeenth-century Holland the envy of rival nations. Sugar, tobacco, coffee, and other colonial produce cultivated by enslaved African laborers were among the "embarrassment of riches" daily consumed in the affluent United Provinces during the early modern era.[145]

Despite their enviable record in extracting wealth from foreign lands, the Dutch colonizers discovered that the realities of the North American frontier seldom, if ever, matched their ideal vision of the New World, which beguiled even the cautious Dutch Calvinist burgher in Amsterdam. The erection of forts for security and trade in a distant territory, the subjugation of hostile natives, and the recruitment of settlers and the importation of a slave labor force for the permanent occupation and improvement of conquered lands made the project of colonization a costly venture. Because the WIC's business enterprise in North America was only a small component of the broader network of supply and market zones that comprised its commercial empire, that joint-stock company invested meager resources in developing New Netherland into a viable settler colony and directed most of its personnel, as well as the greatest part of its venture capital, toward the development of its lucrative trading forts along the Amazon River and the African littoral. By the 1650s, the WIC sent only two ships each year to New Amsterdam.[146]

Moreover, the WIC proved ill equipped to exercise the art of colonial governance. The veteran military officers whom the WIC sent to rule New Netherland not only plunged that Dutch North American colony into a ruinous war against the natives and mishandled border disputes with the settlers in the neighboring colonies of rival nations but also estranged New Netherland's settler population from the colonial government by curtailing the settlers' liberties. Some Dutch Calvinist clerics believed that life on the colonial frontier had transformed the settlers into a lawless people who resembled savages. Writing 30 years after the founding of New Amsterdam, Dominie Johannes Cornelissen Backerus reported on the moral degeneracy of the settlers: "Most of [the settlers] are very ignorant in regard to true religion [Christianity], and very much given to drink."[147] When, in 1638, the WIC banned the sale of guns and ammunition to the natives and, in 1648, outlawed the traffic in alcohol,[148] the settlers ignored these regulations and continued to supply the natives with firearms, gunpowder, and strong liquor. Reviewing the settlers' record of violating the WIC's laws, Director-General Stuyvesant concluded that the settler population must be subjected to stricter measures of discipline. Endowed with broad judicial and governmental powers, Stuyvesant ruled New Netherland by martial law, which he deemed suitable for the project of colony building. His government imposed order by closing New Amsterdam's taverns after nine o'clock at night, punishing public drunkenness and breaking the Sabbath, jailing outspoken critics, and commissioning a police force, known as the Rattle Watch, to monitor New Amsterdam's population and enforce the law. Stuyvesant's policy of law and order widened the rift between the settler population and the WIC.

In 1649, a group of settlers, known as the Nine Men, sent the Estates General a petition, protesting Stuyvesant's autocratic rule and demanding political reforms, including local autonomy for towns, a court system based on the Amsterdam model, and the regular election of public officials in which eligible settlers exercised the right to vote. Following three years of deliberations, the Estates General ordered Stuyvesant to implement the requested reforms. Although other towns in New Netherland had already won a large measure of autonomy—for example, Gravesend in 1645, Breuckelen in 1646, and Hempstead in 1646—the WIC remained reluctant to relinquish its governmental powers, especially concerning New Amsterdam, its most valuable outpost in North America. In the case of New Amsterdam, Stuyvesant had circumvented popular participation in governmental affairs by installing a clique of colonial elites that ruled the fledgling port town as the WIC's puppet government until 1652, when New Amsterdam's settler population won the right to hold municipal elections without interference from the WIC. This political reform came too late to placate disgruntled settlers. Years of hardship under the WIC's quasi-military government had eroded settler loyalty at the United Provinces' only fortress in North America with any chance of repelling foreign invaders.[149]

Internal discord eventually rendered New Amsterdam vulnerable to the rival European nations pressing against New Netherland's borders. Stuyvesant perceived the Swedish colony Fort Christina along the Delaware River as a potential threat to the integrity of New Netherland's southern border, and in 1655 he dispatched a military expedition to subdue the Swedish Lutherans.[150] Some natives seized the strategic advantage presented by the split between competing European invaders and, while the Dutch military forces were away fighting the Swedes, attacked vulnerable Dutch outposts, vandalized houses on Manhattan Island, burned twenty-eight farms in the Pavonia area, and killed fifty settlers along the Hudson River. Faced with this new crisis, known as the Peach Tree War, Stuyvesant appealed to all Europeans in the region—Swedes, Dutch, and English—to resolve their differences and band together in "Christian unity . . . in drawing a line to keep the barbarians in submission or at least quiet."[151] However, Stuyvesant's call for Christian solidarity produced no enduring agreement of interest between the rival European colonizers in North America.

At the time of the restoration of Charles II to the English throne in 1660, England, the United Provinces' most aggressive challenger in the international competition among the European maritime powers, cast a covetous gaze toward the Dutch outposts situated in the midst of the British North American colonies. Despite many setbacks and false starts, the WIC had managed to transform New Amsterdam into an embryonic port town with a stone fort, palisades, windmill, counting house, canals, two rustic churches, and 120 dwellings. The Dutch colony builders were also beginning to develop the surrounding countryside into a productive agricultural hinterland, with the help of European farming families that, during the 1650s, migrated to New Netherland in larger numbers than in previous years.[152] Nevertheless, by 1664, Dutch occupation of the expansive territory of New Netherland was slight, especially compared with the more populous English colonies to the north and the south. For example, at that time Virginia had 40,000 inhabitants and New England had 50,000 inhabitants, while New Netherland had at most 9,000 inhabitants. The United Provinces' claim to New Netherland was tenuous at best, based as it was on the slender occupation of a vast territorial domain. England's King Charles II claimed the region that encompassed New Netherland and, in 1663, granted that territory to his younger brother, the Duke of York. Encouraged by Dutch impassivity toward the English presence within the jurisdiction of New Netherland—for example, on the eastern shore of Long Island and the Hudson Valley frontier—England determined to dislodge the Dutch Republic from its desirable but weakly held North American territory. On August 8, 1664, Richard Nicolls, Charles II's commissioner, entered Nyack Bay and, with the backing of four warships, obtained the bloodless surrender of New Amsterdam on Manhattan Island and the rest of New Netherland.[153] Unanticipated obstacles and unforeseen antagonisms had dissolved the Dutch colony builders' utopian dream of unobstructed conquest, occupation, and exploitation of foreign lands.

"Nothing That Is Necessary Is to Be Discouraged"

IMMIGRATION, LABOR, AND THE PROJECT OF COLONY BUILDING
UNDER ENGLISH RULE, 1664–1774

Instead of placing the project of occupying and developing the recently conquered territory, formerly known as New Netherland and renamed New York, in the hands of a trading company, as the Estates General of the United Provinces had done, the English monarch, King Charles II (1660–85), entrusted that task to his brother, the Duke of York. In its entirety, the Duke's North American province included a tract of land stretching from the Connecticut River to the Delaware River, a coastal area along Long Island, Martha's Vineyard and Nantucket, and part of the present state of Maine between the St. Croix and Kennebec rivers. At the time of the English conquest of New Netherland in 1664, there were only a few colonial outposts in that area, and these settler enclaves—in the Hudson Valley, Long Island, Westchester County, and Manhattan Island—were scarcely sufficient to secure England's claim to such an extensive territorial domain. To establish an incontestable hold on New York, the early English colony builders planned to people that thinly populated region with loyal British subjects. Based on the feudalistic model of colonial Ireland, England's first overseas colony,[1] the initial colonization scheme for New York called for the transportation of numerous British tenants to the North American manorial estates of favored landlords, who had received enormous allotments of land in New York as a reward for their allegiance to the Stuart monarchy. But other than some English colonial officials, adventurers, and traders, few migrants from the British Isles permanently settled in New York during the early years of English rule. The historian Joyce Goodfriend has noted that the high rate of outmigration among these newcomers retarded the growth of the colony's settler population.[2] New York's first colonial governor, Richard

Nicolls (1665–72), explained that British settlers "are blowne up with large designes, but not knowing the knack of trading here to differ from most places, they meet with discouragements and stay not to become wiser."[3] If, as Nicolls suggested, British settlers left New York after only a short stay because they lacked the patience that would have enabled them to learn the colony's particular trading customs and thereby prosper, British newcomers, nonetheless, understood that New York offered them fewer opportunities for an independent life than other British North American colonies, where the transformative dynamics of modernity were elevating penniless peasants, who had been uprooted by the devastations of war, the enclosure of land, high rents, and the deterioration of the cottage industries in their homeland, to the level of independent landowners. However much the early English colony builders hoped to recruit loyal British subjects to occupy and develop the land in New York, they could not rely on their own countrymen to people that overseas colony. To their dismay, nothing like the numerous tenants of the sort that English colony builders had transported to colonial Ireland permanently settled in the Duke of York's North American province.

England valued New York and the other English overseas colonies as vehicles for achieving the mercantilist goal of national self-sufficiency in the context of domestic upheaval, intensifying economic competition, and international war. Writing about the ideal relation between the nation and the colonies, the Bristol merchant John Carey remarked: "I take England and all its plantations to be one great Body, those being so many limbs or countries belonging to it, therefore when we consume their growth we do as it were spend the Fruits of our own Land, and what thereof we sell to our Neighbours for Bullion, or such commodities as must pay for therein, brings a second Profit to the Nation. . . . This was the first design of settling Plantations abroad, that the People of England might better maintain a Commerce and Trade among themselves, the chief Profit whereof was to redound to the centre."[4] According to Carey, the English overseas colonies were subordinate appendages of the nation and should, therefore, serve England's national interest by contributing to the accumulation of wealth in the metropolitan core. To ensure that England's colonial possessions fulfilled their purpose, the English Parliament of the Restoration Era passed several laws that excluded rival maritime nations from the carrying trade to and from the English overseas colonies: The Navigation Act of 1660 granted English merchants a monopoly on the shipping and the marketing of a list of colonial goods; the Staple Act of 1663 ordered that all European manufactured goods must be carried in English sailing vessels and pass through an English port before being shipped to any part of the British Empire; and the Navigation Act of 1673 required merchants in the English overseas colonies to post a bond of indemnity against violations of the commerce laws, as well as pay a "plantation duty" on produce shipped from colonial seaports.[5] In addition, England's Privy Council devised an administrative apparatus for enforcing these regulations and implementing colonial policy. However, the imperial administration lacked effective centralized controls. The result was an absence of coordination on the part of various overlapping and ill-organized jurisdictions, confused policies, opposing agendas, and the rapid turnover of colonial officials, all of which made the cumbersome task of managing the English overseas colonies more, rather than less, unwieldy.

England's Glorious Revolution of 1688–89 and the demise of the Restoration monarchy marked a shift from the social relations of feudalism and the

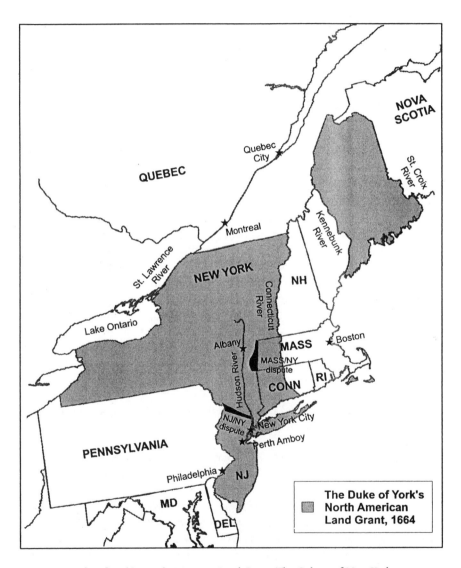

Figure 2.1. Duke of York's North American Land Grant: The Colony of New York

seignorial values of the English aristocracy toward the social relations of capitalist production and the laissez-faire values of the rising English bourgeoisie. Though they remained partly feudalistic in design, the English overseas colonies increasingly became an investment outlet for English capitalists, who now played an influential role in shaping England's domestic and colonial policies. Providing vital services, such as the shipment of goods, the transportation of people, and the transfer of money from one place to another, independent English merchants and their ships, wharves, warehouses, counting houses, and financial networks became the principal articulators linking the scattered territories of the first British Empire.[6]

English colony builders of the post-Restoration era continued to promote British emigration to New York. But prior to the 1770s, most British migrants preferred to settle in other British North American colonies, where they, many believed, had a better chance of attaining personal autonomy than in New York. Consequently, the promoters of colonization had to rely on people from various societies outside the British metropolitan core to populate New York. Stressing the sharp contrast between the population movements that shaped colonial New England and those that molded colonial New York, the historian Bernard Bailyn notes that, by 1700, New England's relatively homogeneous communities had developed out of a single, largely uniform demographic process, while New York's more heterogeneous communities were the product of "diversity of the most extreme kind, and not a single expanding network of communities impelled outward by the dynamic of a distinctive demographic process, but half a dozen different demographic processes moving in different phases at different speeds."[7] Populated by a diverse assortment of people deposited by multiple Eurodiasporic and Afrodiasporic population movements, colonial New York was, as the historian Michael Kammen has noted, unique among the English overseas colonies.[8] Especially notable was the heterogeneity of colonial New York City's population. According to a description of that port town, written in 1670, Dutch, Walloons, English, French, Africans, Swedes, Finns, Germans, and Irish inhabited the seaport at the tip of Manhattan Island. In addition to many Protestant congregations, an untold number of Dunkers, Quakers, Anabaptists, and other sects, as well as a few Jews, Catholics, African conjurors, and atheists, resided in colonial New York City.[9]

Over time, an international labor force of free, indentured, and enslaved laborers transformed colonial New York City from a frontier outpost into a bustling entrepôt. Also, this mixed labor force gradually developed the surrounding hinterland into a commercial farming district, which produced a variety of foodstuffs and other provisions for the city market and for export to England's major seaports, southern Europe, the staple-producing colonies in the English and foreign West Indies, the coast of British North America, Suriname, and Madeira.[10] With its multicultural, polyglot settler population of independent merchants, artisans, and farmers, whose identity was, in large part, anchored in property ownership, including the ownership of enslaved blacks, colonial Manhattan and the adjacent territory scarcely resembled the early English colony builders' initial feudalistic vision of a culturally homogeneous overseas settler colony of numerous loyal British tenants who paid rents to a clique of privileged landlords.

The idea that settlers from a single source—namely, the British Isles—would be a majority of New York's population became less and less realistic, as immigrants from various parts of Europe arrived at the port of New York in numbers that far exceeded the influx of British migrants. In 1687, Governor Thomas Dongan (1682–88) remarked: "I believe for these 7 years past, there has not come over into this province twenty English Scotch or Irish familys. But of French there have since my coming here several familys . . . & a great many more are expected . . . which is another great argument of the necessity of adding to this Government that a more equal ballance may be kept here between his Majesty's naturall born subjects and Foreigners which latter are the most prevailing part of this Government."[11] As Governor Dongan indicated, immigration flows into New York's seaport during the 1680s deposited mostly French-speaking Protestants, also known as Huguenots. Following Louis XIV's revocation of the Edict of Nantes in 1685, these Protestants were forced to flee France to escape persecution under Catholic rule. Before migrating to New York, Huguenot refugees resided for a time in Amsterdam, Geneva, London, and other Protestant strongholds in Europe. Of the several French Protestant exile communities, London's Huguenot enclave contributed the largest number of French Protestants who settled in colonial New York City.[12]

In addition to the Huguenot settlers, several well-to-do families from Jewish exile communities in London, Suriname, and Curaçao disembarked at the port of New York during the early English colonial period, between 1690 and 1710.[13] Descendants of the Sephardim, whom Catholic rulers expelled from Portugal and Spain in 1492, these Jewish immigrants—for example, the Gomez and the Pachecos families—joined the earlier Sephardic settlers—the Levy, the Lucena, and the Israel families—who left Brazil and migrated to Manhattan Island in 1654. Included in the flow of Jewish immigrants from London were some Ashkenazic Jews, such as the Franks and Simson families. Additionally, German-speaking and Polish-speaking Ashkenazim from central Europe arrived at the port of New York during King George's War (1744–48). A final installment of Jewish immigrants, a dozen or so Venetian Jews, settled in New York City on the eve of the American Revolution.[14] Although New York City attracted the largest number of Jewish immigrants of any port town in British North America, there was no massive, sustained influx of Jewish sojourners into New York's seaport during the English colonial era. Jewish immigration flows contributed no more than 200 to 300 settlers to colonial New York's total population; by 1775, only 400 Jews resided in New York City. Like the Dutch colonial authorities in New Netherland, the English colonial rulers in New York imposed political and economic restraints on the Jews. But these restrictions were not the main deterrents to the relocation of

Jews to New York. So few Jews settled in that English overseas colony and other parts of British North America largely because the expansion of commerce in European cities and business opportunities in the Caribbean basin proved to be powerful anchors keeping Jews close to the older Jewish exile communities.[15] Nevertheless, the Jewish shopkeepers, merchants, shippers, and moneylenders who ventured to colonial New York City thrived in that colonial port town and established a small but well-to-do Jewish community, which contributed to the diversity of the city's population.

Besides the Ashkenazic Jews, central Europe yielded another, more substantial influx of immigrants into the port of New York. A considerable number of Protestants from the Palatinate, Mainz, Baden, and Württemberg principalities of Germany and from Kraków, Poland, arrived at New York's seaport during the English colonial period. These newcomers were destitute refugees whose homelands had been devastated by two destructive wars—the War of the League of Augsburg (1689–97),[16] or King William's War, and the War of Spanish Succession (1702–13),[17] or Queen Anne's War. The severe winter of 1708–9 and religious persecution accelerated the Protestant exodus from Europe. Owing to Queen Anne's gift of free passage to the English overseas settler colonies, Protestant refugees from the Rhenish Palatinate looked to British North America as a sanctuary where they might enjoy liberty of conscience without fear of harassment from tyrannical Catholic princes.[18] A sudden and heavy influx of nearly 2,400 Palatines arrived at the port of New York in 1709–10. Disease had overtaken these German-speaking travelers during their transatlantic voyage, and they arrived at New York's seaport in wretched physical condition. New York City's municipal government was ill prepared to attend to the wants of so many distressed newcomers. Citing the health threat that these ailing immigrants posed to the port town, the municipal government prevented the Palatines from entering the city and quarantined them on Governor's Island.[19] During the first month of their confinement, the Palatines lived in tents without proper heating and drainage, a setting that led to the spread of contagious diseases. Some Palatine newcomers never recovered from the maladies that they contracted during the transatlantic passage to New York City and during their internment on Governor's Island. Within a year of their arrival at the port of New York, no fewer than 226 Palatines died of typhus and other ailments. To alleviate the burden of caring for the surviving newcomers, the municipal government sold Palatine orphans and indigent adults into indentured servitude.[20]

Although recruiters assured prospective European immigrants that they would be well treated once they arrived in the English overseas settler colonies, news about the degrading treatment that the German-speaking immigrants received in colonial New York City eventually made its way to the Rhenish Palatinate.[21] It was not until 1722, nearly 15 years after the initial Palatines disembarked at the port of New York, that New York City witnessed another influx of immigrants from the Rhineland—a total of only 40 Palatines. Most of these German-speaking Lutherans soon left the city and removed to the remote Mohawk Valley with their pastor, Reverend John James Ehlig.[22] Between January 1738 and April 1739, just before the War of Jenkin's Ear (1739–43) curtailed the flow of European immigrants across the Atlantic Ocean,[23] 534 German-speaking Lutherans from Swabia arrived at New York's seaport.[24] Some of these newcomers eventually moved to Pennsylvania, while others stayed in New York City. Between October 1753 and October 1754, the port of New York received a heavy influx of 2,006 Palatines.[25] This was the final documented installment of Palatines that entered New York's seaport during the English colonial period. For the most part, these German speakers settled in Pennsylvania, where they became independent farmers, though some were sold into indentured servitude at New York City.[26]

Intermittent flows of Scots-Irish migrants from two northern ports of colonial Ireland—Londonderry and Newry—joined the sporadic influx of immigrants from Europe.[27] Often confused with the indigenous Gaelic-speaking Irish, whom the English colonizers drove from the Ulster plains following victory in the Tyrone War (1594–1603) and the aftermath of a defeated Irish uprising in 1641, the Scots-Irish or Ulster Scots were the Irish-born descendants of Scottish tenants who, beginning around 1609, occupied the lands of the vanquished Celt and Catholic natives.[28] By 1715, the deterioration of the linen industry and ruinous rents prompted an exodus of tenant weavers from Ulster. Although a small number of Gaelic-speaking Catholics migrated to colonial New York City, most newcomers from Ulster were Scots-Irish. In addition to the impetus of economic hardship, Anglican efforts to obstruct the establishment of a presbytery in colonial Ireland precipitated the migration of Scots-Irish Presbyterians to British North America, where Ulster Presbyterians hoped to found their own churches without interference from the Church of England.[29] Writing from New York City in 1737, James Murray, a Scots-Irish settler, asked a kinsman in Ulster to inform the impoverished tenants and weavers in Tyrone County that "God has open'd a Door for their Deliverance" in New York.[30] New York City needed skilled workers, and the *Belfast News Letter* announced: "Sundry artificers—a gunsmith, house carpenter, blacksmith, cooper, brick layer, and a leather dresser"[31] were wanted in that colonial North American port town. When recruiters visited Ulster, they assured the rapidly growing and burdened population that they would find ample opportunities to pursue an independent livelihood and to worship according to the dictates of their consciences, if they settled in New York. Between 1728 and 1754, nearly 900 Ulster Scots responded to these promises and exchanged the proceeds from the sale of their meager belongings for the price of a ticket to New York City.[32] In 1763, nearly two dozen Scots-Irish migrants from Newry and environs disembarked at the seaport of New York; and one year later another 300 Scots-Irish migrants, led by the Presbyterian minister and physician Thomas Clark, arrived at the port town on Manhattan Island. Except for the craftsmen whose skills were at that time in great demand in New York City, these Scots-Irish migrants soon left New York and removed to colonies that offered them better opportunities to become independent farmers. In Ulster, recruiting agents and printed notices advertised the advantages of relocation to Pennsylvania and North Carolina. These British North American colonies successfully recruited Scots-Irish settlers with the enticement of liberal land policies and other attractive incentives.

In contrast, New York remained an unattractive final destination for British migrants prior to the 1770s. In that colony a small number of prominent families—for example, the Bayards, the Livingstons, the Philipses, and the Van Cortlandts—engrossed huge tracts of land, which New York's colonial governors bestowed on them in exchange for their loyalty to the English Crown. As a rule, these landlords preferred to keep their estates intact and leased, instead of sold, land to tenants.³³ Since most British newcomers preferred to cultivate their own farmland rather than work leaseholds, these migrants mostly shunned New York. Although many more immigrants from Europe passed through the port of New York, they, too, mainly resettled outside New York, in British North American colonies that offered them better opportunities to purchase cheap land.

During the years immediately preceding the War for Independence, New York suddenly became a popular destination for British migrants. The British Isles, not Europe, then supplied that colony with permanent settlers. According to Bernard Bailyn, of the total number of British migrants that removed to the settler colonies in British North America between 1773 and 1775, nearly 20 percent settled in New York, of which less than 2 percent came from England and approximately 85 percent came from Scotland.³⁴ The majority of the migrants from England were Yorkshire farming families. Only 40 migrants came from London and the Thames Valley, a location that, in general, contributed mostly young, unmarried men to the flow of British migrants into British North America. Very few artisans from London and the Thames Valley removed to New York City. A majority of the British artisans who arrived at the port of New York on the eve of the Revolution came from the West Lowlands of Scotland, where the decay of the textile industry caused high unemployment rates among Scottish weavers. This circumstance inspired these West Lowlanders to leave their homeland and travel to colonial New York City in search of employment.³⁵ Inhabitants from other regions of Scotland also found removal to New York to be an attractive prospect. Nearly all British migrants who disembarked at the port of New York between 1773 and 1775 were members of farming families from the Highlands and Hebrides of Scotland. Scottish farming families removed to New York to escape straitened economic conditions and dim personal futures in their homeland. They, along with other British migrants, eventually flocked into up-country New York and settled on farmland in the newly opened colonial frontier that encompassed the Mohawk, Schoharie, and Upper Susquehanna river valleys.³⁶ In December 1773, Daniel M'Leod, Esq. of Killmorrie, solicited proposals from New York landlords who wished to recruit Scottish settlers to occupy and cultivate their large parcels of upcountry farmland.³⁷ By the outbreak of the War for Independence, approximately 6,000 to 7,000 tenants, mostly from Scotland, lived in New York. Most tenants obtained favorable leasehold terms and, since tenancy was generally a temporary condition for settlers in New York, many eventually achieved freeholder status.³⁸ All told, the main result of the British migration flow of the 1770s was to transform up-country New York's virgin lands into a flourishing agricultural region. In addition, the arrival of large numbers of British migrants at the port of New York during the

1770s transformed New York City into what Bernard Bailyn calls a "staging center for the distribution of immigrants into the far northern frontier."[39] Although only a small fraction of the total number of British migrants that disembarked at New York's seaport just before the onset of the War for Independence settled in the city, British newcomers doubtless added to the growing ranks of propertyless towndwellers and contributed to the accretion of New York City's permanent population from approximately 22, 000 inhabitants in 1771 to nearly 25,000 inhabitants in 1775.[40]

In contrast to emigrants from London and the Thames Valley, who generally sailed in cargo vessels that carried relatively few passengers, perhaps no more than 20 or 30 travelers,[41] Scottish emigrants were more likely to travel on sailing vessels that specialized in the transport of settlers to the English overseas colonies, seldom carried fewer then 50 passengers, and, on occasion, transported as many as 500 passengers.[42] For some Scottish emigrants, the transatlantic passage was a traumatic adventure, since the merchants who were engaged in the business of transporting British laborers across the Atlantic Ocean did not always hire vessels outfitted with adequate living space and sufficient provisions. Furthermore, the captains and crews sometimes displayed little concern for the welfare of their passengers and at times treated them no better than slaves. On September 17, 1773, approximately 300 migrants from the Highlands of Scotland boarded a brig called the *Nancy* and, from the harbor of Muckle Ferry in the vicinity of Dornoch in Sutherland, began an overseas journey to the port of New York. The newspaper accounts of the *Nancy*'s voyage reported several instances of the mistreatment of the Scottish passengers during their 10-week voyage:

> One Woman, who with a little skillet, was warming some of her Meal and Water at the Fire, by the tossing of the Ship, or some other Accident, happen to spill some of it on Deck, was seized by the shoulders, and dragged over it to wipe it up with her clothes, and the Rest of her Meals thrown over board. Another Woman was struck on the Breast by one of the Men, and so much hurt, that her life [was] in Danger. A poor sick Child, who could not drink the Water afforded them, which stunk intolerably, earnestly begged for a little good warm Water, and not being able to obtain it, continued to call for it till he died. Another poor Child having got to the Fire, the Mate took him up, and dashed him against the Deck, where by he was much hurt, and confined to his bed till he died, about a fortnight after. A young Man who used sometimes to assist the Seamen in working the Vessel, being wanted for that Purpose when he was below, eating his unsavory Meal, the Captain ran to him, seized the Hair of his Head, and by it dragged Him up four Steps to the Deck, throwing him to the Wind a handful of the hair which was left in his Hand.[43]

The Scottish voyagers were tightly packed into a brig that was far too small to accommodate 15 score passengers. Also, that sailing vessel was, in other respects, poorly outfitted for the transatlantic voyage, having inadequate sanitation and cooking facilities on board. During the journey, the Scots were sometimes forced to eat raw meat and to drink putrid water. Because the door adjoining the hold and upper deck was nailed shut, the Scots had no fresh air, except what flowed through the hatches that remained open and during rough seas allowed water to pour into the hold, where the Scots were obliged to lodge on the floor without beds. Due to stormy weather, the *Nancy* made slow progress against a tempestuous sea. Provisions became scarce, and the Scottish Highlanders nearly starved for want of adequate rations. While the captain and his crew enjoyed wholesome victuals, they taunted the starving Scots and, after satiating themselves with food and drink, "order the Bones and Leavings of their Meals to be thrown down into the Hold" to the passengers, whom the crew derisively labeled "the Scotch Negroes." The Scottish passengers' health deteriorated, as they struggled to survive between decks. Approximately a third of the nearly 300 Scottish migrants who began the transatlantic passage perished during the crossing; seven infants were born during the voyage but died at sea. In traversing the border between the old and new worlds, in making the transatlantic passage from Muckle Ferry, Scotland, to the port of New York, the Scottish migrants learned what it could mean to be a "Negro," a slave, a member of a despised and exploited race. For the Scottish Highlanders, their traumatic voyage on the *Nancy* was a harsh introduction to a world in which human beings were subjected to the absolute will of others who had little regard for their humanity.

Miraculously, nearly 200 of the abused Scots survived to tell the story of their ordeal on board the *Nancy*. When the brig finally reached the harbor of New York, many of the passengers were ill with contagious diseases and for this reason were quarantined on Andrew's Island for 10 days. Shortly before Christmas, the Scottish newcomers were allowed to enter New York City; they landed at the city's dock late at night. According to the newspaper reports, the Scots were "weak and emaciated, thinly clad, some of them sickly, most of them without Money, and none knowing where to go, or how to obtain Necessaries, or shelter themselves from the inclemency of the Weather, which was freezing cold, and the Ground covered with Snow, their condition appeared to be truly deplorable." The spectacle of such a large number of distressed Scottish newcomers incited the compassion of the townspeople, who rallied to support the unfortunate migrants with alms until arrangements could be made for the Scots' assimilation into the settler community.

Despite disquieting reports about the mistreatment of the Scottish passengers on board the *Nancy*, Scottish families continued to undertake the hazardous voyage to the port of New York. Constituting the largest group of immigrants entering that seaport on the eve of the American Revolution, Scottish emigrants understood that, although the shippers who specialized in the transportation of settlers to British North America did not always treat their passengers more humanely than slave traders treated their human cargoes, immigrants from the British Isles and Europe, regardless of their social origins, occupied a status in the English overseas settler colonies that was superior to black Africans and their descendants. As white settlers, they occupied an ennobled racial position. That much was guaranteed to the British and European immigrants who ventured to colonial New York.[44] Although during their passage to the port of New York the Scots on board the *Nancy* had been vilified with the epithet "Scotch Negroes" and treated no better than slaves, once they disembarked at colonial New York's seaport, these Scottish newcomers acquired the privileges that obtained to *whiteness*. This meant, among other things, that they had a reasonable opportunity of achieving an independent life in the colonial frontier and, even, of becoming the owners of slaves.

In addition to the erratic influx of British and European immigrants, periodic waves of involuntary immigrants from various parts of the Atlantic world entered the port of New York during the English colonial period and added to the city's diverse constituent peoples. The early New York City slave trader Jacobus Van Cortlandt received small lots of West Indian slaves and sold them on consignment to townspeople and farmers from the surrounding countryside.[45] These human cargoes included some infirm and aged slaves, even though Van Cortlandt advised his West Indian business associates that old and defective slaves were unwanted in colonial New York. On May 16, 1698, Van Cortlandt wrote Miles Mayhew about a female slave whom he was unable to sell for his West Indian correspondent: "I have been very often in despair of Ever selling the woman for our Country-people do not Care to buy old slaves; therefore would advise you or any of your friends to Send no Slaves to this place that exceed 25 Years of age."[46] In another letter, Van Cortlandt informed Barnabas Jenkins that a male West Indian slave with a "distemper about his throat" would not find a ready buyer in New York.[47] The practice of dumping such refuse West Indian slaves on New York City's slave market became so troublesome that, in 1702, the colonial assembly imposed a prohibitive duty on human cargo from the West Indies.[48]

In addition to the traffic in small lots of slaves from the West Indies, the haphazard and illicit trade between pirates and New York City merchants accounts for some of the human cargo that arrived at the port of New York during the early English colonial era. This was the age of piracy, the heyday of plunder for profit. During King William's War (1689–97), New York City became a favorite haunt for pirates, such as the infamous Captain Kidd.[49] Because of the scarcity of capital for financing legitimate commercial ventures, New York City merchants purchased African slaves, along with spices, satins, silks, and other exotic goods, from freebooters at low black market prices and then sold these commodities in the city, sometimes at a substantial profit. Opportunistic New York City merchants—for example, Frederick Philipse, Thomas Marston, Robert Glover, and John Johnson—profited from the piratical traffic in slaves during King William's War, when the threat of naval attacks prevented laborers from the British Isles and Europe from crossing the Atlantic Ocean and the attendant labor shortage in New York and throughout colonial America spiked the price of slaves.[50] Piracy did not always enrich New York City merchants, however. On occasion, they became the hapless victims of crime on the high seas. For example, a newspaper report announced that, in September 1730, a New York City brigantine returned home in ballast after "a crew of Spanish mulatto and Negro pirates" had boarded the vessel and seized its cargo as it sailed from Jamaica through the Windward Passage.[51]

Dependent as it was on mercurial personalities and felonious methods, the piratical traffic in slaves proved to be an unpredictable business involving considerable risk. The slave-trading activities of Frederick Philipse disclose the irregular provenance of the human cargo that entered New York's seaport during the early years of English colonial rule, as well as the gamble that New York City merchants took when they purchased contraband slaves. In 1698, Philipse acquired two shipments of enslaved East Africans through his contacts with Samuel Burgess, an inhabitant of the notorious pirate colony on the island of Madagascar. Philipse exchanged provisions, arms, and munitions for whatever loot the pirate had on hand, including slaves. Although the exact size of the human cargo that Philipse acquired in this deal is unknown, they were large by New York City standards and glutted the city's slave market. Philipse could not find buyers for both shipments of East African slaves and sent one parcel to his manor in Westchester County.[52] Reporting on market conditions at the port of New York in 1698, Jacobus Van Cortlandt wrote a West Indian business correspondent that "the great quantity of slaves are come from Madagascar makes slaves to sell very slow."[53] In addition to the inordinate size of Philipse's enslaved East African cargoes, the abrupt resumption of European immigration flows across the Atlantic Ocean, following the cessation of King William's War and the attendant increase in the availability of laborers from the British Isles and Europe, account for the dull market for slaves in 1698.

New Yorkers preferred British and European laborers. But frequent seasons of war, which repeatedly curtailed the supply of laborers from the British Isles and Europe, produced a cyclical demand for slaves in New York. Between 1715 and 1772, independent merchants delivered no fewer than 4,949 slaves to New York's seaport. Sailing vessels returning from the West Indies brought at a minimum 3,260 slaves in separate shipments of 5 to 6 slaves on average, slavers returning from the African coast carried at least 1,478 slaves in individual shipments of nearly 55 slaves on average, and cargo vessels returning from the Azores, the Spanish colonies, Suriname, coastal North America, and London transported another 211 or so slaves in single shipments of 2 or 3 slaves on average (Table 2.1). Added to the total flow of involuntary immigrants into the port of New York were approximately 40 human prizes, whom privateers seized from enemy sailing vessels, and an estimated 609 slaves, whom slave traders smuggled overland from the seaport at Perth Amboy, New Jersey, and other ports.[54] Forcibly removed from their various homelands and sold into slavery at New York City, these human cargoes augmented the diversity of colonial Manhattan's population.

Sporadic influxes of enslaved human cargoes entered the port of New York during wartime. Queen Anne's War (1702–13) disrupted the transportation of British and European immigrants to the port of New York, and during that war slave traders took advantage of the accompanying labor shortage and rising price of slaves. Between 1701 and 1714, slave traders carried a documented total of 487 slaves to New York's seaport: Slavers returning from the African littoral brought 209 slaves, and sailing vessels returning from the West Indies brought 278 slaves.[55] War sometimes presented an opportunity for slave traders to profit,

TABLE 2.1 Estimated Slave Imports to Port of New York, 1715–1772

Origin	Total	Shipments	Average size	% of total
Africa	1,478	27	54.74	30.0
West Indies	3,260	556	5.86	66.0
Antigua	349	63	5.54	7.0
Barbados	566	90	6.29	12.0
Bermuda	70	33	2.12	1.0
Curaçao	108	38	2.84	2.0
Eustatius	64	9	7.11	1.0
Jamaica	1,384	201	6.98	28.0
St. Christoph	62	15	4.13	1.0
St. Thomas	95	42	2.26	2.0
Other Islands	232	65	3.57	5.0
Unknown	330	64	5.15	7.0
North America	156	52	3.00	3.0
Suriname	16	8	2.00	0.30
New Spain	11	8	1.37	0.20
Compeche	4	1	4.00	
Cartegena	1	1	1.00	
Honduras	4	1	4.00	
Other	2	1	2.00	
Azores	25	8	3.12	0.50
Cape Verde	3	1	3.00	
Madeira	22	7	3.14	
London	3	3	1.00	

Source: Naval Officer's Shipping List and American Inspector General's Ledger.

but more often it obstructed trade of all kinds. In a letter to the London merchant John White, James Van Horne complained about the depressed condition of trade at the port of New York, owing to the frequency of war. "We are in this place much Tir'd with war," Van Horne wrote. "Trade is Intirely stagnated, nothing goes on Among us but privateering."[56] When international war completely blocked the flow of regular commerce through the seaport, including the traffic in slaves, New York City merchants pooled their capital and invested in privateering ventures, which sometimes seized valuable cargo from enemy sailing vessels. A quasi-piratical mode of wealth accumulation and a state-sanctioned contribution to England's national interest in harassing rival nations, privateering operations required a relatively low capital investment and promised a sizeable return in profit. Like New Amsterdam under Dutch colonial rule, English colonial New York City received small lots of human contraband seized from enemy sailing vessels. The Vice-Admiralty Court, the judicial body created in 1686 to adjudicate cases that involved contraband from captured enemy sailing vessels, condemned Negroes, mulattos, and Indians from New Spain as lawful prizes on the principle that their dark skin color constituted prima facie evidence of their slave status, even though some Spanish-speaking captives swore they were free subjects of Spain.[57] Reporting on the sale of Spanish-speaking captives at the port of New York during Queen Anne's War, Governor Robert Hunter (1710–19) remarked: "by reason of their colour which is swarthy, they were said to be slaves and as such were sold among many others of the same colour and country."[58] In this manner, Spanish-speaking slaves were added to colonial Manhattan's increasingly diverse black population, which included a considerable number of East Africans.

Besides the relatively large cargoes of enslaved East Africans that freebooters from Madagascar brought to New York's seaport, few enslaved native Africans disembarked at the port of New York prior to the second decade of the eighteenth century. The Royal African Company (RAC, 1663–98) held a monopoly on the shipment of slaves to English ports, including the English colonial seaports in the Western Hemisphere. However, that trading company brought no slaves to New York. A shareholder in the RAC, the Duke of York, later King James II (1685–88), promoted policies especially designed to encourage the importation and sale of African slaves in colonial New York. But because of the inefficiency of the imperial administration, colonial policies sometimes took several years to actualize, if they were implemented at all. It was not until 1702 that, upon the request of Governor Cornbury (1702–8), the colonial assembly encouraged the sale of African slaves in New York by enacting a discriminatory import duty, setting the impost on slaves from Africa at half the rate collected on slaves from the West Indies.[59] With the cessation of Queen Anne's War and the signing of the Treaty of Utrecht in 1713, England acquired the *asiento*, the coveted contract that granted a single maritime nation the monopoly to the shipping of slaves to New Spain. This award, along with the rising demand for slaves in the Antilles, the nullification of the RAC's trade monopoly on the west coast of Africa in 1689, and the termination of the English East India Company's (1600–1874) monopoly on trade along the East African coast in 1715,[60] paved the way for the ascendancy of independent merchants from England and the English overseas colonies in the transatlantic slave trade.

Following Queen Anne's War, a few independent New York City merchants financed slaving ventures for the purpose of supplying the lucrative slave markets in Brazil, New Spain, and the English West Indies with enslaved native Africans. New York City slaving vessels sometimes reached the Caribbean basin behind other slavers, whose cargoes glutted the target slave markets,[61] and therefore returned to the port of New York with cargoes of surplus native Africans. In 1721, the New York City slaver *Crown Galley* sailed to Madagascar, where it collected 254 East Africans and then departed for Brazil, where it deposited a portion of its human cargo. From Brazil, that slaving vessel sailed to Barbados, its last port of call in the Caribbean basin, where it deposited more slaves before returning to its home port with 117 surplus East African slaves, nearly half of its original cargo.[62] Between 1715 and 1721, New York City merchants brought no fewer than 534 native African slaves to the port of New York.[63] Many, if not most, of these imported slaves were surplus African slaves from human cargo originally intended for sale in the Caribbean basin. Largely because of the importation of these slaves, New York City's black population more than doubled, increasing from 603 in 1703 to 1,362 in 1723.[64]

The Atlantic merchant community received encouraging reports on the transatlantic slave trade. In 1730, a New York City newspaper printed the following inviting prospectus: "The African trade had been the most gainful trade to the English and Dutch, that it was possible for them to find in any part of the world, the returns of Gold and Slaves being had for the meanest Trifles imaginable, such as Bits of Iron, painted Glass, Knives, Hatches, Glass Beads. And the like."[65] Such news doubtless captured the attention of New York City merchants, who were always alert for lucrative trading investments. But for the most part, these merchants waited for more positive incentives to appear in the slave market before entering the capricious business of transporting enslaved African cargoes across the Atlantic Ocean to the Americas. The historian James G. Lydon has noted: "All in all New Yorkers did not seriously enter the African trade until the late 1740s."[66] As the demand for slaves in the burgeoning sugar-producing islands of the English West Indies skyrocketed during the mid-eighteenth century, peaking in the largest islands during the 1760s,[67] New York City merchants began to take a more active part in the traffic in African slaves, undertaking polygonal voyages in which slave traders sailed for the West African coast with guns and provisions, exchanged these goods for African slaves at the trading forts along the Gold Coast—for example, at Elmina, Cape Coast, and Whydah—raced back across the Atlantic to the English West Indies sugar islands, which absorbed enslaved Africans at an astounding rate, then sailed to the Chesapeake region in North America, whose tobacco farmers eagerly awaited shipments of slaves, and finally returned to the port of New York with cargoes of sugar, dyewoods, indigo, tobacco, and incidental lots of slaves.[68] This polygonal trade involved considerable risk to investment capital, and the New York City merchants who participated in the slave traffic were sometimes stuck with African-born slaves who had been intended for sale in the English West Indies, other ports in the Caribbean basin, or the Chesapeake region but found no buyers there. These surplus slaves were eventually carried to New York City. As a consequence, the number of native Africans brought to the port of New York was probably greater than the extant port records of direct shipments from Africa indicate. Throughout the English colonial era, shipments of slaves from

TABLE 2.2 Documented African Slave Imports to the Port of New York, 1715–1721

Date	Number	Merchants
1715	38	Anthony Lynch, Alex. Moore, Anthony Rutgers, & Rip Van Dam
1716	43	Frances Gerbrausen, Alex Moore, Anthony Rutgers, & Rip Van Dam
1717	100	Richard Janeway, Nathanial Simpson, & William Walton
1717	166	Andrew Fresneau, Abraham, Garrett, & John Van Horne
1718	64	Adnrew Fresneau, Abraham, Garrett, & John Van Horne
1718	6	Adolph Phillipse
1721	117	Richard Janeway, Isaac Levy, William Walton, & Nathaniel Simpson

Source: NOSL.

the West Indies brought to New York's seaport by slaving vessels probably included leftover native Africans, whom New York City slave traders could not sell at a Caribbean port of call or in the Chesapeake colonies. Owing in large part to the importation of slaves, people of African descent were 20 percent of New York City's total population by 1746.[69]

Because of the severe business contractions in 1714–16, 1737–44, and 1751–55, New York City witnessed relatively slight economic development until the mid-1750s, when the city and the surrounding countryside experienced a transformative economic boom due to the windfall of income from military expenditures that poured into the region during the French and Indian War (1756–63).[70] New York City now required a reliable source of laborers to handle the swelling volume of tonnage that passed through its port and to boost agricultural production in the nearby farming districts in the context of increased demand for foodstuffs in the city, which was now an overpopulated garrison town that housed hundreds of English troops. However, the imperial administration was incapable of exercising effective control over the British migrants and European immigrants who circulated throughout the first British Empire and was, therefore, unable to direct these labor supplies to New York City and the surrounding countryside, where labor scarcities threatened to stall the economic upturn. Instead of settling in New York, the lion's share of the supply of laborers from the British Isles and Europe settled in other regions of British North America, where newcomers could purchase cheap land. Hence these preferred laborers were seldom available in sufficient numbers to meet the labor demand in New York City and its environs.

During the era of rapid economic development, New Yorkers turned to the seemingly inexhaustible supply of slaves from Africa to satisfy their labor needs. Whereas prior to the late 1740s nearly three of four slaves who arrived at the port of New York were carried in vessels returning from the West Indies, after the late 1740s close to 70 percent of the slaves who entered colonial New York's seaport were transported in slaving vessels returning directly from Africa.[71] Hoping to take advantage of the favorable tariff on native African slaves and to capitalize on the rise in the demand for laborers in New York City and the adjacent farming districts, New York City merchants—for example, Samuel Bridge and John Dwightwith—undertook bilateral slaving voyages between the port of New York and West Africa's Gold Coast. Bridge imported 23 enslaved West Africans in 1754; he and Dwightwith imported another 103 slaves from West Africa in 1763.[72] A rare report documents the middle passage from the West African coast to the port of New York and offers a glimpse at the hardships endured by involuntary African voyagers who were destined for enslavement in colonial New York City and the surrounding countryside. A sailor named Charles Sorisco gave the following description of the harsh treatment that a cargo of enslaved West Africans received while on board the *York*, a New York City slaving vessel. "John Lovel the Chief Mate," Sorisco reported, "beat the Negro slaves on board the said [slaving vessel] in a Cruel Manner with ropes, staves, Hedding, the handle of a broom, and particularly one Walker who afterwards died & a Negro woman, named Neura, who Lovel tied up to the Main shroud and beat her with a tail full of Notches, in a very inhuman manner."[73] Enslaved Africans were not always passive victims. In 1761, the West Africans on board Captain John Nicoll's brig the *Agnes* staged a bloody mutiny shortly after the slaving vessel cleared the Gold Coast. The crewmen killed two score Africans in putting down that uprising. Once order on the brig had been restored, Captain Nicoll resumed his return voyage to the port of New York, only to be captured by a French privateer just off the North American coast.[74]

The New York City slaving vessels that participated in the bilateral African carrying trade usually embarked on voyages in early spring and arrived on the west coast of Africa in six to eight weeks, before the start of the West African littoral's deadly malaria season. On the West African coast, ship captains exchanged rum, firearms, ammunition, and other manufactured goods for slaves, African produce, and, if they were lucky, gold. Departing the coast of West Africa in early summer, the slaving vessels typically returned to the port of New York in July or August.[75] This was fortuitous timing, for it gave native sub-Saharan Africans a lengthy period to acclimate to their new environment before the onset of winter on the eastern seaboard of North America. Nevertheless, the dense concentration of townspeople, combined with the humid climate, made New York City an ideal setting for the spread of contagious diseases. When enslaved newcomers, whose health had been compromised during arduous transatlantic journeys, were introduced to the city's disease environment, they sometimes succumbed to fatal illnesses within a few weeks of their arrival at New York's seaport. Moreover, the spread of communicable diseases gave rise to lethal epidemics—for example, the outbreak of yellow fever in 1702 and the contagion of smallpox in 1756—that depressed overall population growth and, importantly, led to high infant mortality rates. A recent study of the skeletal remains from a portion of colonial New York City's burial ground for its African-descended inhabitants shows that 30 percent of the sample burial population were infants below the age of 2 years and another 10 percent were children between the ages 2 and 12 years. Approximately 60 percent of the sample infant-child burial population displayed dental hypoplasia, a defect of the deciduous dentition or "baby teeth," indicating serious illness during infancy.[76] Colonial New York City's African-descended population did not begin to reproduce at a rate that outpaced deaths until the 1740s, with a modest rate of natural increase during the 1740s and slight rates of natural increase during the 1750s and 1760s.[77] Consequently, slaves born in New York City could not have been a majority of the northern colonial port town's African-descended population much early than the 1760s. Unlike the Chesapeake region, where the early and steady natural increase of the African-descended population produced a slave labor force in which American-born slaves comprised a majority by the 1730s,[78] New York City remained dependent on imported slave labor supplies for most of the colonial era. The nearly fivefold increase in the city's African-descended population between 1703 and 1771 was due, almost entirely, to the importation of slaves born outside New York.[79]

During the severe economic contraction of 1764 to 1769, New York City's slave labor market underwent a precipitous decline, especially when compared with the robust demand for slaves in the English West Indies at that time. Although a few New York City merchants continued to invest in slaving ventures to Africa, they now typically sold their enslaved African cargoes in the West Indies. As late as 1774, Governor William Tryon wrote: "There are a few vessels employed annually in the African Trade, their Outward Cargoes are chiefly Rum and some British Manufactures.—The high price and ready sale they meet with for their Slaves in the West Indies induce them always to dispose of the cargoes among the Islands."[80] Few enslaved human cargoes arrived at the port of New York following the French and Indian War. Between 1770 and 1772, sailing vessels brought 86 enslaved West Africans to the city's docks, but no officially documented shipments of slaves arrived at New York's seaport between 1773 and the outbreak of the War for Independence.[81] As a consequence of the considerable influx of British migrants into the port of New York and the curtailment of the colony's slave trade during the early 1770s, the proportion of African-descended people in the city's total population declined from 17 percent in 1756 to 14 percent in 1771.[82] Nevertheless, enslaved labor remained a significant component of the colonial port town's workforce. In 1774, the Scottish visitor Patrick M'Robert wrote that "it rather hurts an European eye to see so many negro slaves upon the streets."[83] The slave traders who sold enslaved blacks at New York City during the English colonial era had laid the foundation for an enduring legacy of racial domination in that northern port town.[84]

The English colony builders debated the advantages and the disadvantages of slave versus free labor and in doing so broached the issue of the ethnic and racial composition of the colony's labor force. On one side, the advocates of free labor clung to the dream of peopling New York with numerous British tenants or, if British sources of labor proved insufficient to match the colony's labor needs, European immigrants. Free labor proponents argued that the presence of slaves made New York an unattractive final destination for laborers from the British Isles and Europe, who esteemed freedom, sought an independent life in British North America, and increasingly regarded competition from slave labor to be a threat to their livelihood and a debasement of work. The advocates of free labor therefore called on the colonial state to impose a prohibitive duty on slave imports, which would reduce the number of slaves in New York and thereby render that English overseas colony more attractive to British and European settlers. On the other side, some advocates of slave labor insisted that the seemingly inexhaustible pool of slaves from Africa was the only source of laborers that could satisfy New York's unmet labor needs. They therefore argued that as long as the colony faced a labor deficit, the colonial state should do everything in its power to encourage the importation of slaves to the port of New York. This last position was in keeping with the policies of the English Crown and some colonial officials. In a 1726 pamphlet titled *The Interest of the Country in Laying Duties*, the colonial officeholder Cadwallader Colden announced his opposition to a proposed import duty on slaves and made a case for

FROM FRONTIER OUTPOST TO SETTLER COLONY

the exploitation of slave labor in New York. Although Colden registered his belief that in the long run a free labor force would benefit New York more than an enslaved labor force, he argued: "It is true that it were better for the Country, if there were no Negroes in it, and that all could be carried on by Freemen who have greater Interest in promoting the Good of a Country, and who strengthen it more than any number of Slaves can do: Dearness of the Wages of hired Servants makes Slaves at this Time, necessary, nothing that is necessary is to be discouraged."[85] Colden's use of the term "Negroes" references slave labor and does not suggest that an antiblack bias subtends his remarks. Colden framed his discussion on New York's labor needs primarily in terms of the relative cheapness of slave labor versus the high cost of wage laborers. To be sure, English convicts offered another cheap alternative labor supply, but they presented certain disadvantages. Remarking on the character of English convicts, a colonial customs officer warned that "the worst in the world come out of Bridewell and Newgate."[86] In 1734, Governor William Cosby (1732–36) bemoaned New York's failure to compete successfully with adjoining colonies to recruit virtuous white settlers. "I see with concern," Cosby wrote, "that whilst the neighboring Provinces are filled with honest, useful and laborious white people, the truest riches and surest strength of a country, this Province seems, regardless of the vast advantage which such acquisitions might bring them and of the disadvantages that attend the too great importation of [enslaved blacks], to be filled with Negroes and convicts."[87] Cosby assigned a differential value to white laborers, on the one hand, and black laborers, on the other, placing the latter in the category of undesirable laborers, such as convicts, and implicitly endorsing the notion that, with respect to moral disposition, white laborers, excepting the notable anomaly of white criminals, were more desirable than black laborers, who were summarily devalued in being lumped together with convict laborers. In his remarks, Governor Cosby overlooked the invaluable contributions that black workers had already made to the project of colony building in New York, while he wistfully speculated about the value a more numerous white settler population might add to the colony. Cosby thus introduced a racial bias, a high esteem for racial whiteness, in his statement on colonial New York's labor problem.

Yet prior to the 1770s, New York City experienced a chronic shortage of white laborers, as most newcomers from the British Isles and Europe, even those who stayed in New York, settled outside the city, mainly in remote frontier regions, where they had a reasonable opportunity to purchase inexpensive farmland and lead an independent life. Late in the colonial era, Governor Henry Moore observed that most white settlers preferred to pursue a life of "abject poverty" as farmers on the colonial frontier than to live a comfortable life in New York City "by working at the Trades in which they were brought up." Moore added that these white settlers lived, for many years, deplorable lives, but during that time took immense pride in the fact that they were independent American farmers.[88]

The English colony builders who watched the flow of British migrants and European immigrants pass through the port of New York on their way to other parts of British North America remained pessimistic about New York's ability to attract and retain desirable white laborers. These observers understood that some method of compelling white workers to remain in New York would benefit the colony. For this reason, British and European servants, laborers who were white yet bonded to their masters for a prescribed number of years, were regarded as the best solution to New York's labor shortage. But owing to the dearth of laborers, even the poorest white servants were usually able to negotiate contracts that limited their length of service to only a few years. Though a typical indenture agreement required from four to seven years of service, servants and apprentices seldom completed a full term of service.[89] In 1711, the municipal authorities responded to complaints from master craftsmen and lengthened the minimum term of service for New York City apprentices to seven years.[90] However, the continued scarcity of apprentices from the British Isles and Europe made it nearly impossible to enforce that law. Noting the brief terms of service and the high rate of outmigration among servants and apprentices, some colonizers advocated the use of slave labor, pointing out that slaves, unlike other workers, could be forced to labor in New York for as long as they were needed. Thus, even as these English colony builders expressed a preference for peopling New York with settlers from the British Isles and Europe, they continued to encourage the importation of enslaved Africans as a vital necessity. Because of this policy and the fact that prior to the 1770s British migrants and European immigrants were unavailable in sufficient numbers to satisfy New York's labor needs, slave labor remained an integral component of New York's labor system.

In New York City, enslaved porters and stevedores labored at the colonial port town's docks, wharves, slips, and warehouses. These enslaved dockworkers hoisted ponderous cargo, often without the aid of mechanical lifts. A recent analysis of the skeletal remains of a portion of colonial New York City's African-descended population identified injuries that typify humans who regularly haul heavy loads—for example, fractures to the spinous process of the lumbar vertebrae (or lower back) and the thoracic vertebrae (or middle to lower back). In one case, an examination of the skeletal structure of a male who died in his early thirties revealed a hairline fracture of the first cervical vertebra (or neck).[91] This adult male, whose skeletal remains are the only testimony to his life, probably sustained that injury as a consequence of repeated axial overloading, which suggests that he engaged in the practice of head carrying, a common method of transporting materials of moderate to light weight in many West African societies that, when utilized to transport heavy cargo of the kind that entered New York's seaport, could result in serious injury to the neck.[92]

Enslaved West Africans, so-called Guinea Negroes, were a significant component of colonial New York City's labor force by the mid-1750s. Writing from the port of New York during the French and Indian War, a British naval officer observed: "The laborious people in general are the Guinea Negroes, who lie under particular restraints."[93] These enslaved West Africans helped to keep the busy colonial port town moving and could be found loading and unloading cargo at the city's port facilities.

During the French and Indian War, New York City witnessed a boom in the shipbuilding industry and ancillary enterprises.[94] At that time the building, repair, and outfitting of sailing vessels became a lucrative business in the colonial port town. By 1770, New York City merchants owned 60 percent of the ocean-going vessels that passed through the port of New York.[95] Most of these sailing vessels were built at the city's shipyard. Master craftsmen and slaves worked side by side in the city's shipbuilding industry. With the aid of his slave, the New York City ship carpenter Henry Cruger repaired sailing vessels of every class. Together, master and slave earned £3 2s. 6d. for seven days' labor on the repair of the sloop *William & Elizabeth* and another £8 3s. 6d. for a similar job on the *General Gage*, a New York City brig that participated in the provision trade with St. Croix.[96] In addition to the exploitation of slave labor in the city's shipbuilding industry, New York City slaveowners hired out their slaves to work on the construction and repair of port facilities. On March 22, 1770, William and Abraham Beekman engaged two master carpenters, James Reade and William Hutchins, to repair their damaged wharf along the East River. By the terms of their contract with the Beekmans, Reade and Hutchins had "to raise the wharf and restore it to good condition." This demolition and construction job took more than a year to complete. During that time, Reade and Hutchins hired several slaves to aid them in pulling down and rebuilding Beekman's wharf.[97] Male slaves, physically robust and in the prime of life, were needed to undertake such physically strenuous tasks. The New York City slave trader John Watt described the basic characteristics that made a slave suitable for the colonial port town's labor market: "For this market they must be young, if not quite children, those advanced in years will never do. . . . Males are best."[98] The townspeople prized male slaves who had survived childhood diseases yet were young and physically fit enough to merit the initial investment in purchase costs and additional expenditures on feeding and clothing human chattel. For this reason, "seasoned slaves," whose immune systems had made a successful adjustment to New York City's disease environment,[99] were preferred to "new Negroes," recent arrivals who had no acquired immunity to the lethal pathogens that were endemic to the colonial port town.

Cultural factors were an important consideration for New York City artisans who contemplated purchasing slaves and training them in their crafts. Because of the direct relationship between cultural literacy and production efficiency in the skilled trades, master craftsmen preferred to purchase young American-born male slaves who were proficient in a European language and already somewhat familiar with European standards of measurement. Most native Africans could not speak a European language and were generally unfamiliar with European-derived techniques of artisanal production. For this reason, master craftsmen were reluctant to purchase "new Negroes," whose training in the skilled trades involved considerable inefficiency. In colonial New York City, the training of enslaved laborers in the skilled trades brought master craftsmen and slaves into frequent and intimate contact. Slaveowning artisans typically lived under the same roof with their slaves and labored alongside them at work sites about town and in the shops that they usually kept on the street level of their living quarters. Doubtless, some native African newcomers learned European languages at the workshops of New York City artisans and at other work sites. The anthropologist Melville Herskovitz has argued that in the Americas enslaved native Africans who were trained in European-derived crafts underwent an accelerated process of acculturation as a consequence of intensive interaction with artisans from Europe.[100] Of course, months of instruction were required before a novice slave displayed dexterity in an unfamiliar craft, and several years would pass before a master craftsman would begin to receive a return on his investment in slave property. Yet slaves proved to be capable of acquiring artisanal skills, and some became master craftsmen who excelled in the skilled trades.[101] These skilled slaves were not merely "living tools" but were unmistakably "thinking things," capable of mastering complex tasks. Once a young male slave mastered a skilled trade, he became valuable property that produced high-priced finished goods. Apart from the purchase of arable land, ownership of a youthful skilled slave was perhaps the best long-term investment for ambitious settlers. This circumstance enhanced the viability of slavery in port towns like colonial New York City, where skilled journeymen and apprentices from the British Isles and Europe were scarce and commanded high wages.

In colonial New York City, weekly slave auctions were held at the Merchants' Coffee House, the Fly Market, and Proctor's Vendue House. Because slaves typically lived in their masters' houses, prospective buyers were reluctant to purchase slaves of unknown character. Newspaper notices routinely reassured dubious buyers, whenever possible, by vouching for the moral disposition, linguistic competency, and intellectual capacity of advertised slaves.[102] However, as the absence of an informative description of the advertised "new Negro" in the following newspaper notice indicates, it was not always possible to obtain information about enslaved newcomers: "A Likely Negro Girl about 18 Years of Age, and a likely Negro Boy about 16 Years, both born in this City. They can speak good English and Dutch, and are also bred up to all sorts of House-work, and also a new Negro Man. Enquire at the Post-office in New-York."[103] The townspeople were wise to exercise caution when purchasing enslaved newcomers, since unruly slaves who had participated in slave revolts in the West Indies were sometimes transported to the port of New York.[104] For this reason, the settlers preferred to purchase slaves who had been born in New York (or at least raised from childhood in the colony) and were, therefore, familiar with the local customs and presumably well adapted to their life of enslavement. Of course, the purchase of human chattel always involved risk. Two lawsuits aptly illustrate this point. In October 1751, Nathan Levy sued Henry Shaver for trespass on a debt. In his complaint, Levy claimed that Shaver had promised to pay him the sum of £10 (New York currency) for "one Negro Wench." In his answer, Shaver explained that he refused to pay Levy because the slave delivered to him was "infirm and unsound of Mind and Memory" and hence had "neither use nor Value."[105] Several years later, in a similar lawsuit, Richard Hale sued Moses Franks for breach of contract in the sale of a slave. Hale claimed that he had agreed to buy "a Negro Girl Slave that was Compas Montis & Could speak the Language of her native Country." (Bilingual slaves who spoke English in addition to Spanish or a West African language were valuable property in colonial

New York City, whose merchant community engaged in overseas trade in Spanish America and along the West African littoral).[106] According to Hale, the slave he had purchased from Franks turned out to be "unsound & Dumb and Labouring under Great infirmity of mind . . . & could not speak her native Country Tongue."[107] Although both lawsuits were settled in the purchaser's favor, the trials lasted several weeks. Given the length of such lawsuits and the uncertainty of their outcome, most New York City townspeople probably inspected slaves carefully before making purchases.

Living in relatively small dwellings and in a densely populated port town, the townspeople were particularly wary of acquiring female slaves, who were generally assumed to be sexually promiscuous and therefore prone to bring unwanted infants into settler households. Lacking biotechnologies, such as the ones used in present-day neocolonialist campaigns of birth control and sterilization in so-called Third World nations, the colonial state of the early modern era was incapable of regulating female fertility in overseas colonies. Colonial New York City slaveowners were sometimes burdened with the costly expense of feeding and clothing the unwanted offspring of their female slaves. Slave traders were attuned to the concerns of prospective New York City buyers who wished to purchase a single female slave but could not afford to care for unwanted slave children. For this reason, the following newspaper notice announced that the advertised female slave could bear no children: "To Be Sold, a likely barren Negro Wench about 24 years of age, enquire of the Printer hereof."[108] Another advertisement announced: "To Be Sold, a young Wench about 29 years old, that drinks no strong Drink, and gets no Children, a very good Drudge."[109] For some New York City slaveowners, fecundity in producing offspring was such an undesirable trait in female slaves that otherwise exemplary cooks and drudges were sold because of that troublesome characteristic. One newspaper ad stated: "To Be Sold, an excellent Negro Wench, about 20 Years old, with a male Child, about three Months old; the Wench has had the Small-Pox, can cook, wash, and iron, can be well recommended, and is sold for no other Fault than being too fruitful."[110] Owing to the gendered division of labor in colonial New York City, most enslaved women labored in the city's household mode of production, as drudges, cooks, and nurses within the confines of their masters' houses. Female slaves generally acquired skills deemed appropriate to their gender. With early training, young female slaves became accomplished seamstresses, whose dexterity with a needle proved to be an asset in household industries.[111] On market days, female slaves ventured outside the domestic sphere to the marts along the East River, at Coenties slip and Clarke's ferry, where fish, oysters, and country produce were sold.[112] Female slaves were sometimes employed as vendors at these city markets, a practice that would have been familiar to slaves from West Africa, where women typically controlled village markets.

In contrast to enslaved women who, except for market days, were confined to their master's houses, enslaved men were a highly mobile component of colonial New York City's labor force. Male slaves circulated from work site to work site about town and piloted market boats between the city and the farming villages in Long Island and New Jersey. As part of the crews on board oceangoing vessels embarking from the port of New York, some enslaved males traveled overseas. Two male slaves named Bon and Noice sailed on the New York City privateer ship *Duke of Cumberland* during its tour in the Caribbean Sea in the spring and summer of 1759. Free black sailors also belonged to the crews on New York City privateer vessels. Richard Richardson, a free black sailor, took his share of the prize money from a successful privateering venture, when, in 1766, the *Harlequin* returned to New York's seaport after a Caribbean cruise.[113] Ordinary vessels of trade employed enslaved crewmen. In 1775, Captain Samuel Gilford hired Thomas Vardill's male slave, who in that same year sailed with Gilford to Bristol, England, and back to the port of New York on the brigantine *Cornelia's Portage*. That brigantine's crew also included a free black sailor named Colevain.[114]

Besides laboring on board sailing vessels, at the city's port facilities, in artisans' shops, and at construction sites about town, male slaves cultivated farmland in the countryside. Female slaves probably labored alongside male slaves and other male farm laborers, cultivating and harvesting crops, in addition to laboring at the household tasks of cooking, cleaning, and caring for children. During the French and Indian War, New York City became an overcrowded garrison town housing numerous English soldiers. The sudden accretion of the city's population during that war created a great demand for foodstuffs and other country produce. At that time, victualing (or selling food supplies to the army) became an especially lucrative business. Most slaves who disembarked at the port of New York during the French and Indian War were probably employed as farm laborers in the nearby farming district and helped transform the countryside within the city's orbit into a prosperous region of commercial agricultural production. By 1756, 10,000 to 20,000 slaves lived within a 50-mile radius of New York City.[115] At that time slaves comprised 20 to 27 percent of the total population in rural Kings, Queens, Richmond, Westchester, and Suffolk counties, as well as in Bergen County in eastern New Jersey. Male slaves accounted for nearly 60 percent of the total enslaved population in these agricultural regions.[116]

The imperatives of colony building, of transforming the fledgling port town into a thriving entrepôt and its hinterland into flourishing units of commercial agricultural production, necessitated bringing together an assortment of laborers—free, indentured, and enslaved laborers—at work sites in town and country.[117] White workers and enslaved black workers labored side by side in both the agricultural and commercial sectors of the economy. In this mixed labor system, no racialized division of labor protected white laborers from the competition of black laborers. In colonial New York City, most black laborers were slaves. Enslaved laborers who could be rented on a daily, monthly, or even yearly basis for odd jobs and seasonal employment were particularly well suited to the colonial port town's need for a flexible labor force. Published in 1711, the following public notice indicates that the hiring-out system was already an established mechanism of New York City's labor market: "All negro . . . slaves that are let out to hire, within this city, do take up their standing in order to be hired at the market-house [Meal Market] at Wall Street Slip, until such time as they are hired, whereby all persons may know where to hire slaves as their occasion shall require, and all masters discover where their slaves are so hired."[118] The white workingmen of colonial New York City complained that the practice of hiring out slaves endangered their livelihoods. As early as 1686, the city's cartmen submitted a petition to protest that the use of hired slaves in the removal of trash from the city streets and in the carting of goods at the weigh house and markets violated their monopoly on hauling the city's garbage and other materials. The cartmen further complained that competition from hired slave labor threatened to reduce them to poverty. The municipal government redressed the cartmen's grievance by mandating that no hired "Negro or Slave be suffered to work on the [weigh house] as a Porter about any Goods either imported or Exported from or into this City." Finding it cheaper to hire enslaved drayers and porters to haul their goods than to pay the city's cartmen at the fixed rate of 6d. per load, town dwellers ignored this regulation.[119] Although Adam Smith asserted that "the work done by freemen comes cheaper in the end than that performed by slaves. It is found to do so even at Boston, New York, and Philadelphia, where the wages of common labour are so very high,"[120] in colonial New York City hiring slaves proved to be less costly than employing cartmen, whose artificial monopoly, fixed wages, and other archaic privileges rendered them vulnerable to competition from hired slave labor.[121]

Skilled white workers also complained that competition from slave labor diminished their wages. The premium wages paid to craftsmen in colonial New York City drew some journeymen from the British Isles and Europe to the port of New York but never in numbers sufficient to meet the city's demand for skilled workers. Journeymen were so scarce and the wages paid to them so costly that master craftsmen turned to enslaved laborers as a substitute labor force. In colonial New York City, the average price of an adult male slave was, in 1700, approximately £40 and, in 1760, nearly £100, while, as late as 1772, white journeymen earned daily wages of 8s.6d., making slave ownership a cheaper option in the long run than hiring journeymen.[122] For a higher initial expenditure than the cost to hire a journeyman, a master craftsman could purchase a slave who was bonded to him for life, train that slave in his craft, and eventually sell or over time hire out his skilled slave at a profit. In colonial New York City, a substantial proportion of artisans, many more than in colonial Boston and colonial Philadelphia, owned slaves.[123] By 1743, the practice of training slaves in a skilled craft was so common among the artisans of New York City that journeymen in the cooper trade signed a petition that called on the municipal government to prohibit master coopers from training slaves in their craft.[124] At that time a severe economic depression reduced the wages of journeymen, and competition from slave labor threatened to undermine their wages even further. Hoping to offer journeymen some relief, New York's interim Governor George Clarke (1736–43) directed New York's colonial assembly to establish a law that would protect skilled journeymen from the detrimental competition that followed from the practice of training slaves in the skilled trades. Clarke chided the members of that legislative body, some of whom were slaveowners: "The artificers complain and with too much reason of the pernicious custom of breeding slaves to trades whereby the honest and industrious tradesmen are reduced to poverty for want of employ and many of them forced to leave us to seek their living in other countries."[125] Judging from Clarke's statement, the use of slaves in the skilled trades was damaging the material welfare of New York City journeymen and precipitating the outmigration of these tradesmen. Though journeymen suffered from the competition of slave labor, widespread slave ownership among artisans and the practice of hiring out slaves probably had the greatest adverse impact on the livelihood of unskilled white day laborers. By the early decades of the eighteenth century, the typical wage of these workers was approximately 3s. each day, and by the late decades approximately 6s. But as the typical rent of from 2s.6d. to 3s.6d. each day for an unskilled slave indicates,[126] New York City slaveowners were hiring out slaves at a rate that was competitive with, if not ruinous to, the wages of unskilled day laborers.

From the petitions against the slave hiring-out system and the practice of training slaves in the skilled trades, we learn that the historic conflict between the economic interests of slaveowners and white workingmen dates back to the colonial period. At that juncture in New York City's history, white workingmen valued their wages as much as their whiteness. To be sure, white workingmen assumed (or occupied) the subject-position of "not black" and therefore "not slave." In their petitions, white workingmen demanded that the colonial state protect the privileges promised to white settlers—for example, high wages and, in some cases, a monopoly on certain trades.[127] Yet unlike their nineteenth-century counterparts, the white workingmen of colonial New York City instigated no race riots in protest against competition from black workers in the labor market.[128] As a social group, these white workingmen never engaged in overt acts of violence against black laborers, because they understood that such action would have, in most cases, amounted to an assault on the property of slaveowners, a crime that the colonial state was sure to punish.[129] Moreover, these white workingmen understood that the slaveowners, not the slaves, benefited from the exploitation of slave labor. For this reason, their petitions condemned slaveowners who trained slaves in the skilled trades and hired out slaves at rates that proved damaging to the welfare of white workingmen. These remonstrances stopped short of demanding the abolition of slavery, yet evident in them were the stirrings of social antagonisms that during the nineteenth century would develop into a free labor movement that was dedicated to preserving the privileges of white workingmen.[130]

To be sure, class and race were interrelated ingredients of social identity in colonial New York City. The ownership of enslaved blacks was an important basis of social stratification within the settler population; at the same time, a white-black binary marked the distinction between workers who were forced to labor without consent or contract and those workers who labored because they were promised limited terms of indenture and apprenticeship, high wages, and other attractive incentives.[131] Although it was not unusual for white settlers to pass through a period of temporary servitude, most newcomers from the British Isles and Europe, especially those who disembarked at the port of New York prior to the 1770s, managed to become the head of an independent household. "Every servant in the old social world," Peter Laslett has noted, "was probably quite confident that he or she would some day get married and be at the head of a new family, keeping others in subordination."[132] Although many British migrants and European immigrants doubted that colonial New York City was a likely place for them to obtain a life of independence, Laslett's statement also applies to colonial New York City, where a broad segment of the white settler population, artisans as well as wealthy merchants, established independent households and owned slaves.

Located at the southernmost extreme of Manhattan Island, colonial New York City encompassed an area of approximately two and one-half square miles. Because of the density of population and the scarcity of housing, only a few slaveowners provided their slaves with separate living quarters, known as "Negro kitchens" and usually located in the masters' backyards. Together with other household members, most masters and slaves lived under the same roof, in cramped dwellings of no more than two stories, with each floor partitioned into two rooms.[133] At the time of the English takeover in 1664 relatively few adult town dwellers, only 12.5 percent of household heads, owned slaves.[134] By 1703, approximately 41 percent of household heads in New York City owned at least one slave. The census of 1703, wills, inventories, and other household records make possible an informative, though somewhat static, ward-by-ward survey of slave ownership patterns in colonial New York City.[135]

The most instructive place to begin this survey is the East Ward, a municipal jurisdiction bounded by Burgher's Path to the south, Wall Street to the north, Smith Street to the west, and William Street to the east. Located in the East Ward along the East River were the city's shipyard, Beekman's and Schuyler's wharves, Frederick Philipse's warehouse on Queen Street, the crane at the east end of Wall Street (also known as "the Fly"), and the Fly Market at the intersection of Pearl Street and Maiden Lane. Dockworkers, sailors, and transients roamed the wharves along the East River by day and by night. Seafarers generally found temporary lodging in the East Ward boardinghouses that catered to sailors and other travelers. Permanent residents—for example, ship carpenters, sail makers, and mariners—inhabited that ward's maze of crooked streets and narrow alleyways. A few wealthy merchants—for example, Jacobus Van Cortlandt, Stephen Van Cortlandt, and Abraham Van Horne—resided along the southern end of Queen Street near Burgher's Path. Most East Ward residents made a livelihood from maritime occupations and related jobs.[136] Because of the intensive use of slave labor at the port facilities along the East River, the East Ward contained the largest absolute number of black inhabitants of any ward. By 1703, a quarter of the city's total black population lived in East Ward households. In that same year, the East Ward's total population was approximately 883 inhabitants, of whom approximately 665 were white inhabitants and 218 (25 percent) were enslaved blacks. Nearly half of the East Ward households (96 of 212) held at least one slave. Whereas 105 adult male slaves lived in East Ward households, only 60 adult male slaves and 57 adult male slaves lived in Dock Ward and South Ward households, respectively. Male adults were approximately half of the East Ward's total black population. The need for a physically robust labor force that could handle the heavy cargo arriving at the port facilities along the East River explains the preponderance of adult males in that ward's black population. During an ordinary workday, the number of slaves in the East Ward was temporarily augmented by enslaved men who resided in other city wards but were sent to labor at the port facilities along the East River. According to the census of 1703, white inhabitants outnumbered enslaved blacks by three to one in the East Ward. But when the presence of hired slaves and other enslaved laborers who frequented that area of the city in the execution of their masters' business is considered, a closer balance between white workingmen and enslaved black laborers was probably characteristic of the East Ward's demographic landscape during a typical workday.

New York City mariners lived in the East Ward near the city's port facilities. Captain John Theobald resided in the East Ward with two adult white males, three white female children, two adult male slaves, and one adult female slave. Like other East Ward slaveowners, Theobald probably employed his adult male slaves at the port facilities when they did not accompany him on overseas voyages. Since no adult white females lived in the mariner's house, the adult female slave in his household probably performed child-rearing duties as well as housekeeping chores. Theobald's male slaves doubtless had daily contact with other enslaved men who worked in the East Ward, whereas his female slave probably had fewer occasions to interact with slaves outside the domestic space of her master's house. Also located in the East Ward was the dwelling of Captain Nicholas Dumaresq, the son of Elias Dumaresq, a French Huguenot who, in the 1580s, fled religious persecution in France, took temporary asylum in Amsterdam, and, finally, settled in New Amsterdam. In 1701, four children—a daughter named Sarah, an eldest son named Nicholas, a son named Jacob, and a son named John—lived with the widower Nicholas Dumaresq. At that time an enslaved girl also lived in the Dumaresq household.[137] Like the female slave in the Theobald household, Dumaresq's slave girl probably labored in her master's house as a drudge and cook. She also probably performed the duties of nursemaid to her master's motherless children. The English mariner Captain Giles Shelly lived in the East Ward with his wife and an exceptionally large lot of six slaves—one enslaved black woman named Hagar, one enslaved Indian man named Venture, and another enslaved Indian man named Symon, his wife, and his two children.[138] In 1679, the colonial state outlawed the enslavement of members of New York's Indian communities,[139] but Indians from outside New York and their offspring were held in lifelong hereditable bondage. With respect to their living and working conditions, the lives of these enslaved Indians probably differed little from the lives of enslaved blacks.

While the city's East Ward became a multicultural, polyglot neighborhood, which reflected the port of New York's function as a gateway for multiple immigration flows from throughout the Atlantic world, the city's South Ward remained the locus of a close-knit, aging, and relatively homogeneous commu-

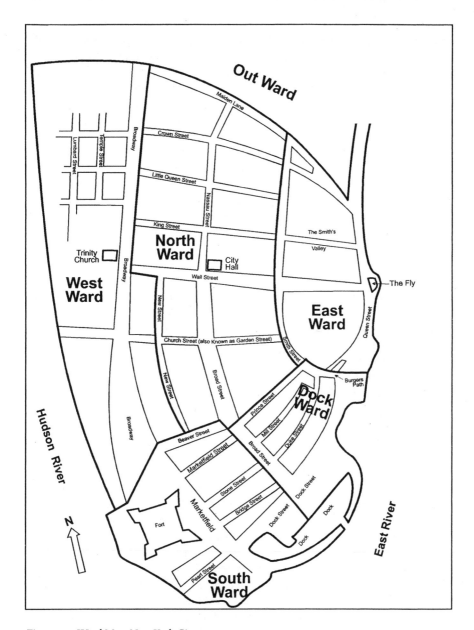

Figure 2.2. Ward Map, New York City, 1703

nity of long-established Dutch-speaking settlers. The site of the early Dutch colonial outpost, known as New Amsterdam and situated at the tip of Manhattan Island, the South Ward was bounded by the Hudson River to the south and to the west, Beaver Street to north, and Broad Street to the east. Located in that ward were the city's oldest landmarks, the fort and the bowling green.[140] Approximately 50 percent of South Ward householders (62 of 118) owned at least one slave. In 1624, Aeffie Peternela Ten Eyck, the widow of an early Dutch-speaking settler named Derrick Ten Eyck, lived in the South Ward on Stone Street, the first paved street in New York City. Aeffie Ten Eyck inhabited a brick dwelling and owned one elderly slave woman.[141] South Ward slaveowners were more likely to own aged slaves than slaveowners in the other city wards. In 1703, approximately 15 percent of the South Ward's slaveowning households kept slaves over the age of 60 years, whereas only 5 percent of the slaveowning households in each of the other wards contained slaves in that age cohort. The elderly South Ward slaves were probably long-time Manhattan residents who had arrived at the colonial seaport before the rise in population density abetted the outbreak of lethal epidemics that resulted in high infant mortality rates. Surviving childhood diseases as youngsters, these slaves enjoyed greater longevity than slaves who disembarked at the port of New York during the period in which the accretion of the city's population produced overcrowding and the environmental conditions for the easy spread of deadly microbes. The households of South Ward slaveowners contained relatively large lots of slaves, three to four on average as opposed to an average of one or two slaves held in other city slaveowning households. Rip Van Dam lived in the South Ward on Stone Street, just a short walk from Aeffie Ten Eyck's house. A wealthy colonial Netherlander, politician, and slave trader, Van Dam prospered under English rule and served as a member of the Governor's Council from 1702 to 1732 and as acting governor from 1731 to 1732.[142] By 1749, Van Dam's household included his second wife, an unmarried adult son and daughter, three sons and two daughters under the age of 16 years, and six slaves—three men, two women, and one boy.[143] The relatively large lot of slaves in Van Dam's household represented a portion of the wealth that the prosperous merchant had accumulated over the years.

By 1703 some of the city's wealthiest merchants, a combination of Anglo, Dutch, and French colonial elites, maintained residences in the Dock Ward, the municipal jurisdiction bounded by Burgher's Path to the east, Broad Street to the west, Prince Street to the north, and the East River to the south. During the English colonial period, the area around the City Dock and the marketplace at Hanover Square in the Dock Ward gradually became the port town's principal business center.[144] In 1703, approximately 731 inhabitants resided in the Dock Ward, with white settlers comprising 75 percent and enslaved blacks accounting for 25 percent of that ward's total population. Each workday, a relatively large slave labor force assembled at the City Dock and Hanover Square. Nearly 70 percent of Dock Ward householders (80 of 124) owned at least one slave, the largest proportion of slaveholding of any ward. The merchant Elias Boudinot, a descendant of Huguenots who fled France to Antigua in the 1680s and then settled in New York City, resided on Dock Street. Elias participated in the provision trade to the West Indies, and he maintained a lasting partnership with his brother, John Boudinot, who lived in Antigua. Elias Boudinot's household contained two slaves,[145] a grouping that corresponded to the pattern of slaveholdings in the Dock Ward and in the city as a whole.

Bounded by Beaver and Prince streets to the south and Maiden Lane to the north, with its westernmost limit at New Street and Broadway and its easternmost extreme at Smith Street,[146] the North Ward was colonial New York City's least affluent neighborhood. The majority of North Ward households were probably headed by white workingmen who could not afford to purchase and maintain slaves. In 1703, approximately 20 percent of North Ward householders owned slaves. Of the 848 inhabitants of the North Ward, only 58 were enslaved blacks. The modest but by no means impoverished households of artisans dominated the southernmost area of the North Ward. The greater part of that ward's black population probably lived in the households of the master crafts-men who resided south of Crown Street. The cordwainer Abraham Kip lived on New Street, a corridor of dwellings that demarcated the northerly movement of the South Ward's Dutch and Walloon populations. Kip was a descendant of French Walloons who, in the fourteenth century, fled their native land and settled in Amsterdam. His grandfather, Hendrick Kip, sailed with Henry Hudson on his 1610 voyage to North America and in 1635 settled in New Amsterdam. By 1703, Abraham Kip had established an independent household, which in-cluded his wife, Catalina (née de la Noy), a son and a daughter, and an enslaved family.[147] Kip obtained a grant of land, known as Kip's Bay Farm and located along present-day Thirty-fifth Street between the East River and Second Ave-nue. As the value of real estate on Manhattan Island soared with population growth and the northward expansion of residential housing, especially during the era of the Industrial Revolution, Kip's Bay Farm became the principal source of the Kip family's wealth.[148]

Bounded by Maiden Lane to the north, Beaver Street to the south, New Street to the east, and the Hudson River to the west, the West Ward remained sparsely populated for much of the English colonial period. Located in the West Ward on the west side of Broadway near the corner of Broadway and Wall Street, Trinity Church, the Anglican house of worship, stood at the crossroads of town and country on Manhattan Island. Trinity Church Farm encompassed most of the land north of King Street and west of Broadway between present-day Chambers and Fulton streets.[149] The Anglican vestry did not commence selling parcels of that farmland until the 1730s, a decision that kept population density low in the West Ward before that time.[150] In 1703, only 622 residents lived in the West Ward, and black town dwellers were no more than 15 percent of that ward's total population. Most West Ward residents were tenant farmers who cultivated Trinity Church Farm.[151] Reverend Pierre Peiret, pastor for the city's French Calvinist congregation from 1688 to 1704, also resided on Trinity Church Farm. For many years, the Anglican vestry supplemented the salaries of the city's Protestant ministers by allowing them to occupy and cultivate parcels of the church's farmland in the West Ward. In 1703, Pieret maintained a relatively large household that included his wife, adult son and daughter, a son under the age of 16 years, and four slaves. Pieret's parcel of land on Trinity Church Farm was probably larger than most city lots and hence allowed the French Calvinist minister to keep more slaves than most New York City slaveowners, who typically lived on small plots of land in a densely populated section of the colo-nial port town. Travelers who trekked southward through the West Ward along Broadway encountered an increasingly congested landscape. The wealthy mer-

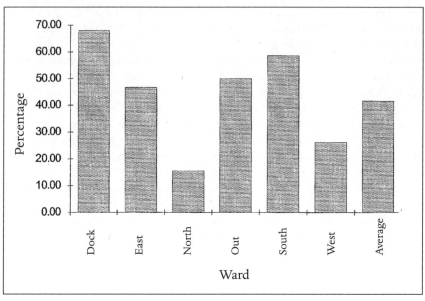

Figure 2.3. Percentage of Slaveowning Households, 1703

chant Peter Bayard resided in the southern sector of the West Ward, at One Broadway on the corner of Broadway and Exchange Place. Bayard's household included his wife, two daughters, and one female slave,[152] a grouping that closely resembled the typical slaveowning household in colonial New York City.

Until the early decades of the nineteenth century, the area on Manhattan Island outside the city limit remained countryside, interrupted by independent family farms and the country seats of wealthy townspeople.[153] The municipal government assigned this underpopulated rural district, which included two farming villages, the Bowery and Harlem, to the loosely defined jurisdiction called the Outward. Established by Peter Stuyvesant in 1651, the Bowery consisted of contiguous farm lots bounded by present-day Fourth Avenue and extending as far north as Eighteenth Street. Originally settled by Dutch and Walloon farmers in 1636 and named Nieuw Haarlem after the Dutch town nearby Amsterdam, English colonial Harlem included a village and a string of farm lots that the settlers laid out from the East River to the Hudson River and northward from its southern boundary at present-day Seventy-fourth Street.[154] In 1703, only 339 inhabitants lived in the Outward. Farmers and their families, many of whom were the descendants of the early Dutch and Walloon settlers, were three-quarters of the Outward's total population, while black inhabitants comprised one-quarter of its total population. Half of the Outward households held slaves. Because the area's agricultural economy placed a premium on the physical strength of farm laborers, men outnumbered women and children in

FROM FRONTIER OUTPOST TO SETTLER COLONY

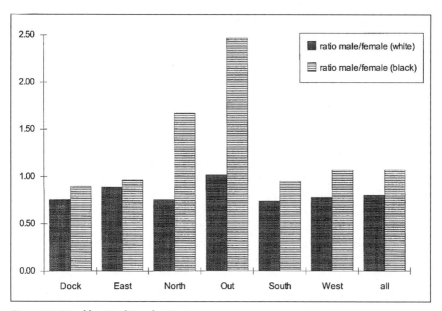

Figure 2.4. Ward-by-Ward Gender Ratios

the Outward's black population. According to the census of 1703, there were only 13 women and 2 children out of a total of 84 black inhabitants in that rural district.

By the first decade of the eighteenth century, long-established settlers had already purchased most of the arable land in the Outward, and these landowners were reluctant to sell this land to newcomers, preferring instead to make gifts of these rural landholdings to their heirs. By 1703, the colonial Netherlander Hendrickus Brevoort had purchased a tract of farmland in the Bowery between present-day Tenth and Eighteenth streets. Upon his death, his eldest son, Hendrickus the younger, inherited his Bowery landholdings. This Hendrickus became a prosperous farmer and eventually built a brick dwelling on the Brevoort farm near present-day Eleventh Street. In addition to farming, he practiced the wheelwright trade and kept a shop in his barn.[155] His two male slaves labored by his side during the early years of his career, at a time when he was improving his farmland and laying the groundwork for his offspring's future prosperity.[156] When Hendrickus the younger died in 1782, his son, Abraham, inherited the Breevoort farm.[156] The Brevoort family pattern of patriarchal land control, of keeping family land intact until the death of the male head of household, resembled the practice of New England patriarchs, which the historian Philip J. Greven documents in his path-breaking study on landholding patterns in colonial Andover, Massachusetts.[157] In colonial New York City and the surrounding farming districts, the practice of patriarchal land control and other customs of traditional patrimonial societies existed alongside capitalist property relations and the bourgeois value of possessive individualism. A general characteristic of colonialism, the coexistence of the archaic and the modern remained a salient feature of colonial Manhattan until the dynamics of modernity finally catapulted its inhabitants into the age of the democratic and industrial revolutions.

Much like the farming districts of eighteenth-century Europe, brewhouses, sawmills, gristmills, slaughterhouses, and bake ovens dotted colonial Manhattan's rural landscape. Outward farmers typically combined commercial agricultural production with food-processing industries, such as bolting, meatpacking, and brewing, as well as the processing of timber into lumber, casks, staves, and naval stores. By the first decade of the eighteenth century, Thomas Codington operated a brewery on his Harlem farm, where he and his eight slaves raised barley and other raw ingredients, which they later processed into beer.[158] While partly produced for household consumption, the bulk of the beer that Codington and his slaves brewed on his farm was probably transported to the city market for sale. The Outward's increasing orientation toward commercial farming and the processing of agricultural produce for the nearby city market reflected the strengthening of the economic link between town and country during the eighteenth century.

Members of the Rutgers family lived in both town and country. Harmanus Rutgers was a descendant of early Dutch settlers who arrived at Manhattan Island in 1646. According to the census of 1703, Harmanus II, an adult male, lived with his father, Harmanus the elder, and two adult male slaves on the north side of Stone Street in the South Ward. In that year his younger adult brother, Anthony Rutgers, lived with one adult female slave in the Dock Ward on Broad Street. Harmanus II eventually left his father's house and moved to the Rutgers family brewery on the north side of Maiden Lane. Upon his father's death, Harmanus II inherited the Rutgers brewery and in his will bequeathed that property, which included a storehouse, malthouse, millhouse, three slaves, and a "Negro kitchen," to his eldest son, Harmanus III. Harmanus II had also purchased Outward farmland, a tract of more than 1,000 acres near present-day Chatham Square. Upon his death, he gave that property to his son Hendrick, who built a brick house on the land and over time made other improvements to the homestead. Like his brother, Anthony Rutgers accumulated property in both town and country. Anthony built a dwelling on Maiden Lane near his brother's house and later moved to a farm located northwest of City Hall, at the intersection of Broadway and present-day Chambers Street. Anthony also inherited Outward farmland, which he leased to white tenants who cultivated barley and sold a share of the harvest to their landlord. At the Rutgers brewery, that grain was distilled into beer and then transported to the city for sale. Over the years, the Rutgers family, which included the founder of Rutgers University, Colonel Henry Rutgers, accumulated a sizeable fortune through market-oriented purchases of real estate in both town and country, the operation of a successful brewery business, and the exploitation of white tenants and enslaved black laborers.[159]

Strung along the Hudson River as far north as Fort Orange, were the manorial estates of wealthy New York gentlemen.[160] New York's royal governors dispensed these large tracts of land to prominent settlers in exchange for their loyalty to the English Crown.[161] These governors also used various forms of patronage to entice men of accomplishment to settle in New York. Lured to New York by the promise of land, prestige, and political influence, Doctor Cadwallader Colden (1688–1776) became a member of the colony's landed elite. Born in Ireland to Scottish parents, Colden had studied medicine in London, considered himself a man of science, and carried on a correspondence with leading intellectuals in Europe, such as the renowned Swedish naturalist Linnaeus. Like Cotton Mather of colonial Massachusetts, Colden defied popular superstition by advocating smallpox inoculation and immunizing his own family. At the invitation of Governor Hunter, Colden left his physician's practice in Philadelphia and, in 1718, settled in New York City. An influential figure in colonial New York politics, Colden was a zealous defender of the Crown's prerogative powers and was rewarded for his loyalty with a number of coveted offices in the colonial government. From 1736 until his death in 1776, Colden held the successive posts of surveyor-general, member of the Governor's Council, and lieutenant governor.[162]

One year after Colden's arrival at New York City, Governor Hunter endowed the Scots-Irish physician with a land grant of 2,000 acres in Orange County, New York. Colden soon purchased an additional 1,000 acres and named his manorial estate Coldenham. Colden moved his wife, Alice, and their children to Coldenham, where he intended to pursue the secure life of a country gentleman on the rental income that he intended to collect from British tenants. Preferring to settle on land they owned, most British migrants shunned leaseholds, however. As his dream of obtaining ample rental income from numerous British tenants proved to be an unrealizable fantasy, Colden turned to enslaved black laborers who, by 1756, cultivated part of his farmland.[163] The owner of slaves and the lord of a manorial estate, Colden was a member of the British colonial elite, which Benedict Anderson has characterized as capitalists in aristocratic drag who were allowed "to play aristocrat off center court: i.e. anywhere in the empire except at home."[164] By the 1720s, the metropolitan government in London had abolished the feudal privileges of New York's colonial elite of wealthy landlords in order to make New York more attractive to settlers from the British Isles and Europe. Colden managed his manorial estate less like a feudal lord and more like a shrewd American businessman. Like other prominent settlers—for example, Frederick Philipse, Robert Livingston, and Stephanus DeLancey—he profited from the English Crown's patronage system of expansive land grants and lucrative monopoly contracts. Whether as landowners, overseas traders, or victuallers for the Royal troops, New York's colonial elite had an economic interest in the colony's commercial development. However much its members wrapped themselves in the trappings of an aristocracy, all but a few owed their social status to wealth alone, which typically consisted of land and slaves.

Enslaved blacks comprised a proportion of the wealth of colonial New York's ruling elite and also of the New York City artisans and the small, independent farmers in the hinterland. These colonists of diverse birthplaces, languages, and religions not only shared a common economic interest in the ownership and exploitation of enslaved labor, but also came to share a sense of communal belonging to a single, distinct race, set apart from the culturally alien race of African descent whose condition of servitude was heritable and perpetual bondage. The multiple population movements that flowed into the port of New York deposited a diverse assemblage of newcomers on Manhattan Island. The project of colony building on that island-peninsula, especially the need for a reliable labor force, involved installing uprooted newcomers in relationally constituted and differentially valued racialized subject-positions. Most Bantu, Malagasy, Akan, and other people from sub-Saharan Africa came to occupy the subject-position "enslaved black," while most English, Dutch, German, and other Western Europeans came to occupy the subject-position "white settler." The following three chapters discuss the process of racial formation and the emergence of antiblack racism as a disciplinary mechanism of colonial governance in the heterogeneous and sometimes volatile port town at the tip of Manhattan Island.

PART II

Racial Formation and the Art of Colonial Governance

"A Difference amongst Ourselves"

DIVISIONS OF RELIGION AND LANGUAGE,
SOLIDARITIES OF RACE AND NATION IN
COLONIAL NEW YORK CITY'S SETTLER POPULATION

Colonial New York City's multicultural, polyglot settler population
was the product of multiple transatlantic population movements originating in
the European diasporas of the post-Reformation era. Religious persecution,
war, poverty, and the dislocations accompanying the advent of modernity
brought to the colonial port town at the tip of Manhattan Island intermittent
flows of sojourners from a wide geographical arch across Europe and the
British Isles, reaching as far east as Kraków, as far west and north as the Hebrides, and as far south as Baden-Württemberg. Enlisted in the project of
colony building on Manhattan Island and in the surrounding countryside as part
of a vital labor force, these immigrants were, of course, more than mere constituents of labor in colonial development; they were, importantly, bearers of
cultures and ideologies that on the colonial frontier competed for dominance
over the settler population, especially the American-born youth.

Minimizing the articulated antagonisms of linguistic, confessional, natal, and
social differences among the settlers while, at the same time, forging a shared
sense of belonging to the English nation from the real and imaginary affinities
between colonial Netherlanders, German-speaking immigrants, French Protestants, and British migrants became the most difficult task confronting the English rulers. For them, practicing the art of colonial governance involved the
extension of English rights to the mainly foreign-born Protestant settler population, the incorporation of these peoples into the political community of loyal
English subjects, and the transplantation of legitimating institutions of English
culture for the cultivation of English civilities in the settlers. This expansion of

the communal boundaries of the English nation amounted to a reterritorializa-tion of Englishness—that is, a movement from defining Englishness as primarily consisting of the external trait of having been born on the soil of England to positing certain internal traits of innate racial disposition as the essence of En-glishness. Crucial to this shift was the myth of the Anglo-Saxon race, which le-gitimated the incorporation of Germanic peoples, including colonial Nether-landers, German speakers from the Rhineland, and even French Protestants, into the English nation. Importantly, the reterritorialization of Englishness gave rise to the privileging of racial purity as the decisive principle of boundary maintenance, for determining not only who would be excluded from but also who would be included in the English nation. Most studies of racial formation stress the process of exclusion, often to the neglect of inclusionary processes. This study departs from that methodology by giving attention to the criteria of inclusion in the racial formation of colonial New York City's settler population and to the problem of self-difference within the city's diverse and factious settler population that together prompted the formation of racial whiteness as an es-sential ingredient of Englishness in the colonial port town.

Inhabited by a collection of foreigners, speaking all kind of languages and professing many types of religious belief, colonial New York City scarcely con-formed to the new English rulers' conception of an ideal society. Reporting on the variety of religions in the colonial port town, Governor Edmund Andros (1674–77 and 1681) wrote in 1678: "There are Religions of all sorts, one Church of England, Several Presbyterians & Independents, Quakers & Anabaptists of Sev-erall sects, some Jews but presbyterians & Independents most numerous & sub-stantiall."[1] In 1686, Governor Dongan called attention to the numerical weak-ness of the major Christian congregations, the comparatively large number of minor religious sects, and the absence of religiosity among most settlers: "Here bee not many of the Church of England, few Catholicks; abundance of Quak-ers preachers men and Women especially; Singing Quakers; Ranting Quakers; Sabbatarians; Antisabbatarians; some Anabaptists; some Independents; some Jews; in short all sorts of opinions there are some, and the most part, of none at all."[2] Writing from the city in 1692, Charles Lodwick complained: "Our chiefest unhappyness here is too great a mixture of nations."[3] And as late as 1760, an En-glish visitor reported that the city's settler population was comprised of so many "different nations, different languages and different religions . . . it is impossible to give them any precise or determinate character."[4]

Significantly, most settlers had little or no previous experience of allegiance to a centralized governmental authority. This characteristic described the settlers who arrived at Manhattan Island during the Dutch colonial period: The colonial Netherlanders came from the Dutch Republic, a geopolitical jurisdiction that more closely resembled a loose confederation of provinces than a single, con-solidated, territorial nation-state, and the Walloon settlers originated in the Bur-gundian or southern Netherlands (present-day Belgium), a war-torn territory and object of a protracted contest between the United Provinces and Spain dur-ing the early modern era. Disembarking at the port of New York during the early years of English rule, the French-speaking Huguenot settlers were Protestant refugees who had fled religious persecution at the hands of France's Catholic monarch, and the German-speaking settlers that flowed into New York's seaport were mostly militant Protestants from various fragmented European provinces ruled by Catholic princes but not yet incorporated into a nation-state or a comparable governmental unit.

The English rulers in colonial New York City had few models to guide them in governing such a culturally varied and politically estranged settler population, which included not only different linguistic and religious groups but also numerous uprooted people who were largely disconnected from the sources of authority in England. Arguably, the New England colonies offered the most successful example of English colonization in North America. But unlike colonial New York City's settler population, colonial New Englanders were mainly English-speaking migrants from the British Isles. In New York City, the art of colonial governance became a matter of making loyal British subjects out of the port town's diverse foreign-born settler population. The English Crown relied on surrogates to fulfill that goal and to project its sovereignty to that distant seaport. Colonial administrators, clergymen, missionaries, and schoolmasters undertook the task of transplanting English cultural institutions and systems of representation, as well as English institutions of governance, in New York City. Yet during the early stages of English rule, neither the English colonial administration nor the Church of England proved to be capable of effectively extending the reach of the English territorial monarchy and its legitimating religious and cultural institutions to that remote colonial port town.

Not surprisingly, the arrival of the news of England's Glorious Revolution (1688–89) in New York City precipitated a crisis of colonial governance that resulted in an uprising known as Leisler's Rebellion (1689–92), a settler revolt that began with the removal of the Crown-appointed colonial officials who ruled New York in the name of the Stuart monarchy and ended in the execution of the rebel leaders. In the wake of Leisler's Rebellion, the English rulers, again, confronted the task of securing the undivided loyalty of the city's factious foreign-born settler population. Endeavoring to minimize linguistic, confessional, and natal differences among the settlers and to foster a shared sense of communal belonging to the English nation among them, the English Parliament eliminated the political disabilities imposed on foreign-born Protestant settlers, while the Society for the Propagation of the Gospel in Foreign Parts, the Church of England's overseas missionary organization, cultivated the civilities and competencies of Englishness among the settlers by providing them with English-language schooling and instruction in the doctrines of Anglicanism. By the middle of the eighteenth century, the rise in conversions to Anglicanism and the nearly universal use of the English language among American-born settlers, along with the widespread practice of settler intermarriage, had produced a relatively homogeneous Anglicized settler population. However, Englishness stood in an uneasy relation to competing bonds of group identity. As late as the 1740s, confessional, linguistic, and natal differences remained sources of antagonism both within the city's settler population and between the English rulers and the settlers.

With the capture of the Dutch fort at the tip of Manhattan Island, the English conquerors confronted the task of peaceably ruling a foreign settler population. The terms of the English takeover, first outlined in the Articles of Capitulation (1664),[5] were designed to appease colonial Netherlanders who, along with other Dutch speakers, were nearly 80 percent of New York City's settler population at the time of the English conquest.[6] The provisions of the Dutch surrender declared colonial Netherlanders to be free denizens with the right to trade within the British Empire, extended liberty of conscience to Dutch Calvinists, promised to respect Dutch customs of inheritance, and released colonial Netherlanders from the obligation to bear arms against England's enemy, the United Provinces. However, the groundwork for what appeared to be an amicable changeover from Dutch to English rule was nearly spoiled when some roguish English soldiers asserted their status as conquerors by seizing the property of Dutch-speaking townspeople and arrogantly defying the authority of the colonial Netherlanders whom the new English rulers had appointed to governmental posts. In retaliation, colonial Netherlanders communicated their hatred of the English military presence by hailing the Royal troops with the epithet "English dogs" or, when their English vocabulary failed them, by raising their fists in anger. On June 19, 1665, mounting antagonisms between Dutch-speaking settlers and English-speaking newcomers erupted into a violent altercation, in which a colonial Netherlander and New York City constable named Hendrick Obe suffered serious bodily injury. Although overt hostility toward the new English rulers had subsided by 1670, some colonial Netherlanders did not conceal their desire to rid themselves of the English conquerors, when Dutch military forces recaptured Manhattan Island in 1673.[7] The Dutch Reconquest was short-lived, however. After only 15 months under the restored Dutch colonial government, Manhattan Island, together with the rest of New York, reverted to England by stipulation of the Treaty of Westminster, which concluded the third Anglo-Dutch War.[8]

Alarmed at the colonial Netherlanders' collaboration with Dutch officials during the Reconquest of 1673 and the refusal of some to pledge an oath of allegiance to the English Crown, New York's Governor Edmund Andros considered a plan for the removal of colonial Netherlanders from New York City and the resettlement of that population to the territory in and around Albany. This scheme also envisioned replacing the relocated population of colonial Netherlanders with loyal settlers from the British Isles. The English colonial government never realized this plan, though some disaffected colonial Netherlanders voluntarily left New York following the Retrocession of 1674. Instead of forcefully relocating potentially disloyal settlers to remote parts of New York, Andros reiterated the English conquerors' demanded that colonial Netherlanders submit a pledge of allegiance to the English Crown. When several Dutch merchants refused to swear fidelity to the English monarch unless Andros confirmed the exemptions listed in the Articles of Capitulation, the English governor brought them to court and tried them as alien interlopers who traded in New York City in violation of the English Navigation Acts. Whereas in previous trials involving Dutch defendants the English colonial authorities had impaneled juries composed of both Dutch and English settlers and, in some cases, took care to convene all-Dutch juries, in the trial against the obstinate Dutch merchants a panel comprised entirely of Englishmen convicted the accused of trespass against the Crown's revenues. As punishment for their crime, the Dutch merchants forfeited their property in England and in the English overseas colonies. This action served as a warning to colonial Netherlanders and other foreigners who resided within the first British Empire: Submit to English rule or lose the liberties granted to them, including the right to own property. To allay growing fears that the English rulers intended to divest all colonial Netherlanders of their liberty, Governor Andros promised that in New York the "Inhabitants of the Dutch nation . . . should participate in the same privileges as those of the English nation."[9] However, implicit in this assurance was a principle of reciprocity—that along with the privilege of English liberties came the obligation to obey English law, disavow all competing political loyalties, and recognize the sovereignty of the English Crown. If the "Dutch nation," a majority of New York City's settler population, refused to submit to English rule, they would be treated as aliens with no claim to English liberties. However, the imperatives of colony building, especially the urgency of attracting and retaining settlers, meant that the English authorities had to expand rather than retract the liberties of colonial New York's settler population.

Although the Duke of York retained his prerogative powers of rule over colonial New York and its inhabitants, in 1683 he granted the settlers a charter of liberties and an elective colonial assembly.[10] As its first piece of business, New York's newly established legislative body enacted a law that extended a range of individual rights and political privileges to all Christian settlers of foreign birth who had resided in New York for at least six years and willingly pledged an oath of fidelity to the English Crown. These liberties included the freedom to conduct trade and practice crafts in New York, as well as the right to own, alienate, and inherit property in the colony, vote in New York elections, and hold public offices. Known as the "Act for Naturalizing all these foreign Nations at Present Inhabiting within this Province and Professing Christianity, and for Encouragement of Others to Come and Settle within the Same" (1683),[11] that law eradicated most political distinctions between foreign-born and English-born settlers. However, the privileges that it bestowed on the Christian settlers of foreign birth did not extend beyond colonial New York's borders. In England, the law maintained a clear distinction between rights-bearing subjects and aliens without rights, and it further divided the rights-bearing population into finer categories of subjecthood—for example, native-born subjects, naturalized subjects, and denizens—with different rights and privileges or, alternatively, varying disabilities. Some foreign-born settlers applied for and received patents of English denizenship, and thereby obtained the right to trade at all English ports; own, devise, and inherit land within the English realm, including England; and bring legal actions before most English courts, but not the right to vote and hold public office in England. Importantly, no political disabilities distinguished the *post-nati* children of denizens from native Englishmen.[12] However, English law limited most rights and privileges of English subjecthood to Christians only. In England, all Jews were barred from voting, holding public office, owning land, and bearing arms in the English realm. Because the extensive intercontinental network of Jewish merchants and moneylenders provided invaluable financial services to the first British Empire, the English state allowed Jews to do business within England's commercial sphere and to reside in England and in the English overseas colonies without interference.[13]

In New York, the early English colonial authorities extended liberty of conscience to all settlers, including the Jewish settlers. The Duke's instructions to Governor Andros stated: "Permit all persons of what Religion soever, quietly to inhabit within the precincts of your jurisdiction, without giving them any disturbance or disquiet whatsoever, for or by reason of their differing opinions in matters of Religion; Provided they give no disturbance to the publique peace, nor doe molest or disquiet others in the free exercise of their religion."[14] New York's Charter of Liberties of 1683 further stipulated that each county would have its own tax-supported church, with that privilege going to the Protestant congregation whose representatives were a majority of the parish vestry. According to the charter, minority Protestant congregations received no tax support but were granted the privilege of holding public worship services and paying their ministers from voluntary donations. The English rulers thus struck a compromise between the extension of religious liberty to all settlers and the establishment of a state church in the amended form of plural tax-supported Protestant churches. While official colonial policy denied Catholic settlers the privilege of holding public worship services, the early English colonial officials tolerated the presence of professing Catholic laypeople but not Catholic priests within the jurisdiction of New York. By permitting the settlers, including Catholics and Jews, to exercise individual liberty of conscience, the English rulers hoped to avoid popular unrest as well as make New York an attractive destination for diverse religious refugees from Europe. But that policy soon reopened the field of contestation in which debate over religious tolerance and the state-church relation divided post-Reformation Englishmen.

With the accession of Charles II to the English throne in 1660, the Episcopacy of London molded the Church of England into a sacral institution for legitimating and extending the dynastic rule of the Stuart monarchy. Catholic-leaning clerics now controlled that ecclesiastical body. Claiming the authority to govern all churches within the English realm and attempting to impose Anglican ministers on dissenting independent congregations throughout the British Isles, the Episcopacy of London ignited a firestorm of popular protest against the Church of England establishment. Once again, dissenting Protestants refused to recognize the authority of the Episcopacy of London over their congregations and defended their independence by continuing to hire ministers of their own choosing, without seeking approval from the Anglican officials.[15] Acting in the name of the English Crown, the Episcopacy of London took on the task of governing souls in the English overseas colonies during an era of internal turbulence in England. Reverend Thomas Bray, founder of several Anglican missionary organizations and rector of St. Botolph in London, wrote the following assessment of the urgent mission facing the Church of England in the overseas territories of the first British Empire: "Some colonies and plantations wholly destitute and unprovided of a maintenance of ministers, many of the subjects of this realm want the administration of God's word and sacraments, and seemed to be abandoned to atheism and infidelity."[16] Church of England officials pledged to fortify the feeble foundations of institutionalized religion on the colonial frontier, but the protests of dissenting congregations in the British Isles and the revolutionary upheavals that followed from them proved to be such a consuming distraction that the English state church was unable to devote much attention to colonial affairs. At the time of the English conquest of New Netherland in 1664, the Episcopacy of London superseded the Classis of Amsterdam as the chief ecclesiastical authority in the conquered territory that the English Crown renamed New York. But that ecclesiastical body sent few ministers to New York during the early years of English rule. It was not until 1694, fully 30 years after the English takeover, that the city's Anglican congregation built its own house of worship. And it was not until 1702, approximately 40 years after the restoration of the Stuart monarchy and more than a decade after the Glorious Revolution, that Bray's Society for the Propagation of the Gospel in Foreign Parts (SPG), an Anglican missionary organization charged with the duty of transplanting Anglicanism in the English overseas colonies, sent missionaries to New York City.

Reverend John Miller, the first Anglican clergyman called to New York City, bemoaned the spiritual condition of that colonial port town's settler population and considered the "wickedness and irreligion of the white settlers to be the foremost evil in the province."[17] In a letter to the Anglican officials in London, written four decades after the English Conquest, Colonel Caleb Heathcote reported on the frailty of institutionalized religion in New York: "I cannot omitt giving you the State of this Country in relation to the Church," he wrote, "& shall begin the History therefore from the Time I first came amongst them, which was about twelve years ago when I found it the most rude & Heathenish country I ever saw in my whole Life, which call'd themselves Christians, there being not so much as the least marks or footsteps of religion of any sort, Sundays being the only time sett apart by them for all manner of vain sports & Lewd Diversions, & they were grown to such a Degree of rudeness that it was Intolerable."[18] Reproaching the SPG missionaries for neglecting the Christian settlers' spiritual well being and devoting a disproportionate share of their attention to the enslaved Africans, an English newcomer warned: "While the very Negroes may be washed and become White by the Gospel, the Christians may be turned into Negroes and become black and polluted."[19] In colonial New York City, where light-skinned Europeans lived in close proximity to dark-skinned Africans, the Manichean dualism, which equated *blackness* with moral pollution and *whiteness* with moral purity, was projected onto the colonial population. In this respect, the medieval Christian symbolism of darkness and light became the basis of reified, binary categories of humankind. Sub-Saharan Africans thus became the living embodiments of *blackness*, ever-present reminders of what the settlers were in danger of becoming: godless savages who dwelled in spiritual darkness.

For the English colonial authorities, the imposition of universal conformity to the Church of England offered one method of establishing a government over the souls of the settlers and saving them from the peril of degenerating to savagery. However, the English rulers worried that the sudden imposition of compulsory adherence to the Church of England would ignite widespread settler opposition to the English colonial government. For this reason, the English state initially pursued a policy of religious tolerance and ordered New York's colonial authorities to refrain from interfering in the settlers' religious affairs. Some zealous Anglicans regarded this policy as an unacceptable concession to the dissenting congregations and an obstacle to the spread of Anglicanism in the newly conquered colony. Finding himself living in a strange land, where Protestant dissenters were a majority of the settler population, an Anglican newcomer lamented: "Though the English grew numerous, the government in their hands and the national laws took place, yet for want of a Temple for the public Worship according to the English Church, this seemed rather like a Foreign Province, than an English Colony, possessed and settled by people of our own Nation."[20] According to the Anglican newcomer, the Church of England was a desperately needed institution of English culture, without which New York would remain an alien country.

New York Anglicans received no immediate remedy from the Episcopacy of London, but the English Crown did take action. Convinced that tolerance of religious pluralism in the English overseas colonies posed a threat to his sovereignty, King James II, previously the Duke of York and successor to the English throne following the death of Charles II in 1685, vetoed New York's Charter of Liberties and advised the colony's royal governor: "Our will and pleasure is that noe minister be preferred by you to any Ecclesiastical Benefice in that our Province, without a Certificát from ye most Reverend the Lord Archbishop of Canterbury of his being conformable to ye Doctrine and Discipline of the Church of England."[21] James II further commanded all New York churches to conform to the Church of England liturgy. Specifically, the Stuart monarch ordered the *Book of Common Prayer* read each Sunday and holiday in every church and the sacraments administered according to Anglican practice. An innovation of Elizabeth I, the *Book of Common Prayer* (1559) set out, in detail, uniform rituals and prayers that were to be performed in all English churches according to a fixed calendar.[22] Each Sunday and holiday all congregations, though scattered throughout the English realm, were expected to recite the same supplications from the *Book of Common Prayer*. Some prayers—for example, the Litany and the Thanksgiving Prayer on the Anniversary of the Monarch's Coronation—were recited in the form of a call-and-response that reinforced the confessional bond between the clerical leader, who delivered the beginning of each line of the prayer, and the members of the congregation, who replied in unison with its ending. In this and other respects, the Church of England's forms of worship iterated the hierarchical order of English society. In addition, the *Book of Common Prayer*'s "Calendar of Lessons" assigned, for each day of the year, a moral principle and two sets of correlative biblical passages that all devout Anglicans were expected to contemplate at morning and evening prayers. From its inception, the primary task of the Church of England and its *Book of Common Prayer* was the production and maintenance of horizontal and vertical identifications that were supposed to cement the bond of national community and secure universal loyalty to the English Crown among disciplined English subjects. Like Elizabeth I, the Stuart monarchs of the Restoration era regarded the national church, which subjected its adherents to the discipline of uniform and regular rituals of worship, as an indispensable institution of governance. When King James II, embattled monarch of England, endeavored to impose universal conformity to the Church of England liturgy on colonial New York's settler population, he did so as a means of extending his sovereignty to the distant and recently conquered colony that his brother, the former king of England, had named in his honor.

James II did, however, respect the proviso of the English takeover that allowed the Classis of Amsterdam to retain authority over the Dutch Reformed churches in British North America. In effect, that provision of the Dutch surrender exempted New York's Dutch Calvinist congregations from James II's imposition of the Church of England liturgy and Anglican ministers on the colony's churches.[23] In view of that special exemption, Dominie Selijns, New York City's Dutch Calvinist minister, reminded his congregation of their exceptional privileges and preached obedience to the English civil authorities: "We are in a foreign country, and also governed by the English nation. . . . We must exercise much prudence in order to preserve the liberties granted us," he advised.[24] Having witnessed the stern punishment that Governor Andros meted out to refractory Dutch merchants in 1675, most wealthy congregants heeded the Dutch Calvinist clergyman's advice. These colonial Netherlanders had already reconciled themselves to the political realities of English rule, submitted oaths of loyalty to the English Crown, and agreed to obey the English Navigation Acts in exchange for English liberties.

Additionally, the English Crown bestowed gifts of patronage on influential colonial Netherlanders—for example, the Bayards, the Philipses, and the Van Cortlandts—as reward for their collaboration in governing New York. As a result of this system of favoritism, a rift of social inequality emerged within New York City's settler population during the years following the English Conquest, "a cleavage felt nowhere more strongly," the historian Randall Balmer has noted, "than in the Dutch community."[25] While a privileged segment of colonial Netherlanders prospered during the early years of English rule, most Dutch-speaking Calvinist settlers were never admitted to the colonial ruling class. By the late 1680s, a clique of Anglo-Dutch elites monopolized appointed offices and other forms of Crown patronage, such as generous land grants and lucrative government contracts. The growing political clout and social prestige of that upper stratum of New York City's population could not be easily disarticulated from the exclusion of most Dutch-speaking Calvinists from the city's narrow circle of privilege, influence, and wealth. Now positioned as a conquered and increasingly marginalized population with respect to determining the political and economic affairs of the colony that they helped build, some long-established colonial Netherlanders suspected King James II, and the Catholic-leaning officials he sent to New York to rule on his behalf, of plotting to install a despotic government over them.

The Stuart monarch seemed to confirm these suspicions when, in 1686, he asserted his claim to the divine right of absolute rule by vetoing New York's Charter of Liberties, vacating the separate charters of the New England colonies, dissolving the colonial assemblies, placing all powers of colonial governance in the hands of Crown-appointed officials, consolidating the New England colonies into a supracolony called the Dominion of New England, and, later, annexing New York to that jurisdiction. By these sweeping autocratic acts, James II aimed to bring the English overseas colonies under stricter control and, through the better regulation of colonial trade, increase the Crown's revenues from the collection of duties on tobacco, sugar, and other colonial produce.[26] The settlers protested against James II's colonial policy and the abrogation of the liberties that the English state had promised them. Writing from New York City, Governor Thomas Dongan observed with alarm: "The people growing every day more numerous & they generally of a turbulent disposition."[27] Meanwhile, a combination of the Stuart monarch's adversaries in England launched a decisive challenge to his sovereignty.

In 1688, James II's enemies, many of whom had opposed his accession to the English throne, invited Prince William of Orange and his wife, Mary, James II's daughter, to invade England and seize the English Crown. With the landing of Prince William's army at Trobay in Devonshire and the desertion of his own troops, James II fled to Catholic France. Known as the Glorious Revolution (1688–89), the flight of James II and the installation of the Protestants William III and Mary II as joint sovereigns of England resulted in historic constitutional reforms, including the prohibition against the accession of any Catholic to the English throne, the English Declaration of Rights and Bill of Rights, the abolition of the royal prerogative to nullify English law and suspend the English Parliament, and the elimination of the monarch's right to levy taxes and maintain a standing army without parliamentary consent. In this respect, the Glorious Revolution marked a shift from feudal to modern institutions of governance and announced the ascendancy of the Lockean conception of sovereignty. The ideals of the Glorious Revolution resonated throughout the settler colonies of British North America. Once news of England's Glorious Revolution radiated outward from the metropolitan center to the colonial frontier, restive settlers defied the authority of colonial officeholders who owed their appointments to the recently deposed Stuart monarch, James II.[28]

While elsewhere in British North America the settlers quickly united to seize the colonial governments, the disunited settlers in New York quarreled over the issue of who should lead. By the late 1680s, the proliferation of social and religious antagonisms had created a fault line that divided New York City's settler population into two opposing political camps. On the one side, the city's privileged clique of Anglo-Dutch elites reluctantly recognized the accession of William of Orange to the English throne but insisted that James II's appointees remain at their colonial posts, unless recalled by the new monarch. This group consisted of the lieutenant governor and his council, the heads of New York City's municipal government, prominent clergymen, including Dutch Calvinist ministers, and the wealthy merchants and landlords who had materially benefited from the patronage that James II had bestowed on his loyal supporters. On the other side, their opponents insisted that the overthrow of James II meant that his colonial appointees no longer ruled New York. This faction consisted of a cross section of the city's settler population—for example, common laborers, artisans, ambitious shopkeepers, and a few wealthy merchants. Even though it is impossible to ascertain the precise linguistic and religious composition of the opposition faction, the historian Thomas Archdeacon has argued that New York City's Dutch-speaking Calvinist majority, two-thirds of the city's total population on the eve of the Glorious Revolution, supported the overthrow of James II's colonial appointees.[29] In New York City, the settlers from Holland welcomed the accession of their countryman, William of Orange, to the English throne. Not all of the early Dutch-speaking Calvinist settlers were, however, natives of Holland; nearly half had been born elsewhere, mainly in the areas of Europe that witnessed bloody battles between Catholics and Protestants during the Thirty Years War (1618–48).[30] Displaced by the devastation of that war, these Protestant refugees fled to Calvinist strongholds in the Netherlands, where they lived for some time. In the Netherlands, Protestant exiles, especially the younger generation, mastered the Dutch language and adopted other Dutch habits. They also learned to cherish their deliverance from Catholic tyranny and the liberties that they enjoyed under the protection of the Dutch Republic and the Dutch Reformed Church. The Dutch West India Company transported a segment of the United Provinces' Protestant refugee community to New Netherland, and when England captured that Dutch colony, the English conquerors inherited a settler population with a Dutch-speaking Calvinist majority. Although originating from different homelands, these settlers shared a common language and, above all, a common antipathy against Roman Catholicism.

Not surprisingly, New York City's Dutch-speaking Calvinist majority viewed the world through the optic of post-Reformation politics and regarded any alliance with papists as a betrayal of the Protestant cause. When these anti-Catholic settlers observed the incipient alliance between the clique of wealthy Anglo-Dutch elites and the colonial officeholders who owed their appointments to the professed Catholic James II, they perceived a dangerous conspiracy to impose Catholic tyranny on New York.[31] For this reason, they called for the removal of the deposed Stuart monarch's colonial surrogates, whom they now openly accused of infecting New York with the pestilence of Roman Catholicism. Prominent New York Anglicans were, these settlers alleged, false Protestants who secretly worshiped idols and perpetuated popery. In addition, anti-Catholic alarmists circulated the rumor that James II intended to retain control over New York by joining with Catholic France to invade and conquer the colony. Questioning Lieutenant Governor Francis Nicholson's loyalty to England's new monarch, supporters of the Glorious Revolution in New York City demanded that Nicholson read a public proclamation acknowledging the accession of William of Orange to the English throne. Nicholson reluctantly acquiesced to this ultimatum but soon fled New York for fear that, if he remained in the colony, he would be imprisoned as a papist conspirator. The lieutenant governor's sudden exit set the stage for Leisler's Rebellion (1689–91), a coup d'état against New York City's colonial officeholders and Anglo-Dutch ruling elite.

On October 23, 1689, some restive settlers seized the fort at the tip of Manhattan Island, declared martial law, jailed James II's royal designees, and installed the militia captain and zealous Dutch-speaking Calvinist Jacob Leisler as head of the interim military government. The son of a Palatine minister and born in Frankfurt am Main in 1640, Leisler migrated to New Amsterdam in 1660 and served as a military officer for the Dutch West India Company until the English Conquest of 1664. While in the WIC's employ, Leisler engaged in trading ventures for his own profit and eventually married the widow of a prominent colonial Netherlander. In this and other matters, Leisler followed the typical path of early settlers who began their careers in Manhattan under Dutch rule. Although Leisler assisted the restored Dutch colonial government during the Reconquest of 1673, he remained on favorable terms with the English rulers following the Retrocession of 1674. The English takeover did not hamper Leisler in his ambition to become a wealthy merchant. Rather, the Dutch-speaking Calvinist from Frankfurt am Main and former officer in the WIC military forces prospered under English colonial rule. As a naturalized English subject, Leisler took advantage of new business opportunities within the English commercial sphere and shifted the focus of his maritime trading ventures to the British North American coast, specifically the lucrative Chesapeake tobacco trade. All told, Leisler held no grievances against the English rulers on account of any damage that he sustained to his material estate as a consequence of the English conquest. At the time of the Glorious Revolution, Leisler was one of New York City's wealthiest merchants. In consideration of his social status, the English rulers attempted to recruit him into the ranks of New York's Anglo-Dutch ruling class. Leisler accepted appointments to minor government posts, but for the most part he maintained a guarded distance from the narrow circle of Anglo-Dutch placeholders that ruled New York.[32]

"Governance, for Leisler," the historian David Voorhees has stressed, "was a spiritual as well as civic duty."[33] It was at the intersection of politics and religion that Leisler distinguished himself from New York City's Anglo-Dutch elite. Around 1685, Leisler left the city's Dutch Calvinist Church in protest against Dominie Selijns's refusal to condemn the preaching of heterodoxy in New York. Instead of joining the city's Anglican Church, as other wealthy Calvinist merchants had done, Leisler joined the city's French Calvinist Church, where he worshiped with Huguenot congregants who had recently fled France to escape Louis XIV's persecution of Protestants following the revocation of the Edict of Nantes (1685). Leisler's family had ties to the Huguenot congregation in Frankfurt, and Leisler himself had spent a portion of his personal fortune to finance the relocation of

Huguenot refugees from Europe to New York City. A zealous Calvinist and generous benefactor to the Protestant victims of Catholic tyranny, Leisler remained alert to the threat that the Catholic monarch King James II posed to Protestantism in the English overseas colonies, as well as in England. As Captain Leisler later explained, he and his followers commandeered the colonial government in order to extend the Protestant victories of the Glorious Revolution to New York.[34] It was on behalf of England's new Protestant monarch and the greater Protestant cause against Catholic despotism that Leisler agreed to lead New York City's settler revolt against James II's placemen.

In December 1689, a vessel arrived at the port of New York with instructions from England's new monarch. These orders were addressed to Francis Nicholson or, as the documents stated, "such as for the time being take care of Preserving the Peace and administrating the Lawes in our said Province of New York in America."[35] Because Nicholson no longer resided in New York, Jacob Leisler interpreted the royal missive to mean that he, as commander of the military forces at Fort William, should remain in charge of the colony's interim military government until King William III appointed a new governor. The ousted members of Nicholson's council objected to Leisler's interpretation of the king's instructions, decried his assumption of authority, and declared that the militia captain and his associates were in rebellion against the English Crown. Although Liesler's loudest enemies had earlier fled New York City and retreated to Albany to avoid imprisonment, some of his foes had returned to the city by 1690. At that time, Leisler incarcerated two of his most vocal opponents, Nicholas Bayard and William Nicolls, on the charge of fomenting a riot and, later that same year, claimed to have discovered a "popish plot" to incinerate the city.[36]

During the course of addressing these and other internal intrigues against his government, Leisler all but neglected the important political deliberations on New York's future that were taking place in London. Leisler's enemies had sent emissaries to the metropolis to denounce him. In their meeting with King William III, Leisler's adversaries accused him of ruining New York's trade, revoking the liberties of the English Crown's loyal subjects in New York, and usurping the monarch's authority. They even broadcast the rumor that Leisler, a Dutch-speaking Calvinist and ex-military officer for the WIC, intended to exterminate the English settlers and surrender New York to the United Provinces. Seeking confirmation of his government, Leisler eventually sent two supporters, Joost Stol and Benjamin Blagge, to London to lobby on his behalf. Leisler's ambassadors were strangers to English metropolitan politics and in their interview with William III did an inadequate job of defending Leisler's government. Ultimately, the new Protestant monarch refused to condone the overthrow of James II's appointed officials in New York, even if such action had been taken to secure his own accession to the English throne. The new monarch's colonial policy was clear. While England's Glorious Revolution announced a shift from the investiture of absolute power in the person of a single monarch unbound by law to a new governmental economy of the supremacy of law over autocratic rulers and a balanced constitution of shared governmental powers between the

Crown, Parliament, and common lawyers in which the governed participated in the formulation of law, the achievements of the Glorious Revolution did not annul the lawful authority of the Crown's designated surrogates in the British Empire; on no occasion were the settlers to take the law into their own hands and forcibly remove Crown-appointed officials from their colonial posts. Leisler and his supporters had misjudged the temper of the Glorious Revolution, King William III, and the Compromise of 1689. They would soon pay a severe price for their miscalculation.

When, in 1691, New York's newly appointed royal governor, Henry Sloughter, arrived at the port of New York, he immediately ordered Captain Leisler to deliver the fort at the tip of Manhattan Island to him. Leisler at first refused to obey Sloughter's directive but eventually surrendered the fortress, which he had renamed Fort William in honor of England's new Protestant monarch. Acting on the advice of Leisler's enemies, who now occupied seats on the governor's council, Sloughter arrested Leisler and several of his followers on the charge of treason. Leisler and his son-in-law, John Milbourne, were soon convicted of that capital crime. Following the sentencing, Leisler's wife and other members of his family begged Sloughter to spare the lives of the condemned men. But the governor remained unmoved by their pleas for leniency and, as a warning to disaffected settlers of what would happen to them should they dare to defy New York's English colonial rulers, executed the two overzealous supporters of the Glorious Revolution.[37] Governor Sloughter performed this bloody deed in the name of the English monarch, who, despite the constitutional limitations on his authority in England, still possessed the sovereign power "to *take* life or *let* live" within the realm of empire.[38]

On May 16, 1691, a large crowd assembled to witness Leisler's execution. At the appointed hour, English soldiers carted Leisler to the gallows, where an executioner hanged the convicted traitor by the neck and then beheaded him.[39] With this public spectacle of punishment, the English colonial rulers intended to pacify widespread opposition to their government. But the brutal execution served only to redouble the resentment of Leisler's numerous supporters. In his last statement from the gallows, Leisler called for an end to the discord that divided New York City's settler population from the city's ruling elite.[40] Yet as the final deathblow extinguished his life, the onlookers could be heard uttering recriminations against the English colonial rulers. Before dispersing, the crowd sang Psalm 79 in unison. With that mass performance of psalmody, Leisler's supporters achieved an "unisonality" that at that moment constituted them as a community united against a common oppressor.[41] The mass singing of Psalm 79 was an especially resonant mode of protest against the colonial officeholders, whom many settlers regarded as the enemies of true religion. That passage from the Bible recalled the heathens' destruction of Jerusalem, the biblical Jacob's martyrdom, and God's impending wrath.[42] Leisler's mourners seemed to be warning that God would surely punish colonial New York's bloodthirsty rulers for the injustice that they had done to their martyred hero.

Leisler's Rebellion and its aftermath exposed the volatility of a settler population that was riven by confessional, linguistic, natal, and social antagonisms. In view of this precarious situation, the English colonial rulers soon took steps to appease the restive settlers and, in 1692, acquiesced to the demands of English-speaking settlers who clamored for a new charter of liberties and the reinstatement of the elective colonial assembly.[43] Other settlers also coveted English liberties. For the settlers from Europe who had experienced unjust taxation and religious persecution in their homelands, English liberties appeared in an especially favorable light. Colonial Netherlanders were, of course, eager to preserve their liberties. But instead of referring to English rights, some pointed with pride to the Dutch revolt against tyrannical Catholic Spain in 1568, the founding of the Dutch Republic in 1580, and the unique freedom of the people in the United Provinces. Moreover, these colonial Netherlanders regarded the English colonial rulers as usurpers of liberty, who ruled New York by right of violent conquest rather than popular consent. As the historian John Murrin has noted, some colonial Netherlanders interpreted the restoration of New York's Charter of Liberties and its colonial assembly as an act of "ethnic aggression,"[44] the gift horse of English Trojans who used the lure of English rights to further a secret despotic design to impose a corrupted Church of England establishment on New York's dissenting congregations.

Governor Benjamin Fletcher (1692–98), a William and Mary appointee, seemed to confirm this suspicion when he launched an attack against religious pluralism in New York by securing the passage of the Ministry Act (1693) from the newly reconvened colonial assembly, now dominated by prominent New York Anglicans. That statute obliged all taxpayers in New York, Richmond, Queens, and Westchester counties to support the Church of England and the Anglican clergymen whom the Episcopacy of London sent to New York.[45] A steadfast supporter of England's national church, Governor Fletcher equated religious pluralism with disorder and expressed his contempt for New York City's factious settler population, remarking: "I find them a divided, contentious, impoverished people."[46] Fletcher soon provoked a renewed surge of settler opposition to New York's English colonial government when, in 1694, he named Reverend John Miller, the Anglican chaplain for the English soldiers at the fort on Manhattan Island, to the coveted post of New York City's tax-supported minister. Like Fletcher, Reverend Miller harbored contempt for the city's settler population and in his description of the townspeople wrote: "As to their religion, they are very much divided; few of them intelligent and sincere, but the most part ignorant and conceited, fickle and regardless as to their wealth and disposition thereto. . . ."[47] Comprised of dissenting Protestants who chafed under the government of Jacob Leisler's state executioners, New York City's vestry opposed Miller's appointment and insisted on hiring their own candidate. Hoping to appease his opponents and to avert another settler revolt, Fletcher agreed to appoint a compromise candidate.[48]

Fallout from Leisler's Rebellion polarized New York City's political life for more than a decade after Leisler's execution. Writing from the city in 1695, Reverend Miller observed: "These injuries done by either side to their opposites have made a most unhappy division & breach among them which will hardly of a long time admit a cure."[49] Hostility between the Leislerians and the anti-

Leislerians or, as they were sometimes called, the "Black Party" and the "White Party" persisted until the 1710s.[50] Lord Cornbury, royal governor of New York from 1702 to 1708, opined that the Leslerians (or "Black Party") "will never be reconciled to an English governor, unless they can find one who will betray the English laws . . . and interest to the Dutch."[51] New York City's Dutch Reformed Church became the arena for acts of revenge against the Leislerians' most despised enemies—namely, Calvinists who had sided with Governor Sloughter and joined the Anglo-Dutch ruling elite in calling for Leisler's execution. On that score, nobody was more detested than Dominie Selijns, the city's Dutch Reformed minister. In retaliation against Selijns, the Leislerian majority in the city's Dutch Calvinist congregation arranged to withhold his salary. Outrage against Selijns was so vehement and pervasive that as late as 1698 nearly 90 percent of the city's Dutch Calvinist congregation abstained from the Lord's Supper that Selijns officiated over at the Dutch Reformed Church.[52] Political fallout from Leisler's execution and the punishment of his supporters extended far beyond New York City and eventually reached across the Atlantic Ocean. In London, the Leislerians' emissaries demanded that Parliament repeal the writ of attainder against their victimized leader and order the return of the property that Governor Sloughter had confiscated from Leisler's family and followers. Connected to influential Hollanders by the bonds of kinship and marriage, the Leislerians used transatlantic networks to enlist ambassadors at The Hague to negotiate on their behalf. The use of diplomacy proved to be an effective strategy for obtaining redress of their grievances. In 1694, England's Privy Council pardoned Leisler's followers and ordered the return of their estates. The following year, the English Parliament annulled the writ that charged Leisler and his son-in-law Jacob Milbourne with treason.[53]

After a delay of several years, the Privy Council finally ordered New York's royal governor to permit the Leislerians to stage a public funeral in honor of Leisler and Milbourne, whose corpses had been buried in a remote area of New York City that the municipal government reserved for the burial of paupers, strangers, criminals, and slaves. In 1698, a delegation of Leislerians exhumed the physical remains of their heroes from that ignominious burial place and prepared them for a dignified reburial. During the weeks immediately preceding the reinterment ceremony, the physical remains lay in state at the Dutch Reformed Church. Outside that house of worship, throngs of mourners waited in line to pay tribute to Leisler and Milbourne. On Sunday, October 20, 1698, nearly six years after the execution of Jacob Leisler and his son-in-law, no fewer than 1,200 mourners gathered at the Dutch Calvinist churchyard to witness the reinterment of two members of their community whom the English rulers had executed as traitors. The assembly of such a large crowd of Leislerians so alarmed the ruling elite that during the days of mourning they and their families absented the city for fear that the outpouring of grief would incite another rebellion.[54] In 1698, New York City's Dutch-speaking Calvinist settler majority and the English colonial rulers were no more united than they had been at the time of the Glorious Revolution.

Soon after his arrival at the port of New York, Governor Robert Bellomont

(1698–1699) wrote about the Anglo-Dutch division and the role his predecessor played in perpetuating that divide:

> the late Governor [Fletcher] made advantage to divide the people by supposing a Dutch and English interest to be different here . . . , he supported a few rascally English who are a scandall to their nation and the Protestant religion, and here great opposers to the Protestant religion, and who joined him in the worst methods of gain and severely used the Dutch except some few merchants, whose trade he favoured. . . . I discourage all I can these distinctions of Dutch and English which is set on foot by the factious people of this town [New York City], and I tell 'em those are only to be acknowledged Englishmen that live in obedience to the laws of England.[55]

With this last pronouncement, Bellomont, like Governor Andros before him, promoted a political order in which all settlers were called on to transcend their differences and unite as obedient English subjects. But with the recall of Bellomont and the appointment of Edward Hyde, Viscount Cornbury, to the office of royal governor of New York, an Anglican zealot headed the colonial government. Governor Cornbury (1702–8) soon imposed Anglican clergymen on several independent Protestant congregations in New York and some time later refused to recognize the ordination credentials of Reverend Francis Mackemie, who had moved to New York City to organize a presbytery, the elected consistory of church elders that govern the Presbyterian churches in a particular district.[56] Seeking redress before colonial New York's Court of Chancery, Reverend Mackemie accused Governor Cornbury of violating the Presbyterian settlers' right to liberty of conscience, which, he argued, included the right to found congregations and select ministers without interference from the Church of England and state authorities. After hearing Mackemie's complaint, the court declared that New York's royal governors held authority over the colony's Anglican congregations only. To render the meaning of its ruling perfectly clear, the court affirmed the settlers' privilege to call ministers of their own choosing, as long as those clergymen could present credentials that verified their ordination in a Protestant church.[57] This court decision was an important victory for colonial New York's independent congregations and the principle of religious pluralism. However, the Church of England faction in New York's colonial assembly later defeated a bill that would have allocated a portion of the Crown's revenues for the support of all Protestant clergymen called to New York.[58] Nevertheless, the court's earlier ruling had secured liberty of conscience for all Protestant settlers. A multiplicity of independent Protestant denominations remained a leading feature of colonial New York City's religious and cultural landscape.[59]

Whereas some settlers brought the sectarian antagonisms of post-Reformation Europe with them to colonial New York City, other settlers, perhaps a majority, desired nothing more ardently than to coexist in peace with their fellow Protestants and to follow the dictates of individual conscience, free from the molestation of the Roman Catholic Church and other centralized ecclesiastical authorities. Enticed by the promise of religious freedom, some Protestant exiles from Europe settled on Manhattan Island and in other parts of colonial New York. Although this circumstance did not conform to the English colonizers' plan for peopling that conquered territory with migrants from the British Isles, some observers maintained that European Protestants made model settlers. Writing in the 1750s, William Smith praised the contributions that Protestant refugees from the Rhineland had made to the project of colony building in New York. "Queen Anne's liberty to these people, was not more beneficial to them, than serviceable to this colony," Smith wrote. "They have behave themselves peaceably and lived with great industry. Many are rich, all are Protestants, and well affected to the government."[60] In Smith's judgment, these foreign-born Protestants had proved to be a great benefit to the English colonization scheme in New York and therefore had earned the rights and privileges that New York's Naturalization Act of 1683 granted to Christian settlers of foreign birth who met the New York residency requirement and had sworn an oath of allegiance to the English Crown.

Because the rights and privileges listed in that law extended no farther than the borders of colonial New York, some foreign-born settlers applied for English denizenship, a political status that allowed them to exercise a limited set of freedoms within the entire English realm, including England. Moreover, the Stuart monarchs granted individual patents of English denizenship to Christian settlers of foreign birth, including Catholics. However, this ad hoc procedure was not part of any overarching naturalization plan. A more systematic policy of incorporating foreign-born Protestant settlers into the national community began during Queen Anne's reign. Combining political and confessional conceptions of national identity, this naturalization policy took shape in the context of the parliamentary deliberations on the Act of Union of 1707[61] and in consideration of the task of colonial governance.[62] In 1706, Parliament passed "An Act for Naturalizing Foreign Protestants," which granted English liberties to all foreign-born Protestants who had resided in the English realm, including the English overseas colonies, for at least seven years, verified that they were true Protestants by passing a sacramental test, and willingly pledged allegiance to the English Crown. Determined to govern a subject population no longer confined to the territory of England but dispersed throughout the British Isles and the far-flung colonies of the first British Empire, Parliament, for the most part now purged of Roman Catholic officeholders,[63] promoted a conception of national identity predicated in no small measure on the presumption that Protestantism and English liberties constituted a foundation of shared values uniting the settler population in the distant overseas colonies with the population in England, Wales, and Scotland. Although debates over the proper form of church polity, the meaning of grace, the doctrine of predestination, and the relevance of the sacraments divided Protestants into several denominations,[64] more fundamental Protestant precepts—for example, belief in the individual worshiper's direct relationship with God and the primacy of the Scripture—united them. Furthermore, the provisions in the English Bill of Rights (1689) and the Act of Settlement of 1701 that guaranteed a Protestant succession to the English throne forged a bond of shared confessional identity between the English Crown and its rights-bearing Protestant subjects. Even though England's Naturalization Act of 1706 did not provide Protestant settlers of foreign birth and other settlers in the English overseas colonies with representation in the national Parliament and therefore did not fully incorporate them into the emergent political community of British subjects,[65] it did minimize the political distinctions between the Protestant subjects who inhabited the British Isles, soon to be consolidated, with the notable exception of Ireland, into the United Kingdom of Great Britain, and other Protestant subjects who were scattered throughout the first British Empire. Moreover, the Naturalization Act of 1706 also minimized the political distinctions that divided the Protestant settlers in the English overseas colonies. The elimination of the political disabilities imposed on Protestant settlers of foreign birth meant that a broad segment of colonial New York City's mostly Protestant population now shared a common political status.

In addition, the high frequency of cross-denominational marriage minimized the importance of the confessional divisions that differentiated the city's several Protestant congregations. Although determining a ritual affiliation for a cross-denominational marriage was a potential source of conflict, disagreement, when it did arise, was usually resolved through interfamilial negotiation, which served as the first step toward uniting the families of the bride and the groom as an extended family. The city's privileged circle of Anglo-Dutch elites formed a close-knit network of extended family units. This colonial ruling class maintained their status and wealth by marrying among themselves. Likewise, the bonds of kinship and marriage united the wider settler population. Because of the widespread practice of settler endogamy, a broad segment of the city's settler population came to share common ancestors, if traceable only through one or two generations.

Early modern racial mythology encouraged the practice of settler endogamy by promoting the belief that the city's settler population of British migrants, German immigrants, and long-established colonial Netherlanders were descendants of the same ancient Germanic stock and naturally coalesced because of primordial affinities. Well suited to cultivating a shared sense of communal belonging among the settlers who colonized Manhattan Island, the myth of the Anglo-Saxon race traced the origin of the English people to ancient Germanic tribes and therefore established a consanguineous bond between Englishmen and the branches of Germanic people in Europe—for example, the inhabitants of the Rhineland and the Netherlands. According to legend, the Germanic tribes known as the Angles, the Saxons, and the Jutes colonized England during the fifth century and, marrying among themselves only while living in that alien land, propagated a pure and noble race on England's shores.[66] The practice of endogamy among the Germanic invaders who conquered fifth-century England presumably accounted for the apparent resemblance between the English people and the Germanic people of Europe. From the Venerable Bede to John Hare, antiquarian historians crafted legends that taught Englishmen to take pride in their pure Germanic ancestry and the innate gifts of that racial inheritance.[67] Writing in 1647, the English Saxonist John Hare extolled the virtues of the ancient Germanic ancestors: "Our Progenitors that transplanted themselves from Germany hither, did not commixe themselves with the ancient inhabitants of the Countrey the Britaines (as other Colonies did with the Natives in those places where they came) but totally expelling them, they took the sole possession of the Land to themselves, thereby preserving their blood, lawes, and languages uncorrupted."[68] According to Hare's version of the Anglo-Saxon legend, the English people had lived in a state of freedom under the ideal political institutions that their Germanic progenitors had bequeathed to them until 1066, when Norman conquerors imported the foreign institution of autocratic rule. With the extraction of the Magna Charta from King John in 1215, the English people regained their liberties and proved that they were a race innately endowed with the capacity to preserve their freedom against the innovations of tyrannical rulers. The descendants of the ancient German tribes, true Englishmen were a racially pure, culturally homogeneous, and free people.[69] Disavowing the mixed character of the English people, Hare's Anglo-Saxonist chronicle excluded both the Norman conquerors and the aboriginal Britons from the English lineage. To that end, he cast the Normans in the role of villainous corruptors of English liberty and banished the native Britons from the annals of English history on the pretext of their putative paganism. Additionally, the Gothicist version of the Anglo-Saxon myth not only denied that the English nation was a mixture of various peoples but also claimed that the English people followed the true religion of Noachidian monotheism and were, in fact, the direct descendants of Gotar, the grandson of the progenitor of the isles of Gentiles, Japheth, none other than the son of Noah. In 1605, the English Gothicist chronicler Richard Verstegan wrote: "And whereas some do call us a mixed nation by reason of these Danes and Normans coming among us, I answer . . . that the Danes and the Normans were once one same people with the Germans, as were also the Saxons; and we not to be accompted mixed by having only some such joined unto us again, as sometimes had one same language, and one same original with us."[70] Verstegan's Gothicist account of the origin of the English people acknowledged that the Romans, the Danes, and the Normans had conquered England but insisted that these conquerors were Germanic peoples, with the exception of the Roman pagans, who had been swept away by the ancient Germanic tribes (i.e., the Goths—the Angles, the Saxons, and the Jutes). With the fifth-century invasion of the so-called Goths and the expulsion of the Romans, England became a clean slate for the propagation of a pure race cleansed of paganism and tyranny.

The articulation of racial purity, true religion (Noachidian monotheism), and free political institutions structured the discourse of English national identity during much of the early modern era. At that time, England's imperial tasks of peopling its overseas colonies and governing its settler populations, such as colonial New York City's mostly foreign-born settler population, involved the forging of a national community that imagined itself as racially pure yet open to the assimilation of similar peoples from other lands.

The myth of the Anglo-Saxon race posited a culturalist conception of race, which assigned Germanic peoples, including the English people, to a distinct (or pure) racial category whose members share unique hereditary traits—especially the capacity to preserve liberty uncorrupted by tyranny and the moral disposition of devotion to true religion (or Noachidian monotheism). Drawing on that myth during an epoch of colonial expansion into foreign territories, the discourse of English national identity no longer privileged birth in England as the primary criterion for defining a rights-bearing English subject but now advanced a revised conception of "Englishness," a set of unique, internalized traits, to define membership in the national community. In this respect, the imperative of reconciling empire and nation found resolution in the reterritorialization of Englishness. English national identity now migrated from the external frontiers of soil (or geography) to the internal frontiers of race, language, religion, and political values.[71] In this way, Englishness became an internalized condition of being. Affirming that Englishness was rooted less in being born on the soil of England than in innate racial qualities, early modern representations of the English people relied on earthy metaphors of arborescent racial descent, which sustained the value of rootedness in English heritage in the face of the challenges of displacement, diaspora, and exile. Carrying a portable, interiorized Englishness within them during a period of domestic turbulence and overseas expansion, early modern Englishmen could be confident that they would always remain English in essence, whether they lived in England or in a foreign land and regardless of the external vicissitudes that beset them. Moreover, this conception of Englishness opened the boundaries of the English national community to the influx of peoples who were not born on English soil but allegedly shared common Germanic ancestors and inborn traits with the English people. The Anglo-Saxon legend enabled the project of colony building on Manhattan Island, for that myth accommodated the incorporation of the colony's majority foreign-born Protestant settler population of colonial Netherlanders, immigrants from the Rhineland, and other Protestants of Germanic descent into the English nation without compromising the putative racial purity of the English people.

However, in the long run the project of colony building and the task of colonial governance severely tested idealized, essentialist notions of Englishness and primordial racial affinity. While the English people might be thought of as carrying an immutable natural disposition within them, Englishness was hardly *an autogenetic trait passed down from one generation to the next like some kind of eternal omneity.* If the distinctive traits of the English national character were to be preserved in the Englishmen who transplanted themselves in the foreign soil of empire, the sustaining institutions of English culture had also to be transplanted with them. Moreover, cultivating a sense of national belonging among the settlers who had been born outside the British Isles and clung to the particular languages and customs of their birthplaces required the zeal of dedicated missionaries. For these reasons, the English colony builders enlisted the SPG, the Church of England's chief missionary organization, in the task of inculcating English civilities in the overseas settler populations.

From 1702 through to the outbreak of the War for Independence, the SPG sent missionaries to New York City. Their chief assigned task was to proselytize among the settlers, convert as many as possible to Anglicanism, and in the process of doing so teach them the English language. SPG missionaries used printed manuals of religious instruction known as catechisms to educate youths and win converts.[72] Potential converts who could not comprehend English sometimes received Anglican catechisms printed in their native languages. Nevertheless, the Church of England valued an informed laity that could read the English language and comprehend the King James Bible, the *Book of Common Prayer*, and other devotional texts printed in English. Hence, teaching proselytes whose native tongue was not English how to read the English language was one of the primary goals of the SPG missionaries. In the SPG classroom at New York City, missionaries taught English as a second language from elementary textbooks such as *The English and Low-Dutch School-Master* (1730), *A Complete Guide to the English Tongue* (1745), and *The New-York Primer* (1746).[73] In polyglot New York City, English-language schooling became a means of shaping American-born and other foreign-born youths into model British subjects. According to the early modern conception of Englishness, a common English language would weld empire and nation into a unitary linguistic community, as the everyday practice of speaking the English language brought English-speakers into unbroken communication with other English-speakers regardless of where they lived. The city's Anglican Chaplain, John Sharpe, advocated the extension of England's nascent system of national education to the English overseas settler colonies. Mastery of the English language gave youngsters in the colonies a sense of belonging to the English nation and even encouraged them to join the Church of England. In his proposal for improving English-language schooling in New York City, Sharpe observed: "There is hardly anything which is more wanted in this Colony than learning there being no place I know in America where it is either less encouraged or regarded. This City is so conveniently situated for Trade and the Genius of the people so inclined to merchandise, that they generally seek no other Education for their children than writing and Arithmetick." New York City youths ought to be given a standardized English education, Sharpe advised, for "the Regular or Academical formation of their principles and manners. This would reconcile them early to the National Church and we might hope that in the rising Generation there would be Unity, Uniformity, Loyalty, and Brotherly Love."[74] Sharpe's proposal thus reflected the dream of creating a uniform British culture that would compact the settler populations scattered throughout the first British Empire with the national community in England. The Anglicization programs of Reverend Sharpe and the SPG did not achieve overnight success, however.

In colonial Manhattan, the English takeover did not result in the immediate ascendancy of the English language and other expressions of English culture. As the historian David Narrett has noted, the English "might command the government but they were not a dominant social or cultural presence for many years."[75] English culture asserted itself gradually and, at first, in the limited sphere of state affairs. In the multicultural, polyglot port town at the tip of the island, competing cultures vied with English culture in a contest for sovereignty over American-born youths. While most settlers were willing to obey English law in order to merit the rights and privileges of British subjecthood, some clung to the traditions of their forefathers and endeavored to hand down their particular religion, language, and customs to their offspring. Even though the United Provinces relinquished political control over the territory renamed New York in 1664, Dutch-speaking Calvinists were a majority of New York City's settler population until the 1730s; some colonial Netherlanders and foreign-born settlers strove to retain their particular traditions.[76]

Catechetical schooling became a crucial yet controversial institutional vehicle for the process of English enculturation as well as preserving the distinctive competing cultures of colonial New York City's diverse settler population. In 1633, the Dutch Reformed Church founded a short-lived school for teaching American-born youths the Dutch language and the doctrines of Calvinism. But the Dutch school received meager financial support from the Classis of Amsterdam, the central ecclesiastical governing body of the Dutch Reformed Church, and as a consequence of inadequate funding closed its doors in 1637, just four years after its founding.[77] For several decades thereafter, the settler youths, except for the few who had private tutors, received little formal education of any kind. The opening of the SPG school around 1702 changed that situation. Voluntary contributions and income derived from sugar plantations in Barbados supported the SPG schools in the English overseas colonies,[78] but their chief source of funding came from the financial allocations of the colonial assemblies and tuition payments.[79] In 1723, Dr. Bray's Associates, a state-funded SPG organization, opened an English-language charity school, for the benefit of children whose parents could not afford to pay the SPG's modest tuition fees, let alone hire private tutors to educate their children. At that time, some colonial Netherlanders in New York City opposed the SPG's English-language curriculum, insisting that state-funded schooling should not be limited to English-language instruction, since Dutch-speakers comprised a majority of the city's taxpayers. Several Dutch-speaking townspeople demanded that the English rulers hire a schoolmaster charged with the duty of teaching their children the Dutch language. Because financing Dutch-language instruction did not serve the English state's agenda of cultivating English civilities in the city's settler population, the English rulers rejected the Dutch-speakers' petition. Recognizing that the English rulers would not provide state funding for Dutch-language schooling, the city's Dutch Reformed Church commenced a fund-raising campaign and with the aid of private donations reopened its school in 1725. Dutch-speaking Lutherans enrolled their children in the Calvinist-sponsored Dutch school. But it was not long before the Lutheran parents accused the Dutch Calvinist schoolmaster of inculcating the doctrines of Calvinism in their children without parental approval. These parents threatened to withdraw their children from his care and found their own school, whose curriculum would include instruction in the doctrines of Lutheranism as well as the Dutch language. However, the Lutheran Dutch-speakers were too poor to hire their own schoolmaster and never acted on their threat. In contrast, the city's Jewish community, though only a tiny fraction of the colonial port town's settler population, had sufficient financial resources to maintain a Hebrew school without state and other outside support. Although New York's colonial assembly imposed numerous political disabilities on the Jewish settlers, that discriminatory policy did not prevent the city's synagogue, Temple Shearith Israel, from opening, in 1682, a school for instructing children in Hebrew.[80] Private contributions from wealthy Jewish settlers and Jewish enclaves outside New York City sustained the city's Hebrew school and thus compensated for the absence of a Jewish state that supported institutions of Jewish culture.

The English takeover and the attendant loss of financial support from the United Provinces, without adequate offsetting donations of colonial Netherlanders, undermined the ability of New York City's Dutch Reformed Church to minister to the needs of its congregants. As the historian John Murrin has shown, "No institution suffered more from the [English] conquest than the Dutch Reformed Church."[81] In part because of the frailty of the Dutch Reformed Church and other institutions of Dutch culture, especially Dutch-language schooling, the American-born offspring of colonial Netherlanders gradually abandoned the traditions of their forefathers. Reverend Henry Mühlenberg explained: "Dutch children forget their mother tongue and learn English. Since they cannot hear English in their own church [Dutch Reformed Church] they go over to the other [the Anglican Church] to hear what they understand and like."[82] By the middle of the eighteenth century, English was not only the official state language but also the lingua franca of the city's counting-houses, taverns, marketplaces, and most settler households. According to the historian Joyce Goodfriend, the gradual decline of Dutch cultural institutions and the progressive ascendancy of English institutions of culture in colonial New York City gave rise to heightened "ethnic consciousness" among some colonial Netherlanders.[83] As Dutch-speaking Calvinists witnessed their children master the English language, join the Anglican Church, and adopt other English customs, they became aware that the preservation of the particular customs of a people who had transplanted themselves in a foreign land depended upon the active transmission of culturally learned behavior to their descendants. For this reason, the city's Dutch Reformed Church reopened its Dutch school after a suspension of nearly 90 years.[84] But the colonial Netherlanders had, in a contemporary observer's opinion, acted too late and were guilty of "a wretched carelessness of necessary things, [and] have now for some years neglected to have their children receive instruction in the Netherlandish tongue."[85]

In a defensive response to the erosion of Dutch cultural influence over their American-born offspring and the city's broader settler population, some colonial Netherlanders entrenched themselves in sectarian exclusivism. Citing fidelity to their parent culture and the preservation of the distinctive doctrines and practices of the Dutch Calvinist Church as its goal, the church council banned, in 1727, the use of the Lutheran and the Anglican burial rituals at the Dutch Calvinist cemetery. Although that exclusionary policy marked a departure from the spirit of cooperation between the city's several Protestant churches regarding burials, the city's Anglican ministers agreed to abide by the new rule and quietly discontinued the practice of performing the Church of England sacrament for Anglicans who were buried alongside family members at the Dutch Calvinist burial ground. Contrastingly, Reverend Wilhelm Christoph Berkenmeyer, the city's Lutheran pastor, ordered his entire congregation, including those Lutherans who had married members of the Dutch Reformed Church, to abstain from using the Calvinist cemetery altogether.[86] In defense of his act of retaliation, Reverend Berkenmeyer argued:

> If they allow us to make use of their churchyard, bells and grave-digger, how can they forbid us the use of our service? If it be said: By your acting this way, friendship and peace are broken, then we answer: We enjoy little friendship from them. They were not willing to help in the erection of our church building, [an action] which is the opposite of universal love and Christian duty. Their ministers forbade the schoolteachers to teach our Lutheran children from Lutheran books. Now they refuse us to use our burial service, with the result that our dead are not accepted [in their churchyard]. For it is certain that one thing follows another. Consequently, it is the Reformed who break the peace, not we, and this [way of acting] is certainly very poor evidence of friendship. It cannot be respected, and knowledge of it will get around in the Christian community.[87]

Besides disturbing the peace within New York City's broader Protestant community, the Dutch-speaking elders who controlled the Dutch Calvinist church council were party to the outbreak of factionalism within their own congregation. In 1740, an unmistakable shift in the linguistic composition of the city's Calvinist congregation gave rise to an internal schism—involving, on the one side, a vocal majority who demanded that their ministers conduct a portion of the Calvinist services in the English language and, on the other side, an inflexible minority of Dutch-speaking elders who refused to submit to the majority's will. The English-speaking Calvinists had historical precedent on their side. During the 1680s, qualified ministers performed separate French-language and English-language services at the Dutch Reformed Church without opposition from the Dutch-speaking congregants, who at that time were a majority of the city's Calvinist congregation. In 1683, Dominie Selijns described the spirit of collegiality that existed among the city's Calvinist ministers: "Pierre Daillé, former professor at Salmurs (Saumur, France) has become my colleague. He exercises his ministry in the French Church here. He is full of zeal, learning and piety. Exiled for the sake of his religion, he now devotes himself here to the cause of Christ with untiring energy. Rev. John Gordon has come over from England to perform service for the English. His English service is after my morning service, and the French service is after my afternoon service."[88] For Dominie Selijns, the qualities of "zeal, learning and piety," not proficiency in the Dutch language, were the most important criteria for evaluating a clergyman's fitness to occupy the post of Calvinist minister in New York City. By the 1740s, a majority in the city's Dutch Reformed Church congregation understood the English language perfectly but could barely, if at all, comprehend the Dutch language. Nevertheless, the culturally embattled Dutch-speaking elders refused to permit the reintroduction of English-language services in the city's Dutch Reformed Church. The elders' exclusionary policy gave expression to the anxieties of colonial Netherlanders who witnessed the decline of Dutch cultural authority over the Calvinist congregation and the city that Dutch-speaking Calvinists once dominated.

The language controversy embroiled New York City Calvinists in a dispute of several years' duration. During the 1740s, so many English-speaking settlers left the factious Dutch Reformed congregation and converted to Anglicanism that, by 1751, a single house of worship could no longer hold the city's entire Anglican congregation. William Smith explained that the increase in the number of Anglicans in the city could be accounted for "partly by the arrival of strangers from Europe, but principally by proselytes from the Dutch church."[89] Watching the split within his congregation widen and defections to the Anglican Church mount, the city's Calvinist minister pleaded with the feuding factions to set aside their differences and unite: "We enjoy the free exercise of our religious services in every respect, although there is not the least provision made for our church by the civil authority. Hence mutual affection, and unity in faith and piety are the only means of preserving our Christian churches, and of making them prosperous."[90] Declining membership rolls and the need to placate the English-speaking majority of congregants finally forced the church council to hire a minister who could deliver Calvinist services in the English language. In 1764, Pastor Archibald Laidlie, a Scottish Calvinist who had received his ordination credentials from the Classis of Amsterdam, accepted the call to minister to New York City's Dutch Reformed congregation. Laidlie resuscitated that flagging congregation and, within five years of his arrival, officiated at a public ceremony commemorating the completion of the city's second Dutch Reformed house of worship, named the Dutch North Church and located on the west side of William Street between Fulton and Ann streets. Pastor John Henry Livingston, a New Yorker who had studied Calvinist theology in Holland, now presided over the old Dutch Church, and Laidlie ministered to the new Dutch North Church. Although these Calvinist churches retained the name "Dutch" in their official monikers, that term functioned as a vestigial placeholder of little meaningful connection to the unique traditions of Holland. Laidlie and Livingston now performed Calvinist services in the English language for an English-speaking majority of congregants whose Psalter, catechism, and liturgy were printed in English.[91] "Once the common dialect of this Province," William Livingston observed, "[the Dutch language] is now scarcely understood, except by its most ancient inhabitants."[92] By accommodating the majority's demand for English-language services, the Dutch-speaking elders rescued New York City's Dutch Reformed Church from total collapse—but in doing so, they acknowledged the termination of Dutch cultural dominance over the city's Calvinist congregations, as well as its broader settler population. In the city some members of the Dutch Reformed congregation had married members of the Anglican congregation, and increasing numbers of the American-born offspring of the colonial Netherlanders joined the Anglican Church. The widespread adoption of the English language, along with the pervasive practice of endogamy among the settler population and mounting defections to the Anglican Church, gradually eroded the cultural particularities that had once delimited the group boundary of the city's Dutch-speaking Calvinist community.

A history of exile in England made the city's Huguenot population especially prone to assimilate English ways. As refugees in London and other English towns, these French-speaking Calvinists began a process of Anglicanization (or conversion to Anglicanism) and a broader process of Anglicization (or adoption of English customs) later completed in the English overseas settler colonies. In colonial New York City, a schism within the French Reformed Church precipitated a wave of Huguenot defections to the city's Anglican Church, but that split had little to do with a defensive reaction against the decline of French culture among New York City Huguenots. The rupture occurred in 1724, when, one year after his first wife's death, the French Calvinist minister Reverend Louis Rou announced that he intended to wed 14-year-old Renée Marie Gougeon. The Huguenot elders raised doubts about the propriety of the proposed marriage, citing Renée Marie's relatively young age as their principal objection to the union. When Jean Joseph de Moulinaar, Rou's assistant at le Temple du Saint-Esprit, sided with the church elders and refused to marry the couple, Rou turned to his Dutch Calvinist colleague, who agreed to solemnize the union and married the Huguenot minister and his youthful bride in a wedding ceremony held at the Dutch Reformed Church. Later, during the French Reformed Church council elections, Rou campaigned against the aged parishioners who had opposed his second marriage. Triumphant in their reelection bid, the church elders retaliated against Rou by revoking his salary and appointing his assistant to the post of head minister. In response, Rou rallied the women and the poor in the French Reformed congregation to his defense. Additionally, Rou asked Governor William Burnet (1720–28) to intervene on his behalf in his salary dispute with the Huguenot elders. At this juncture, the elders suggested that the feuding factions engage the city's Dutch Calvinist minister to act as a mediator. When Rou rejected their proposal, his enemies accused him of promising to impose the Anglican mode of worship on the French Calvinist congregation in exchange for an official order of reinstatement from the English colonial rulers. Finally, Governor Burnet forced the Huguenot church council to reinstate Rou and pay his salary. Declaring their unwillingness to accept Reverend Rou as their spiritual leader, the Huguenot elders and their followers left the French Calvinist congregation and defected to the Anglican Church.[93] By merging with the Anglicans, instead of joining the declining Dutch Calvinist Church or, alternatively, remaining in the French Calvinist Church with the poor and the female parishioners, the Huguenot elders and their wealthy supporters confirmed the ascendancy of English institutions of culture in colonial New York City. The Huguenot elders, unlike the Dutch Calvinist elders, readily adopted English ways. Their earlier condemnation of Rou's alleged plan to impose the Anglican form of worship on the French Calvinist congregation proved to be a mere tactic in their campaign against a minister whom they deemed morally unfit to lead them.

New York City's French Calvinist Church never recovered from the exodus of its wealthiest members, even though Reverend Rou faithfully ministered to the city's French-speaking Calvinists until his death in 1750. Nearly four years later, Reverend Jean Carle, a Calvinist minister and a native of France, undertook the duties of pastor for the floundering Huguenot congregation, now mostly elderly women and the poor. Carle soon discovered that the membership subscriptions to le Temple du Saint-Esprit were insufficient to pay his salary and, in view of that fact, advised his congregation to join the Anglican Church, which, he observed, was stronger in numbers and could support his ministry. Although Carle assured his parishioners that the Anglicans were eager to have Huguenots join their congregation and that the Anglican vestrymen had agreed to allow him to hold French-language services at the Anglican house of worship, the remnants of the French Calvinist congregation rejected his advice. In 1763, Carle finally tired of struggling to survive on a meager salary and deserted New York City's French Calvinist congregation. Lacking adequate resources to hire a permanent minister, much less to employ a schoolmaster to teach the French language to their American-born offspring, the Huguenot townspeople drifted away from the particular traditions of their forefathers. Writing in the middle of the eighteenth century, William Smith Jr. observed: "The French church by the contentions of 1724, and the disuse of the [French] language, is now reduced to an inconsiderable handful."[94] By the eve of the War for Independence, only a few aged parishioners remained in the city's French Calvinist Church.[95]

German-speaking immigrants achieved greater success in transmitting their native language and particular traditions to their American-born offspring than any other group of settlers from outside the British Isles. According to the historian A. G. Roeber, the establishment of the German-language press in the British North American colonies was an important contributing factor to that accomplishment. The German-language newspapers provided German-speaking immigrants from fragmented central Europe with a regular conduit of communication and a common cultural resource previously unavailable to them. "The mélange of German-speakers," Roeber has pointed out, "eventually enjoyed a more unified experience in North America than they had known in Europe."[96] Even though German-speaking immigrants constituted a distinct linguistic community and endeavored to preserve the traditions of their forefathers, they were keenly aware that the achievement of prosperity in a foreign land required successful adaptation to novel conditions of life. Some German-speakers who disembarked at the port of New York were destitute refugees of war,[97] penniless "redemptioners" who sold themselves into servitude in exchange for passage to New York City. As a consequence of their poverty, these German-speakers were scarcely in a position to reject the dominant culture of the host colony. Prior to 1730, Dutch customs dominated New York City's cultural life, and the German-speaking immigrants who at that time settled in the city learned some Dutch and adopted some Dutch habits to ensure their material survival. The German-speaking newcomers who settled in New York City after 1730 also faced pressures to adopt foreign customs. By that time, however, there was little doubt that the assimilation of English ways held greater social advantages for newcomers than the adoption of the once dominant but increasingly marginal Dutch culture.

Between January 1738 and April 1739, just before the outbreak of the war of Jenkins Ear (1739–1743), nearly 540 Lutherans from Swabia (i.e. Baden-Württemberg, a southwestern state of present-day Germany) settled in New York City. Like earlier German-speaking immigrants, the Swabian newcomers endeavored, as best they could, to preserve their traditions while adapting to their new life in a foreign land. Upon arriving at New York City, the German-speaking Lutherans from Swabia joined the city's Lutheran church. In doing so, they altered the linguistic composition of that congregation and transformed it from one with a Dutch-speaking majority of long-established settlers to one with a German-speaking majority of recent immigrants. The shift in the linguistic balance of the city's Lutheran congregation led to an internal schism known as the Lutheran language controversy. Whereas prior to the 1730s a German-speaking minority quietly abided by the will of a Dutch-speaking majority to offer Lutheran services in the Dutch language only, by the 1740s a German-speaking majority protested that practice. Given the pressures to adopt foreign customs in the arena of worldly affairs, the use of German-language services in the city's Lutheran church became a privileged index of group boundary maintenance for the Lutheran newcomers from Swabia.[98] The use of Dutch-language services was just as crucial to the preservation of group identity among long-established Dutch-speaking Lutherans, who, during the 1730s and 1740s, witnessed the decline of Dutch culture in New York City. Importantly, the church-language link sustained group cohesion in the case of the monolingual Lutheran congregations in Baden, Württemberg, and nearby principalities. But the nexus of language and church became a site of rupture in the case of colonial New York City's Lutheran congregation, with its two competing linguistic groups.

An irreparable schism within the Lutheran congregation erupted in 1742, when the Lutheran German-speakers asked their pastor to deliver half of the Lutheran services in the German language. Before migrating to New York City, some German-speaking Lutherans had lived for a time in Amsterdam, and they now justified a request for German-language services by pointing out that Amsterdam's Lutheran church held Dutch-language and German-language services alternately. Lending his support to the German-speakers in his congregation, New York City's Lutheran pastor, Reverend Michael Christian Knoll, explained: "Since this province was formerly under the Dutch, and also that as late as 20 years ago most everything was still Dutch, the Germans had little trouble in learning the Dutch language. But since that time everything seems to have turned to English. . . . From among the Germans who have been settling in these parts in the past ten years, more than 100 souls could have come to the Holy Supper, but they have neither here nor in the country the opportunity to learn Dutch, since even in the homes of the Dutch only English is spoken."[99] Knoll warned that if German-language services were not offered at the city's Lutheran church, the Swabian newcomers would desert Lutheranism and join the Anglican Church, where they would at least benefit from learning the language of the ruling elite. Although Dutch-speaking elders controlled the Lutheran Church council, that governing body agreed to a compromise and permitted Knoll to deliver one-third of the Lutheran services in the German language. But after a trial period, the Lutheran church council canceled the German-language services on the pretext that too few parishioners attended these services. The Swabian parishioners begged the Dutch-speaking church elders to reinstate the German-language services but were told that they must learn Dutch as earlier German-speaking Lutherans had done.

In 1749, following several years of futile protests, the Lutheran German-speakers threatened to found their own church. Fearing that a mass exodus from his congregation would result in the reduction of his salary, Reverend Knoll made one last attempt to broker a lasting compromise that would satisfy the entire Lutheran congregation. After reaching an impasse in his negotiations, Knoll informed the Lutheran church council that, in the event of a permanent schism, he would preserve his livelihood by serving both the German-speaking and the Dutch-speaking congregations in their separate houses of worship. Outraged at Knoll's plan, the church elders reminded the Lutheran pastor that the original terms of his employment called him to minister to the city's Dutch-speaking Lutheran congregation only and, furthermore, required him to preach in the Dutch language. They warned that, if he elected to serve another congregation, they were no longer obliged to pay any part of his salary. This admonition opened an unbridgeable breach between the Lutheran pastor and the elders. And in 1750, Knoll resigned his post. In that same year, the German-speaking Lutherans founded their own church named the Christian Lutheran Church. The newly organized congregation hired Reverend Johann Ries, a German-speaking minister who had received Lutheran ordination at Halle University. In founding their own Lutheran congregation, the German-speakers echoed Martin Luther's declaration: "I thank God that I am able to hear and find my God in the German language, whom neither I nor you would ever find in Latin or Greek or Hebrew."[100] To be sure, neither Luther nor New York City's German-speaking Lutherans believed that only German-speakers could find salvation. Rather, they expressed a belief shared by all Lutherans, that the individual members of a linguistic community found God through hearing his Word in the vernacular (or native language) of their homeland.

By 1751, the "Old Lutherans" (or Dutch-speaking Lutheran congregation) had hired Reverend Melchior Mühlenberg to preach to them in the Dutch language for a few months each year. Although the long-established Dutch-speaking Lutherans managed to retain Dutch-language services in their church and the Swabian newcomers founded their own separate German-speaking Lutheran congregation, these accomplishments were achieved at the cost of dividing New York City Lutherans into two hostile camps. Commenting on the incessant bickering among New York City Lutherans, Mühlenberg complained: "It is a deplorable thing when such strifes arise in congregations, since the members are almost without exception interwoven with one another by marriage, relationships, and the like, and the disaffected will not rest, but continue to agitate to gain a following."[101] Mühlenberg soon tired of his parishioners' waspish temperament and, after only two years of ministering to a quarrelsome congregation, abandoned his part-time post in New York City. Increasingly, American-born Lutherans left the city's contentious Lutheran churches. Over time, the offspring of long-time Dutch-speaking Lutheran settlers, as well as the children of German-speaking Lutheran newcomers, learned the English language, intermarried with other English-speakers, and abandoned the Lutheran congregations to join the Anglican congregations or, more often, shunned institutionalized religion altogether. Reverend Berkenmeyer expressed his dismay at the spiritual condition of "Lutherans" in chattel-oriented, English-ruled colonial New York City and the spirit of possessive individualism among the "Lutheran" settlers when he observed:

> They work only for a livelihood, for fields, for property. Occupied with these troubles and, like depraved people, craving for other [material] goods and chattel, they did not know or had forgotten how to seek for heavenly things. Now that they have been supplied with an abundance of food, and while even their situation as slaves has changed to that of masters, they bear so little any yoke that they are not at all ashamed to throw off the yoke of Christ. . . . Life to them is, so to speak, simply like the sun going down and coming up again at daybreak. The children of these people (also the children of those who are considered the pillars of the Church and who expected it least of all from their own children) are lured by the convenience of the strange ruling English language or rejoice over the idle hope of certainly becoming happier through it. They are set in motion like a spinning top by a kind of twist of the evil spirit within them, which is unfathomable to me. They publicly get rid of the pastor of the religion of their fathers, or, if shame prevents them in doing this, they give next to nothing to support the Church, by using the excuse of a mixed marriage. . . . Through this they claim not to be Lutherans at all. . . . Here in this country there is no community of Lutherans; by far the majority are merely a crowd of fickle people. They are the people who, when asked if this one or that one is a Lutheran by birth, have a ready answer: "He is nothing."[102]

Dominie Gualthrus Du Bois discovered that the factious New York City Calvinists were also abandoning their religious traditions. Du Bois complained: "So many conventicles exist. Hence so many are perplexed and misled; while others neglect and scoff at the divine service not to speak of those who, on various pretexts, entirely abstain from the Lord's Supper."[103] Though Dominie Du Bois bemoaned the decline of the Dutch Reformed religion in New York City, he openly advocated accommodation to English cultural ascendancy in other arenas of life and warned his Dutch Calvinist colleagues that in a colonial port town, where English was the common language of the settler population and so many Dutch Reformed congregants had intermarried with Anglicans, the reassertion of sectarian exclusivism would result in families being "torn asunder, where now, for the most part hands are joined."[104] Even as Du Bois remarked on the familial and linguistic ties that by the middle of the eighteenth century united Anglicans and Calvinists, he remained mindful of the fragility of these bonds.

While the social and political advantages of religious fellowship with the

English-speaking ruling elite led increasing numbers of American-born settlers to join the Anglican Church,[105] the eruption of internal schisms within the city's dissenting Protestant congregations led others to seek sanctuary from sectarian antagonisms in the quietude of indifference to institutionalized religion. As the settlers struggled to transform the frontier outpost on Manhattan Island into a thriving entrepôt surrounded by a prosperous hinterland of commercial agricultural production, religion appeared to be gradually receding into the background of daily life. New York City ministers, especially clergymen who had been educated at the centers of pietism in Europe, deplored the apparent decline of religious piety in the colonial port town and endeavored to rekindle the flame of faith within the townspeople.[106] Between 1739 and 1741, the movement of evangelical Protestantism known as the Great Awakening sparked brief religious revivals throughout British America. In New York City, revival meetings attracted thousands of townspeople and rural folk, though, as the historian Michael Kammen has pointed out, "The Awakening may have had less impact in New York than in any colony north of the Carolinas."[107] The city's orthodox ministers condemned the intrusion of pietistic outsiders and banned the evangelist George Whitefield from preaching in their houses of worship during his visit to the city in 1739. But Whitefield secured a podium when Reverend Ebenezer Pemberton broke ranks with his colleagues and invited the controversial evangelist to deliver a sermon at the Presbyterian meetinghouse. Internal opposition to the invitation that Reverend Pemberton had extended to Whitefield created a disturbance within the city's English-speaking Presbyterian congregation, now divided between pietistic parishioners, called "New Lights," and orthodox parishioners, called "Old Lights." The spectacle of the crowd that packed into the Presbyterian house of worship to hear Whitefield preach vindicated Pemberton and the New Light Presbyterians. Later, during two visits to New York City in 1740, Whitefield preached to outdoor gatherings, reaching a total of 5,000 to 7,000 eager souls. Remarking on the spiritual starvation of the townspeople, Whitefield wrote, "I find that little of the work of God has been in it [New York City] for many years."[108] The pietistic minister Theodorus Jacobus Frelinghusen placed the blame for the settlers' spiritual impoverishment on his Dutch Calvinist colleagues, who, he claimed, preached the doctrine of justification (or the achievement of spiritual salvation through worldly deeds) and in doing so discouraged their parishioners from trusting in the power of God's irresistible grace.[109] Noting the spiritual lethargy of the city's Dutch-speaking Lutheran congregation, Reverend Melchior Mühlenberg remarked: "These poor souls have been lulled and consoled for so many years that they consider a two-hour service in church on Sunday as quite sufficient for justification . . . whatever is said that does not sound like the old doctrine, but which urges conversion to God and living faith in the Lord Jesus, seems dangerous to them."[110] Orthodox clergymen dismissed these unfavorable assessments of their ministry, complaining that pietistic preachers from outside New York City had fueled anticlerical hostilities and renewed baleful factionalism within the city's Protestant congregations.

A shared faith in the basic doctrines of Protestantism, along with a common English language, political status, and Germanic ancestry, proved to be insufficient to unite colonial New York City's settler population, which remained divided by, as a member of the Anglo-Dutch colonial elite put it, "a difference amongst ourselves."[111] To be sure, sectarian conflicts of the post-Reformation era faded with the passage of time, for the elimination of political distinctions between settlers of foreign birth and native-born English settlers, the Anglo-Saxon myth, settler endogamy, the pervasive use of the English language, and widespread conversion to Anglicanism set in motion a process of Anglicization that gradually minimized and subordinated confessional, natal, and linguistic differences among the settlers. But as Leisler's Rebellion and the schisms within the city's several Protestant congregations revealed, sectarian antagonisms involving natal, religious, and linguistic differences could resurface and, once reanimated, were articulated with volatile political and social antagonisms. It was precisely the problem of forging the colonial port town's internally riven Anglo-Saxon Protestant settler population into a fully sutured national community of loyal British subjects that accounts for the role that antiblack racism played in colonial governance.

"One and the Same Interest"

ANTIBLACK RACISM AND COLONIAL DOMINATION
WITH AND WITHOUT HEGEMONY

Fighting among themselves and defying church and state authorities, colonial New York City's settler population proved to be difficult to govern and rarely united around a common cause, except when frightened by some perceived threat. In the wake of the Slave Revolt of 1712, the city's black population became such a phobogenic object. At that time, the English rulers, the Anglo-Dutch colonial elite, and the broader settler population united around a shared interest in the violent subjugation of enslaved blacks and free blacks.[1] The art of colonial governance now combined the incorporation of foreign-born Protestant settlers into a community of loyal, rights-bearing British subjects with antiblack racism, which became a disciplinary mechanism that not only minimized the black population's opportunities to foment and execute a successful rebellion but also became integral to governing the city's settler population. Whereas before a deep cleavage existed between the English rulers and the broader settler population, which was divided within itself by confessional, linguistic, natal, and social distinctions, solidarity now prevailed between the English colonial authorities and the settlers and, importantly, within the settler community. Whereas the colonial state was once broadly perceived as the tyrannical foe that had committed the crime of judicial murder against a respected member of the settler community, it was now widely regarded as the vigilant protector that exercised the legitimate use of violence against the city's black population, a dangerous and alien presence that for the most part had not converted to Christianity and, though living in close physical proximity to the settlers, remained strangers in their midst.

Colonial New York City's black population was at once an object of fear and an object of benevolence. The early English colonizers considered the "civilizing" mission of converting the so-called heathens to Christianity to be a primary goal of colonial expansionism. In *A Discourse Concerning Western Planting*, published in 1584, Richard Hakluyt, a leading propagandist for English colonization schemes, cited biblical authority in proposing that the personnel of English colony building in the Americas include missionaries who would proselytize among the natives. Hakluyt wrote:

> The blessed Apostle Paule, the converter of the Gentiles, Rom: 10. writeth in this manner: Whosoever shall call on the name of the Lorde shall be saved. But howe shall they call on him in whom they have not believed? and howe shall they believe in him of whom they have not hearde? and how shall they heare withoute a preacher? and howe shall they preache excepte they be sente? Then it is necessary for the salvation of those poore people which have sitt so longe in darkenes and in the shadowe of deathe, that preachers should be sent unto them.[2]

It was not until the first decade of the eighteenth century that the Church of England dispatched Society for the Propagation of the Gospel in Foreign Parts (SPG) missionaries to New York City, however.[3] These missionaries at first worked among the remnants of the coastal Indian population but, like the Dutch Calvinist clergymen who preceded them, shifted their attention to the city's black population, which held the promise of becoming a numerous flock of converts because of the influx of involuntary immigrants from Africa and other parts of the black Atlantic world into the port of New York. Reporting from New York City in 1721, a SPG missionary observed: "A ship from Madagascar hath brought 120 of them [enslaved Malagasy] since three weeks. The number doth increase daily and the spiritual harvest would be great."[4]

Although New York City was a promising site for the SPG's missionary work,[5] an average of only 13 black converts received the Anglican baptism each year for a 69-year period between 1704 and 1773.[6] Slaveowner opposition partly explains the SPG's unimpressive slave conversion record. In addition to a small number of free blacks, colonial New York City's black population was comprised of slaves whose masters, for the most part, refused to have their slaves baptized because too many uncertainties surrounded the status of Christianized slaves. The question of whether Christians ought to be enslaved was a moral dilemma dating back to the founding of the first Christian churches. That question was resolved in most regions of Western Europe with the decline of slavery in that part of the world during the early Middle Ages. In addition to socioeconomic factors, such as transformations in the rural economy[7] and the collapse of centralized authority,[8] the biblical injunction that prohibited Christians from enslaving their coreligionists accounts for the demise of slavery and the rise of serfdom in Western Europe between the sixth and the eleventh centuries.[9] As increasing numbers of peasants submitted to externally imposed codes of "civilized" behavior, including professing, if not practicing, Christianity, the enslavement of the European peasantry became untenable. In keeping with Christendom's prohibition against the enslavement of fellow Christians and their offspring, the Christian colony builders of the seventeenth century claimed to enslave only non-Christians, so-called heathens. Even though Christendom acknowledged the shared humanity of all people, the discourse of missionary colonialism assigned the Christian colonizers to the rank of superior race and relegated the non-Christians to the rank of inferior race. During the early modern era, the averred cultural and moral superiority of Christians legitimated New World slavery, an ostensibly benevolent institution that was supposed to benefit the enslaved by bringing them under the government of Christian enslavers.[10] In this respect, Christendom's "civilizing" mission among the heathens in foreign lands was an extension of the process of pacification that Christendom imposed on the European peasantry during medieval times.[11]

Modeled on Leviticus 25:38, 45–46 and intended principally as a means of assuring prospective settlers from the British Isles and Europe that they would not be subjected to enslavement upon arrival at the port of New York, colonial New York's law of slavery reiterated the biblical injunction against Christians enslaving coreligionists and simply stated: "No Christian shall be kept in Bondslavery."[12] That statute would have been sufficient to seal the fate of the involuntary immigrants from the West Indies and Africa who disembarked at New York's seaport, but for the fact that it failed to anticipate the contingency of slave conversion, which produced the undecidable category "Christian slave" and threatened to undo the binarism free Christian/enslaved heathen inscribed in the colonial law.[13] The colonialist goal of slave conversion thus transferred to the New World the very dilemma that had contributed to the demise of slavery in Western Europe. New York City slaveowners worried that the colonial institution of slavery might go the way of slavery in Europe and for this reason resisted the SPG's efforts to convert their slaves to Christianity.

As part of a broader pattern of slaveowner disapproval of the SPG's proselytizing activities among the black populations in British North America, opposition to the SPG's missionary work in colonial New York City mounted with the rise of slave ownership in the city's settler population.[14] Most New York City slaveowners were Christians whose religious obligations included the duty of converting their slaves to Christianity. However, these slaveowners were hardly exemplary Christians. Writing from the city, Governor Dongan noted: "It is the endeavor of all persons here to bring up their children & servants in that opinion which themselves profess; But this I observe that they take no care of the conversion of their slaves."[15] Recognizing that colonial New York's institution of slavery was predicated on the presumption that slaves were not Christians, most slaveowners renounced their Christian duty and prevented SPG missionaries and other clergymen from proselytizing among their slaves and baptizing slaves who had converted to Christianity. An SPG missionary explained that his labor among the slaves was pointless unless the city's slaveowners received a guarantee from the English rulers that conversion to Christianity would not alter the slave's condition of lifelong bondage. "I know very well that many people—look upon it as a very Great Difficulty that when they [Negroes] are Baptised, they will cease to be Slaves. . . . If there were a law which permitted the Inhabitants to cause their Negroes to be Instructed and Baptised," he advised, "I believe that would be great Advantage provided nevertheless that the slaves might have no right to pretend to a Temporal Liberty because that would be a great Injury to the Plantations which are only supported by the Labour of those People."[16] In an effort to remove the main cause of slaveowner opposition to its Christian "civilizing" mission, the SPG successfully lobbied New York's colonial assembly to pass a law ensuring that enslaved converts remained in bondage for their entire lives.

Enacted in 1706 and titled "An Act to Incourage the Baptising of Negro, Indian and Mulatto Slaves," that statute unequivocally stated: "Be it Exacted by the Governour, Council and Assembly, and it is hereby Enacted by the Authority of the same, That in the Baptizing of any Negro, Indian, Mulatto or Mestee Slave shall not be any cause or reason for the setting them or any of them at liberty."[17] In a final coup de grâce, colonial New York's amended law of slavery comprehensively defined a slave as "all and every Negro, Indian, Mulatto and Mestee Bastard Child and Children who is, are, and shal be born of any Negro, Indian, Mulatto or Mestee, shall follow ye State and Condition of the Mother and be esteemed reputed taken and adjudged a Slave and Slaves to all intents and purposes whatsoever."[18] The term *Negro*, along with the terms *Indian, Mulatto,* and *Mestee*, now supplanted the phrase *no Christian* in the legal construction of the category *slave*. By precisely enumerating the people who were lawfully held in the condition of lifelong bondage, something that the earlier law defined solely in negative relation to the term *Christian*, the Law of 1706 acknowledged the unreliability of the binarism free Christian / enslaved heathen. The category *slave* now shifted from an ascribed identity principally defined by the criterion of religion to one defined by the criterion of heredity—specifically, matrilineal descent. Invoking the ancient Roman law dictum *partus sequitor ventrum* to construct a hereditary condition of bondage determined by matrilineal descent, the Law of 1706 thus replaced a potentially contestable condition of bond-slavery with a seemingly incontrovertible condition of bondage.

Of course, no law could anticipate all the contingencies that might render the institution of chattel slavery vulnerable to contestation. Nevertheless, each term and combination of terms in colonial New York's amended law of slavery was calculated to close loopholes and eradicate ambiguities that threatened to undermine the slaveowner's right to slave property. For example, whereas prior to the enactment of the Law of 1706 the terms *Mulatto* (a person of European and African ancestry) and *Mestee* (a person of European and Amerindian ancestry) were anomalous categories, they now specified the intermixtures of peoples eligible for enslavement. In this way, the revised law of slavery eliminated many, but not all, uncertainties regarding the status of children born of mixed unions.[19] In addition, the term *bastard* confirmed the exclusion of the conjugal bonds of slaves from the legally recognized institution of marriage and, importantly, divested all fathers, enslaved and free, of paternal rights over offspring born of a slave woman.[20] Lastly, the term *Mulatto* paired with the term *bastard*, as well as the term *Mestee* coupled with the term *bastard*, made it clear that all children born of a union between a Negro slave woman and a Caucasian male (or, alternatively, between an Indian slave woman and a Caucasian male) were slaves and hence the uncontested property of the mother's owner. In this way, the Law of 1706 replaced the permeable boundary that previously separated free Christians from enslaved heathens with a seemingly impervious boundary grounded in the presumably infallible rule of making the individual's assignment to the category *slave* dependent on being born of an enslaved woman. Enslaved women thus became the progenitors of a servile lineage, which over the generations no longer necessarily displayed any of the particular cultural and physiognomic traits originally ascribed to the enslaved—for example, heathenism and dark skin color. While an offspring of a slave woman might convert to Christianity and exhibit none of the visible bodily characteristics ascribed to, for example, the category "Negro" in the racial classification system of early-modern natural history, no individual could alter the fact of having been born of a slave woman. By defining lifelong bondage as a heritable condition transmitted from mother to child, the Law of 1706 smuggled in the imprimatur of Mother Nature and in doing so naturalized the legal institution of chattel slavery and its social relation of property. The "Negro, Indian, Mulatto, and Mestee," the law insinuated, did not become slaves as a result of any historical process, but were natural-born slaves. Importantly, the use of the criterion of heredity in the legal construction of colonial New York's institution of slavery marks a crucial juncture in the history of racial formation, a point at which the discursive construction of *race* began to take on its modern biologized form under a racist state apparatus. In colonial New York, the legal condition of perpetual hereditary bondage was made to resemble an innate, immutable condition of the "Negro, Indian, Mulatto, and Mestee."[21] In this respect, the making of the modern institution of slavery was continuous with the making of the modern conception of race.

On the whole, the Law of 1706 solved the problem of slave conversion and eradicated many of the ambiguities surrounding the status of mulattoes and mestees. However, that law did not reassure slaveowners who worried that the SPG's recognition of the slaves' spiritual equality encouraged slaves to abhor their enslavement and rebel against their worldly masters. Hoping to persuade skeptical slaveowners that baptizing the slaves, and thereby bringing them into the spiritual community of Christians, was a prudent course of action, England's influential Anglican Bishop William Fleetwood argued: "What a security will this be to their masters when those [slaves] that they [slaveowners] now fear more than an enemy are in one and the same interest, when there will be a mutual trust and confidence, and they that are now watched and guarded for fear of doing mischief will be safeguarded to their masters for preventing it."[22] In New York City, Governor Hunter endorsed the missionary work of SPG catechist Elias Neau and issued the following proclamation: "That in the City of New-York, where the Venerable Society for the Propagation of the Gospel in Foreign Parts have in their Zeal for the Enlargement of Christ's Church appointed Mr. Elias

Neau, a person well qualified with Piety and Knowledge, to Catechize and Instruct Children, Servants, Negro and Indian Slaves in the Knowledge of Jesus
Christ, That all parents Masters and Mistresses of Families be assisting in the ac-
complishing of a Work so good and commendable, by sending and encouraging
to go to such School of Instruction, their Children and Servants, Negro and Indian Slaves."[23] Having secured a law that encouraged masters to have their slaves
baptized and obtained endorsements from an Anglican official in England and
New York's royal governor, the SPG had cleared the way for Neau's missionary
work in colonial New York City, except for the notable obstruction of lingering
slaveowner opposition to slave conversion.

Neau began his career as New York City's first SPG catechist in 1703, even
though he did not receive his official appointment to that post until 1705.[24] Writing from the colonial port town to the SPG authorities in London, Neau observed: "There are here a great number of slaves which we call Negroes of both
sexes & of all ages, who are without God in the world and of whom there is no
manner of Care taken, 'tis worthy of the Charity of the Glorious Body of the
Society to Endeavour to find out some methods for their instruction."[25] Neau's
black pupils attended rudimentary worship services, where they heard his sermons on biblical texts, such as the Gospel of St. John, and listened to his exhor-
tations on the doctrines of Protestantism and the reformation of the "true
church."[26] Neau reported: "I also read to them from time to time the principal
stories of the Holy Scriptures that I may give them an Historical notion of the
Creation and redemption of the World. In a word I conceal nothing from them
that is proper to bring them to Salvation: I set before their eyes the promises and
threatenings. God grant them Grace to make good use thereof. . . ."[27] Neau's
method of preparing catechumens for baptism also consisted of having his
pupils memorize and recite basic Christian tenets. For example, his black pupils
memorized the Lord's Prayer and recited the correct responses to a simple
question-and-answer catechism, all in the English language.[28] Neau briefly ex-
perimented with a pedagogic method that probably appealed to these catechumens, many of whom had been raised in the vibrant oral cultures of sub-
Saharan Africa and the West Indies. Neau explained: "I have changed the
method I took in the beginning a little, or rather changed nothing, but have
added a few things as prayers and singing of Psalms, that encourages both them
and me, for I represent to them that God placed them in the World only for his
Glory; and that in praying and singing those divine Praises one doth in part
obey his commands. I observe with pleasure that they strive who shall sing
best."[29] Neau's singing Negroes attracted curious townspeople, who gathered
outside the SPG classroom to enjoy the Negroes' performance of the Psalms.

However, the SPG authorities in London opposed Neau's experimental teaching methods, insisting that the Lord's Prayer and the 39 Articles of the Church
of England Confession "ought not to be Invoked by a people who know it
not."[30] The Episcopacy of London insisted that an understanding of Christian
doctrine must precede any testament of faith and that the rote recitation of
prayers and the Anglican catechism was by itself insufficient evidence that catechumens, including enslaved blacks, fully comprehended the Scripture, had ob-

tained God's grace, and thus qualified for admission to the holy sacrament of Baptism. In this respect, the Anglican authorities rejected the notion that the mere utterance of a statement, such as "I believe in God the Father Almighty, Creator of heaven and earth," is somehow identical to the speaker actually doing the act the statement implies—in this case, believing that the Christian God is the single, omnipotent creator. In response to the criticism of his superiors, Neau defended his method of pedagogy but agreed that "knowledge ought to go before the Invokation [and] tis necessary that God should intervene by his Grace in the Instructions that shall be given to those people." "I believe," he added, "that in representing to them before I make them pray, that God is their Father by the right of their Creation & Protection that I may very well teach them this Prayer without any Danger."[31] The Anglican authorities perceived a grave danger, however. In their view, Neau's teaching practices ran the risk of giving the slaves the false impression that a profession of faith was identical to faith itself. After receiving a final rebuke from his superiors, Neau returned to a more conventional pedagogic method, which emphasized teaching his pupils how to read and comprehend English and encouraging them to study the Bible and Anglican devotional texts printed in the English language as preparation for salvation or the infusion of God's grace.

For the most part, New York City's SPG catechists acceded to the SPG authorities' standards for admission to the sacrament of Baptism and therefore privileged mastery of reading skills and study of the written word over memorization and recitation in instructing their black pupils. Neau ordered Akan-language and Mandingo-language transcriptions of the Lord's Prayer to aid him in his labors among native Africans.[32] In addition, the SPG catechist ordered Dutch-language, Spanish-language, and French-language editions of the Lord's Prayer and the Anglican catechism, because some black catechumens could read one or more of these languages. However, the SPG authorities in London insisted that the ability to read English was the most important prerequisite to a sound Anglican catechism. Hence, teaching the black catechumen how to read English well enough to study the English-language Bible, Anglican catechism, and other devotional texts was a primary duty of the SPG catechists. Using Dyche's *Spelling Book*, the SPG catechists instructed their black pupils in the rudiments of reading the English language. Once these pupils had mastered English sufficiently to read elementary English-language texts, the catechists introduced them to simplified statements of Anglican doctrine such as Lewis's *Exposition of the Church Catechism, Or the Church-Catechism Broke into Short Questions*, Worthington's *Scripture Catechism*, and Doctor Woodward's *Short Catechism*.[33] The SPG catechists also encouraged their pupils to take the beginner's catechism, with the alphabet printed on the back cover, home for private study.[34] Once these texts left the SPG classroom, the means of acquiring the cultural tool of English literacy became available to a larger proportion of New York City's black population than the tiny fraction that regularly attended the SPG classes. Neau suspected that some black pupils attended the SPG catechism "only for the books."[35]

Nevertheless, Neau predicted that his missionary work would yield a "good harvest" of black converts.[36] Anticipating a large flock of black proselytes, the SPG catechist furnished a classroom on the second floor of his dwelling with benches sufficient to seat 200 to 300 pupils.[37] Actual attendance rates fell far short of Neau's initial expectation, however. The number of black catechumens who attended the SPG classes rarely exceeded 60 pupils—in two years only, 1708 and 1771, when it was reported that in each of these years there were more than 200 black catechumens in attendance.[38] Some enslaved blacks wished to convert to Christianity but, as Neau complained, "upon desiring the approbation of their Masters to be baptised they [the slaves] are either threatened to be sold to Virginia or else to be sent into the Country if they come any more to School; Good God! What sort of religion have these people [the masters]? For my part I can't help saying that they have none at all."[39] Many New York City slaveowners remained unconvinced that Christianized slaves made more tractable servants than enslaved "heathens" and therefore prohibited their slaves from attending the SPG catechism, this time on the pretext that the SPG catechist scheduled classes at times that interfered with their slaves' work routine. Initially, Neau held his classes on Mondays, Wednesdays, and Fridays at 4 P.M. but soon re-scheduled them for Wednesdays, Fridays, and Saturdays at 5 P.M. The revised schedule resulted in no significant increase in attendance rates, however. In the long run, perhaps so few blacks attended the SPG catechism because enslaved blacks could no longer hope that by converting to Christianity they would be liberated from bondage.

In his history of the SPG's overseas missionary work, the SPG secretary David Humphreys gave the following account of the settler population's lack of concern for the spiritual condition of New York City's black population:

The Negroes were much discouraged from embracing the Christian religion, upon account on the very little regard shewn them in any religious respect. Their marriages were performed by mutual consent only, without the blessings of the Church: they were buried by those of their owne country or Complex-ion in the common field, without any Christian office; perhaps some ridiculous Heathen rites were performed at the Grave by some of their own people. No notice was given of their being sick, that they might be visited, on the contrary, frequent Discourses were made in Conversation that they had no souls and per-ished as the Beasts.[40]

In 1712, Reverend John Sharpe reported that "not above ye tenth" of the city's black population attended the SPG catechism.[41] Neau eventually despaired at the slow progress that his black pilgrims were making on the road to salvation and conceded that while he endeavored "to make them comprehend the ne-cessity of baptism, . . . their hearts [were] desperately corrupted." "I observe with sorrow," he added, "that the knowledge they acquire makes but little Im-pression, that corruption reigns and which, like a Torrent overflows all our Country, serves only to strengthen them in the unfortunate practice of vice."[42] Investing years of tireless labor in his missionary work among the black town dwellers, Neau had saved few souls and reported in 1712: "The greatest part of the black people in New York remain unbaptised."[43]

For most of the English colonial period, unacculturated foreign-born slaves from the East African coast, Madagascar, the Guinea coast of West Africa, Angola, the Congo, and the West Indies were a majority of New York City's diverse black population. Opponents of the importation and exploitation of enslaved black laborers feared that the culturally alien and increasingly numerous African population posed a threat to the city's safety and for that reason supported schemes for the encouragement of the importation of laborers from the British Isles and Europe to replace the enslaved Africans. The fear of black insurgency materialized on Sunday, April 1, 1712, at around 2 A.M., when roughly two dozen black town dwellers, armed with guns, hatchets, knives, and other stolen weapons, gathered in the orchard at the rear of a house in the city's East Ward, broke into a nearby outhouse, set fire to that building, and ambushed the settlers who rushed to extinguish the blaze. With the aid of reinforcements, the settlers soon prevailed in the ensuing skirmish, but not before 8 of their number had been killed and 12 others wounded. While the settlers appraised the damage from the early morning battle, the rebels took refuge in hiding places about town and in the woods outside the city's limit. Governor Hunter ordered the militia to pursue the fugitives, and before long the search party captured the rebels who remained inside the city. Preferring death to capture, the rebels who had escaped to the countryside committed suicide before the armed settlers could arrest them.[44]

The English colonial authorities jailed a total of 70 suspected rebels, and during a two-month period following the rebellion, special courts tried and convicted 21 accused rebels. Governor Hunter pardoned three convicted insurrectionaries, arguing that one convicted black man named Mars had been judged guilty on insufficient evidence and that two condemned Spanish-speaking Indians named José and Juan deserved reprieves because the uncertainty surrounding the lawfulness of their enslavement and the possibility that they were free subjects of Spain amounted to an extenuating circumstance. Swayed by these arguments, the English Crown confirmed Hunter's pardons. Even though vengeful townspeople clamored for mass retaliation and some municipal authorities suspected many more slaves of conspiracy, the English colonial rulers executed only 18 convicted rebels, who were subjected to horrific exemplary punishments intended to instill terror in the city's broader black population. The executioners burned some condemned rebels at the stake, hanged others, beheaded all, and left their mutilated bodies outdoors to rot from exposure.[45]

Shortly after the revolt, Governor Hunter addressed New York's colonial assembly and advised that legislative body to enact more effective laws for policing the enslaved population. "The Late Hellish Attempt of yor Slaves," he remarked, "is sufficient to convince you of the necessity of putting that sort of men [the slaves] under better regulation by Some good law for that Purpose, and to take away the Root of that Evill to Encourage the Importation of White Servants."[46] The colonial assembly heeded Governor Hunter's advice and enacted the Black Code of 1712, which codified a series of statutes first promulgated between 1682 and 1707.[47] The Black Code (1) reiterated that slaves had no claim to freedom by virtue of conversion to Christianity and that the status of slave was a lifelong heritable condition of bondage transmitted from slave mother to her offspring; (2) reconfirmed the separate slave penal code that outlined special procedures by which slaves were to be tried, convicted, and punished; (3) reaffirmed the prohibition against many types of social and economic intercourse between slaves and free men and women; and (4) restated the statuary restrictions on the manumission of slaves.[48] The Black Code also reiterated the disabilities imposed on free blacks, including the statuary prohibition, enacted in 1707, against recently emancipated blacks owning, devising, and inheriting land. Governor Hunter vetoed the restrictions on the free blacks' property rights, and the Privy Council later approved a revision of the Black Code that omitted the prohibition against free blacks' owning land but included the interdiction against recently manumitted blacks inheriting and devising land to their heirs.[49] In colonial New York, both enslaved blacks and free blacks were now subjected to severe regulations.[50]

In the wake of New York City's Slave Revolt of 1712, some settlers accused the SPG catechist Elias Neau of introducing the slaves to incendiary ideas and thereby inspiring them to revolt against their masters.[51] Writing from New York City in June 1712, Chaplain John Sharpe reported: "This barbarian Conspiracy of the Negroes, which was first thought to be general, opened the mouth of many against Negroes being made Christians. Mr. Neau durst hardly appear; his School was blamed as the main occasion of it."[52] Pointing out that only two of the convicted insurrectionaries were Christianized slaves, Sharpe vigorously defended Neau and the SPG's proselytizing activities among the black town dwellers. As in the case of most New World slave rebellions prior to the 1760s, unacculturated native Africans were the leaders and principal participants in the New York City Slave Revolt of 1712. Sharpe reported that native Akan had led the revolt in New York City: "Some Negro Slaves here of ye Nations of Cormantee [Coromantee] & Pappa [Pawpaw] plotted to destroy all the whites in order to obtain their freedom and kept their Conspiracy secret that there was not the least suspicion of it (as formerly there had been) till it came to its execution."[53] A subdivision of the Akan people, the Coromantees, resided at Koromantin, the site of an English trading fort located on the Gold Coast of Africa (or present-day Ghana) between Elmina and Accra and several miles down the coast from Moree. The Pawpaws, also a subdivision of the Akan, lived up the coast from Whydah, at Great and Little Popo, the site of two English trading forts.[54] Although the exact date of entry is unknown, the Coromantee and Pawpaw rebels probably arrived at the port of New York City between 1710 and 1712, a period when a total of 185 involuntary immigrants from the Gold Coast of West Africa disembarked at New York's seaport.[55] Thousands of miles separated Manhattan Island from Koromantin and Popo, and this geographical distance mirrored the cultural estrangement that the Coromantee and Pawpaw strangers doubtless experienced in their new environment. For these enslaved native Africans, forced migration to New York City involved a traumatic rupture from the familiar old world of Akan culture and violent integration into the strange new world of an English-ruled settler colony.

The Akan newcomers would have found little odd in the settlers' practice of enslaving strangers, exchanging persons as articles of trade, and determining slave status by matrilineal descent, since slavery on the Gold Coast displayed similar features.[56] But they would have found other fundamental features of colonial New York's institution of slavery incompatible with their own culturally ingrained values concerning human bondage. Most West African cultures had a set of well-defined laws prescribing the legitimate master-slave relation and the just treatment of slaves. Suzanne Miers and Igor Kopytoff have written: "Africa stands out *par excellence* in the legal precision, the multiplicity of detail and variation, and degree of cultural explicitness" of its laws of slavery.[57] In Akan society, there was a finely differentiated continuum of slave statuses. The lowest rank was the *akyere*, a convicted criminal who served as a slave because his or her capital punishment had been postponed until there arose a need for a human sacrifice at the funeral of a dignitary. Next to the *akyere* was the *odonko*, or foreign-born slave. Because the *odonko* was a kinless stranger, he or she could be sold as an article of trade. Describing the *odonko*, A. Norman Klein has written, "Having no lineage membership, hence no corporate protection, he was an isolated 'solitary creature' who could be depersonalized and treated as a commodity."[58] With regard to status and treatment, the *odonko* resembled the condition of the slave under colonial New York's law of slavery. However, unlike the slave in New York, the faithful *odonko* in Akan society was entitled to an endowment of land and the products of his or her own labor. On the next rung up from the *odonko* was the *awowa* or pawn, a clan member who had been temporarily forfeited to another clan to work off a communal liability or as collateral against a debt. Akan clans sometimes made restitution for crimes or reparation for the ravages of war by transferring one or more of their own people to the injured party. Clans could not always redeem pawned lineage members. In such cases, the unfortunate *awowa* was debased to the status of kinless stranger and became what was known as an *akao pa*. The status of the *akao pa* was now identical to the *odonko*, for both had become kinless slaves who could be sold and whose offspring were also slaves. Like the obedient *odonko,* the loyal *akao pa* was also entitled to land, as well as to the fruits of his or her own labor. An Akan proverb prescribes the "just" treatment of the faithful *akao pa* as follows: *Akoa nim som a, ofa ne ti ade di,* or "When a slave knows how to serve [his master well], he is permitted to take his own earnings."[59] A slave who served well sometimes inherited part of his or her master's estate. Another Akan proverb stipulates: *Akoa onim som di ne wura ade,* or "A slave who knows how to serve succeeds to his master's estate." Although English translations are incapable of conveying the exact meaning of the Akan proverbs about slavery, they offer a useful approximation of the Akan-speaking peoples' normative expectations with respect to the "just" treatment of slaves and the "legitimate" exercise of authority over them. In their relations with unacculturated native Africans, New York City enslavers often struggled with the problem of translation. It was perhaps the impossibility of translating the English concepts "justice" and "legitimacy" into the Akan language that proved to be an insurmountable obstacle to the establishment of slaveowner hegemony over the Coromantee and Pawpaw newcomers who, in 1712, revolted against their subjection to unfamiliar relations of domination.

In all likelihood, these Akan slaves rebelled against their masters not so much to overthrow colonial New York's institution of slavery and assert their belief in the value of freedom[60] as to restore themselves to familiar forms of Akan sociality or, failing that objective, to escape their enslavers through committing suicide, which, for them, meant reunion with their ancestors. Certainly, the condition of natal alienation that the Coromantee and Pawpaw rebels endured during their enslavement in colonial New York City was an affront to the value Akan people placed on communal belonging. On the Gold Coast, the offspring of enslaved strangers, beginning with the second or third generation, were adopted into the clan network of their enslavers through the system of kinship and marriage. With tribal adoption, enslaved foreigners ceased to be strangers. Moreover, slavery on the Gold Coast did not denigrate the cultural heritage of enslaved captives. When the Asante clans defeated the southern Akan and enslaved these conquered people, they incorporated elements of southern Akan culture. The end product of this fusion was a rich and complex culture.[61] The culturally specific expectations of Coromantees, Pawpaws, and other Akan people with respect to the "legitimate" use and "just" treatment of slaves doubtless shaped their response to New World slavery. In a letter to the Lords of Trade, Christopher Codrington, an Antiguan planter, described how enslaved Coromantees comported themselves on his plantation:

> They [Coromantees] are not only the best and most faithful of our slaves, but are really all born Heroes. There is a difference between them and all other Negroes beyond what 'tis possible for yr Lordships to conceive. There never was a raskal or coward of that nation, intrepid to the last degree, not a man of them but will stand to be cut to pieces without a sigh or groan, but implacably revengeful when ill treated. My father who had studied the genius and temper of all kinds of Negroes 45 years with a very nice observance, would say, noe man deserved a Corramante [Coromantee] that would not treat him like a friend rather than a slave.[62]

Although Codrington had never visited the Gold Coast of Africa and therefore had no first-hand knowledge of Akan ethics concerning the master-slave relation, he correctly understood that Coromantee slaves expected to be rewarded for faithful service with "just" treatment.[63] Not only that, they expected specific entitlements, such as the right to the use of land, the products of their own labor, and even tribal adoption. Perhaps Codrington had a dim comprehension of these expectations when he stated that a Coromantee ought to be treated like a "friend rather than a slave."

In colonial New York City, the English rulers rarely enforced the laws against slave abuse. Thus the treatment of slaves varied according to the arbitrary will of individual slaveowners. A contemporary report on the Slave Revolt of 1712 stated that the Coromantee and Pawpaw rebels were motivated to revolt by "some hard usage they apprehended to have received from their masters."[64] From the perspective of these involuntary Akan immigrants, the slaves in New York City were subject to "hard usage," for, even if they served their masters well, slaves were not entitled to land and the products of their own labor, and they received nothing like a tribal adoption into their masters' families and the broader settler community. In short, the slaves "belonged to" individual settlers, but they did not "belong in" the settler community. In contrast to the slave in the Akan kingdom, the slave in colonial New York was not only held in perpetual and heritable bondage but also relegated to the condition that Orlando Patterson has called "social death."[65] This condition of natal alienation was fundamentally at odds with the normative expectations of the Coromantee and Pawpaw rebels, who during their childhood and early adult years had been preparing for full integration into Akan society. No effort seems to have been made to provide these native African strangers with an adjustment (or seasoning) period, during which they would have been gradually introduced to colonial New York's laws and customs and integrated into its labor system. Thrust into an unfamiliar world without the slightest preparation, the Coromantee and Pawpaw newcomers rebelled against their new masters within two years of their arrival at the port of New York.

Although the Coromantee and Pawpaw rebels were recent newcomers, these "New Negroes" did not act alone in rising against their enslavers. Other slaves, from equally distinctive societies and cultures, joined them. As in the case of the Akan-speaking rebels, ingrained, culturally specific ideals guided these slaves in their response to the unfamiliar relations of domination that they confronted in colonial New York City. The careers of two Spanish-speaking Indians named Juan and José illustrate this point. Sold into slavery as prize goods from a captured Spanish privateer in 1706, José and Juan participated in the Slave Revolt of 1712. Throughout their captivity, the two men claimed to be free subjects of Spain, members of the captured Spanish sailing vessel's crew and not part of its human cargo. However, these Spanish-speaking Indians could not document their claim, and the Vice-Admiralty Court, whose duties included adjudicating disputes involving captives from enemy sailing vessels, condemned Juan and José to lifelong bondage. Having no nonviolent avenue of redress available to them, the Spanish-speaking Indians joined the slave uprising and on the morning of April 1, 1712, set fire to an outhouse owned by José's master in protest against colonial New York City's binary regime of black/white, slave/not slave, which had assigned them to a racial subject-position identical to the one enslaved blacks occupied.[66]

Bilingual blacks probably acted as interpreters for the rebels, who, taken as a whole, shared no common language. During the trial proceedings following the revolt, the court engaged bilingual blacks to act as interpreters for the Spanish-speaking Indians and the Akan-speaking Africans accused of murdering their masters.[67] Colonial New York City newspaper advertisements document the presence of black town dwellers who spoke at least two languages. Black men who spoke both Spanish and English were hired on New York City privateering vessels headed for the Caribbean Sea, and others who spoke both Akan and English were valuable members of the crews on board New York City slavers that sailed to the Gold Coast of Africa. Most New York City trading vessels visited ports of call where crewmembers encountered a variety of languages. The seafaring life encouraged sailors to learn a second and perhaps a third language and even to create new languages, such as pidgin, a simplified language invented to facilitate communication where initially there is no common language. After journeying several months at sea, sailors returned to their home ports and likely introduced pidgin to town dwellers who worked at the docks.[68] As Peter Linebaugh has noted, "By the mid-eighteenth century there were pidgin speaking communities in Philadelphia, New York, and Halifax. . . . Pidgin became an instrument, like the drum or the fiddle, of communication among the oppressed: scorned and not easily understood by 'polite' society."[69] Given the early emergence of colonial New York City's polyglot culture, it is likely that a pidgin community existed in that port town long before the middle of the eighteenth century.

In any event, the Slave Revolt of 1712 emerged out of the linguistic environment of a colonial seaport where some black town dwellers spoke more than one language. Bilingual blacks were more readily accessible at the port of New York than they were in the surrounding countryside, where the typical rural black was a slave who lived on a relatively isolated farm and therefore had few opportunities to acquire a European language other than the one spoken in his or her master's household. While traveling through rural New York in 1744, more than 30 years after the Slave Revolt of 1712, Alexander Hamilton, an English-speaking physician from Annapolis, Maryland, and his English-speaking slave named Dromo encountered a Dutch-speaking slave girl from the Long Island countryside. But because of the language barrier, Hamilton and his slave were unable to have any meaningful communication with her.[70] Had the two English-speaking travelers from Maryland encountered the slave girl in New York City, rather than in the countryside, they could have easily found a bilingual town dweller, as likely to be a black resident as a white townsperson, who spoke both Dutch and English to act as a translator for them. Bilingual blacks doubtless facilitated communication across the linguistic borders of the city's polyglot black population. Historians often include the linguistic diversity of enslaved populations among the list of factors that deterred slave conspiracy in early America. But New York City provided an environment that allowed urban slaves to overcome the language barriers that divided them. In that colonial port town, urban slaves lived in densely populated polyglot neighborhoods and therefore had far greater opportunity than isolated rural slaves to learn a second and possibly a third language, which would aid rather than hamper them in spreading discontent and communicating plans for an uprising throughout the city's broader polyglot black population. Through the conduit of bilingual interpreters, some of whom had crisscrossed the Atlantic world, black town dwellers who had lived their entire lives in New York City perhaps learned about distant societies and cultures[71]—for example, that in New Spain Indians and Negroes could attain the rights of Spanish subjecthood and that in Akan society the slaves, beginning with the second or third generation, were adopted into the clan network of their enslavers through the system of kinship and marriage. Such knowledge perhaps broadened the horizons of confined black town dwellers and motivated some to rebel against their masters.

The Slave Revolt of 1712 took place during a period when political fallout from Leisler's Rebellion had not yet abated and at a moment when new political antagonisms over the Crown's revenues and the governor's salary created further discord in the settler colony. Commenting on the political climate in colonial New York on the eve of the slave uprising, William Smith wrote, "Our publick affairs never wore a more melancholy aspect than at this juncture."[72] The timing of the revolt suggests that acculturated blacks, who had been born in New York or at least had lived in the colony long enough to have acquired an understanding of the settlers' political affairs, contrived to take advantage of internal factionalism within the settler population. To be sure, other factors militated against the success of a slave revolt.[73] First, the settler population greatly outnumbered the enslaved population, by a margin of five to one for most of the colonial era. Second, in that eighteenth-century garrison town, the colonial authorities could quickly mobilize the English soldiers and the armed settler majority to defeat any slave uprising. Third, the city's slave labor force did not, as a rule, work in large gangs and live in segregated slave quarters. Under such conditions, restive black town dwellers could not easily organize and carry out a successful mass rebellion. Nevertheless, New York City's Slave Revolt of 1712 was the first slave uprising in British North America undertaken by more than three or four slaves. On two separate occasions—in 1702 and in 1708—a few New York slaves were executed for the murder of their masters, but no widespread conspiracy seems to have been part of these isolated attacks.[74] In contrast, at least 21 rebels secretly planned and carried out the 1712 uprising. Such an airtight conspiracy doubtless involved the cooperation of the city's broader black population.

In 1712, New York City's total population numbered at least 6,307 inhabitants, of whom no fewer than 945 or 15 percent were black town dwellers.[75] Most black town dwellers worked in crowded city neighborhoods. The Slave Revolt of 1712 took place in the East Ward, the city's most densely populated neighborhood, and all but three of the rebels lived in crowded parts of the city.[76] Like prisoners on work furloughs, the slaves left their masters' houses each morning and congregated in large numbers at work sites about town—for example, at the port facilities along the East River. In an effort to prevent slave conspiracy, the municipal authorities enacted, in 1683, an ordinance that prohibited the unsupervised assembly of more than four slaves at a single time and place within the city's limit,[77] and later, in 1702, the colonial authorities reduced the number of slaves allowed to congregate within the city's limit to three.[78] But given the labor-intensive activity at the city's docks, wharves, warehouses, and shipyard, that regulation proved impossible to enforce. Hence, restive black town dwellers had daily opportunities to spread the contagion of discontent to other black town dwellers. In addition to the colonial port town's everyday work environment, officially sanctioned holidays—for example, annual celebrations of the New Year, St. Patrick's Day, and the English monarch's coronation and birthday—provided occasions for the unmonitored gathering of large crowds of slaves. The rebels of 1712 assembled to finalize the plan for their revolt during the city's New Year's Day festivities,[79] a fixed holiday when the municipal government temporarily suspended its restriction on the number of slaves allowed to amass within the city's limits. During such mass public festivals, dangerous conspirators could not be easily distinguished from harmless revelers.

The cultural practices of urban slaves resist the imposition of a single meaning on them and have proved to be difficult to interpret, not only for the contemporary enslavers who endeavored to suppress servile insurrection but also for present-day scholars who study the history of slave culture and its political implications. In separate studies, the historians Sterling Stuckey and Shane White offer opposing interpretations of the parades that the black populations in New York City and Albany held during the observance of Pentecost (or Whitsuntide), a vernal holiday that Dutch-speakers called Pinkster.[80] Pointing out that the black Pinkster pageants of kings and queens closely resembled processions staged by black communities in West Africa, Cuba, New England, and other parts of the black Atlantic world, Stuckey argues that the black Pinkster parades in New York City and Albany masked an African-derived cultural practice and therefore should be regarded as a mode of subaltern resistance to the imposition of the dominant culture of New York's ruling class.[81] In contrast, White argues that in New York City and Albany the mock pageants of black royalty, though infused with some African elements, clearly resembled European-derived rituals of status inversion and expressed the "syncretization of African and Dutch culture," clear evidence, White adds, of the black population's assimilation of dominant cultural practices in the context of enslavement in a white settler colony.[82] Both interpretations have substantial merit and, when considered together, not only disclose the resemblance between certain Africa-derived and European-derived folk traditions but also, importantly, call attention to the difficulty of determining with certainty whether the cultural practices of early black urban populations camouflaged resistance to the dominant culture or revealed accommodation to it.

When during fixed holidays the colonial rulers tolerated status inversion rituals, whether derived from Africa or Europe, they did so, as Ranajit Guha has noted, "precisely in order to prevent such inversions from occurring in real life."[83] Of course, officially sanctioned rituals of status inversion did not always contain subaltern insurgency within safe and predictable temporal intervals, such as fixed holidays; that mechanism of governance always involved the risk of servile unrest spilling over into everyday life and, without warning, igniting a violent revolt. A close analysis of the sudden and violent irruption of subaltern insurgency that awoke the settlers in New York City on Sunday morning, April 1, 1712, only one week after the city's mass New Year's Day celebration, reveals that a cross section of the city's black population could not accommodate an integral feature of the dominant culture and, from various perspectives, regarded the settler colony's institution of slavery as an intolerable injustice, an unbearable affront to their own ideals of "justice" and "legitimacy."

While New York City slaveowners accused the SPG catechist Elias Neau of fueling slave unrest and igniting the Slave Revolt of 1712, the SPG catechist James Wetmore later argued that the settlers shared the blame for the prevalence of insubordination among the black town dwellers. Noting that the deplorable example of errant Christian settlers had made a far deeper impression on the city's black population than the model of Christian virtue he and other SPG catechists had provided the black town dwellers, Wetmore concluded that the SPG was fighting a losing battle: "One doesn't notice any change. There is not one in ten that comes to the catechism. They [Negroes] are naturally libertines and those to whom they belong do not bother themselves much about their welfare so long as they serve well. Thus it is as much the fault of the masters as that of the Negroes if their Slaves are not good men. Furthermore, the bad examples of the whites confirm the Negroes only too much in their impenitence and in their corruption." Wetmore was far from convinced that the white settlers were a morally superior people who justly enslaved black Africans, and he questioned the theory that asserted black Africans (so-called Negroes) were slaves because they bore the Noachidian curse. He remarked: "I have been told that the Negroes bear on their foreheads the marks of the reprobation and that their color and their condition confirms that opinion. I always cry out against the temerity that dares fouiller in the impenetrables of God, and furthermore I do not see that the turpitude of their crimes is more atrocious than that of the whites because we are only too often scandalized by the horrors that the Christians commit. I know, sir, that the evil of one doesn't excuse that of the other, but at least these wretches are in some sort more excusable."[84] Wetmore's indignation at the "temerity that dares fouiller in the impenetrables of God" referenced the tortuous interpretations of postdiluvian history that construed dark skin color as a visible mark of Noah's blight on the descendants of Ham and, since the sixth century, designated parts of Africa as the homeland of Hamites.[85] Biblical genealogies, such as the Hamites, became an integral part of early modern discourses of race and antiblack racism, legitimating Christendom's fantasies about the inferiority of black Africans and the enslavement of these dark-skinned people. As was the case for other educated Europeans of the early modern era, Wetmore's encounter with black Africans filled him with contradictory feelings of sympathy and aversion. In this respect, Wetmore's ambivalence toward black Africans occupied what the historian Robin Blackburn has called the "meeting-point between prejudice and respectable learning."[86] Although the learned SPG catechist remained reluctant to attribute the myth of the Noachidian curse to black Africans and their descendants, he nevertheless subscribed to other popular antiblack prejudices. Writing about colonial New York City's black population, Wetmore remarked: "Most of them [Negroes] are so vicious that people don't care to trust them in companies together, and some have under the pretense of going to catechizing taken opportunity to [be] absent from their masters service many days."[87] Once regarded as a worthy object of Christendom's "civilizing" mission, the colonial port town's black population was now viewed as an alien and untrustworthy presence that imperiled the safety of the settler colony.

Owing to the increase in the importation of enslaved native Africans beginning in the late 1740s and overall negligible rates of natural increase among black towndwellers, a shift from an unacculturated native African majority to an acculturated American-born majority in colonial New York City's black population probably occurred later than historians have generally supposed, probably no earlier than the 1760s.[88] Prior to that time, only a tiny fraction of the city's black population fully embraced the Christian belief system. This circumstance attests to the black town dwellers' generally low level of acculturation during the pre-1760s period. Excluded from the city's Christian community, most black town dwellers were denied a Christian burial and instead were buried at the Negros Burial Ground, an isolated cemetery of approximately six acres, located on the common just north of present-day City Hall Park. Using current street designations, the borders of the Negros Burial Ground included Duane Street on the north, Chambers Street on the south, Centre and Lafayette streets on the east, and Broadway on the west.[89] Whereas the colonial rulers deemed the area encompassing the Negros Burial Ground to be a convenient location for the disposal of toxic waste and the burial of outsiders, such as paupers, criminals, and slaves,[90] black town dwellers valued that same land, with its wooded landscape of gradually sloping hills and adjacent pond, as a sacred burial place. In use for an 83-year period between 1712 and 1795 and perhaps longer,[91] the Negros Burial Ground provided the colonial port town's black population with a semi-autonomous social space, where several generations of black town dwellers performed a fundamental ritual of communal life, the veneration of the dead.[92] The municipal government pursued a policy of minimal interference in the burial rites that the black town dwellers conducted at the Negros Burial Ground. Although in 1722 the municipal authorities imposed an after-dark curfew on burials at the Negros Burial Ground and restricted the number of black mourners permitted to attend funerals there to 12,[93] they never revoked the black town dwellers' customary privilege of burying their dead according to their own beliefs and practices. Reverend John Sharpe reported that in New York City "[Negroes] were buried in the Common by those of their country and complexion without office [i.e., without the supervision of a Christian clergyman]; on the contrary the Heathenish rites are performed at the grave by their countrymen."[94] The city's black population performed their own communal burial rituals and in doing so forged a distinct moral community set apart from the city's Christian settler community. Importantly, the racially segregated cemetery became an incubator for the retribalization of diverse African peoples who were brought together by the externally imposed and shared experience of forced migration and enslavement in a foreign land.[95] Put differently, the semi-autonomous space of colonial New York City's Negros Burial Ground became the site of the formation of racial blackness, a process that involved a dialectic of inclusion and exclusion, centripetal and centrifugal forces in counterpoint to the formation of racial whiteness.

The historian Lawrence Levine has pointed out: "For Africans, as for other people, the journey to the New World did not inexorably sever all associations with the Old World; that with Africans, as with European and Asian immigrants, aspects of the traditional cultures and worldviews they came with may have continued to exist not as mere vestiges but as dynamic, living, creative parts of group life in the United States."[96] Colonial New York City's black population was closer to African cultures than the U.S. black populations that existed after 1807, when the official closure of the transatlantic slave trade curtailed the flow of native Africans to the United States. As long as native Africans continued to disembark at the port of New York, beliefs and practices of African derivation remained an available source of moral authority for the colonial port town's black population. African-derived ideals and customs probably cemented the bond between the diverse assortment of rebels that participated in the Slave Revolt of 1712. According to a contemporary report, an African conjuror, a free black man called "Peter the Doctor," officiated over a rite of invincibility in which he dusted the rebels' bodies with a white powder that, the insurrectionaries believed, protected them from bodily injury. That same document also states that the rebels symbolized their solidarity by cutting themselves, mixing together the blood that poured from their separate wounds, and ingesting the mixture.[97] These rituals resemble elements of the African-derived magico-religious practice known as obeah and performed among the black populations of the British West Indies and other English overseas colonies, where the continuous influx of native Africans supported the retention of Africanisms.[98]

In addition to evidence of the practice of African-derived rituals on the part of the rebels of 1712, both written and archeological evidence indicates that the basic ritualistic features of the funerals that black town dwellers conducted at the Negros Burial Ground, what Reverend Sharpe characterized as "Heathenish rites," were derived, at least in part, from traditional West African religious practices.[99] Prior to the prohibition against after-dark burials, some settlers complained that feverish drumming and chanting emanated from the Negros Burial Ground late into the night and disturbed their sleep. To be sure, such ecstatic mourning rituals were hardly unique to West African burial ceremonies. However, material artifacts uncovered during the 1991 excavation of a portion of the Negros Burial Ground[100] suggest that at least a segment of colonial New York City's black population were Akan peoples and that they not only followed African-derived burial practices but also at one time or another practiced particular burial customs derived from the Akan culture of the Gold Coast (present-day Ghana). For example, that archeological excavation found human skeletons whose incisors had been modified into an hourglass shape, an indication that the deceased had been captured from the Akan peoples, who were known for the practice of filing teeth into that distinctive pattern.[101] In addition, the same archeological investigation unearthed corpses with coins placed over their eyes, human remains interred with glass beads, an infant with a string of eight white beads around the neck, an adult female skeleton with an elaborate girdle of glass beads and cowries wrapped around her hip, and other burial features that bear a resemblance to Akan and other West African burial customs.[102]

Finally, the archeological excavation of the Negros Burial Ground discovered a coffin lid displaying the heart-shaped Sankofa symbol, sign for the Akan belief that a "return to the past is the path to the future."[103] The appearance of Sankofa in the decorative art uncovered at the Negros Burial Ground indicates that a trace of the Akan belief system, if only as a dim vestige of that ancient African cosmology, survived the native Africans' enslavement in colonial New York City.

The lack of affinity between African religious cosmologies and the city's dominant Christian belief system militated against the penetration of Christianity into the city's black population.[104] Dutch Calvinist ministers proselytized among Manhattan Island's earliest black inhabitants, and the island's free black population joined the Dutch Reformed Church. However, the particular interpretation of Christianity known as Calvinism made only a slight impression on the island's mostly native African enslaved population. Calvinism attracted few adherents among native Africans partly because its foundational tenets—the doctrines of original sin and divine election—were incompatible with African religious beliefs. Calvinists believed that, since the time of Adam and Eve's expulsion from paradise, the whole of humankind inherited their ancestors' original sin and were doomed to endure a life of unceasing toil. While the general notion of an ancestral inheritance would have been familiar to native Africans, the Calvinist belief in the innate sinfulness of humankind was fundamentally at odds with the African conviction that all human beings entered the world without guilt or shame and that the imperfections of humankind, along with the hardships of the world in which they lived, reflected the original creation. Moreover, whereas Calvinism pointed to the judgment of a single, irate God when explaining the cause of human suffering, the African theory of causality accommodated a multiplicity of supernatural forces when accounting for the origin of human adversity. Writing from New Amsterdam in 1664, a Dutch cleric offered this characteristically Calvinist explanation for the English Conquest: "The Lord begins to deal in judgment with his people . . . it appears as if God were punishing this land for its sins—a terrible comet in the west."[105] According to this Calvinist theory of causality, the calamities that had befallen the Dutch colonial outposts in North America were God's retribution against sinners; the comet on the horizon was an awful portent of more punishment to come. Native Africans would have found this account of the Dutch colony's demise to be a perfectly acceptable causal explanation—but, instead of passively submitting to the judgment of a single, angry God, native Africans appealed to a pantheon of deities. Each deity in its own unique sphere of influence held the power to intervene in the world on behalf of its devotees and reverse earthly misfortune.[106] The worship of a plurality of gods was absolute anathema to Calvinists, as was the African belief that worshipers could sway the will of the gods with lavish offerings and thereby achieve their own worldly ends. Importantly, Calvinism's idealization of the transhistorical, providential authority of God to determine the course of worldly events and its doctrine of original sin narrowed the Calvinist conception of human agency. During the ruinous Indian war, a Dutch Calvinist clergyman implored the settlers "with one accord and low and humble hearts

[to] call on the name of the Lord, to pray and beseech His divine Majesty to cause the floods of His anger and clouds of his indignation . . . to cease and to change into streams of His antient favor and Mercies."[107] During hard times, the ascetic Calvinists held no sumptuous feasts to appease angry deities, as native Africans might have done, but instead declared days of fasting and humiliation, meekly repented their sins, and begged God for mercy. Although native Africans acknowledged the existence of a Supreme Being,[108] the Calvinist doctrine of divine election—belief that a single, omnipotent God endowed only a select few with true grace and hence admitted only a small number of predestined, saved souls into heaven—directly contradicted the African conviction that all spirits return to a celestial homeland to which the dead, the living, and the not-yet born belonged. Finally, the encounter between African cosmologies, on the one hand, and Calvinism, on the other, amounted to a confrontation between fundamentally incommensurable worldviews. Although a few free blacks converted to Calvinism, the lack of affinity between these distinctive belief systems meant that few articulatory channels opened the way for the effective penetration of Calvinism into the religious life of the native Africans who were a majority of Dutch colonial Manhattan's black population.

Following the English conquest of 1664, cargoes of native Africans continued to disembark at the port of New York, and each fresh infusion of slaves from Africa re-Africanized colonial New York City's black population. To be sure, native Africans who had mastered the English language would have had little trouble comprehending the basic Christian beliefs redacted in Elias Neau's short call-and-response catechism—namely, that God was the omnipotent, eternal Supreme Being, the creator and ruler of heaven and earth, that he makes himself known to humankind through his works on earth, and that true believers come to understand (or obtain faith in God) through the infusion of the Holy Spirit in them. However, a chief obstacle to the SPG's proselytizing mission among native Africans was the Protestant concept of salvation, that only faithful Christians, who prepared for the infusion of grace by studying God's Word (the Holy Scriptures), were admitted into heaven. Native Africans believed that after death the spirits (or souls) of all but a few people, not merely the "saved," returned to the spirit world and joined the ancestors there. Some, perhaps most, native Africans shunned Calvinism and Anglicanism, because the particulars of these religious belief systems were fundamentally at odds with West African religious beliefs.

Religious practice and belief are mutually reinforcing foundations of culture. But when transplanted in foreign lands without institutional anchors, they seldom subsist in equal measure. Taking this and other factors into account, the historian Jon Butler has argued: "African slaves in the British mainland colonies experienced a spiritual holocaust that effectively destroyed traditional African religious *systems*, but not all particular or discrete religious practices."[109] While some African religious practices survived the traumatic rupture of the middle passage, the absence of African institutional supports in New York City militated against the preservation of fully coherent African belief systems in that port town. Though the black town dwellers probably incorporated elements of

African cosmologies, such as Sankofa, into their religion, the destructuration of traditional African religious systems made, in the long run, receptivity to new religious worldviews an ontological necessity for native Africans and their descendants.[110] Neither entirely Christian nor the totality of any single African belief system, the religion of the city's black population was in the process of *becoming*. What native Africans and their descendants underwent during their enslavement in colonial New York City was not a "spiritual holocaust" but a spiritual transformation, arising out of their confrontation with novel conditions of life and loss. To the questions What shall we do? How shall we live? new prophets, new gods, and new values responded to the city's black population.

Christianity began to make inroads into the hearts and minds of the black town dwellers during the 1740s—roughly, at a time when the city's black population achieved a modest level of natural increase and acculturated American-born blacks began to be a significant segment, though far from a majority, of that population. In 1740, the SPG catechist Richard Carlton stated that some of his black pupils were creditable students and "might make many white people (who have had more happy opportunities of instruction) blush, were they present at their examinations."[111] Arriving at the port of New York in 1748, the SPG catechist Reverend Samuel Auchmuty obtained greater success in the task of converting black town dwellers to Christianity than did his predecessors, who had proselytized among a predominantly unacculturated native African population.[112] Whereas the early SPG catechist Elias Neau had complained that his black catechumens refused to accept the Christian God as the Supreme Being because they believed "the god of their country is as great as ours,"[113] Auchmuty could boast that his black pupils readily accepted the Christian God. Auchmuty's black pupils probably spoke English, however imperfectly, and were probably better prepared to master English reading skills and comprehend the basic tenets of Christianity than native Africans and other unacculturated blacks. Reporting on the progress of his black pupils, Auchmuty wrote that they "read well" and "make no small proficiency in the Christian religion."[114] In addition to teaching his black pupils how to read English well enough to study the Holy Scriptures, the Anglican catechism, and other devotional texts printed in English, Auchmuty organized a Sabbath-day worship service and lecture series for the black townspeople. Each Sunday a small congregation of black town dwellers heard an English-language sermon. When other duties prevented Auchmuty from officiating at these worship services, a trusted black convert substituted for him. In Auchmuty's estimation, many of the adult black converts would "soon become qualified to instruct their children."[115] Auchmuty taught his black pupils that Christianity obligated all servants to obey their masters and had them memorize the following excerpt from an English-language primer: "ser-vants to be o-be-di-ent unto their Mas-ters. . . . Ser-vants o-bey in all things your master ac-cording to the Flesh."[116] Praising the Christianized blacks, Auchmuty wrote: "They are in general exemplary in their conduct and behavior. It affords me no small pleasure to reflect that not one single black that has been admitted by me to the Holy Communion has turned out bad."[117]

In 1764, the Episcopacy of London promoted Reverend Auchmuty to the rectorship of Trinity Church, New York City's Anglican house of worship. His successor to the post of SPG catechist for the city's black population, Reverend Charles Inglis, performed his duties until the War for Independence suspended the SPG's missionary work in North America. Inglis followed Auchmuty's example and each Sunday led some black townspeople in a public worship service, which included the singing of hymns as well as the recitation of the Anglican catechism, the Communion prayer, and a benediction.[118] By the eve of the war, a cohort of acculturated blacks, who in all likelihood had been born in New York City, spoke English as their native tongue, and during childhood had perhaps attended the SPG catechism and Sabbath worship services, resided in New York City. Some of these black town dwellers had probably mastered the basic tenets of Christianity and the Anglican catechism well enough to merit baptism and Christian burial. Reverend Auchmuty officiated at the funeral of an Anglicanized slave girl named Mary. The slave girl's master, Evert Bancker, paid the expenses associated with her funeral, including the cost of a burial plot in the Anglican churchyard, a gravedigger, white gloves for the pallbearers, the ringing of the Anglican church bells, and other trappings of a burial befitting a member of the Anglican Church.[119] Buried in the winter of 1773–74, Mary was one of the last black Anglicans interred at Trinity Churchyard. Soon after her funeral, the Anglican vestrymen decided to enforce a church ordinance authored nearly a century earlier. That rule stipulated: "no Negros be buried within the bounds & Limits of the Church yard of Trinity Church."[120] In July 1774, the vestrymen finalized plans for opening a separate cemetery for black Anglicans near the Negros Burial Ground and to that end appropriated a piece of land bound by Church, Reade, and Chapel streets, along with a portion of Anthony Rutgers's adjacent landholdings.[121] With the establishment of the "whites only" and "blacks only" burial grounds, the vestrymen inaugurated a policy of racial segregation that would lead to the founding of a separate black Anglican congregation in the early nineteenth century.[122]

Anglicanism and Calvinism were not the only versions of Christianity available to black town dwellers. The presence of enslaved captives from New Spain in colonial New York City suggests that elements of Catholicism, perhaps already fused with African-derived religious beliefs and practices, might have been introduced to the port town's black population.[123] Apart from contact with slaves from New Spain, the city's black population had slight exposure to Catholicism because in 1691 the English rulers banished Roman Catholic priests from New York.[124] Of the various interpretations of Christianity transported to British North America, evangelical Protestantism harvested the largest number of black converts. Because few racially mixed congregations of evangelical Protestants existed during colonial times and black evangelical churches were not organized until the Revolutionary era,[125] these black converts had few opportunities to participate in institutionalized modes of evangelical Protestantism. During the series of regional revivals known as the Great Awakening, George Whitefield delivered sermons to huge outdoor gatherings at New York City in 1739, 1740, and 1741.[126] Although Whitefield did not advocate the abolition of slavery,[127] the evangelist introduced the black audience that gathered in the open field outside the city's limits to a version of Christianity that displayed an affinity with the ideals of equality and freedom that would become the leading values of the age of democratic revolutions.[128] While the unique configuration of doctrines that made evangelical Protestantism a meaningful worldview could not have been completely understandable to native Africans who did not comprehend the English language, English-speaking, American-born blacks and acculturated native Africans were certainly capable of grasping the basic principles of the Christian belief system[129] and even of apprehending the fundamental distinction between the doctrines of ascetic Protestantism, which commanded the enslaved to "obey and suffer," and the doctrines of evangelical Protestantism, which privileged spiritual autonomy over absolute obedience to worldly authority figures.

Among the socially marginalized groups that were likely to embrace evangelical Protestantism were acculturated black youths who were born or at least raised in New York City during 1740s and reached adulthood two decades later. By the 1760s, American-born and other acculturated blacks were a larger proportion of New York City's black population than ever before. These black townspeople were probably better prepared to comprehend the essential doctrines of Christianity than their parents and grandparents. Nonetheless, language barriers and other obstacles continued to erect roadblocks that hampered the penetration of Christianity into the city's black population. The historian Ira Berlin reports that, of the runaway slaves whose language proficiency was described in New York City newspaper advertisements during the post-1760s period, in excess of one-quarter spoke "English badly, if at all."[130] At about the time that the numbers of American-born town dwellers in colonial New York City approached a historic high point, the city's black population underwent a process of re-Africanization because of the relatively large cargoes of enslaved native Africans that, beginning in the late 1740s, arrived at the port of New York. African-derived religious beliefs continued to be an available and competing source of moral authority for the city's black population.

"What a slave child learned," the historian Herbert Gutman has noted, "always depended upon what that child was taught and who taught that child."[131] In colonial New York City, slave children grew up in a world where Christian authority figures vied with black adults, some of whom were native Africans, for the decisive role in instructing young slaves on how to conduct themselves as moral subjects. In his classic study, *Slave and Citizen*, the historian Frank Tannenbaum writes, "Slavery was not merely a legal relation; it was a moral one."[132] In *Roll, Jordan, Roll*, the historian Eugene Genovese argues that a "paternalistic compromise" between masters and slaves provided the moral basis for the master-slave relation in the antebellum plantation South. In that same study, Genovese contends that this bargain involved the slaves' acceptance of the obligation to obey their masters in exchange for the masters' recognition of the slaves' humanity, a concession that gave to the slaves certain customary privileges, such as the privilege to choose their spouses, name their children, and tend, in their spare time, small garden plots. On the plantations of the ante-bellum South, slaveowner paternalism was a mechanism of hegemonic domination, which cloaked the violence inherent in the institution of slavery under a veil of benevolence and consent.[133] In *The Black Family, 1750–1820,* Herbert Gutman questions whether a "paternalistic ethos" among southern slaveowners could have existed early enough for the slave-owning class to establish hegemony over their slaves. Gutman argues: "But 'the living space' within which slaves—individually and collectively—asserted their identity and acted upon their beliefs existed before any 'paternalistic compromise' could have occurred. . . . Much in the behavior of slaves was affected and even determined by their regular interaction with owners and other whites, but these and other choices had their origins within the slave experience."[134] According to Gutman, the master-slave relation was not the only social relation in the slave's "experience"; other significant relationships, rooted in the black family of the segregated slave quarters, were integral to the slave's experiential reality and provided the slaves in the plantation South with alternative models of moral authority, which successfully contested the slaveowners' claim to represent the interest of the slaves. Genovese and Gutman have little to say about the master-slave relation in the colonial North. Yet, as Jon Butler has shown, the SPG promoted the twin ethics of paternalistic slave ownership and absolute slave obedience throughout the British North American colonies.[135] This moral economy was of paramount importance to the master-slave relation in colonial New York City, where masters, along with the members of their families, shared the same living space with household slaves.

In that colonial port town, the obligations of paternalistic slave ownership sometimes extended from the cradle to the grave. Inventories and account books indicate that New York City slaveowners looked after the basic material welfare of their slaves, supplying adult slaves, along with the slave children born in their households, with food, clothing, and shelter.[136] Besides these meager prerequisites of life, slaveowners also paid the cost of inexpensive yet decent burials for deceased slaves.[137] Few New York City slaveowners rewarded their slaves with the gift of freedom. In a rare act of voluntary manumission, the widow Christiana Cappoens stipulated in her will that after her death Isabell, her female slave, should be freed from bondage and receive manumission papers documenting her free status. Cappoens also left Isabell several items of modest value: one small gold hoop ring, one iron pot, one kettle, a bed, and pillows.[138] In his will, William Walton, a wealthy New York City merchant, made a more generous bequest to his household slaves, ordering that after his wife's death they should receive their freedom papers, £25 for setting up in a trade, and an additional annual stipend of £14.[139] Another slaveowner, Teneke Bensen of Harlem, stipulated in his last testament that, if after his death his female slave named Lane did not wish to stay with his sister-in-law Elizabeth, she was to be sold to a new master meeting with her approval or, failing that, allowed to purchase her own freedom for a reasonable sum.[140] In this way, Bensen not only granted Lane a decisive role in any arrangements for her sale after his death but also acknowledged the possibility that his slave wished to be a free woman.

Executors and heirs did not always honor such provisions in the wills of slave-owners. During the 1750s, Juan Miranda, a Spanish-speaking slave, sued his master's heirs, who kept him in bondage in violation of his master's last testament, which stipulated that the heirs allow Miranda to purchase his freedom. Miranda's case ambled through the court system for nearly a decade and was never brought to a final decision, at least as far as the extant records show.[141] Miranda's lawyer, New York's Attorney-General John Tabor Kempe, handled at least two additional freedom suits, the cases of Manuel de Cumana, a Spanish-speaking Indian who claimed to be a free subject of Spain, and Simon Moore, an enslaved black man who claimed that he was born of a free woman and therefore unlawfully enslaved.[142] During the early eighteenth century, colonial New York's Supreme Court advised lawyers to desist from representing slaves in freedom suits and further warned that such actions created unrest in the broader enslaved population.[143] However, international law required the colonial administration to consider petitions and freedom suits that lawyers presented on behalf of captives of war who claimed to be free subjects of rival nations. In accordance with the international law that governed the treatment of prisoners of war, England's Board of Trade ordered, in 1750, the release of 45 subjects of Spain who had been sold into slavery at the port of New York during King George's War.[144] Such intervention was rare and occurred only in the cases where the plaintiff's claim had been verified by documentary evidence and the testimony of diplomats. In colonial New York City, the majority of slaves had no access to freedom through voluntary manumission, self-purchase, petitions, court suits, and diplomatic channels. As a consequence, free blacks were only a tiny fraction of the city's total black population throughout the English colonial period.[145]

A legacy of Dutch colonial rule and located north of present-day Prince Street and south of present-day Astor Place between the east side of Lafayette Street and the west side of a wagon road called Old Bowery Road, which ran diagonally from present-day Chatham Square to the intersection of Fourth Avenue and Eighth Street, the area known as the "Free Negro Lots" was the site of the only separate enclave of free black landowners on Manhattan Island during the colonial period.[146] In 1664-65, the early English colonial rulers confirmed the individual deeds of colonial Manhattan's free black landowners, a total of 30 deeds.[147] Nevertheless, the English colonial government relegated free blacks, including the owners of the Free Negro Lots, to the status of aliens and denied them the political privileges of English subjecthood. At the time of the Dutch Reconquest of 1673, free blacks probably enjoyed a short-lived reprieve from the disadvantages imposed on them by English colonial law. With the return to English colonial rule in 1674, free blacks were again consigned to the status of aliens. Nearly a decade later, in 1683, some free black landowners sold their landholdings on Manhattan Island to white settlers—for example, the Tucker, Dyckman, Bleecker, and Hertzing families[148]—departed the island with the outmigration of some colonial Netherlanders, and settled in Brooklyn, New Utrecht, and New Jersey.[149] Through the practice of intermarriage, godparent-ing, and the adoption of orphans from their free black community,[150] the re-maining black landowners on Manhattan Island managed to transmit their land to their heirs, who held on to the landholdings until the 1710s and 1720s. At the time of his death in 1694, Salomon Petersen bequeathed his land to his wife, Maritie, the daughter of Anthony Portugees, one of the first landholders in the Free Negro Lots. Except for £4, which he left to his eldest son, Salomon Peters, he divided the remainder of his humble estate, 18 shillings, some tools, and firearms, between his sons. For years, Maritie Petersen clung to the land con-veyed to her by her husband, Salomon Petersen, a free black landowner in the Free Negro Lots and son of Pieter Santome, one of the first enslaved blacks brought to Manhattan Island in 1626 and one of the black petitioners to obtain freedom and land in 1644. In 1716, Maritie sold her land to John Horne, a white settler.[151] By the late 1720s, all the parcels of land in the Free Negro Lots had fallen into the hands of white settlers.[152] During the early decades of the eigh-teenth century, New York City's free black population became a pariah class, liv-ing outside the master-slave relation and sinking deeper and deeper into poverty. As if to ensure that free blacks became mired in a life of poverty, New York's colonial assembly enacted a law that prohibited ex-slaves, who were man-umitted after 1702, from owning land.[153] In 1706, the metropolitan authorities in London disallowed that colonial statute. In response, the colonial assembly swiftly enacted a law that did not nullify the right of free blacks to own land but prohibited ex-slaves, who were manumitted after 1707, from inheriting land and devising land to their heirs.[154] Incorporated into the Black Code of 1712, that prohibition effectively prevented newly manumitted free blacks from passing on their land and independent status to their offspring. The colonial assembly also included in the Black Code of 1712 a statute that prohibited the manumission of aged and helpless slaves, whom callous slaveowners sometimes abandoned be-cause they were no longer productive laborers.[155] The colonial assembly claimed that other restrictions on manumission and the free black population were necessary, asserting: "It is found by Experience that the free Negroes in this colony are an Idle Slothful people and prove very often a charge on the place where they are."[156] In September 1738, an example of the fate of free black families appeared before the city's churchwardens and vestrymen. Lucas Pe-tersen, the son of Pieter Lucasse and the great-grandson of Pieter Santome, was born free in colonial New York City. By the late 1730s, he had been reduced to the condition of dire privation. No longer able to support his ailing wife, Lucas sent her to the vestrymen for alms.[157] Cases of indigence among the city's free black population seemed to substantiate the colonial assembly's claim that free blacks were incapable of leading independent lives.[158]

The Black Code of 1712 required slaveowners who manumitted their slaves to post a £200 bond of surety and an additional £20 each year against the indigence of each emancipated slave.[159] That antimanumission measure placed a nearly insurmountable obstacle in the way of slaves who desired to purchase their free-dom and of free blacks who wished to purchase their enslaved loved ones and thereby liberate them from bondage. Nevertheless, John Fortune, a free black cooper of New York City, had, by 1724, saved enough money to purchase an enslaved woman named Marya, whom he later married, and her son, perhaps his own offspring.[160] Furthermore, the antimanumission law did not deter the mariner John Sarly from manumitting his slave woman, Janie. He, along with the merchant Samuel London and the baker John Bergen, paid the mandatory surety bond.[161] Sarly liberated Janie in 1767, at a time when the settlers began to debate the merits of independence from England and when the rate of voluntary manumissions in British North American began a precipitous rise, owing to the pressure settlers felt to bring their behavior in alignment with their religious convictions and their ideological commitments to the ideals of republicanism and the Enlightenment. In colonial New York, voluntary manumissions were rare occurrences, even during the Revolutionary era.[162] Slaves were costly investments, and except for some conscientious Quakers,[163] colonial New York City slaveowners seldom liberated valuable slaves.

Owing to the relatively high price that slaves commanded in the city's labor market, slaves were regularly subjected to sale, usually through private transactions and occasionally at public auctions.[164] Sale was not the only method by which slaves passed from one master to another. Slaveowners sometimes transferred slaves to their kin through the mechanism of gifts of inheritance. That legal device enabled slaveowners to keep household slaves within their families and to assign a slave or a group of slaves to a particular heir. In this manner, a tradition of slaveholding was, in some settler families, handed down from one generation to the next.[165] Over time, slaveholding became a tradition in the Colden family. In his will, dated December 16, 1774, Alexander Colden left his wife, Elizabeth, an enslaved woman named Florah, a female slave whom his father, Cadwallader Colden, had bequeathed to him in that same year, another enslaved woman named Nanny, an enslaved fellow named Dick, and six slave children—Mary, Ann, Sarah, Phebe (alias Cookoo), Magdalen (alias Monkey), and Peter. Alexander instructed his wife to distribute equal shares of his remaining estate to his offspring, except for several items set aside for his eldest son, John. Among these items were an enslaved fellow named Tom, an enslaved woman named Arnot, and an enslaved lad named Will.[166] In this way, Alexander kept his household slaves within the Colden clan.

To ensure that his household slaves would not be sold outside the family circle after his death, Abraham Van Horne arranged a private family auction of these slaves. His last testament stipulated: "Itemized in order to prevent my Negroes from falling into the hands of strangers or any other than my four—children (To witt) David and Samuel & Margaret & Anna Van Horne. I do hereby will—order and direct that all my Negro slaves as well as male as female shall be sold & bought amongst my four last aforementioned children and to the highest bidder or bidders to them in a private venue or sale to be had and held among themselves only."[167] By directing that his slaves were be sold in a private auction among his four children only, Van Horne spared his household slaves the dehumanizing trauma of being sold to strangers whose character was unknown. The seemingly beneficent provision of Van Horne's will was probably his way of rewarding his household slaves for their faithful service. Yet, what in the estimation of Van Horne's slaves was the value of their master's reward?

From the perspective of these slaves, was a private family auction any more humane than a public auction? Although Van Horne's paternalistic gesture suggests that he considered his slaves to be members of his household, these same slaves experienced nothing like an adoption into their master's family. Rather, the slaves in Van Horne's estate were treated like cherished family heirlooms. In the Van Hornes' case, property in slaves constituted a large proportion of the family's wealth. Nevertheless, the long-term retention of household slaves within the Van Horne family provided the necessary stability for the formation of familial ties among the Van Horne household slaves, and these bonds were acknowledged and preserved in later transfers of slaves within the Van Horne clan. In his last testament James Van Horne, Abraham Van Horne's eldest son, recognized the familial bonds among his household slaves. James bequeathed one-half of his estate to his eldest son, John Van Horne, together with several slave families: "Old Dick and Betty his wife, Jack and Cattleen his wife, Mary her daughter, young Jack brother of Benjamin Morell, Bristol and Diana, and finally, Phil or the boy or man I shall exchange him for with his mother."[168]

The Van Hornes were not the only slaveowners who acknowledged the familial attachments among their household slaves. When financial necessity required the sale of slave families, New York City slaveowners endeavored to preserve the mother-child bond by selling slave mothers with their offspring. Some benevolent slaveowners even granted their slaves a voice in the arrangement of their sale, which usually amounted to granting these slaves veto power over their sale to buyers who lived outside New York City and its environs. In 1763, the New York City slave trader John Watts complained: "It is an invariable indulgence here to permit slaves of any kind to chose those masters, there is no persuading them to leave their country (if I may call it so) their acquaintance & friends, to explore what to their narrow minds appears a new world."[169] After many years of experience as a slave trader, Watts had come to resent the limitations that local custom placed on the right of individual slaveowners to dispose of their slave property as they wished. But what that New York City slave trader perceived as an "indulgence" was, in fact, a necessity. Watts seems not to have understood what the Van Hornes, the Coldens, and other New York City slaveholding families knew well: that slaveowners must endeavor to temper the harshness inherent in the institution of chattel slavery, if they were to remain the masters of the slaves in their households. Put differently, these slaveowners understood that the gift of paternalistic benevolence was a means of imposing an obligation of obedience on their slaves.

The task of managing the domestic relations in his household was the penultimate test of the slaveowner-patriarch's moral authority. While away on business in New York City, Cadwallader Colden sent letters of instruction for the governance of his household to his wife at Coldenham Manor. In a letter dated August 29, 1744, Colden wrote: "Pray remember me affectionately to Jenny, Kathy, & David. Tell the last that I expect a great deal from him now in my absence because I hope he no longer looks on himself as a Child & that he'l be ashamed to play about the Doors with the Negro Children."[170] Like the Old

Testament patriarch Abraham, Colden forbade his son from mingling with the Ishmaels of his household. An attempt at distancing his family from the enslaved blacks on his manorial estate, Colden's commandment to his son betrays his anxiety over the specter of "creolean degeneracy," which, according to European pundits such as Count Buffon, Abbé Raynal, and Cornelius De Pauw, rendered the American-born offspring of transplanted Europeans inferior to native-born Europeans in physical, intellectual, and moral capacities.[171] Colden mapped the intersecting norms of gender and race on the spatial boundaries of his manor house. The doorway to that dwelling became a figure for the threshold marking his son's passage into white manhood, a passageway haunted by the enslaved black children who provoked in Colden the apprehension that life on the North American frontier had exposed his own son to the peril of arrested development or perpetual childhood. David Colden was 11 years of age when he received his father's commandment to cease his childlike relations with his black playmates. Putting childhood behind him, David eventually accepted the responsibilities of white manhood, which included assuming the role of slave master while his father was away on business. When Cadwallader Colden died in 1776, he left his Spring Hill mansion on Long Island to his son David, along with a voluminous library, some surveying instruments, a riding and hunting outfit, as well as several slaves—that is, all the appurtenances of a gentleman's life in colonial New York.[172]

Having grown up in slave-owning households, the Colden and the Van Horne heirs were never truly first-time slaveowners, and they assumed the role of slave master as if it were a "natural" part of becoming an adult. By the time the Colden and the Van Horne children crossed the threshold to adulthood, they had already lived for many years with their families' household slaves. During their childhood years, these New York slaveowners established intimate relationships with household slaves that would be permanently altered when they reached adulthood, established their own slaveowning households, and, in some cases, became the masters of slaves who were once their childhood playmates and surrogate mothers. Such transitions involved the renegotiation of power relations. Living together under the same roof, slaveowner-patriarchs, their families, and their household slaves negotiated what Genovese calls "paternalistic compromises," invented codes of etiquette that allowed the enslavers and the enslaved to live side by side in apparent harmony.

However, the fusion of racial domination and sexual desire within the domestic space of these slave-owning households severely tested this moral economy. In the colonialist imaginary, the master-slave relation sometimes assumed the aspect of a fierce power struggle between rapist and victim, what Thomas Jefferson described as "the whole commerce between master and slave [that was] a perpetual exercise of the most boisterous passions, the most unremitting despotism on the one part, and degrading submission on the other."[173] Defined as an act of sexual violence against the person of another, rape has much in common with the institution of chattel slavery, which involves the violent seizure of a person's body. Because the relations of domination in colonial New York City's slave-owning households depended on the interlocking regimes of patriarchy and white supremacy, the fear of slave rebellion intersected with the fantasy of the black male rapist and the exaggerated vulnerability of white womanhood to interracial rape.[174] When an enslaved black male was accused of rape, he was not uncommonly charged with directing the alleged sexual assault against a female member of his master's immediate family—for example, his master's wife or daughter.

On Monday, January 21, 1733, court proceedings began against Cato, an enslaved black man accused of raping his master's daughter.[175] Throughout his interrogation, Cato declared his innocence. Additionally, the testimony of white witnesses was introduced into evidence on both sides of the case. After two weeks of deliberation, a panel of five white male settlers and two or three justices of the peace acquitted Cato of the crime of rape. But owing to lingering suspicions, the court offered to have Cato transported out of New York at the colonial state's expense. Momentarily caught between the contending imperatives of his patriarchal obligation to protect his daughter, on the one hand, and his interest in preserving his financial investment in his male slave, on the other, the slaveowner-patriarch chose economic self-interest. Sylvester's decision to keep his male slave suggests that he remained confident in his authority to quiet any future tempest within his household on Shelter Island, where both Cato and his daughter continued to live. Endowed with sovereignty over his household, the patriarch-slaveholder Sylvester ruled a petty and sometimes turbulent kingdom within the larger kingdom of the first British Empire.

Another incident provides a striking example of the volatile fusion of interracial sexual desire and domestic violence in colonial New York City's slave-owning households. On July 20, 1737, Jonnoau, an enslaved black man, was indicted on the charge of attempting to rape Anne Carr, his master's wife. Then as now, evidence of rape was not always sufficient to convict accused rapists; attempted rape was even more difficult to prove. Lacking evidence to convict Jonnoau of attempted rape, the jury acquitted the accused of that crime but found him guilty of the lesser crime of battering.[176] Although the minutes of the court do not disclose the provocation for the alleged attack, William Carr, Jonnoau's master, later accused his wife of having a voluntary sexual liaison with his male slave. Carr's accusation suggests that the alleged assault was perhaps the result of a lovers' quarrel between his slave, Jonnoau, and his wife, Anne Carr. The following public announcement of William Carr's divorce from his wife appeared in the New York City newspaper:

Whereas Anne, the Wife of William Carr of the City of New York, has behaved herself in an indecent and Wicked manner, by being too familiar with a Negro Man, as was proved in Open Court on Wednesday last, whereby she has broken the Marriage Contract; and he being informed, that he is not under any Obligation to live with or support her in her wickedness and also drinking to excess. These are therefore to desire all shop-keepers Publick-House-keepers, and all other Persons, not to Trust nor to Give the said Anne Carr Credit on the said Carr's account. . . .[177]

Such were the "boisterous passions" that destroyed the Carrs' conjugal bond. As the alleged violation of the gendered and racialized codes of etiquette in the Carr household suggests, the specter of domestic violence and interracial sexual desire threatened to break through the "barriers of civility within which," as Elizabeth Fox-Genovese has put it, "slaveholding conventions tried to contain it."[178] In colonial New York City, where slaveowners and their families lived under the same roof with enslaved blacks, the volatile fusion of desire and violence seemed to present an ever-present danger to the settler family and the national community in that overseas settler colony.

Whereas in early colonial Virginia the uneven sex ratio in the settler population made an explicit law against interracial marriage vital to the establishment of white family units,[179] in early colonial New York an explicit statutory decree against miscegenation seemed unnecessary since the balanced sex ratio in the settler population promoted the establishment of white settler families. In colonial New York, an internalized taboo on miscegenation, rather than a law against interracial sex and marriage, became a vital mechanism for regulating society. In this respect, that northern settler colony began to resemble a normative society in which internalized controls are supposed to manage the behavior of self-disciplined individuals. Although it proved to be an imperfect disciplinary mechanism, the prohibition against miscegenation (i.e., the rule of endogamy) controlled, to some extent, interracial sexual desires that threatened to dismantle the boundary separating the white settler population from the black population. As the English rulers opened the border of national community and admitted all foreign-born Protestant settlers and their offspring to the English nation through a nearly boundless process of settler assimilation, the intergroup boundary of the settler population migrated to the threshold of nation. At that point, the taboo on miscegenation became the "principle of closure, of exclusion" that demarcated the limit of national belonging.[180] In this way, the application of the miscegenation taboo in colonial New York became integral to intergroup boundary maintenance in the settler population and, importantly, the racialization of the concept "nation" in that overseas settler colony.

The policing of white female sexuality became vital to intergroup boundary maintenance in the settler population. Endowed with the power of procreation, the white female settlers of childbearing age were charged with the responsibility of reproducing a racially pure national community on the foreign soil of empire. For their part, the adult white male settlers exercised a monopoly on the traffic in white females and performed the duty of confining that commerce within the barriers of civility that protected white settler families and, by extension, the national community from racial contamination. As the episode in the Sylvester household shows, slaveowner-patriarchs were not always willing to protect, at any cost, the white women in their households against the alleged sexual aggressions of black men.[181] The white women who lived in the slave-owning households of colonial New York City learned that the relations of racial domination could not only sever the familial ties among slaves but could also damage the affinal bonds in their own families. To be sure, lurid episodes of sexual and racial violence were not confined to the southern colonies. Doubtless, the grandmothers and great-grandmothers of nineteenth-century New York City abolitionist women had firsthand knowledge of the "monstrous system," in which scandals of interracial desire rent the fabric of slave-owning families and harsh judgments ruined the reputations of white women, plunging them into the abyss of poverty and ill repute. As the Carr family intrigue indicates, white women who were merely suspected of engaging in voluntary sexual relations with black men were thought to have committed a crime against civilization. These women paid a high price for their alleged betrayal, banishment from the protection of white male authority figures and the nation. When the white female settler forgot that she was a member of the master race and, more important, the guarantor of its reproduction and racial purity, she was punished with a cruel reminder that she was also a member of the subjugated sex.

In colonial New York City, the black female was a member of both a subjugated sex and a subjugated race. Even though the balanced sex ratio in the adult cohort of the city's settler population encouraged white men to establish respectable conjugal unions with white females of marriageable age and the gendered and racialized norms of the city's settler community stigmatized concubinary relations between white males and black females,[182] patriarchy and white supremacy combined to make black females vulnerable to sexual exploitation at the hands of white men. Colonial New York City newspaper advertisements for the sale of mulatto children born of enslaved black women offer evidence that such acts of sexual exploitation occurred in New York City and elsewhere in colonial New York.[183] In that northern settler colony, the colonial authorities and other white male authority figures fell under no obligation, either statutory or customary, to protect black females from sexual abuse, for popular representations of black female sexuality depicted black females as promiscuous creatures who were more likely to be the seducers of white men than the victims of sexual mistreatment.[184]

Like the black female, the black male was a member of a subjugated race, but unlike her, he was a member of the dominant sex and a rival in the homosocial male contest of mastery over women. In the colonialist imaginary, the black male was a dangerous rebel and rapacious sexual predator. When convicted of either raping or attempting to rape a white female, the black male received the severest punishment. In 1743, a New York City court convicted an unnamed black man of the crime of attempted rape and sentenced him to burn alive. The New York City newspaper published an account of his public execution, reporting: "On Tuesday last he was burnt accordingly, in the presence of a numerous Company of Spectators, great part of which were of the Black Tribe. By the Inspection of the Justice inflicted on this Negro, it is hoped it may be a Means to deter others from attempting such wicked crimes for the Future."[185] Thus, the colonial state intervened to punish a black male in a public spectacle of exemplary corporal punishment intended to terrorize the entire black population into submission.

With respect to governing colonial New York City's black population, the English colonial rulers exercised domination without hegemony. The repressive and negative aspect of the law, and the violence that subtended it, took over where the ostensibly benevolent civilizing activity of SPG missionaries and paternalistic slaveowners failed. To be sure, the SPG's effort to teach the ruling English language and Anglican doctrine to the black town dwellers remained crucial to the imposition of hegemonic domination over them. But only a tiny fraction of the city's black population attended the SPG classes. There could be no persuasion without a common language, and no hegemony, or "one and the same interest," without persuasion. If the black town dwellers did not comprehend the meaning of the word "o-bey," then the whip, the hangman's noose, and the stake would have to be employed to teach them. Racial domination in colonial New York City increasingly rested on harsh civil codes that prescribed severe corporal punishment for disobedient blacks, enslaved and free.[186] In contrast to the resort to overt physical violence in subjugating the city's black population, the English colonial rulers increasingly relied on nonviolent measures to govern the city's settler population and secure settler allegiance to the English Crown. This policy involved cultivating a sense of belonging to the English nation among the Protestant settlers of foreign birth. To that end, the Naturalization Act of 1706 granted most of the rights and privileges of British subjects to foreign-born Protestants who had resided in the British Empire, including British North America, for a stipulated number of years and pledged allegiance to the English Crown. Moreover, the Anglo-Saxon legend, which traced the origin of the English people to ancient Germanic tribes, forged a racial bond between the English rulers and the Germanic peoples from the Netherlands and elsewhere in Europe who were a majority of New York City's settler population for most of the colonial period. In addition, the Church of England's missionary organization, the SPG, provided the settlers' offspring with English-language schooling and indoctrination in the tenets of Anglicanism. Over time, the colonial policies of the English rulers forged the city's settler population into a relatively homogeneous Anglicized community. The English rulers even tolerated the presence of Jews and Catholics, as long as these minority settler populations obeyed English law and did not protest the political disabilities imposed on them.

As the natal, linguistic, and confessional antagonisms within the settler population drifted into the background, social conflict moved to the foreground. In an effort to make colonial New York a more attractive place of settlement for servants from the British Isles and Europe and, equally important, to minimize the danger of social unrest within the settler population and to promote the widest possible settler consent to English rule, the early English colonial rulers stripped indentured servitude of many of its harsh features and promulgated statutes that made a clear distinction between the status of white servants, on the one hand, and enslaved blacks, on the other.[187] Later, in the same year of the enactment of the Naturalization Law of 1706, New York's colonial assembly revised the colony's law of slavery, transforming bond-slavery from a potentially alterable condition predicated on the unreliable criterion of the slave's religious difference to a seemingly immutable, heritable condition passed down from the enslaved Negro, mulatto, Indian, or mestee mother to her offspring. Moreover, with the promulgation of the Black Code of 1712, all blacks, enslaved and free, were firmly relegated to the status of permanent aliens. Although the city's free black population retained the right to own land, they were now prohibited from inheriting land and devising land to their heirs, a disability that hindered the ability of free blacks to transmit their independent status over several generations. In contrast, most white settlers, including propertyless white servants, were elevated to the status of rights-bearing English subjects who occupied an ennobled position above the subjugated black population. In this way, the English colonial rulers attempted to subordinate social conflict, as well as confessional, linguistic, and natal antagonisms, to racial difference. "Colonial racism," Benedict Anderson writes, "was a major element in the concept of 'Empire' which attempted to weld dynastic legitimacy and national community."[188] Whereas violent coercion became the means by which the English rulers governed the black population, persuasion, in the guise of antiblack racism, became a vital means by which they obtained settler consent to their colonial government and settler allegiance to the English Crown.[189] In this respect, the English rulers reformulated the obstacles against establishing hegemony over an alien black population as an advantage in obtaining hegemony over the white settler majority. For the English rulers in colonial New York City, governance meant securing domination with and without hegemony.

"The Most Natural View of the Whole"

DISCOVERING THE "PLOT OF 1741–42" AND THE
DISCURSIVE CONSTRUCTION OF THE "DANGEROUS OTHER"
IN THE COLONIALIST DISCOURSE OF CONSPIRACY

Even though the disciplinary mechanism of antiblack racism mini-mized and subordinated the differences that divided the city's settler population, white solidarity was not something the English rulers could take for granted. Besides having to take precautions against servile insurrection, the English rulers also had to contend with the proliferation of political antagonisms within the ranks of the colonial elite. "Factional strife was," the historian Patricia U. Bonomi has noted, "an almost endemic condition of the colony's public life."[1] The historian Carl L. Becker states, "Prior to 1765, the central fact in the political history of New York was the contest between opposing factions of the colonial elite."[2] This political rivalry took the form of a competition for control over the colonial assembly, in which an opposition party of prominent settlers endeav-ored to gain a majority of the seats in the colony's elective legislative body and to array its powers against the prerogatives of the Crown-appointed governor and the ruling party of influential settlers that supported the royal governor in exchange for lucrative land grants and appointments to governmental offices.

During the winter of 1741–42, rival factions within the colonial elite clashed in a bitter power struggle over who should govern New York. At the same time, rumors of a Spanish invasion and a general alarm over a disturbing crime wave weakened the ruling party's support among the broader settler population—that is, the intermediate stratum of colonial New York's population, a majority of the colony's voters and therefore key to control over the colonial assembly and the colony's political affairs. It was during this crisis that the ruling party claimed to have discovered a sinister plot against English colonial rule. This con-spiracy, the colonial authorities alleged, involved a dangerous combination of enslaved blacks, free blacks, and white outsiders who, together, planned to burn New York City, murder the respectable white townspeople, and establish a renegade regime under the protection of England's enemy, Catholic Spain. Through a series of arrests and showcase trials, the ruling party convinced anxious white town dwellers that recent unsolved crimes were not unconnected events, as they had been initially perceived, but instead were evidence of a deliberate design to destroy the settler colony. In view of the intensifying public alarm over this purported security threat, the colonial elite temporarily set aside their differences and, together with the broader settler population, now galvanized into a unified community that rallied behind the ruling party's program for purging traitors inside the colony. Since widespread belief in the existence of a conspiratorial menace to the public safety had effectively neutralized its political rivals, the ruling party endeavored to prolong the state of emergency. As late as December 1742, nearly 10 months after the initial investigation into the alleged plot began, prosecutors were bringing forth indictments against suspected traitors. By that time, factionalism within the ranks of the colonial elite had resurfaced. The opponents of the ruling party now began to criticize the court proceedings against the convicted conspirators, charging that the Crown-appointed magistrates of the court had rushed to judgment and, on inadequate evidence, ordered the execution of innocent slaves and white people. Hence, the charge of judicial murder became a leading issue in the reinvigorated opposition faction's campaign to remove members of the ruling party from governmental office.[3]

In a document entitled *Journal of the Proceedings in the Detection of the Conspiracy Formed by Some White People in Conjunction with Negro and Other Slaves for Burning the City of New-York in America and Murdering the Inhabitants*, Daniel Horsmanden, Crown-appointed justice of New York's Supreme Court from 1736 to 1747, defends the ruling party against the charge of judicial murder.[4] Published in 1744, Horsmanden's *Journal* iterates the colonialist discourse of conspiracy, which during the emergency of 1741–42 aspired to install a permanent social war (or binary division of society) and thereby produce two vital ingredients of governance—consent and common sense.[5] The colonialist discourse of conspiracy deployed a binary logic of identity and difference that established commonsensical criteria for distinguishing between, on the one side, "loyal subjects" who were united in allegiance to the English colonial rulers by their shared fear of subaltern insurgency and, on the other side, disloyal subjects whose deviance from the norms of whiteness, Protestantism, and property holding assigned them to the category "dangerous other." The discursive construction of that phobogenic object became a tool in the art of colonial governance, allowing the ruling elite to claim that it represented the interest of the broader settler population and enabling the ruling elite to gain voluntary acquiescence to its government from the city's rights-bearing white Anglo-Saxon Protestant settler majority of propertied merchants, mariners, artisans, and shopkeepers. Focused on the danger from below, this intermediate stratum of the city's settler population coalesced as a unified community along a horizontal axis of identification and as loyal subjects of the English Crown along a vertical axis of identification. In brief, the fantasy of the "dangerous other" gave phantasmatic support to the horizontal and vertical identifications constitutive of colonial governance.

The settlers were not always vigilant against the threat of conspiracy from below. Between 1735 and 1741, political factionalism within the ranks of the colonial elite monopolized their attention.[6] In 1735, they were preoccupied with the Zenger trial, a dramatic court case that originated in a salary dispute between William Cosby, the royal governor of New York from 1732 to 1736, and Rip Van Dam, a prominent New York City merchant whom Governor Cosby had ousted from his council.[7] The turbulence had not subsided from that contest when, in March 1736, the sudden death of Governor Cosby precipitated a political crisis that brought New York to the brink of civil war. When Cosby died, Van Dam claimed the post of interim governor. Lieutenant Governor George Clarke, a Crown appointee, also coveted the executive office. With the assistance of his supporters among the colonial elite, Clarke occupied the fort at the tip of Manhattan Island, as well as the government buildings inside that fortress, and took charge of the colony's affairs. Challenging Clarke's authority, Van Dam and his opposition faction accused the lieutenant governor of usurping the powers of government. Animosity between the Van Dam faction and the Clarke faction had neared the point of armed conflict when, in 1737, a vessel arrived at the port of New York with a letter from the English monarch, appointing Lieutenant Governor Clarke interim head of colonial New York's government. According to the king's instructions, Clarke was to continue as chief executive of the colony until Cosby's permanent replacement could be named. The news of Clarke's temporary appointment left Van Dam and his backers with no alternative but to yield to the Crown's wishes. They remained, however, outspoken critics of the lieutenant governor and waited for an opportunity to bring public disfavor on him and his ruling party.[8]

By 1737, the fiscal powers of government in New York had shifted from the English Crown and its appointed officials to the popularly elected colonial assembly. Although the English Crown selected New York's royal governor, an elected body of colonial representatives now controlled the allocation of his salary. This new balance of governmental powers meant that the Crown-appointed governor could no longer ignore the arena of popular politics, in which competing factions of the colonial elite vied for the support of the numerous intermediate stratum of property-holding adult white male settlers who exercised the vote and elected representatives to the colonial assembly.[9] Nevertheless, the succession of governors who ruled colonial New York in the name of the English Crown shunned the practice of overt electioneering. In sharp contrast, factions within the colonial elite resembled nascent political parties and conducted vigorous election campaigns, which stimulated political participation on the part of the relatively large segment of adult white male property owners that voted in New York elections. As Bonomi has noted, the Van

Dam faction was foremost in the vanguard of devising techniques of popular politics.[10] In an effort to establish an anti-Clarke majority in the colonial assembly and offset the interim governor's executive powers, the Van Dam faction (the opposition party) portrayed the Clarke administration (the ruling party) as the enemy of the common man, while styling itself as the protector of the public interest. The opposition party achieved a notable victory in the spring elections of 1737, when James Alexander and Garret Van Horne of the Van Dam faction defeated Adolph Philipse and Stephen DeLancey of the Clarke faction in a contest for the New York City seats in the colonial assembly.

Hoping to forestall further erosion of his political influence, interim Governor Clarke negotiated a rapprochement with the Van Dam camp and incorporated that faction within the ruling party. This new coalition was, however, based on a precarious alliance between long-standing political rivals. England's war against Spain and the attendant economic depression rendered that coalition all the more fragile. During the War of Jenkin's Ear (1739–42), New York City merchants suffered because of the disruption of the provisions trade to the West Indies, economic competition from Pennsylvania, and the scarcity of cash. At about the same time, the New York City coopers complained that the practice of hiring out slaves in the skilled trades was ruining their livelihood. Also, the city's dissenting Protestant churches were embroiled in internal controversies. Moreover, the harsh winter of 1740–41 and the subsequent bakers' strike in protest of the high price of wheat led to shortages of food that weighed heavily on impoverished town dwellers.[11] In addition to the material hardships visited on the poor, the deployment of military forces from Manhattan Island to the Caribbean theater of war left New York City vulnerable to servile insurrection and foreign invasion. (Many of the colonial port town's long-time residents could remember the Slave Revolt of 1712. In addition, local folklore doubtless preserved the memory of the English Conquest of 1664 and the Dutch Reconquest of 1673.) As hostilities against Spain mounted and rumors of a Spanish invasion circulated throughout British North America, the townspeople became anxious for their safety. In view of England's escalating war against Spain and the prospect of a Spanish assault against the nearly defenseless port town, interim Governor Clarke asked New York's colonial assembly to allocate public funds for financing the construction of desperately needed fortifications and other defense preparations. But the reanimated anti-Clarke majority in that legislative body denied Clarke's request.

Thus, the crises of war, economic depression, controversies within some Protestant churches, and the immiseration of the poor established the conditions for the return of internal antagonisms within the colonial elite and a renewed challenge to Clarke's ruling party. In his brief history of the Clarke administration Cadwallader Colden recalled that during this period of crisis Clarke's ruling party "lost every day ground with the people & [was] divided among themselves."[12] Suddenly, in the winter of 1741–42, an unsolved crime wave and a rash of mysterious fires struck New York City, adding to Clarke's troubles. It was in these disturbing yet seemingly unrelated events that the ruling party perceived a dangerous conspiracy against English colonial rule and discovered the "plot of 1741–42."

On February 28, 1741, the first unsettling event unfolded. Late that night, unknown culprits burglarized Robert Hogg's shop in the city's North Ward. Stolen from that shop were several coins, a couple of silver candlesticks, and some linen. A few days later, the colonial authorities arrested Caesar, a male slave of John Vaarck, for possession of Hogg's stolen property. Vaarck had found the purloined items underneath the floor of the "Negro kitchen" in his back yard and remanded Caesar and the stolen goods to the sheriff in charge of the city jail. Because Prince, one of Caesar's comrades, was a reputed ringleader of a black brotherhood, known as the "Geneva Club" after their conviction for stealing a barrel of Geneva gin from a New York City shopkeeper in 1736,[13] the colonial authorities jailed that enslaved black man on suspicion of having burglarized Hogg's shop and interrogated him about the recent break-in. Prince denied any involvement in that crime. Since the colonial authorities had no concrete evidence to implicate Prince in the Hogg burglary, they returned him to his owner, who had posted bail for the release of his slave. Caesar, on the other hand, remained in the city jail.

Because it was rumored that Caesar and Prince were patrons of a certain tavern in the city's West Ward, the proprietor of that pub, John Hughson, and his wife, Sarah, were brought before the sheriff for questioning about the Hogg robbery. Popular resorts, such as Hughson's tavern, had long been suspected of harboring black-market exchanges in stolen goods.[14] Hughson, his wife, and his four daughters had migrated from Westchester County to New York City in 1739. At that time, Hughson opened a dry goods store in the city's Montgomerie Ward and at that shop sold "penny drams" of liquor to slaves. The newcomer eventually moved to the city's West Ward, where he leased a tavern at the upper end of Broadway. Settling on the fringes of New York City's respectable community of merchants, shopkeepers, artisans, and other white settlers who conducted more reputable businesses, Hughson and his family soon became the object of town gossip. It was rumored that at Hughson's tavern large numbers of slaves amused themselves with strong liquors, drumming, fiddling, and the company of white women. In 1740, the constables raided Hughson's tavern and found that the proprietor was conducting a "disorderly house," where enslaved blacks and white servants gathered without permission from their masters. The colonial authorities convicted Hughson of illegally "entertaining Negro slaves." Because this infraction of the law was the tavern keeper's first such offense, he received a warning from the court instead of a fine. In his second brush with the law, Hughson once again got off lightly. Even though the newcomer was suspected of involvement in the burglary of Hogg's shop, he and his wife were freed after a search of their tavern and dwelling failed to uncover any incriminating evidence. As the investigation of John Hughson indicates, the colonial authorities devoted considerable effort to solving the Hogg burglary. But they initially perceived nothing extraordinary about that crime. In subsequent weeks, anxiety-ridden town dwellers witnessed an unnerving outbreak of fires, which aroused the authorities' suspicion that a more dangerous threat than some cunning burglars imperiled the city and its inhabitants.

On March 18, 1741, the day after a disorderly St. Patrick's Day celebration, the first in a series of mysterious fires destroyed most of the buildings inside the fort, including the chapel, the lieutenant governor's residence, and several barracks. The destruction of the fortress, the symbol of the English military presence in colonial New York, underscored the vulnerability of the tinderbox town. An official inquiry into the destructive fire established that the most likely cause of the combustion was the negligence of a plumber, who, on the morning before the blaze erupted, had repaired a leak at the chapel inside the fort and, in his haste to finish his work, left behind a live coal from his soldering equipment. This construction of events was deemed the most plausible explanation for the inferno, but the possibility of arson was not ruled out.[15] During the following three weeks, the townspeople witnessed nine additional fires.[16] Because slaves were the ready-made suspects for the crime of arson, the panic-stricken white town dwellers now cast a suspicious gaze over the city's enslaved black population, which included a significant number of fairly recent newcomers. Between 1732 and 1754, more than 35 percent of the immigrants who disembarked at the port of New York were slaves, mostly native Africans.[17] As early as 1737, an anxious town dweller warned: "Too great a Number of that Unchristian and barbarous People [were] being imported."[18] Although white New Yorkers were preoccupied with internal political divisions, they were not entirely insensible to the danger of servile insurrection.[19] Some town dwellers recalled the Slave Revolt of 1712, which involved native African newcomers who set fire to some buildings and ambushed the townspeople who arrived at the scene of the fire in order to put out the blaze. Linking the recent arsons to slave revolt, some frightened white townspeople exclaimed that the Negroes were rising against them. In response to this alarm, white vigilantes seized slaves in the streets and carried them to the city jailer. In light of the current hostilities with Spain and the participation of enslaved Spanish-speakers in the Slave Revolt of 1712, some Spanish-speaking slaves of the city's East Ward—Antonio de San Bendito, Antonio de la Cruz, Augustine Gutierrez, Juan de la Sylva, and Pablo Ventura Angél—were also jailed.[20] These enslaved Spanish-speakers had arrived at the port of New York in 1740.[21] Despite the physical evidence of arson found at several of the burnt buildings and the arrest of 20 or so slaves on suspicion of having intentionally set the recent fires, the colonial authorities made little progress on tying the combustions to a slave uprising. Nevertheless, they were now convinced that the mysterious blazes were somehow connected to more sinister crimes.

Twelve days after the conflagrations of April 6, the colonial authorities made several arrests in connection with the Hogg burglary. Acting on a tip from Mary Burton, John Hughson's indentured servant, the sheriff and several deputies searched Hughson's tavern and dwelling for a second time. That inspection uncovered stolen goods underneath the floor of Hughson's house. With this discovery, the colonial authorities imprisoned the tavern keeper and his wife. They also incarcerated Prince for possession of stolen goods—some beeswax and indigo, allegedly pilfered from Abraham Meyers Cohen's house. By this time, Caesar, Prince's comrade, had spent nearly seven weeks in jail. The colonial authorities now quickly prosecuted Caesar, Prince, and the Hughsons on charges of burglary. But at this juncture in the official investigation, the colonial authorities had no tangible evidence to implicate the accused thieves in the crime of arson, which, they believed, was part of a more serious criminal plot. On May 1, 1742, Caesar and Prince were brought before the court on two counts of burglary each. The prosecuting attorney surmised that, on the instructions of their white accomplices, thievish slaves had used arson as a subterfuge to enter the homes of unsuspecting townspeople and steal valuable property on the pretext of saving these items from the flames. With these allegations, the colonial authorities proclaimed they had eradicated an organized burglary ring, a previously hidden part of the city's criminal underworld. The prosecution's only evidence against the accused was the stolen property from Hogg's shop and Cohen's house. But after a brief deliberation, the court found Caesar and Prince guilty of burglary. The court magistrates immediately sentenced the black men to hang by the neck until dead. Justice Frederick Philipse summoned the two condemned slaves before the bench and asserted his conviction that they were somehow involved in the recent outbreak of fires. Philipse advised them to tell what they knew for the salvation of their souls, but Caesar and Prince made no confession of guilt.

On May 11, 1742, the townspeople witnessed the execution of the condemned slaves. The object of exemplary punishment, Caesar's corpse was left outdoors until it had decomposed. Justice Horsmanden stated that the public display of Caesar's rotting body was intended "to break the knot [of silent conspirators], and to induce some of them to unfold this mystery of iniquity, in hopes of thereby recommending themselves to mercy." As a further inducement, the colonial authorities offered a reward of £100 to any settler who could provide useful information about the mysterious rash of arsons. Soon after, they advertised a reward of freedom to any slave who could name the arsonists.[22] In the weeks following the executions and the publication of the rewards to informants, scores of slaves were brought before official examiners and interrogated. Under the pressure of examination, these slaves poured forth a cascade of incriminating and self-incriminating confessions. Doubtless, some informants committed perjury in order to obtain the reward of freedom, while others merely wished to save their lives. One informant told constable John Schultz that many slaves had made false confessions of grandiose dimension because they feared that "if they didn't they'd be hanged." The coerced nature of the confessions did not, however, invalidate the testimony of informants who confirmed the colonial authorities' belief that they had discovered an elaborate plot against English rule. The transcripts of coerced confessions and the trial testimony of terrified informants enabled the prosecution to convict and execute 31 enslaved blacks and four white outsiders for their putative roles in a grand conspiracy to burn New York City, murder the respectable white townspeople, and overthrow the English colonial government. Another 70 enslaved blacks and seven white outsiders were transported out of the colony as punishment for their alleged role in the conspiracy.[23]

For 16 weeks after the execution of Caesar and Prince, from May 11 to August 31, 1742, the colonial authorities focused the attention of the townspeople on a series of showcase trials, in which the mysterious crime wave and series of fires were represented as a diabolic plot of Spanish origin. By placing this nefarious scheme before the numerous intermediate stratum of property-holding, voting white townspeople, Clarke's ruling party, which perhaps genuinely feared an intrigue against English colonial rule, forestalled popular protest against its government. Animosities that could have been directed upward against the ruling party were channeled downward toward New York City's increasingly numerous and alien black population, as well as white outsiders who consorted with blacks. During the court proceedings, the factious white settlers were temporarily united around the discovery and suppression of a dangerous conspiracy from below; their attention was diverted from the internal conflicts that divided them. Furthermore, the political enemies of the lieutenant governor dared not challenge his authority during the conspiracy trials for fear of being accused of putting self-interest ahead of the public interest or, worse, of being implicated in the plot itself.

Declaring a state of emergency and placing the city's entire populace under martial law, Clarke's ruling party reasserted its authority over colonial affairs. The colonial authorities also secretly determined to conduct a general search throughout the port town. In perhaps the most expansive exercise and coordination of police power in the history of New York prior to the Revolutionary era, the colonial rulers authorized the city's aldermen, councilmen, and constables to search and seize the property of ordinary white town dwellers. Daniel Horsmanden described the secret plan:

> The proposal was approved of, and each alderman and his common councilman, with constables attending them, undertook to search his respective ward on the south side of the fresh water pond; and the Monday following was the day fixed upon for making the experiment. This scheme was communicated to the governor, and his honour thought fit to order the militia out that day in aid of the magistrates, who were to be dispersed through the city, and sentries of them posted at the ends of streets to guard all avenues, with orders to stop all suspected persons that should be observed carrying bags or bundles, or removing goods from house to house, in order for their examination; and all this was to be kept very secret till the project was put in execution.

The "general search" of May 13, 1742, uncovered no evidence of a plot against English colonial rule.[24]

Throughout the summer of 1742, English troops maintained a regular military watch over the city, monitoring the comings and goings of long-time residents and newcomers alike.[25] During the summer months, the colonial authorities also began a crackdown on the city's numerous taverns, tippling houses, and dramshops, especially those establishments that catered to the city's enslaved population. During the conspiracy trials, one of the prosecutors, Joseph Murray, stated that the city's tavern life posed a threat to public order and that tavern keepers and shopkeepers who continued to sell strong liquor to slaves should be punished, for "under the pretense of selling what they call a penny dram to a negro, [tavern keepers and shop owners] will sell to him as many quarts or gallons of rum, as he can steal money or goods to pay for." Justice Horsmanden added: "The many fatal consequences flowing from the prevailing and wicked practice are so notorious and so nearly concern us all that one would be almost surprised to think there should be a necessity for a court to recommend a suppressing of such pernicious houses." Horsmanden also noted that the unwarranted amount of leisure time and unregulated mobility of the port town's slave labor force posed an additional danger. He pointed to the example of Cuffee, the enslaved man of the aged Adolph Philipse: "It was notorious Cuff had a great deal of idle time upon his hands, perhaps more than any negro in town, consequently was much at large for making frequent daily or nightly visits at Hughson's, and therefore indeed must of course have become personally acquainted with a greater number of the conspirators, than others who had fewer of the like opportunities." At another juncture in the conspiracy trials, the prosecutor William Smith remarked on the hazard presented by unsupervised gatherings of enslaved blacks in the streets on the Sabbath: "It appears that this horrid scene of iniquity has been chiefly contrived and promoted at meetings of negroes in great numbers on Sundays. This instructive circumstance may teach us many lessons, both of reproof and caution, which I only hint at, and shall leave the deduction of the particulars to every one's reflection." The correct deduction, which law-abiding townspeople were supposed to draw from the discovery of the "plot of 1741–42," was that New York City's enslaved population should be brought under stricter regulation and that effective methods should be devised to achieve that end. Yet the emergency measures of the summer of 1742 were temporary expedients only. The colonial authorities never instituted fully effective mechanisms for policing the city's enslaved population. The bulk of the responsibility for disciplining the port town's slave labor force continued to fall on the shoulders of individual slaveowners. For this reason, the preface to Horsmanden's *Journal* reminds New York City slaveowners "to keep a very watchful eye over [their slaves], and not to indulge them with too great liberties, which we find they make use of to the worst purpose, caballing, and confederating together in mischief in great numbers."

The city's white servant population proved more difficult to police than its enslaved black labor force, for in an effort to attract white laborers to New York the colonial authorities granted white servants privileges and liberties that gave them greater freedom of movement and assembly than enslaved blacks and free blacks enjoyed. Although the War of Jenkin's Ear curtailed the flow of immigrants from the British Isles and Europe into the port of New York, that war did not totally halt the haphazard influx of white strangers into the port town. While the colonial authorities worried that the unregulated assembly of transients, enslaved blacks, and white servants in the city's streets, docks, and taverns posed a threat to the public safety, they were incapable of effectively monitoring the city's subaltern population. Fear of an interracial conspiracy among the propertyless stratum of the colonial port town's social hierarchy was hardly an irrational apprehension. Poor whites and enslaved blacks had ample opportunities to congregate in secret and plot against their superiors. Taking this undeniable factor into account, the colonial authorities surmised that the recent mysterious crime wave and rash of fires were not random, unrelated events but the manifestation of a conspiracy that existed among a dangerous combination of enslaved blacks and white outsiders.

"Conspiratorial interpretations—attributing events to the concerted designs of willful individuals—became," the historian Gordon Wood has noted, "a major means by which educated men in the early modern period ordered and gave meaning to their world."[26] Daniel Horsmanden's *Journal* (1744) provides an instructive example of the way in which educated men—in this instance, a party of politically embattled colonial elite in eighteenth-century New York City—constructed a meaningful world and disseminated their worldview to the common man. The following discussion analyzes the discursive conventions of narration deployed in Horsmanden's *Journal* in order to discern how the ruling elite's discourse of conspiracy became common sense.

A vehicle for legitimating the ruling party's use of the death penalty to restore law and order during the emergency of 1741–42, Horsmanden's *Journal* is first and foremost a political document. A member of the Governor's Council, a justice of New York's Supreme Court, and the recorder for that court from 1733 to 1747, Horsmanden had a political stake in defending the ruling party's acts of judgment against the hostile counterjudgments of its political enemies. In addition to the ruling party's political foes in New York, detractors from outside the colony also questioned the validity of the court proceedings against the suspects convicted of and executed for the crime of conspiracy. In a letter addressed to Cadwallader Colden and dated July 23, 1742, an anonymous New Englander accuses New York's ruling party of staging a witch-hunt and likens New York City's recent conspiracy trials to the Salem Witchcraft Trials of 1692. Casting doubt on the trustworthiness of the coerced confessions that New York's colonial authorities extracted from terrified black town dwellers and used to convict accused conspirators, Colden's correspondent remarks: "It makes me suspect that your present case, & ours heretofore are much the same, and that Negro & spectre evidence will turn out alike."[27] In addition, appearing in New York City and Philadelphia around 1743 were several printed broadsides that characterized the Crown-appointed officials who presided over New York's conspiracy trials as bloodthirsty executioners bent on destroying the lives of innocent slaves and white people.[28] Hence, the pressing political motive of defending the Clarke administration against the charge of judicial murder led Horsmanden to publish his *Journal*. Horsmanden's *Journal* and the printed attacks that necessitated its publication disclose the rising force of public supervision over the English rulers in eighteenth-century New York City. As early as the 1690s, the political reforms of the Glorious Revolution allowed some New York City town dwellers to call into question the divine right of the monarch to take life and also enabled them to obtain the revocation of the writ of attainder against the executed leaders of Leisler's Rebellion from the English Parliament. By the 1740s, the representation of the ruling party as an extension of monarchical sovereignty was hardly an unassailable defense against the accusation of judicial murder. By that time, the imperatives of popular politics in the settler colony required the ruling party to convince the public of the lawfulness of its actions.[29] Instead of sending an administrative report to the metropolitan authorities in London or writing a passionate rebuttal addressed to the ruling party's political enemies among the colonial elite, Horsmanden wisely appealed to the court of public opinion—that is, to the settler majority of literate freeholders who voted in colonial New York's elections.

The historian Thomas J. Davis has noted, "As a document of the time, [Horsmanden's *Journal*] stands on its internal structure and ought to be judged thereon."[30] In his *Journal*, Horsmanden adheres to the discursive conventions of eighteenth-century print culture, privileging impersonal utterance, the authoritative mode of public communication or publicity. Through the cultural matrix of the print medium, Horsmanden's unmarked narrator addresses an abstract public of undifferentiated readers that scrutinizes the ruling party's conduct of governmental affairs during the emergency of 1741–42. Cloaked in the veil of disinterested recorder of historical events, Horsmanden published a seemingly straightforward, day-by-day account of the events leading to the conspiracy trials and executions.[31] In the preface to his *Journal*, the judge turned historian asserts the impartiality of the kind of text he has brought before the public:[32]

A *journal* would give more satisfaction, inasmuch as in such a kind of process, the depositions and examinations themselves, which were the ground-work of the proceedings, would appear at large; which most probably would afford conviction to such as have a disposition to be convinced and have *in reality* doubted whether any particular convicts had justice done them or not, notwithstanding they had the opportunity of *seeing* and *hearing* a great deal concerning them; and others, who had no such opportunities, who were prejudiced at distance in their disfavour, by frivolous reports, might the readier be undeceived: for as the proceedings are set forth in the order of time they were produced, the reader will thereby be furnished with the most natural view of the whole and be better enabled to conceive the design and dangerous depth of this *hellish project*, as well as the justice of the several prosecutions.

While Horsmanden gives the impression of letting the evidence speak for itself, so that his readers can examine for themselves the unembellished facts, the depositions, interrogations, and other printed records appear in his text after an "Introduction" that offers his own narration of the events of 1741–42. The facts do not, then, "appear at large," as Horsmanden claims, but instead are framed by a historical narrative that confers meaning upon the unsystematic compilation of documents assembled during the official investigation and the conspiracy trials.[33] While a few scattered sources, such as brief newspaper reports and fragmentary records, provide bits and pieces of information on the disturbing burglaries and rash of fires, the official investigation into the mysterious crime wave, and the conspiracy trials,[34] Horsmanden's narrative is the only full account of the alleged conspiracy. In short, Horsmanden's *Journal* is the "plot of 1741–42."

Horsmanden's narrative imposes a coherent meaning on the baffling events of 1741–42. As his narrative unfolds, the reader discovers the logical connection between seemingly random occurrences. Here, the production of knowledge is an effect of the power of narration: A single impersonal narrator performs the task of presenting the reader with *the gradual disclosure of meaning* as *the dispensation of a telos* or, as the narrator puts it, the "most natural view of the whole."[35] It is, then, the production of knowledge through narrative representation that invests Horsmanden's text with authority, prescience, and coherence. Narrative sentences—that is, the narration of events that could not have been witnessed (or perceived) in the manner described, because they reference integral future events that could not have been known to the observer at the time of the occurrence of the events being described[36]—endow Horsmanden's narrator with the faculty of omniscience. In Horsmanden's text, such narrative sentences are accompanied by supplementary phrases of the following sort: "as was discovered and will appear more fully hereafter." In this way, Horsmanden underscores the device of omniscient narration by drawing attention to the imperfect knowledge of the common man—his implied reader—who attributed the outbreak of fires to a variety of causes, ranging from sheer caprice to arson, but did not apprehend the more sinister design against English colonial rule. Horsmanden's omniscient narrator observes:

> The five several fires, viz. at the fort, captain Warren's house, Van Zandt's storehouse, Quick's stable, and Ben Thomas's kitchen, having happened in so short a time succeeding each other; and the attempt made of a sixth on Mr. Murray's haystack, it was natural for people of any reflection, to conclude that the fire was set on purpose by a combination of villains, and therefore occasioned great uneasiness to every one that had thought; but upon this supposition nobody imagined there could be any further design; than for some wicked wretches to have the opportunity of making a prey of their neighbor's goods, under pretence of assistance in removing them for security from the danger of flames; for upon these late instances, many of the sufferers had complained of great losses of their goods, and furniture, which had been removed from their houses upon these occasions.

While the anxious town dwellers perceived an ulterior and fraudulent motive in apparently altruistic gestures, they did not, according to Horsmanden's narrator, fathom the more ominous plot hidden still deeper beneath the surface of events. In contrast, Horsmanden's omniscient narrator assumes the position of an imperial subject that possesses knowledge that the ordinary town dweller does not possess.

Although Horsmanden's narrator calls attention to the incomplete knowledge of the bewildered townspeople, his narrative portrays them as a cohesive community of loyal subjects who rush to the lieutenant governor's aid when an inferno engulfs his residence inside the fort. "Upon the chapel bells ringing," the narrator tells the reader, "great numbers of people . . . came to the assistance of the lieutenant governor and his family; and as the people of this city, to do them justice, are very active and diligent upon these occasions. . . ." At another point, the narrator describes a social drama in which a black villain is carried to jail "upon the people's shoulders." During the emergency of 1741–42, the factious hive of white town dwellers, the narrator reports, cast aside their quarrels and, drawing more closely together as the "people," acted in a common interest against a common enemy. Horsmanden's narrative thus depicts the vertical and horizontal identifications that bound the intermediate stratum of white settlers into a cohesive community of loyal subjects. When the evidence contradicts this idealized image of the city's white settler community, it is dismissed. According to Horsmanden's narrative, the colonial authorities reject the allegation of treason directed against John Romme, the cousin of a prominent city councilman. Having learned that Romme has been convicted of receiving stolen goods from the Hogg robbery and sentenced to hang, Mary Burton, an indentured servant from John Hughson's household, makes what Horsmanden's narrator calls an "ingenious confession." Mary's confession is "ingenious" in a double sense: First, it reveals knowledge of events unknown to the reader; second, it attempts to arrange the particulars of the "plot" in a fashion that displaces guilt from the Hughsons and herself and onto John Romme. To that end, Mary places the meetings of the conspiratorial cabal at Romme's workplace, where he had operated a dramshop frequented by slaves, instead of at Hughson's tavern, where she had lived. Luckily for Romme, his guilt in the crime of plotting to commit treason could not be assimilated in the colonial authorities' theory of conspiracy, which portrayed the city's intermediate stratum of propertied white settlers—artisans, merchants, and shopkeepers—as loyal subjects of the English Crown. The colonial authorities therefore dismiss Mary's story about Romme's central role in the conspiracy, and the examiners persuade the female servant to recant her accusations against the well-connected shopkeeper. Exonerated of the charge of conspiracy and instead convicted of the lesser crime of receiving stolen goods, Romme receives leniency from the court and is spared his life on the condition that he leave the colony. According to Horsmanden's narrative, Mary also attempts to incriminate members of New York City's colonial elite or, as she referred to them, "some people in *ruffles*." The colonial authorities dismiss her accusations against these prominent settlers, whom they characterize as loyal British subjects "of known credit, fortunes and reputations, and of religious principles superior to a suspicion of being concerned in such destestable practices."

With its unsolved crime wave and its constables and robbers, Horsmanden's narrative reads like a detective mystery story. After retelling the mysterious events of 1741–42, the narrator announces: "Who did it was a question remained to be determined." John Hughson, the tavern keeper, is eventually branded ringleader of the conspiracy. According to Horsmanden's reprint of the trial records, a prosecutor points to Hughson and declares to the jury: "Gentlemen, behold the author and abettor of all the late conflagrations, terrors, and devastation that have befallen this city." The prosecutor adds: "This is the man!—this that grand incendiary!—that arch rebel against God, his king, and his country!—that devil incarnate, and chief agent of the old Abaddon of the infernal pit, and Geryon of darkness!" The prosecutor's allusions to the apocalyptic visions told in the Book of Revelation[37] cast Hughson in the role of the chief agent of destruction. The tavern keeper's disastrous career in colonial New York City becomes an instructive example of the destiny of those who succumb to the forces of evil in the Manichean struggle between darkness and light. During Hughson's sentencing, Justice Philipse calls the condemned tavern keeper before the bench and asserts: "Miserable Wretch! How he has plunged himself and family into that pit which he had dug for others, and brought down upon his own pate that violent dealing which he contrived and in part executed against his neighbors. . . . I know not which is the more astonishing, the extreme folly, or wickedness of so base and shocking a conspiracy. . . . What could it be expected to end in, in the account of any rational and considerate person among you, but your own destruction." The execution of Hughson and his wife cautioned other white townspeople against transgressing the racialized norms of bourgeois respectability. According to Horsmanden's narrative, it is the Hughsons' association with enslaved blacks that at first marks the tavern keeper and his wife as targets of suspicion.[38] At the Hughsons' sentencing, Chief Justice James DeLancey remarks that "disorderly houses," such as Hughson's tavern, subvert the city's biracial hierarchy of white over black and that the condemned white traitors are "guilty of not only making Negroes their equals but even their superiors by waiting upon, keeping with, and entertaining them." Perhaps Hughson, his wife, and the other white outsiders who were executed for the crime of treason were guilty of nothing more.

An anti-Catholic bias subtended the colonialist discourse of conspiracy, and during the emergency of 1741–42 Roman Catholics became targets of suspicion. Accustomed to identifying Irishmen with Roman Catholicism and rebellion,[39] the colonial authorities arrested several Irish soldiers on suspicion of participating in the purported "popish" plot to murder the Protestant townspeople.[40] Although these Irish soldiers were never brought to trial, the prosecutors appealed to popular anti-Catholic sentiment during the court proceedings against other accused conspirators. In his address to the jury, a prosecutor stated: "They [Roman Catholics] hold it not only lawful but meritorious to kill and destroy all that differ in opinion from them, if it may any ways serve the interest of their detestable religion; the whole scheme of which seems to be a restless endeavour to extirpate all other religions whatsoever, but more especially the protestant religion, which they maliciously call the Northern heresy." The prosecutor added, "Then they have their doctrine of transubstantiation, which is so big with absurdities that it is shocking to the common sense and reason of mankind; for were that doctrine true, their priests by a few words of their mouths, can make a God as often as they please: but then they eat him too, and this they have the impudence to call honouring and adoring him. . . . These and many other juggling tricks they have in their hocus pocus, bloody religion." Denouncing the Roman Catholic doctrine of transubstantiation and reputed belief in the magical power of words, the prosecutor draws an implicit identification between Catholicism and the "black arts"—for example, heathen superstition, magic, witchcraft, and sorcery—that resonated with the anti-Catholic prejudices of the city's white Protestant settler population and therefore served to bolster the ruling party's claim that Roman Catholics had, in league with culturally alien blacks who also allegedly practiced magic, conspired to murder the white Protestant townspeople.

Horsmanden's *Journal* calls attention to Catholic Spain's long history of conspiring against Protestant nations and presents quotes from printed histories that relate the infamous papist plots against Protestant England's Queen Elizabeth I and King William III. According to Horsmanden's narrative, General James Oglethorpe of Georgia inflames the Catholic scare throughout British North America when, on May 16, 1742, he issues a security alert, warning the English colonial authorities that Catholic Spain has sent agents provocateurs to infiltrate the English overseas colonies and that "priests were employed [for this purpose], under pretended appellations of physicians, dancing-masters," and the like. For colonial New York City's Protestant majority, the Catholic priest was the perfect symbol of conspiracy. Horsmanden's narrative casts John Ury, a white newcomer who allegedly held unorthodox religious views, in the role of conspiratorial Catholic priest. Like other young men of meager fortune, Ury had migrated to British North America to improve his lot in life. According to his diary, Ury arrived in New York City on November 2, 1741, after having traveled through Maryland and Pennsylvania. This stranger soon found himself in the wrong place at the wrong time. Following a brief period of unemployment in the city, Ury began to teach Greek and Latin to the children of wealthy townspeople. Town gossips circulated the rumor that the young schoolmaster and newcomer professed the Roman Catholic faith and since his arrival in the city had convened several secret meetings attended by crypto-Catholics. It was also alleged that Ury had quoted certain biblical texts upon which the Church of Rome based its claim that it was the only true church and that priests were authorized to forgive sin. When this news reached the colonial authorities, they immediately arrested Ury on suspicion of being a Catholic priest.[41]

Following his arrest, Ury and several informants were brought before colonial inquisitors, who conduct an official investigation into his religious beliefs and complicity in the suspected plot to overthrow English rule in colonial New York City and erect a "Negro regime" in alliance with Catholic Spain.[42] Two informants, Sarah, John Hughson's daughter, and William Kane, an Irish soldier, implicate Ury in the crime of conspiracy. These informants tell the colonial authorities that Ury is, in fact, a Catholic priest who had not only attempted to convert several poor whites and enslaved blacks to Catholicism but also endeavored to enlist them in a papist conspiracy to murder the Protestant townspeople. Both informants claim to have witnessed Ury perform the rite of a Roman Catholic Baptism, which allegedly served to seal the covenant among the conspirators who pledged to keep their plot secret. In her deposition, Sarah states: "He [John Ury] used to christen negroes there [in her father's house], crossed them on the face, and had water and other things; and he told them he would absolve them from all their sins." During his cross-examination of Sarah in court, Ury attempts to prove that the prosecution's star witness cannot distinguish a Catholic baptismal ceremony from an Anglican christening service. In reply to Ury's interrogation, Sarah recalls only faint images from the ritual that, she insists, the young stranger performed. Finally, Sarah admits that Ury had spoken in a language she could not comprehend. Sarah was no expert witness on the liturgical practices of the Catholic Church and was incompetent to identify the unique features of a Roman Catholic Baptism. Then as now, Baptism was so fundamental to the practice of Christianity that the ceremony was nearly identical in all Christian churches. The prosecutor John Chambers proves to be more learned than Sarah Hughson with regard to the unique liturgical practices and doctrines of the Roman Catholic Church. In a statement before the jury, Chambers asserts that performing "his priest's office in latin, his baptising with salt, his use of the crucifix, his exposing the sacrament by lighted candles, his preaching upon those texts upon which papists pretend to found the Pope's supremacy, and his declared power to forgive sins as well as God Almighty will undoubtedly fix the brand of a Roman priest upon [Ury]." In his attempt to persuade the jury that Ury is beyond doubt a Catholic priest, Chambers correctly identifies elements of the Roman Catholic rite of Baptism that distinguish it from the Anglican sacrament of Baptism—specifically, the exhortation in Latin, the Jesuit tradition of using salt as a sacramental trapping, and the more general Catholic tradition of passing a lighted candle to the godparent or parent of the baptized infant.[43] None of the eyewitnesses to the Baptism that Ury was supposed to have performed could testify to the Catholic derivation of these particulars, however.

According to Horsmanden's narrative, some time before Ury's arrest, John Hildreth, an Anglican missionary, engaged in several theological disputations with the newcomer. In his deposition, Hildreth testifies that Ury "believed it was through the great encourgement the negroes had received from Mr. Whitefield [George Whitefield], we had all the disturbance, and that he believed Mr. Whitefield was more of a Roman than anything else, and he believed he [Whitefield] came abroad [in 1740] with no good design." Hildreth further testifies that Ury rejected the doctrine of free grace as well as the doctrine of predestination. Ury's opposition to these two extreme positions on the doctrinal spectrum of the post-Reformation era did not make him a Roman Catholic; along that continuum was a multiplicity of finely differentiated religious doctrines. During his trial, Ury insists that he is a nonjuring Anglican, not a Roman Catholic priest.[44] In his closing statement before the court, Ury argues that his is a case of mistaken identity. "Gentlemen," he argues, "the mistake the major part of the world lies under is their apprehending that a non-juring priest must be a popish priest whereas there is no truer protestant." With regard to the charge of conspiracy to murder the Protestant townspeople and to overthrow the English colonial rulers, Ury insists that "the doctrine they [nonjuring priests] assert and stand by is non-resistance and passive disobedience." He goes on to insist that there are "no truer subjects of King George" than nonjuring priests. This last speech of John Ury notwithstanding, the jury finds the young stranger guilty of treason and sentences him to hang by the neck until dead.

In addition to the white outsiders John Hughson, Mary Hughson, and John Ury, 31 enslaved blacks were executed for conspiring to destroy colonial New

York City. During the conspiracy trials, Sandy (or Sawney), Thomas Nisblet's slave and one of the prosecution's key witnesses, testifies that during clandestine meetings at Gerardus Comfort's dwelling house in the city's East Ward a separate all-black clique of conspirators had, without the encouragement and assistance of white agitators, concocted their own plan to set the town on fire and murder the white townspeople. Swearing themselves to secrecy, the black conspirators, Sandy reports, organized themselves into two incendiary units of 100 blacks each and then divided the town into two districts, which they intended to burn to the ground. According to Sandy's testimony, one unit included the members of the black brotherhood known as the Long Bridge Boys, and the other unit was comprised of the members of the Smith Fly Boys, also a black brotherhood. Although Sandy's disclosure of a separate plot among black town dwellers opened a window onto troubling aspects of the urban blacks' collective life that were largely hidden from the view of white authority figures, Horsmanden's narrative discounts this alarming contingency and refrains from representing the black town dwellers as having any agency of their own. Horsmanden's narrative presents instead a drama in which black town dwellers are transfigured into incendiary marionettes that are manipulated from behind the scene by the invisible hand of white saboteurs. For example, Horsmanden's account of the burglary into Hogg's shop credits a white lad named Wilson with masterminding that robbery. Moreover, Horsmanden's narrator describes the more dangerous conspiracy as "a scheme of villainy in which white people were confederated with negroes and most probably were the first movers and seducers of the slaves." Stressing this point, Horsmanden's narrator portrays the white traitors as the offspring of Belial, the fallen angel from Milton's *Paradise Lost* who mobilizes a dark legion of Satan's followers to do battle in the war of good against evil.[45] According to Horsmanden's narrator, the black town dwellers are motivated to act only "in combination with the most flagitious, degenerated, and abandoned, and scum and dregs of the white people, and others of the worst hearts, if possible, because of abler heads, who entitled themselves to be ten times more the children of Belial, than the negroes themselves." Thus in Horsmanden's "plot of 1741–42," white outsiders, like John Hughson, John Ury, and the youngster Wilson, are the primary agents of conspiracy. The black town dwellers are therefore not truly his dramatis personae. By depriving colonial New York City's mostly enslaved, black population of agency, Horsmanden's narrative attempts to disavow what the historian Eugene Genovese has called "the fundamental contradiction in chattel slavery" or "the impossibility of the slaves ever becoming the things they were supposed to be."[46] Horsmanden's account of the events of 1741–42 exposes this contradiction for, even as his narrative denies the enslaved blacks any volition of their own, it warns the reader about the danger posed by the unregulated movement and assembly of disloyal slaves who possess subtle intelligence and abuse the informal privileges that indulgent slaveowners granted them to conspire against their superiors.

Contradiction and heterogeneity play a crucial "facilitating role," Homi Bhabha points out, "in the construction of authoritarian practices and their strategic, discursive fixations."[47] Grappling to comprehend a world of contingency, to confer a fixed meaning on the seemingly random events of 1741–42, the colonialist discourse of conspiracy imposes the terrifying name of monstrosity on the blacks of colonial New York City. According to Horsmanden's reprint of a conspiracy trial transcript, Joseph Murray, one of the prosecutors, questions the humanity of the black townspeople by stressing the monstrous nature of their alleged crimes: "No scheme more monstrous could have been invented," Murray declares, "nor can anything be thought of more foolish, than the motives that induced these wretches to enter into it! . . . It is hard to say whether the wickedness or the folly of this design is the greater; and had it not been in part executed before it was discovered, we should with great difficulty have been persuaded to believe it possible, that such a wicked and foolish plot could be contrived by any creatures in human shape." Furthermore, the imputation of bestiality to the blacks served to support the prosecution's contention that they are capable of monstrous acts of cruelty. According to Horsmanden's reprint of an interrogation transcript, an examiner describes a black woman named Sarah as "one of the oddest animals amongst the black confederates. . . . When she was first interrogated upon this examination about the conspiracy, she . . . threw herself into the most violent agitations; foamed at the mouth, and uttered the bitterest imprecations." During the court proceedings, a witness offered further proof of the inhumanity of the blacks, claiming that "Diana (Mr. Machado's negro woman) in a passion, because her mistress was angry with her, took her own young child from her breast, and laid it in the cold, that it froze to death." Such accusations of infanticide seemed to confirm that black women lacked the nurturing maternal instincts attributed to the female sex of the human species. During the sentencing phase in the trial of two condemned blacks, Justice Philipse betrays the court's tendency to conflate black criminality with monstrosity: "Crimes, gentlemen, so astonishingly cruel and detestable, that one would think they never could enter into the minds, much less the resolution of any but a conclave of devils to execute; and yet such monsters in iniquity are these two criminals and the rest of their confederates." Even though Philipse asserts that the condemned blacks are monsters, he refers to their souls and the punishment of everlasting damnation: "Yet [ye] cannot be so stupid, surely, as to imagine, that when ye leave this world, when your souls put off these bodies of clay, ye shall become like the beasts that perish, that your spirits shall only vanish into the soft air and cease to be. No, your souls are immortal, they will live forever, either to be eternally happy, or eternally miserable in the other world, where you are now going." Announcing his concern for the souls of black folks whose bodies he has just ordered destroyed and who during their enslavement in colonial New York City had been exploited like beasts of labor, Justice Philipse exposes his own ambivalent attitude toward the blacks. Such ambivalence did not, however, prevent the colonial authorities from acting swiftly and authoritatively in executing black town dwellers for conspiring against English rule.

The guilty verdicts in the cases of all but a few blacks were founded on coerced confessions of ambiguous meaning. In the preface to his *Journal*, Horsmanden complains that during the interrogation phase of the official investigation he and other officers of the court were faced with the nearly insurmountable task of extracting the truth from black suspects who spoke English imperfectly and perhaps contrived to confuse their inquisitors with ambiguous speeches. "The difficulty of bringing and holding them to the truth, if by chance it starts through them," Horsmanden explains, "is not to be surmounted, but by the closest attention; many of them have a great deal of craft; their unintelligible jargon stands them in great stead, to conceal their meaning; so that the examiner must expect to encounter with much perplexity, grope through a maze of obscurity, be obliged to lay hold of broken hints, lay them carefully together, and thoroughly weigh and compare them with each other, before he can be able to see light, or fix those creatures to any certain determinate meaning." Owing to their inability to comprehend the fragmented speech patterns (or broken English) of some black town dwellers, the colonial officials sometimes engaged interpreters to aid them in extracting confessions from black suspects. During the interrogation session of a black man named Jack, the colonial authorities entrusted two white laborers with the grave duty of deciphering the meaning of the suspect's words. Horsmanden's narrator explains: "There were two young men, sons-in-law of Jack's master, who were aware Jack would not be understood without their aid, and they signified their desire of being by when he was examined, from a supposition that they might be of service in interpreting his meaning, as he had been used to them, having often worked in the same shop together at the cooper's trade, whereby he was so familiarized to them, they could make a shift to understand his language."[48] Doubtless, the official transcript of Jack's confession and the incriminating declarations of other black suspects were translations of dubious authority, which fixed a "certain determinate meaning" on ambiguous, puzzling words.

For New York City slaveowners, the ingratitude of their slaves presented the most perplexing puzzle of all. Certain that they had been benevolent masters, these slaveowners could not understand why there were not more Ariels and Fridays among the enslaved blacks of colonial New York City. Pondering that riddle, Justice Philipse opines:

> The monstrous ingratitude of this black tribe is what exceedingly aggravates their guilt. Their slavery among us is generally softened with great indulgence: They live without care and are commonly better fed and clothed than the poor of most Christian Countries. They were indeed slaves, but under the protection of the law, none can hurt them with impunity. They are really more happy in this place than in the midst of the continual plunder, cruelty, and rapine of their native countries. Notwithstanding all the kindness and tenderness with which they have been treated among us, yet this is the second attempt of the same kind that this brutish and bloody species of mankind have made within one age.

Struggling to comprehend the disloyalty of slaves who, in his judgment, had been treated with kindness and lived under the mildest form of bondage, Philipse calls two condemned black men before the bench and asks them to explain why they had committed such horrific crimes. The magistrate asks, "What then could prompt you to undertake so vile, so wicked, so monstrous, so execrable and hellish a scheme, as to murder and destroy your own masters and benefactors? Nay, to destroy root and branch, all the white people of this place, and to lay the whole town in ashes." Standing before the bench of judgment, the two black men offered no answer to Judge Philipse's question. They and other black town dwellers remained puzzling enigmas.

Nevertheless, Horsmanden's narrative strives to eliminate indeterminacy by imposing a fixed meaning on the ambiguous words and gestures of unacculturated blacks. His narrator relates the story of Quaco and two other black men who had been strolling up Broadway toward Trinity Church on Sunday, April 5, 1742, the same day that live coals were found in a haystack and only one day before the fort caught fire. Like many other unacculturated black town dwellers, these black men roamed the city streets on Sundays while the Christian settlers attended worship services. Upon looking out a window from the upper floor of a building fronting Broadway, a white woman named Abigail Earle spies the three black men and, Horsmanden's narrator reports, overhears Quaco "with a vaporing sort of air [say], 'Fire, Fire, Scorch, Scorch, A LITTLE, damn it, BY-AND-BY,' and then throw up his hands and laughed." At that moment, the sentence fragments and abrupt gesticulation of the unacculturated black man cried out to be interpreted. According to Horsmanden's narrative, Mrs. Earle "conceives great jealousy" in Quaco's broken English. Determined to fill the gaps in the intercepted snatches of Quaco's conversation with his comrades, the colonial authorities assert that Mrs. Earle has placed "the natural construction upon her apprehensions" of the jargon and strange "airs and graces" of the black suspect and that Quaco is without doubt guilty of conspiracy. In other words, the colonial authorities conclude that although Quaco spoke the language of his English masters imperfectly, that Caliban of colonial New York City had, nonetheless, learned how to curse them with it.

During his trial, Quaco denied that his short speech held a conspiratorial meaning. A court reporter transcribed Quaco's declaration of innocence into proper English syntax. The printed transcript reports that the accused told the court that he and his comrades had been "talking of admiral Vernon's taking Porto Bello; and that he thereupon signified to his companions, that he thought that was but a small feat to what his brave officer would do by-and-by, to annoy the Spaniards, or words tantamount." Quaco's spoken testimony failed to establish, beyond doubt, his allegiance to England in its war against Spain. Subsequently, the court magistrates condemned the black man to death for the crime of conspiracy. The death sentence imposed on Quaco discloses the peril unacculturated black town dwellers faced when their fragmentary speech acts were exposed to the interpretation of English-speaking judges. At the time of Quaco's execution, unacculturated African-born slaves from a variety of African homelands were 30 percent of New York City's black population.[49] Although Quaco's birthplace is unknown, his name was in common usage among the Akan people and indicates that he, a parent, or other kin had ties to that part of West African society and through naming practices endeavored to retain some connection to West African culture. A pidgin-speaking community of black town dwellers almost certainly existed in colonial New York City, and most native African newcomers and other unacculturated blacks, in fact, spoke poor English. This circumstance had grave consequences for these unacculturated blacks during the investigation into the alleged conspiracy of 1741–42. In *Black Skin, White Mask*, Frantz Fanon writes: "To speak means to be in a position to use a certain syntax, to grasp the morphology of this or that language, but it means above all to assume a culture, to support the weight of a civilization."[50] In Quaco's case, his imperfect mastery of the English language rendered him incapable of persuading the English colonial court of his innocence, of assuming the position of a loyal British subject. In a fundamental respect, Quaco and other unacculturated black suspects were unable to speak in self-defense, for the colonialist discourse of conspiracy established the conditions for the intelligibility of speech and identified the foreign, broken speech patterns of unacculturated blacks with conspiracy. In sharp contrast, their judges possessed the power to speak, to constitute a meaningful world by virtue of their mastery over the ruling English language. Fanon writes: "A man who has a language consequently possesses the world expressed and implied by that language. What we are getting at becomes plain: Mastery of language affords remarkable power."[51] The power of Horsmanden's narrative depended, in large part, on the deployment of language or the syntagmatic composition of a meaningful world expressed in seemingly natural (or common sense) constructions of thought.

Horsmanden's narrative presents its implied reader, the baffled white town dweller of colonial New York City, with a commonsensical structure of explanation that confers a meaningful order on puzzling events—specifically, that for every effect there is a cause,[52] that latent in mysterious events is a willful design, and that the hidden character of persons will be revealed in and through their deviance from the normal (or expected) sequence of human behavior. The historian Thomas J. Davis notes: "Random human behavior was not something most New Yorkers [white settlers] in 1741 accepted. In their worldview everything had a cause and purpose and happened for a reason. Either God was sending a message of good or ill, or evil was besieging them. . . . Perplexed and frustrated people visualized a common strand in their troubles."[53] It was "common practice," the historian Gordon Woods adds, "to look beneath the surface of persons and of things for hidden meaning."[54] The narrative construction of apparent random events and human behavior into a coherent causal explanation made meaning and judgment possible. As Horsmanden's narrative of conspiracy unfolds, the hidden design underlying the mysterious events of 1741–42 becomes manifest. Eventually, black town dwellers and white outsiders are exposed as a "villainous confederacy of latent enemies."

Colonial New York City was part of the early modern world of disguise[55]—and in that port town, people wore masks. The convicted conspirator Peggy Kerry assumed the alias Margaret Salingburgh when, sometime before the discovery of the "plot of 1741–42," she disembarked at the port of New York. Peggy's use of an alias typified the practice of assuming a fictive identity that gave untold numbers of European immigrants a new lease on life in the overseas colonies. Enslaved blacks also wore masks. Caesar, one of the slaves convicted of burglarizing Hogg's shop, was known by the alias John Gwin. In Caesar's case, an assumed name was perhaps used to hide his involvement in the city's criminal underworld. In addition, several other slaves convicted of participating in the conspiracy were known by more than one name, and they were not unusual in this habit. Runaway slaves often masked their identity by using aliases. These fugitives probably found it easier to fashion new identities amid colonial New York City's heterogeneous and dense population than in more homogeneous and less densely populated port towns. More broadly, the formation of racial alterity in colonial New York City imposed upon Africans and their descendants a veil of blackness that rendered them disturbing enigmas to the white townspeople. Throughout the official investigation into the purported conspiracy, the colonial authorities endeavor to penetrate that veil and to comprehend the mystery that, they suspected, lay beneath it.

Horsmanden's narrator relates a case of mistaken identity that discloses the pitfalls of relying on surface appearance to discern hidden truths. Yet far from rejecting the notion that there exists a correspondence between exterior aspect and interior moral disposition, Horsmanden's narrator wishes only to caution against hasty judgment. During the official investigation into the alleged conspiracy, an enslaved black man named Cork is, according to Horsmanden's narrative, mistaken for an enslaved black man named Patrick and imprisoned at the city jail for examination. A white female named Peggy Kerry, alias Margaret Salingburgh, is brought before a lineup of black men and asked to identify Patrick, whom she has accused of joining in the conspiracy. Upon inspecting the lineup, Peggy immediately informs the colonial authorities that they have arrested the wrong black man. Horsmanden's narrator explains why Cork was taken into custody but promptly cleared of suspicion:

> Cork was unfortunately of a countenance somewhat ill-favoured, naturally of a suspicious look and reckoned withal to be unlucky too. His being sent for before the magistrates in such a perilous season might be thought sufficient to alarm the most innocent of the negroes and occasion appearance of their being under some terrible apprehensions. But it was much otherwise with Cork, and notwithstanding the disadvantage of his natural aspect, upon being interrogated concerning the conspiracy, he showed such a cheerful, open, honest smile upon his countenance (none of your fictitious, hypocritical grins) that everyone that was by and observed it (and there were several in the room) jumped in the same observation and opinion, that they never saw a fellow look so handsome: Such an efficacy have truth and innocence that they even reflect beauty upon deformity!

The colonial authorities finally apprehend Patrick, the fugitive suspect, and imprison him in the city jail for examination. In the following passage, Horsmanden's narrator contrasts Cork's innocent appearance to Patrick's guilty countenance:

> On the contrary, Patrick's visage betrayed his guilt. Those who are used to negroes may have experienced that some of them, when charged with any piece

of villainy they have been detected in, have an odd knack or (it is hard what to call or how to describe it) way of turning their eyes inwards, as it were, as if shocked at the consciousness of their own perfidy; their looks, at the same time, discovering all the symptoms of the most inveterate malice and resentment. This was Patrick's appearance, and such [was] his behavior upon examination, as served to induce one's credit to what Peggy had declared so far at least that he was present at a meeting when the conspiracy was talked of and was one of the persons consenting to act a part in that infernal scheme.

According to Horsmanden's tale of mistaken identity, the confessions of the flesh divulge Patrick's guilt. Likewise, visible and decipherable marks on Cork's bodily surface evince his innocence. Specifically, Cork's "handsome" face and "honest" smile save him from the hangman's noose. Cork's inner qualities of honesty and innocence even have the effect of rendering the "deformed" physiognomic traits that ostensibly typify the Negro race or, as the narrator puts it, the Negro's "natural aspect" beautiful in the eyes of the beholding colonial inquisitors. In judging Cork to be both deformed and beautiful, the colonial authorities betray their simultaneous aversion and attraction to the "colonized other."[56]

Significantly, ambivalence, indeterminacy, and undecidability structure the colonialist discourse of conspiracy and enable its production of knowledge. For instance, the colonial authorities initially find themselves in the embarrassing situation of having failed to name and to classify Negroes correctly. That a servant girl calls attention to their error only adds to their chagrin. At this juncture, Horsmanden's narrative reconstitutes the authoritative knowledge of the colonial officials by diminishing the servant girl's role in pointing out their mistake and, more important, recuperates the imperial subject's power to impose a fixed meaning on the Negro's bodily surface by disavowing the problem of indeterminacy altogether. According to Horsmanden's story, the inspection of the Negro's bodily surface in lineups and interrogation rooms renders the inner character of the Negro perfectly legible. In this respect, Horsmanden's narrative anticipates the theory of Johann Caspar Lavater (1742–1801), who, believing that the soul impresses itself on the face and other regions of the bodily surface, studied human physiognomy in order to establish the inner moral and intellectual dispositions of human beings and on that basis assign them to distinct classifications.[57] Moreover, Horsmanden's narrative resonates with theories of biblical exegesis, later grouped under the term *hermeneutics*, and the episteme of British empiricism. The basic premise of biblical exegesis asserts that even seemingly enigmatic texts contain a determinate meaning whose recovery is made possible through a method of interpretation that decodes what is initially unintelligible into a meaningful pattern understandable to human intelligence, while the intellectual system of British empiricism is predicated on the assertion that human understanding comes about as the product of sensory experience leaving impressions on the mind.[58] As Horsmanden's story unfolds, inner truths, which initially reside beyond the horizon of human sensory perception, eventually become perceptible to the naked eye and hence accessible to human understanding.

Like the ecclesiastical authorities of an earlier era, the eighteenth-century jurist Daniel Horsmanden claims the authority to read signs and ascribe meaning to them. Referring to the habitus (or ingrained bodily disposition) that supposedly typifies guilty Negroes, Horsmanden, in sharp contrast to his admission that he is incapable of comprehending the speech fragments of unacculturated black suspects, boasts about his expertise in deciphering the meaning of the visible signs that allegedly appear on the Negro's bodily surface and in the Negro's bodily gestures. "When charged with any piece of villainy," Horsmanden's narrator observes, "[guilty Negroes] have an odd knack or . . . way of turning their eyes inwards." Finally, there are, according to Horsmanden's discourse of conspiracy, good and bad Negroes, handsome and grotesque Negroes, innocent and guilty Negroes. And this is certain because, under the regime of visual examination, all Negroes eventually become transparent. In this respect, Horsmanden's narrative produces what Homi Bhabha terms "the colonized as a social reality which is at once an 'other' and yet entirely knowable and visible."[59] In Horsmanden's *Journal*, the enigmatic bodily surface of the Negro becomes pure transparency and hence bears a fixed meaning. Thus, the Negro is denied the attribute of self-difference—that is, of true subjecthood. In this way, Horsmanden's narrative disavows the problem of indeterminacy not only as an integral condition of the process of giving meaning to the world but also as a source of subaltern agency.[60]

For the colonial authorities, the solution to the problem of policing the city's population of enslaved blacks, free blacks, and propertyless white outsiders became a matter of subjecting individuals and their bodies, gestures, and speech to examination in lineups and interrogation rooms.[61] Yet without a declared state of emergency, such access to the subaltern population would have been impossible to achieve. During the early modern era, the disciplinary mechanisms of surveillance remained limited in scope and therefore could not guarantee the effective penetration of power into the colonial port town's dense and opaque subaltern population. To be sure, there were schools, barracks, jails, and a few hospitals, but as yet no professional police, integral surveillance, and panopticism. Colonial New York City's ruling elite was just beginning to enter the Enlightenment dream of living in a totally "transparent society, visible and legible in each of its parts, the dream of there no longer existing any zones of darkness."[62] Throughout the colonial period, the city's many alleyways, docks, taverns, and other dimly lit spaces continued to provide spawning grounds for a shadowy underworld populated by "dangerous others." To render the inhabitants of these dark zones visible, transparent, and legible, Horsmanden's *Journal* and the broader colonialist discourse of conspiracy drew a cognitive map that equated deviance from the white Anglo-Saxon Protestant bourgeois norm with conspiracy against English colonial rule, whether disloyalty qua difference is embodied in the form of Negroes, Catholic priests, or propertyless white outsiders.

Detecting white traitors proved to be a more difficult task than identifying black conspirators, whose dark skin immediately marked them as suspect. The rumor that agents of Spain, Catholic priests incognito, had secretly infiltrated

New York City with the intent to murder white Protestants alerts the anxious white townspeople to another hidden and sinister presence in their midst. In John Ury's case, religious heterodoxy, though more difficult to discern than dark skin color, becomes yet another sign of guilt. In the case of other condemned whites, no religious and surface bodily difference immediately mark them as disloyal subjects. Nonetheless, their guilt eventually becomes manifest, for their "fair" skin is revealed to be the disguise of dark agents of destruction. For example, Horsmanden's narrator informs the reader that Hughson's "crimes have made him blacker than a negro: the scandal of his complecion, and the disgrace of human nature." In Horsmanden's narrative, Hughson's interior blackness or hidden moral depravity becomes manifest with the appearance of a legible form of blackness on his bodily surface. The reader is told that following Hughson's execution his corpse is displayed at the battery so that the townspeople can observe the fate of those who challenge the colonial rulers. As the result of many days of exposure outdoors, Hughson's body rapidly decays. Horsmanden's narrator reports, "The town was amused with a rumor that Hughson was turned Negro . . . [his] face, hands, and neck, and feet—were of a deep shining black, rather blacker than the Negro placed by him who was one of the darkest hue of his kind. The hair of Hughson's beard and neck—his head could not be seen for he had a cap on—was curling like the wool of a Negro's beard and head. And the features of his face were of the symetry of a Negro beauty: the nose broad and flat, the nostrils open and extended, the mouth wide, lips full and thick." Taken for a visible confirmation of his guilt or moral blackness, Hughson's darkened and rotten corpse seemed to resemble the ideal Negro type (or "beauty").[63] Here, a logic of noncontradiction structures Horsmanden's narrative in that it disavows self-difference or the possibility that Hughson can be both guilty and truly white. Hence, the moral of Horsmanden's story is that the bête noire of colonial New York City might at first appear to be white but in time the truths hidden within the interior moral space of suspected conspirators will become visibly manifest as an exterior or legible form of blackness that, in the colonialist imaginary, is associated with guilt.

The theme of guilt by association with the city's black population structures the colonialist discourse of conspiracy and directs antiblack racism not only at enslaved blacks and free blacks but also as actively at the city's lowly stratum of propertyless white outsiders who mingled with blacks in the colonial port town's taverns, tippling houses, and dramshops. Moreover, Horsmanden's representation of the events of 1741–42 plays on the colonialist fear of miscegenation and the threat that interracial sexual desire posed to the racial purity of the colonial port town's white settler community. His narrator iterates this racist fantasy, reporting that black conspirators had plotted to destroy the colonial port town and exterminate the white settler population, except for the white women, whom the black conspirators intended to hold as captives in harems. Doubtless, the colonial authorities executed the unmarried white female named Peggy Kerry, alias Margaret Salingburgh, not only for the crime of conspiracy against the English colonial state but also as a punishment for her transgression of the prohibition against miscegenation. According to Horsmanden's narrative, the fact that Peggy has been impregnated by Prince, the black man convicted of burglarizing Hogg's shop, and has given birth to a "babe largely partaking of a dark complecion" confirms her disloyalty. Peggy's dark-skinned offspring is thus taken as a visible omen that bears witness to her impure and traitorous inner disposition.

According to the Manichean symbolism of darkness and light, whiteness symbolizes moral purity, and blackness moral pollution. In medieval Europe, the criminalization of the laboring poor involved the imputation of blackness to the servile population. For example, it was said that the serfs harbored an inner blackness that was bone deep.[64] By the early modern era, the similes "black as Satan" and "black as Cham" were essential elements of the English vernacular, a basic part of the parole of the common man in the first British Empire. Moreover, the similes "black as a Moor" and "black as a Negro" signified something very real to the white Christian settlers in the English overseas colonies, for Western Christendom's encounter with the Berber and Arab people of Northwest Africa (the Moors) and the people of sub-Saharan Africa (the Negroes) provided them with phobogenic objects upon which they projected age-old beliefs that equate blackness with evil, guilt, and sin.[65] Even though the Enlightenment was beginning to discredit belief in omens, portents, and other superstitions, many educated men of the early modern era continued to subscribe to the Manichean symbolism of darkness and light, to equate blackness with moral degeneracy, and even to give scientific rationalizations for the belief in the inherent inferiority of dark-skinned people. As the historian David Brion Davis has persuasively argued, the culturally ingrained responses of early modern Europeans to dark-skinned people were among the several factors that account for the subjection of black Africans to forced migration and enslavement in the New World.[66] In colonial New York City and other English overseas settler colonies where white settlers lived in close proximity to enslaved blacks, the Negro became the living embodiment of blackness. Unlike the "scabby Negro" of Benedict Spinoza's dream, who held for that inhabitant of seventeenth-century Amsterdam little more than a phantom existence,[67] the presence of an increasingly numerous black population was an everyday reality for the white townspeople of colonial New York City, who also dreamed of dark specters yet awoke only to live their own worst nightmares. For these anxious town dwellers, blackness attained a certain facticity; the empirical realities of daily life seemed to approximate their nocturnal and fantastic fears of blackness.

Over time, vulgar similes that posited the Negro as a figure of comparison (or resemblance) in representations of evil, sin, and guilt were sublated in more powerful metaphors that held lethal consequences for dark-skinned people. "Metaphors," Hayden White writes, "are crucially necessary when a culture or social group encounters phenomena that either elude or run afoul of normal expectations or quotidian experiences."[68] For the anxious townspeople of colonial New York City, the Negro became a seductive metaphor for evil, corruption, and calamity, a key figure that, when subjected to interpretation, conferred meaning on the mysteries of 1741–42. That breach of routine led the colonial authorities to search for a hidden explanation woven into the fabric of puzzling events. Dark skin color and other signs of deviance from the norms of white-ness, Protestantism, and property holding became the principal criteria for iden-tifying "dangerous others" and determining the cause of the baffling crime wave and rash of fires. Here, the binary logic of sameness and difference man-aged ambiguity, indeterminacy, and ambivalence. By constructing Manichean oppositions of darkness and light and offering the bewildered townspeople a simplistic, black-and-white explanation for mysterious events, the colonialist discourse of conspiracy seemed to abolish the troubling complexity of social reality.

A tale suspended between the white settlers' real and imaginary worlds, Horsmanden's "plot of 1741–42" resonated with popular belief in omens, por-tents, and prodigies. The colonialist discourse of conspiracy borrows much of its vocabulary, as well as its logic and grammar, from the language of marvels and wonders dating back to the Middle Ages.[69] As the historian David Hall stresses in his influential study on popular religion in seventeenth-century New England, educated clergymen accommodated the folk beliefs of the common man. In doing so, that segment of the colonial elite, Hall demonstrates, took a leading role in interpreting bizarre events such as monster births, catastrophic storms, and destruction by fire.[70] In like manner, New York City's ruling elite took up the task of interpreting the mysteries that beset the city during the emergency of 1741–42. Judge Daniel Horsmanden, along with other jurists and court officials, assimilated the common man's beliefs in omens, marvels, and wonders to the colonialist discourse of conspiracy, bringing them into articula-tion with other popular prejudices—for example, anti-Catholicism and an-tiblack racism—and with ingrained patterns of perception and cognition, such as the Manichean dualism of darkness and light and the binary logic of identity and difference.[71] In this way, colonial New York City's ruling elite constructed the common sense of colonial governmentality, which allowed them to govern by consent of the governed, the intermediate stratum of propertied white free-hold electors.

By discovering the "plot of 1741–42"—namely, a dark threat to the city's security in the guise of a dangerous combination of enslaved blacks, free blacks, Catholic priests, and white outsiders who had allegedly conspired to in-cinerate the city, exterminate the white Protestant townspeople, and found a renegade colony in alliance with England's enemy, Catholic Spain—Lieutenant Governor Clarke and his ruling party claimed the leadership role of protector of the people, neutralized the opposition party, and united the broader white Protestant settler population during a time of internal political crisis and inter-national war. The ruling party's response to the emergency of 1741–42 rein-forced the horizontal axis of identification among the property-holding white Protestant Anglo-Saxon settlers, as well as the vertical axis of identification of loyal British subjects with the English rulers. In doing so, the ruling party forti-fied the fragile structure of colonial governance in New York City and managed to avert a settler revolt of the sort led by Jacob Leisler following the Glorious Revolution. By late 1742, however, the opposition party began to criticize the court proceedings against accused conspirators. At that juncture, the ruling party could not risk giving the appearance that it was governing too much and therefore terminated its showcase conspiracy trials and exercise of extraordinary police powers.[72] Consequently, the primary responsibility for policing the city's subaltern population fell, once again, to the intermediate stratum of propertied white Protestant Anglo-Saxon settlers.

PART III

Subaltern Insurgency and the Breakdown of Colonial Governance

6

"We Shall Never Be Quite Safe"

POLICING THE FUGITIVE BODY OF COLONIAL NEW YORK CITY'S
SERVILE POPULATION

During the colonial period, the port of New York remained a largely open gateway, through which outsiders could enter undetected. To be sure, the colonial authorities attempted to keep an account of the strangers who disembarked at the seaport, ordering the captains of sailing vessels to submit lists of passengers and requiring all newcomers who planned to stay in the city for more than a few weeks to register with the mayor.[1] These regulations advised strangers that they were being watched. But the compilation of passenger lists and the registration of newcomers alone could not solve the problem of everyday acts of subaltern insurgency—for example, petty theft, trafficking in stolen property, the appropriation of leisure time, unsupervised assembly, interracial socializing in the dramshops, taverns, and tippling houses, unauthorized visits to friends and loved ones, and running away. Over time, policing the city's servile population became more and more a matter of subjecting servants and slaves, their bodies and their movements, to a pervasive visual regime of individualizing surveillance. However, no single, centralized authority kept watch over the city's servile population, and the mobile body of fugitive servants and slaves often eluded the discontinuous gaze of the colonial state.

To a great extent, the detection of runaways depended on the vigilance of the free white townspeople. Most colonial New York City newspapers carried notices for runaway servants and slaves, and these printed advertisements aspired to inculcate the habit of watchfulness in the free white townspeople and to constitute that intermediate stratum of the city's settler population as a vigilant public endowed with the capacity of supervision over the port town's servile population. Even though a small percentage of settler households subscribed to a newspaper, the casual circulation of broadsheets, coupled with the practice of reading published news aloud at home and in storefronts, taverns, coffeehouses, and other gathering places, meant that ads for runaways reached a much wider audience than the documented number of newspaper subscribers.[2] Because the fundamental basis of sociality in colonial New York City was face-to-face visual contact between town dwellers, public alertness to the distinguishing visible characteristics of individual runaways became indispensable to the task of apprehending fugitives. Although colonial New York City newspaper advertisements for runaways rarely included pictorial illustrations,[3] they skillfully combined print technology's capacity for the dissemination of information with the mimetic capabilities of the written word to imitate visual observation. These newspaper ads were designed to conjure a visual image of the body of each advertised fugitive in the minds of the townspeople. This visual regime of individualizing surveillance produced a mind-body duality that assigned the faculty of rational intelligence to the free white settler population and ascribed the property of objectified corporeality to the fugitive population of runaway servants and slaves. Miming visual observation, printed newspaper advertisements for fugitives represent the servile population as objects, the chattel of possessive individual subjects. Just as the descriptions of individual items of personal property listed in wills and probate records served as a means of verifying the ownership of that chattel, the descriptions of runaway servants and slaves in newspaper notices provided crucial information for identifying a specific fugitive and establishing to whom that particular runaway belonged.[4]

Owing to the descriptive information contained in them, the newspaper ads for runaways reveal as much about the sex, age, and other visible characteristics of fugitives as they do about early modern techniques of individualizing surveillance. Colonial New York City newspaper advertisements for runaways indicate that the vast majority of fugitive servants and slaves were young male adults: males were approximately 90 percent of the runaway sample population for this study, and the median age of these runaways was 23.5 years.[5] In addition to generic characteristics such as the fugitive's sex and age, the newspaper ads for runaways often included descriptions of visible infirmities, remarkable bodily dispositions, and other peculiar marks that served to individualize the fugitive body of each advertised runaway. On August 27, 1733, the following advertisement appeared in the *New-York Gazette*:

> Ran away the 18th of August, 1733 from Jacobus Van Cortlandt of the city of New York, a Negro Man Slave, named Andrew Saxon, a very tall Fellow, walks lamish with his Left Leg; the Thumb of his left Hand is somewhat stiff by a wound he had in his Hand formerly: the shirts he had with him and on his Back are marked with a cross on the left Breast; He professeth himself to be a Roman Catholic, speaks very good English, is a Carpenter and Cooper by Trade, and has the Tools for both Trades with him; he had on a pair of

Trousers, but 'tis uncertain what other clothes he has with him. Whoever takes up and secures the said Negro man, and gives Notice thereof to Said Master so as he may be had again shall have Forty Shillings if Taken within Ten miles of the city of New-York and Three pounds if further, as a reward, all reasonable charges paid by Jacobus Van Cortlandt.[6]

By drawing attention to the fugitive's visible bodily infirmities—for example, his crippled left leg and sickly left hand—this ad attempted to render the runaway legible against the background of the city's aggregate black population. Similarly, descriptive detail disaggregated individual white runaways from the city's white settler majority. A range of distinctive visible bodily characteristics individualized the fugitive body of a "lame" white servant named Timothy Sheels, who, according to the newspaper ad for his arrest, was "much pitted with the small-pox" and known for walking with a "down look" and "shutting his eyes" when he laughed.[7] Physical infirmities and bodily idiosyncrasies did not exhaust the inventory of individualizing marks itemized in runaway ads. Like the newspaper advertisements for the sale of servants and slaves, advertisements for runaways often called attention to attributes of physique that attested to the fugitive's exceptional physical well-being. On January 9, 1735, the *New-York Weekly Journal* carried the following ad, highlighting a runaway's robust health, tall stature, and erect posture:

Runaway from Mary Bisset of the City of New-York, widow, a Negro Man named George (calls himself George Goldin) he is a lusty tall Fellow, very straight limb'd, and walks very upright, he had on when he went away, a light colour'd Great-Coat, and a blue Jacket, he formerly followed Chimney-Sweeping in this City. Whoever takes up and secures him, so that his mistress may have him again, shall have 20s.[8]

Runaway ads also included descriptions of noncorporeal peculiarities—for example, the fugitive's exceptional occupational skills and unorthodox religious beliefs. The newspaper advertisement for his capture indicated that the runaway slave Andrew Saxon had mastered two crafts during his enslavement in British America and, unlike his enslaver, adhered to the doctrines of Roman Catholicism. Besides noting the advertised fugitive's religious beliefs and occupational skills, the runaway ads sometimes referenced distinguishing personal habits—for example, the fugitive's fondness for strong drink, tobacco, cursing, or favorite pastimes, such as fiddling, dancing, or singing.[9]

Importantly, ads for runaway servants mention, whenever possible, the fugitive's birthplace and native language, particularistic marks of ethnicity that denied white runaway servants the invisibility that the camouflage of whiteness might have otherwise afforded them.[10] A large proportion of fugitive servants, approximately 46 percent of the total documented runaway servant population, were natives of Ireland. Servants from England, Scotland, and Wales were approximately 23 percent of that runaway servant population, while servants from continental Europe and Scandinavia were another 16 percent. American-born servants accounted for 14 percent of advertised fugitive servants. The major part of both the documented runaway English, Scottish, and Welsh servants (25 of 48) and American-born servants (20 of 30) appeared in newspaper advertisements published after 1765. Ads for runaway slaves rarely mention the fugitive's ethnicity, but the following colonial New York City newspaper announcement for the capture of an Angolan runaway suggests that particular cultural traits sometimes individualized fugitive slaves: "Runaway from Samuel Willis of Middletown in Connecticut, a well-set Angola, Negro fellow aged about 20 years, a Little bow-leg'd, and his Toes spread pretty much, he has small scratches each side of his face, sometimes has a Bobb in his Ear, and is a good Cook."[11] This ad describes arresting marks of both cultural and physical particularity—the fugitive's Angolan origin, the scratches, perhaps tribal markings,[12] on each side of his face, and his habit of wearing an earring, possibly an artifact of Angolan custom or the seafaring culture.[13] Regardless of the origin and intended cultural significance of the Angolan's peculiar marks, they now identified him as a runaway slave. Native Africans were less than 10 percent of this study's sample runaway slave population. American-born slaves, who had lived in close contact with the settlers for many years and who spoke at least one European language, ran away in larger numbers than less acculturated native African slaves. Notably more unacculturated slaves seem to have absconded from their masters after 1760.[14]

Because the law required slaves to carry a pass or written permission from their masters when traveling beyond the city's limit,[15] fugitives who could forge their masters' signatures on such documents had a better chance of escaping than fugitives who could not duplicate their masters' handwriting and produce forged passes.[16] Some slaveowners suspected untrustworthy settlers and servants of forging passes for runaway slaves.[17] Although most slaves could not write, most fugitive slaves spoke at least one European language, if only imperfectly. A majority of the documented runaway slave population spoke English, nearly 20 percent spoke Dutch, and 5 percent spoke another European language. Approximately 6 percent were bilingual and typically spoke both English and Dutch.[18] A few runaway slaves spoke as many as three European languages with varying degrees of proficiency. Colonial New York City newspaper advertisements for runaways often rated the fugitive's oral language skills along a scale of "very good" (fluent) to "very broken" (poor) speaking proficiency.[19] In the autumn of 1727, Captain Matthew Norris, resident of New York City, offered a 40-shilling reward for the capture and return of an adult male slave named John Henricus, who, Norris noted, spoke "very good" English in addition to the Welsh dialect.[20] In the spring of 1760, Captain William Fitzherbert offered a three-pound reward for the capture and return of a Negro boy named Glasgow who, Fitzherbert pointed out, spoke "very broken" English.[21] By 1760, the documented runaway population was less rather than more acculturated with respect to English language skills, a trend that was largely the result of the influx of unacculturated enslaved native Africans into the port of New York from the late 1740s through to the early 1770s. The historian Ira Berlin has noted that during the post-1760 period more than 25 percent of the documented fugitive slaves spoke poor English, if any at all.[22]

In colonial New York City newspapers, usage of the term *broken* to indicate poor proficiency in a spoken language was not limited to descriptions of black fugitives' language skills. Newspaper ads for runaways described white servants who spoke "broken" English, Dutch, German, and other European languages. White servants born in the British Isles were not always fluent English speakers. Daniel Macraw and John Ross, Scottish Highlanders who ran away from their master in 1746, spoke "broken English."[23] Primarily drawn from the multiethnic British Isles and Europe, colonial New York City's servant population exhibited linguistic diversity and bilingualism. Approximately 11 percent of the documented runaway servant population spoke two or more languages. Bilingual runaway servants, like bilingual runaway slaves, most often spoke English and Dutch. For many white servants in colonial New York City, English was not a native language but a second language acquired after several years of living in the English overseas colony. A New York City newspaper ad noted that the Danish runaway servant John Christophers spoke some English, while his accomplice and fellow countryman spoke no English.[24] The runaway ads generally used the terms *high Dutch* when referring to the German language. The term *low Dutch* became a linguistic marker indicating that the fugitive was born in the colonies, where colonial Netherlanders generally spoke a *lingua rustica* or provincial mode of the Dutch language.[25] Newspaper ads for fugitives included some Irish servants who spoke English with a distinctive accent or brogue,[26] as well as some Scottish Highlanders who spoke a dialect that even the English-speaking settlers found unintelligible.[27]

Colonial New York City newspaper ads for runaways often included a detailed description of each advertised fugitive's habit of dress, as well as a complete itemization of the clothes the fugitive had on his back and carried away.[28] When Andrew Saxon absconded from his master, he was wearing a shirt embellished with a cross on the left breast. In addition to its meaning as a religious symbol, the cross on Saxon's shirt branded him as a runaway slave. In an era of sumptuary laws that stipulated the proper mode of attire for each social rank (e.g., plain clothes for the laboring classes and more elegant apparel for their social superiors), clothing became a visible code, differentiating gentlemen and masters from servants and slaves.[29] Slaveowners sometimes required unruly slaves, especially those who were habitual runaways, to wear clothing that displayed visible insignias of their servile status. Yet, as Anne McClintock has noted, "Clothes are the visible signs of social identity but are also permanently subject to disarrangement and symbolic theft."[30] In attempting to elude his enslavers, Saxon might have worn his shirt inside out or traded it for apparel befitting a free man.[31]

Runaway slaves could shed their clothing but not their skin. In ancient slave societies, brands, tattoos, and shaved heads differentiated the enslaved from the free population in a context where no visible physiognomic trait distinguished the slaves. In colonial British America, enslavers rarely inflicted such legible marks on the slave's bodily surface, though slaveowners sometimes branded habitual runaways with the mark RN.[32] In British North America, dark skin color became prima facie evidence of slave status, as well as a justification for the enslavement of sub-Saharan Africans. European enslavers regarded, David Brion Davis has noted, "darkness of skin as a brand which God or nature impressed upon inferior people."[33] Moreover, during the Enlightenment the increasingly influential scientific discourse of natural history selected dark skin color as a privileged trait for assigning individuals to its abstract racial typology designated "Negro" after the Spanish word for "black." Written documents from the colonial period, including New York City newspaper advertisements, often used the designation *Negro* as a synonym for slave. In December 1737, the *New-York Gazette* printed the following notice: "Ran away from John Bell of the City of New York, Carpenter, one Negro Woman, named Jenney, aged about 14 or 15 years, she was born in New York, speaks English, and some Dutch. She has a flat Nose, thick Lips, and full Face."[34] The use of the term *Negro* in this ad was all that was needed to indicate that Jenney was a slave. But, for added definition, the same newspaper notice cited visually observable facial features that the racial classification schema of the early modern era ascribed to the ideal Negro (or Ethiopian) type.[35] In this way, the colonial New York City newspaper advertisements for fugitive slaves did not merely describe. As media, they communicated, through iteration, ascriptive categories of race and servile status and, in complex and contradictory ways, contributed to the process of racial formation and its articulation with the exploitation of labor.

Importantly, the mysteries of human diversity rendered questionable the reliability of skin color and other visible physiognomic traits as signifiers of servile status and called into question the logic of sameness and difference that structured the early modern racial classification schema. In 1735, a New York City newspaper reported that a female slave had given birth to twins, one with "white" skin and the other with "black" skin.[36] Both father and mother were probably classified as Negroes, since, if the twins had been the product of a known interracial union, the newspaper report would have referred to them as mulattoes. The "white" sibling was likely an albino. Although albinos were scientific curiosities, for the general public the main wonder was the birth of twins of opposite skin types, one of perfect "white" and the other of perfect "black." Such "miraculous births" troubled the logic of noncontradiction that mandated like must produce like; here was a perplexing case in which like produced both sameness and difference. Naturalists of the early modern era were uncertain whether the distinguishing marks of a particular racial type were immutable traits or whether they were the product of environmental conditions and hence likely to change when the descendants of a racial group moved to new climates. In any event, the binary logic of the classification system that separated humankind into distinct yet relationally constituted races could be misleading, since it constructed ideal taxonomies of race that eliminated the messy reality of human diversity.[37] Then as now, the permutations of the human genetic code produced a range of skin pigmentations between the two reductive extremes of "black" and "white."[38] On July 3, 1738, the weekly edition of the New York City newspaper printed an advertisement for the arrest of a "lusty Madagascar Negro Man, of yellowish Complexion" and another ad for the return of a "lusty well-sett Negro Man, of Brownish complecion."[39] Epidermal heterogeneity also characterized the documented runaway servant population, and the newspaper ads for these fugitives noted observable features of the runaway's bodily surface that deviated from the physiognomic norms ascribed to the ideal Caucasian type. On August 26, 1734, the New York City newspaper reported that two Irish servants had absconded from their master and that "the one named Michael Highland . . . is a tall lusty thick well set Fellow, brown complecion," while "the other named John Whilen . . . is of middle stature, fair complecion . . . and [has] thick lips."[40] Some newspaper advertisements for runaway servants and slaves thus reminded the settlers of the marvel of human variation and the puzzle of indeterminacy presented by the diverse human beings who populated colonial New York City. In this way, these newspaper ads alerted the public to the unreliability of skin color and other visible physiognomic traits as indexes to servile status and thus discouraged overconfidence in the use of simplistic stereotypes of "free white" and "enslaved black" to identify and apprehend fugitives.

Doubtless, some light-skinned slaves passed into the free white world.[41] On October 9, 1738, the New-York Gazette printed the following advertisement:

> Run-away on the 16th of September, from Charles Decker, of Richmond County upon Staten Island, a Mulatto Slave named Harry, about 24 Years of Age, of Middle Stature, blew eyes, blackish Hair, a Fair Skin for a Mulatto, he speaks good Dutch but his English is sometime Broken: He had on when he went away a lightish Duroy Coat, blew grey kersey Jacket, a narrow brimm'd Beaver Hat, gray wollen stockings, new round toe'd Shoes, and Silver Buckels.[42]

The attention brought to Harry's "fair" skin and blue eyes suggests that instead of fleeing the white settler colony he might have attempted to pass into the realm of the master race. Harry's visible bodily surface provided him with a kind of camouflage that probably rendered him invisible against the background of colonial New York City's white settler majority. In this respect, the act of racial passing can be regarded as a disappearing act. David Theo Goldberg has noted that "visibility and invisibility each can serve contextually as weapons, as defensive or offensive strategy, as a mode of self-determination or denial of it."[43] In Harry's case, strategic invisibility offered the passport that he needed to gain entrance into the free world. It did not, however, fully guarantee his emancipation. For the light-skinned Harry, the feat of racial passing probably depended as heavily on his ability to narrate a credible autobiography of his life as a free man as on his strategic use of the invisibility that his light skin color afforded him. By necessity, such fictional self-fashioning would have to include a story of being born of a free woman, a tale of his accomplishment of self-purchase, or some other account of his emancipation that encouraged a *misrecognition*, whereby Harry's individualizing bodily marks, which in the runaway ad identify him as a light-skinned mulatto slave, become unremarkable. For Harry, successful escape depended, in the broadest sense, on his subjection to the norms of whiteness. Other mulatto fugitives doubtless took advantage of their anomalous position and escaped through the blind spots in the binary regime of visuality that coded bodies as either black and unfree or white and free. The artful dodger Charles Roberts, a male mulatto servant known by the alias "German," ran away from his master on April 12, 1762. His master offered the following description of Roberts's talents at deception and mischief:

> His behavior is excessively complaisent, obsequious, and insinuating; he speaks good English smoothly and plausibly, and generally with a cringe and a smile, he is extremely artful, and ready at inventing specious pretences to conceal villainous Actions and Designs. He plays on the Fiddle, can read and write tolerably well, and understands a Little Arithmetic and Accounts. I have reason to believe some evil-minded Persons in town have encouraged and been Accomplices in his villainous Designs; it is probable he will contrive the most specious forgeries to give him the appearance of a free man.[44]

Notably, the visual regime of individualizing surveillance could not foreclose the threat of trespass that Harry, the talented Charles Roberts, and other light-skinned mulatto runaway servants and slaves posed to the settler colony's biracial social hierarchy.[45] A rigid binarism of free white/unfree black structured commonsensical patterns of seeing and knowing and admitted no contradiction. For precisely this reason, some light-skinned fugitive slaves, especially those who were verbally adept and skilled at manipulating the preconceptions of others, passed through the guarded yet permeable borders of the free white world, evading the imperfect disciplinary mechanisms created to contain them in their assigned subject-position.

Free blacks posed a greater threat to the settler colony's biracial social hierarchy than light-skinned slaves and the act of racial passing. The anomalous subject-position of free blacks called into question the reductive binarism of free white/enslaved black. An incident in the life of a young black girl suggests that the free black presence in colonial New York City opened an avenue of escape for enslaved blacks. In 1763, a dispute arose over the sale of a black girl who claimed that, although of dark complexion, she had been born free and unlawfully sold into slavery. The existence of free blacks in the colony lent credibility to her story, and as a consequence the colonial authorities could not dismiss the truth of her assertion without legally valid evidence to the contrary. The black girl's mere claim to having been born free entangled New York City slave traders in legal uncertainties for several months. Captain Isaac Youngblood insisted that, while he had no written proof that the black girl had been born to a slave woman, he had, in good faith, bought the female youth from Captain Hunter, who had sold her on consignment for Nicholas Bayard. Hoping to substantiate his property right in the person of the black girl in question, the mariner inquired to Nicholas Bayard about the black girl's mother, whose servile status was, by mandate of colonial New York's law of slavery, passed on to her daughter, regardless of the child's skin color and other physiognomic traits. Bayard hired a lawyer, Archibald Carey, to obtain proof that the black girl's mother was, in fact, a slave. On December 13, 1763, Carey wrote to his client: "You may be assured that she was Borne a slave, the father & mother are now Living in the same family, Mr. Bostherth, who lived near my father's

Country Seat & his best neighbors & friend. Brought her up. Also, born in his family. I could send you proofs of it." Once documentary evidence of her mother's slave status was submitted to the court, Captain Youngblood was certain to receive clear title to the black girl he had purchased from Captain Hunter.[46]

Like most female slaves, that young black girl did not make a bid for freedom by running away from her master. Female slaves account for only 6 percent of the documented fugitive slave population. Confined to their masters' houses, except for weekly trips to the city markets, and subjected to almost constant surveillance, female slaves were presented with few opportunities to escape. Moreover, enslaved mothers bore the custodial responsibility of caring for their young offspring, and flight from slavery with a helpless infant diminished their chances of successful escape.[47] Female slaves sometimes eloped with adult male accomplices; and when female slaves fled alone, they sometimes impersonated males, as in the case of a female Indian slave named Kate, who, the newspaper ad for her capture stated, "in all probability will equip herself in men's clothes, and inlist for a soldier."[48] Female servants comprised only 4 percent of the documented fugitive servant population. Female servants rarely absconded alone; all but a few ran away in the company of men. By eloping with a male accomplice or, more boldly, assuming the identity of a male, female runaways enhanced their chances of escaping detection in a world where women who traveled without a male companion were instant objects of suspicion.

While men who traveled alone were less likely to attract suspicion than single female sojourners, a significant proportion of the documented male fugitive population—approximately 22 percent—eloped with accomplices. The daily gathering of the city's male labor force at urban work sites doubtless encouraged servants and slaves to conspire to run away in the company of other laborers. In 1689, around the time of Leisler's Rebellion, a group of fugitive slaves from New York City rampaged through the farming village of Harlem.[49] Although enslaved black males and white male servants labored side by side at New York City work sites, they seldom absconded together. The colonial penal code discouraged such collaboration. Any fugitive servant convicted of running away in consort with a slave paid a double penalty for his or her crime. Following his failed attempt to escape in the company of a runaway slave, Robert Bowman, a white indentured servant, was ordered to complete the term of five years' service that he owed his master. As punishment for his crime, Bowman received 39 lashes on his naked back and was required to labor six months for his accomplice's master in compensation for the labor time lost during the runaway slave's absence. The court took no action against Bowman's accomplice and instead remanded the ex-fugitive slave to his master for correction.[50] When white servants ran away in groups, they generally escaped in the company of other servants from their homelands. On Saturday evening, April 19, 1765, Timothy Sullivan, Timothy McCarthy, and Phillip McCardell, indentured servants and natives of Ireland, ran away from their masters after spending only five months in New York City;[51] and on Friday evening, April 11, 1768, Johannes Finckenfor absconded from his master in the company of two other German servants.[52]

Indian runaways account for only a tiny fraction of the sample runaway population, approximately 3 percent of runaway slaves and less than 1 percent of runaway servants. These fugitives usually escaped alone and probably headed for the Northwest Territory, where they were likely to receive asylum from the native inhabitants of that remote region or from the renegades, vagabonds, and bandits who had established isolated maroon communities on the frontier. The French explorer Sieur de Villiers reported that, during his 1690 expedition southward from Lake Ontario into the Canisteo River valley, he discovered an "outlaw village of longhouses" inhabited by Indians, Frenchmen, Dutchmen, Englishmen, and runaway slaves. In 1762, Sir William Johnson sent a military expedition to destroy that maroon community and to apprehend a couple of its inhabitants, Long Coat and Squash Cutter, who had been accused of murdering two Englishmen.[53] After 1705, New York's penal code imposed the death penalty on runaways who were captured more than 40 miles north of Albany.[54] The colonial authorities deemed this harsh deterrent a vital security measure, for in times when England was at war against France, slaves and servants who escaped to the northwest frontier might carry military intelligence to the French enemies or their Indian allies and thus imperil the safety of the English colonies. During the French and Indian War, enslaved black males were enlisted in the New York militia through the substitution and hiring-out systems. Though few in number, black soldiers and other enslaved black males accompanied English troops to New York's distant frontier and were, therefore, familiar with that territory. In 1765, a male slave named Robbin and a pregnant female slave named Rose ran away from their master, who believed that the couple was headed for the northwest frontier because, some years earlier, Robbin had traveled with a military expedition to that region.[55]

While the Northwest Territory attracted some runaways, the open Atlantic Ocean beckoned other fugitives. In 1749, four slaves from New Spain murdered the crew of a sloop moored at the port of New York, hijacked that sailing vessel, and escaped by sea.[56] In all likelihood, these Spanish-speaking runaways were sailors and therefore capable of navigating the commandeered sloop homeward. Because of the indiscriminate hiring practices of mariners, untold numbers of runaways secured passage on sailing vessels embarking from New York's seaport. Newspaper advertisements for runaways often included a warning reminding mariners that the law forbade "harboring, concealing or carrying off" fugitives.[57] Colonial New York City slaveowners sometimes hired out their male servants and slaves to mariners who employed hired laborers for voyages of varying durations, extending from a few weeks to more than a year. Newspaper advertisements for fugitives generally noted when a runaway had experience at sea, because servants and slaves who had tasted the seafaring life sometimes attempted to escape by sea after returning to New York City. Policing the revolving gateway of the port of New York, which not only allowed undetected strangers into the city but also enabled unknown numbers of the city's servants and slaves to escape, proved to be an impossible task.

During the colonial period, no regular salaried police force monitored New York City.[58] Instead, a night watch, dating back to Dutch rule and drawn from the ranks of the adult white male property holders, conducted irregular patrols through the port town's neighborhoods. But the presence of night watchmen in the streets after sunset was an ineffective mechanism for policing the city's servile population. The colonial authorities relied on masters to keep a vigilant watch over their bondsmen and to punish insubordinate servants and slaves. At the same time, the colonial authorities urged masters to use restraint when punishing unruly bondsmen. The colonial laws made the murder of a slave a capital crime and imposed a fine of £40 on masters who mutilated their slaves.[59] Nevertheless, masters sometimes inflicted severe bodily damages on bond laborers. In a New York City newspaper announcement, several destitute white women publicized their misgivings about entering into contracts of indenture with abusive masters and appealed to public opinion and the moral authority of household mistresses for protection from mistreatment at the hands of brutal masters. "It is proper the World should know our Terms," the women wrote. "We think it reasonable we should not be beat by our Mistresses Husband, they being too strong, and perhaps may do tender Women mischief. If any Ladies want Servants, and will engage for their Husbands, they shall be soon supplied."[60] Unlike female servants, male servants could not lay claim to the vulnerabilities of the weaker sex when appealing to the public for protection from tyrannical masters, and abused slaves, regardless of their gender, had extremely limited recourse to public opinion. New York City slaveowners sometimes used lethal force when punishing their bondsmen. In December 1733, a newspaper report described the fatal beating that a New York City master inflicted on the body of his male slave: "Last night being the 21st the Jury of Inquest taken before the High Sheriff (in the Coroner's absence) found that said [William] Petit . . . with his Fists and Feet, beat, wounded, kick'd and bruised the Negro [Joe] on his Breast, Head, and other Parts of his Body to the Degree, that thereof he instantly died."[61] Following this preliminary finding, a jury convicted Petit of manslaughter or recklessly taking the life of his slave. In a similar incident, the New York City blockmaker John Van Zandt horsewhipped his slave until his victim fell unconscious and died. The city coroner supported the medical opinion of Doctor Braine and Doctor DuPuy, the physicians who performed the initial autopsy of the deceased slave's corpse. In his final report, the coroner stated: "The correction given by the Master was not the cause of his Death, but it was by the visitation of God."[62] By attributing the slave's death to "natural causes," to use the parlance of present-day forensic medicine, the coroner's report exempted Van Zandt from an indictment on the charge of murder.

Both Van Zandt and Petit had fatally injured their slaves in the act of punishing them for taking time off from work without permission. Colonial New York City offered servants and slaves numerous diversions from drudgery. The city markets became popular gathering spots, where the port town's servile population congregated with the regularity of the conduct of trade. Each workday, dancing, drumming, fiddling, and singing intermingled with the din of maritime commerce. During the colonial period, the port of New York became a crucible for a vibrant black urban culture. Commerce stimulated cultural production and sometimes transformed the recreational activities of enslaved black laborers into a means of getting paid. Within the public space of the city markets and its matrix of exchange, slaves who had a talent for fiddling soon became street performers, earning income from the donations of appreciative town dwellers, who deposited coins in the fiddler's hat or cup and, in doing so, became consumers of black urban cultural production. Whereas black culture in the rural South took shape within the comparatively insular space of the racially segregated slave quarters, black culture in colonial New York City developed in the relatively open, multiethnic, market-oriented space of a port town and merged with the city's broader urban working-class culture. For urban black laborers, the value-making activity of commerce coincided with the value-making activity of the bricoleur, whose improvisational reworking of bits and pieces of everyday artifacts transformed material culture into cultural material for a poetry of the marketplace.

By the early nineteenth-century, New York City's black vendors shouted street cries dating back to the colonial period.[63] Like the work songs of the early slaves in the rural South, the cries of the city's black street vendors transformed routine labor activity into an expressive form that gave a measure of dignity to the lives of exploited workers. This functional similarity should not, however, obscure the dissimilarities of form and content between the rural work songs and the urban street cries. Whereas the formal structure of antiphony and the thematic stress on spiritual liberation from a life of strenuous labor in the work songs of rural slaves emerged from the conditions of gang labor and the seasonal work routine of agricultural production on the southern staple-crop plantations, the short refrains of solicitation and the thematic of consumption in the street cries of urban slave vendors reflected the process of commodification taking place at the urban marketplace. A peach was worth 10 pence on the city streets, the slave vendor cried, because its taste magically satisfied the appetite for fresh things. Although the street cries did not explicitly reference rural sites of agricultural production— for example, the nearby truck farms in the surrounding countryside and the distant sugar plantations in the West Indies where exploited laborers cultivated crops destined for consumption in urban centers throughout the Atlantic world—they did, for those passersby whose ears and eyes were open to it, call attention to exploitative labor practices in colonial port towns, where enslaved street vendors in tattered clothing and bare feet sold agricultural produce for their masters at inflated prices. Among the street vendors were enslaved females who escaped the tedium and confinement of housework by setting up carts and stalls at the city's outdoor markets. At the urban marketplace, otherwise isolated female slaves participated in the collective life of the city's servile population.

The urban market for agricultural produce brought rural blacks to the city, where they sold fruits and vegetables to the town dwellers. At the city markets, these "country Negroes" interacted with urban blacks who frequented the outdoor marketplaces while on errands or during stolen leisure time. In addition to agricultural produce, rural blacks from Long Island and Eastern Jersey brought their own brand of culture to the city. Elements of rural black culture were doubtless incorporated into black urban culture. The reverse was also true, as the cultural practices of urban blacks probably made an impression on rural black culture. Both enslaved and free blacks from other parts of the Atlantic world also contributed to colonial New York City's black urban culture and to the formation of a broader black Atlantic culture, whose fluid and hybrid expressive forms migrated from port town to port town and from these transshipment points of international commerce into the countryside. As already noted, the transatlantic slave trade brought native Africans to the port of New York, and these involuntary immigrants surely infused the city's black culture with cultural idioms imported directly from Africa. The commingling of diverse cultures and their circulation make it difficult to state with certainty the exact provenance of many of the expressive forms urban blacks performed in the port towns of British North America. Thomas De Voe attributed a dance, known as the "jig or breakdown" and performed in the streets of early New York City, to rural slaves from Long Island.[64] But sailors and other maritime workers performed similar dances at the port of London.[65] An estimated 3,000 seaman were registered at the port of New York on the eve of the War for Independence.[66] More than a few of these sailors were black men; by the eighteenth century, black sailors were approximately 40 percent of the British merchant marine.[67] Constituted as a modern nomadic subject by a life of maritime travel, the black seafarer became a black Atlantic flâneur embued with the attributes of hybridity and mobility that characterized the emergent cosmopolitan international maritime working class of the early modern era. Circumnavigating the Atlantic world, traveling from port town to port town along the Atlantic littoral and the Caribbean basin, endowed the black Atlantic flâneur with the panoramic perspective of a mobilized gaze. At seaports such as the port of New York, this black sailor and others like him narrated tales of their seafaring lives and adventures in distant lands, thus broadening the horizon of the relatively sedentary and confined black town dwellers whom they encountered during shore leave.[68] These black seafarers also brought new expressive forms to the port towns they visited. Just as the nexus of trade between town and country facilitated cultural exchange between urban and rural blacks, the integrally related and much wider overseas trade became the channel for the dissemination of various cultural styles between the port of New York and other seaports along the Atlantic littoral. Set afloat on the currents of maritime commerce, particularistic cultural expressions soon found their way to distant ports.[69] At these maritime theaters of cultural exchange, mimicry and appropriation quickly transformed exotic yet portable cultural practices into recognizable features of a cosmopolitan urban working-class culture. Colonial New York City's black urban culture was not only an enduring feature of that port town's working-class culture but also probably a component of the broader culture of the international working class of the early modern era.

During the summer months, the poorest segments of colonial New York City's laboring class, along with the large numbers of transient sailors who took shore leave at the port of New York during the late summer and early autumn, gathered at the docks along the East River, where they amused themselves far into the night. Some townspeople complained that this boisterous activity disturbed their sleep, but the colonial authorities seldom enforced the city curfew or otherwise curtailed the laborers' nighttime revelries. As the following episodes reveal, sailors had their own rules of decorum and methods of punishing offenders. One evening in July 1743, a black sailor, who had become unruly or "a little to[o] hot," received a dunking from his crew mates in order "to cool his Courage."[70] Two weeks later, some sailors discovered that a white woman had disguised herself in men's clothing and hired herself on board a privateering vessel named the *Castor and Pollux*. As punishment for attempting to appropriate the prerogatives of the masculine seafaring trade, the all-male crew subjected the unfortunate woman to the punishment of dunking and other corrections: "They seized upon the unhappy Wretch," the New York City newspaper reported, "and dunk'd her three Times from the Yard-Arm, and afterwards made their Negroes Tarr her all over from Head to Foot, by which cruel Treatment, and the Rope that let her into the Water having been indiscreetly fastened, the poor Woman was very much hurt, and continues now ill."[71] Though female prostitutes were welcome companions to sailors and other transients who inhabited the docks, most women who ventured into the male-dominated waterfront along the East River risked public humiliation and bodily injury.[72]

The street life around the East River waterfront fostered fraternal bonds among male slaves. Named for the dock-area landmarks where they ordinarily gathered, the Long Bridge Boys and the Smith Fly Boys were black brotherhoods that became notorious for their exploits. Resisting the biracial hierarchy that allowed black males few prerogatives of manhood, the members of these black confraternities demonstrated their manliness during nighttime adventures in which, as a colonial official reported, they "junket[ed] together at night . . . upon the produce of the spoils of their pilfering." Although the colonial penal code imposed the death penalty on defendants convicted of burglary, in some cases the colonial magistrates ordered lighter correction for valuable servants and slaves whose masters were willing to compensate the crime victims for the loss of their property and other damages.[73] Because criminal activity typically occurred under the cover of darkness, the colonial authorities imposed a curfew, requiring all blacks, enslaved and free, above the age of 14 years to carry a lantern or candle when on the streets after sunset.[74] This "Negro illumination law" and other measures for detecting and preventing the clandestine movement of slaves at night proved to be difficult to enforce in a colonial port town where there was no professional police force or regular military watch. To encourage individual masters to exercise greater control over their slaves, the colonial authorities fined slaveowners whose bondsmen were arrested for street brawling, insobriety, and other incidents of disturbing the peace and reckless behavior.[75] Slaveowners were not always vigilant overseers, however. Unruly slaves continued to evade surveillance, roamed the city streets at night, and mingled with the servants, sailors, vagabonds, and other transients who populated the dock area.

The New York City clergy complained to the colonial authorities about the presence of rowdy slaves in the city streets on the Sabbath. The SPG catechist Elias Neau pointed out that "on Sundays while we are at our Devotions, the Streets are full of Negroes who dance & divert themselves. . . ."[76] This unsupervised activity disquieted the colonial authorities, who recognized that the city was especially vulnerable to slave revolt during the hours of Christian worship services. For this reason, they enacted a municipal ordinance that prohibited black town dwellers from breaking the Sabbath.[77] In addition to faulting their servants and slaves for Sabbath-breaking, New York City masters cited the servile population's fondness for drink as the principal cause of insubordination, sloth, and criminal activity among servants and slaves. A New York City newspaper carried the following report on the alleged addiction of the laboring class to Geneva gin, a strong liquor imported from Holland: "It is with deepest Concern your Committee observe the Strong Inclination of the Inferior sort of People to these destructive Liquors . . . the constant use of strong-waters, and particularly Geneva, never fails to produce an invincible aversion to work and Labour. [It] raises the most violent and outrageous passions, renders them incapable of hard Labour . . . besides the fatal effects it has on their morals and religions."[78] Suspecting that servants and slaves resorted to stealing and other crimes to support their drinking habits, New York's colonial assembly prohibited tavern keepers from selling intoxicating drinks to unfree laborers.[79] Long known for its many taverns, colonial New York City witnessed the proliferation of drinking establishments with the military buildup that accompanied the French and Indian War.[80] Many of these taverns catered to the city's servile population, even though colonial law prohibited that practice. Servants and slaves also frequented the city's dramshops, typically located in dry goods stores, where shopkeepers sold liquor by the dram (or one-eighth ounce). At these storefronts, patrons could purchase as much liquor as they could imbibe at one sitting. Robert Livingston vowed to sell a troublesome slave from his New York City household into the countryside, explaining that "here [New York City] there are so many Little Dram Shops that ruin half the Negroes in town."[81] In addition to the taverns and dramshops, some free townspeople operated tippling houses, private residences where hosts sold liquor to their guests. Intended as a measure to reduce drunkenness and idleness among servants and slaves, a colonial law prohibited the keeping of such "disorderly houses," as well as the practice of entertaining unfree laborers without permission from their masters. According to that statute, any white settler convicted of entertaining a servant or a slave without authorization paid a £5 fine.[82] In 1716, the court convicted Thomas Noble, a free white resident of the South Ward, of keeping a tippling house and unlawfully entertaining two enslaved men, the slave of Cornelius Schulyer, resident of the South Ward, and the slave of August Jay, resident of the Dock Ward.[83] During the early years of English rule, the colonial law imposed harsh penalties on free blacks who entertained unfree laborers without permission from their masters. On March 7, 1671, Domingo and Manuel Angola were brought before the court and charged with illegally entertaining some servants and slaves. The court record stated: "The free Negroes were from time to time entertaining sundry of the servants and negroes belonging to the Burghers and inhabitants . . . to the great damage of their owners." The colonial magistrate warned the free blacks that they would forfeit their freedom should they again appear before the court on a similar charge. The magistrate also ordered Domingo and Manuel to communicate his warning to other free black town dwellers.[84] According to a subsequent law, free blacks convicted of illicitly entertaining servants and slaves no longer forfeited their freedom but instead paid a fine double the sum imposed on white settlers convicted of the same crime.[85] In February 1714, Peter the Doctor, a free black town dweller who two years earlier had been indicted for but later exonerated of participating in the Slave Revolt of 1712, was convicted of entertaining Sarah, the enslaved woman of William Wharton, a resident of the Dock Ward. Consistent with the law, a colonial magistrate ordered Peter to pay a fine in the amount of £10.[86] Despite these and similar convictions, free townspeople continued to entertain servants and slaves in their homes.

The prevalence of "disorderly houses," such as taverns, dramshops, and tippling houses, provided the city's servile population with a screen from surveillance and doubtless contributed to insobriety and tardiness among servants and slaves. The spatial and temporal structures of labor in the colonial port town militated against rigorous regulation of the city's workforce. The lack of rigid separation between work and leisure spaces made it impossible to enforce a strict work routine of the kind later imposed on the industrial labor force under the factory system. Although respectable society increasingly condemned the pursuit of idle amusements as a threat to the value of labor, colonial New York City's servants and slaves persistently and, to a large degree, successfully valorized leisure pastimes and transformed recreational activity into expressive forms of a vibrant urban working-class culture. In this way, servants and slaves evaded the colonial port town's exploitative labor system without ever leaving New York City. During the day, the city's servile population stole leisure time and amused themselves in the streets, at the city markets, and at the dramshops. After sunset and on Sundays, they haunted the docks along the East River, frequented the many taverns and tippling houses that catered to servants and slaves, and visited the homes of free townspeople. During these ephemeral interludes and within these compact spaces, the city's laboring class forged solidarities across the color line. The colonial authorities deemed interracial commingling among the city's servile population a particularly dangerous trend. But owing to the weaknesses of official surveillance and the poor resolution of its image of the densely populated port town's social body, they had little chance of eradicating the many dimly lit recesses within the city, where propertyless servants, slaves, and outsiders conducted illicit traffic of all sorts.

Unlike wage laborers, servants and slaves received no monetary reward for their labors and, as a consequence, had little or no access to cash. For unfree laborers, theft was one way of getting paid. Some laborers from the British Isles and Europe regarded the act of appropriating small pieces of their masters' property as a customary privilege rather than outright theft. The colonial authorities surmised that the practice of allowing servants and slaves to conduct trade encouraged propertyless laborers to steal from their masters and other propertied town dwellers and to engage in black market exchanges of stolen goods. For this reason, the colonial assembly enacted an antitrafficking law that required any free person who had been convicted of purchasing stolen goods from a servant or a slave to pay the owner triple the value of the pilfered merchandise in addition to a fine of £5.[87] But this and other laws proved to be an ineffective deterrent against the crimes of theft and receiving stolen goods. Nevertheless, the colonial authorities continued to bring servants and slaves before the criminal court on the charge of petty larceny, as well as selling and holding stolen goods. When accused of crimes, white servants were entitled to due process of law, including a trial by 12 jurors. In this regard, they enjoyed the rights of British subjects. The Court of Quarter Sessions of the Justices of the Peace was the central apparatus of the criminal justice system in colonial New York, and that court had jurisdiction over criminal cases against servants. Slaves were not afforded the rights of British subjects; and according to the Black Code of 1712, three justices of the peace, along with five prominent freeholders, were empowered to sit as a special panel that rendered judgments in cases involving slaves charged with infractions of the law.[88] Slaveowners often punished their slaves without benefit of a court trial. Nonetheless, Douglas Greenberg's study on crime in colonial New York shows that enslaved blacks were brought to court for thievery almost twice as often as white settlers, including white servants and apprentices. In colonial New York, the court convicted 81 percent of black defendants, while it convicted less than 40 percent of white defendants.[89] Typically, both servants and slaves were convicted of stealing low-bulk valuables that could be pilfered and sold with ease. Defendants convicted of petty larceny, stealing goods valued under 10 pence, received from 9 to 29 lashes.[90] The colonial authorities usually administered this corporal punishment at the public whipping post, located just inside the palisade at the city's northern limit. On occasion, guards carted convicts through the city streets, stopping at the busiest intersections to inflict on the criminal's body the installment of lashes that the court had prescribed as punishment. With these and other public rituals of corporal punishment, the colonial authorities attempted to disperse power across the city landscape, but this diffusion of power was incapable of penetrating the hidden recesses where lawbreakers planned and often committed their crimes.

In colonial New York City, acts of theft rarely resulted in bodily injury to the crime victim. Violent crimes, such as assault and battery, were occasionally connected with acts of overt defiance against the ruling elite. According to Greenberg, colonial Netherlanders were charged with contempt of authority more often than any other segment of New York's population.[91] Although colonial Englishmen generally pursued nonviolent, legalistic channels in seeking redress for their grievances against the ruling elite, unruly Englishmen sometimes tested the limits of the law by defying the authority of colonial Netherlanders who were members of the city's night watch. At two o'clock in the morning on

January 2, 1737, Abraham Van Horne Jr. and James Van Horne, colonial Netherlanders, long-time city residents, and night watchmen, discovered John Smith, an English newcomer, roaming the West Ward. Smith resisted their attempt to remove him from the street, and a minor brawl ensued. Later, Smith brought a lawsuit against the Van Hornes, charging them with assault and "abusing the Watch."[92] Smith's initial defiance and subsequent accusations against the Van Hornes in court perhaps registered his contempt for colonial Netherlanders who presumed to exercise authority over Englishmen. Certainly, the English newcomer's lawsuit reminded the Van Hornes and other colonial Netherlanders that they no longer ruled Manhattan and were now a conquered people who must submit to English law.

Free blacks did not enjoy the political and legal rights of British subjects and as a consequence had few protections against abusive authority figures. For the most part, free black town dwellers seem to have successfully avoided violent entanglements with the municipal authorities and other white townspeople. A rare but infamous case of assault occurred in 1696, when Prince, a male slave, struck, with his bare hand, New York City Mayor William Merritt during a confrontation between an illegal assembly of slaves and the municipal authorities who ordered the slaves to disperse. As punishment for his crime, Prince received a series of lashes on his naked back at every major street intersection in town.[93] This method of exemplary public punishment doubtless served as a deterrent to black town dwellers who, when provoked in some way, contemplated committing similar assaults. Another notable exception was the case of Shadrack, a free black man who, in 1774, was convicted of assault and battery on a white man with his bare hands.[94] Shadrack's crime was typical in another respect, however, for on occasions when black town dwellers assaulted white townspeople they seldom used lethal weapons. Although both enslaved and free blacks were prohibited from owning and carrying firearms, some blacks who lived in the white settler households had access to guns. On April 25, 1743, a New York City newspaper carried the following report: "On Friday last, a Negro Boy belonging to Abraham Akerman of the Place, taking his Master's Gun, and (as is supposed) thinking it not loaded, fired it off, and thereby shot one of his Master's Children dead on the Spot, and wounded a Negro Boy (his own brother) in the Head so that 'tis thought he can't recover."[95]

Because colonial New York City was a tinderbox town, the townspeople were especially frightened of uncontrollable blazes.[96] Anxiety-ridden townspeople were quick to suspect enslaved blacks of intentionally setting fires, even though little or no evidence implicated them in the crime of arson.[97] Such suspicions were not entirely irrational apprehensions. The slaves who revolted in 1712 set fire to a building. In 1736, a suspicious blaze damaged John Roosevelt's stable, bolting-house, and other buildings in the East Ward, where the Slave Revolt of 1712 had taken place. Newspaper coverage of that fire surmised that arsonists had used live coals to ignite the combustion. The news item explained that the alleged acts of arson were likely the design of disgruntled slaves, including a female slave who belonged to the owner of the charred buildings.[98] When a mysterious rash of fires erupted during the winter of 1741–42, the white townspeople at first attributed the blazes to some restive slaves who planned to revolt against their masters. That explanation for the troubling series of fires reflected the trepidation of enslavers who lived in close quarters with enslaved people, whom they feared as domestic enemies and hostile property. The colonial authorities regarded the accretion of the city's black population as a grave threat to the public safety. During the emergency of 1741–42, William Smith expressed this worry when he remarked: "I fear, gentlemen, that we shall never be quite safe till that wicked race are under restraint or their number greatly reduced within the city."[99] The English colony builder's dream of reducing the number of enslaved blacks and peopling the colony with numerous loyal British settlers proved to be difficult to realize. New York City did not witness some relief from its reliance on the labor of enslaved blacks until the 1770s, when relatively large numbers of laborers from the British Isles disembarked at the port of New York. For much of the eighteenth century, New York City held the largest percentage and the second largest absolute number of enslaved blacks of any port town in British North America. For this reason, the colonial authorities continued to worry that the city's black population, in combination with poor white newcomers of doubtful loyalty to the English colonial government, would foment a conspiracy from below and undertake a violent revolt against their rulers.

As early as 1766, the ruling elite complained that too many impoverished white newcomers were settling in New York. In the same year, the colonial assembly passed an "Act for the Regulation of Servants," reflecting the ruling elite's desire that only white people of property migrate to the settler colony.[100] However, some New Yorkers placed the blame for the rise in poverty in New York on the ruling elite, whom they characterized as a callous social class that profited from the labor of the working poor. In August 1767, an anonymous New Yorker wrote: "It is to the meaner Class of Mankind, the industrious Poor, that as many of us are indebted for these goodly Dwellings we inhabit, for that comfortable Substance we enjoy while others are languishing under disagreeable sensations of Penury and Want."[101] Following the cessation of the French and Indian War in 1764, the port of New York suffered a severe postwar trade contraction. During the 1770s, New York City offered white newcomers few opportunities to improve their material circumstances, yet during the early years of that decade, large numbers of migrants from the British Isles disembarked at the port of New York. A majority of these newcomers soon moved to upcountry New York—but the poorest immigrants remained in New York City. More than ever, the English colonial rulers now gambled that the psychological benefits of whiteness would be incentive enough to command the loyalty of the city's population of propertyless newcomers from the British Isles and other parts of Europe.[102]

At that time, the English Parliament and the Hanoverian monarchy boldly asserted sovereignty over the English overseas colonies, demanding, with the enactment of new strict regulations, that the settlers assume a subordinate position within the first British Empire and faithfully serve England's interest in the exploitation of its colonial possessions for the purpose of raising national revenues. In this respect, the white settlers in British mainland America occupied the subject-positions of both colonizer and colonized, of agent of colonialism and subjugated object of colonial domination.[103] The proliferation of political antagonisms between the settlers and the English colonial rulers over various new regulations of the English Parliament—for example, the Stamp Act of 1765, the Quartering Act of 1765, the Townshend Act of 1767, the Tea Act of 1773, and the Intolerable Acts of 1774—fostered a climate of unrest in the British North American colonies. In revolutionary New York City, unruly crowds, sometimes with the endorsement of wealthy merchants, defied the English troops garrisoned at the port town, erected liberty poles in support of the growing independence movement, burned effigies of English authority figures, dismantled the statue of King George III on the Bowling Green, damaged property, and threatened the lives of loyalists who collaborated with the English colonial government.[104] "Crowd action," the historian Edward Countryman has noted, "stretched and rent the fabric of New York society."[105] One of the frayed threads of colonial New York's social fabric, and of British North American society as a whole, was white solidarity. The solvent of antiblack racism and the fear of conspiracy from below could no longer avert the breakdown of colonial governance.

As early as the 1750s, an opposition faction of the colonial elite rallied the broader settler population against Crown-appointed colonial authorities and the segment of the colonial elite that supported them in exchange for lucrative rewards. This time, popular discontent against the colonial government would mature into a social movement for independence and the preservation of English liberties. Published in the first issue of New York City's *The Independent Reflector*, an editorial declared: "Vice and Folly ought to be attacked where-ever they are met; and especially when in high and conspicuous stations."[106] Another editorial observed that settlers who voted for the clique of placemen in corrupt colonial elections were acting "more like a Herd of Slaves, than a Society of Freemen." "When a People are reduced to such a miserable State of Depravity," the anonymous author warned, "it is almost impossible they should long preserve that Love of Liberty, which always was, and I hope ever will be, the distinguishing Characteristic of *Englishmen*." In a final appeal to the settlers, the author pleaded: "Dare to think for yourselves, and scorn to be bought and sold."[107] For the proponents of American independence, the enslaved blacks presented, as Bernard Bailyn has noted, "only a more dramatic, more bizarre variation of the condition of all who lost the power of self-determination."[108] Put differently, the enslaved blacks offered a magnified mirror image of what the white settlers were in danger of becoming. For white settlers who lived and worked among slaves, the condition of enslaved blacks closely approximated the nightmare of their own enslavement at the hands of tyrannical English rulers. Though not the debased condition of bondage imposed on black Africans and their descendants, political slavery was, the leaders of the mounting white settler independence movement asserted, a detestable condition of utter incapacity and lack of desire to preserve liberty that would surely overtake the English people, once their secret enemies had destroyed the balance of their constitution.

By the seventh and eighth decades of the eighteenth century, the white settlers kept a close watch on the designs of corrupt ministers in England and Crown-appointed officials in the colonies who, the settlers increasingly believed, conspired to enslave them not only by destroying their material prosperity but also by taking away their liberties.[109] The discovery of a ministerial plot against the white settlers' liberties seemed credible to enslavers who themselves kept in captivity men and women who had only a dark skin, if that, to merit their subjection to lifelong and heritable bondage. This reformulation of common sense called into question the legitimacy of English colonial rule and finally propelled the white settlers into the War for Independence. In New York City, on July 9, 1776, the settlers gathered to hear a public reading of the Declaration of Independence, cheer the parade of the Continental troops, and affirm that New York had existed as an independent republic since April 20, 1775, the day after the Battle of Lexington. Focused on a conspiracy from above rather than from below, the city's intermediate stratum of respectable, propertied white Anglo-Saxon Protestant settlers joined the wider British North American settler revolt against English colonial rule.

"The Happiness of Liberty of Which I Knew Nothing Before"

PASSPORTS TO FREEDOM AND THE BLACK EXODUS
FROM POST-REVOLUTIONARY NEW YORK CITY

At the time that the settlers were debating the merits of independence from England in colonial newspapers and pamphlets, literate slaves were pressing their own claim to freedom. Most notably, the writings of Phillis Wheatley (1753–84) and the 1773–77 petitions of her black contemporaries in Boston presented incisive remonstrances against the institution of racial slavery.[1] Exploiting the intensifying antagonism between the English rulers and the settlers, the Boston petitioners submitted their grievances to both sides of the Anglo-American conflict: the Massachusetts General Court and the commander in chief of the British military forces in North America. Illiterate slaves also took advantage of the political crisis and revolted against their masters. In 1774, amid violent scenes of loyalist reprisals against American patriots in the streets of New York City, two slaves murdered their masters, known "supporters of liberty," and then ran away.[2] Servile insubordination had been building momentum since 1765 and, by the onset of the white American War for Independence (1775–83), the "contagion of rebellion" had spread among the enslaved masses throughout British America.[3] Given its intercolonial scope and the considerable number of slaves involved, black insurgency during the Anglo-American war constituted one of the largest and most significant slave uprisings prior to the Haitian Revolution.[4]

Slave uprisings in the late eighteenth century differed from previous slave rebellions, whose ultimate aim, according to Eugene Genovese, was not so much to overthrow the institution of slavery in the New World as to restore the rebels to traditional forms of African communal life. Whereas the ideal of individual autonomy seldom, if ever, inspired the earlier "restorationist" slave revolts led by native Africans, that liberal democratic value propelled acculturated native Africans, like Phillis Wheatley, and American-born blacks, who reached adulthood during the 1760s and 1770s, to expand and radicalize modern democratic culture.[5] Prior to the age of democratic revolutions and the advent of modernity, black slavery went largely unquestioned and did not become a matter of sustained public debate until the Enlightenment intervened to reorient Western culture toward the ideal of human progress.[6] Measuring the West against the yardstick of its own values, Phillis Wheatley called attention to the ethical dilemma posed by the perpetuation of slavery in modern times. A native West African who, at the age of eight years, was kidnapped from her homeland, shipped to Boston, and enslaved in that northern colonial port town, Wheatley is best known as the first African to publish a book of poems in the English language. The content of several poems and letters expressed Wheatley's opposition to racial slavery. In a letter to Reverend Samson Occom, dated February 11, 1774, Wheatley pointed out the "strange Absurdity" in the American philosophes' effort to reconcile human bondage with human emancipation. "How well the Cry of Liberty, and the reverse Disposition for the exercise of oppressive Power over others agree," she wrote, "I humbly think it does not require the Penetration of a Philosopher to determine."[7] In Wheatley's view, the American philosophes more closely resembled ancient Egyptian pagans than modern men of enlightenment. Arguing that slavery is absolutely incompatible with the modern ideals of freedom and human progress, Wheatley was in the vanguard of radical political thinkers. She and other enslaved blacks of her generation embraced the newly emerging democratic values of modernity and in doing so forwarded the modern impulse toward human emancipation.[8]

Although most settlers did not anticipate the wave of unrest that would spread among the enslaved masses in British North America and then expand and radicalize the social movement that initially coalesced in the American Revolution, some perspicacious white Americans did predict such an outcome, variously figuring the rise of black insurgency as a "snowball, in rolling," a "wolf by the ears," and a "fire-bell in the night." As thousands of enslaved blacks absconded from patriot slaveowners and fled to the British side during the white American War for Independence, black insurgency became a palpable threat to the survival of the new republics. "Slave flight quickened during the War of Independence," the historians Graham Hodges and Allen E. Brown have noted. "Whether inspired by political debate, inspired by abolitionist appeals of the Society of Friends, opportunistically following the warring armies, slaves fled their masters in greater numbers than ever before."[9] In British North America, the split between the American rebels and the English colonial rulers opened avenues of escape for thousands of enslaved blacks. According to the most reliable estimate, between 80,000 to 100,000 of the half million enslaved blacks that inhabited the 13 British mainland colonies—or, nearly one-fifth of British North America's total enslaved population—ran away from their masters during the Anglo-American war.[10] Black insurgency threatened to push the American Revolution beyond the limits that the white settlers initially assigned to it.

Positioned at the center of mainland British America, the port of New York was the geographical linchpin tying the rebel colonies together; for this reason, holding that centrally located seaport became a key objective in the British war strategy of dividing the American patriots and achieving a speedy victory. After invading the surrounding countryside, the British army occupied New York City on September 15, 1776, and remained there until the end of the war.[11] Having earlier abandoned their homes in the wake of mob violence directed against them, loyalist residents returned to the city when news of the British military occupation reached them. Additional loyalists from nearby farming districts soon followed. This installment of war refugees was only a prelude to the flood of homeless sojourners that poured into the city during subsequent phases of the war. With each military defeat, the British army lost crucial ground, until it was finally reduced to a few strongholds, including its military headquarters at New York City.[12] The ensuing influx of military personnel, white loyalists, and fugitive slaves into the occupied port town enlarged the city's already swollen population of displaced people and converted the once bustling entrepôt into an overcrowded garrison town, loyalist refugee camp, and runaway slave community.[13]

Besides functioning as the British military headquarters and strategic stronghold, New York City became a haven for fugitive slaves from many parts of British America. According to a British military census of 1779, no fewer than 12,000 runaway slaves inhabited the city, where they found a temporary sanctuary and, at that time, constituted the largest fugitive slave community in North America, with the exception, perhaps, of East Florida. By 1782, at least 4,000 runaway slaves, including nearly 1,000 black soldiers, remained in New York City.[14] An early wartime influx of runaway slaves into New York City was the result of Lord Dunmore's November 7, 1775, proclamation, declaring "all indentured Servants, Negroes, or others (appertaining to Rebels) free that are able, and willing to bear Arms, they joining His Majesty's Troops, as soon as may be, for the more speedily reducing the Colony to a proper sense of their duty, to his Majesty's Crown and Dignity."[15] An estimated 800 tidewater slaves, of which the vast majority were fugitives from patriot plantations, responded to Dunmore's appeal. To the horror of the American rebels, Dunmore armed the able-bodied male runaways and enlisted them, along with white loyalists, in a military campaign against the patriots of the tidewater region. After months of skirmishes in open fields, guerilla warfare, and other intrigues, Dunmore's depleted and demoralized army could no long muster a fight; and in November 1776, the exiled governor of Virginia, along with his band of white loyalists and runaway slaves, fled to New York City.[16] Among the military personnel who embarked from the tidewater region with Dunmore were 100 black soldiers, the remnants of his Ethiopian Regiment.[17] That military unit of runaway slaves was absorbed into the Black Brigade of New York City, a corps of black troops attached to the larger regiment of British regulars known as the Queen's Rangers.[18]

In British-occupied New York City, black soldiers, together with their families, lived in racially segregated barracks at 18 Broadway, 10 Church Street, 18 Great George Street, 8 Skinner Street, and 36 St. James Street.[19] By the winter of 1776–77, an estimated 800 black soldiers were being trained for military service on Staten Island.[20] Discipline among the black troops proved less problematic than was the case for white soldiers, since many of the black recruits, unlike white enlisted men, had been enslaved laborers in the plantation South and were already accustomed to the routinization and group cooperation required of soldiers. Desertion among black soldiers on both sides of the war was a rare occurrence. Many of the same factors that made enslaved blacks a more dependable labor force than white servants—for example, the imposition of longer terms of service and more severe punishment for misconduct—made black soldiers a more reliable fighting force than white soldiers. Moreover, few black soldiers had farms of their own to tend during harvest season, a time when the desertion rate among the white troops in the state militias and Continental Army soared. Black soldiers fought for exceptionally high stakes. The Ethiopian Regiment's slogan—"Liberty to Slaves"—declared the black soldiers' motivation in taking up arms on the British side.[21] By appropriating the guiding concept of the white American War for Independence, black soldiers, from the South and the North, expanded and radicalized the meaning of liberty to encompass the black struggle to abolish slavery.

Fearing just such a turn of events, New York patriots at first refused to arm slaves. According to a provision in New York's Militia Act of 1775, enslaved blacks, but not free blacks, were excluded from the New York militias. As a consequence of this restriction, New York enlisted fewer than a dozen black soldiers during the early years of the war. But to meet its quota of fresh recruits, the New York State Assembly later revoked its initial prohibition against arming slaves. Despite the possibility that the enslaved black population, once armed, would convert the white American War for Independence into a struggle against racial slavery, the assembly accepted that risk as an expedient solution to the military manpower shortage that arose during the protracted war and passed a law granting freedom to adult male slaves who joined the state militia. The American patriot General Philip Schuyler of the New York militia later complained that the black recruits "disgrace our arms."[22] Some New York loyalists opposed the British wartime policy of arming black men. From the British headquarters in New York City, the loyalist military officer and slaveowner Brigadier General Oliver DeLancey issued an order declaring "all Negroes Mulattos and other Improper Persons who have been admitted to the Corps be immediately discharged."[23] British officers ignored DeLancey's directive and accepted volunteers from the lowest echelon of New York's social hierarchy, including its black population. Denouncing the British practice of enlisting "irregular troops," the patriot sympathizer Henry M. Mühlenberg wrote that the "so-called Tories have assembled from various nationalities— for example, a regiment of Catholics, a regiment of Negroes, who are fitted for and inclined towards barbarities . . . lacking in human feeling and are familiar with every corner of the country."[24] British military commanders deployed black soldiers, alongside loyalist militia units, in military operations throughout Westchester County and eastern New Jersey. In 1777, the Black Brigade of New York City fought in the indecisive Battle of Monmouth. Many of the most intense battles of the war took place in the so-called neutral ground of eastern New Jersey, where a deep split between patriots and loyalists, guerrilla warfare, night raids, and other disruptions of war allowed New Jersey blacks to escape from slavery.[25] Colonel Tye, a "Jersey negro" and the leader of the Black Brigade, was more familiar with the territory of eastern New Jersey than his British commanders. In 1779 and 1780, Tye and his black troops raided patriot farms in eastern New Jersey, carried away badly needed provisions to the British side, and liberated dozens of slaves who followed their black emancipators to the environs of New York City, where they joined the community of black war refugees from other parts of British North America.[26]

Alarmed by the epidemic of slave defections and rumors of slave insurrection, New York patriots heightened their vigilance over the rebel colony's restive enslaved population.[27] Albany's Committee on the Detection and Defeating of Conspiracies imposed severe penalties on captured runaways and offered rewards to anyone who apprehended fugitive slaves and to informants who reported slave conspiracies. On June 14, 1778, the committee received a letter from Robert Yates, stating that Thomas Anderson, a white blacksmith residing on Livingston Manor, had been accused of "encouraging Negroes to desert their masters and to go over to the enemy and was also forging passes for runaway slaves under the signature of Captain Solomon Strong." The committee promptly issued a warrant for Anderson's arrest; and by June 16, 1778, Anderson was confined in Albany's jail. One year later, the committee received a rumor that Tom, the slave of Henry Hogan, was presently "endeavouring to Stir up the minds of the Negroes against their Masters and raising Insurrections among them." According to another intelligence report, Tom had been some time earlier arrested for "seducing a number of Negro slaves to join the enemy" at New York City but was subsequently released from prison and remained at large. On June 4, 1779, the committee issued a warrant for Tom's arrest, but the fugitive was never apprehended.[28]

The actions of vigilance committees did little to stem the rise of black insurgency. As the Anglo-American conflict entered its fourth year, the battle between the American patriots and the British military for the loyalty of enslaved blacks became a crucial war front. The British tendered a comprehensive offer to enslaved blacks on June 30, 1779, when Sir Henry Clinton published his Phillipsburg Proclamation, calling on the slaves of American rebels to defect to the British side in exchange for security to take up gainful employment in the British occupied territories. Clinton's declaration made an important distinction between contraband slaves who had been captured by the British army and runaway slaves who had voluntarily eloped from their patriot masters. According to that British wartime policy, the British government promised to purchase slaves who had been captured during British military campaigns and raids on patriot estates but stipulated that runaway slaves who voluntarily defected to the British side could no longer be held in bondage or sold as slaves. The Phillipsburg Proclamation stated:

> Whereas the enemy have adopted a practice of enrolling Negroes among their troops, I do hereby give Notice that all Negroes taken in Arms or upon any military Duty shall be purchased for the public service at a stated price; the money to be paid to the captors. But I do most strictly forbid any Person to sell or claim right over any Negroes the property of a Rebel who may take refuge with any part of this Army. And I do promise to every Negro who shall desert the Rebel Standard full Security to follow within the Lines any occupation which he may think proper.[29]

Clinton's appeal to the slaves threatened to deprive American patriots of their most valuable property by precipitating the mass flight of enslaved blacks to British strongholds. In an effort to contain black insurgency, patriot slaveowners warned the enslaved black population that the Phillipsburg Proclamation was a subterfuge calculated to deceive them. But this warning fell on deaf ears. Enslaved blacks interpreted Clinton's decree as an emancipation proclamation and, whenever possible, rushed to join the British side. On November 27, 1780, the *New York Mercury* nervously reported that "a desire of obtaining freedom unhappily reigns throughout the generality of slaves at present."[30] The enslaved blacks, Henry Mühlenberg remarked, "secretly wished the British army might win, for then all Negro slaves will gain their freedom. It is said that sentiment is universal amongst all the Negroes in America."[31] Although the Phillipsburg Proclamation posed no ethical objection to the institution of slavery,[32] in practical terms the British policy of offering sanctuary to runaway slaves destabilized the long-standing colonial relation of domination that had confined slave revolts to untenable, sometimes suicidal, acts of defiance. While Clinton's appeal made no explicit reference to the abolition of slavery and the opprobrium of holding human beings in lifelong, heritable bondage, it had the effect of emancipating any enslaved blacks who voluntarily deserted their patriot masters and crossed over to the British side. Facing military manpower shortages and the possibility of mass slave defections to the British side, the American patriots determined that the best course of action would be to offer freedom to some in order to secure the subordination of many. In 1779, the American Congress therefore revoked its initial policy and offered enslaved black men individual grants of freedom as a reward for enlisting in the Continental Army.[33] By 1781, black troops comprised approximately one-quarter of the Continental forces at White Plains, New York.[34] Unlike British military officers, who made more sweeping overtures to the slaves, the American Congress never issued a wholesale appeal to the entire enslaved popula-tion, for such a policy, they feared, would have been tantamount to abolishing slavery.[35]

A direct appeal to the entire enslaved population in the rebel colonies, Clinton's Phillipsburg Proclamation promised that once a fugitive slave arrived behind British lines the runaway could no longer be sold as chattel and was free to earn an independent livelihood. With this policy, the British military commander dramatically transformed the circumstances of runaway slaves. Instead of living as outlaws, fugitive slaves now found an asylum in British-occupied strongholds, where they worked as wage laborers, reunited with kin, formed new affinal and consanguineal relationships, and established independent households. Following Clinton's decree, so many slaves absconded from their masters and fled to the already overcrowded British military camps and British-occupied port towns that the flood of black refugees of war soon threatened to cripple the British war effort. In response, British military officers in New York City ordered ferrymen to deny transportation to fugitive slaves seeking passage to the city and Refugeetown at Staten Island.[36] The majority of the runaway slaves residing in New York City during the Anglo-American conflict never fought for the British military but instead aided the British war effort as civilian laborers. The Phillipsburg Proclamation, inviting runaways to take up residence behind British lines and to pursue gainful employment there, was part of Clinton's attempt to remedy the city's wartime labor shortage. The occupying army needed workers to rebuild sections of the city that were damaged when, on September 21, 1776, American incendiaries infiltrated the tinderbox town and set fire to buildings in several locations. That conflagration destroyed one-quarter of the city, including Trinity Church, the Lutheran Church, and more than 1,000 other buildings in the West Ward.[37] In addition to rebuilding the city, black refugees improved the garrison town's fortifications and labored in other tasks that were crucial to the ongoing British military operations deployed from the port of New York. As teamsters, drivers, and wagoners, they carted armaments and provisions from the city docks to magazines and storehouses about town. During the winter months, when vital goods were in short supply, the British Commissary and the Forage and Provisions Departments sent "black pioneers" on foraging expeditions in the surrounding countryside. Black pilots, who were familiar with the rivers, narrows, and bay, steered small boats to landings along riverbanks, where foraging parties collected provisions and loaded them onto vessels returning to New York City.[38] For most black refugees, wartime employment presented their first opportunity to earn wages for their labors. Black civilian laborers generally received lower wages than their white counterparts, but black soldiers and English troops received equal pay by the war's end.[39]

The contingencies of war brought together black families who had been separated under slavery and provided the conditions for the creation of new family units. With each military campaign, slaves living in the vicinity of battle took advantage of the attending confusion and escaped from their masters. A large number of runaway slaves were southerners who fled to the British strongholds of Norfolk, Savannah, and Charleston, during the disruptions of war and remained in those occupied port towns until the retreating British military forces transported them to various locations, including Bermuda, East Florida, Jamaica, maritime Canada, London, and New York City. The runaway slaves whom the British military relocated to the port of New York were housed on Staten Island in a tent city of temporary shelters known as Refugeetown and on Manhattan Island in another tent city known as "Canvas Town," located in the burnt area of the West Ward.

During the final months of the British evacuation of New York City, between April 23 and July 31, 1783, approximately 81 oceangoing vessels carried 3,000 black refugees of war from the harbor of New York.[40] The majority of these black refugees, roughly 74 percent, were transported to Nova Scotia and New Brunswick, where they founded free black communities.[41] Nearly half were southerners from the tidewater region of Virginia and Maryland and the coastal areas of South Carolina and Georgia; roughly 21 percent were from New York and New Jersey; another 9 percent were from other English colonies, mainly New England.[42] Most of the adults were in the prime of life: The mean age of adult males was 28 years, and for adult females it was 22 years. Nearly one-third of the black refugees who migrated to maritime Canada traveled in family units, a remarkable proportion, given that these families had united or reunited during the chaos of war.[43] In crossing the border dividing patriots from loyalists, enslaved from free, the flow of black refugee families into Nova Scotia and New Brunswick following the American War for Independence marked a brief yet notable reversal of the African-descended people's history of forced migration to and enslavement in the Americas. During the British evacuation, New York City continued to serve the port town function of dispersal site for population movements, notable at that time the exodus of ex-slaves to maritime Canada.

On July 31, 1783, an exemplary group of black refugees—33 men, 53 women, and 44 children—left the harbor of New York for Port Roseway, Nova Scotia, aboard the HMS *L'Abondance*. These black refugees had journeyed along similar paths that during the war converged at British-occupied New York City and at the war's end took them to the wilderness of maritime Canada. The Moore family was one of the newly constructed black families that departed on *L'Abondance*. Daniel Moore, the family head, left North Carolina in 1776, soon after the Battle of Moore's Creek Bridge, in which a patriot militia defeated a regiment of British regulars and Governor Martin's band of white loyalists and runaway slaves.[44] At that time, the British transported Daniel, along with 238 other black refugees of war, to New York City. Although Daniel adopted the surname of his former master, John Moore, he embraced his new life of independence. Daniel, age 27, married Tina, age 22, soon after his arrival at the port of New York. His wife, a fugitive slave from Portsmouth, Virginia, had escaped from her master in 1776 and in that same year left the tidewater region with other evacuees the British carried to New York City. Born free behind British lines, their daughter, Elizabeth, was only 6 years old when she traveled to Nova Scotia with her parents in 1783. Sailing with the Moores on *L'Abondance* were Cyrus Speir and his family. Daniel Moore and Cyrus followed nearly identical itineraries during the war. Like Daniel, Cyrus took advantage of the disruptions of war and made a bid for freedom. At the age of 33, he fled to the British side during the Battle of Moore's Creek Bridge, a bloody skirmish that took place near his master's farm at Cross Creek, North Carolina, in 1776 and ended with a patriot victory over British troops, white loyalists, and slaves. Also like Daniel, Cyrus kept his former master's surname and married a tidewater refugee. Following the British evacuation of Wilmington, North Carolina, in November 1781, Cyrus, now age 38, moved to New York City, where he married Judith, a fugitive slave who, at the age of 26, absconded from her master's estate near Nansemond, Virginia, during the Collier-Matthews invasion of tidewater Virginia in 1779 and in that same year traveled with her son, Frank, age 5, to New York City. In 1782, Cyrus and Judith had a daughter of their own named Patty.

A few elderly blacks sailed with the youthful black families on *L'Abondance*. Among the most noteworthy were the Hallsteads, James, age 65, and Sally, age 60, who were described as having "feeble" bodies. Responding to Lord Dunmore's appeal to the enslaved blacks of Virginia's tidewater region, James deserted his patriot master, Samuel Hallstead of Norfolk County, Virginia, and Sally left her owner, Edward Mosely of Princess Ann County, Virginia. Dunmore had addressed his appeal to able-bodied runaways who were capable of bearing arms, not elderly slaves like James and Sally Hallstead. The presence of aged and infirm runaway slaves within the British lines hampered the British war effort, as the British army was ill prepared to care for elderly and sickly refugees of war. Not surprisingly, nearly half of the total number of fugitive slaves who fled to the British side perished before the war's end. James and Sally were among the fortune runaways who survived wartime hardships. In late 1776, the Hallsteads, possibly husband and wife or perhaps brother and sister, departed Virginia with Lord Dunmore, his army, and a cadre of loyalists, temporarily resettled in New York City, and nearly seven years later sailed from the port of New York to Port Roseway, Nova Scotia, with 128 other black refugees of war. The remarkable resilience of this elderly couple and their willingness to undertake hazardous journeys in the midst of war and in the twilight of their lives attest to their enduring desire for freedom.

Like the Hallsteads, Cloe Walker, a single mother and age 23, answered Dunmore's appeal and absconded from her master, James McKay, during the loyalist retreat from Norfolk in late 1776. Soon after, Cloe and her son, Sam, age 6, were transported to New York City, where Cloe gave birth to a female infant named Lydia. The Walker family was among the 11 percent of black female-headed families that departed the harbor of New York with the British military forces at the conclusion of the war. The relatively large proportion of women among the passengers sailing on *L'Abondance* was indicative of the rise in the proportion of women in the runaway slave population during the war. Approximately 30 percent of the black refugees listed in the passenger rolls of the British sailing vessels that left the port of New York during the final days of the British evacuation were female adults,[45] whereas adult females account for no more than 6 percent of this study's sample prewar runaway slave population. Cloe Walker, other single female adults, and their children joined the phalanx of male-headed black settler families that would struggle for survival in the wilderness of maritime Canada. As ex-slaves from the plantation South, the Walkers, the Moores, the Speirs, and the Hallsteads shared a common past—and they would share a common future as the founders of the Black Atlantic communities in Nova Scotia and New Brunswick.

Northern blacks accompanied the black southerners on the voyage to maritime Canada. They, too, had constructed and reconstructed families during the Anglo-American war. The head of the Lawrence family, York, age 30, escaped from Albany, seat of New York's rebel government in 1777; his wife, Dinah, age 26, ran away from the patriot slaveowner Peter Shanerhorn of New York in that same year. By the time the young couple left New York City in 1783, they had two daughters: Betsy, age 3, and Gabriel, age 18 months. In 1778, Cornelius Van Sayl and his wife, Catherine, ran away from their patriot masters and fled to British-occupied New York City. In all probability, these fugitive slaves from Monmouth County, New Jersey, absconded from their masters during the Battle of Monmouth, in late June 1778, or perhaps during one of the loyalist raids into eastern New Jersey. Unlike many of his southern counterparts, Cornelius discarded the surname of his former master, John Lloyd, and adopted instead the Dutch patronym Van Sayl. He likewise dispensed with his English first name, James, and took the name Cornelius, a first name in common usage among Dutch-speaking settlers. Like other blacks from eastern New Jersey, the Van Sayls had contact with Dutch-speaking settlers during their enslavement and probably spoke some Dutch, if only imperfectly. Catherine's former master, John van der Veer, was a descendant of early Dutch-speaking settlers. Some time before her escape, Catherine gave birth to a female infant named Mary. This child was, perhaps, the offspring of a previous union between Catherine and Cornelius, evidence of the conjugal bond they maintained while living in separate slave-owning households. Once behind British lines, the Van Sayls united as an independent family. Only two months before their departure for Nova Scotia, Cornelius, age 30, and Catherine, age 26, had a male infant named Peter.[46] The Van Sayls, the Lawrences, and other black families from the northern colonies joined their southern counterparts on the trek to the Canadian wilderness. While a common subjection to colonial relations of domination did not efface all differences of language, religion, and other cultural particularities between the ex-slaves who built the Black Atlantic communities in Nova Scotia and New Brunswick, that shared history did forge a chain of equivalence uniting the black settlers. Finally, it was not so much *a condition in common as a consciousness in common*, a shared high regard for the value of freedom, that bound the black settlers of maritime Canada into cohesive communities.

How, then, did these ex-slaves conceptualize freedom? Published in 1798, the memoirs of Boston King—ex-slave, black refugee of war in British-occupied New York City, Methodist preacher, and leader of the Black Atlantic community at Birchtown, Nova Scotia, and, later, at Freetown, Sierra Leone—trace the journey of a modern black subject whose life intersected with the historic transformations attending the age of democratic revolutions. In this respect, his memoirs offer an insight into the concept of freedom embraced by fugitive slaves who made their way to British-occupied New York City during the war and sailed for maritime Canada at the war's end.[47] King was born in South Carolina around 1760, and by 1780 he was an enslaved apprentice living in the household of a master carpenter who moved from Charleston, South Carolina, to the countryside shortly before the British occupation of the southern port town. Not long after the British captured Charleston, a white indentured servant in his master's household rode away on a horse, which King had borrowed from a neighbor, and failed to return. King's life as a slave had taught him that slaves were defenseless against arbitrary authority. He therefore feared that he would be accused of stealing the horse and unjustly punished. King reports: "This involved me in the greatest perplexity, and I expected the severest punishment, because the gentleman to whom the horse belonged was a very bad man, and knew not how to show mercy." Rather than accept punishment for a crime he did not commit, King ran away. "To escape his cruelty," King writes, "I determined to go to Charles-Town, and throw myself into the hands of the English. They received me readily, and I began to feel the happiness of liberty of which I knew nothing before." King was among the documented 7,163 blacks that the British military forces took with them during the British evacuation of Charleston in late 1782. The majority of these black refugees of war—no fewer than 6,540 blacks—were shipped to Jamaica and East Florida, where most remained in bondage.[48] King was more fortunate, for the British transported him to New York City, where, for the first time in his life, he earned a wage as a free laborer. Though his wages were meager and sometimes nonexistent, King managed to survive in the overcrowded port town. There, he met another runaway slave named Violet, whom he married. The couple established their own household, and on July 31, 1783, they sailed for Port Roseway, Nova Scotia, on *L'Abondance* with other recently emancipated black settler families.

King's life as a free man was interrupted when some time in 1782, one year prior to his departure to maritime Canada, patriot forces captured and reenslaved him. Writing about his life as a slave in the northern town of Brunswick, New Jersey, King reports: "My master used me well as I could expect; and indeed the slaves about Baltimore, Philadelphia, and New-York, have as good victuals as many of the English; for they have meat once a day, and milk for breakfast and supper; and what is better than all, many of the masters send their slaves to school at night, that they may learn to read the Scriptures. This is a privilege indeed. But alas, all these enjoyments could not satisfy me without Liberty!" The lesson of reenslavement in a northern town taught King to regard slavery, however mild, as the antithesis of freedom. In his memoirs, King insists that he preferred a life of liberty with all its hardships to the comfortable life of the most fortunate slave. Nevertheless, he sometimes wavered in his determination to regain his freedom. When wracked with doubts, King turned to God for guidance and awaited His instructions. "As I was at prayer one Sunday evening," King writes, "I thought the Lord heard me, and would mercifully deliver me. Therefore putting my confidence in him, about one o'clock in the morning I went down to the river side, and found the guards were either asleep or in the tavern." Interpreting this opportunity to escape as a sign of divine deliverance, King crossed the river and from the shore headed for New York City, where, a short time later, he was reunited with his wife. From that moment forward, King never faltered in his conviction that God had endowed him and all human beings with a natural and inalienable right to life, liberty, and the pursuit of happiness. King credited God alone, not enlightened men, with the dispensation of civil and religious liberty.

The ideals of evangelical Protestantism, in articulation with the ideals of the Enlightenment, informed King's conceptualization of freedom and that of other acculturated American-born blacks, enslaved and free, who reached adulthood during the age of democratic revolutions.[49] The conceptualization of freedom as a divine dispensation and natural right of all humankind is iterated in nearly every slave narrative published prior to and after King's memoirs first appeared in print.[50] Importantly, the posture of humility assumed by King and other early black writers should not be confused with fatalism but was central to what Barbara Johnson calls "covert strategies of protest."[51] Concealed under the cover of their self-effacing modesty was the secret agency of black writers whose sly civility laid bare the contradictions of enlightened enslavers who professed to value freedom while keeping one-half million blacks in bondage. Like King, a substantial proportion of the enslaved black population in British North America embarked upon a journey from slavery to freedom during the white American War for Independence. In discussing the metaphors of travel through which Phillis Wheatley's poems represent the history of Africans in British North America, Johnson observes: "The voyage from life to death, from Paganism to Christianity, and from English rule to American rule are all described in terms of a passage from slavery to freedom."[52] King's memoirs replicate these homologous registers of transformative migration, except for one critical difference: The transition from English rule to American rule is no longer analogous to the passage from slavery to freedom. The geopolitical movements of runaway slaves during the white American War for Independence altered the neat parallelism structuring Wheatley's travel metaphors. For King and other black refugees of war like him, it was their relocation to the British side, not the long march toward the fulfillment of liberal democracy in the United States, that paralleled the passage from slavery to freedom. Tens of thousands of enslaved blacks were, as Wheatley had warned, "impatient of Oppression" at the hands of tyrannical slaveowners. Trusting that the Anglo-American conflict was God's sign that the moment of deliverance from bondage had arrived, they did not wait patiently for the American philosophes to manumit them but instead made their own bid for freedom by crossing over to the British side during the disruptions of war. Even blacks who were either born free or manumitted prior to the war elected to leave the new republics during the several British evacuations at the conclusion of the war rather than stay in a nation that claimed to esteem liberty yet perpetuated slavery.[53] To be sure, the black refugees of war who departed the shores of New York for Nova Scotia and New Brunswick could not be certain about their future under the English colonial government in maritime Canada and, in fact, confronted exclusionary barriers during their journey toward the attainment of full subject status in the British Commonwealth. Nevertheless, they were also acutely aware that the American victory had already brought about the reassertion of slaveowner control over the enslaved black population in the new republics.

With the American military victory, the legal status of black refugees of war became the object of controversy in the final contest of power between the Americans and the British. In the midst of the British evacuation of

New York City, patriot slaveowners rushed to the port of New York to claim runaway slaves who either had already boarded or were waiting to board British vessels scheduled to leave the shores of the new republic. The appearance of the American slaveowners, Boston King writes, "filled us with inexpressible anguish and terror, especially when we saw our old masters coming from Virginia, North-Carolina, and other parts, and seizing upon their slaves in the streets of New-York, or even dragging them from their beds. Many of the slaves had very cruel masters, so that the thoughts of returning home with them embittered life to us. For some days we lost our appetite for food, and sleep departed from our eyes."[54] This violent seizure of black refugees threatened to turn the British evacuation of New York City into a drama of anarchy and despair. Demanding the return of the runaway slaves who were preparing to depart New York's harbor on British sailing vessels, American slaveowners reminded the British military authorities that the Treaty of Paris forbade the British from removing any enslaved blacks belonging to American citizens. Article Seven of the Treaty of Paris stipulated: "His Brittanic Majesty shall with all convenient speed, and without causing any destruction or carrying away any Negroes or other property of the American inhabitants, withdraw all his armies, garrisons and fleets from the said United States, and from every port, place and harbour within the same."[55] Though the terms of the evacuation were clear, they ran counter to the wartime proclamations that promised freedom to runaway slaves who voluntarily defected to the British side.[56] Writing from New York City on June 17, 1783, Adjutant General Carl Leopold Baurmeister of the Hessian forces reported: "General Clinton's repeated proclamations while he was the chief in command permitted the negroes to leave their plantations and follow the army. Half of them are no longer alive, and the greater part of the rest have gone on board the ships. The small number still here refuse to be delivered in so unwarrantable a manner. They insist on their rights under the proclamation, and General Carleton protects these slaves, although those who desire to return may do so."[57] Sir Guy Carleton, the Commander-in-Chief in charge of the British evacuation, insisted that all blacks who had taken up residence behind the British lines before November 30, 1782, the date on which the Americans and the British signed the preliminary provisions of the Treaty of Paris, were exempt from the peace accord's stipulation requiring the British to return the Americans' slave property. In short, Carleton maintained that the blacks in question had been emancipated by the several British proclamations before any pact between the Americans and the British had been signed.[58] Anticipating this policy, British military officers had already issued travel certificates (or passports) to blacks who stated that they had voluntarily fled to the British side before November 30, 1782. Known as "Birch Certificates," these documents read: "This is to certify to whomsoever it may concern, that the Bearer hereof _____ a Negro, resorted to the British Lines, in consequence of the Proclamations of Sir William Howe, and Sir Henry Clinton, late Commanders in Chief in America; and that the said Negro has hereby his Excellency Sir Guy Carleton's Permission to go to Nova-Scotia, or wherever else _____ may think proper. By Order of Brigadier General Birch."[59]

Having received several letters protesting the British intent to carry away runaway slaves, General George Washington, commander of the victorious Continental Army, requested a meeting with General Carleton. On May 6, 1783, the two military leaders met at Orangetown, New Jersey, to discuss the disputed runaway slaves. In that conference, General Washington complained about the indiscriminate distribution of passports allowing blacks to embark with the British fleet and demanded the return of runaway slaves whom American slaveowners claimed as their property. In response to Washington's ultimatum, Carleton insisted that the British army's liberation of runaway slaves conformed to recognized rules of war and reaffirmed his intention to honor the several British proclamations promising freedom to runaway slaves who escaped to the British lines, adding his assurance that, should the British government later repudiate his decision, American slaveowners would be compensated for the loss of their slave property.[60] Carleton had already convened a joint board of American and British commissioners empowered to hear and adjudicate the claims of slaveowners who alleged the British were protecting runaway slaves who had not arrived behind British lines before November 30, 1782, and were, nonetheless, preparing to leave with the British fleet. New York State Attorney-General Egbert Benson, Lieutenant-Colonel William Smith, and Daniel Parker Esq. represented the American slaveowners' interest; Captain Armstrong, Major Phillips, and Captain Coke represented the British interest in keeping their pledge to the black loyalists. The board of inquiry convened at Fraunces Tavern on Wednesdays between 10 and 2 o'clock.[61]

On July 24, 1783, Gerard Beeckman, an American patriot and resident of New York City, petitioned the board of inquiry for the return of his slave property—a boy named Peter and a girl named Elizabeth. These children, along with their father, Samuel Dobson, had boarded a British vessel waiting for permission to embark for Nova Scotia. Beeckman submitted a deed for the two children, substantiating his claim to ownership. The document showed that Beeckman's father-in-law, Pierre Van Cortlandt of the Manor Van Cortlandt in Westchester County, had, in 1777, given Peter and Elizabeth to his daughter Cornelia, the claimant's wife. Beeckman informed the board that, in April 1778, Samuel Dobson had kidnapped the children from Van Cortlandt Manor, where Beeckman's wife and slaves had resided during the war, and that Dobson had brought the youngsters to New York City. Because Beeckman presented a legal title to the black children and because Dobson confirmed that he had removed the youths from the Van Cortlandt estate, the board ordered that Beeckman be "permitted to take and dispose of them as he may think proper." In this summary manner, the Dobson family, only recently reunited, was separated once again.

Nine days earlier, Dobson was himself the object of a case before the board of inquiry. On July 15, 1783, Doctor Abraham Teller of Westchester County, New York, petitioned the board for the return of his slave, Samuel Dobson. Four witnesses appeared before the board on the claimant's behalf. Samuel Hake testified that, in April 1782, he had told Teller that he desired to purchase a slave and that Teller had responded that he owned a black man whom he wished to dispose of. Hake also testified that, one month later, he made a further inquiry to the claimant's brothers regarding the legal status of the black man Teller had proposed to sell him and that the claimant's brothers, then loyalist residents of New York City, confirmed that Dobson was the claimant's property. A second witness, Stephen Stephens, stated that he had resided in the same house with Abraham Teller from 1778 to 1782, and during that time Dobson had lived under Teller's care and worked for the claimant as a slave. According to Stephens's testimony, Dobson had gone on a privateering cruise with the claimant's consent. Two of Abraham Teller's long-time acquaintances also testified that Dobson was the claimant's slave. One of these witnesses, William Miller, stated that nearly 12 years earlier he had inoculated Dobson against smallpox at Teller's farm in Westchester County and that he had "always looked upon [Dobson] to belong to the claimant [Teller]." Finally, Teller asserted that together, as master and slave, he and Dobson had moved to New York City and that he had later given his slave permission to join the crew of a British privateering vessel.

Dobson never denied that he had been a slave, but his narrative and, in particular, his account of how he arrived behind British lines differed from the claimant's story in several crucial details. Dobson explained that he was not the property of Abraham Teller but the slave of Teller's mother, Allida Teller of Teller's Point in Westchester County, New York. Dobson claimed that Abraham Teller departed Westchester County alone some time before April 1778. He also claimed that he had been left to care for the farm at Teller's Point and that he had been "ill used" by the local patriots and, as a consequence of these abuses, had determined to flee to the British lines at New York City. He further testified that his mistress had given him permission to quit Teller's Point and that, in April 1778, he had boarded a British galley commanded by Captain Clarke. Finding that the vessel was headed upriver, he later boarded a sloop tethered to the *Phoenix*, a British man-of-war headed downriver to the city. Dobson admitted that Abraham Teller happened to be on the same sloop but added that he had been on the vessel for three days before he became aware of Teller's presence there and that he had no communication with his ex-mistress's son during the trip to the city. Dobson's counternarrative thus rested on his assertion that he had left his former mistress on his own volition, that he had relocated to British-occupied New York City alone, not in the company of Abraham Teller, and that he had arrived behind the British lines before November 30, 1782. The contested facts of this case made a judgment difficult. After the witnesses had been heard, one of the American commissioners, Lieutenant-Colonel Smith, asked Teller whether he considered himself a subject of Great Britain or a citizen of the new republic. Teller answered that he considered himself a subject of the King of England. Upon hearing Teller's profession of loyalty to the English monarch, the American commissioners indicated that they had no interest in the claim of a loyalist. The board, then, referred the dispute to the discretion of Brigadier General Samuel Birch, the commandant of New York City under British occupation, who subsequently refused to nullify the passport previously issued to Samuel Dobson. The ex-slave was, therefore, free to leave New York—but, as the fate of young Peter and Elizabeth would have it, without his two children.

Black refugees also initiated cases brought before the joint commission. On

May 30, 1783, A. [Toney] Bartram petitioned the board of inquiry for the release of his daughter, Nancy, who at that time was being detained by Henry Rogers in a dwelling on Queen Street. Bartram and his two daughters—Nancy and Flora—held passports issued by Captain Nathan Hubell of the British army some time after July 1779, when the Bartram family fled to the British side. But in the summer of 1783, Rogers seized Nancy in order to return the girl to her former master in Connecticut. Rogers was one of the many opportunists who had taken up the occupation of "Negro catcher," a lucrative vocation during the final months of the British evacuation.[62] In view of the fact that Rogers presented no evidence to discredit the assumption that Nancy had arrived within the British lines prior to November 30, 1782, and that she had done so on her own volition, the commissioners ordered the slave catcher to set the black girl at liberty and "not to detain her any longer contrary to her Inclinations." Far luckier was A. [Toney] Bartram than Samuel Dobson, who lost his children to an American slaveowner.[63]

The criteria used in the validation of the coveted passports are also evident in cases initiated by white loyalists. For example, William Ferrer, a loyalist, claimed that Dinah Archer was his property and ought to be surrendered to him. At the hearing before the board of inquiry, Dinah submitted her passport, which stated: "The Bearer Dinah Archer being a free Negro has the Commandant's permission to pass from this Garrison to whatever Place she may think Proper." Upon examination by the members of the board of inquiry, Dinah confessed that she, in truth, had been formerly the slave of John Bayne of Crane Island in Norfolk County, Virginia, and that she had been sold to William Ferrer, the claimant, in whose household she had resided for nearly three years before Ferrer abandoned her and moved to England.[64] After Ferrer's departure, Dinah inquired about her legal status to Bayne, her previous owner. Bayne informed Dinah that he had not given Ferrer a bill of sale for her and then compelled the black woman to return to his household, where she remained until 1780, when she ran away from her captor and fled to a nearby British camp. In 1779, Dinah, along with other tidewater blacks, left Virginia for New York City with Sir George Collier and General Matthews of the British army. After hearing Dinah's revised story, the board of inquiry referred the dispute between the runaway slave and William Ferrer to the British commandant of New York City, who subsequently refused to invalidate Dinah's passport. In accordance with British policy, Dinah was entitled to the benefits of the British proclamations regarding runaway slaves, because she now stated that she had left her master *proprio motu*, on her own volition, and had arrived behind British lines before November 30, 1782. Since Dinah had confessed to having lied about her previous condition of servitude, the British military authorities perhaps doubted the veracity of her most recent story. But the British commandant's belief in Dinah's credibility was a less decisive factor in his final judgment than the fact that Dinah's narrative, whether true or false, conformed to the logic allowing the British military authorities to validate the passports granted to black refugees.[65]

All of the cases before the board of inquiry turned on the issue of volition and timing. If the black refugee could effectively narrate a tale of self-emancipation and of timely self-removal to the British side prior to November 30, 1782, then the passport granting the black refugee permission to leave the port of New York with the British fleet remained valid. It was, therefore, this generalizable narrative representation of the black wartime experience that secured fugitive slaves the benefits of the British proclamations and the travel certificates that would become their passports to freedom. During the final phase of the British evacuation of New York City, fugitive slaves became free subjects in and through the narration of stories of wartime flight from slavery that conformed to the legal-rational logic governing the validation of passports that the British military authorities issued to black refugees of war.[66] In this respect, fugitive slave narratives constituted an emancipatory discourse that installed the runaway slave as a modern subject endowed with the faculty of reason and hence the capacity for rational self-determination.

The fugitive slaves who sided with the British during the Anglo-American conflict did so not principally out of loyalty to England or any other nation but out of a high esteem for the value of freedom forged during a history of enslavement and subjection to other relations of domination in the English overseas colonies. Though dubbed "followers of the Army and Flag," these black war refugees belonged to no nation. The historical trajectory of the Black Atlantic communities that they founded in maritime Canada and later in Sierra Leone exceeded the boundaries of the modern nation-state even as, at crucial junctures, they crisscrossed and intersected with that emerging geopolitical formation. The recently emancipated black settlers who migrated to the Canadian wilderness at the war's end were but a fraction of the tens of thousands of slaves who either defected to the British side, escaped over land to the northwest frontier, or fled on sailing vessels to unknown destinations during the Anglo-American war. Even though the British military leaders who authored the appeals addressed to the enslaved black population in British North America never intended to emancipate so many slaves, they were powerless to determine the meaning enslaved blacks would draw from their proclamations and to curtail the wave of black insurgency precipitated by the war. Similarly, the American patriots never intended their slogan of liberty to extend further than the white settler revolt against English colonial rule. Yet by taking up the cause of liberty, thousands of enslaved blacks disregarded the American patriots' intention and pursued their own bid for freedom. Liberty, like a sponge not yet saturated with the plenitude of finite and fixed meaning, expanded to buoy the radical freedom struggle of enslaved blacks during the War for Independence and beyond. Because the victory of the white American independence movement did not result in the thorough dissolution of colonial relations of domination in the newly constituted republics that would soon become the United States, future emancipatory practices in that modern nation-state would crucially involve challenges to the perpetuation of black slavery, the binary racial formation of white over black, and other enduring legacies of the nation's colonial past.

Epilogue

"What to the Slave Is the Fourth of July?"

THE APORIA OF AMERICAN DEMOCRACY AND
THE PERMANENCE OF RACISM

The ex-slaves who evacuated New York City at the war's end left behind kinfolk and friends who remained in bondage in the new republics that would become the United States of America. The perpetuation of slavery in the former British North American colonies called into question the fledgling nation's dedication to the Enlightenment values of freedom and human progress, and soon opened a field of hegemonic struggle between proslavery and antislavery blocs. Whereas Vermont swiftly outlawed human bondage in 1777, the other northern states, including New York, dismantled the institution of slavery gradually, over several decades and only after protracted deliberations. With the exception of Virginia, whose citizens debated doomed legislation for the abolition of slavery and the slave trade, the southern states firmly rejected proposals for the emancipation of the South's numerous and valuable slave property. Because separate state legislatures and, in the case of Massachusetts, a state court determined the status of slavery in the individual states, an undivisive national policy on slavery proved difficult to achieve.[1]

During the summer of 1787, the states, except Rhode Island, sent representatives to Philadelphia, where the delegates drafted a federal constitution that guaranteed, its advocates argued, the nation's future stability. Of the several compromises reached at the Philadelphia convention, none revealed the aporia of American democracy, the contradictory gap between the philosophical premises of its foundational text and the statements contained in that same text, more aptly than the compromise inscribed in Article I, Section 2 of the U.S. Constitution. That article stipulated: The slaves counted as three-fifths of persons in the formula for computing the numerical apportionment of state seats in the House of Representatives and three-fifths of property in the formula for determining direct taxes.[2] In the debate over the so-called three-fifths clause, Gouverneur Morris, delegate from Pennsylvania and opponent of slavery, pointed out the apparent illogic of the controversial article and in doing so underscored the contradiction of perpetuating slavery in an averred modern democratic nation. "Upon what principle is it that the slaves be computed in the representation? Are they men?" he asked. "Then make them citizens & let them vote. Are they property? Why then is no other property included?"[3] Recognizing the import of Morris's trenchant questions yet urging the ratification of the proposed federal constitution, James Madison defended the logic of the seemingly troublesome clause and exposed the fallacy of reductive arguments that assumed slaves must be either only chattel, having no personality under the law, or persons, having the right to vote as citizens: "But we must deny the fact that slaves are considered merely as property, and in no respect whatever persons. The true state of the case is that they partake of both these qualities: being considered by our laws, in some respect as persons, and in others as property."[4] To assure the public that the authors of the Constitution had not compounded the national dilemma of slavery, Madison argued that Article I, Section 2 followed sound reasoning by applying the rule of context to resolve the apparent conundrum of the slaves' "mixed character." He pointed out that in the context of representation the article assigned the slaves to the single category "persons" and in the context of taxation to the distinct category "property." In this way, the article wisely included, Madison added, the opposing interests of the slave and the free states, a mechanism of "control and balance" that would guarantee, he predicted, the future stability of the nation.[5] Madison's brilliant arguments in this and other constitutional debates prevailed; and by 1788, the states, except for North Carolina and Rhode Island, had ratified the U.S. Constitution. However, some prominent white Americans believed that by failing to abolish slavery the framers of the federal constitution had not only compounded a troubling contradiction but also tolerated a national sin that would be punished by a national disaster.

From the early national period through to the Civil War, an escalating crisis over the territorial expansion of human bondage in the United States and the specter of slave insurrection cast doubt on the survival of the nation and the credibility of American democracy. Moreover, the future geopolitical development of the United States involved the exclusion of free blacks from the rights of U.S. citizenship, the appropriation of Native American lands, and the conquest of Mexican territory with westward expansion, as well as the accumulation of wealth through the exploitation of enslaved black laborers. Thus the history of the United States in the guise of "manifest destiny" remained entangled with the history of colonialism and its relations of racial domination. Nevertheless, most white citizens confidently celebrated their freedom and prosperity, just as their forefathers had done during the earliest days of independence from English colonial rule.

A little-known commemorative engraving discloses the entailments of colonialism that patriotic celebrations of national independence ceremoniously disavowed.[6] That engraving depicts a parade along Broadway, held on November 25, 1783, to welcome General Washington and the victorious Continental Army into New York City following the final British evacuation. At the engraving's center, a heroic George Washington, mounted on horseback, leads his troops down the "Great White Way."[7] Assembled along each side of the street, a crowd of American patriots and their families frames the military procession. This scene would convey an uninterrupted image of a racially homogeneous nation, united in celebration of its unfettered freedom, but for two visible reminders of colonialism's legacy of the racial subordination of Native Americans and African Americans. Near the bottom left edge of the engraving, a lone Indian, clearly differentiated from the crowd by his native costume, squats on the street. This particularized image of the Native American—specifically, the representation of the Indian's dress and posture—recalls the native population's resistance to cultural assimilation and subsequent marginalization on the fringes of the dominant white society. In the midst of the crowd, on the opposite side of the street, stands another figure, dressed in ordinary workingmen's attire and differentiated from the mass assemblage of citizens only by his darker skin color. Representing the black presence in the United States, the figure of the black workingman disrupts the otherwise continuous image of white patriots rejoicing at the birth of a new nation. With these contrasting figures—the Indian and the Negro—the engraving suggests that the black population is insinuated within the nation in a way the native population is not. Consigned to the oblivion of timeless myth, the "(ig)noble savage" takes no active part in celebrating the nation's present and, by implication, creating its future.[8] On the other hand, the black workingman is at once integral to yet potentially disruptive of the new nation and its unfolding destiny.

Interestingly, the Evacuation Day engraving anticipates famous passages from Alexis de Tocqueville's *Democracy in America*, in which the French aristocrat and social commentator expresses his misgivings about the future of a democratic society divided into three separate races—African, European, and Indian.[9] "Chance has brought them together on the same soil," Tocqueville writes, "but they have mixed without combining, and each follows a separate destiny."[10] Addressing the status of the Indian and the African in the United States, Tocqueville observes: "Both occupy an equally inferior position in the land where they dwell; both suffer the effects of tyranny, and, though their afflictions are different, they have the same people to blame for them." According to Tocqueville, the Indians successfully resisted cultural imperialism but sustained devastating military defeat and finally retreated to the margins of American society, where they spent a largely autonomous yet uncivilized life. "The moral and physical condition of these peoples," he writes, "has constantly deteriorated, and in becoming more wretched, they have also become more barbarous. Nevertheless, the Europeans have not been able to change the character of the Indians entirely, and although they can destroy them, they have not been able to establish order or to subdue them." In Tocqueville's view, the African suffered a vastly different yet equally tragic fate: "The United States Negro has lost even the memory of his homeland; he has abjured their religion and forgotten their mores. Ceasing to belong to Africa, he has acquired no right to the blessings of Europe; he is left in suspense between two societies and isolated between two peoples, sold by one and repudiated by the other; in the whole world there is nothing but his master's hearth to provide him with some semblance of a homeland." For Tocqueville, the North American Indian was a race condemned to an abject existence outside the boundaries of the dominant white society and culture, while the U.S. Negro was a race stranded between two worlds.

Turning to the glaring contradiction of American democracy, Tocqueville insists that white Americans had erred in keeping the Negro race in bondage in the midst of a democratic society: "They first violated every right of humanity by their treatment of the Negro and then taught him the value and inviolability of those rights. They have opened their ranks to their slaves, but when they tried to come in, they drove them out again with ignominy. Wishing to have servitude, they have nevertheless been drawn against their will or unconsciously toward liberty, without the courage to be either completely wicked or entirely just." Alluding to the threat of slave insurrection and the impending national crisis of civil war, Tocqueville predicts that the United States cannot resolve the subversive aporia of the coexistence of slavery and freedom without violent conflict. "Slavery, amid the democratic liberty and enlightenment of our age," he writes, "is not an institution that can last. Either the slave or the master will put an end to it. In either case great misfortunes are to be anticipated." A witness to the French Revolution and its terror, Tocqueville was able to make a number of astute observations about the dangers facing democracies, including the difficulty of abolishing the artificial inequalities that were deeply sedimented in the mores of the people. Reasoning from analogy, Tocqueville draws a comparison between, on the one hand, the French aristocracy and, on the other, white Americans, whose superior privileges were not only codified in law and legitimated as age-old tradition but also grounded in naturalized racial hierarchies. "If inequality created by the law alone is so hard to eradicate, how is one to destroy that which also seems to have immovable foundations in nature herself?" he asks. "I plainly see," he adds, "that in some parts of the country [the United States] the legal barrier between the two races is tending to come down, but not that of mores. I see that slavery is in retreat, but the prejudice from which it arose is unmovable." If the citizens of the United States were to achieve an uncompromised democracy, they must, Tocqueville concludes, not only abolish the legal institution of slavery but also the customary privileges that conferred upon white Americans a status akin to a hereditary aristocracy.

Tocqueville published his famous passages on the U.S. racial dilemma in 1835. Eight years earlier, the New York State Assembly passed a statute outlawing slavery within the jurisdiction of New York. But in 1835 a black man named Caesar was still enslaved in a New York family whose custom of owning slaves was, like an aristocratic privilege, passed from one generation to the next. Caesar's condition of bondage was never merely a matter of law but was also a matter of the traditional prerogatives of a social class habituated to exercising mastery over racially subordinated others. Born a slave in 1737, on a manorial estate known as Bethlehem and located eight miles south of Albany, Caesar became a trusted household slave who, in addition to his daily chores, drove the sleigh that each year transported his master's family to New York City for the winter holiday. At age 30, Caesar was entrusted with the duty of caring for his master, who, at the age of 60, lapsed into senility and slept in a sturdy oak cradle over six feet long. After his master's accidental drowning, Caesar became the slave of his late master's eldest son, who died in 1817. By that time, Caesar was 80 years old. A quite elderly man yet robust in health, Caesar lived another 35 years as the slave of his first master's grandson. Caesar's third master relieved him of his duties but never informed him that an act of the New York State Assembly had freed him, effective July 4, 1827. Caesar lived out the rest of his life unaware of the demise of slavery in New York and in 1852, at the age of 115 years, died in the place of his birth.[11]

Eleven years after Caesar's death, the U.S. Civil War brought about the emancipation of the nearly four million enslaved blacks who, by the 1860s, resided in the southern states. On April 14, 1865, when triumphant Union troops raised the federal flag over Fort Sumter, defeated citadel of the Confederacy, and marched through the streets of Charleston, South Carolina, that city's black population celebrated the long-awaited deliverance from bondage. That same day, Corporal C. J. Howard befriended a 109-year-old black man, who had been born a slave in the Carolina low country. A near contemporary of Caesar, the New York slave from Bethlehem Manor, the elderly black southerner told Corporal Howard that "he had served his master's children's children, that he had been praying 75 years for the war to come and God had answered his prayers at last."[12] Only 20 years old at the time of the publication of the Declaration of Independence on July 4, 1776, the date that white Americans commemorated during the annual celebrations of their freedom from British tyranny, he would have to wait four score and nine years to celebrate his own liberation from the tyranny of the white American slaveocracy.

What value, then, did slaves, like Caesar and Corporal Howard's southern friend, attach to patriotic celebrations of the nation's liberty prior to the abolition of slavery throughout the United States?

In a caustic oration, delivered in Rochester, New York, on July 5, 1852, to commemorate the twenty-fifth anniversary of the abolition of slavery in New York, Frederick Douglass, ex-slave and black abolitionist, posed the question: "What to the Slave Is the Fourth of July?"[13] Putting himself in the position of the slave,[14] Douglass stated: "I shall see this day and its popular characteristics from the slave's point of view. Standing here, identified with the American bondman, making his wrongs mine, I do not hesitate to declare, with all my soul, that the character and conduct of the nation never looked blacker to me than on this Fourth of July. Whether we turn to the declarations of the past, or to the professions of the present, the conduct of the nation seems equally hideous and revolting. America is false to the past, false to the present, and solemnly binds herself to be false to the future." Douglass thus observed that, from the slave's vantage point, American democracy was a fraud perpetrated from the moment of its founding. It would remain so, he insisted, as long as the nation preserved slavery in any part of its territory. In his oration, Douglass invited the audience to follow his example and enter into a process of identification with the slave and, from the slave's standpoint, critically assess the limits of the nation's commitment to democratic principles.[15] Refusing to lend dignity to the proslavery argument, which asserted that the Negro lacked the capacity to reason, was hence not truly a human being, and therefore justly enslaved, Douglass refrained from directly arguing the contrary and instead pointed out that the slave's humanity had already been recognized in the laws of the southern states.[16] Douglass noted: "It is admitted in the fact that Southern statute-books are covered with enactments, forbidding under severe fines and penalties, the teaching of the slave to read or write. When you can point to any such laws in reference to the beasts of the field, then I may consent to argue the manhood of the slave." In this way, Douglass exposed the aporia of American democracy.

Regarded as *anticitizens*, whose presence at white Independence Day festivities was deemed to be a desecration of the pure body politic that enjoyed the pleasures of full national belonging,[17] black New Yorkers transformed their exclusion from patriotic celebrations into a political weapon. Standing before the Rochester audience on July 5, Douglass delivered his oration as if he were speaking on the Fourth of July and thereby demonstrated that white Americans did not monopolize the capacity for holding freedom in high esteem and paying tribute to its blessings. Although the process of gradual emancipation in New York State commenced on July 4, 1799, and the abolition of slavery in New York was officially completed on July 4, 1827,[18] black New Yorkers postponed by one day their annual freedom observances and set aside July fifth to celebrate and, importantly, to stage public critiques of a nation that professed to value liberty yet countenanced the enslavement of millions of southern blacks and the extension of slavery into newly organized territories of the United States. By doing so, they called attention to the deferral of universal freedom in the United States. Black New Yorkers of the antebellum era not only criticized the dominant white political culture but also displayed transnational identifications by holding annual celebrations of Haitian Independence Day (January 1, 1804), the abolition of the African slave trade by England, Denmark, and the United States (January 1, 1808), and the emancipation of the slaves in the British West Indies (August 1, 1834).[19] Within nineteenth-century New York's black political culture, watershed events in the expansion of democracy taking place outside the geopolitical borders of the United States were just as worthy of commemoration as seemingly local events, such as the abolition of slavery in New York State and John Brown's raid on Harper's Ferry. In this respect, black New Yorkers linked their political struggle with a broader history of progress and human emancipation. This articulation of local and global democratic movements would become a hallmark of black radicalism in New York and throughout the Black Atlantic world.[20]

With the ratification of the Thirteenth Amendment to the Constitution, which in 1865 abolished slavery in the entire territory of the United States, and subsequent civil rights amendments, which were promulgated to protect the liberty of recently emancipated black citizens and their descendants, many contemporaries believed that the nation had finally aligned its laws with its philosophical foundations and thereby eliminated the aporia of American democracy. Yet during the postemancipation period, evidence of the intransigence of antiblack racism—for example, the rise of lynching and the introduction of Jim Crow laws—engendered real doubts about the nation's devotion to democratic principles and set the stage for the proliferation of volatile political antagonisms during the twentieth century. By the 1960s, the United States, the same nation that had fought two costly wars to save democracy in Europe, was paradoxically engaged in an imperialist war in Vietnam and seemed reluctant to ensure the expansion of democracy at home. In an essay titled "Fifth Avenue, Uptown: A Letter from Harlem" and published in 1960, the black New Yorker and expatriate writer James Baldwin calls attention to the use of military manpower to enforce U.S. domestic and foreign policies of white supremacy. Drawing an analogy between the white policeman in Harlem and the invading U.S. soldier in a foreign territory, Baldwin writes: "He moves through Harlem, therefore, like an occupying soldier in a bitterly hostile country; which is precisely what, and where, he is, and is the reason he walks in two and threes. And he is not the only one who knows why he is always in company; the people who are watching him know why, too. Any street meeting, sacred or secular, which he and his colleagues uneasily cover, has as its explicit or implicit burden the cruelty of white domination. And these days, of course, in terms increasingly vivid and jubilant, it speaks of the end of that domination. The white policeman standing on a Harlem street corner finds himself at the center of the revolution now occurring in the world."[21] In Baldwin's view, the white policeman in Harlem faced a native liberation movement against internal colonialism within U.S. domestic borders. Just as the black abolitionists of the antebellum era had linked the freedom struggle in the United States with the Haitian Revolution, Baldwin regarded the twentieth-century independence movements in Africa, Asia, and Latin America and the U.S. black civil rights and black power movements of the post–World War II era as a continuous anticolonial revolution.

During his 1962 tour of six major West African cities, Baldwin became acutely sensible to the complex and pervasive entailments of colonialism. After completing that trip, Baldwin wrote "Down on the Cross," an essay condemning the West's colonialist legacy of race-thinking and its obstruction of alternative formations of peoplehood throughout the world: "What one would not like to see again," Baldwin writes, "is the consolidation of peoples on the basis of their color. But as long as we in the West place on color the value that we do, we make it impossible for the great unwashed to consolidate themselves according to any other principle. Color is not a human or a personal reality; it is a political reality. But this is a distinction so extremely hard to make that the West has not been able to make it yet."[22] Baldwin insisted that white Americans must first re-examine their values and undergo a radical transformation of consciousness amounting to the abolition of the racial binarism of white over black, before the United States could accomplish any good in undertaking its expansive role in world affairs. Baldwin believed that the color line, which W. E. B. Du Bois famously called the "problem of the twentieth century," was a "fearful and delicate problem, which compromises, where it does not corrupt, all the American efforts to build a better world—here, there, or anywhere." Convinced that racism had distorted American democracy in the realm of foreign as well as domestic policy, Baldwin lamented: "The American dream has therefore become something much more resembling a nightmare, on the private, domestic, and international levels." Baldwin therefore urged Americans, both blacks and whites, "to end the racial nightmare, and achieve our country, and change the history of the world."

Despite the achievements of the U.S. black civil rights and black power movements, the color line, grounded in centuries-old beliefs and customs, proved more difficult to abolish than racial domination, grounded in law alone. Whereas the legal institution of slavery and Jim Crow laws once assured white Americans, regardless of their class position, a status akin to an aristocracy of skin color, the customary privileges of whiteness, deeply rooted in the mores of the nation and transplanted everywhere the United States implemented imperialist policies, were now primarily maintained by a racist culture, not by statute. Ending what Baldwin called the "racial nightmare" thus appeared as an ever-receding horizon. The apparent intransigency of racist culture in the late twentieth century led some intellectuals of that era to conclude that antiblack racism is a permanent bulwark stabilizing U.S. liberal democracy in spite of gross imbalances in the distribution of wealth.[23] The eminent law professor Derrick Bell has written: "Racism in America is not a curable aberration—as all believed at some earlier point. Rather, it is a key component in this country's stability. Identifying vicariously with those at the top, obsessed with barring blacks from eroding their racial priority for jobs and other resources, most whites accept their own relatively low social status. This acceptance is a major explanation why there is neither turmoil nor much concern about the tremendous disparity in income, wealth, and opportunity separating those at the top of the economic heap and the many, many down toward the bottom."[24] Bell's point is not that the permanence of racism reflects a natural disposition of humankind. Rather, antiblack racism is, in Bell's view, a disciplinary mechanism of elite rule, which sustains U.S. liberalism and its global expansion in the face of flagrant social inequality throughout the world. This is not to say that all conceptions of race are inescapably racist. After all, the discursive construction of a hierarchy of superior and inferior races that naturalizes social inequality is a contingent rather than a necessary feature of race-thinking. Antiracist movements have sometimes embraced the concept "race" as the foundation of their political struggles without endorsing racism. But, as Bell points out, "If we are to seek new goals for our struggles, we must first reassess the worth of the racial assumptions on which, without careful thought, we have presumed too much and relied on too long."[25]

Although the biological validity of race has been largely discredited, the political value of race remains severely inflated. It is, perhaps, precisely because race no longer means something biological but something political that race-thinking continues to operate as a seemingly indispensable way of knowing the world. Paul Gilroy writes, "Raciology has saturated the discourse in which it circulates. It cannot be readily re-signified or de-signified, and to imagine that its dangerous meanings can be easily re-articulated into benign, democratic forms would be to exaggerate the power of critical and oppositional interests. In contrast, the creative acts involved in destroying raciology and transcending 'race' are more than warranted by the goal of authentic democracy to which they point. The political will to liberate humankind from race-thinking must be complemented by precise historical reasons why these attempts are worth making."[26] Problematizing the history of race-thinking is especially crucial to the prospects of emancipatory projects in liberal democracies that disavow the salience of race and consign racism to the past, even as it surreptitiously operates as a durable instrument of elite rule. Positioned at the exit of the twentieth century and gazing out at the opening of the twenty-first, the distinguished historian David Brion Davis observed, "Although political rhetoric often conceals this truth, as we complete the twentieth century and prepare to enter a new millennium, no issue in America is as sensitive, potentially explosive, and resistant to resolution as the issue of race. To understand the meaning of race in the future, we must first uncover the historical and cultural contexts of the past in which separate human races were conceived."[27] In keeping with that project, the aim of this study has been to interrogate the history of racial formation in New York City during the early modern era of colonialist expansionism and the rise of merchant capitalism. This study shows that the enslavement of black Africans and the installation of the enslaver and the enslaved into relationally constituted racial subject-positions was not an "unthinking decision," as Winthrop Jordan has characterized it,[28] but a failure to think in any terms except the reductive categories of black and white. The broader goal of this monograph has been to problematize that familiar way of knowing by disclosing how, historically, the commonsensical construction of superior and inferior races legitimated social inequality in colonial New York City and how antiblack racism operated as a disciplinary mechanism of governance that stabilized colonial rule in that factious port town.[29]

Although the discourse of American exceptionalism disavows this fact, a historical stemma connects our neocolonial present to our colonial past. In contemporary New York City, the entailments of colonialism and its material and ideal relations of domination sustain a racist culture, in which a ruling elite exercises power on a truly global scale, governs according to the pure reason of capitalist profit, and obtains the consent of the governed through disciplinary mechanisms, some new and others centuries old. Although we have entered a new epoch of global capitalism and transnational migration, "the net of racial politics," Arjun Appadurai observes, "is now cast wider than ever before on the streets of the urban United States."[30] As the Haitian, Colombian, and West African immigrants of present-day New York City well know, compulsory identifications still assign newcomers to binary racial categories. Certainly, breaking the white/black binary, which has for so long structured much of U.S. race-thinking, requires more than plugging the nonwhite immigrants of the post-1960s period into the equation of U.S. multiculturalism or wrapping the old politics of liberal pluralism in a new hybridized ideological integument. Even alternative racial classification systems that posit intermediate and mixed racial positions produce their own binary formations.[31] As Lewis Gordon points out, "Every 'in-between' is a whiteness or a blackness waiting to emerge. . . . Either one is categorized as white due to one's apparent distance from blackness or one is categorized as black due to one's apparent distance from whiteness."[32] Such are the historical entailments of the colonial past and its legacy of binary, black-and-white race-thinking. Given the hold binary race-thinking has on the political imaginary, it seems reasonable to propose that liberating the imagination from that way of knowing the world is one of the most urgent tasks of the twenty-first century. This emancipatory abolitionist project not only involves a critique of the systems of representation that structure word-object and word-image associations as polar oppositions but also requires a critical interrogation into the specific histories of colonialism that gave rise to racial hierarchies and the relations of racial domination that sustain today's neocolonial racist cultures.

Of course, such hegemonic struggles will take place in a world where the old identificatory schema of racial classification has been upgraded. In the new millennium, the filmmaker in Hollywood and the digital game maker in Silicon Valley work in collaboration with the census taker in New York City and the INS officer in Miami to classify and contain the increasingly diverse inventory of phantasmagoric threats to the national security and the pure body politic—for example, the Arab terrorist, the Colombian drug smuggler, and the Chinese spy. For the transnational "others" of the late-modern political imaginary, the imagination has not only become a "social practice"[33] but also become an ever more hazardous terrain. The realm of the imagination has become such a perilous environment precisely because its processes of identification are, like a Nintendo game, now programmed to perform irrevocable judgments within a fraction of a second.[34] So that, in the time it takes to discharge 41 rounds of ammunition from a rapid-fire pistol, certain irretrievable identifications have taken place while others have been foreclosed. Not enough time, perhaps, to think: That's a wallet, not a gun. Too late to ask: What's in that wallet? And to ascertain the answer: an identification card and money, two items no worldly citizen of present-day New York City would be caught dead without. Awaking to the murderous legacies of the global city's colonial past is a vital imperative of present-day emancipatory projects.

Appendix A: Elias Neau's Short Question-and-Answer Catechism

(1)
Q: How long is it since God has his beginning?
A: From all eternity.

(2)
Q: How long will He continue to be?
A: For ever & ever.

(3)
Q: By whom does He subsist?
A: By himself.

(4)
Q: On whom does he depend?
A: On nobody.

(5)
Q: Where is God?
A: Everywhere.

(6)
Q: Where is He Chiefly?
A: In heaven.

(7)
Q: What does He do there?
A: He governs things.

(8)
Q: Who is with him?
A: The saints and the angels.

(9)
Q: What is his throne?
A: Heaven.

(10)
Q: What is his footstool?
A: Earth.

(11)
Q: How did God make himself known at first?
A: By his works.

(12)
Q: How afterwards?
A: By his words.

(13)
Q: Who taught us to understand?
A: The Holy Spirit.

(14)
Q: How many works are there of God?
A: Two amongst others.

(15)
Q: What is the first?
A: The work of creation.

(16)
Q: What is the second?
A: The work of redemption.

Source: Letter from Elias Neau to Dr. Woodward dated September 5, 1705 in Letterbook of the SPG. [Microfilm] Widener Library. Harvard University.

Notes

Introduction

1. For two excellent studies on capitalism's realization of global supremacy, see Kern, *The Culture of Time and Space*, and Sassen, *Losing Control?* Of course, the phenomenon of globalization in our own time is the product of historical forces dating back to the early modern era. Stuart Hall writes, "Again, globalization is not new. European exploration, conquest and colonization were early forms of the same secular, historical process." See Hall, "Conclusion: The Multi-Cultural Question," 214. For the capitalist world-system theory, see Wallerstein, *The Modern World System*, Vol. 1, and *The Capitalist World Economy*. For a critique of Wallerstein's world-system thesis on the grounds that it places the emergence of capitalism in the sixteenth century when it properly belongs in the eighteenth century, see Brenner, "Origins of Capitalism."

2. For an influential study on the new urban formation that arose with the most recent stage in globalization, see Sassen, *The Global City*.

3. In the ancient Greco-Roman world, colonialism referred to the transplantation of people in new territories for the purpose of bringing that land under cultivation. More recently defined as the conquest and occupation of a foreign territory and the subjugation of its native inhabitants in order to exploit its resources for the benefit of the invaders and their sponsors, colonialism has produced various structures of domination, ranging from colonies with native majority populations governed by foreign colonizers, in some cases, and the native elite, in others—for example, colonial South Africa and colonial India—to colonies with settler majority populations governed by colonial officials from the imperial center or, alternatively, by colonial elites drawn from the settler population, for example, colonial Australia and colonial Virginia. See Emerson, "Colonialism"; Verlinden, *The Beginnings of Modern Colonization*; and Denoon, "Understanding Settler Colonies."

Immanuel Wallerstein writes, "Colonialism in the age of capitalism differed from previous imperial systems in that it came to encompass the entire world. Launched from

Europe in the 15th century, it reached its zenith in the 19th century, by which time all nations and territories had been assigned a place in 'the modern world system.'" See Wallerstein, *The Modern World System*, 2:3. For a critique of world-systems theory, see Blussé, Wesseling, and Winius, *History and Underdevelopment*.

4. For influential theories of racial formation, see Omi and Winant, *Racial Formation in the United States*, and San Juan, *Racial Formations/Critical Transformations*.

5. For superb studies on the concept "race," see Malik, *The Meaning of Race*; Smedley, *Race in North America*; Banton, *The Idea of Race*; Gould, *The Mismeasurement of Man*, esp. chapter 2; and Gossett, *Race*.

6. For nonbiological conceptions of race, see Hodgen, *Early Anthropology in the Sixteenth and Seventeenth Centuries*. Even though the natives of Ireland were in surface bodily appearance indistinguishable from the English people, the early modern English colonizers regarded the indigenous population of Ireland as an alien and inferior race, whose religion and kinship and marriage customs were barbarous. See Rich, *Race and Empire in British Politics*.

7. It was not until the late eighteenth century that physiognomic traits gained primacy over cultural and environmental criteria in the classificatory procedure that divided human beings into separate categories called races. Before that time, the set of truth claims asserted by the biological sciences were simply unavailable as a knowledge base for legitimating racial classifications. The historian Michel Foucault writes, "Historians want to write histories of biology in the eighteenth century; but they do not realize that biology did not exist, that the pattern of knowledge that has been familiar to us for a hundred and fifty years is not valid for a previous period." See Foucault, *The Order of Things*, 127. Once scientific inquiry moved beyond the study of human anatomy to explore human biology and to discover the key biological mechanisms of human heredity, the term *race* assumed the guise of a biogenetic category and came to refer to a distinct group of people whose shared genetic traits are transmitted from one generation to the next. That is, *race* now denoted a distinct population (or gene pool) that exhibits a certain frequency of genetic markers. For general overviews of the history of the biological and biogenetic sciences and their relation to the ideological construction of race, see Lewontin, *Biology as Ideology*, and Kevles, *In the Name of Eugenics*. As genetically determined traits became the core content imputed to race, the displaced cultural content gradually came to define what is nowadays known as *ethnicity*, a term that first appeared in the English language around 1953. It is important to keep in mind that prior to the late nineteenth century, the concept "race" was scarcely dependent on the availability of the biological and biogenetic sciences for validation. Well before the founding of these sciences, theology and natural history produced discourses of race. For much of its history, the meaning of race encompassed nation, culture, language, tribe, and related categories. See Guillaumin, "The Idea of Race and Its Elevation to Autonomous Scientific and Legal Status," and Tonkin, McDonald, and Chapman, "History and Ethnicity."

8. Carolus Linnaeus, *System naturae* [1735]. Quoted in Foucault, *The Order of Things*, 159.

9. The earliest known use of taxonomies of race appears in a travel account of François Bernier (1620–88), "Nouvelle division de la Terre par les différérates espèces ou races d'hommes qui l'habitent, envoyée par un fameux voyaguer."

10. For a general account of the procedure of early modern natural history, see Foucault, *The Order of Things*, 125–62.

11. Ibid., 138.

12. Ibid., 132, 134.

13. Blumenbach, *On the Natural Variety of Mankind*, in Bernasconi and Lott, *The Idea of Race*, 27–37.

14. Although Kant was not the earliest Western European thinker to use taxonomies of race, he was the first to make a clear distinction between the categories *race* and *species*. Addressing the problem of reconciling the unity of the human species with the idea of separate races, Kant writes, "Proceeding in this way, Negroes and whites are clearly not different species of human beings (since they presumably belong to one line of descent), but they do comprise two different races." In Kant's classification schema, the term *race* is by no means an identity category ascribed to nonwhites only. Rather, the categories "Negro race," "Hun race (Mongol or Kalmuck)," and "Hindu or Hindustani race" are relationally constituted identities that derive their meaning in and through their apparent differences from the category "white race," which, according to Kant, diverges least from the "lineal root genus" of the human species and therefore logically serves as its proxy in the calibration of the degree to which all other categories of race deviate from the "original human form." See Kant, "Of the Different Human Races," in Bernasconi and Lott, *The Idea of Race*, 8–27.

15. For an influential essay on the historically contingent formation of race in the United States, see Fields, "Slavery, Race, and Ideology in the United States."

16. According to Elazar Barkan, scientific discourse began to repudiate the biological validity of race as early as the 1920s. See Barkan, *Retreat from Scientific Racism*, 4. The renowned anthropologist Ashley Montagu was in the forefront of Western intellectuals who, during World War II and the postwar era, discredited the biological validity of race and warned that further disastrous consequences would follow from the continued usage of that concept in the social sciences and social policy. See his *Man's Most Dangerous Myth* and his *Statement on Race*. For overviews of the changing fortunes of the concept *race* in the discourse of the biological sciences, see Steve Jones, *The Language of Genes*; Gilman and Stepan, "Appropriating the Idioms of Science"; and Shipman, *The Evolution of Racism*.

17. Omi and Winant, *Racial Formation*, 60.

18. For a useful theoretical essay on relations of domination and racial formation, see Stuart Hall, "Race, Articulation and Societies Structured in Domination."

19. The Dutch seaborne empire can be mapped along the overseas trading routes linking the Baltic, the Mediterranean, the Levant, Archangel in Russia, Africa, Southeast Asia, Nagasaki in Japan, Recife in Brazil, Curaçao, New Amsterdam on Manhattan Island, and the seaports of the Netherlands. See D. W. Davies, *A Primer of Dutch Seventeenth-Century Overseas Trade*; Boxer, *The Dutch Seaborne Empire, 1600–1800*; Aymard, *Dutch Capitalism and World Capitalism*; and Jonathan Israel, *Dutch Primacy in the World Trade, 1585–1740*.

20. See Fanon, *Black Skin, White Masks*, 109.

21. For colonial port town functions, see Price, "Economic Function and the Growth of American Port Towns in the Eighteenth Century," and Ross and Telkamp, *Colonial Cities*, esp. 1–6.

22. For the foundational texts of the American exceptionalism thesis in U.S. liberal nationalist historiography, see Frederick Jackson Turner, *The Frontier in American History*; Beard and Beard, *The Rise of American Civilization*; Boorstin, *The Genius of American Politics*; Potter, *People of Plenty*; and Hartz, *The Liberal Tradition in America*. For recent debates over the American exceptionalism thesis, see Shafer, *Is America Different?* These texts often define American exceptionalism by way of a comparison: When compared with the history of Europe, the history of the United States is exceptionally free from class division, revolutionary upheaval, and authoritarianism.

23. For an overview of the scholarly debate over the merits of the American exceptionalism thesis, see Kammen, "The Problem of American Exceptionalism." The following offer noteworthy critiques of that dominant thesis in the historiography on U.S. society and culture: Veysey, "The Autonomy of American History Reconsidered"; Dorothy

Ross, "Historical Consciousness in Nineteenth-Century America"; Iriye, "The Internationalization of History"; and Tyrrell, "American Exceptionalism in an Age of International History." For two timely reflections on the myth of American exceptionalism and its role in enabling the new world order of global capitalism, see Spiro, "The New Sovereigntists," and Fukuyama, "The End of American Exceptionalism."

24. Jack P. Greene, *Pursuits of Happiness*, 3–4.

25. Ibid., 5, 168, 138. James McPherson argues that until the Civil War era the northern states were generally regarded as anomalous sectors within the United States. See McPherson, "Antebellum Southern Exceptionalism."

26. Engaged in the competition between the descendants of Cavaliers, Yankees, and Knickerbockers over the title of progenitor of uniquely American political institutions and exceptional material prosperity, prominent nineteenth-century New Yorkers wrote histories that challenged the primacy of New England and Virginia as the source of the U.S. national character. See William Dunlap, *History of the New Netherlands Province of New York and State of New York*, and Curry, *New-York*.

27. Hopkins, "Back to the Future."

28. Balibar, "The Nation Form," 89.

29. Orlando Patterson has argued that the great importance attributed to freedom in Western culture was occasioned by the presence and proliferation of slavery. It was in the West, Patterson argues, that freedom first acquired an overriding social significance. Freedom attained an exalted value earlier in the West because it was there that the concept first served the political interest of a ruling elite who, by the expansion of slavery abroad, extended democracy at home. According to Patterson, it was during the imperial period of ancient Greek history that freedom initially emerged as the penultimate social value for the West. During the campaigns of conquest and the proliferation of slavery, from the Persian Wars to the era of Alexander, the exaltation of freedom became the basis of social identification between the masses of Athenian citizens and the ruling elite. At that time, the enslavement of alien others—in this case, Armenians, Arabs, Palestinians, Egyptians, and Ethiopians (but also Italians, Illyrians, Thracians, Scythians, and Phrygians)—fostered a shared high regard for freedom among the ancient Greeks. Freedom thus attained not only an exalted but also a hegemonic value, one that assisted the Athenian rulers in forestalling domestic unrest. Patterson writes: "The demos accepted the rulership of the traditional ruling class because they saw its members as kinsmen, kith and kin against a world of unfree barbarians. It was slavery that created this conception of the world, one shared by rulers and demos alike." In the same way, the enslavement of foreign-born others—Greeks, Sardinians, Spaniards, Gauls, Germans, Carthaginians, and many of the same people the Greeks had enslaved—assisted the ruling elite of the late Republican Era and Principate in securing the allegiance of Roman citizens. For the paradoxical connection between slavery and freedom in the ancient West, see Orlando Patterson, *Freedom*, Vol. I. See also Westerman, "Slavery and the Elements of Freedom in Ancient Greece"; Fisher, *Slavery in Classical Greece*; and Bradley, *Slavery and Society at Rome*. For a skeptical yet tempered evaluation of Patterson's thesis, see Haskell, "Review of *Freedom*."

The paradoxical complicity between the valorization of freedom and the enslavement of alien others, which produced a bond of kinship among the demos of the Athenian city-state and, subsequently, the citizens of Rome, would, centuries later, be closely approximated by the bond of racial identification among citizens of the *herrenvolk* democracy eventually established in the United States. See Edmund S. Morgan, *American Slavery, American Freedom*; and Oakes, *The Ruling Race* and *Slavery and Freedom*. For the concept of *herrenvolk* democracy (or the ideological-political regime that confers the political rights of citizenship on a "master race" while denying racialized others access to these rights), see van den Berghe, *Race and Ethnicity*. For the history of *herrenvolk* democracy in the United States, see Fredrickson, *The Black Image in the White Mind*, esp. 90–94.

30. In this respect, colonial New York City and its hinterland was not quite a slave society but closely resembled one. The historian Ira Berlin writes: "In some places, the North itself took on the trappings of a slave society, with an economy that rested upon the labor of enslaved Africans and African Americans." See Berlin, *Many Thousand Gone*, 177.

31. Ibid., 8.

32. By shifting to an enslaved black labor force, wealthy planters in colonial Virginia reduced the southern staple-crop colony's dependence on land-hungry settlers who resisted the colonial elite's attempts to check settler expansion into Indian territory. At the same time, the colonial elite instituted a number of egalitarian reforms that gave the masses of settlers a voice in the colony's political affairs. Colonial Virginia's representative assembly promulgated, according to Edmund S. Morgan, "measures to align white men of every rank against colored men of every tent." Ordinary settlers were "allowed not only to prosper," Morgan adds, "but also to acquire social, psychological, and political advantages that turned the thrust of exploitation away from them and aligned them with the exploiters" of enslaved blacks. In this way, antiblack racism fostered white solidarity by erecting a "screen of racial contempt" that not only separated "dangerous free whites from dangerous slave blacks" but also obscured the social inequalities that divided white Virginians. See Morgan, *American Slavery, American Freedom*, 346, 344, 328.

Carl Becker (*The History of Political Parties in the Province of New York, 1760–1776*), Patricia Bonomi (*A Factious People*), and Milton Klein (*The Politics of Diversity*) have written important books covering the influence of ethnic diversity and social stratification on the evolution of politics in colonial New York; but none of these studies considers, in depth, the impact of black slavery and antiblack racism on colonial governance in that northern settler colony. For a brief reference to the function of antiblack racism in minimizing ethnic conflict within colonial New York City's settler population, see Archdeacon, *New York City, 1664–1710*, 145.

33. Edmund S. Morgan, *American Slavery, American Freedom*, 381.

34. For an excellent study that draws important connections between the material culture of eighteenth-century tidewater Virginia and republicanism, see Breen, *Tobacco Culture*.

35. Edmund S. Morgan, *American Slavery, American Freedom*, 368–69.

36. For foundational texts in British North American community studies, see Powell, *Puritan Village*; Rutman, *Winthrop's Boston*; Demos, *A Little Commonwealth*; Lockridge, *A New England Town*; Greven, *Four Generations*; Zuckerman, *Peaceable Kingdoms*; Wolf, *Urban Village*; Kross, *The Evolution of an American Town*; and Heyrman, *Commerce and Culture*. For an overview of British North American community studies, see Rutman, "Assessing the Little Communities of Early America."

37. Nash, *Forging Freedom*; Shane White, *Somewhat More Independent*; and Hodges, *Root and Branch*. These monographs augment earlier studies on the laws of slavery in the northern settler colonies. See Lorenzo J. Greene, *The Negro in Colonial New England*; McManus, *A History of Negro Slavery in New York*; and Edward Raymond Turner, *The Negro in Pennsylvania*.

38. For an exception to the general neglect of in-depth analysis of master-slave interactions in the historiography of the northern settler colonies, see Goodfriend, *Before the Melting Pot*.

39. For the evolution of the laws of slavery in the British North American colonies, see Leon A. Higginbotham, *In a Matter of Color*.

40. For a superb analysis of slaveowner paternalism in the colonial South, see Philip D. Morgan, *Slave Counterpoint*, 284–96.

41. The historian Richard Wade (*Slavery in the Cities*) iterates Frederick Douglass's famous assertion that "slavery dislikes a dense population" and, therefore, the urban environment undermines the institution of slavery, whereas Claudia Goldin (*Urban Slavery in the American South*) has uncovered a good deal of evidence that refutes Douglass's claim. This study argues that slavery and the urban environment are hardly incompatible and that, although urban labor routines and demographic patterns in colonial New York City established conditions for contestation between masters and slaves, these factors by no means led to the demise of slavery in that colonial port town.

42. Archdeacon, *New York City*, 46–47; Nash, *Urban Crucible*, 108–9; "Slaves and Slaveowners in Colonial Philadelphia," 226; *Forging Freedom*, 33; and Lorenzo J. Greene, *The Negro in Colonial New England*, 19.

43. Lee, "The Problem of Slave Community in the Eighteenth-Century Chesapeake," 344.

44. For colonial Charleston, South Carolina, see Philip D. Morgan, "Black Life in Eighteenth-Century Charleston." Charleston slaveowners held larger lots of slaves on average than their New York City counterparts. See Philip D. Morgan, *Slave Counterpoint*, 41, 78.

45. Goodfriend, *Before the Melting Pot*, 6.

46. Edmund S. Morgan, *American Slavery, American Freedom*, 386.

47. Heckscher, *Mercantilism*; Wallerstein, *The Modern World System*, Vol. 2; and Buraway, "Race, Class, and Colonialism," 546.

48. The scramble for empire and competition in world trade between England and Holland precipitated the Anglo-Dutch Wars (1652–54, 1665–67, and 1672–74). See J. R. Jones, *The Anglo-Dutch Wars of the Seventeenth Century*.

49. For a general account of the role of independent merchants in the spread of capitalism and slavery, see Fox-Genovese and Genovese, *Fruits of Merchant Capitalism*.

50. In this study, the term *English* is used in contexts that antedate the 1707 Act of Union, except in the case of descriptions of migrants from the British Isles, excluding England, where the term *British* is used. The term *English rulers* refers to the metropolitan government in England and its surrogates in British America.

51. Said, *Orientalism*, 327.

Chapter 1

1. The Wappinger, also known as the Weckquaesgeek, were a chieftaincy within the Munsee, a subdivision of the loose Lenape confederation that also included the Unalachtigo and the Unami. At the time of the European invasion, the southernmost extreme of Manhattan Island was dotted with a few canoe embarkments and campsites of the Canarsee, who inhabited present-day Brooklyn and other parts of western Long Island. See Goddard, "Delaware"; Kraft, *The Lenape*; Bolton, *Indian Life of Long Ago in the City of New York*, 16; and Kammen, *Colonial New York*, 7.

2. For Hudson's expeditions in North America, see Asher, *Henry Hudson the Navigator*, 45–93. Besides Hudson, two earlier European explorers, Giovanni da Varranzano in 1524 and Esteban Gomez in 1525, made voyages to the region. It is also likely that fishermen from Newfoundland ventured as far south as Manhattan Island prior to Hudson's voyages. See Quinn, *North America from Earliest Discovery to the First Settlements*, 154–58, 380.

3. Following a successful revolt from Catholic Spain in 1580, the Protestants of northern Netherlands achieved independence. Organized as a confederation of seven provinces and eleven cities but dominated by the wealthy maritime provinces of Holland and Zeeland, the Dutch Republic, known as the United Provinces of the Free Netherlands, possessed a small territory and population yet accumulated enormous per

capita wealth through its engagement in overseas commerce. See Geyl, *The Revolt of the Netherlands, 1555–1609*, and Jonathan Israel, *The Dutch Republic*.

4. The joint-stock company became the instrument of Dutch colonial expansionism in Asia also. The Estates General granted the Dutch East India Company (1602–1798) a monopoly on the Dutch overseas trade east of the Cape of Good Hope and west of the Strait of Magellan. From its headquarters in Batavia (present-day Jakarta, Indonesia), this joint-stock company conducted a trade in spices, silk, tea, and other exotic goods from Asia. For an overview of the role of merchant capitalism in Dutch colonial expansionism, see Boxer, *Dutch Seaborne Empire*.

5. Rink, *Holland on the Hudson*, 34, 42.

6. In North America the WIC also erected Swaanendael, Fort Nassau, and Fort Casimir along the Delaware River, Fort Hope along the Connecticut River, Eastdorp or Vreeland (later Westchester) along the Harlem River, Bergen on the Jersey shore, and Breuckelen (later Brooklyn), Ameersfoort, Midwout, and New Utrecht in western Long Island.

7. Because few European traders as yet spoke Algonquian, the language of the coastal, woodland, and river Indians, they became dependent on the expertise of Algonquian-speaking middlemen from the Mahican of the upper Hudson River. Although the Mahican enjoyed the privileged status of key articulators in the early Amerindian-European trade, the natives soon began to fight among themselves for primacy in the trade with the European newcomers. Using firearms that European traders sold to them, the assertive Haudenosaunee-speaking Mohawk expanded their control over the interior, where fur pelts were most plentiful, and eventually displaced the Mahican as the chief intermediaries in the Amerindian-European trade. For a description of the fur trade in New Netherland, see Condon, *New York Beginnings*, and Rink, *Holland on the Hudson*. For a recent comparative study on Amerindian-European relations, see Nan A. Rothschild, *Colonial Encounters in a Native American Landscape*.

8. For a superb study on the introduction of alcohol into Amerindian cultures, see Mancall, *Deadly Medicine*.

9. *NNN*, 22.

10. For ceremonial gift giving at treaty signings and other official meetings between Indian sachems and Dutch leaders, see Gehring and Grumet, "Observations of the Indians from Jasper Danckaerts' Journal, 1679–80," 108.

11. For the natives' use of alcohol to induce dreams, see Tooker, *Native North American Spirituality of the Eastern Woodlands*, 120–25; and Axtell, *The Invasion Within*, 64–65.

12. Mancall, *Deadly Medicine*, 64–67, 70, 75. See also Hudson, *Black Drink*.

13. Quoted in Gehring and Grumet, "Observations of the Indians from Jasper Danckaerts' Journal," 108.

14. Fernow, *Records of New Amsterdam from 1653 to 1674 Anno Domini*, 1:22, 5:97; O'Callaghan, *Laws and Ordinances of New Netherland, 1638–1674*, 10–12.

15. Scott and Stryker-Rodda, *New York Historical Manuscripts*, 4:4 (hereafter cited as *NYHM:D*).

16. *NNN*, 340.

17. Van der Donck, *A Description of the New Netherlands*, 86–87; *NNN*, 109. For corrections to the English translation of van der Donck's *Beschrijvinge van Nieuw Nederlandt* [1655], see van Gastel, "Van der Donck's Description of the Indians," 411–21.

18. *NNN*, 106.

19. Ibid., 174.

20. For superb studies on gender and sexuality in Native American cultures, see Klein and Ackerman, *Women and Power in Native North America*; Jacobs, Thomas, and Lang, *Two-Spirited People*; Brown, "The Anglo-Algonquian Gender Frontier," and Natalie Zemon Davis, "Iroquois Women, European Women."

21. *NNN*, 108.

22. Ibid., 273.

23. Ibid., 213.

24. Ibid., 216.

25. Kammen, *Colonial New York*, 12.

26. *NYHM:D*, 4:124–25.

27. Quoted in Kammen, *Colonial New York*, 61. For the trade jargon invented for the Dutch-Amerindian commerce, see Feister, "Linguistic Communication between the Dutch and Indians in New Netherland, 1609–1664."

28. For a history of the transition from the precapitalist to the capitalist conception of property, see Marx, *Pre-Capitalist Economic Formations*.

29. Van Gastel, "Van der Donck's Description of the Indians," 418.

30. For the conception of protection and tribute (or rent), see Lane, *Profits from Power*.

31. Rink, *Holland on the Hudson*, 217.

32. O'Callaghan, *Documentary History of the State of New York*, 2:556–57 (hereafter cited as *DHNY*). *NNN*, 91, 94.

33. Trelease, *Indian Affairs in Colonial New York*.

34. *NNN*, 57.

35. *Genesis* 1:28 KJV.

36. O'Callaghan and Fernow, *Documents Relative to the Colonial History of the State of New York* (hereafter cited as *DRHNY*), 1:150.

37. *DRHNY*, 1:151.

38. *NNN*, 228, 280–82.

39. Ibid., 283–84.

40. Ibid., 214.

41. *DRHNY*, 1:190.

42. Quoted in Rink, *Holland on the Hudson*, 221.

43. For an archeological investigation into the changes in the coastal Indians' material culture, see Ceci, *The Effect of European Contact and Trade on the Settlement Pattern of Indians in Coastal New York, 1524–1665*. In many respects, the Wappinger shared the fate of the native population along the coast of southern New England. See Cronon, *Changes in the Land*; Mancall, *Deadly Medicine*, 50, 116–17.

44. Rink, *Holland on the Hudson*, 99–100.

45. Kammen, *Colonial New York*, 33, 37, 46–47; Bachman, *Peltries or Plantations*.

46. *DRHNY*, 1:152.

47. For a discussion of the "Freedoms and Exemptions" [1628] and the revised list of privileges, see Rink, *Holland on the Hudson*, 100–101, 137.

48. *DRHNY*, 1:114, 119.

49. Rink, *Holland on the Hudson*, 158.

50. *NNN*, 89.

51. Ibid., 132.

52. *DHNY*, 1:596.

53. *DRHNY*, 1:154. For the high cost of enticing indentured servants to New Netherland, see also van den Boogaart, "The Servant Migration to New Netherland, 1624–1664."

54. For the Dutch slave trade, see Postma, *The Dutch in the Atlantic Slave Trade, 1600–1815*.

55. Ibid., 19–20.

56. For documentation on the Dutch slave entrepôt at Curaçao, see Donnan, *Documents Illustrative of the History of the Slave Trade*, 3:406–10; Gehring and Schiltkamp, *Curacao Papers, 1640–1665*, Vol. 17.

57. For the capture of human cargo later sold in New Amsterdam as prize goods, see O'Callaghan, *Calendar of Historical Manuscripts in the Office of the Secretary of State of New York*, 1:73; Donnan, *Documents Illustrative*, 3:405, 416–17, 426–27.

58. *DRHNY*, 1:151, 182.

59. To eliminate a potential obstacle to the resumption of peaceful trade relations with the indigenous population, the WIC fined settlers who refused to pay wages to Indian laborers. See *NYHM:D*, 4:566.

60. Donnan, *Documents Illustrative*, 3:444.

61. Wagman, "Corporate Slavery in New Netherland"; Swan, "First Africans into New Netherland, 1625 or 1626?"

62. Hodges, *Root and Branch*, 16.

63. Kea, *Settlements, Trade, and Politics in the Seventeenth-Century Gold Coast, 1469–1682*, chap. 2.

64. Postma, *The Dutch Atlantic in the Atlantic Slave Trade*, 17–18; Emmer, "The Dutch and the Making of the Second Atlantic System."

65. Blackburn, *The Making of New World Slavery, From the Baroque to the Modern, 1492–1800*, 211.

66. For the successful petition of independent traders for the abolition of the WIC's monopoly on the African slave trade, see O'Callaghan, *Laws and Ordinances of New Netherland*, 81, 127; and Donnan, *Documents Illustrative*, 3:413–14.

67. Paulo d'Angola, Symon Congo, Pieter Santome, and Anthony Potugese were among the first slaves brought to New Amsterdam in 1626. See Donnan, *Documents Illustrative*, 3:405.

68. For the export of slaves from Brazil to New Amsterdam, see Donnan, *Documents Illustrative*, 3:406, 410.

69. For the use of interpreters in a case involving a slave named Jan Angola, see Fernow, *Records of New Amsterdam*, 5:337.

70. Quoted in Donnan, *Documents Illustrative*, 3:421.

71. McManus, *History of Negro Slavery in New York*, 4. Enslaved blacks also built the Dutch fort at Oyster Bay. See Cox, *Oyster Bay Town Records*, 2:697–98.

72. *DRHNY*, xiv:18; Hodges, *Root and Branch*, 9.

73. *DRHNY*, 1:415.

74. Stokes, *Iconography of Manhattan Island, 1648–1909*, 2:297–98, 408; 4:96; 6:73–77, 120–24, 136–37. See also Vingboom Map–Eÿland Manatùs [1639] in Stokes, *Iconography*, 2:183–86; Wagman, "Corporate Slavery in New Netherland," 35; and *DRHNY*, 14:18.

75. *NYHM:D*, 1:123.

76. Wagman, "Corporate Slavery in New Netherland," 36–37.

77. *DRHNY*, 1:110–15.

78. *NYHM:D*, 1:23; 4:35, 53, 62, 208–9; Rink, *Holland on the Hudson*, 160–61.

79. Stokes, *Iconography*, 4:82; Berlin, *Many Thousands Gone*, 51–52. It is likely that these five slaves were the same enslaved workers who received wages for their labor on the fort in 1639. See Hodges, *Root and Branch*, 10.

80. Wagman, "Corporate Slavery in New Netherland," 38.

81. As in the case of the early Virginia colony, there was no single social position reserved for the African-descended people of New Netherland. See Leon A. Higginbotham, *In the Matter of Color*, 111.

82. *DRHNY*, 1:156.

83. Ibid., 1:415.

84. The 11 male slaves granted half-freedom on February 25, 1644, were Paulo d'Angola, Groote Manuel, Little Manuel [aka Manuel Minuit], Manuel de Gerrit de Reus, Symon Congo, Anthony Potugees, Garcia Domingo, Pieter Santome, Jan Francisco, Little Anthony [aka Anthony Minuit], and Jan Fort Orange. For the confirmation of these grants of half-freedom, see O'Callaghan, *Laws and Ordinances of New Netherland*, 36–37, 60.

85. For additional grants of half-freedom to slaves in New Netherland, see O'Callaghan, *Calendar of Dutch Historical Manuscripts*, 1:256; *NYHM:D*, 4:326–28.

86. For the grants of full freedom, see O'Callaghan, *Calendar of Dutch Historical Manuscripts*, 1:242, 256, 269.

87. Ibid., 1:87, 105, 269. The "free Negro lots" appear on the Vingboom Map–Eÿland Manatùs [1639]. See Stokes, *Iconography*, 2:183–86. For additional references to these lots, see Stokes, *Iconography*, 4:99 and 6:71, 74, 123–24; Christoph, "The Freedmen of New Amsterdam"; Hoff, "A Colonial Black Family in New York and New Jersey."

88. For the Roman *colonus*, see Perry Anderson, *Passage from Antiquity to Feudalism*, 128–72; Wickman, "From the Ancient World to Feudalism," 34.

89. Christoph, "Freedmen of New Amsterdam," 142–43.

90. O'Callaghan, *Calendar of Dutch Historical Manuscripts*, 1:268, 289, 293, 307, 331.

91. Berlin, *From Creole to African*, 269.

92. Ibid., 144.

93. Edwin T. Corwin, *Ecclesiastical Records, State of New York* (hereafter cited as *Ecclesiastical Records*), 1:488–89.

94. Of the documented 25 marriages of black couples performed by New Amsterdam's Dutch Calvinist clergy, all but one probably involved free blacks. See "Marriages in the Dutch Reformed Church of New Amsterdam and New York City, 1639 to 1801." Of the documented 49 black children baptized under the offices of the colonial outposts' Dutch Calvinist clergy, a majority were likely the offspring of free blacks. See "Baptisms in the Dutch Reformed Church of New Amsterdam and New York City, 1639 to 1730."

95. Hodges, *Root and Branch*, 15.

96. *DRHNY*, 2:248, 54.

97. For the commutation of death penalties in cases involving slaves convicted of capital crimes, see *NYHM:D*, 4:97–100, 326–28.

98. *DRHNY*, 2:248.

99. Quoted in Kammen, *Colonial New York*, 37.

100. Van den Boogaart, "The Servant Migration to New Netherland."

101. Ibid.

102. Ibid., 52.

103. Robert J. Swan, "The Black Presence in Seventeenth-Century Brooklyn." For two additional inhabitants of mixed ancestry, see Hodges, *Root and Branch*, 10–11; and Hershkowitz, "The Troublesome Turk."

104. Quoted in Kammen, *Colonial New York*, 63.

105. Oliver Rink, "The People of New Netherland; Cohen, "How Dutch Were the Dutch of New Netherland?" 54–55.

106. Marcus, *The Colonial American Jew, 1492–1776*, 1:216.

107. *NNN*, 392.

108. Quoted in Marcus, *The Colonial American Jews*, 1:217.

109. Ibid., 1:218–19.

110. O'Callaghan, *Laws and Ordinances*, 12.

111. *Ecclesiastical Records*, 1:530.

112. Ibid., 1:142.

113. Quoted in Kammen, *Colonial New York*, 59.

114. *Ecclesiastical Records*, 1:494.

115. Ibid., 1:398–99.

116. Ibid., 1:398.

117. Ceci, *Effect of European Contact*, 71–77, 83–86.

118. Van der Donck, *A Description of the New Netherlands*, 86–87. See also *NNN*, 223–24.

119. Ibid., 73–74.

120. Quoted in van Gastel, "Van der Donck's Description of the Indians," 417.

121. For European perceptions of Native Americans and early modern discourses on

race, see Chaplin, "Natural Philosophy and an Early Racial Idiom in North America"; and Brown, "Native Americans and Early Modern Concepts of Race."

122. Ibid.

123. Stuart Hall, "Conclusion: The Multi-cultural Question," 223. See also Dirks, *Colonialism and Culture*.

124. Kidd, *British Identities before Nationalism*, 24.

125. Young, *Colonial Desire*, 27.

126. Stoler, *Race and the Education of Desire*, 27.

127. *NNN*, 128.

128. Ibid., 127.

129. Ibid., 126–27.

130. David Brion Davis writes: "A double standard in judging Negroes and Indians enabled colonists of various nationalities to channel moral concern toward the aborigine, whose freedom was often essential for commercial and military security, and to screen off the critical center of the American dilemma" (*The Problem of Slavery in Western Culture*, 10). While the colonizers in New Netherland enslaved few natives, a combination of military, labor, and logistical factors led them to direct moral concern toward the black Africans and away from the coastal Indians, whom they increasingly feared and eventually exterminated.

131. *Ecclesiastical Records*, 1:142.

132. *NNN*, 409.

133. The term "Reformed churches" refers to the Protestant communions originally founded on the doctrines of John Calvin and Huldreich Zwingli.

134. At the Dordrecht (Dort) meeting in 1618, the Reformed churches discussed "heathen baptism" and formulated a policy that gave slaveowners the power to deny their slaves access to baptism.

135. *Ecclesiastical Records*, 1:548.

136. "Baptisms in the Reformed Dutch Church."

137. Allison Blakey, *Blacks in the Dutch World*, 4–5.

138. Dutch sailing vessels brought occasional cargoes of slaves to Holland's ports, but slave traders never managed to establish a market for slaves in the Dutch Republic because of the Netherlanders' resistance to the introduction of African bondage in their homeland. As late as 1656, the municipal authorities in Middleburg freed a cargo of enslaved Africans that a Dutch sailing vessel brought to that Dutch port town. See Drescher, *Capitalism and Antislavery*, 15, 137.

139. Blackburn, *The Making of New World Slavery*, 189–90, 192–94; George I. Smith, *Religion and Trade in New Netherland*, 126–27.

140. *DRHNY*, 1:302, 343.

141. *NNN*, 329–30; *DRHNY*, 1:335, 343.

142. *NNN*, 408–9.

143. Quoted in Kammen, *Colonial New York*, 62.

144. Prior to 1589, there was, according to the historian Benjamin Braude, considerable disagreement and ambiguity in both the Christian and the Jewish interpretations of Genesis 9–10, which recounts the story of the curse of Ham. Between 1589 and 1625, proponents of the enslavement of black Africans, Braude argues, constructed an interpretation of these biblical passages in which they trace the lineage of sub-Saharan Africans to the sons of Ham, regard the sub-Saharan Africans' "black" skin color as the visible mark of the curse of Ham, and consider the black Africans' perpetual bondage as a punishment from God. Braude, "The Sons of Noah," esp. 135–38, 142.

145. The historian Thomas Holt has noted that the consumption of goods fabricated from the raw produce cultivated by enslaved black laborers in the overseas colonies engendered a heightened sense of racial consciousness among Western Europeans who

never traveled to Asia, Africa, or the Americas. Holt, "Marking"; Schama, *The Embarrassment of Riches.*

146. Blackburn, *The Making of New World Slavery*, 203.

147. Fernow, *Records of New Amsterdam*, 1:9–10; O'Callaghan, *Laws and Ordinances of New Netherland*, 34–35, 182–83.

148. *Ecclesiastical Record*, 1:142.

149. Kammen, *Colonial New York*, 52–55.

150. For a history of the Swedish colonial outposts along the Delaware River, see Amandus Johnson, *The Swedish Settlements on the Delaware, 1638–1664.*

151. Quoted in Kammen, *Colonial New York*, 67.

152. Rink, *Holland on the Hudson*, 165–68.

153. The WIC officially surrendered its fort on Manhattan Island on September 15, 1664. The English conquest of New Amsterdam was part of the challenge ambitious Englishmen of the Restoration era waged against the United Provinces' dominance in overseas commerce. British mercantilist policies, such as the Navigation Law of 1660, were intended to end the Dutch carrying trade to the British West Indies and precipitated three Anglo-Dutch wars.

Chapter 2

1. As the historian Nicholas Canny has shown, English colonization of Ulster and Munster provided models for the English project of colony building in North America. See his "The Ideology of English Colonization," *The Elizabethan Conquest of Ireland*, and *Kingdom and Colony.*

2. Goodfriend, *Before the Melting Pot*, 52.

3. Quoted in ibid.

4. Quoted in Sachs, *The Widening Gate*, 268–69.

5. The several English navigation acts precipitated the Anglo-Dutch wars of the seventeenth century. Enacted to eliminate the Dutch carrying trade with English ports, the earliest such law, the Navigation Act of 1651, codified England's mercantilist policy, which the overseas commerce laws of the Restoration era would later expand. See Farnell, "The Navigation Act of 1651, the First Dutch War, and the London Merchant Community."

6. Rabb, *Enterprise and Empire*; Hancock, *Citizens of the World.*

7. Bailyn, *The Peopling of British North America*, 95.

8. Kammen, *Colonial New York*, 75.

9. Denton, *A Brief Description of New-York*; DHNY, 1:91; DRHNY, 3:415.

10. For general descriptions of colonial New York's overseas trade, see DHNY, 1:714–21, 727–28.

11. DHNY, 1:161.

12. Approximately 20,000 to 50,000 Huguenot refugees from northern and western France eventually crossed the English Channel to London and Bristol, and of these exiles nearly 2,000 eventually resettled in British North America. See Butler, *The Huguenots in America*, esp. 27, 46, 49, 55, 151, 177.

13. The English Crown expelled the Jews from England in 1290, but, beginning in the sixteenth century, economic competition with rival nations contributed to a climate of tolerance for Jews, whose international network of moneylenders and traders provided vital services to the first British Empire.

14. Marcus, *The Colonial American Jew*, 1:308–11, 284.

15. Fortune, *Merchants and Jews.*

16. England entered the War of the League of Augsburg to halt France in its bid to seize control over central Europe.

17. In the War of the Spanish Succession, England and the United Netherlands contested Louis XIV's claim to the Spanish Crown.

18. The Rhenish Palatinate included an area that stretched along both banks of the Rhine River and its branches, the Main and the Neckar rivers, from the confluence of the Moselle and the Rhine southward to Basle, Switzerland, from Zweibrücken, on the border of Lorraine, westward along the Main am Baireuth, flanking the Upper (or Bavarian) Palatinate. See Knittle, *The Early Eighteenth Century Palatine Emigration*, 2. In 1708, England's Queen Anne offered asylum to Protestant refugees from areas of Europe devastated by the War of Spanish Succession. Several thousand Swiss and Palatine refugees temporarily settled in England and later relocated to the colony of New York. In December 1708, approximately 58 Palatines from the areas of Landau and Frankfurt arrived at the port of New York. They spent the winter in the city, and in the spring Governor Lovelace (1708–10) resettled 15 German-speaking Lutherans from the Rhenish Palatinate on land grants 50 miles north of New York City, near the mouth of Quassaick Creek at the present-day site of Newburgh, New York. See *DHNY*, 3:543; and Emigrants, CO 323/6, 56, PRO.

19. For the quarantine of the Palatines on Governor's Island, see *DHNY*, 3:559.

20. For the apprenticing of Palatine orphans, see *DHNY*, 3:566–67. For the sale of indentured servants from the Rhenish Palatinate, see Knittle, *Early Eighteenth Century Palatine Emigration*, 111–42.

21. Sypher, "Voices in the Wilderness"; Roeber, "'The Origins of Whatever Is Not English among Us,'" 241; Benson, *Peter Kalm's Travels in North America*, 142–43.

22. Knittle, *Early Eighteenth Century Palatine Emigration*, 159.

23. Only one sailing vessel brought European immigrants to the port of New York during the War of Jenkin's Ear—60 Palatines in 1641. See Naval Officer's Shipping List for the Port of New York, 1715–1765, CO 5/1222–1229, PRO (hereafter cited as NOSL).

24. NOSL; *New York Gazette*, April 17 to April 23, 1739.

25. NOSL; *New York Mercury*, October 14 to October 20, 1754; *New York Weekly Post-Boy*, July 15 to July 21, 1754.

26. The *New York Weekly Post-Boy* announced: "To Be Sold, A German Servant man, with his Wife and Son, of about Six years old, who are to serve five Years, he is as compleat a Gardner as any in America; understands a Flower and Kitchen Garden to Perfection." Also cited in McKee, *Labor in Colonial New York, 1664–1776*, 107.

27. Dickson, *Ulster Emigration to Colonial America, 1718–1775*, 103–4.

28. By 1622, at least 8,000 Scottish tenants labored on Ulster plantations. For the history of the colonization of Ulster, see Perceval-Maxwell, *The Scottish Migration to Ulster in the Reign of James I*; Leyburn, *The Scots-Irish*.

29. Miller, *Emigrants and Exiles*.

30. Letter from James Murray to Rev. Baptist Boyd in *New York Gazette*, November 7 to November 13, 1737.

31. Quoted in Dickson, *Ulster Emigration*, 88.

32. Between June 1728 and April 1729, approximately 353 Scots-Irish migrants arrived at the port of New York; nearly a decade later, between May 1737 and April 1739, an additional 268 Scots-Irish settlers disembarked at the port; in 1741, shortly before the War of Jenkin's Ear hampered transatlantic travel from British ports, another 229 Scot-Irish servants landed at New York City; and on August 30, 1754, approximately 40 Ulster Scots made their way to New York before the start of the French and Indian War. See the *New-York Weekly Journal*, June 4 to June 10, 1739; May 25 to May 31, 1741; and the *New York Mercury*, June 10 to June 16, 1754.

33. Favored families owned more than 2 million acres of colonial New York's most fertile farmland. See Kim, *Landlords and Tenants in Colonial New York: Manorial Society, 1665–1775*, esp. 4–43.

34. Bailyn, *Voyagers to the West*, 12–16, 204–18. Between 1773 and 1775, a total of 3,232 British migrants from England and Scotland arrived at the port of New York. See Register of Emigrants, 1773–76 (hereafter cited as Register). During that same period, New York City newspaper announcements document the arrival of an additional 1,278 passengers who traveled to the port of New York on 13 unregistered vessels from British ports. See Bailyn, *Voyagers to the West*, 206, 575.

35. A total of 365 West Lowlanders disembarked at the port of New York between 1773 and 1775. See Bailyn, *Voyages to the West*, 216–18.

36. Ibid., 176, 582–85, 588–89, 597–600.

37. *New York Gazette*, December 20 to December 26, 1773.

38. Kim, *Landlords and Tenants in Colonial New York*, 129–280.

39. Bailyn, *The Peopling of British North America*, 53.

40. Nash, *The Urban Crucible*; Mohl, "Poverty in Early America"; Rossiter, *A Century of Population Growth from the First Census of the United States to the Twelfth, 1790–1900*, 183.

41. For a newspaper notice announcing the arrival of a shipload of 30 English passengers, see the *New York Mercury*, January 3 to January 9, 1774. The bulk of the cargo space in English vessels departing from London was usually devoted to freight.

42. Bailyn, *Voyagers to the West*, 94–103.

43. *New York Weekly Journal*, January 13 to January 19, 1774; January 20 to January 26, 1774. Descriptions of the *Nancy*'s voyage were reported in the *Scots Magazine*, March 1774. See Bumsted, *The People's Clearance*, 21.

44. To make life in New York attractive to prospective settlers, the English colonial rulers established laws that made a clear distinction between the status of enslaved Africans (or Negroes), on the one hand, and white servants and apprentices, on the other. For colonial New York's law of slavery, see *Colonial Laws of New York from the Year 1664 to the Revolution*, 1:19–20; for the laws governing apprenticeships and indentured servitude, see 1:18, 47–48, 157–59.

45. Letter from Jacobus Van Cortlandt to Richard Heigh, New York, April 15, 1698; Letter from Jacobus Van Cortlandt to John Roe, New York, May 28, 1698; Letter from Jacobus Van Cortlandt to Mr. [Miles] Mayhew, New York, June 23, 1698; and Letter from Jacobus Van Cortlandt to William Sherwin, New York, July 14, 1698, in Letterbook of Jacobus Van Cortlandt, 1698–1700. For additional references to the difficulty of finding New York buyers for aged West Indian slaves, see Letter from Jacobus Van Cortlandt to Thomas Nicoll, New York, July 16, 1698, and Letter from Jacobus Van Cortlandt to Richard Heigh, New York, August 18, 1698.

46. Letter from Jacobus Van Cortlandt to Miles Mayhew, New York, July 16, 1698, in Letterbook of Jacobus Van Cortlandt, 1698–1700.

47. Letter from Jacobus Van Cortlandt to Barnabas Jenkins, New York, July 16, 1698, in Letterbook of Jacobus Van Cortlandt, 1698–1700.

48. *Colonial Laws of New York*, 1:675–77. New York's colonial assembly reaffirmed this discriminatory duty in 1718. See O'Callaghan, *Journal of the Legislative Council of the Colony of New York*, 1:433.

49. Lydon, *Pirates, Privateers, and Profits*, 18, 36–59. Colonial New York City can be added to the list of societies where, as Marx has noted, "Merchant's capital, when it holds a position of dominance, stands everywhere for a system of robbery, so that its development among the trading nations of old and modern times is always directly connected with plundering, piracy, kidnapping slaves, and colonial conquest." Marx, *Capital*, 3:331.

50. Donnan, *Documents Illustrative*, 3:442. See also Judd, "Frederick Philipse and the Madagascar Trade."

51. For the seizure of the brigantine, see *New York Gazette*, September 6 to September 12, 1730.

52. McManus, *History of Negro Slavery in New York*, 28. For an additional reference to the glutted New York City slave market resulting from two large shipments of slaves from Madagascar and another from the Guinea Coast, see Letter from Jacobus Van Cortlandt to Richard Heigh, New York, June 4, 1698, in Letterbook of Jacobus Van Cortlandt, 1698–1700.

53. Letter from Jacobus Van Cortlandt to Mr. [Barnabas] Jenkins, New York, April 15, 1698, in Letterbook of Jacobus Van Cortlandt, 1698–1700.

54. Donnan, *Documents Illustrative*, 3:444, 511–13; NOSL; American Inspector General's Ledgers for the Board of Customs and Excise Imports and Exports, America, 1768–73 (hereafter cited as AIGL). James Lydon's study on colonial New York's slave trade offers a higher overall estimate of the total number of slaves brought to the port of New York than the estimate presented in this study. See Lydon, "New York and the Slave Trade," 287. Lydon possibly double-counted some single shipments of slaves, which appear in the official port records under the actual date of arrival and, owing to delays in newspaper reporting, also in newspaper notices published on a later date. To avoid the problem of double-counting in calculating an estimated total number of slaves carried to the port of New York, I have omitted data on enslaved human cargoes contained in newspaper accounts. This procedure resulted in a conservative estimate, which in no way detracts from the historical significance of colonial New York's slave trade.

55. *DHNY*, 1:707; Donnan, *Documents Illustrative*, 3:444.

56. Letter from James Van Horne to John White (London). For Governor Robert Hunter's report on the stoppage of colonial New York's provisions trade to New Spain during and in the immediate aftermath of Queen Anne's War, see *DHNY*, 1:713.

57. Occasional cargoes of contraband slaves entered the port of New York during Queen Anne's War (1702–13), the War of Jenkin's Ear (1739–42), King George's War (1744–48), and the French and Indian War (1756–63). See List of Prize Goods. See also Hough, *Reports of Cases in the Vice Admiralty Court*, 29–32.

58. *DRHNY*, 5:342.

59. *Colonial Laws of New York*, 1:675–77. As already noted, this discriminatory duty also discouraged the dumping of "refuse" West Indian slaves on New York City's slave market. For an early directive ordering the governor of New York to encourage the African slave trade, see *DRHNY*, 5:136. That instruction made reference to the role the Royal African Company was supposed to play in supplying New York with slaves. The port of New York did not receive a single shipment of slaves from the RAC, however.

60. K. G. Davies, *The Royal African Company*; Platt, "The East India Company and the Madagascar Slave Trade."

61. As late as 1726, slave traders glutted the slave markets in Jamaica, Barbados, and Curaçao. See *New York Gazette*, March 13 to March 19, 1726.

62. NOSL; Hodges, *Root and Branch*, 78.

63. The New York City merchants Abraham Van Horne, John Van Horne, and Andrew Fresneau reexported 45 surplus East African slaves to Virginia. See NOSL.

64. For a general overview of colonial New York City's population growth, see Rosenwaike, *Population History of New York City*, 8; Greene and Harrington, *American Population before the Federal Census of 1790*, 88–112.

65. *New York Gazette*, July 20 to July 26, 1730.

66. Lydon, "New York and the Slave Trade," 377.

67. Curtin, *The Slave Trade*; Rawley, *The Transatlantic Slave Trade*.

68. Donnan, *Documents Illustrative*, 3:345.

69. Rossiter, *A Century of Population Growth*, 182.

70. By 1770, New York City still lagged behind Philadelphia, Boston, and Charleston in the amount of tonnage passing through its port. But the city's overseas commerce was

more diversified and evenly distributed than that of the other colonial port towns in British North America, allowing it to achieve a more favorable balance of trade. See Albion, *The Rise of the Port of New York, 1815–1860*, 5; Shepard and Walton, *Shipping, Maritime Trade and the Economic Development of Colonial North America*, 191.

71. Lydon, "New York and the Slave Trade," 387.

72. NOSL.

73. Deposition of a Sailor Concerning the Cruel Treatment of Negro Slaves on Board the Snow York.

74. Donnan, *Documents Illustrative*, 3:452–53. For New York City newspaper reports on slave mutinies, see *New York Weekly Post-Boy*, April 30 to May 6, 1753; March 18 to March 24, 1754; August 21 to August 27, 1766.

75. While not the only pattern, direct trade with a single region was eighteenth-century New York City's dominant pattern of commerce. See Davisson and Bradley, "New York Maritime Trade."

76. Michael L. Blakey, "Notes from the Howard University Biological Anthropology Laboratory," 6.

77. This study uses child-woman ratios (children per 100 women) as a proxy for natural increase. The child-woman ratio for New York City's African-descended population reached 203 by 1746, indicating a modest natural increase during the 1740s. For previous decades, the child-woman ratios indicate that natural increase made no contribution to the growth of the city's African-descended population. The child-woman ratio of 131 by 1756 and 103 by 1771 suggest slight natural increases during the 1750s and the 1760s. The smallpox epidemic of 1756 probably carried away many black infants and children, thus eradicating the gains in natural increase for the city's black population during the 1750s. The child-woman ratios for this study are based on data drawn from Rossiter, *A Century of Population Growth*, 170, 181–83.

78. By the 1730s, a stable reproducing creole majority contributed to the natural increase of the Chesapeake region's black population. See Kulikoff, "A 'Prolifick' People," 405; Menard, "The Maryland Slave Population, 1658 to 1730," 32.

79. Greene and Harrington, *American Population before the Federal Census of 1790*, 88–112.

80. *DHNY*, 1:757.

81. AIGL.

82. Greene and Harrington, *American Population before the Federal Census of 1790*, 88–112.

83. Quoted in Shane White, *Somewhat More Independent*, 3.

84. For information on individual New York City slave traders, see Matson, *Merchants and Empire*, 60–62, 202–3.

85. Colden, "The Interest of the Country in Laying Duties."

86. Quoted in Hodges, *Root and Branch*, 79.

87. Quoted in McKee, *Labor in Colonial New York*, 91.

88. *DRHNY*, 7:888.

89. "Indentures and Apprentices, 1694–1707"; "Indentures and Apprentices, 1718–1727." See also Haar, "White Indentured Servants in Colonial New York."

90. Osgood, *Minutes of the Common Council of the City of New York, 1675–1776*, 1:454–55 (hereafter cited as *MCC*).

91. Mack and Hill, "Recent Research Findings Concerning the African Burial Ground Population."

92. For a description of the practice of head carrying among enslaved black laborers in early New York City, see De Voe, *The Market Book*, 1:244–45.

93. Quoted in Bridenbaugh, *Cities in Revolt*, 88.

94. McKee, *Labor in Colonial New York*, 46.

95. Wilkenfeld, "New York City's Shipowning Community," 62.

96. John Cruger, Waste [Account] Book of Henry and John Cruger. See also John Taylor, Captain John Taylor's Account and Memoranda Book.

97. For the construction contract for Beekman's landing, see Beekman and Beekman, Receipts of William and Abraham Beekman for Sums Paid for the Repair of a Wharf, 1770.

98. Watt, "Letterbook of John Watt," 31.

99. The following newspaper advertisement in the *New York Gazette*, August 4 to August 10, 1729, offers a "seasoned" (adapted) slave for sale: "A Negro girl of about 17 or 18 years of Age who is well seasoned to the Country, and can do all sorts of House-work, is to be Sold. Enquire of the Printer here."

100. Herskovitz, *The Myth of the Negro Past*, esp. 101, 140–41.

101. In this study's sample population of slaves whose occupational expertise was reported in colonial New York City newspaper advertisements for slave sales, nearly 23 percent (78 of 342) were skilled slaves.

102. *New York Gazette*, August 30 to September 5, 1731.

103. Ibid., October 12 to October 18, 1730.

104. For the practice of dumping unruly slaves at the port of New York, see McManus, *History of Negro Slavery in New York*, 35.

105. Minutes of the Mayor's Court, August 7, 1750–December 17, 1751, 474–76 (hereafter cited as Mayor's Court Records).

106. For Spanish-speaking slaves embarking on New York City privateering and other sailing vessels, see *New York Weekly Post-Boy*, October 2 to October 8, 1749; June 27 to July 4, 1748; *New York Mercury*, October 28 to November 3, 1776. For the presence of African seafarers on European sailing vessels that traversed the Atlantic Ocean during the eighteenth century, see Bolster, *Black Jacks*, 52–53, 56, 62.

107. Mayor's Court Records, August 7, 1750–December 17, 1751, 474–76.

108. *New York Mercury*, February 8 to February 14, 1768. Also cited in McKee, *Labor in Colonial New York*, 123.

109. *New York Weekly Post-Boy*, December 19 to December 26, 1748. Also cited in McKee, *Labor in Colonial New York*, 123. For a similar advertisement, see *New York Mercury*, April 8 to April 14, 1776. Quoted in McManus, *History of Negro Slavery in New York*, 45.

110. *New York Weekly Post-Boy*, May 27 to June 1, 1751. For a similar advertisement, see *New York Weekly Post-Boy*, May 17 to May 23, 1756. Quoted in McManus, *History of Negro Slavery in New York*, 45.

111. *New York Gazette*, October 8 to October 14, 1733. This newspaper advertisement indicates that from an early age female slaves began to master the art of sewing: "A very likely Negro Girl to be Sold, brought up here in Town, Speaks very good English, aged about Ten Years, has had the Small-pox and measles, and begins to handle her needle. Enquire of the Printer hereof."

112. For colonial New York City markets, see *MCC*, 1:139–40. See also De Voe, *The Market Book*, 1:242–335; Rothschild, *New York City Neighborhoods*, 56–66.

113. Logbook of a Privateer . . . the Duke of Cumberland; and Logbook of a Privateer . . . the Harlequin.

114. Samuel Gilford, Shipping and Personal Papers.

115. Hodges and Brown, *"Pretends to Be Free,"* xix.

116. McManus, *History of Negro Slavery in New York*, 199.

117. For a general description of the system of labor in British America and the various conditions of servitude—slavery, indentured servitude, and apprenticeship—see Morris, *Government and Labor in Early America*, esp. 72–98.

118. *MCC*, 2:458. See also De Voe, *The Market Book*, 1:242; Booth, *The History of the City of New York*, 270–71; and McKee, *Labor in Colonial New York*, 117–19, 129.

119. For the cartmen of the city of New York, see *MCC*, 1:179, 219–20, 224, 245, 376; 2:195, 196, 354; 3:4. See also Morris, *Government and Labor in Early America*, 183; Hodges, *The New York City Cartmen, 1664–1850*.

120. Adam Smith, *An Inquiry into the Nature and Causes of the Wealth of Nations*, 1:90.

121. For the cartmen's monopoly, see *MCC*, 1:137, 179, 219.

122. McManus, *A History of Negro Slavery in New York*, 43; McKee, *Labor in Colonial New York*, 11–12, 21–61.

123. Archdeacon, *New York City*, 47.

124. Morris, *Government and Labor in Early America*, 159–60, 182–83.

125. Quoted in McKee, *Labor in Colonial New York*, 127.

126. Ibid., 25–26; Hodges, *Root and Branch*, 108.

127. Writing about the U.S. labor movement, W. E. B. Du Bois remarked: "It must be remembered that the white group of laborers, while they received a low wage, were compensated in part by a sort of public and psychological wage." Du Bois, *Black Reconstruction*, 700. For an elaboration of Du Bois's observation, see Roediger, *The Wages of Whiteness*. The white workingmen of colonial New York City seem to have found the "public and psychological" wages of racial whiteness inadequate compensation for low monetary wages. They did, however, seem to have considered the privileges that the colonial state granted to white settlers as a sort of property in whiteness. For an influential discussion of the right to property in whiteness, see Cheryl Harris, "Whiteness as Property."

128. For contemporary reports on the violent assaults against black workingmen on the part of white laborers during the New York City dockworkers' strikes in 1855 and 1863 and the New York City draft riots in 1863, see *New York Tribune*, January 18, 1855, and April 14, 1863; *New York Herald*, January 18, 1855, and April 14, 1863. For historical analysis of these events, see Ernst, *Immigrant Life in New York City, 1852–1863*, 107–11; Man, "Labor Competition and the New York Draft Riots of 1863"; Berstein, *The New York City Draft Riots*, 25–42.

129. For the economic interest of slaveowners in protecting their slave property from white working-class violence and the vulnerability of black workingmen to brutal attacks in the post-Emancipation period, see Wells, "A Red Record," 7.

130. Eric Foner, *Free Soil, Free Labor, Free Men*.

131. For the early statutory regulation of indentureship contracts in colonial New York, see *Colonial Laws of New York*, 1:18.

132. Laslett, *The World We Have Lost*, 67.

133. For a description of the typical dwelling in early-eighteenth-century New York City, see Bridenbaugh, *Cities in the Wilderness*, 308. By the mid–eighteenth century, New York City witnessed an acute housing shortage, and town dwellers lived in less and less commodious spaces. See *New York Journal, or General Advertiser*, October 16 to October 22, 1766.

134. Goodfriend, "Burghers and Blacks," 142–43; Archdeacon, *New York City*, 47.

135. The following discussion is primarily based on the 1703 household census for the County of New York, a jurisdiction that included New York City, two farming villages on Manhattan Island, the Bowery and Harlem, as well as the small islands in the East River. For the County of New York Census of 1703, see Rossiter, *A Century of Population Growth*, 170–81. The census of 1703 divides the population into three age cohorts: inhabitants 16 to 60 years of age, inhabitants under 16 years of age, and inhabitants over 60 years of age. In the following discussion, references to adults indicate inhabitants assigned to the age cohort of 16 to 60 years; references to children indicate inhabitants assigned to the age cohort of under 16 years; and references to the elderly indicate inhabitants assigned to the age cohort over 60 years. In the census of 1703, the designation "white" does not appear as a legible "identity category" but functions as an ex-

nominated (implicit) norm. The census assigns all inhabitants falling outside that norm to the category "Negro." Importantly, this binarism Negro/not Negro renders mulattoes, mustees, and Indians illegible, though newspapers and other archival sources refer to these racial groupings. Historical records suggest that only a small number of free blacks and black indentured servants lived in New York City and the adjacent countryside during the colonial period. It is likely that all but a tiny fraction of the inhabitants assigned to the category "Negro" in the census were slaves. In the following discussion, inhabitants assigned to the category "Negro" are referred to as slaves and enslaved blacks. Finally, all entries in the census have a recorded head of household, and all but three entries strongly suggest that the household head falls in the category of either an adult white male or an adult white female 16 years of age or older.

136. For a description of the East Ward, see Stokes, *Iconography*, 5:658–59. The Dongan Charter of 1686 partitioned New York City into six wards: the South, Dock, East, North, West, and Outward. At that time Wall Street marked the city limit, though the city's population eventually expanded northward beyond Wall Street to the City Common and later to Maiden Lane. With the Montgomerie Charter of 1730, the municipal government added a jurisdiction called Montgomerie Ward. See *MCC*, 1:102–13 and 2:108, 115, 122, 440; Stokes, *Iconography*, 1:192, 251–61 and 6:658; Rothschild, *New York City Neighborhoods*, 31–32, 68, 80; Carl Abbott, "The Neighborhoods of New York City, 1760–1775"; Wilkenfeld, "New York City Neighborhoods, 1730," 171–72. Following the French and Indian War, a period when radically altered economic conditions called attention to the existence of social inequality within the city's settler population, the wealthy townspeople were concentrated in the East, Dock, and South wards, while the poorest townspeople were mostly found north of Warren Street. The increasing concentration of poor townspeople in the colonial port town's northernmost sector inaugurated a long-term trend of spatial segregation that separated rich and poor.

137. Will of Nicholas Dumaresq (1701) and Inventory of the Estate of Nicholas Dumaresq (NYC).

138. Will and Inventory of the Estate of Captain Giles Shelly (1718).

139. For the law abolishing Indian slavery, see *Colonial Laws of New York*, 1:40–42.

140. Stokes, *Iconography*, 5:658–59.

141. Inventory of the Estate of Peternela, widow of Derrick Ten Eyck, dated November 15, 1724. For a history of the Ten Eyck family of New York, see Ten Eyck, *Ten Eyck Family Record*.

142. For a discussion of Van Dam's political career and, in particular, his role in the salary dispute with Governor Cosby, see Katz, *Newcastle's New York*, 63–70, 74–75, 89–90, 115–19; Bonomi, *A Factious People*, 106–10.

143. Inventory of the Estate of Rip Van Dam (1749). See also Inventory of the Goods & Chattels of Rip Van Dam dated September 1, 1753.

144. Stokes, *Iconography*, 5:658.

145. Helen Burr Smith, "Early American Silversmiths."

146. Stokes, *Iconography*, 5:658.

147. See "Kip Family History"; *Historical Notes of the Family Kip of Kipsburg and Kip's Bay*; Frederick Ellswork Kip, *History of the Kip Family in America*.

148. *Historical Notes of the Family Kip of Kipsburg and Kip's Bay*, 127.

149. Queen Anne ceded the land that became Trinity Church Farm to New York City's Anglican Church. See Stokes, *Iconography*, 5:659; Valentine, *History of the City of New York*, 69–70.

150. For population growth in the West Ward after 1730, see *MCC*, 3:475–76.

151. Trinity Parish Leases for the Church Farm, 1704, 1732, 1750–65.

152. General Jason Grant Wilson, "Colonel John Bayard (1738–1807) and Bayard Family of America: An Address."

153. Country seats on Manhattan Island: Lady Warren's "Greenwich"; Oliver De-Lancey's "Bloomingdale"; Colonel Clarke's "Chelsea"; John Morin Scott's "Hermitage"; and Charles Ward Anthorp's "Elmwood."

154. Stokes, *Iconography*, 5:659–60.

155. Purple, "Contributions to the History of the Ancient Families of New York."

156. Will of Henry [Hendrickus] Brevoort.

157. For a pattern of patriarchal land control in a colonial New England town, see Greven, *Four Generations*.

158. Inventory of the Estate of Captain Thomas Codrington (1710).

159. Cosby, "The Rutgers Family of New York"; Will of Anthony Rutgers (1746). See also Bruckbauer, *The Kirk of Rutgers Farm*.

160. Kim, *Landlords and Tenants*, 188.

161. *DHNY*, 1:749–50.

162. For a detailed portrait of Colden's career, see Keys, *Cadwallader Colden*. See also Purple, "Notes, Biographical and Genealogical of the Colden Family, and Some of its Collateral Branches in America."

163. Inventory of the Estate of Cadwallader Colden (1756).

164. Benedict Anderson, *Imagined Communities*, 150.

165. For a comparative analysis of the Spanish, English, and French models of colonization and their greater and lesser reliance on feudal institutions, see Pagden, *Lords of All the World*. For the ascendancy of the bourgeoisie and the rise of possessive individualism, see MacPherson, *The Political Theory of Possessive Individualism*.

Chapter 3

1. *DRHNY*, 2:262; and quoted in Kammen, *Colonial New York*, 86.

2. *DRHNY*, 1:423.

3. Letter from Charles Lodwick to the Royal Society.

4. Quoted in Kammen, *Colonial New York*, 245.

5. *DRHNY*, 2:250–53.

6. Archdeacon, *New York City*, 27.

7. For Anglo-Dutch relations in colonial New York following the English Conquest, see Fernow, *Records of New Amsterdam*, 5:208, 211–12, 232, 260–63, 338; and Murrin, "English Rights as Ethnic Aggression," 59–60.

8. An episode in the third Anglo-Dutch War (1672–74), the Dutch Reconquest lasted from July 30, 1673, to February 9, 1674.

9. Quoted in Murrin, "English Rights as Ethnic Aggression," 63.

10. *Colonial Laws of New York* 1:115; *DHNY*, 3:317–18. For earlier efforts to obstruct the establishment of an elective colonial assembly in New York, see *DRHNY*, 2:230–31.

11. *Colonial Law of New York*, 1:123–24.

12. For a general historical account of naturalization law in British North America and the conceptualization of U.S. citizenship, see Kettner, *The Development of American Citizenship*, 4, 30–36. See also Carpenter, "Naturalization in England and the American Colonies"; and Hoyt, "Naturalization under the American Colonies."

13. In late-eighteenth-century England, proposals for incorporating Jews into the political community of rights-bearing British subjects aroused anti-Semitic prejudices. In response, Great Britain's Jewish community and their supporters reminded the British state of the Jew's loyal service to the British Empire. See Birnbaum and Katznelson, *Paths of Emancipation*; Liedtke and Wendehorst, *The Emancipation of Catholics, Jews, and Protestants*.

14. Quoted in Kammen, *Colonial New York*, 86.

15. Earlier, during the rule of Elizabeth I (1558–1603), the Church of England was called on to forge a consensus among post-Reformation Englishmen who were divided into

opposing factions of Protestants and Catholics. To that end, Queen Elizabeth I and her advisers crafted "Ecclesia Anglicana" out of a set of doctrinal and liturgical compromises between Protestants and Roman Catholics. Militant Protestants regarded the final settlement as a corruption of the true church and protested against the prerogatives of the Church of England establishment. Subsequent controversies over the church-state relation and religious tolerance became the source of an irremediable conflict between embattled English monarchs and their nonconformist foes. Finally, the tumult of the English Revolution (1642–48) and the Interregnum (1649–59) prevented the Church of England from fulfilling its task of uniting the English people. Hill, *A Century of Revolution, 1603–1714*.

16. Quoted in Humphreys, *An Account of the Endeavours Used By the Society For the Propagation of the Gospel in Foreign Parts* (hereafter cited as Humphreys, *Account of the SPG*), 21.

17. Miller, *A Description of the Province and City of New York*, 208.

18. Letter from Colonel Heathcote to the Secretary, the Manor of Scarsdale, April 10, 1704 in Letterbooks of the SPG.

19. *Ecclesiastical Records*, 2:1118.

20. *DRHNY*, 4:526.

21. Ibid., 3:372.

22. Lathbury, *A History of the Book of Common Prayer*.

23. *Ecclesiastical Records*, 2:952–53. Later, New York City's Lutheran and French Protestant churches won similar exemptions. See *Ecclesiastical Records*, 2:884; and *DHNY*, 3:406.

24. *Ecclesiastical Records*, 2:755.

25. Balmer, *A Perfect Babel of Confusion*, 36.

26. Steele, *Politics of Colonial Policy*, 42–68.

27. *DRHNY*, 2:418.

28. For the political crisis in the British North American settler colonies attending the Glorious Revolution, see Lovejoy, *The Glorious Revolution in America*. Historians have offered different explanatory models for the response to the Glorious Revolution in colonial New York. Jerome Reich (*Leisler's Rebellion*) attributes colonial New York's initial political impasse to an ideological conflict between settlers dedicated to democracy and those dedicated to aristocratic rule, whereas Lawrence H. Leder (*Liberty and Authority*) attributes it to a contest between two competing factions of ambitious colonial elites who were more concerned with gaining social prestige and political influence for themselves than with the expansion of liberty. In separate studies Thomas Archdeacon ("'Distinguished for Nation Sak'") and Charles H. McCormick (*Leisler's Rebellion*) have emphasized the competing economic interests that divided New York's settler population on the eve of the Glorious Revolution. Other studies have recognized the importance of cultural differences among the settlers in colonial New York. John M. Murrin ("English Rights as Ethnic Aggression," 57) argues, for example, that the split within New York's settler population following the Glorious Revolution was fundamentally "an ethnic Dutch reaction to the English conquest." Murrin's study offers a persuasive account of the politics of culture in early colonial New York.

29. Archdeacon, "Distinguished for Nation Sak.'"

30. Cohen, "How Dutch Were the Dutch of New Netherland?" 54–55.

31. In 1672, the Duke of York, later King James II, publicly professed his adherence to Roman Catholicism. In 1682, the Duke appointed the Irish Catholic Thomas Dongan to the post of governor of New York.

32. Voorhees, "The 'fervent Zeale' of Jacob Leisler."

33. Ibid., 461.

34. *DHNY*, 2:378–89.

35. Quoted in Leder, "'Like Madmen through the Streets.'"

36. Ibid.

37. Leder, "Records of the Trials of Jacob Leisler and His Associates."

38. Michel Foucault describes the powers of the absolute sovereign: "The sovereign exercised his right of life only by exercising his right to kill, or by refraining from killing; he evidenced his power over life only through the death he was capable of requiring. The right which was formulated as the 'power of life and death' was in reality the right to *take* life or *let* live." Foucault, *The History of Sexuality*, 136.

39. The initial death sentence ordered that Leisler and Milbourne were to be "sever-all[y] hanged by the Neck and being Alive their bodys be Cutt Downe to the Earth that their Bowells be taken out and they being Alive burnt before their faces that their heads shall be struck off and their Bodys Cutt in four parts. . . ." Although the English penal code allowed multiple punishments for a single crime, especially in cases of high treason and regicide, such executions were scarcely ordinary occurrences. In the case of Leisler and Melbourne Governor Sloughter commuted the most horrific punishments, perhaps out of trepidation that the prolonged torture of the condemned men would incite a riot. See Leder, "Records of the Trials of Jacob Leisler and His Associates," 454. See also Voorhees, "The 'fervent Zeale' of Jacob Leisler," 447.

40. *DHNY*, 2:380.

41. Benedict Anderson has suggested that the mass singing in unison of, for example, poetry, songs, and national anthems is constitutive of a "special kind of contemporane-ous community." Anderson, *Imagined Communities*, 145.

42. Balmer, *A Perfect Babel of Confusion*, 43.

43. First enacted in 1683, colonial New York's Charter of Liberties, along with its provi-sion for a popularly elected colonial assembly, was disallowed by King James II in 1686. See *Colonial Law of New York* 1:226–31, 244–53, 255–57.

44. Murrin, "English Rights as Ethnic Aggression," 57.

45. For the Ministry Act of 1693, see *Colonial Laws of New York* 1:328–31.

46. Quoted in Balmer, *A Perfect Babel of Confusion*, 50.

47. Miller, *A Description of the Province and City of New York*, 69.

48. Balmer, *A Perfect Babel of Confusion*, 83–85.

49. Miller, *A Description of the Province and City of New York,* 69.

50. *DRHNY*, 4:1071.

51. Ibid.

52. *Ecclesiastical Records*, 2:1071–72, 1092, 1103. See also Balmer, *A Perfect Babel of Confu-sion*, 45, 50.

53. *DRHNY*, 4:83; *DHNY*, 2:435–37.

54. *DHNY*, 4:400–401, 523, 620–21; *Ecclesiastical Records*, 2:1242.

55. *DRHNY*, 4:312, 325.

56. Reverend Francis Mackemie founded the first presbytery in North America at Philadelphia in 1706.

57. Kammen, *Colonial New York*, 85–86, 136–37, 157.

58. Ibid., 221.

59. During the last half of the eighteenth century, members of evangelical denomina-tions, large and small, built churches in New York City. For example, in 1752 the Mora-vians erected a house of worship at Fulton Street, and in 1770 the Methodist congrega-tion erected a meetinghouse at John Street between Nassau and Williams streets.

60. William Smith, *History of the Province of New-York*, 1:138.

61. The Act of Union of 1536 had already united England and Wales. The Act of Union of 1707 consolidated England, Wales, and Scotland into the single geopolitical unit known as the United Kingdom of Great Britain. According to that act, Great Britain had uniform laws, its subjects obtained representation in a national Parliament, and English became the official state language. Ireland was not incorporated into Great Britain until the Act of

Union of 1801. Infamously, that act imposed political disabilities on Ireland's Catholic population. See Hugh F. Kearney, *The British Isles*; Linda Colley, *Britons*. Robert Young has argued that the term "British" betrays the asymmetrical power relation between nation and empire, the metropolitan and colonial societies. That term was coined "to mask the metonymic extension of English dominance over the other kingdoms with which," Young writes, "England had constructed illicit acts of union." See Young, *Colonial Desire*, 3.

62. Kathleen Wilson, *The Sense of the People*; Steele, *Politics of Colonial Policy*, 42–68.

63. Haydon, *Anti-Catholicism in Eighteenth-Century England*.

64. The Protestant churches trace their origin to the Reformation and are divided into two main branches: the Reformed churches founded on the doctrines of John Calvin and Huldreich Zwingli (e.g., the Calvinist Church) and the Evangelical churches founded on the doctrines of Martin Luther (e.g., the Lutheran Church).

65. During the sixth and seventh decades of the eighteenth century, the political distinction between subjects with representation in the national Parliament and subjects without such representation became an intractable constitutional controversy that gave rise to the settler revolt in British North America known as the American War for Independence. That settler uprising resulted in the founding of the 13 republics that initially comprised the United States.

66. The seventeenth-century chroniclers of the Anglo-Saxon legend relied on the works of the historian Cornelius Tacitus (55–117)—specifically, his *Germania* and *Agricola*—for their primary source of historical information on the ancient Germanic tribes. These classical texts, along with exegetical analysis of the biblical accounts of postdiluvian history, became the foundation of the Anglo-Saxon racial myth. By the late nineteenth century, a biologicized conception of race had displaced the historical-textual underpinnings of Anglo-Saxonism. Nevertheless, the construction of race in the discourse of the biological sciences has always been culturally determined and, in crucial respects, has legitimated rather than refuted the traditional historiographical foundations of racial mythologies, including the myth of the Anglo-Saxon race.

67. For the importance of racial mythology in the construction of early modern English national identity, see MacDougall, *Racial Myth in English History*, 31–70. In contrast to MacDougall's account of the rise of nationalism, Martin Thom traces the emergence of nationalism in Western Europe to the transition from Enlightenment thinking to Romanticism and its reaction against the Terror of Thermidorian Paris. Largely based on late-eighteenth- and nineteenth-century continental European sources, Thom's periodization of the rise of nationalism in Western Europe discounts earlier discourses of national identity, especially those arising from the nation-empire relation. See Thom, *Republics, Nations, and Tribes*.

68. Quoted in MacDougall, *Racial Myth in English History*, 60; and in Kidd, *British Identities before Nationalism*, 77.

69. Racial mythologies are apt to change with shifts in national and international politics. During England's late-nineteenth-century rivalry with Germany, English nationalists celebrated the hybridity of the English peoples and counterposed the culture of the reputedly mixed English people to the culture of the presumably pure German Saxon, which had stagnated, according to the English propagandists, because of its insularity. These English nationalists now insisted that the superiority of the English peoples derived from the mixture of Celts, Saxons, Normans, and Danes, which produced the superior racial hybrid known as the Anglo-Saxon race. See Young, *Colonial Desire*, 17.

70. Quoted in Kidd, *British Identities before Nationalism*, 77.

71. For the centrality of language and religion in earlier European conceptions of peoplehood, see Bartlett, *The Making of Europe*.

72. During the early modern era, memorization and recitation of the state-church catechism was imposed on diverse peasant populations in central Europe to bring

about the uniformity of culture integral to nation building. See Sabean, *Power in the Blood*, 111.

73. Kammen, *Colonial New York*, 248.

74. Sharpe, "Proposals for Erecting a School," 341.

75. David E. Narrett, "From Mutual Will to Male Prerogative," 1.

76. For a study of inheritance practices in colonial New York, see Narrett, *Inheritance and Family in Colonial New York* and "From Mutual Will to Male Prerogative," 1–4.

77. Kilpatrick, *The Dutch Schools of New Netherland and Colonial New York*, 39–40.

78. Bennett, *Bondsmen and Bishops*.

79. Letter from Mr. Huddleston to the Secretary, New York, February 23, 1711 in Letterbooks of the SPG.

80. Founded in the same year, New York City's Temple Shearith Israel was originally located at present-day St. James Place.

81. Murrin, "English Rights as Ethnic Aggression," 61. See also Balmer, *A Perfect Babel of Confusion*, 26.

82. Henry M. Mühlenberg, *Journals of Henry Mühlenberg*, 1:278.

83. Goodfriend, *Before the Melting Pot*, 6.

84. Kammen, *Colonial New York*, 248.

85. Quoted in ibid., 236.

86. *Protocol of the Lutheran Church in New York City, 1702–1750*, 110–14 (hereafter cited as *Lutheran Protocol*).

87. *Lutheran Protocol*, 114.

88. *Ecclesiastical Records*, 1:866–67. As early as 1628, the Dutch Calvinist minister in New Amsterdam offered French-language services to the Walloon settlers. See *NNN*, 125; and *Ecclesiastical Records*, 1:53–54.

89. William Smith, *History of the Province of New-York*, 1:204–5.

90. Quoted in Kammen, *Colonial New York*, 239.

91. Balmer, *A Perfect Babel of Confusion*, 144; Kammen, *Colonial New York*, 236.

92. Quoted in Balmer, *A Perfect Babel of Confusion*, 112.

93. Butler, *Huguenots in America*, 192–93.

94. William Smith, *History of the Province of New-York*, 1:208. See also Maynard, *The Huguenot Church of New York*, 301–3.

95. Le Temple du Saint-Esprit, New York City's French Calvinist church, dissolved in 1833.

96. Roeber, "'The Origin of Whatever Is Not English among Us,'" 221.

97. Successive waves of impoverished German-speaking refugees arrived at Manhattan Island in the aftermath of the Thirty Years War (1618–48), the War of Palatine Succession (1688–97), and the War of Spanish Succession (1709–13).

98. For influential theories of group boundary maintenance, see Barth, *Ethnic Groups and Boundaries*; Eriksen, *Ethnicity and Nationalism*.

99. *Lutheran Protocol*, 323. The following discussion of the language controversy in colonial New York City's Lutheran Church is based on *Lutheran Protocol*, 269–70, 295–96, 305–13, 320–21.

100. Quoted in MacDougall, *Racial Myth in English History*, 44. An advocate of the use of the vernacular in Protestant worship services, Martin Luther had his Wittenberg Protest (1517) translated into German.

101. Mühlenberg, *Journals*, 1:251.

102. *Lutheran Protocol*, 176–77.

103. Quoted in Balmer, *A Perfect Babel of Confusion*, 122.

104. Quoted in ibid., 131.

105. Whereas Anglicans were only 5 to 10 percent of New York City's total settler population in 1720, they were a near majority of that colonial port town's settler popula-

tion by 1775. See Balmer, *A Perfect Babel of Confusion*, 91, 93–94; Richard W. Pointer, *Protestant Pluralism and the New York Experience*, 146n.

106. For an excellent history of pietism in the middle colonies of British North America, see Balmer, *A Perfect Babel of Confusion*, esp. 120–30.

107. Kammen, *Colonial New York*, 230.

108. Whitefield, *George Whitefield's Journals*, 483–86.

109. Pietistic preachers alleged that clergymen preached the doctrine of justification when they encouraged their parishioners to believe that instead of relying on the infusion of God's free grace and faith alone they could achieve assurance of their salvation by diligently attending to their worldly callings.

110. Mühlenberg, *Journals*, 1:231.

111. Colden, "A Memorial to his Excellency."

Chapter 4

1. For brief references to the efficacy of antiblack racism in subordinating and minimizing divisiveness within the settler population, see Jordan, *White over Black*, 119–20; Archdeacon, *New York City*, 145–46; and Thomas J. Davis, "'These Enemies of Their Own Household,'" 133.

2. Hakluyt, "A Discourse Concerning Western Planting in the Year 1584."

3. See Klingberg, *Anglican Humanitarianism in Colonial New York*, for a historical overview of Anglican missionary activities in colonial New York.

4. Letter from Elias Neau to David Humphreys, New York, June 22, 1721 in Letterbooks of the SPG.

5. Klingberg, "The S.P.G. Program for Negroes in Colonial New York."

6. The annual average of slave conversions is calculated from the SPG catechists' reports: Letter from Reverend Vesey to the Secretary, New York, September 5, 1704; Letter from Elias Neau to John Chamberlayn, New York, November 16, 1714; Letter from Elias Neau to David Humphreys, New York, January 22, 1720; Letter from Thomas Colgan to David Humphreys, New York, May 20, 1727; Letter from Thomas Colgan to David Humphreys, New York, December 23, 1728; Letter from Richard Charlton to the Secretary, New York, June 5, 1733; Letter from Reverend Auchmuty to Daniel Burton, New York, April 25, 1771; and Letter from Joseph Hildreth to Richard Hind, New York, November 7, 1773, in Letterbooks of the SPG.

The city's Lutheran church converted a few black town dwellers. By 1705, Arie Van Guinee, a free black from Suriname, and his wife, Jora, were members of the city's Lutheran congregation, and in that same year the Lutheran minister baptized their daughter, Maria. In 1726, the Lutheran minister administered Holy Communion to two black town dwellers, Jan Louis and his wife. See Goodfriend, *Before the Melting Pot*, 126.

7. Bloch, *Slavery and Serfdom in the Middle Ages*; Duby, *The Early Growth of the European Economy*.

8. Dockès, *Medieval Slavery and Liberation*.

9. With the crucial exception of Latin Europe, the institution of slavery had disappeared from most parts of Western European by the twelfth century. Medieval legal scholars invented the institution of serfdom to take its place, but within three centuries even that mitigated form of bondage had all but vanished. See Bonnaisse, *From Slavery to Feudalism in South-Western Europe*.

10. For the early Spanish invasion of the Americas and its enabling discourse of missionary colonialism, see Todorov, *The Conquest of America*.

11. Elias, *The Civilizing Process*.

12. Leviticus 25:45–46 states: "Moreover of the children of the strangers that do so-

journ among you, of them shall ye buy, and of their families that *are* with you, which they begat in your land: and they shall be your possession. And ye shall take them as an inheritance for your children after you, to inherit *them for* a possession; they shall be your bondmen for ever: but over your brethren the children of Israel, ye shall not rule one over another with rigour." Following the model of Leviticus, colonial New York's law of "Bond-slavery" states: "No Christian shall be kept in Bond-slavery, villenage or Captivity, except such who shall be Judged thereunto by Authority, or such as willingly have sould, or shall sell themselves." See *Colonial Laws of New York*, 1:18. Also modeled on Leviticus, the Massachusetts law of "Bond-slavery" (1641) states: "there shall never be any bond-slavery, villenage or captivitie amongst us; unless it be lawfull captives taken in just warrs, and such strangers as willingly sell themselves, or are solde to us." See Farrand, *The Laws and Liberties of Massachusetts*, 4.

13. In this respect, the category "Christian slave" presented a dilemma akin to the problem of the *conversos* in Inquisition Spain, where the ecclesiastical authorities feared that the conversion of Jews and Muslims to Christianity destabilized the social hierarchy based on the dominance of the so-called Old Christians—or, Christians who claimed a seamless family tradition of adherence to the doctrines of the Roman Catholic Church. In sixteenth-century Spain, the problem of the *conversos* was ostensibly solved with the extension of the concept *limpieza de sangre* from a privileged criterion for establishing membership in the aristocracy to one that defined membership in the broader national community. For a discussion of the problem of the *conversos* in Inquisition Spain, see Kamen, *Inquisition and Society in Spain in the Sixteenth and Seventeenth Centuries*, 100–133. Interestingly, the application of the criterion "purity of the blood" for determining national belonging in Inquisition Spain bears a close resemblance to the solution to the problem of slave conversion in colonial New York, where, together, the valorization of the racial purity of the settler population and the emphasis on biological heredity in defining the category "slave" established the boundaries of national community.

14. For a general overview of slaveowner opposition to the Anglican civilizing mission among the slaves of British North America, see Bonomi, *Under the Cope of Heaven*, 16.

15. DRHNY, 2:156.

16. Letter from Elias Neau to the Secretary, New York, July 4, 1704, in Letterbooks of the SPG.

17. *Colonial Laws of New York*, 1:429, 597–98.

18. In an effort to construct an exhaustive, airtight law of slavery, New York's colonial assembly included Indians in the list of peoples eligible for enslavement, even though the settlers enslaved few Indians as a consequence of the Law of 1679, which prohibited the enslavement of Indians born in New York. See *Colonial Laws of New York*, 1:21, 40–42.

19. In 1677, William Corvan, a mulatto, took advantage of the ambiguity surrounding the status of mulattoes in colonial New York at that time. Corvan claimed that he was born free and that he was an indentured servant and not a slave, as his master claimed. See O'Callaghan, *Calendar of Historical Manuscripts*, 2:56.

20. Colonial Virginia's 1662 law of slavery included a similar provision that, according to the feminist legal historian Kathleen Brown, "reflected significant innovations in English traditions of marriage, family, and paternal authority." See Brown, *Good Wives, Nasty Wenches, and Anxious Patriarchs*, 135. For a brilliant essay on the impact that the statutory denegation of the father's paternal rights over his offspring born of an enslaved woman had on the historical development of African American culture, see Spillers, "Mama's Baby, Papa's Baby."

21. For the construction of racial subjects in legal discourse, see Haney-López, *White by Law*. In Butts v. Penny (1677) and Gelly v. Cleve (1694), the English courts ruled that enslaved blacks were "lesser breeds without the law" and therefore excluded from the

rights of Englishmen and lawfully held as chattel. See Shyllon, *Black Slaves in Britain*, 24–25.

22. William Fleetwood, *Relative Duties of Parents and Children, Husbands and Wives, Masters and Servants*, 273, 277, 289, quoted in Klingberg, *Anglican Humanitarianism*, 16. For a superb analysis of the Anglican conception of "absolute obedience" and "slaveowner paternalism," see Butler, *Awash in a Sea of Faith*, 135–49.

23. Quoted in Letter from Elias Neau to the Secretary, New York, February 21, 1711, in Letterbooks of the SPG.

24. Reverend William Vesey, rector of New York City's Anglican church, delayed Neau's appointment, objecting that because the French-speaking lay minister lacked sufficient English language skills and knowledge of Anglican doctrine he should not be entrusted with the duties of SPG catechist. After considering Vesey's objections, the SPG authorities in London confirmed Neau's appointment. See Letter from Reverend William Vesey to the Secretary, New York, October 26, 1704, in Letterbooks of the SPG. For a sketch of Neau's life, see Cohen, "Elias Neau, Instructor of New York's Slaves."

25. Letter from Elias Neau to Mr. Hodges, New York, July 10, 1703, in Letterbooks of the SPG.

26. Letter from Elias Neau to Secretary, New York City, February 27, 1709, and Letter from Elias Neau to Secretary, New York City, July 5, 1709, in Letterbooks of the SPG.

27. Letter from Elias Neau to Secretary, New York, July 9, 1709, in Letterbooks of the SPG.

28. For Elias Neau's Question-and-Answer Catechism, see Appendix A.

29. Letter from Elias Neau to John Chamberlain, New York, July 24, 1707, in Letterbooks.

30. Letter from Elias Neau to John Camberlayn, New York, November 28, 1706, in Letterbooks of the SPG.

31. Ibid.

32. Klingberg, *Anglican Humanitarianism*, 144.

33. Letter from Elias Neau to the Secretary, New York, March 1, 1705–6, in Letterbooks of the SPG.

34. Letter of Elias Neau to Chamberlayne, New York, August 24, 1708, and Letter of Elias Neau to the Secretary [N.D.] in Letterbook of the SPG. William Huddleston, the SPG catechist for New York City's black population following Neau's death in 1722, reported: "Swarms of Negroes come about my door and asking if I would be pleased to teach them and build on Mr. Neau's foundation." Quoted in Hodges, *Root and Branch*, 85. Like Neau's black pupils, these black town dwellers were as interested in acquiring literacy as a means of improving their worldly condition as they were in achieving spiritual salvation. Bray's Associates, an SPG educational institution, sent schoolteachers to colonial New York City. At Bray's School, black children received instruction in English-language reading and writing skills. In addition, black girls received instruction in sewing. For the school's curriculum, see also Letter from Joseph Hildreth to the Secretary, New York, October 18, 1768, in Letterbooks of the SPG.

35. Letter of Elias Neau to the Secretary, New York, June 16, 1715, in Letterbook of the SPG.

36. Letter from Elias Neau to John Chamberlain, New York, July 24, 1707, in Letterbooks of the SPG.

37. Letter from Reverend Vesey to the Secretary, New York, September 5, 1704; Letter from Thomas Colgan to David Humphries, New York, May 20, 1727; Letter from Thomas Colgan to David Humphries, New York, December 23, 1728; Letter from Richard Charlton to the Secretary, New York, June 5, 1733; Letter from Reverend Auch-

muty to Daniel Burton, New York, April 25, 1771; and Letter from Joseph Hildreth to Richard Hind, New York, November 7, 1773, in Letterbooks of the SPG.

38. Letter from Elias Neau to John Chamberlayn, New York, August 24, 1708, in Letterbooks of the SPG.

39. Humphreys, *An Account of the SPG*, 238.

40. Letter from John Sharpe to Secretary, New York, June 23, 1712, in Letterbooks of the SPG.

41. Letter from Elias Neau to John Chamberlayn, New York, June 11, 1719, in Letterbooks of the SPG.

42. Letter from Elias Neau to Secretary, New York City, February 21, 1712. in Letterbooks of the SPG.

43. For a detailed account of New York City's Slave Revolt of 1712, see Scott, "The Slave Insurrection in New York in 1712." See also Foote, "'Some Hard Usage.'" In other parts of the Americas, enslaved Coromantee committed suicide in the belief that after death their spirits returned to their homelands. See Philip D. Morgan, *Slave Counterpoint*, 641.

45. Minutes of the Court of Quarter Sessions, August 7, 1694, to 1731, 212–24, 228–48; Minutes of the Supreme Court of Judicature, June 6, 1710–June 5, 1714, 399–400, 417, 426, 429. See also Coroner's Inquisition, April 9, 1712; *DRHNY*, 5:356–57; and *Boston Weekly News-Letter*, April 7 to April 13 and April 14 to April 20, 1712. At the time of the revolt, the *Boston Weekly News-Letter* was the only newspaper published in British North America.

46. O'Callaghan, *Journal of the Legislative Council*, 1:133.

47. Leon A. Higginbotham, *In the Matter of Color*, 116–23.

48. *Colonial Laws of New York*, 1:761–67. See also Olson, "The Slave Code in Colonial New York," 147–65.

49. *DRHNY*, 5:357.

50. In contrast to colonial New York's Black Code of 1712, statutes in colonial Virginia, beginning in 1705, granted free blacks some privileges of British subjecthood. But with the rise of the free black population in the towns around 1723 and mounting fears of a conspiracy involving slaves and free blacks, Virginia's colonial assembly stripped free blacks of their privileges and enacted statutes for the strict regulation of free black men and women. See Brown, *Good Wives, Nasty Wenches*, 275–322.

51. Letter from Mr. Thomas Barclay to the Secretary, New York, May 31, 1712, in Letterbooks of the SPG; and Letter from Elias Neau to the Secretary, New York, October 15, 1712, in Letterbooks of the SPG.

52. Letter from John Sharpe to the Secretary, New York, June 23, 1712, in Letterbooks of the SPG.

53. Letter from John Sharpe to the Secretary, New York, June 23, 1712, in Letterbooks of the SPG. Enslaved Akan were notorious for instigating and carrying out slave rebellions, skill in the tactics of guerrilla warfare, and success in establishing maroon communities. In addition to the early slave uprisings in Antigua in 1701 and in New York City in 1712, enslaved Akan led at least five slave revolts in Jamaica between 1673 and 1690. See Craton, *Testing the Chains*, 57, 75.

54. Fage, "A New Check List of the Forts and Castles of Ghana," iv.

55. Between 1710 and 1712, all documented slaves brought to the port of New York, a total of 185 West African newcomers, were natives of the Gold Coast of Africa, also called Guinea. Captain Jarrat brought the 1711 shipment of slaves from the Gold Coast, but before he arrived at Manhattan he stopped at Boston, where he deposited 19 slaves. Donnan, *Documents Illustrative*, 3:444.

56. Eugene Genovese has argued that the differences between slavery in the Americas and human bondage in Africa likely registered with native Africans as differences of de-

gree rather than kind. See Genovese, *From Rebellion to Revolt*, xiv. While acknowledging that the institutions of slavery in West Africa and in the Americas shared some common features, this study stresses the fundamental differences between the two systems of slavery.

57. Miers and Kopytoff, *Slavery in Africa*, 11. See also Rattray, *Ashanti Law and Constitution*, v.

58. Anatole Norman Klein, "West African Unfree Labor Before and After the Rise of the Atlantic Slave Trade," in Foner and Genovese, *Slavery in the New World*, 90.

59. This and other Akan proverbs, as well as their English translations, are drawn from Rattray, *Ashanti Proverbs*. The seventeenth-century Akwamu, an Akan Empire headquartered on the Gold Coast, preceded the Asante, another Akan Empire, and had earlier disseminated these proverbs. Osei Tutu and Okomfo Anokye, credited with founding the Asante state in the eighteenth century, learned statecraft from the Akwamu, including lawmaking. The laws of the Popo and Koromantin communities probably stemmed from long-term contact between the two groups and the Akwamu and were later reinforced by the Asante, whose hegemony as an imperial power later made them culturally influential on the Gold Coast. See Wilkes, "The Mossi and Akan State, 1500 to 1800," 434; Hampton, "The Continuity Factor in Ga Music."

60. The sociologist Orlando Patterson writes, "There is nothing at all self-evident in the idea or, more properly, the high esteem in which we in the West hold freedom. For most of human history, and for nearly all of the non-Western world prior to Western contact, freedom was, and for many still remains, anything but an obvious or desirable goal. Other values and ideals were, or are, of far greater importance to them." Patterson *Freedom*, 1:x.

61. Wilks, *Forests of Gold*.

62. Quoted in Kenneth Scott, "The Slave Insurrection of 1712," 46–47.

63. The historian Eugene Genovese has noted, "Africans brought with them as many commitments to and preconceptions of justice and legitimacy as their captors did." Genovese, *From Rebellion to Resistance*, xvi.

64. *DRHNY*, 5:341.

65. Patterson, *Slavery and Social Death*, esp. 1–14.

66. Minutes of the Court of Quarter Sessions, August 7, 1694, to 1731, 214–46, 248.

67. Ibid.

68. Rediker, *Between the Devil and the Deep Blue Sea*.

69. Linebaugh, "All the Atlantic Mountain Shook," 111.

70. Bridenbaugh, *Gentlemen's Progress*, 40–41. See also Warner, *The Letters of the Republic*, 13; Shane White, *Somewhat More Independent*, 190.

71. For the role of overseas news and rumors in fueling the Haitian Revolution, see Julius S. Scott, "The Common Wind."

72. William Smith, *History of the Province of New-York*, 1:147.

73. Richard Wade has argued that the urban environment was incompatible with the institution of chattel slavery. In contrast, Claudia Goldin has argued that the urban setting supported slavery and militated against the success of slave uprisings. See Wade, *Slavery in the Cities*, and Goldin, *Urban Slavery in the American South*. This study shows that even though the density of the city's population and the slaves' flexible work routines gave rise to problems of slave control, the environment of colonial New York City in general did not undermine the institution of slavery, but instead generated a demand for slave labor and in this respect enhanced the viability of chattel slavery.

74. Aptheker, *American Negro Slave Revolts*, 168–69. In 1702, New York's colonial assembly enacted the colony's first law exclusively aimed at the regulation of the enslaved population. *Colonial Laws of New York*, 1:519–21.

75. Rossiter, *A Century of Population Growth*, 181.

76. Only three convicted rebels had lived in the thinly populated West Ward, and none had lived in the sparsely populated North Ward and Outward. See Minutes of the Court of Quarter Sessions, August 7, 1694, to 1731, 212–24, 228–48; Minutes of the Supreme Court of Judicature, June 6, 1710–June 5, 1714, 399–400, 417, 426, 429.

77. *MCC*, 1:134.

78. *Colonial Laws of New York*, 1:519–21.

79. Letter from John Sharpe to the Secretary, New York, June 23, 1712, in Letterbooks of the SPG.

80. The black town dwellers continued to observe Pinkster well into the nineteenth century, long after the descendants of the colonial Netherlanders discontinued the practice. For a description of Albany's black Pinkster Day celebration, see Eights, "Pinkster Festivities in Albany Sixty Years Ago." For a fictional account of a New York City black Pinkster Day festival, see Cooper, *Satanstoe*, 50–78.

81. Stuckey, *Slave Culture*, 80–83. For a comparable interpretation of the black Pinkster parades, see Williams-Meyers, "Pinkster Carnival." For a discussion of similar black festivals, see Reidy, "'Negro Election Day' and Black Community Life in New England, 1750–1860"; Lorenzo J. Greene, *The Negro in Colonial New England*, 245–48; and Reid, "The John Canoe Festival."

82. Shane White, *Somewhat More Independent*, 98. See also Shane White, "Pinkster in Albany, 1803"; "'It Was a Proud Day'"; and "Pinkster." For an influential study on status inversion rituals, see Victor Turner, *The Ritual Process*, esp. chapters 3–5. For rituals of status reversal in early modern Europe, see Natalie Zemon Davis, *Society and Culture in Early Modern French Society*, esp. 128–29, 130–31, 143; and Burke, *Popular Culture in Early Modern Europe*, esp. 183, 188–89, 199–204. For status inversion rituals in African cultures, see Gluckman, *Custom and Conflict in Africa*, esp. 109–36; *Rituals of Rebellion in South-East Africa*, esp. introduction and chapter 5.

83. Guha, *Elementary Aspects of Peasant Insurgency in Colonial India*, 30.

84. Letter from James Wetmore to the Secretary [n.d.] in Letterbooks of the SPG.

85. For the biblical passages most often cited as evidence that black Africans were the descendants of the sons of Ham, see Genesis 9:18–27; 10:6–14. For a useful discussion of early modern interpretations of postdiluvian history, see Kidd, *British Identities before Nationalism*, 19–33

86. Blackburn, *The Making of New World Slavery*, 72.

87. Letter from James Wetmore to the Secretary, New York, December 3, 1726, in Letterbooks of the SPG.

88. According to the historian Philip D. Morgan, native Africans comprised a majority in the Carolina low country's black population not much earlier than the 1770s. See Morgan, "Black Society in the Lowcountry, 1760–1810," 89; *Slave Counterpoint*, 82–83. In contrast to the black populations in the colonial Carolina low country and in colonial New York City, American-born blacks comprised a majority of the colonial Chesapeake region's black population as early as the 1730s. See Kulikoff, "A 'Prolifick' People," 405; Menard, "The Maryland Slave Population, 1658 to 1730," 32. In the Caribbean basin, native Africans were a majority of the black population for a longer period than was the case for British mainland America. In Jamaica, the emergence of an American-born black majority most likely occurred between the 1770s and the 1820s, later than in most black populations of British mainland America. See Brathwaite, *The Development of Creole Society in Jamaica, 1770–1820*.

89. Another convenient way of locating the Negros Burial Ground is to find block numbers 153, 154, and 155 on the official NYCMAP for the Borough of Manhattan, New York City.

90. Valentine, "History of Broadway," 567.

91. Though the exact date is unknown, colonial New York City's black population

probably began burying their dead at the Negros Burial Ground no later than 1712. See Sharpe, "Proposals for Erecting a School," 355. The practice of burying the dead on the land called the Negros Burial Ground probably ceased in 1795, when that parcel of real estate was divided among the heirs of the original landowners. See Liber Deeds and Conveyances. At that time the municipal government began to make arrangements for the establishment of a black cemetery on Chrystie Street. See *MCC*, 2:137.

92. The historian John S. Blassingame has emphasized the importance of semi-autonomous social space, such as separate slave quarters, in the formation of rural slave cultures on the plantations of the antebellum South. See Blassingame, *Slave Community*. In colonial cities, semi-autonomous social space—for example, Congo Square in New Orleans and the separate slave districts in Bridgetown, Barbados; Rio de Janiero, Brazil; and Havana, Cuba, and the Negros Burial Ground in colonial New York City—enabled the development of urban slave cultures.

93. *MCC*, 3:296, 4:447.

94. Sharpe, "Proposals for Erecting a School," 355. Conjurors (or root doctors)—for example, Peter the Doctor, a free black from New York City's East Ward, and Doctor Harry, a free black from Nassau, Long Island—may well have presided over these burial rites.

95. For an excellent study of the processes of detribalization and retribalization undergone by people of African descent in the southern colonies of British North America and the plantation South of the United States, see Gomez, *Exchanging Our Country Marks*.

96. Levine, *Black Culture and Black Consciousness*, 5.

97. Letter from John Sharpe to the Secretary, New York, June 23, 1712, in Letter-books.

98. Williams, *Voodoos and Obeahs*; Hedrick and Stephens, *It's a Natural Fact*; Morrish, *Obeah, Christ and Rastaman*; and Sheridan, *Doctors and Slaves*.

99. For black burial associations in nineteenth-century New York City and their retention of African-derived burial practices, see Craig Steven Wilder, *In the Company of Black Men*, 9–35.

100. In 1991, during the construction of the 34-story tower for the federal office building at 290 Broadway, a team of archeologists excavated 435 burials in the northeast portion of colonial New York City's Negros Burial Ground (a segment of present-day Block 154 only). Protected for nearly three centuries by 16 to 25 feet of landfill, colonial New York City's Negros Burial Ground is the best preserved and oldest urban black burial site uncovered in the Americas to date and is estimated to contain approximately 20,000 separate skeletal remains. Largely undisturbed burials lay underneath the building structures at 14–16 Reade Street, 51 Chambers Street, 21 Duane Street; the northern portion of the Court Square Building at the corner of Reade and Lafayette streets; and the northern portion of the A. T. Stewart Store Building at 280 Broadway. Some partially disturbed burials lay beneath other areas of Chambers, Reade, and Duane streets. The digging of subway tunnels along Centre Street, Lafayette Street, and Broadway destroyed many burials. For an overview of the 1991 excavation on Block 154, see Hansen and McGowan, *Breaking Ground, Breaking Silence*. St. Peter's Cemetery in New Orleans is the only other eighteenth-century urban black burial ground excavated in the Americas. Only 29 skeletal remains were uncovered at that site. See Owsley, "Demography and Pathology of an Urban Slave Population from New Orleans."

101. Of the 435 burials excavated from colonial New York City's Negros Burial Ground, archeologists have identified 16 human remains with modified teeth, some displaying an hourglass pattern. For a textual reference to a black town dweller with filed teeth, see *New York Weekly Post-Boy*, October 14 to October 20, 1762. Archeologists have discovered evidence of the practice of tooth mutilation or filing in other slave burial

populations in the Americas. See Stewart and Groome, "The African Custom of Tooth Mutilation in America"; Handler, Corrucini, and Mutaw, "Tooth Mutilation in the Caribbean."

102. The people of West Africa interred burial goods with human remains. Burial goods have also been uncovered at slave graveyards in the Caribbean basin and in the southern United States. See Thompson, *Flash of the Spirit*, 132–42; Philip D. Morgan, *Slave Counterpoint*, 642.

103. For a discussion of Sankofa, see Tedla, *Sankofa*.

104. For affinities and incompatibilities between African cosmologies, on the one hand, and Western European cosmologies, on the other, see Horton, *Patterns of Thought in Africa and the West*. No single, uniform religious cosmology dominated the cultures of sub-Saharan Africa during the era of the transatlantic slave trade. Rather, the various clan groups in that region of Africa each adhered to its own distinct belief system and worshiped its own particular pantheon of deities. For the diversity of African religions, see Ranger, "Recent Developments in the Study of African Religions and Cultural History and Their Relevance for the Historiography of the Diaspora," 21. Native Africans did, however, share some basic beliefs. See Mbiti, *African Religions and Philosophies*; Mintz and Price, *An Anthropological Approach to the Afro-American Past*, 23.

105. Quoted in Balmer, *A Perfect Babel of Confusion*, 5.

106. Mbiti, *African Religions and Philosophies*, 57.

107. Fernow, *Records of New Amsterdam*, 2:41.

108. Mbiti, *African Religions and Philosophy*, 30–31.

109. Butler, *Awash in a Sea of Faith*, 153.

110. For the receptivity of African religious cosmologies to new worldviews, see Mbiti, *African Religions and Philosophy*, 138.

111. Quoted in Klingberg, *Anglican Humanitarianism*, 144–45.

112. A review of the SPG's slave conversion record in colonial New York City indicates that as late as the 1730s its missionary work had reduced only slightly the cultural alienness of the city's black population; but, beginning in the 1740s, the SPG began to improve its conversion record, especially among black youths. See Letter from Reverend Vesey to the Secretary, New York, September 5, 1704; Letter from Elias Neau to John Chamberlayn [n.d.]; Letter from Elias Neau to John Chamberlayn, New York, August 24, 1708; Letter from Thomas Colgan to David Humphreys, New York, May 20, 1727; Letter from Thomas Colgan to David Humphreys, New York, December 23, 1728; Letter from Richard Charlton to the Secretary, New York, June 5, 1733; Letter from Reverend Auchmuty to the Secretary, New York, October 2, 1751; Letter from Reverend Auchmuty to Daniel Burton, New York, April 25, 1771; and Letter from Joseph Hildreth to Richard Hind, New York, November 7, 1773, in Letterbooks of the SPG.

113. Quoted in Goodfriend, *Before the Melting Pot*, 123.

114. Quoted in Klingberg, *Anglican Humanitarianism*, 149.

115. Quoted in Hodges, *Root and Branch*, 120.

116. Quoted in ibid., 119.

117. Letter from Samuel Auchmuty to the Secretary, New York, August 22, 1748, in Letterbooks of the SPG.

118. Klingberg, *Anglican Humanitarianism*, 151.

119. House Expense Book of Evert Bancker, 1760 to 1775.

120. For the early prohibition against the burial of blacks in Trinity Churchyard, see Trinity Church Vestry Minutes, October 25, 1697, 1:11.

121. For the arrangements for opening the separate cemetery for black Anglicans, see Trinity Church Vestry Minutes, September 15, 1773, 1:377–78; Trinity Church Vestry Minutes, July 7, 1774, 1:385.

122. DeCosta, *Three Score and Ten*, 14–21.

123. Privateers sold Spanish-speaking Indian and mulatto captives into slavery at the port of New York during the War of Jenkin's Ear (1739–42), King George's War (1744–48), and the French and Indian War (1756–63). In the slave cultures of the Caribbean basin, the fusion of compatible African and Catholic religious beliefs and practices resulted in the formation of syncretic slave religions—for example, Candomblé in Brazil, Santería in Cuba, and Vodun in Haiti. For an influential discussion of syncretic New World slave religions, see Bastide, *African Civilisation in the New World*.

124. *Colonial Laws of New York*, 1:428–30.

125. For a reference to a few racially mixed evangelical congregations in colonial New York, see Hodges, *Root and Branch*, 86. For the early black evangelical congregations, see Bonomi, *Under the Cope of Heaven*, 119; Boles, *Masters and Slaves In the House of the Lord*; Jackson, "Early Strivings of the Negro in Virginia"; and Frey, *Water from the Rock*, 37.

126. *New York Gazette*, November 12 to November 18, 1739. See also Whitefield, *George Whitefield's Journals*, 345–46.

127. Slaveowner opposition to the preaching of egalitarian ideals would force evangelical ministers to temper their emphasis on equality and formulate an accommodation to slavery. See Essig, *The Bonds of Wickedness*, 73–96; Oakes, *The Ruling Race*, 108.

128. George Whitefield did not advocate the abolition of slavery, but instead called for better treatment of slaves. See Stein, "George Whitefield on Slavery."

129. For the influence of evangelical Protestantism on an acculturated native African and his conversion experience, see Gronniosaw, *A Narrative of the Most Remarkable Particulars*, 45–47.

130. Berlin, *Many Thousands Gone*, 184.

131. Gutman, *The Black Family in Slavery and Freedom, 1750–1925*, 261.

132. Tannenbaum, *Slave and Citizen*, vii.

133. Genovese, *Roll, Jordan, Roll*, esp. 5.

134. Gutman, *Black Family*, 316.

135. Butler, *Awash in a Sea of Faith*, 137–44.

136. For receipts for the purchase of apparel for slaves, see House Expense Book of Evert Bancker, 1760 to 1775. See also Receipt Book of Nicholas Bayard, April 20, 1762–August 11, 1772; Ledger of Accounts of Charles Nicoll for the Sale and Repair of Shoes. Nicoll's business records show the accounts of 21 New York City slaveowners whose slaves frequented his shop: Captain James Creighton, John Watts, and Stephen Delancey were among the slaveowners who maintained accounts with Nicoll. Between 1759 and 1763, Nicoll took in a total of £37 for the sale and repair of "Negros' shoes."

137. Abraham Van Horne sold "Negro coffins" to New York City slaveowners. His busiest season occurred in 1756, when a smallpox epidemic struck the densely populated port town. The price of the coffins for enslaved adults ranged from 11s. to 14s. each, including rosin and screws. The price of an enslaved child's coffin ranged from 4s. 6d. to 10s. each, depending on its dimensions. See Day Book of Abraham Van Horne, 1753 to 1756.

A majority of the burial population from the excavated portion of colonial New York City's Negros Burial Ground had been wrapped in shrouds. Stain outlines in the earth indicate that at least 77 percent of the 435 burials uncovered during the 1991 excavation had been interred in inexpensive nondecorative hexagonal coffins made of woods native to the environment surrounding the city during colonial times—for example, pine, cedar, and spruce. The initial preparation of human remains for burial probably marked the limit of New York City slaveowners' involvement in most slave burials. Because decaying corpses presented a health hazard to the inhabitants of the densely populated port town, human remains were doubtless buried as expeditiously as possible. It is therefore likely that the owner of a deceased slave quickly transferred the human remains, already wrapped in a cerement and laid in a coffin, to the deceased slave's family and friends. Once in possession of the corpse, these mourners probably conveyed the human remains to the Negros Burial Ground, where a gathering of black town dwellers participated in the burial ceremony.

138. Inventory of the Estate of Christiana Cappoens [Goschersen], December 19, 1693.

139. Hodges, *Root and Branch*, 72.

140. Will of Teneke Bensen, February 21, 1753.

141. Petition of a Negro for Freedom; *New York Weekly Post-Boy*, July 24 to July 30, 1758. A Spanish-speaking captive from New Spain, Juan Miranda had been seized from a Spanish sailing vessel, condemned as a prize good, and sold into slavery at New York City. Miranda was perhaps familiar with the system of *coartación*, a legal mechanism in New Spain that allowed master and slave to enter into an agreement, generally arbitrated through the court, whereby the slave arranged to purchase his or her freedom at a fixed price, often with installments paid over a set period of time. According to David Brion Davis, the system of *coartación* originated in Cuba and then migrated to other Spanish colonies. See Davis, *Problem of Slavery in Western Culture*, 266–67. See also Aimes, "Coartación."

In 1746, New York's Vice-Admiralty Court judged six of nine Indians, mulattoes, and Negroes, earlier seized from a Spanish sailing vessel and brought to the port of New York for sale, to be lawful prize goods. At that time the court ordered that the condemned captives be allowed to purchase their freedom, perhaps in consideration of New Spain's system of *coartación*. See Hough, *Reports of Cases in the Vice Admiralty Court*, 29–33, 199; *Colonial Laws of New York*, 1:429. Juan Miranda was perhaps one of the unlucky captives condemned to slavery in 1746. If this was the case, then, the Vice-Admiralty Court had promised Miranda that he would be allowed to purchase his freedom, a court order that Miranda's master perhaps attempted to honor in his last testament.

142. Hodges, *Root and Branch*, 130. For additional freedom suits, see Edwin V. Morgan, *Slavery in New York*, 11–12; *New-York Weekly Gazette*, July 18 to July 24, 1763.

143. Goodfriend, *Before the Melting Pot*, 125.

144. Hodges, *Root and Branch*, 130–31.

145. The historian Shane White guesses that no more than 100 free blacks lived in New York City during the colonial period. White, *Somewhat More Independent*, 153.

146. In 1659–60, WIC Director-General Petrus Stuyvesant confirmed the deeds of 10 free black landowners, who in 1644 acquired land as a reward for faithful service to the WIC during the Indian war, and another three free black landowners, who received land in 1647. These contiguous parcels of land became known as the "Free Negro Lots." Beside the "Free Negro Lots" in the vicinity of present-day Astor Place, there were additional free black homesteads scattered about lower Manhattan. For example, free blacks resided on the city's Anglican Church farm. The 1703 household census for the County of New York does not include free black householders, though other historical records document the presence of free blacks on Manhattan Island. See Trinity Parish Leases for the Church Farm. Only seven censuses taken in New York before 1790 included the category "free Negro" or "free Black": New Utrecht in 1698, Westchester in 1698, Eastchester in 1698, Fordham in 1698, Bedford in 1698, and Oysterbay in 1755 and 1781.

147. For the English confirmation of these separate deeds, see O'Callaghan, *Calendar of Historical Manuscripts*, 1:126, 128; Stokes, *Iconography*, 6:123.

148. Stokes, *Iconography*, 6:123.

149. Fabend, "The Yeoman Ideal," 94; Hodges, *Root and Branch*, 35.

150. Hodges, *Root and Branch*, 17, 71; Christoph, "Freedmen of New Amsterdam," 116–17; and O'Callaghan, *Calendar of Dutch Historical Manuscripts*, 1:222, 256.

151. For the landholdings and genealogical records of Pieter Santome and his descendants, see Hoff, "A Colonial Black Family in New York and New Jersey," 101–34.

152. Christoph, "Freedmen of New Amsterdam," 148–49.

153. *Colonial Laws of New York,* 1:519–21.

154. New York's colonial assembly reintroduced the 1702 statute in the Black Code of 1712. The Privy Council again disallowed that statute, but allowed the colonial assembly to replace it with the 1707 statute. See *DRHNY,* 5:457; *Colonial Laws of New York,* 1:761–67.

155. *Colonial Laws of New York,* 1:761.

156. Quoted in Hodges, *Root and Branch,* 67.

157. For the charity case involving Mary, Lucas Petersen's wife, see New York City, Charities, Church Wardens and Vestrymen. The record also indicates that the church wardens gave Mary a pauper's burial on September 14, 1738.

158. For court cases involving indigent free blacks, see Minutes of the Mayor's Court, November 28, 1710–May 17, 1715; Minutes of the Mayor's Court, June 22, 1714–December 24, 1717; Minutes of the Mayor's Court, May 6, 1718–November 23, 1720; and Minutes of the Mayor's Court, February 17, 1735/36–August 3, 1742.

159. For the decline in manumissions, see Kruger, "Born to Run," 593.

160. Yoshpee, "Record of Slave Manumission in New York during the Colonial and Early National Period."

161. Bond of Surety for Manumission, May 7, 1767. Minutes of the Court of Quarter Sessions, January 1, 1722–January 5, 1772.

162. Hodges, *Root and Branch,* 143.

163. Between 1718 and 1771, an antislavery movement gained influence among Quakers in New York. In 1718, the New York Quaker William Burling wrote an early antislavery tract, later published in Benjamin Lay's *All Slave-Keeper's That Keep the Innocent in Bondage Apostates,* 6–11. Before that time, the Burling family had participated in the slave trade and owned slaves. By the 1720s, the Burlings had renounced trafficking in slaves and had divested themselves of their slave property. In 1771, the New York Yearly Meeting announced that it would disown all Quakers who persisted in trading and keeping slaves. By 1782, New York Quakers had freed all but two slaves held captive in their community. See Drake, *Quakers and Slavery in America,* 134, 170–72; Worrall, *Quakers in the Colonial Northeast,* 157–63.

164. The colonial New York City newspapers each issue printed an average of six notices advertising the sale of slaves. Account books and probate records also document the sale of slaves. See Journal of Evert Bancker Recording the Sales and Dry Goods; Inventory of the Estate of Captain Giles Shelly; and Inventory of the Estate of Rip Van Dam.

165. Will of Joseph Reade, July 23, 1761; Inventory of the Estate of Rip Van Dam.

166. Will of Alexander Colden, December 16, 1774; Will of Elizabeth Colden [n.d.].

167. Will of Abraham Van Horne.

168. Will of James Van Horne.

169. Letterbook of John Watts, 17.

170. Letters and Papers of Cadwallader Colden, 213.

171. In an effort to refute the theory of "creolean degeneracy," the Americans Thomas Jefferson, Benjamin Franklin, and Aaron Burr sent specimens of American plant and animal life to European correspondents. Gerbi, *The Dispute of the New World*; Ceaser, *Reconstructing America.*

172. Will of Cadwallader Colden, March 15, 1779. New York State Archives, Albany.

173. Jefferson, *Notes on the State of Virginia,* 162.

174. For two excellent historical studies on the topic of rape in the southern slave regime, see Hodes, *Sex Across the Color Line*; Jacquelyn Dowd Hall, "'The Mind that Burns in Each Body.'" For an exceptionally insightful analysis of the much neglected topics of rape, gender, and race in the colonial North, see Dayton, *Women Before the Bar,* 265.

175. At that time Shelter Island was part of the legal jurisdiction of New York County. For the case against Cato, see Minutes of the Court of Quarter Sessions, August 7, 1694,

to 1731. See also *New York Gazette,* January 21 to January 27, 1733, and January 28 to February 3, 1733; and *New-York Weekly Journal,* January 28 to February 3, 1733.

176. Dom Rex v. Jonnoau, a Negro Man Slave, July 20, 1737, in Minutes of the Court of Quarter Sessions, May 2, 1732 to August 4, 1762.

177. *New York* Gazette, July 25 to July 31, 1737.

178. Fox-Genovese, *Within the Plantation Household,* 263.

179. Colonial Virginia's Antimiscegenation Law of 1691 punished white setters who married a Negro, mulatto, or Indian with banishment from the colony. See McIlwaine, *Legislative Journals of the Council of Colonial Virginia,* 1:262; Edmund S. Morgan, *American Slavery, American Freedom,* 335.

180. The sociologist Etienne Balibar has convincingly argued that a "principle of closure, exclusion" is always a necessary component of a cohesive national community. See Balibar, "The Nation Form," 100–102.

181. The slaveowner-patriarch's interest in preserving his slave property sometimes saved male slaves from the death penalty. In 1749, John Murray obstructed the official court proceedings charging his male slave with the rape of a white woman, a capital crime. See McManus, *A History of Negro Slavery in New York,* 96.

182. For colonial societies where concubinary relations were tolerated and even encouraged, see Verena Martinez-Alier, *Marriage, Class and Colour in Nineteenth-Century Cuba;* Stoler, "Carnal Knowledge and Imperial Power," in di Leonardo, *Gender at the Crossroads of Knowledge;* and Lovejoy, "Concubinage and the Status of Women Slaves in Early Colonial Northern Nigeria."

183. In this study's sample population of enslaved children advertised for sale in colonial New York City newspapers, nearly 13 percent (21 out of 164) were designated "mulattoes." The sample population does not include enslaved children from outside colonial New York.

184. For a brilliant analysis of the discursive construction of the black female seductress (or black "Jezebel" stereotype), see Hartman, *Scenes of Subjection.*

185. *New York Weekly Post-Boy,* April 25 to May 1, 1743. In 1763, a bloodthirsty crowd of New York City townspeople stoned and dragged through the streets a black man named Tom, who was accused of the attempted rape of a white child. Tom was soon arrested, convicted of that crime, and executed. See *New York Mercury,* December 5 to December 11, 1763.

186. The historian Philip D. Morgan writes, "A defining characteristic of slavery was its highly personal mechanism of coercion: the whip, rather than the law, was its indispensable and ubiquitous instrument." Morgan, *Slave Counterpoint,* 265. The sociologist Orlando Patterson adds, "Violence was the ultimate sanction." Patterson, *Slavery and Social Death,* 12.

187. *Colonial Laws of New York,* 1:18, 47–48, 157–59; 4:924–25.

188. Benedict Anderson, *Imagined Communities,* 150.

189. For the deployment of antiblack racism as a disciplinary mechanism of elite rule over propertyless whites, see Allen, *The Invention of the White Race,* esp. 19, 23.

Chapter 5

1. Bonomi, *A Factious People,* 78.

2. Becker, *The History of Political Parties in the Province of New York,* 5.

3. For studies on this episode in colonial New York City's history, see Clarke, "The Negro Plot of 1741"; Szasz, "The New York Slave Revolt of 1741"; Thomas J. Davis, *Rumor of Revolt;* and Peter Hoffer, *The Great New York Conspiracy of 1741.*

4. Horsmanden, *Journal of the Proceedings in the Detection of the Conspiracy.* The follow-

ing discussion relies on the reprint of Horsmanden's *Journal* in Thomas J. Davis, *The New York Conspiracy by Daniel Horsmanden*.

5. For an influential definition of *common sense* and its relation to *hegemony* (or the attainment of the consent of the governed to elite rule, involving a battle of conflicting social groups to determine what is historically true and culminating in the worldview of a particular group becoming dominant), see Gramsci, *Selections from the Prison Notebooks*, 325–43.

6. Bonomi, *A Factious People*, 130–35.

7. For a discussion of the Zenger Trial, see Levy, *Freedom of the Press from Zenger to Jefferson*, esp. xxvi–xxxvii.

8. The rivalry between the Van Dam and Clarke factions was reminiscent of the internal divisions that gave rise to Leisler's Rebellion of 1689–92, the power struggle that followed the death of Governor Bellomont in 1701, and the dispute between New York's landed elite and merchants over the royal revenues and the allocation of the governor's salary in 1712. See Bonomi, *A Factious People*, 103–39.

9. Colonial New York's law defined a voter (or freehold elector) as an adult white male inhabitant who possessed an unencumbered estate (land and/or tenements) worth at least £40 per annum. See *Colonial Laws of New York*, 1:74.

10. Bonomi, *A Factious People*, 91.

11. Thomas J. Davis, *Rumor of Revolt*, 27–30.

12. Colden, "History of Gov. William Cosby's Administration."

13. Due to the dearth of documentary references to them, the black brotherhoods of colonial New York City have received scant scholarly attention, whereas colonial Brazil's black urban brotherhoods, known as *irmandades*, have been the focus of several detailed studies. These studies indicate that the black brotherhoods in the cities of Brazil date back to the eighteenth century and that these confraternities organized the burial of slaves and free blacks, as well as other mutual aid activities for colonial Brazil's black urban communities. See Russell-Wood, "Black and Mulatto Brotherhoods in Colonial Brazil"; Scaran, *Devoçao e escravidão*; Mulvey, "The Black Lay Brotherhoods of Colonial Brazil; and Boschi, *Os leigos e o poder*. Documentary references to colonial New York City's black brotherhoods do not indicate that they served as mutual aid organizations for the city's black community but instead tend to criminalize these confraternities, stressing the involvement of their leaders in burglaries and other infractions of the law. Black men did, however, organize mutual aid societies in nineteenth-century New York City. See Wilder, *In the Company of Black Men*, 9–35.

14. The historian Douglas Greenberg suggests that before the crime wave of 1741–42 struck New York City a connection between theft and "disorderly houses," such as taverns, already existed in the minds of the settlers. See Greenberg, *Crime and Law Enforcement in the Colony of New York*, 52–53.

15. For a description of the fire at the fort, see *New-York Weekly Journal*, March 23 to March 29, 1741–42.

16. For a description of these fires, see *New-York Weekly Journal*, April 13 to April 19, 1742. See also *Boston Weekly News-Letter*, May 7 to May 13, 1742.

17. McManus, *History of Negro Slavery in New York*, 25; Lydon, "New York and the Slave Trade," 387.

18. *New-York Weekly Journal*, March 22 to March 28, 1737.

19. New York City newspapers reported slave rebellions and conspiracies that occurred outside New York, as well as mutinies on slaving vessels. See *New York Gazette*, November 30 to December 6, 1730; September 4 to September 10, 1732; September 23 to September 29, 1734; February 22 to February 28, 1837; and *New-York Weekly Journal*, October 14 to October 20, 1734; July 29 to August 4, 1734; and May 28 to June 3, 1739.

20. Some witnesses in the conspiracy trials seem to have been familiar with the tactics of the enslaved rebels who during the Slave Revolt of 1712 set fire to buildings and ambushed white town dwellers in the night. For example, Sarah, an enslaved female informant, testified: "they [the alleged black conspirators] used to say that when they set fire to the town, they'd do it in the night and as the white people came to extinguish it, they'd kill and destroy them."

21. Hough, *Reports of Cases in the Vice Admiralty Court*, 17.

22. For the announcement of the rewards offered to informants, see *New-York Weekly Journal*, April 18 to April 24, 1742. See also *MCC*, 5:16–18.

23. A List of White Persons Taken into Custody on Account of the Conspiracy and List of Negroes Committed on Account of the Conspiracy [1741] in Thomas J. Davis, *New York Conspiracy*, 467–673.

24. For a newspaper report on the "general search," as well as Lieutenant Governor Clarke's proclamation of a day of "public fasting and humiliation," see *New-York Weekly Journal*, April 19 to April 25, 1742.

25. For the establishment of the military watch over New York City during the summer of 1742, see *MCC*, 5:43–44.

26. Gordon S. Wood, "Conspiracy and the Paranoid Style," 411.

27. Letter from Province of the Massachusetts Bay to Cadwallader Colden, Boston, [July 23?], 1741 in "Letters and Papers of Cadwallader Colden," 270–72.

28. Thomas J. Davis, *Rumor of Revolt*, 237.

29. This shift was symptomatic of the transformation of the public sphere, involving, on one hand, the contraction of the realm wherein a monarch represented himself as the embodiment of the divine authority of God and, on the other hand, the dilation of the domain wherein privatized individuals coalesced as an abstract public endowed with the capacity of supervision over governmental officials. The decisive mark of this "new domain of the public," Jürgen Habermas has noted, was the published word. See Habermas, *The Structural Transformation of the Public Sphere*, esp. 1–88.

30. Thomas J. Davis, *New York Conspiracy*, xxiii.

31. In commenting on the official documentation of subaltern conspiracy and rebellion in British colonial India, Ranajit Guha notes: "Drafted into the service of the regime as a direct instrument of its will it did not even bother to conceal its partisan character. Indeed, it often merged, both in its narrative and analytic forms, into what was explicitly official writing. For administrative practice turned it almost into a convention that a magistrate or a judge should construct his report on a local uprising as a historical narrative." See Guha, *Elementary Aspects of Peasant Insurgency*, 3. The colonial rulers in New York City also turned to the convention of historical narrative to document the "plot of 1741–42," but the transformation of the public sphere in that white settler colony required that they follow the conventions of print culture and conceal, as much as possible, their partisan biases. For a superb discussion of print culture in British North America, see Warner, *The Letters of the Republic*.

32. For the discursive conventions, the logic of cause and effect, and the evidentiary protocols shared by judges and historians, see Ginzburg, "Checking the Evidence."

33. Hayden White provides a useful review of the distinction modern historians generally make between three basic categories of historical representation—the annals, the chronicle, and history proper (historical narrative). White notes that for a historical representation to fall into the category of history proper, "events must be not only registered within the chronological framework of their original occurrence but narrated as well, that is to say, revealed as possessing a structure, an order of meaning, that they do not possess as mere sequence." See White, *Content of the Form*, 5. Horsmanden's "Introduction" offers just such a narration, for it confers a meaningful structure on the sequence of puzzling events that occurred during the winter of 1741–42. In his "Preface"

Horsmanden claims to forgo historical narration and announces that he will present instead a journal or diary, something akin to the annals. Yet only a few pages later, he acknowledges that he offers both a journal and a narrative. In this chapter, I use the phrase "Horsmanden's narrative" to refer to the historical narration contained in his "Introduction." I treat Horsmanden's reprint of the official interrogations, confessions, and court proceedings as extended footnotes or supporting evidence for his narrative. These reprinted documents are, therefore, drawn into my analysis of Horsmanden's narrative. The anthropologist Victor Turner has argued that "legal procedures generate narratives from brute facts." See Turner, "Social Drama and Stories about Them," 153. For important historical studies based on a narratological analysis of legal documents, see Ladurie, *Montaillou*; Ginzburg, *The Cheese and the Worms* and *Night Battles*; and Natalie Zemon Davis, *The Return of Martin Guerre* and *Fiction in the Archives*.

34. The original court records and other official transcripts have been destroyed. For the newspaper coverage of the conspiracy trials, see *New-York Weekly Journal*, March 22 to March 28, 1741–42, September 14 to September 20, 1742; October 12 to October 18, 1742; and *Boston Weekly News-Letter*, May 7 to May 13, 1742; July 15 to July 21, 1742; and August 12 to August 18, 1742. See also English Manuscripts.

35. Fredric Jameson notes that conspiracy theories involve a claim to comprehending the whole. See Jameson, *Postmodernism, or, The Cultural Logic of Late Capitalism*, 38.

36. Danto, *Narration and Knowledge*, xii, 143–81.

37. Abaddon (in Hebrew) or Apollyon (in Greek): "angel of the bottomless pit." See Rev. 9:11.

38. John Hughson's father (pardoned on condition of departing the colony), his four brothers (pardoned on condition of departing the colony), his wife (convicted of conspiracy and hanged), and his daughter (pardoned) all fell under suspicion because of their familial ties to John Hughson and their alleged association with enslaved blacks.

39. In the wake of the Jacobite Uprising of 1715, New York's colonial assembly enacted a law that imposed several restrictions on Catholics who resided within the colony, including prohibiting them from carrying firearms and requiring them to post a bond of surety for their good conduct and loyalty. *Colonial Laws of New York*, 1:858. See also *DRHNY*, 4:160.

40. The colonial authorities jailed four Irish soldiers—Edward Kelly, William Kane, Edward Murphey, and Andrew Ryan—but released them after the prosecution failed to uncover sufficient evidence to bring them to trial. See "A List of White Persons Taken into Custody on Account of the Conspiracy [1741]" in Thomas J. Davis, *New York Conspiracy*, 467. Earlier, in 1700, New York's Royal Governor Bellomont, a William and Mary appointee, described recent immigrants from Ulster as the "very scum of the army in Ireland and several Irish papists amongst 'em." *DRHNY*, 4:770.

41. Ury was reported to have preached on Matthew 16:18–19. See Thomas J. Davis, *Rumor of Revolt*, 200. For the statute that banished Catholic priests from colonial New York and imposed life imprisonment on Catholic priests who were discovered in the colony, see *Colonial Laws of New York*, 1:428–30.

42. At this juncture, the official investigation into the "plot of 1741–42" begins to resemble the Spanish Inquisition and its localized auto-da-fé, whose goal was to eliminate heterodoxy among professed Christians—particularly among *conversos* (the suspect category of Jews and Muslims who had converted to Christianity). Like the Spanish inquisitors, the authorities in colonial New York City endeavored to purge hidden heretics—in this case, crypto-Catholics who could not be distinguished from the white Protestant settler population by any particular visible mark.

43. Kavanagh, *The Shape of Baptism*.

44. Following England's Glorious Revolution, the term *nonjuring priest* referred to an Anglican cleric who, in 1689, refused to take an oath of allegiance to William and Mary

after James II had been deposed from the throne of England. At that time nonjuring priests asserted their belief in the divine right of monarchs to absolute rule and pledged to protest the new political order through passive disobedience only. See Ollard, *A Dictionary of English Church History*, 410–14.

45. Milton, *Paradise Lost*, 2:108–15, 117–18, 226–27.

46. Genovese, *Roll, Jordan, Roll*, 5. See also David Brion Davis, *Problem of Slavery in Western Culture*, 223, 248.

47. Bhabha, *The Location of Culture*, 80.

48. The colonial port town's workplaces, especially the shops of New York City craftsmen, were sites of the acquisition of translation skills and the manufacture of cultural hybridity, as well as the acquisition of artisanal skills and the production of finished commodities.

49. Nash, "Forging Freedom," 294. Nash notes the use of West African day-names in eighteenth-century New York City's black population. For naming patterns in the southern black populations, see Kulikoff, *Tobacco and Slaves*, 325–26; and Peter H. Wood, *Black Majority*, 181–86.

50. Fanon, *Black Skin, White Mask*, 17–18.

51. Ibid., 18.

52. For a useful discussion of the cultural logic of cause and effect, see Gasking, *Language, Logic, and Causation*.

53. Thomas J. Davis, *New York Conspiracy*, xix.

54. Gordon S. Wood, "Conspiracy and the Paranoid Style," 407.

55. For a discussion of the fear of deception, false identity, and theatricality in early modern Anglo-American culture, see Agnew, *Worlds Apart*.

56. For an influential theorization of the colonizer's ambivalent attitude toward the "colonized other," see Young, *Colonial Desire*.

57. Stemmler, "The Physiognomical Portraits of Johann Caspar Lavater"; Shookman, *The Faces of Physiognomy*.

58. For the significance of the hermeneutic tradition in Western European thought, see Palmer, *Hermeneutics*. For the intellectual tradition of British empiricism, see Thomas, *The British Empiricists*; Law, *The Rhetoric of Empiricism*. For empiricism as a condition of the formation of value, see Bracken, "Essence, Accident, and Race."

59. Bhabha, *Location of Culture*, 70–71.

60. For the disavowal of subaltern agency in the discourse of conspiracy in colonial India, see Guha, *Elementary Aspects of Peasant Insurgency*, 80.

61. Michel Foucault has noted in a more general context that the solution to the problem of disciplining populations is a matter of "gaining access to individuals themselves, to their bodies, their gestures and all their daily actions." See Foucault, *Power/Knowledge*, 151–52.

62. Ibid., 152.

63. In Horsmanden's narrative, the term *beauty* operates simultaneously as both an aesthetic and a cognitive category.

64. Kolchin, *Unfree Labor*, 170.

65. For a recent debate about the disposition of Europeans toward darker-skinned people and the origin of antiblack racism, see Vaughan and Vaughan, "Before *Othello*"; Bartels, "*Othello* and Africa"; Braude, "The Sons of Noah and the Construction of Ethnic and Geographical Identities in the Medieval and Early Modern Periods"; and Sweet, "The Iberian Roots of American Racist Thought."

66. David Brion Davis, *Problem of Slavery in Western Culture*, 446.

67. For a description of Spinoza's dream, see Ferrer, "The Dream of Benedict de Spinoza." Although Amsterdam had a small but visible black population since the seventeenth century, it is unlikely that Spinoza ever actually encountered the Negro of his

dreams. For a general discussion of the black presence in early modern Amsterdam, see Allison Blakey, *Blacks in the Dutch World*.

68. Hayden White, *Tropics of Discourse*, 184.

69. For the status of marvels and wonders in the Western intellectual tradition, see Burns, *The Great Debate on Miracles*; Daston, *Wonders and the Order of Nature*.

70. David D. Hall, *Worlds of Wonder, Days of Judgment*, esp. 71–116.

71. Following David Brion Davis's lead, this analysis has studied the colonialist discourse of conspiracy as "a special language or cultural form" that brings into articulation various strands of preexisting and emergent intellectual traditions and popular beliefs. See David Brion Davis, *The Fear of Conspiracy*, xv.

72. Admiral George Clinton arrived from England in 1743 and replaced George Clarke as interim Governor of New York. In the following year, Clinton removed Daniel Horsmanden from his post of Supreme Court justice. See Bonomi, *Factious People*, 149–66.

Chapter 6

1. *Colonial Laws of New York*, 1:507–8, 2:51–61.

2. For a survey of newspaper subscriptions in the British North American colonies, see Mott, *American Journalism*, 59.

3. For generic pictorial illustrations of runaways in colonial New York City newspaper advertisements, see *New-York Weekly Journal*, August 30 to September 5, 1756; *New York Weekly Post-Boy*, October 27 to November 2, 1763; and *New York Journal, or General Advertiser*, August 13 to August 19, 1767.

4. For a discussion of the resemblance of runaway ads to wills and probate records, see Prude, "To Look upon the 'Lower Sort,'" 137. The following analysis of colonial New York City newspaper advertisements for runaways is indebted to the example of Prude's superb study.

5. The sample runaway population for this study was compiled from 241 ads appearing in the following newspapers: *New York Gazette* (1726–41, 1744, and 1747–51); *New-York Weekly Journal* (1733–73); *New York Weekly Post-Boy* (1743–71); *New York Mercury* (1753–83); *New York Journal, or General Advertiser* (1766–75); and *Royal Gazette* (1777–82). This runaway sample population includes 249 fugitive slaves and 312 fugitive servants—a total of 561 runaways. Another 671 advertised runaways—fugitive slaves whose sex and/or age is unknown, fugitive servants whose sex and/or age and birthplace are unknown, and all runaways whose masters lived outside New York and the countryside surrounding New York City—are excluded from this study's runaway sample population. For reprints of 662 newspaper advertisements for runaways covering colonial New York and colonial New Jersey, see Hodges and Brown, *"Pretends to Be Free."*

6. *New-York Weekly Journal*, August 27 to September 2, 1733. For additional newspaper descriptions of physical infirmities, bodily dispositions, and other peculiar marks that individualized the fugitive body, see *New York Weekly Post-Boy*, July 10 to July 16, 1749; *New York Mercury*, July 1 to July 7, 1754, and July 17 to July 23, 1758.

7. *New York Mercury*, July 17 to July 23, 1758. Studies of runaway populations in the southern colonies generally attribute the peculiar bodily disposition known as the "down look" to enslaved blacks, but colonial New York City newspaper ads for runaways describe white servants who exhibited that same body posture. For the "down look" among the white runaway servants, see *New York Weekly Post-Boy*, August 28 to September 3, 1749; *New York Mercury*, June 26 to July 2, 1758, July 17 to July 23, 1758, July 2 to July 8, 1764; *New York Journal, or General Advertiser*, June 4 to June 10, 1768, July 9 to July 15, 1768, August 4 to August 10, 1768, March 23 to March 29, 1769, and March 25 to March 31, 1773.

8. *New-York Weekly Journal*, January 9 to January 15, 1735.

9. *New York Gazette*, May 17 to May 23, 1736; *New York Weekly Post-Boy*, April 10 to April

16, 1749; *New York Journal, or General Advertiser*, January 14 to January 20, 1768, August 4 to August 10, 1768; November 17 to November 23, 1768, August 22 to August 28, 1771; November 5 to November 11, 1772, and July 28 to August 3, 1774.

10. In the runaway servant sample for this study, only 1 percent of fugitive servants (2 out of 217) have no designated birthplace or nationality.

11. *New York Gazette,* October 29 to November 4, 1744.

12. For references to other runaway slaves who displayed tribal markings, sometimes referred to as "Guinea cuts," see *New-York Weekly Journal*, August 24 to August 30, 1730; and *New York Weekly Post-Boy*, April 1 to April 7, 1754, July 28 to August 3, 1763, December 10 to December 16, 1770, and January 4 to January 10, 1773.

13. Customs of bodily adornment, including ear piercing, were hardly exclusive to African cultures. In maritime culture, for example, European sailors pierced their ears and sported earrings. For a fascinating overview of the history of ear piercing in the West, see Steinbach, *The Fashionable Ear*, chaps. 25–27. For an additional example of a runaway slave with a pierced ear, see *New York Weekly Post-Boy*, September 30 to November 6, 1762.

14. Berlin, *Many Thousands Gone*, 184.

15. *Colonial Laws of New York*, 1:94.

16. For runaway slaves suspected of carrying forged passes and indentures, see *New York Gazette*, August 12 to August 18, 1728, and June 23 to June 29, 1729; *New York Weekly Post-Boy*, May 1 to May 7, 1749; *New York Mercury*, July 31 to August 6, 1758, August 21 to August 27, 1758, and September 24 to September 30, 1764; and *New York Journal, or General Advertiser*, January 16 to January 22, 1772, May 6 to May 12, 1773, and November 3,to November 9, 1774.

17. *New York Weekly Post-Boy*, October 15 to October 11, 1753.

18. For the persistence of bilingualism among black New Yorkers during the early national period, see Shane White, *Somewhat More Independent*, 190. See also Kruger, "Born to Run," 86–87.

19. For approximately 70 percent of the sample runaway slave population and nearly 75 percent of the sample runaway servant population, newspaper advertisements rated the fugitive's proficiency in spoken language(s) along a scale of "very good" (fluent) to "broken" (poor) speaking proficiency.

20. *New York Gazette*, August 28 to September 3, 1727.

21. *New York Weekly Post-Boy*, March 17 to March 23, 1760.

22. Berlin, *Many Thousands Gone*, 184.

23. *New York Weekly Post-Boy*, October 13 to October 19, 1746. For additional examples of the usage of the term *broken* to describe the language skill of runaway servants in colonial New York City newspaper ads, see also *New York Journal, or General Advertiser*, March 14 to March 20, 1768, April 29 to May 4, 1773, and October 6 to October 12, 1774.

24. *New York Mercury*, July 8 to July 14, 1765. See also *New York Journal, or General Advertiser*, March 5 to March 11, 1767.

25. *New York Journal, or General Advertiser*, November 5 to November 11, 1772.

26. *New York Weekly Post-Boy*, August 15 to August 21, 1748; *New York Mercury*, April 22 to April 28, 1765, and September 16 to September 22, 1765; *New York Journal, or General Advertiser*, June 23 to June 29, 1768, and August 12 to August 18, 1773.

27. *New York Journal, or General Advertiser*, December 24 to December 30, 1772, and October 27 to November 2, 1774; *Royal Gazette*, May 15 to May 21, 1777.

28. In his study on advertisements for runaways from both the northern and southern colonies, Jonathan Prude concludes that runaway ads "did not depict body features consistently or meticulously" and that clothing was "the most powerful signifier in runaway ads." However, Prude notes: "Northern runaways of all kinds were usually more elaborately described than their southern counterparts." See Prude, "To Look upon the 'Lower Sort,'" 142, 150–51.

29. Bushman, *The Refinement of America*, 69–74.

30. McClintock, *Imperial Leather*, 67.

31. For ads indicating that runaways had changed their clothing, see *New York Mercury*, July 23 to July 29, 1753, and October 8 to October 14, 1764.

32. For a description of a runaway slave who had been branded with mark *RN*, see *New York Gazette*, August 24 to August 30, 1730. In addition to habitual runaways, other criminals were branded with marks signifying their particular crimes. For a description of a white female servant with the brand mark *B* for bigamy, see *New York Journal, or General Advertiser*, May 11 to May 17, 1769. For additional brands, see *New York Weekly Post-Boy*, June 26 to July 2, 1766; and *Royal Gazette*, January 3 to January 9, 1778.

33. David Brion Davis, *Problem of Slavery in Western Culture*, 49.

34. *New York Gazette*, December 12 to December 18, 1737.

35. For foundational primary sources in the eighteenth-century discourse of race and its racial classification schema, see Bernasconi, *Concepts of Race in the Eighteenth Century*.

36. *New-York Weekly Journal*, January 27 to February 2, 1734. For a reference to a similar "miraculous birth" in colonial New York City, see Jordan, *White over Black*, 250–51.

37. Because some visible bodily traits attributed to particular racial classifications were thought to be mutable, changing with climate and other environmental conditions, the category "race" was rendered unstable in the scientific discourse of the early modern era. See Foucault, *The Order of Things*, 308–9.

38. For a discussion of early modern theories about the original skin color of humankind and the causes of variation in skin pigmentation within the human species, see Jordan, *White over Black*, 248–52.

39. *New York Gazette*, July 3 to July 9, 1738.

40. *New-York Weekly Journal*, July 13 to July 19, 1730. For additional examples of the range of skin pigmentation among runaway servants, see also *New-York Weekly Journal*, August 26 to September 1, 1734; *New York Mercury*, November 24 to November 30, 1760, and April 19 to April 25, 1762; *New York Journal, or General Advertiser*, September 9 to September 16, 1769.

41. For newspaper ads describing light-skinned mulatto slaves who might be mistaken for free whites, see *New York Journal, or General Advertiser*, December 8 to December 14, 1774; and December 22 to December 28, 1774.

42. *New York Gazette*, October 2 to October 8, 1738. Harry remained at large in 1743. See *New York Weekly Post-Boy*, July 25 to July 31, 1743.

43. Goldberg, *Racial Subjects*, 82.

44. *New York Weekly Post-Boy*, April 29 to May 5, 1762.

45. For additional newspaper advertisements for the capture of mulatto runaway servants and slaves, see *New York Weekly Post-Boy*, August 27 to September 2, 1759, June 18 to 24, 1762, and March 18 to March 24, 1771.

46. Letter from Nicholas Bayard to Archibald Carey (attrny), New York, December 13, 1763, and Letter from Nicholas Bayard to Capt. Youngblood, New York, December 13, 1763, in Letterbook of Nicholas Bayard, 1763. Enslaved Indians also resisted enslavement by claiming to have been born free, as most Indians were. In 1711, an Indian woman named Sarah Robins[son] did just that. Like the claim of the young black girl in 1763, Sarah's assertion to freedom entangled her would-be owner Captain Robert Walters, resident of New York City, in a protracted legal dispute. For details on this incident, see Goodfriend, *Before the Melting Pot*, 114–15.

47. For a rare example of an enslaved mother who ran away with an infant, presumably her own offspring, see *New York Mercury*, June 26 to July 2, 1758.

48. *New York Mercury*, June 12 to June 18, 1758.

49. Hodges, *Root and Branch*, 52.

50. Kenneth Scott, *Minutes of the Mayor's Court of New York*, 40–50.

51. *New York Mercury*, April 22 to April 28, 1765.

52. *New York Journal and General Advertiser*, April 14 to April 20, 1768.

53. De Villier reported that the village was said to have existed for 40 years before he discovered it. See *Canisteo Centennial, 1873–1973*.

54. *Colonial Laws of New York*, 1:582–84.

55. *New York Mercury*, October 10 to October 16, 1765. See also *New York Journal, or General Advertiser*, September 24 to September 30, 1772.

56. *New York Weekly Post-Boy*, January 23 to January 29, 1749. For a later attempt by Spanish-speaking slaves to escape by sea, see *New York Weekly Post-Boy*, April 3 to April 9, 1749. See also McManus, *History of Negro Slavery in New York*, 88.

57. See *New York Weekly Post-Boy*, October 2 to October 8, 1749, June 18 to June 24, 1753, October 10 to October 16, 1757, March 6 to March 12, 1758, and December 18 to December 24, 1758; and *New York Mercury*, October 28 to November 3, 1778, for fugitives presumed to be headed for the sea.

58. New York City's professional police force was not founded until 1845. For a history of the professionalization of the NYPD, see Richardson, *The New York City Police*.

59. *Colonial Laws of New York*, 1:119, 157–59.

60. *New-York Weekly Journal*, January 28 to February 3, 1733.

61. *New York Gazette*, December 17 to December 23, 1733.

62. *New-York Weekly Journal*, January 5 to January 11, 1735. Present-day coroner's reports replace the phrase "a visitation by God" with the nomenclature "natural causes."

63. For watercolor paintings depicting New York City slave vendors and their street cries, see Prints Collection, New York Historical Society.

The French scholar Claude Lévi-Strauss (*The Savage Mind*, esp. 16–36) first introduced the term *bricolage* to the field of anthropology. See also de Certeau, *The Practice of Everyday Life*, esp. xiii–xv.

64. De Voe, *The Market Book*, 1:344. See also Watson, *Annals and Occurrences of New York City and State in the Olden Time*, 171.

65. Linebaugh, *The London Hanged*, 135.

66. Abbott, "Neighborhoods of New York City," 50.

67. Linebaugh, *The London Hanged*, 134.

68. For the concept of the "mobilized gaze" as a defining attribute of the flâneur, see Friedberg, *Widow Shopping*, esp. 2–5, 12–13. For the cosmopolitan working-class culture of the early modern era, see Linebaugh, "All the Atlantic Mountain Shook," and Linebaugh and Rediker, "The Many-Headed Hydra."

69. Rediker, *Between the Devil and the Deep Blue Sea*.

70. *New York Weekly Post-Boy*, July 11 to July 17, 1743.

71. Ibid., July 25 to July 31, 1743.

72. The historian Timothy Gilfoyle identifies the neighborhood surrounding George Street and located nearby the East River wharves as a late-eighteenth-century prostitution district. See Gilfoyle, *City of Eros*, 25.

73. *Dom Rex v. Fortuno*, a Negro Man Slave of John Yorworth, May 6, 1724, in Minutes of the Court of Quarter Sessions, August 4, 1694, to 1733; *Dom Rex v. Joseph Loggings*, a free Negro [mariner], May 16, 1738, in Minutes of the Court of Quarter Sessions, May 2, 1732–August 4, 1762; and *Dom Rex v. Juan*, a Negro Man Slave of Charles Beekman, December 4, 1751, in Minutes of the Supreme Court of Judicature, 1766–96.

74. *MCC*, 3:30–31; 4:51–52, 86–87, 254.

75. Ibid., 9:89, 92.

76. Letter from Elias Neau to Mr. Hodges, July 10, 1703, in Letterbooks of the SPG.

77. *MCC*, 1:134, 276–77; *Colonial Laws of New York*, 1:35–57. Other English overseas colonies also feared the Sunday uprising of slaves. In South Carolina, around the time of the Stono Rebellion of 1739, the colonial assembly enacted a statute requiring all white

men to carry a firearm to Sunday worship services. See Peter H. Wood, *Black Majority*, 313. No law required the white Christian settlers in colonial New York to take such precautions on the Sabbath. The demographic dominance of the settler population and the presence of a standing army at the fort perhaps gave white New Yorkers greater confidence in their ability to suppress a slave rebellion than their counterparts in South Carolina, who comprised a demographic minority.

78. *New York Gazette*, May 2 to May 8, 1726.

79. *Colonial Laws of New York*, 1:761–67, 519–21; 3:379–81, 756–60; and 5:583–84.

80. Bridenbaugh, *Cities in Revolt*, 157.

81. Quoted in Hodges, *Root and Branch*, 166.

82. *Colonial Laws of New York*, 1:147–48, 519–21.

83. *Dom Rex v. Thomas Noble*, November 1716, in Minutes of the Court of Quarter Sessions August 7, 1694, to 1733. For a similar case against Mary Weekham, tavernkeeper, see NYC Misc. Mss. [Box 4; #10], Manuscripts Collection, New York Historical Society. See also *Dom Rex v. Henry Slyck*, February 5, 1735, in Minutes of the Court of Quarter Sessions May 2, 1732, to August 4, 1762; *Dom Rex v. Catherine O'Neal* [N.D.] in Minutes of the Court of Quarter Sessions January 1, 1722–January 5, 1772.

84. Fernow, *Records of New Amsterdam*, 6:286.

85. *Colonial Laws of New York*, 1:761–67.

86. *Dom Rex v. Peter*, a Negro Man [alias Peter the Doctor], laborer, February 2, 1714, in Minutes of the Court of Quarter Sessions, August 7, 1694, to 1733. For a similar case against a free black, see also *Dom Rex v. Tom*, a Negro (commonly called Tom Franconneur) in Minutes of the Court of Quarter Sessions, January 1, 1772–January 5, 1742.

87. *Colonial Laws of New York*, 1:519–21, 3:679–88. See also *MCC*, 4:497. For court cases related to alleged infractions of these laws, see *Dom Rex v. Phillis & Lena*, two Infants & Slaves & Matthew Doadman, July 19, 1737, in Minutes of the Court of Quarter Sessions, August 7, 1694, to 1733; and *Dom Rex v. Dick*, a Negro Man Slave belonging to John Van Zandt, February 5, 1752; *Dom Rex v. John Van Zandt*, August 2, 1758; *Dom Rex v. John Van Zandt*, November 5, 1760, in Minutes of the Court of Quarter Sessions, May 2, 1732– August 4, 1762. The antitrafficking laws did not apply to selling fish, fruits, and other country produce. The colonial authorities suspected that gambling, a popular pastime among the slaves, encouraged slaves to steal from their masters and other townspeople. For the municipal ordinances that prohibited slaves from gambling, see *MCC*, 3:277–78.

88. Olson, "The Slave Code in Colonial New York," 157.

89. Greenberg, *Crime and Law Enforcement*, 58 (Table 6), 89.

90. *Colonial Laws of New York*, 2:745–47, 5:644. For cases involving defendants indicted and convicted for petty larceny, see also *Dom Rex v. Betty*, a Negro Slave, August 4, 1719; *Dom Rex v. Franc*, a free Negro Woman, August 4, 1719; *Dom Rex v. William Norris, Charles Arrowsmith, Thomas Lawrence, and Elinor Blackington*, February 2, 1725, in Minutes of the Court of Quarter Sessions August 7, 1694, to 1733; and *Dom Rex v. James McKensey*, August 4, 1742, in Minutes of the Court of Quarter Sessions May 2, 1732–August 4, 1762.

91. Greenberg, *Crime and Law Enforcement*, 64–67. For violent confrontations between English newcomers and colonial Netherlanders, see *DRHNY*, 3:601–2, 747–48. See also Murrin, "English Rights as Ethnic Aggression," 58–60.

92. *Dom Rex v. Abraham Van Horne, Jr. and James Van Horne*, April 7, 1737, in Minutes of the Court of Quarter Session, January 1, 1722–January 5, 1772.

93. Hodges, *Root and Branch*, 53.

94. *Dom Rex v. Shadrach*, a free Negro, August 5, 1774, in Minutes of the General Court of the Peace, November 4, 1760–February 6, 1772. For another violent altercation between a black man—in this case, a runaway slave—and a white settler, see Goodfriend, *Before the Melting Pot*, 118.

95. *New York Weekly Post-Boy*, April 25 to March 1, 1743.

96. For a concerned town dweller's plea that the colonial authorities purchase a fire engine for New York City, see *New York Gazette*, February 4 to February 10, 1728, and February 18 to February 24, 1728.

97. Olson, "The Slave Code in Colonial New York," 159.

98. *New York Gazette*, January 10 to January 16, 1736, and January 17 to January 23, 1736.

99. Quoted in Thomas J. Davis, *Rumor of Revolt*, 93.

100. *Colonial Laws of New York*, 4:924–25.

101. *New York Gazette*, August 13 to August 19, 1767.

102. For a general account of the rise of poverty and the deepening of social inequality in the port towns of British North America during the seventh and eighth decades of the eighteenth century, see Henretta and Nobles, *Evolution of American Society, 1600–1820*, 72; Nash, "Urban Wealth and Poverty in Pre-Revolutionary America."

103. For the relation of domination between the nation and the colonies and the "dialectical process of 'othering,'" see Spivak, "The Rani of Simur."

104. For a detailed discussion of the mounting social tensions in the port towns of British North America on the eve of the American Revolution, see Nash, *Urban Crucible*.

105. Countryman, *A People in Revolution*, 71.

106. *The Independent Reflector*, No. 1, November 30, 1752.

107. Ibid., No. 32, July 5, 1753.

108. Bailyn, *The Ideological Origins of the American Revolution*, 234. For a study that draws a direct relationship between the enslavement of black Africans and their descendants in British North America and the American pamphleteers' concept of political slavery, see Okoye, "Chattel Slavery as the Nightmare of the American Revolutionaries."

109. Bernard Bailyn has persuasively argued that belief in a secret ministerial plot against English liberty structured the white settlers' "logic of rebellion" against English colonial rule. See Bailyn, *The Ideological Origins of the American Revolution*, esp. 94–159. For a related discussion of the Anglo-American political theory, see Robbins, *The Eighteenth-Century Commonwealthman*; and Pocock, "Machiavelli, Harrington, and English Political Ideologies in the Eighteenth Century."

Chapter 7

1. Wheatley, *The Collected Works*; Akers, "'Our Modern Egyptians'"; Aptheker, *Documentary History of the Negro People in the United States*, 1:1–16; Kaplan, "The Domestic Insurrections of the Declaration of Independence"; and Thomas J. Davis, "Emancipation Rhetoric, Natural Rights, and Revolutionary New England."

2. Hodges, "Black Revolt in New York City and the Neutral Zone," 27.

3. For an overview of black insurgency during the white American War for Independence, see Quarles, *The Negro in the American Revolution*; Peter H. Wood, "The Dream Deferred" and "'Liberty is Sweet'"; and Frey, *Water from the Rock*.

4. Black insurgency during the age of democratic revolutions was by no means confined to British America. As C. L. R. James has shown, the enslaved blacks of San Domingo expanded and radicalized the French Revolution, first in overthrowing slavery on that sugar island and then by pressing Robespierre and the Mountain to have the abolition of slavery in the French colonies confirmed by the French National Assembly. See James, *Black Jacobins*.

5. Genovese, *From Rebellion to Revolution*, xviii–xx. See also Mullin, *Africa in America*.

6. David Brion Davis, *Problem of Slavery in Western Culture*, 13.

7. Wheatley, *The Poems of Phillis Wheatley*, 204.

8. "Black critiques of modernity," Paul Gilroy writes, "may also be, in some significant senses, its affirmation." Gilroy, *The Black Atlantic*, 49. For excerpts from the writings of

eighteenth-century blacks, see Potkay and Burr, *Black Atlantic Writers of the Eighteenth Century*.

9. Hodges and Brown, *"Pretends to Be Free,"* xxxii.

10. Frey, *Water from the Rock*, 211.

11. For a brief account of the battles that resulted in the British military occupation of New York City and a discussion of the British military strategy during the Anglo-American conflict, see Bliven, *Battle of New York*.

12. By the terms of the Treaty of Paris, England ceded East Florida to the Americans. That British-occupied territory was not evacuated until August 29, 1785. For the several British evacuations in British North America, see Frey, *Water from the Rock*, 172–93.

13. On the eve of the war, 25,000 civilians lived in New York City, and nearly 33,000 civilians resided in that British stronghold at the conclusion of the war in 1783. Abbott, "Neighborhoods of New York City, 1760–1775"; Barck, *New York City during the War for Independence*, 76, 78.

14. Hodges, "Black Revolt in New York City and the Neutral Zone."

15. Quoted in Quarles, *Negro in the American Revolution*, 19.

16. Ibid., 28–31.

17. Letter from Nathaniel Green to George Washington, July 21, 1776.

18. Quarles, "Lord Dunmore as Liberator," 503.

19. List of Barrack Houses in the Garrison of New York.

20. Wallace, *Appeal to Arms*, 8–11; Don Higginbotham, The *War of American Independence*, 133.

21. Quarles, *Negro in the American Revolution*, 28.

22. Quoted in ibid.,12. See also "Muster Rolls of the New York Provincial Troops, 1755–1764," 60, 182, 284, 364, 385, 398, 402, 406, 418, 420, 426, 427, 440, 442, 498. For a discussion of the use of black troops in the colonial militias, see Quarles, "The Colonial Militia and Negro Manpower." See also Don Higginbotham, *War of American Independence*, 394–97, 401, 416n.

23. Quoted in Don Higginbotham, *War of Independence*, 395.

24. Mühlenberg, *Journals of Henry Melchoir Mühlenberg*, 3:105.

25. Hodges, "Black Revolt in New York City and the Neutral Zone," 24, 34–38.

26. For Colonel Tye's raids into eastern New Jersey, see Hodges, "African-Americans in Monmouth County during the Age of the American Revolution." Some blacks from Bergen County, New Jersey, crossed the Hudson River from Bull's Ferry to Manhattan. See Hodges, *Root and Branch*, 152–53.

27. For black unrest on the New York frontier during the Anglo-American conflict, see Simms, *The Frontiersmen of New York*, 2:176.

28. Sullivan, *Minutes of the Albany Committee of Correspondence, 1775–1778*, 1:24, 649–50; and *Minutes of the Albany Committee on the Detection and Defeating of Conspiracies*, 1:70,142–43, 146, 178, 202, 279, 304; 2:704.

29. Quoted in Lindsay, "Diplomatic Relations between the United States and Great Britain Bearing on the Return of Negro Slaves, 1783–1828," 393.

30. Quoted in Hodges, "Black Revolt in New York City and the Neutral Zone," 21.

31. Mühlenberg, *Journals of Henry Melchoir Mühlenberg*, 3:53, 105.

32. Frey, *Water from the Rock*, 114.

33. Quarles, *Negro in the American Revolution*, 68–110.

34. Wallace, *Appeal to Arms*, 53–54.

35. Maslowski, "National Policy towards the Use of Black Troops in the Revolution"; Philip Foner, *Blacks in the American Revolution*, 42–46.

36. Hodges, "Black Revolt in New York City and the Neutral Zone," 24.

37. In the winter of 1777, another blaze incinerated much of New York City. See Barck, *New York City during the War for Independence*, 74.

38. Rolls of the Quarter Master General's Department for the Wagonmaster or the Forage and Provision Departments of the Army. See also Barck, *New York City during the War for Independence*, 85, 107, 110–11.

39. Hodges, "Black Revolt in New York City and the Neutral Zone," 32. See also Voucher in the Account of Negro Laborers' Employed in the Quarter Master & Commissary General's Department.

40. A total of 3,000 blacks—1,336 men, 914 women, and 750 children—are listed in the Book of Negroes Registered & Certified (hereafter cited as Book of Negroes), a port record documenting the exodus of black refugees of war who during the final days of the British evacuation of New York City, between April 23 and July 31, 1783, left the harbor of New York on British sailing vessels. Of the black émigrés whose condition of servitude is known, 1,135 blacks were declared free under the several British wartime proclamations, 366 blacks were the slaves of white loyalists and veterans of war, 29 blacks were indentured servants, another 620 blacks were either born free, manumitted by their masters, freed as reward for military service on the American side, or had obtained freedom upon their masters' death. Of the 30,000 loyalists resettled in Canada following the Anglo-American conflict, 10 percent were black refugees of war. See Winks, *The Black Loyalists in Canada*, 29–30; Frey, *Water from the Rock*, 193.

41. These black refugees of war founded the free black settler communities of Birchtown, Brindley Town, and Little Tracadie. In Preston near Halifax, Port Roseway (later Shelburne) along the rugged coastline, and other towns, black settlers coexisted alongside Nova Scotia's white settler population. Blacks faced overt antiblack prejudice in maritime Canada and were denied the full rights of British subjects. Only a fraction of the black war refugees received the 20-acre bounty of land that the British government promised them, and those who did obtained barren land. Due to these obstacles, some free black settlers were demoted to indentured servitude and even reenslaved, while others barely maintained their independence. For the story of the black settlers' travail, see Winks, *The Black Loyalists in Canada*, esp. 24–26; Ellen Gibson Wilson, *Loyal Blacks*, esp. 135–256; and T. Watson Smith, "The Slave in Canada." Approximately 26 percent of the black refugees of war who departed from the port of New York during the British evacuation did not journey to Nova Scotia and New Brunswick but instead sailed for other destinations, including Cat Island and Abaco in the Bahamas, Quebec, the Downs in the English Channel between North Foreland and South Foreland, Spithead off the coast of England between Portsmouth and the Isle of Wight, and Germany. See Book of Negroes.

In 1792, a total of 1,196 free black settlers from maritime Canada migrated to the so-called Grain Coast of Africa, where, under the auspices of English opponents of the African slave trade, they founded Freetown, Sierra Leone. For a history of the free black settler migration to Sierra Leone, see Fyfe, *A History of Sierra Leone*; Peterson, *Province of Freedom*; St. Walker, *The Black Loyalists*; Clifford, *From Slavery to Freetown*; and Pullis, *Moving On*.

42. No previous place of residence is documented for nearly 20 percent of the black refugees. Book of Negroes.

43. Ibid.

44. For a brief account of this military battle, see Rankin, "The Moore's Creek Bridge Campaign, 1776." See also Crow, *The Black Experience in Revolutionary North Carolina*, 27–28, 55–56.

45. Book of Negroes.

46. For another brief account of the Van Sayl family's wartime experience, see Hodges, *The Black Loyalist Directory*, xx.

47. The following discussion is based on King, "Memoirs of the Life of Boston King, a Black Preacher."

48. Frey, *Water from the Rock*, 63, 177–82.

49. Like Boston King, other black leaders of the ex-slave communities in maritime Canada—for example, David George and Thomas Peters—emerged out of the evangelical and the Enlightenment milieu. See George, "An Account of the Life of David George"; Grant Gordon, *From Slavery to Freedom, The Life of David George*; and Fyfe, "Thomas Peters."

50. Several slave narratives appeared prior to the publication of Boston King's memoirs—for example, Hammon, *A Narrative of the Uncommon Sufferings, and Surprizing Deliverance of Briton Hammon. A Negro Man*; Gronniosaw, *A Narrative of the Most Remarkable Particulars in the Life of James Albert Ukawsaw Gronniosaw*; Marrant, *A Narrative of the Lord's Wonderful Dealings with Johan Marrant, a Black*; Cugoano, *Thoughts and Sentiments on the Evil of Slavery*; Equiano, *The Interesting Narratives of the Life of Olaudah Equiano*; and Mountain, *Sketches of the Life of Joseph Mountain, a Negro*.

51. Barbara Johnson, *The Feminist Difference*, 91.

52. Ibid., 97, 99.

53. Though a far larger number of free blacks probably left the new republics at the war's end, no fewer than 409 black war refugees, either born free or manumitted before the onset of war, departed the port of New York on sailing vessels headed for maritime Canada and other destinations during the British evacuation of New York City. See Book of Negroes.

54. King, "Memoirs."

55. Quoted in Lindsay, "Diplomatic Relations," 395.

56. British nonobservance of Article Seven of the Treaty of Paris remained a topic of diplomatic correspondence between the United States and Great Britain until 1827, when the U.S. government agreed to accept more than $1.2 million from the British government in compensation for the loss of slave property incurred by American slaveowners during the War for Independence. See Lindsay, "Diplomatic Relations," 418–19.

57. Baurmeister, *The Revolution in America*, 569.

58. Carlton Papers.

59. Birch Certificate.

60. Letter from Sir Guy Carleton to Lord North, August 8, 1783 and Memo. See also Quarles, *Negro in the American Revolution*, 169–70.

61. The following discussion is based on the board of inquiry cases appended to the Book of Negroes. The board of inquiry heard a total of 14 cases before the American commissioners resigned in protest.

62. For the activity of Negro catchers in New York City during the British evacuation, see Hodges, *Black Loyalist Directory*, xvii.

63. At least, this is what the transcripts of the cases before the board of inquiry suggest. However, the list of black refugees aboard the British brig *Concord* indicates that on November 30, 1783, A. [Toney] Bartram sailed to Port Mattoon, Nova Scotia, without his daughters. See Book of Negroes.

64. Because slaveowners could not be certain of the legality of slavery in England, especially in the face of the Somerset Case of 1772, white loyalists who resolved to resettle in England sometimes abandoned or otherwise disposed of their slaves before leaving the British overseas colonies for England.

65. On September 22, 1783, Dinah Archer, age 42 , sailed for Port Roseway, Nova Scotia, on the *Clinton*. See Book of Negroes.

66. The historian Joan Scott has pointed out that it is the "historical processes that, through discourse, position subjects and produce their experiences. It is not individuals who have experience, but subjects who are constituted through experience." See Scott, "'Experience,'" 25–26.

Epilogue

1. Zilversmit, *The First Emancipation*.

2. This section of the U.S. Constitution, along with Article I, Sections 8, 9, and 10, Article IV, Sections 2 and 4, and Article V, have been interpreted as implicit endorsements of slavery. See Wiecek, *The Sources of Antislavery Constitutionalism*, 62–63.

3. Farrand, *The Records of the Federal Constitution of 1787*, 222.

4. Hamilton, Jay, and Madison, *The Federalist Papers*, 336–37. Separately authored but published under the single pseudonym "Publius," the 85 letters known as the Federalist Papers first appeared in New York City newspapers between October 1787 and March 1788. They advocated the speedy ratification of the federal constitution drafted at the Philadelphia Convention during the summer of 1787.

5. *Federalist Papers*, 341.

6. Evacuation Day—Washington's Entrance into New York, November 25, 1783. Prints Collection, New-York Historical Society. For recent studies on popular political culture during the early national era, see Newman, *Parades and the Politics of the Streets*; Travers, *Celebrating the Fourth*; Waldstreicher, *In the Midst of Perpetual Fetes*; Ryan, "Ceremonial Spaces" and "The American Parade"; and Conzen, "Ethnicity as Festive Culture."

7. The 1783 Evacuation Day parade took place along lower Broadway. Today, Broadway extends northward from Bowling Green at the tip of Manhattan Island to 262nd Street in the Bronx. Here, I use the term "Great White Way," which ordinarily refers to the strip of theaters along the midtown section of present-day Broadway just above Time Square, as a figure for the continuation of white domination in postrevolutionary New York City. For a history of the most famous street in New York City, possibly the world, see David W. Dunlap, *On Broadway*; Jenkins, *The Greatest Street in the World*.

8. For an interesting study on the appropriation of Native American symbols and customs in the construction of white American national identity, see Deloria, *Playing Indian*. See also Berkhofer, *The White Man's Indian*.

9. For two recent reassessments of Alexis de Tocqueville's commentary on the U.S. racial dilemma, see Glazer, "Race and Ethnicity in America," and Lieske, "Race and Democracy."

10. The following discussion is based on Alexis de Tocqueville, *Democracy in America*, 1:317–63.

11. Biography of a Slave by Dunkin M. Sill, March 18, 1924.

12. Quoted in Shearer, "The Massachusetts 54th Colored Infantry."

13. First published in 1852 as *Oration, Delivered in Corinthian Hall, Rochester, July 5th, 1852*. See also Douglass, "What to the Slave Is the Fourth of July?" in Andrews, *The Oxford Frederick Douglass Reader*.

14. In this passage from his oration, Douglass uses the rhetorical device *ethopoeia*, or putting oneself in the place of another, so as to understand and express that person's feelings more vividly.

15. When posing the question, "What to the Slave Is the Fourth of July?" Douglass attempts to stimulate the moral faculty of the white citizenry and the related capacity for empathetic identification with the slave. But more than this, Douglass's question seeks to motivate his audience to take an active role in the abolitionist struggle.

16. At this point in his oration, Douglass uses the rhetorical device *argumentum ex concessis*, or reasoning from the premises of one's opponents.

17. Roediger, *Wages of Whiteness*, 57.

18. For New York's Gradual Emancipation Act of 1799, see New York State, *Laws of New York State*, 22nd Session, chapter 62. That law freed all children born to slave women after July 4, 1799, but indentured them to their mothers' masters until they reached the age of 28, if male, and 25, if female. According to a law enacted in 1817, all slaves born

before July 4, 1799, were freed as of July 4, 1827. See New York State, *Laws of New York State*, 40th Session, chapter 137.

19. Waldstreicher, *In the Midst of Perpetual Fetes*, 316–17, 324–25. See also Horton and Horton, *In Hope of Liberty*; Gravely, "The Dialectic of Double Consciousness in Black Freedom Celebrations, 1808–1863"; Rael, *Black Identity and Black Protest in the Antebellum North*; Wiggins, *O' Freedom!*; and Litwack, *North of Slavery*.

20. The articulatory practices of black radicalism encouraged both local and global identifications of black solidarity. For two important assessments of black radicalism, see Robinson, *Black Marxism*; and Stauffer, *The Black Hearts of Men*.

21. Baldwin, *Nobody Knows My Name*, 66–67. "Fifth Avenue, Uptown: A Letter from Harlem" was first published in the July 1960 issue of *Esquire*.

22. Baldwin, *The Fire Next Time*, 103–4. "Down on the Cross" was originally published in the November 17, 1962, issue of *The New Yorker* under the title "Letter from a Region in My Mind."

23. For the symbiosis of liberal democracy and racism in the United States, see Hochschild, *The New American Dilemma*; Goldberg, *Racist Culture*.

24. Bell, *Faces at the Bottom of the Well*, x. Bell echoes W. E. B. Du Bois, who in 1933 observed that instead of staging a "revolt against capitalism," the white worker in the United States engaged in a "wild and ruthless scramble of labor groups over each other in order to climb to wealth on the backs of black labor and foreign immigrants." See Du Bois, "Marxism and the Negro Problem."

25. Bell, *Faces at the Bottom of the Well*, 14.

26. Gilroy, *Against Race*, 12.

27. David Brion Davis, "Constructing Race," 7.

28. Jordan, *White over Black*, 44–98.

29. Zygmunt Bauman writes, "To classify, in other words, is to give the world a structure: to manipulate its possibilities; to make some events more likely than others." See Bauman, *Modernity and Ambivalence*, 1. In this study I have argued that racial classification structured the world of colonial New York City, making racial domination in that settler colony possible and foreclosing other possibilities of alternative social and political developments.

30. Appadurai, *Modernity at Large*, 170. See also Werbner and Modood, *Debating Cultural Hybridity*; Cordero-Guzmán, *Migration, Transnationalization and Race in a Changing New York*; Anthias and Hoyd, *Rethinking Anti-Racisms*; Bhattacharyya, Gabriel, and Small, *Race and Power*; and San Juan, *Racism and Cultural Studies*.

31. For example, binary race-thinking structures contemporary discourses on interracialism and multiracialism in that both discourses posit intermediate positions in relation to the polarities of black and white. For an astute analysis of the alternative racial classification schemes proposed in recent debates about revising the 2000 U.S. Census questionnaires, see Perlmann, "Reflecting the Changing Face of America."

32. Lewis R. Gordon, *Her Majesty's Other Children*, 5.

33. Appadurai, *Modernity at Large*, 31.

34. Of course, humans are capable of performing cognitive operations many times faster than all but a few of the most sophisticated computers—for example, IBM's Deep Thought and Deep Blue. Invented by the British mathematician Alan Turing in 1948, the Turing machine is the prototype of the electronic digital computer, which operates according to algorithmic computation logic (or base two number system). The binary logic of race-thinking resembles the algorithmic logic of the digital computer in that it copes with difference, exception, and indeterminacy by reducing such remainders to the nearest whole or identity. For the limitations of the algorithmic logic machine, see Penrose, *The Emperor's New Mind*.

Bibliography

Unpublished Primary Sources

Archival Documents

American Inspector General's Ledgers for the Board of Customs and Excise Imports and Exports, America, 1768–73. CUST. 16/1. PRO.

Bancker, Evert. House Expense Book of Evert Bancker, 1760 to 1775. BV. Bancker, Evert. Manuscripts Collection. New-York Historical Society.

———. Journal of Evert Bancker Recording the Sales and Dry Goods . . . plus some Receipts and Disbursements, 1771 to 1775. BV. Bancker, Evert. Manuscripts Collection. New-York Historical Society.

Bayard, Nicholas. Letterbook of Nicholas Bayard, 1763. BV. Sec. Bayard. Manuscripts Collection. New-York Historical Society.

———. Receipt Book of Nicholas Bayard, April 20, 1762–August 11, 1772. BV. Bayard. Manuscripts Collection. New-York Historical Society.

Beekman, William. Receipts from the Business of William Beekman, 1760 to 1765. Manuscripts Collection. New-York Historical Society.

——— and Abraham Beekman. Receipts of William and Abraham Beekman for Sums Paid for the Repair of a Wharf, 1770. Beekman Papers, Box 23, No. 4. Manuscripts Collection. New-York Historical Society.

Bensen, Teneke. Will of Teneke Bensen, February 21, 1753. Harlem Papers, 1701–75. Manuscripts Collection. New-York Historical Society.

Biography of a Slave by Dunkin M. Sill, March 18, 1924. Manuscripts Collection. New-York Historical Society.

Birch Certificate. National Archives. Microfilm Collection.

Book of Negroes Registered & Certified after Having Been Inspected by the Commissioners Appointed by His Excellency Sr. Guy Carleton R. B. General and Commander-in-Chief on Board Sundry Vessels in Which They Were Embarked Previous to the Time of Sailing from the Port of New York between 23 April and 31 July both Days Included (1783). British Headquarters Papers [Photocopy]. Manuscripts Division. New York Public Library.

Brevoort, Henry. Will of Henry Brevoort [n.d.]. New York State Archives. Albany.

Cappoens, Christiana [Goschersen]. Inventory of the Estate of Christiana Cappoens [Goschersen], December 19, 1693. New York State Archives. Albany.

Carlton Papers. CO 30/8/344/109–11. PRO.

Codrington, Thomas [Captain]. Inventory of the Estate of Captain Thomas Codrington (1710). New York State Archives. Albany.

Colden, Alexander. Will of Alexander Colden, December 16, 1774. New York State Archive. Albany.

Colden, Cadwallader. The Interest of the Country in Laying Duties (1726). [Photocopy]. Kress Reading Room. Baker Library. Harvard School of Business.

———. A Memorial to his Excellency, Drawn by Colden. BV Rutherford, Box 1, #57, Manuscripts Division. New-York Historical Society.

———. Inventory of the Estate of Cadwallader Colden (1756). New York State Archives. Albany.

———. Will of Cadwallader Colden, March 15, 1779. New York State Archives. Albany.

Colden, Elizabeth. Will of Elizabeth Colden [n.d.]. New York State Archive. Albany.

Coroner's Inquisition, April 9, 1712. Misc. MSS. NYC, Box 4, #13. Manuscripts Collection. New-York Historical Society.

Cruger, John. Waste [Account] Book of Henry and John Cruger, June 28, 1762–January 15, 1768. BV Cruger. Manuscripts Collection. New-York Historical Society.

———. Letter from John Cruger to Dainel Hewlett, New York City, June 18, 1766. Misc. MSS. Cruger, John. Manuscripts Collection. New-York Historical Society.

Deposition of a Sailor Concerning the Cruel Treatment of Negro Slaves on Board the Snow York on Her Late Voyage to the Coast of Africa, Sworn before Mayor White-head Hicks, 7 July 1773. Manuscripts Collection. New-York Historical Society.

Dumaresq, Nicholas. Will of Nicholas Dumaresq (1701) and Inventory of the Estate of Nicholas Dumaresq (NYC). New York State Archives. Albany.

Gilford, Samuel. Shipping and Personal Papers of Samuel Gilford, 1755–1842. BV Gilford. Manuscripts Collection. New-York Historical Society.

Letter from Sir Guy Carleton to Lord North, August 8, 1783, and Memo [n.d.]. CO 5/8, 113–15 [Microfilm]. New York Public Library.

Letter from Nathaniel Green to George Washington, July 21, 1776. Force Papers. Library of Congress.

Letterbooks of the Society for the Propagation of the Gospel in Foreign Parts [SPG]. [Microfilm]. Widener Library. Harvard University.

Liber Deeds and Conveyances, Liber 195, 405–20. Office of the Register. County of New York.

List of Barrack Houses in the Garrison of New York [n.d.]. British Headquarters Papers [Photocopy]. Manuscripts Division. New York Public Library.

List of Prize Goods, New York, December 25, 1739–September 21, 1746. CO 5/1061Gg, 125–219. PRO.

Logbook of a Privateer Sailing from the City of New York on Two Cruises in the W. Indies, Ship, The Duke of Cumberland, 1758–60. Manuscripts Collection. New-York Historical Society.

Logbook of a Privateer Sailing from the City of New York. The Harlequin, 1764–66. Manuscripts Collection. New-York Historical Society.

Naval Officer's Shipping List for the Port of New York, 1715–65. CO 5/1222–29. PRO.

New York City. Charities. Church Wardens and Vestrymen. Minutes, 1694 to 1747 [Transcript]. Manuscripts Collection. New-York Historical Society.

Nicoll, Charles. Ledger of Accounts of Charles Nicoll for the Sale and Repair of Shoes, 1759 to 1765. BV. Nicoll. Manuscripts Collection. New-York Historical Society.
———. Misc. Mss., Box 4, No. 10. Manuscripts Collection. New-York Historical Society.
Palatine Emigrants. CO 323/6, 56. PRO.
Petition of a Negro for Freedom, Addressed to Attorney General Kempe of New York. John Tabor Kempe Papers. NY. Legal Mss, 1750–55. Manuscripts Collection. New-York Historical Society.
Reade, Joseph. Will of Joseph Reade, July 23, 1761. Alexander Papers, Box 46. Manuscripts Collection. New-York Historical Society.
Register of Emigrants, 1773–76. Treasury Papers. T/47/9–12 Vols. I–IV. PRO.
Rolls of the Quarter Master General's Department for the Wagonmaster or the Forage and Provision Departments of the Army [n.d.]. British Headquarters Papers [Photocopy]. Manuscripts Division. New York Public Library.
Rutgers, Anthony. Will of Anthony Rutgers (1746). Archives of the City of New York. New York Surrogate's Court Building.
Shelly, Giles [Captain]. Will and Inventory of the Estate of Captain Giles Shelly (1718). New York State Archives. Albany.
Taylor, John [Captain]. Captain John Taylor's Account and Memoranda Book, Expenses of the Brig, Charming Sally. BV Taylor. Manuscripts Collection. New-York Historical Society.
Ten Eyck, Peternela. Inventory of the Estate of Peternela, widow of Derrick Ten Eyck, November 15, 1724. New York State Archives. Albany.
Trinity Church Vestry Minutes, October 25, 1697, I, 11. Trinity Church Archives. New York City.
Trinity Church Vestry Minutes, September 15, 1773, I, 378; and, Trinity Church Vestry Minutes, July 7, 1774, I, 385. Trinity Church Archives. New York City.
Trinity Parish Leases for the Church Farm, 1704, 1732, 1750–65. Trinity Church Archives. New York City.
Van Cortlandt, Jacobus. Letterbook of Jacobus Van Cortlandt, 1698–1700. BV Van Cortlandt. Manuscripts Collection. New-York Historical Society.
Van Dam, Rip. Inventory of the Estate of Rip Van Dam (1749). Misc. Ms. V. Manuscripts Collection. New-York Historical Society.
———. Inventory of the Goods & Chattels of Rip Van Dam, September 1, 1753. Misc. Ms. V. Manuscripts Collection. New-York Historical Society.
Van Horne, Abraham. Day Book of Abraham Van Horne, 1753 to 1756. Joshua Delaplaine Papers. Manuscripts Collection. New-York Historical Society.
———. Will of Abraham Van Horne (1740). New York State Archives. Albany.
Van Horne, James. Letter from James Van Horne to John White (London) [n.d.]. Misc. MSS. Van Horne, James. Manuscripts Collection. New-York Historical Society.
———. Will of James Van Horne, September 1783. Misc. MSS. Van Horne. Manuscripts Collection. New-York Historical Society
Voucher in the Account of Negro Laborers' Employed in the Quarter Master & Commissary General's Department, July 1, 1780–September 30, 1780, Inclusive. British Headquarters Papers [Photocopy]. Manuscripts Division. New York Public Library.

Court Records

Minutes of the Court of Quarter Sessions, August 7, 1694, to 1733. Archives of the City of New York. New York Surrogate's Court Building.
Minutes of the Court of Quarter Sessions, January 1, 1722–January 5, 1772. Archives of the City of New York. New York Surrogate's Court Building.
Minutes of the Court of Quarter Sessions, May 2, 1732–August 4, 1762. Archives of the City of New York. New York Surrogate's Court Building.

Minutes of the General Court of the Peace, November 4, 1760–February 6, 1772. Hall of Records. Office of the Clerk of New York County.

Minutes of the Mayor's Court, November 28, 1710–May 17, 1715. Archives of the City of New York. New York Surrogate's Court Building.

Minutes of the Mayor's Court, June 22, 1714–December 24, 1717. Archives of the City of New York. New York Surrogate's Court Building.

Minutes of the Mayor's Court, May 6, 1718–November 23, 1720. Archives of the City of New York. New York Surrogate's Court Building.

Minutes of the Mayor's Court, February 17, 1735/36–August 3, 1742. Archives of the City of New York. New York Surrogate's Court Building.

Minutes of the Mayor's Court, August 7, 1750–December 17, 1751. Archives of the City of New York. New York Surrogate's Court Building.

Minutes of the Supreme Court of Judicature, June 6, 1710–June 5, 1714. Hall of Records in the Office of the Clerk of the County of New York.

Published Primary Sources

Newspapers and Other Periodicals

Boston Weekly News-Letter (1704–76).
Crisis (1933).
Independent Reflector (1751–53/54).
New York Gazette (1726–40/41, 1744, 1747–51).
New York Herald (1855 & 1863).
New York Journal, or General Advertiser (1766–76).
New York Mercury (1752–68).
New York Tribune (1855 & 1863).
New-York Weekly Journal (1733–73).
New York Weekly Post-Boy (1743–73).
Royal Gazette (1777–83).
Scots Magazine (March 1774).

Manuscripts

Andrews, William L., ed. *The Oxford Frederick Douglass Reader*. New York: Oxford University Press, 1996.

Aptheker, Herbert, ed. *Documentary History of the Negro People in the United States*. 4 vols. New York: Citadel Press, 1951.

Asher, Georg M., ed. *Henry Hudson the Navigator: The Original Documents in Which His Career is Recorded, Collected, Partly Translated, With an Introduction by G. M. Asher*. Hakluyt Society Publications, 1st ser., vol. 27: 45–93. London, 1863.

Baldwin, James. *The Fire Next Time*. New York: Dial, 1963.

———. *Nobody Knows My Name*. New York: Dial, 1961.

"Baptisms in the Dutch Reformed Church of New Amsterdam and New York City, 1639 to 1730." *New York Genealogical and Biographical Society Record* 2 (1890): 10–41.

Baurmeister, Carl Leopold. *The Revolution in America. Confidential Letters and Journals, 1776–1784, of Adjutant General Baurmeister of the Hessian Forces*. Trans. Bernhard A. Uhlendorf. New Brunswick, N.J.: Rutgers University Press, 1957.

Benson, Adolph B., ed. *Peter Kalm's Travels in North America: The English Version of 1770*. New York: Dover, 1937.

Bernier, François. "Nouvelle division de la Terre par les differérates espèces ou races d'hommes qui l'habitent, envoyée par un fameux voyaguer." *Journal de sçavans* 12 (1684): 133–40.

Blumenbach, Johann Friedrich. *On the Natural Variety of Mankind* [3d. ed., 1795]. In *The Idea of Race*, edited by Robert Bernasconi and Tommy L. Lott. Indianapolis: Hackett, 2000.

Colden, Cadwallader. "History of Gov. William Cosby's Administration." In "Letters and Papers of Cadwallader Colden." *New-York Historical Society Collections* 68 (1935): 283–355.

———. "Letters and Papers of Cadwallader Colden." *New-York Historical Society Collections* 67 (1934).

Colonial Laws of New York from the Year 1664 to the Revolution. Including the Charters to the Duke of York, the Commission and Instructions to Colonial Governors, the Duke's Laws, the Laws of Dongan and Leisler Assemblies, the Charters of Albany and New York, and the Acts of the Colonial Legislatures, 1691 to 1775, Inclusive. 5 vols. Albany, N.Y.: J. B. Lyons, 1896.

Cooper, James Fenimore. *Satanstoe.* 1811. Reprint, New York: American Book Company, 1937.

Corwin, Edward T., ed. *Ecclesiastical Records, State of New York. Published by the State under the Supervision of Hugh Hastings, State Historian.* 7 vols. Albany, N.Y.: J. B. Lyon, 1901–16.

Cox, John, ed. *Oyster Bay Town Records,* 2 vols. New York: Tobias A. Wright, 1916–24.

Cugoano, Ottobah. *Thoughts and Sentiments on the Evil of Slavery.* London, 1787.

Defoe, Daniel. *An Essay upon Projects.* Edited by Joyce D. Kennedy, Michael Seidel, and Maximilian E. Novak. 1697. Reprint, New York: AMS Press, 1999.

Denton, Daniel. *A Brief Description of New-York.* 1670. Facsimile, New York: Columbia University Press, 1937.

De Tocqueville, Alexis. *Democracy in America.* Edited by J. P. Mayer. 2 vols. 1848. Reprint, Garden City, N.Y.: Anchor, 1969.

De Voe, Thomas F. *The Market Book Containing a Historical Account of the Public Markets of the Cities of New York, Philadelphia and Brooklyn, With a Brief Description of Every Article of Human Food Sold Therein, the Introduction of Cattle in America, and Notices of Many Remarkable Specimens.* 2 vols. New York, 1862.

Donnan, Elizabeth, ed. *Documents Illustrative of the History of the Slave Trade.* 4 vols. Washington, D.C.: Carnegie Institute, 1930–35.

Equiano, Olaudah. *The Interesting Narratives of the Life of Olaudah Equiano, or Gustavus Vassa, the African, written by Himself.* London, 1789.

Farrand, Max, ed. *The Laws and Liberties of Massachusetts.* Cambridge: Harvard University Press, 1929.

———, ed. *The Records of the Federal Constitution of 1787.* New Haven: Yale University Press, 1937.

Fernow, Berthold, ed. *Records of New Amsterdam from 1653 to 1674 Anno Domini.* 7 vols. New York: Knickerbocker, 1897.

Fleetwood, William. *Relative Duties of Parents and Children, Husbands and Wives, Masters and Servants.* 1705. 2d ed. London: Printed for John Hooke, 1716.

Gehring, Charles T., and Jacob A. Schiltkamp, eds. *Curacao Papers, 1640–1665: New Netherland Documents,* Vol. 17. Translated by Charles T. Gehring. 18 vols. Interlaken, N.Y.: Heart of the Lakes, 1987.

George, David. "An Account of the Life of David George, from Sierra Leone in Africa; Given by Himself in a Conversation with Brother Rippon and Brother Pearce of Birmingham." *The Baptist Annual Register for 1790–93,* 473–84. London, 1793.

Gronniosaw, James Albert Ukawsaw. *A Narrative of the Most Remarkable Particulars in the Life of James Albert Ukawsaw Gronniosaw, an African Prince.* Bath, England: W. Gye, 1770.

Hakluyt, Richard. "A Discourse Concerning Western Planting in the Year 1584." In *The Original Writings and Correspondence of the Two Richard Hakluyts*, 2: 214–15. Edited by E. G. R. Taylor. 2 vols. London: Hakluyt Society, 1935.

Hamilton, Alexander, John Jay, and James Madison. *The Federalist Papers with an Introduction, Table of Contents, and Index of Ideas by Clinton Rossiter*. New York: New American Library of World Literature, 1961.

Hammon, Briton. *A Narrative of the Uncommon Sufferings, and Surprizing Deliverance of Briton Hammon. A Negro Man,—Servant to General Winslow, of Marshfield, in New England: Who Returned to Boston*. Boston: Green and Russell, 1760.

Historical Notes of the Family Kip of Kipsburg and Kip's Bay. Albany, N.Y., 1871.

Hodges, Graham, ed. *The Black Loyalist Directory: African Americans in Exile after the American Revolution*. New York: Garland, 1996.

Horsmanden, Daniel. *Journal of the Proceedings in the Detection of the Conspiracy Formed by Some White People in Conjunction with Negro and Other Slaves for Burning the City of New-York in America and Murdering the Inhabitants*. New York: James Parker, 1744.

Hough, Charles M., ed. *Reports of Cases in the Vice Admiralty Court of the Province of New York and in the Court of Admiralty of the State of New York, 1715–1788. With Historical Introduction and Appendix*. New Haven: Yale University Press, 1925.

Humphreys, David. *An Account of the Endeavours Used by the Society for the Propagation of the Gospel in Foreign Parts Containing Their Foundation, Proceedings, and the Success of Their Missionaries in the British Colonies, to the Year 1728*. 1728. Facsimile, New York: Arno Press and New York Times, 1969.

"Indentures and Apprentices, 1694–1707." *New-York Historical Society Collections* (1885): 565–622.

"Indentures and Apprentices, 1718–1727." *New-York Historical Society Collections* (1909): 113–99.

Jameson, J. Franklin, ed. *Narratives of New Netherland, 1609–1664*. New York: Charles Scribner, 1909.

————, ed. *Privateering and Piracy in the Colonial Period: Illustrative Documents*. New York: Macmillan, 1923.

Jefferson, Thomas. *Notes on the State of Virginia*. Edited by William Peden. Chapel Hill: University of North Carolina Press, 1955.

Kant, Immanuel. *Of the Different Human Races* [originally published in 1775]. In *The Idea of Race*, edited by Robert Bernasconi and Tommy L. Lott. Indianapolis: Hackett, 2000.

King, Boston. "Memoirs of the Life of Boston King, a Black Preacher, Written by Himself, during his residence at Kingswood-School." *Arminian Magazine* 21 (March, 1798).

Klingberg, Frank J. *Anglican Humanitarianism in Colonial New York*. Philadelphia: Church Historical Society, 1940.

————. "The S.P.G. Program for Negroes in Colonial New York." *Historical Magazine of the Protestant Episcopal Church* 8 (1939): 306–71.

Lay, Benjamin. *All Slave-Keeper's That Keep the Innocent in Bondage Apostates*. Philadelphia, 1737.

Linnaeus, Carolus. *Systema naturae, sive, Regina tria naturæ systematice proposita per classes, ordines, genera, & species*. 1735.

Lodwick, Charles. "Letter from Charles Lodwick to the Royal Society" [May 20, 1692]. *New-York Historical Society Collections*, 2d ser., 2 (1849): 244.

Marrant, John. *A Narrative of the Lord's Wonderful Dealings with John Marrant, a Black (Now Going to Preach the Gospel in Nova Scotia) Born in New York, in North America. Taken*

Down from His Own Relation, Arranged, Corrected, and Published by the Reverend Mr. Aldridge. London, 1785.

"Marriages in the Reformed Dutch Church of New Amsterdam and New York City, 1639 to 1801." *New York Genealogical and Biographical Society Record* 9 (1901).

McIlwaine, H. R., ed. *Legislative Journals of the Council of Colonial Virginia*. 9 vols. Richmond, Va., 1918.

Miller, John. *A Description of the Province and City of New York; With Plans of the City and Several Forts as They Existed in the Year 1695, Or New York Considered and Improved, With Introduction and Notes by Victor Hugo Paltsits*. Cleveland, Ohio: Burrows Brothers, 1903.

Milton, John. *Paradise Lost*. Edited by Scott Elledge. 2d ed. New York: Norton, 1993.

Mountain, Joseph. *Sketches of the Life of Josheph Mountain, a Negro, Who Was Executed at New Haven, on the 20th Day of October, 1790, for a Rape, Committed on the 26th Day of May Last*. New Haven, Conn.: T. and S. Green, 1790.

Mühlenberg, Henry Melchoir. *Journals of Henry Melchoir Mühlenberg*. Edited by Theodore G. Tappert and John Doberstein. 3 vols. Philadelphia: University of Pennsylvania Press, 1942–58.

"Muster Rolls of the New York Provincial Troops, 1755–1764." *New-York Historical Society Collections* 24 (1892).

New York State. *Laws of New York State*. Albany: State of New York, 1901.

O'Callaghan, Edmund B., ed. *Calendar of Historical Manuscripts in the Office of the Secretary of State of New York*. 2 vols. Albany, N.Y.: Weed, Parsons, 1865–66.

———, ed. *Documentary History of the State of New York; Arranged under the Direction of the Hon. Christopher Morgan, Secretary of State*. 4 vols. Albany, N.Y.: Weed, Parsons, 1850–66.

———, ed. *Journal of the Legislative Council of the Colony of New York*. 2 vols. Albany, N.Y.: Weed, Parsons, 1861.

———, ed. *Laws and Ordinances of New Netherland, 1638–1674*. Albany, N.Y.: Weed, Parsons, 1868.

———, and Berthold Fernow, eds. *Documents Relative to the Colonial History of the State of New York; Procured in Holland, England, and France by John Romeyn*. 15 vols. Albany, N.Y.: Weed, Parsons, 1856–87.

Osgood, Herbert Levi, ed. *Minutes of the Common Council of the City of New York, 1675–1776*. 12 vols. Albany, N.Y.: Weed, Parsons, 1901.

Protocol of the Lutheran Church in New York City, 1702–1750. Translated by Simon Hart and Harry J Kreider. New York: Synod of New York City, 1958.

Rossiter, W. S., ed. *A Century of Population Growth from the First Census of the United States to the Twelfth, 1790–1900*. Washington, D.C.: U.S. Bureau of the Census, 1975.

Scott, Kenneth, ed. *Minutes of the Mayor's Court of New York, 1674–1675*. Baltimore: Genealogical Publishing, 1983.

———, and Ken Stryker-Rodda, eds. *New York Historical Manuscripts: Dutch*. Translated by A. J. F. van Laer. 5 vols. Baltimore: Genealogical Publishing, 1974.

Sharpe, [Reverend] John. "Proposals for Erecting a School, Library and Chapel at New York City [1712/13]." *New-York Historical Society Collections* 13 (1880): 341–63.

Smith, William. *History of the Province of New-York*. 1757. 2 vols. Ed. Michael Kammen. Reprint, Cambridge: Harvard University Press, 1972.

Stokes, Isaac Newton, ed. *The Iconography of Manhattan Island, 1648–1909*. 6 Vols. New York: R. H. Dodd. 1915–28.

Sullivan, James, ed. *Minutes of the Albany Committee of Correspondence, 1775–1778*. 2 vols. Albany: University of the State of New York, 1887.

———, ed. *Minutes of the Albany Committee on the Detection and Defeating of Conspiracies*. 2 vols. Albany: University of the State of New York, 1888.

Sypher, F. J., trans. "Voices in the Wilderness: Letters to Colonial New York from Germany [1726–37]." *New York History* 67 (1986): 331–52.

Ten Eyck, Albert M. *Ten Eyck Family Record.* 1949.

Van der Donck, Adriaen. *A Description of the New Netherlands.* 1655. Translated by Jeremiah Johnson and edited by Thomas F. O'Donnell. Syracuse, N.Y.: Syracuse University Press, 1968.

Watt, John. "Letterbook of John Watt." *New-York Historical Society Collections* 61 (1928).

Wheatley, Phyllis. *The Collected Works of Phyllis Wheatley.* Ed. John C. Shields. New York: Oxford University Press, 1988.

———. *The Poems of Phillis Wheatley.* Ed. Julian D. Mason Jr. Chapel Hill: University of North Carolina Press, 1989.

Whitefield, George. *George Whitefield's Journals, 1737–1741.* Reprint, Gainesville: University of Florida Press, 1969.

Secondary Sources

Abbott, Carl. "The Neighborhoods of New York City, 1760–1775." *New York History* 55 (1974): 35–54.

Agnew, Jean-Christophe. *Worlds Apart: The Market and the Theater in Anglo-American Thought, 1550–1750.* Cambridge: Cambridge University Press, 1986.

Aimes, Herbert H. S. "Coartación: A Spanish Institution for the Advancement of Slaves into Freedom." *Yale Review* (February 1909): 412–31.

Akers, Charles W. "'Our Modern Egyptians': Phillis Wheatley and the Whig Campaign against Slavery in Revolutionary Boston." *Journal of Negro History* 60 (July 1975): 397–410.

Albion, Robert G. *The Rise of the Port of New York, 1815–1860.* New York, 1939.

Allen, Theodore W. *The Invention of the White Race: Racial Oppression and Social Control.* Vol. 1. London: Verso, 1994.

Anderson, Benedict. *Imagined Communities: Reflections on the Origin and Spread of Nationalism.* London: Verso, 1983.

Anderson, Perry. *Passage from Antiquity to Feudalism.* London: Verso, 1978.

Anthias, Floyd, and Cathy Hoyd, eds. *Rethinking Anti-Racisms: From Theory to Practice.* New York: Routledge, 2002.

Appadurai, Arjun. *Modernity at Large: Cultural Dimensions of Globalization.* Minneapolis: University of Minnesota Press, 1996.

Aptheker, Herbert. *American Negro Slave Revolts.* New York: Columbia University Press, 1943.

Archdeacon, Thomas J. "'Distinguished for Nation Sak': The Age of Leisler in New York City." In *Colonial America: Essays in Politics and Social Development,* edited by Stanley N. Katz, 143–54. Boston: Little Brown, 1976.

———. *New York City, 1664–1710: Conquest and Change.* Ithaca, N.Y.: Cornell University Press, 1976.

Axtell, James. *The Invasion Within: The Contest of Cultures in Colonial North America.* New York: Oxford University Press, 1985.

Aymard, Maurice, ed. *Dutch Capitalism and World Capitalism.* Cambridge: Cambridge University Press, 1982.

Bachman, Van Cleaf. *Peltries or Plantations: The Economic Policies of the Dutch West India Company in New Netherland.* Baltimore: Johns Hopkins University Press, 1969.

Bailyn, Bernard. *The Ideological Origins of the American Revolution.* Cambridge: Harvard University Press, 1967.

———. *The Peopling of British North America: An Introduction.* New York: Alfred A. Knopf, 1986.

————. *Voyagers to the West: A Passage in the Peopling of America on the Eve of the Revolution.* New York: Knopf, 1987.

Bakker, Peter. "First African into New Netherland, 1613–1614." *De Halve Maen* 68 (Fall 1995): 50–53.

Balibar, Etienne. "The Nation Form: History and Ideology." In *Race, Nation, Class: Ambiguous Identities*, edited by Etienne Balibar and Immanuel Wallerstein, 86–106. London: Verso, 1991.

Balmer, Randall. *A Perfect Babel of Confusion: Dutch Religion and English Culture in the Middle Colonies.* New York: Oxford University Press, 1989.

Banton, Michael P. *The Idea of Race.* London: Tavistock, 1977.

Barck, Oscar T. *New York City during the War for Independence, with Special Reference to the Period of British Occupation.* Port Washington, N.Y.: Ira J. Friedman, 1966.

Barkan, Elazar. *Retreat from Scientific Racism: Changing Concepts of Race in Britain and the United States between the World Wars.* Cambridge: Cambridge University Press, 1992.

Bartels, Emily C. "*Othello* and Africa: Postcolonialism Reconsidered." *William and Mary Quarterly*, 3d ser., 56 (January 1997): 45–64.

Barth, Fredrik, ed., *Ethnic Groups and Boundaries: The Social Organization of Cultural Differences.* Boston: Little, Brown, 1969.

Bartlett, Robert. *The Making of Europe: Conquest, Colonization, and Cultural Change.* Princeton, N.J.: Princeton University Press, 1993.

Bastide, Roger. *African Civilisation in the New World.* Translated by Peter Green. New York: Harper & Row, 1971.

Bauman, Zygmunt. *Modernity and Ambivalence.* Ithaca, N.Y.: Cornell University Press, 1991.

Beard, Charles, and Mary Beard. *The Rise of American Civilization.* New York: Macmillan, 1927.

Becker, Carl. *The History of Political Parties in the Province of New York, 1760–1776.* Madison: University of Wisconsin Press, 1909.

Bell, Derrick. *Faces at the Bottom of the Well: The Permanence of Racism.* Paperback edition. New York: Basic Books, 1992.

Bennett, Harry J. Jr. *Bondsmen and Bishops: Slavery and Apprenticeship on the Codrington Plantations of Barbados, 1710–1838.* Berkeley: University of California Press, 1958.

Berkhofer, Robert E. Jr. *The White Man's Indian: Images of the American Indian from Columbus to the Present.* New York: Alfred Knopf, 1978.

Berlin, Ira. *Many Thousand Gone: The First Two Centuries of Slavery in North America.* Cambridge: Harvard University Press, 1998.

Bernasconi, Robert, ed. *Concepts of Race in the Eighteenth Century.* Bristol: Thoemmes, 2001.

Berstein, Iver. *The New York City Draft Riots: Their Significance for American Society and Politics in the Age of the Civil War.* New York: Oxford University Press, 1990.

Bhabha, Homi. *The Location of Culture.* London: Routledge, 1994.

Bhattacharyya, Garci, John Gabriel, and Stephen Small. *Race and Power: Global Racism in the Twenty-first Century.* London: Routledge, 2002.

Birnbaum, Pierre, and Ira Katznelson. *Paths of Emancipation: Jews, States, and Citizenship.* Princeton, N.J.: Princeton University Press, 1995.

Blackburn, Robin. *The Making of New World Slavery, From the Baroque to the Modern, 1492–1800.* London: Verso, 1997.

Blakey, Allison. *Blacks in the Dutch World: The Evolution of Racial Imagery in a Modern Society.* Bloomington: Indiana University Press, 1993.

Blakey, Michael L. "Notes from the Howard University Biological Anthropology Laboratory." *Newsletter of the African Burial Ground & Five Points Archaeological Projects* 1 (Winter 1966): 6.

Blassingame, John S. *Slave Community: Plantation Life in the Antebellum South.* New York: Oxford University Press, 1972.

Bliven, Bruce Jr. *Battle of New York.* New York: Holt, 1955.

Bloch, Marc. *Slavery and Serfdom in the Middle Ages: Selected Essays.* Translated by William R. Beer. Berkeley: University of California Press, 1975.

Blussé, Leonard, H. L. Wesseling, and G. D. Winius, eds. *History and Underdevelopment: Essays on Underdevelopment and European Expansion in Asia and Africa.* Leiden: Leiden Center for the History of European Expansion, 1980.

Boles, John B., ed. *Masters and Slaves in the House of the Lord: Race and Religion in the American South, 1740–1870.* Lexington: University of Kentucky Press, 1988.

Bolster, W. Jeffrey. *Black Jacks: African American Seamen in the Age of Sail.* Cambridge: Harvard University Press, 1997.

Bolton, Reginald P. *Indian Life of Long Ago in the City of New York.* New York: Schoen, 1934.

Bonnaisse, Pierre. *From Slavery to Feudalism in South-Western Europe.* Translated by Jean Birrell. Cambridge: Cambridge University Press, 1991.

Bonomi, Patricia U. *A Factious People: Politics and Society in Colonial New York.* New York: Columbia University Press, 1972.

———. *Under the Cope of Heaven: Religion, Society, and Politics in Colonial America.* New York: Oxford University Press, 1986.

Boorstin, Daniel. *The Genius of American Politics.* Chicago: University of Chicago Press, 1953.

Booth, Mary L. *The History of the City of New York, From its Earliest Settlement to the Present Time.* New York: W. R. C. Clark and Meeker, 1857.

Boschi, Caio César. *Os leigos e o poder: Irmandades leigos e politica colonizadora em Minas Gerais.* São Paulo: Editora Atica, 1986.

Boxer, Charles R. *The Dutch Seaborne Empire, 1600–1800.* London: Hutchinson, 1965.

Bracken, Harold M. "Essence, Accident, and Race." *Hermathena* 116 (Winter 1973): 81–96.

Bradley, Keith. *Slavery and Society at Rome.* Cambridge: Cambridge University Press, 1994.

Brathwaite, Edward K. *The Development of Creole Society in Jamaica, 1770–1820.* Oxford: Oxford University Press, 1971.

Braude, Benjamin. "The Sons of Noah and the Construction of Ethnic and Geographical Identities in the Medieval and Early Modern Periods." *William and Mary Quarterly,* 3d ser., 56 (January 1997): 103–42.

Breen, Timothy H. *Tobacco Culture: The Mentality of the Great Tidewater Planters on the Eve of the Revolution.* Princeton, N.J.: Princeton University Press, 1985.

Brenner, Robert. "Origins of Capitalism." *New Left Review* 104 (July–August 1977): 25–93.

Bridenbaugh, Carl. *Cities in Revolt: Urban Life in America, 1743–1776.* New York: Knopf, 1955.

———. *Cities in the Wilderness: First Century of Urban Life in America, 1625–1742.* New York: Ronald, 1938.

———, ed. *Gentlemen's Progress: The Itinerarium of Dr. Alexander Hamilton.* Pittsburgh: University of Pittsburgh Press, 1992.

Brown, Kathleen M. "The Anglo-Algonquian Gender Frontier." In *Negotiators of Change: Historical Perspectives on Native American Women,* edited by Nancy Shoemaker, 26–46. New York: Routledge, 1995.

———. *Good Wives, Nasty Wenches, & Anxious Patriarchs: Gender, Race, and Power in Colonial Virginia.* Chapel Hill: University of North Carolina Press, 1996.

———. "Native Americans and Early Modern Concepts of Race." In *Empire and Others:*

British Encounters with Indigenous Peoples, 1600–1850, edited by Martin Daunton and Rick Halpern, 79–100. Philadelphia: University of Pennsylvania Press, 1999.

Bruckbauer, Frederick. *The Kirk of Rutgers Farm*. New York, 1919.

Bumsted, J. M. *The People's Clearance: Highland Emigration to British North America, 1770–1815*. Edinburgh: Edinburgh University Press, 1982.

Buraway, Michael. "Race, Class, and Colonialism." *Social and Economic Studies* 24 (December 1974): 3–21.

Burke, Peter. *Popular Culture in Early Modern Europe*. Rev. ed. Brookfield, Vt.: Ashgate, 1994.

Burns, Richard M. *The Great Debate on Miracles: From Joseph Glanville to David Hume*. Lewisburg, Pa.: Bucknell University Press, 1981.

Bushman, Richard. *The Refinement of America: Persons, Houses, Cities*. New York: Knopf, 1992.

Butler, Jon. *Awash in a Sea of Faith: Christianizing the American People*. Cambridge: Harvard University Press, 1990.

———. *The Huguenots in America: A Refugee People in New World Society*. Cambridge: Harvard University Press, 1983.

Canisteo Centennial, 1873–1973. Canisteo, N.Y.: Historical Society of Steuben County, 1973.

Canny, Nicholas P. *The Elizabethan Conquest of Ireland: A Pattern Established, 1565–76*. New York: Barnes & Noble, 1976.

———. "The Ideology of English Colonization: From Ireland to America." *William and Mary Quarterly*, 3d ser., 31 (October 1973): 575–98.

———. *Kingdom and Colony: Ireland in the Atlantic World*. Baltimore: Johns Hopkins University Press, 1988.

Carpenter, A. H. "Naturalization in England and the American Colonies." *American Historical Review* 9 (1971): 288–303.

Ceaser, James W. *Reconstructing America: Symbol of America in Modern Thought*. New Haven: Yale University Press, 1997.

Ceci, Lynn. *The Effect of European Contact and Trade on the Settlement Pattern of Indians in Coastal New York, 1524–1665: The Archeological and Documentary Evidence*. New York: Garland, 1990.

Chaplin, Joyce E. "Natural Philosophy and an Early Racial Idiom in North America: Comparing English and Indian Bodies." *William and Mary Quarterly*, 3d ser., 54 (January 1997): 229–52.

Christoph, Peter. "The Freedmen of New Amsterdam." *Journal of the Afro-American Historical and Genealogical Society* 4 (Fall 1983): 139–54.

Clarke, T. Wood. "The Negro Plot of 1741." *New York History* 25 (1941): 167–81.

Clifford, Mary Louise. *From Slavery to Freetown: Black Loyalists after the American Revolution*. Jefferson, N.C.: McFarland, 1999.

Cohen, David S. "How Dutch Were the Dutch of New Netherland?" *New York History* 62, 1 (January 1981): 43–60.

Cohen, Sheldon S. "Elias Neau, Instructor of New York's Slaves." *New-York Historical Society Quarterly* 55, 1 (1971): 7–27.

Colley, Linda. *Britons: Forging the Nation, 1707–1837*. New Haven: Yale University Press, 1992.

Condon, Thomas J. *New York Beginnings: The Commercial Origins of New Netherland*. New York: New York University Press, 1968.

Conzen, Kathleen Neils. "Ethnicity as Festive Culture: Nineteenth-Century German Americans on Parade." In *The Invention of Ethnicity*, edited by Werner Sollors, 44–76. New York: Oxford University Press, 1989.

Cordero-Guzmán, Héctor R., ed. *Migration, Transnationalization, and Race in a Changing New York*. Philadelphia: Temple University Press, 2001.

Cosby, Ernest H. "The Rutgers Family of New York." *New York Genealogical and Bio-graphical Society Record* 17 (1886): 12–15.

Countryman, Edward. *A People in Revolution: The American Revolution and Political Society in New York, 1760–1790.* New York: W. W. Norton, 1981.

Craton, Michael. *Testing the Chains: Resistance to Slavery in the British West Indies.* Ithaca, N.Y.: Cornell University Press, 1982.

Cremin, Lawrence A. *American Education: The Colonial Experience, 1607–1783.* New York: Harper & Row, 1970.

Cronon, William. *Changes in the Land: Indians, Colonists, and the Ecology of New England.* New York: Hill & Wang, 1983.

Crow, Jeffrey J. *The Black Experience in Revolutionary North Carolina.* Raleigh: Division of Archives and History, North Carolina Department of Cultural Resources, 1977.

Curry, Daniel. *New-York: Historical Sketches of the Rise and Progress of the Metropolitan City of America.* New York: Carlton & Phillips, 1853.

Curtin, Philip D. *The Slave Trade: A Census.* Madison: University of Wisconsin Press, 1969.

Danto, Arthur C. *Narration and Knowledge, Including the Integral Texts of Analytical Philosophy of History.* New York: Columbia University Press, 1985.

Daston, Lorraine. *Wonders and the Order of Nature, 1150–1750.* Cambridge: MIT Press, 1998.

Davies, D. W. *A Primer of Dutch Seventeenth-Century Overseas Trade.* The Hague: Nijhhoff, 1961.

Davies, K. G. *The Royal African Company.* London: Longmans, Green, 1957.

Davis, David Brion. "Constructing Race: A Reflection." *William and Mary Quarterly,* 3d ser., 54 (January 1997): 7–18.

———. *The Problem of Slavery in Western Culture.* Ithaca, N.Y.: Cornell University Press, 1966.

———, ed. *The Fear of Conspiracy: Images of Un-American Subversion from the Revolution to the Present.* Ithaca, N.Y.: Cornell University Press, 1971.

Davis, Natalie Zemon. *Fiction in the Archives: Pardon Tales and Their Tellers in Sixteenth-Century France.* Stanford, Calif.: Stanford University Press, 1987.

———. "Iroquois Women, European Women." In *American Encounters: Natives and New-comers from European Contact to Indian Removal,* edited by Peter Mancall and James H. Merrell, 97–118. New York: Routledge, 2000.

———. *The Return of Martin Guerre.* Cambridge: Harvard University Press, 1983.

———. *Society and Culture in Early Modern French Society: Eight Essays.* Stanford, Calif.: Stanford University Press, 1975.

Davis, Thomas J., ed. "Emancipation Rhetoric, Natural Rights, and Revolutionary New England: A Note on Four Petitions in Massachusetts, 1773–1777." *New England Quarterly* 62 (1989): 248–63.

———. *The New York Conspiracy by Daniel Horsmanden.* Boston: Beacon, 1971.

———. *A Rumor of Revolt: The "Great Negro Plot" in Colonial New York.* New York: Free Press, 1985.

———. "'These Enemies of Their Own Household': A Note on the Troublesome Slave Population in Eighteenth-Century New York City." *Journal of the Afro-American Historical and Genealogical Society* (October 1984): 133–47.

Davisson, William I., and Lawrence J. Bradley, "New York Maritime Trade: Ship Voyage Patterns, 1715–1765." *New-York Historical Society Quarterly* 60 (1971): 314–15.

Dayton, Cornelia Hughes. *Women Before the Bar: Gender, Law, & Society, 1639–1789.* Chapel Hill: University of North Carolina Press, 1995.

De Certeau, Michel. *The Practice of Everyday Life.* Translated by Steven Rendall. Berkeley: University of California Press, 1984.

DeCosta, B. F. *Three Score and Ten: The Story of St. Philip's Church, New York City. A Dis-*

course Delivered in the New Church, West Twenty-fifth Street at Its Opening. New York: The Parish, 1889.

Deloria, Philip J. *Playing Indian: Otherness and Authenticity in the Assumption of American Indian Identity.* New Haven: Yale University Press, 1999.

Demos, John. *A Little Commonwealth: Family Life in Plymouth Colony.* New York: Oxford University Press, 1970.

Denoon, Donald. "Understanding Settler Colonies." *Historical Studies* 18 (July 1973): 511–27.

Dickson, R. J. *Ulster Emigration to Colonial America, 1718–1775.* London: Routledge and Kegan Paul, 1966.

Dirks, Nicholas B. *Colonialism and Culture.* Ann Arbor: University of Michigan Press, 1991.

Dockès, Pierre. *Medieval Slavery and Liberation.* Translated by Arthur Goldhammer. Chicago: University of Chicago Press, 1982.

Drake, Thomas E. *Quakers and Slavery in America.* New Haven: Yale University Press, 1950.

Drescher, Seymour. *Capitalism and Antislavery: British Mercantilism in Comparative Perspective.* Oxford: Oxford University Press, 1987.

Du Bois, W. E. B. *Black Reconstruction: An Essay Toward a History of the Part Black Folk Played in the Attempt to Reconstruct Democracy in America.* New York: Russell & Russell, 1935.

Du Bois, W. E. B. "Marxism and the Negro Problem," *Crisis* 40 (1933): 104.

Duby, Georges. *The Early Growth of the European Economy: Warriors and Peasants from the Seventh to the Twelfth Century.* Translated by Howard B. Clarke. London: Weidenfeld and Nicolson, 1974.

Dunlap, David W. *On Broadway: Journey Uptown over Time.* New York: Rizzoli, 1990.

Dunlap, William. *History of the New Netherlands Province of New York and State of New York.* New York: Carler & Thorp, 1839–40.

Eights, James. "Pinkster Festivities in Albany Sixty Years Ago." *Collections on the History of Albany* 2 (1867): 323–27.

Elias, Norbert. *The Civilizing Process.* Vol. 1, *The History of Manners.* Translated by E. Jephcott. Oxford: Basil Blackwell, 1978.

Emerson, R. "Colonialism." In *International Encyclopedia of Social and Behavioral Sciences,* 4:2232–44. 26 vols. New York: Macmillan, 1961.

Emmer, P. C. "The Dutch and the Making of the Second Atlantic System." In *Slavery and the Rise of the Atlantic System,* edited by Barbara Solow, 75–96. Cambridge: Cambridge University Press, 1991.

Eriksen, Thomas Hylland. *Ethnicity and Nationalism: Anthropological Perspectives.* London: Pluto, 1993.

Ernst, Robert. *Immigrant Life in New York City, 1852–1863.* New York: King's Crown, 1949.

Essig, James D. *The Bonds of Wickedness: Evangelicals Against Slavery, 1770–1800.* Philadelphia: Temple University Press, 1983.

Fabend, Firth. "The Yeoman Ideal: A Dutch Family in the Middle Colonies, 1650–1800." Ph.D. diss., New York University, 1985.

Fage, F. D. "A New Check List of the Forts and Castles of Ghana." *Transactions of the Historical Society of Ghana,* 1 (1959).

Fanon, Frantz. *Black Skin, White Masks.* New York: Grove, 1967.

Farnell, J. E. "The Navigation Act of 1651, the First Dutch War, and the London Merchant Community." *Economic History Review,* 2d ser., 16 (April 1964): 439–51.

Feister, Lois M. "Linguistic Communication Between the Dutch and Indians in New Netherland, 1609–1664." *Ethnohistory* 20 (1973): 25–38.

Ferrer, Lewis S. "The Dream of Benedict de Spinoza." *The American Imago* 14 (1957): 225–42.

Fields, Barbara. "Slavery, Race, and Ideology in the United States." *New Left Review* 181 (May–June 1990): 95–118.

Fisher, Nicholas R. *Slavery in Classical Greece*. London: Bristol Classical Press, 1993.

Foner, Eric. *Free Soil, Free Labor, Free Men: The Ideology of the Republican Party before the Civil War*. New York: Oxford University Press, 1970.

Foner, Philip. *Blacks in the American Revolution*. Westport, Conn.: Greenwood, 1976.

Foote, Thelma Wills. "'Some Hard Usage': The New York City Slave Revolt of 1712." *New York Folklore* 18 (August 2000): 147–60.

Fortune, Stephen. *Merchants and Jews: The Struggle for British West Indian Commerce, 1650–1750*. Gainesville: University of Florida Press, 1984.

Foucault, Michel. *The History of Sexuality*. Vol. 1: *An Introduction*. New York: Random House, 1978.

———. *The Order of Things: An Archaeology of the Human Sciences*. New York: Vintage, 1970.

———. *Power/Knowledge: Selected Interviews & Other Writings, 1972–1977*. Edited by Colin Gordon and translated by Colin Gordon, Leo Marshall, John Mepham, and Kate Soper. New York: Pantheon, 1980.

Fox-Genovese, Elizabeth. *Within the Plantation Household: Black and White Women of the Old South*. Chapel Hill: University of North Carolina Press, 1988.

Fox-Genovese, Elizabeth, and Eugene Genovese. *Fruits of Merchant Capital: Slavery and Bourgeois Property in the Rise and Expansion of Capitalism*. Oxford: Oxford University Press, 1983.

Fredrickson, George M. *The Black Image in the White Mind: The Debate on the Afro-American Character and Destiny*. New York: Harper & Row, 1971.

Frey, Sylvia R. *Water from the Rock: Black Resistance in a Revolutionary Age*. Princeton, N.J.: Princeton University Press, 1991.

Friedberg, Anne. *Window Shopping: Cinema and the Postmodern*. Berkeley: University of California Press, 1993.

Fukuyama, Francis. "The End of American Exceptionalism." *New Perspectives* 18 (Fall 2001): 40–42.

Fyfe, Christopher H. *A History of Sierra Leone*. London: Oxford University Press, 1962.

———. "Thomas Peters: History and Legend." *Sierra Leone Studies* 1 (1953): 4–13.

Gabriel, John, and Stephen Small. *Race and Power: Global Racism in the Twenty-first Century*. London: Routledge, 2002.

Gasking, Douglas. *Language, Logic, and Causation: Philosophical Writings of Douglas Gasking*. Ed. I. T. Oakley and L. J. O'Neill. Carlton South, Vic.: Melbourne University Press, 1996.

Gehring, Charles T., and Robert S. Grumet. "Observations of the Indians from Jasper Danckaerts' Journal, 1679–80." *William and Mary Quarterly*, 3d ser., 44 (1987).

Genovese, Eugene. *From Rebellion to Revolt: Afro-American Slave Revolts in the Making of the New World*. Baton Rouge: Louisiana State University Press, 1979.

———. *Roll, Jordan, Roll: The World the Slaves Made*. New York: Vintage, 1976.

Gerbi, Antonello. *The Dispute of the New World: The History of a Polemic, 1750–1900*. Translated by Jeremy Moyle. Pittsburgh: University of Pittsburgh Press, 1973.

Geyl, Pieter. *The Revolt of the Netherlands, 1555–1609*. London: Ernst Benn, 1932.

Gilfoyle, Timothy J. *City of Eros: New York City, Prostitution, and the Commercialization of Sex, 1790–1920*. New York: W. W. Norton, 1992.

Gilman, Sander L., and Nancy L. Stepan. "Appropriating the Idioms of Science: The Rejection of Scientific Racism." In *The Bounds of Race: Perspectives on Hegemony and Resistance*, edited by Dominick La Capra, 72–103. Ithaca, N.Y.: Cornell University Press, 1991.

Gilroy, Paul. *Against Race: Imagining Political Culture Beyond the Color Line*. Cambridge: Harvard University Press, 2000.

———. *The Black Atlantic: Modernity and Double Consciousness*. Cambridge: Harvard University Press, 1993.

Ginzburg, Carlo. "Checking the Evidence: The Judge and the Historian." *Critical Inquiry* 18 (Autumn 1991): 79–92.

———. *The Cheese and the Worms: The Cosmos of a Sixteenth-Century Miller*. Translated by John and Anne Tedeschi. New York: Penguin, 1982.

———. *Night Battles: Witchcraft and Agrarian Cults in the Sixteenth and Seventeenth Centuries*. Translated by John and Anne Tedeschi. Baltimore: Johns Hopkins University Press, 1983.

Glazer, Nathan. "Race and Ethnicity in America." *Journal of Democracy* 2 (January 2000): 95–102.

Gluckman, Max. *Custom and Conflict in Africa*. Glencoe, Ill.: Free Press, 1959.

———. *Rituals of Rebellion in South-east Africa*. Glencoe, Ill.: Free Press, 1954.

Goddard, Ives. "Delaware." In *Handbook of North American Indians: Northeast*, edited by William C. Sturtevant, 15: 213–39. 15 vols. Washington, D.C.: Smithsonian Institute, 1978.

Goldberg, David Theo. *Racial Subjects: Writing on Race in America*. New York: Routledge, 1997.

———. *Racist Culture: Philosophy and the Politics of Meaning*. London: Basil Blackwell, 1993.

Goldin, Claudia. *Urban Slavery in the American South, 1830–1860*. Chicago: Chicago University Press, 1976.

Gomez, Michael A. *Exchanging Our Country Marks: The Transformation of African Identities in the Colonial and Antebellum South*. Chapel Hill: University of North Carolina Press, 1998.

Goodfriend, Joyce. *Before the Melting Pot: Society and Culture in Colonial New York City, 1664–1730*. Princeton, N.J.: Princeton University Press, 1992.

———. "Burghers and Blacks: The Evolution of Slave Society at New Amsterdam." *New York History* 59 (1978): 125–44.

Gordon, Grant. *From Slavery to Freedom, The Life of David George: Pioneer Black Baptist Minister*. Hantsport, Nova Scotia: Lancelot, 1992.

Gordon, Lewis R. *Her Majesty's Other Children: Sketches of Racism from a Neocolonial Age*. Lanham, Md.: Rowman & Littlefield, 1997.

Gossett, Thomas F. *Race: The History of an Idea in America*. New York: Schocken, 1965.

Gould, Stephen Jay. *The Mismeasurement of Man*. New York: Norton, 1981.

Gramsci, Antonio. *Selections from the Prison Notebooks*. Translated and edited by Quintin Hoare and Geoffrey Nowell Smith. New York: International Publishers, 1971.

Gravely, William B. "The Dialectic of Double Consciousness in Black Freedom Celebrations, 1808–1863." *Journal of Southern History* 54 (1988): 674–75

Greenberg, Douglas. *Crime and Law Enforcement in the Colony of New York, 1691–1776*. Ithaca, N.Y.: Cornell University Press, 1976.

Greene, Evarts B., and Virginia Harrington. *American Population before the Federal Census of 1790*. New York: Columbia University Press, 1934.

Greene, Jack P. *Pursuits of Happiness: The Social Development of Early Modern British Colonies and the Formation of American Culture*. Chapel Hill: University of North Carolina Press, 1988.

Greene, Lorenzo J. *The Negro in Colonial New England, 1620–1776*. New York: Columbia University Press, 1942.

Greven, Philip J. Jr. *Four Generations: Population, Land, and Family in Colonial Andover, Massachusetts*. Ithaca, N.Y.: Cornell University Press, 1970.

Guha, Ranajit. *Elementary Aspects of Peasant Insurgency in Colonial India*. Delhi: Oxford University Press, 1992.

Guillaumin, Collette. "The Idea of Race and Its Elevation to Autonomous Scientific and Legal Status." In *Sociological Theories: Race and Colonialism*. Paris: UNESCO, 1980.

Gutman, Herbert G. *The Black Family in Slavery and Freedom, 1750–1925*. New York: Random House, 1976.

Haar, Charles M. "White Indentured Servants in Colonial New York." *Americana* 34 (1940): 370–92.

Habermas, Jürgen. *The Structural Transformation of the Public Sphere: An Inquiry into a Category of Bourgeois Society*. Translated by Thomas Burger with the assistance of Frederick Lawrence. Cambridge: MIT Press, 1991.

Hall, David D. *Worlds of Wonder, Days of Judgment: Popular Religious Belief in Early New England*. Cambridge: Harvard University Press, 1989.

Hall, Jacquelyn Dowd. "'The Mind That Burns in Each Body': Women, Rape, and Racial Violence." In *Powers of Desire: Politics of Sexuality*, edited by Ann Snitow, Christine Stansell, and Sharon Thompson, 328–49. New York: New York Monthly Review Press, 1983.

Hall, Stuart. "Conclusion: The Multi-Cultural Question." In *Un/Settled Multiculturalisms: Diasporas, Entanglements,Transruptions*, edited by Barnor Hesse, 211–41. London: Zed, 2000.

———. "Race, Articulation and Societies Structured in Domination." In *Sociological Theories: Race and Colonialism*, 305–45. Paris: UNESCO, 1980.

Hampton, Barbara. "The Continuity Factor in Ga Music." *Black Perspective in Music* 6 (1978): 33–48.

Hancock, David J. *Citizens of the World: London Merchants and the Integration of the British Atlantic Community, 1735–1785*. Cambridge: Harvard University Press, 1995.

Handler, Jerome S., R. S. Corrucini, and R. J. Mutaw. "Tooth Mutilation in the Caribbean: Evidence from a Slave Burial in Barbados." *Journal of Human Evolution* 11 (1982): 297–313.

Handler, Jerome S., and Frederick W. Lange. *Plantation Slavery in Barbados: An Archaeological and Historical Investigation*. Cambridge: Harvard University Press, 1978.

Haney-López, Ian. *White by Law: The Legal Construction of Race*. New York: New York University Press, 1996.

Hansen, Joyce, and Gary McGowan. *Breaking Ground, Breaking Silence: The Story of New York's African Burial Ground*. New York: Holt, 1998.

Harris, Cheryl. "Whiteness as Property." *Harvard Law Review* 106 (June 1993): 1709–91.

Hartman, Saidiya V. *Scenes of Subjection: Terror, Slavery, and Self-Making*. New York: Oxford University Press, 1997.

Hartz, Louis. *The Liberal Tradition in America: Interpretation of American Political Thought since the Revolution*. New York: Harcourt Brace, 1955.

Haskell, Thomas L. "Review of *Freedom. I. Freedom in the Making of Western Culture*. By Orlando Patterson." *Journal of Interdisciplinary History* 25 (Summer 1994): 95–102.

Haydon, Colin. *Anti-Catholicism in Eighteenth-Century England*. Manchester: University of Manchester Press, 1993.

Heckscher, Eli F. *Mercantilism*. 2 vols. London: G. Allen & Unwin, 1935.

Hedrick, Basil C., and Jeanette E. Stephens. *It's a Natural Fact: Obeah in the Bahamas*. Greeley: University of Northern Colorado Press, 1977.

Henretta, James, and Gary H. Nobles. *Evolution of American Society, 1600–1820*. Lexington, Mass.: D. C. Heath, 1987.

Hershkowitz, Leo. "The Troublesome Turk: An Illustration of Judicial Process in New Amsterdam." *New York History* 46 (1965): 299–310.

Herskovitz, Melville J. *The Myth of the Negro Past*. Boston: Beacon, 1929.

Heyrman, Christine L. *Commerce and Culture: The Maritime Communities of Colonial Massachusetts, 1690–1750*. New York: W. W. Norton, 1984.

Higginbotham, Don. *The War of American Independence: Military Attitudes, Policies, and Practice, 1763–1789*. New York: Macmillan, 1971.

Higginbotham, Leon A. *In a Matter of Color: The Colonial Period*. New York: Oxford University Press, 1978.

Hill, Christopher. *A Century of Revolution, 1603–1714*. Edinburgh: T. Nelson, 1961.

Hochschild, Jennifer. *The New American Dilemma: Liberal Democracy and School Desegregation*. New Haven: Yale University Press, 1984.

Hodes, Martha E. *Sex across the Color Line: White Women and Black Men in the American South*. Chapel Hill: University of North Carolina Press, 1993.

Hodgen, Margaret T. *Early Anthropology in the Sixteenth and Seventeenth Centuries*. Philadelphia: University of Pennsylvania Press, 1964.

Hodges, Graham. "African-Americans in Monmouth County during the Age of the American Revolution." In *Monmouth County Park System 1990 Black History Celebration*, 18–23. Lincroft, N.J.: New Jersey Historical Commission, 1990.

———. "Black Revolt in New York City and the Neutral Zone: 1775–83." In *New York in the Age of the Constitution, 1775–1800*, edited by Paul A. Gilje and William Pencak, 20–47. Cranbury, N.J.: Associated University Press, 1992.

———. *The New York City Cartmen, 1664–1850*. New York: New York University Press, 1986.

Hodges, Graham, and Allan Edward Brown, eds. *"Pretends to Be Free": Runaway Slave Advertisements from Colonial and Revolutionary New York and New Jersey*. New York: Garland, 1994.

———. *Root & Branch: African Americans in New York & East Jersey, 1613–1863*. Chapel Hill: University of North Carolina Press, 1999.

Hoff, Henry B. "A Colonial Black Family in New York and New Jersey: Pieter Santome and His Descendants." *Journal of the Afro-American Genealogical and Historical Society* 9 (Fall 1988): 101–34.

Hoffer, Peter. *The Great New York Conspiracy of 1741: Slavery, Crime, and Colonial Law*. Lawrence: University Press of Kansas, 2003.

Holt, Thomas. "Marking: Race, Race-Making, and the Writing of History." *American Historical Review* 100 (February 1995): 1–28.

Hopkins, A. G. "Back to the Future: From National to Imperial History." *Past & Present* 164 (August 1999): 198–243.

Horton, Oliver, and Lois F. Horton. *In Hope of Liberty: Culture, Community, and Protest among Northern Free Blacks, 1700–1860*. New York: Oxford University Press, 1997.

Horton, Robin. *Patterns of Thought in Africa and the West: Essays on Magic, Religion, and Science*. Cambridge: Cambridge University Press, 1993.

Hoyt, Edward A. "Naturalization under the American Colonies." *Political Science Quarterly* 67 (1952): 248–66.

Hudson, Charles M., ed. *Black Drink: A Native American Tea*. Athens: Georgia University Press, 1979.

Iriye, Akira. "The Internationalization of History." *American Historical Review* 94 (February 1989): 1–10.

Israel, Jonathan. *Dutch Primacy in the World Trade, 1585–1740*. Oxford: Clarendon, 1989.

Israel, Joseph. *The Dutch Republic: Its Rise, Greatness and Fall*. New York: Oxford University Press, 1995.

Jackson, Luther P. "Early Strivings of the Negro in Virginia." *Journal of Negro History* 16 (1931): 168–239.

Jacobs, Sue-Ellen, Wesley Thomas, and Sabine Lang, eds. *Two-Spirited People: Native American Gender Identity, Sexuality, and Spirituality*. Urbana: University of Illinois Press, 1997.

James, C. L. R. *Black Jacobins: Toussaint L'Ouverture and the San Domingo Revolution*. New York: Vintage, 1963.

Jameson, Fredric. *Postmodernism, or, The Cultural Logic of Late Capitalism*. Durham, N.C.: Duke University Press, 1991.

Jenkins, Stephen. *The Greatest Street in the World: The Story of Broadway, Old and New, from the Bowling Green to Albany*. New York: G. P. Putnam's Sons, 1911.

Johnson, Amandus. *The Swedish Settlements on the Delaware, 1638–1664*. 2 vols. New York: D. Appleton, 1911.

Johnson, Barbara. *The Feminist Difference: Literature, Psychoanalysis, and Gender*. Cambridge: Harvard University Press, 1998.

Jones, J. R. *The Anglo-Dutch Wars of the Seventeenth Century*. London: Longmans, 1996.

Jones, Steve. *The Language of Genes: Biology, History and the Evolutionary Future*. London: Harper Collins, 1993.

Jordan, Winthrop. *White over Black: American Attitudes Toward the Negro, 1550–1812*. Chapel Hill: University of North Carolina Press, 1968.

Judd, Jacob. "Frederick Philipse and the Madagascar Trade." *New-York Historical Society Quarterly* 55 (1971): 354–74.

Kamen, Henry. *Inquisition and Society in Spain in the Sixteenth and Seventeenth Centuries*. Bloomington: Indiana University Press, 1985.

Kammen, Michael. *Colonial New York: A History*. New York: Charles Scribner's Sons, 1975.
———. "The Problem of American Exceptionalism: A Reconsideration." *American Quarterly* 45 (March 1993): 1–44.

Kaplan, Sidney. "The Domestic Insurrections of the Declaration of Independence." *Journal of Negro History* 61 (1976): 249–50.

Katz, Stanley M. *Newcastle's New York: Anglo-American Politics, 1732–1753*. Cambridge: Harvard University Press, 1968.

Kavanagh, Aidan. *The Shape of Baptism: Rite of Christian Initiation*. New York: Pueblo, 1978.

Kea, Ray. *Settlements, Trade, and Politics in the Seventeenth-Century Gold Coast, 1469–1682*. Athens: University of Georgia Press, 1979.

Kearney, Hugh F. *The British Isles: A History of Four Nations*. Cambridge: Cambridge University Press, 1989.

Kemp, Webb. *Support of Schools in Colonial New York by the SPG*. New York: Arno, 1970.

Kern, Stephen. *The Culture of Time and Space, 1880–1918*. Cambridge: Harvard University Press, 1983.

Kettner, James H. *The Development of American Citizenship, 1608–1870*. Chapel Hill: University of North Carolina Press, 1978.

Kevles, Daniel J. *In the Name of Eugenics: Genetics and the Uses of Human Heredity*. New York: Knopf, 1985.

Keys, Alice M. *Cadwallader Colden: A Representative Eighteenth-Century Official*. New York: AMS Press, 1967.

Kidd, Colon. *British Identities before Nationalism: Ethnicity and Nationhood in the Atlantic World, 1600–1800*. Cambridge: Cambridge University Press, 1999.

Kilpatrick, William H. *The Dutch Schools of New Netherland and Colonial New York*. New York: Arno Press, 1969.

Kim, Sung Bok. *Landlords and Tenants in Colonial New York: Manorial Society, 1665–1775*. Chapel Hill: University of North Carolina Pres, 1978.

"Kip Family History." *New York Genealogical and Biographical Society Record* 8 (1921): 67–133.

Kip, Frederick Ellswork. *History of the Kip Family in America*. Montclair, N.Y., 1928.

Klein, Anatole Norman. "West African Unfree Labor before and after the Rise of the Atlantic Slave Trade." In *Slavery in the New World: A Reader in Comparative History*, edited by Laura Foner and Eugene Genovese, 87–95. Englewood Cliffs, N.J.: Prentice-Hall, 1969.

Klein, Laura F., and Lillian A. Ackerman, eds. *Women and Power in Native North America*. Norman: University of Oklahoma Press, 1995.

Klein, Milton M., ed. *The Politics of Diversity: Essays in the History of Colonial New York*. Port Washington, N.Y: Kennikat, 1974.

Knittle, Walter A. *The Early Eighteenth Century Palatine Emigration: A British Government Redemptioner Project to Manufacture Naval Stores*. Philadelphia: Dorrance, 1937.

Kolchin, Peter. *Unfree Labor: American Slavery and Russian Serfdom*. Cambridge: Harvard University Press, 1987.

Kraft, Herbert C. *The Lenape: Archaeology, History, and Ethnography*. Newark: New Jersey Historical Society, 1986.

Kross, Jessica. *The Evolution of an American Town: Newtown, New York, 1624–1775*. Philadelphia: Temple University Press, 1983.

Kruger, Vivian. "Born to Run: The Slave Family in Early New York, 1626–1827." Ph.D. diss. Columbia University, 1985.

Kulikoff, Allen. "A 'Prolifick' People: Black Population Growth in the Chesapeake Colonies, 1700–1790." *Southern Studies* 16 (1977): 391–428.

Ladurie, Emmanuel Le Roy. *Montaillou: The Promised Land of Error*. Translated by Barbara Bray. New York: G. Braziller, 1978.

Lane, Frederick. *Profits from Power: Readings in Protection, Rent, and Violence-Controlling Enterprises*. Albany, N.Y., 1979.

Laslett, Peter. *The World We Have Lost*. New York: Scribner, 1971.

Lathbury, Thomas. *A History of the Book of Common Prayer and other books of authority, with an attempt to ascertain how the rubrics and canons have been understood and observed from the Reformation to the Accession of George III; also an account of the State of Religion and Religious parties in England from 1640–1660*. Oxford: John Henry and James Parker, 1859.

Law, Jules D. *The Rhetoric of Empiricism: Language and Perception from Locke to I. A. Richards*. Ithaca, N.Y.: Cornell University Press, 1993.

Leder, Lawrence H. *Liberty and Authority: Early American Political Ideology*. Chicago: Quadrangle, 1968.

———. "'Like Madmen through the Streets': The New York City Riot of June 1690." *New-York Historical Society Quarterly* 39 (October 1955): 405–15.

———. "Records of the Trials of Jacob Leisler and His Associates." *New-York Historical Society Quarterly* 36, 4 (October 1952): 431–57.

Lee, Jean Butenhoff. "The Problem of Slave Community in the Eighteenth-Century Chesapeake." *William and Mary Quarterly*, 3d. ser., 43 (1986): 333–61.

Levin, Harry. *The Power of Blackness: Hawthorne, Poe, Melville*. New York: Knopf, 1958.

Levine, Lawrence W. *Black Culture and Black Consciousness: Afro-American Folk Thought from Slavery to Freedom*. New York: Oxford University Press, 1977.

Lévi-Strauss, Claude. *The Savage Mind*. Translated by George Weidenfeld and edited by Julian Pitt-Rivers and Ernest Gellner. Chicago: University of Chicago Press, 1966.

Levy, Leonard. *Freedom of the Press from Zenger to Jefferson: Early American Libertarianism*. New York: Bobbs-Merrill, 1966.

Lewontin, Richard C. *Biology as Ideology: The Doctrine of DNA*. New York: Anansi, 1991.

Leyburn, James G. *The Scots-Irish: A Social History*. Chapel Hill: University of North Carolina Press, 1962.

Liedtke, Rainer, and Stephan Wendehorst. *The Emancipation of Catholics, Jews, and Protestants: Minorities and the Nation State in Nineteenth-Century Europe*. New York: St. Martin's Press, 1999.

Lieske, Joel. "Race and Democracy." *Political Science & Politics* 32 (June 199): 217–25.

Lindsay, Arnett G. "Diplomatic Relations between the United States and Great Britain Bearing on the Return of Negro Slaves, 1783–1828." *Journal of Negro History* 5 (October 1920): 391–419.

Linebaugh, Peter. "All the Atlantic Mountain Shook." *Labour/Le Travaileur* 10 (Autumn 1982): 82–121.

———. *The London Hanged: Crime and Civil Society in the Eighteenth Century.* Cambridge: Cambridge University Press, 1992.

Linebaugh, Peter, and Marcus Rediker. "The Many-Headed Hydra: Sailors, Slaves, and the Atlantic Working Class in the Eighteenth Century." *Journal of Historical Sociology* 3 (1990): 225–52.

Litwack, Leon F. *North of Slavery: The Negro in the Free States, 1790–1860.* Chicago: University of Chicago Press, 1961.

Lockridge, Kenneth A. *A New England Town, the First Hundred Years: Dedham, Massachusetts, 1636–1736.* New York: W. W. Norton, 1970.

Lovejoy, David S. *The Glorious Revolution in America.* New York: Harper & Row, 1972.

Lovejoy, Paul E. "Concubinage and the Status of Women Slaves in Early Colonial Northern Nigeria." In *"We Specialize in the Impossible": A Reader in Black Women's History,* edited by Darlene Clark Hine, Wilma King, and Linda Reed, 77–123. Brooklyn, N.Y.: Carlson, 1995.

Lydon, James G. "New York and the Slave Trade, 1700 to 1774." *William and Mary Quarterly,* 3d ser., 35 (1978): 375–94.

———. *Pirates, Privateers, and Profits.* Upper Saddle River, N.J.: Gregg, 1970.

MacDougall, Hugh A. *Racial Myth in English History: Trojans, Teutons, and Anglo-Saxons.* Hanover, N.H.: University of New England Press, 1982.

Mack, Mark E., and M. Cassandra Hill. "Recent Research Findings Concerning the African Burial Ground Population." *Newsletter of the African Burial Ground & Five Points Archaeological Projects* 1 (Fall 1995): 3–4.

MacPherson, C. B. *The Political Theory of Possessive Individualism.* Oxford: Clarendon, 1962.

Malik, Kenan. *The Meaning of Race: Race, History and Culture in Western Society.* New York: New York University Press, 1996.

Man, Albion Jr. "Labor Competition and the New York Draft Riots of 1863." *Journal of Negro History* 34 (1951): 386–402.

Mancall, Peter C. *Deadly Medicine: Indians and Alcohol in Early America.* Ithaca, N.Y.: Cornell University Press, 1995.

Marcus, Jacob R. *The Colonial American Jew, 1492–1776.* 2 vols. Detroit: Wayne State University Press, 1970.

Martinez-Alier, Verena. *Marriage, Class and Colour in Nineteenth-Century Cuba: A Study of Racial Attitudes and Sexual Values in a Slave Society.* Ann Arbor: University of Michigan Press, 1974.

Marx, Karl. *Capital.* Vol. 3: *The Process of Capitalist Production as a Whole.* Edited by Frederick Engels. 3 vols. 1894. Reprint, New York: International Publishers, 1967.

———. *Pre-Capitalist Economic Formations.* Translated by Jack Cohen. New York: International Publishers, 1964.

Maslowski, Peter. "National Policy Towards the Use of Black Troops in the Revolution." *South Carolina Historical Magazine* 72 (1972): 1–17.

Matson, Cathy. *Merchants and Empire: Trading in Colonial New York.* Baltimore: Johns Hopkins University Press, 1997.

Maynard, John A. F. *The Huguenot Church of New York: A History of the Church of Saint Esprit.* New York, 1938.

Mbiti, John S. *African Religions and Philosophies.* New York: Doubleday, 1969.

McClintock, Anne. *Imperial Leather: Race, Gender, and Sexuality in the Colonial Contest.* New York: Routledge, 1995.

McCormick, Charles H. *Leisler's Rebellion.* New York: Garland, 1989.

McKee, Samuel. *Labor in Colonial New York, 1664–1776.* New York: Columbia University Press, 1935.

McManus, Edgar J. *A History of Negro Slavery in New York*. New York: Syracuse University Press, 1966.

McPherson, James M. "Antebellum Southern Exceptionalism: A New Look at an Old Question." *Civil War History* 29 (September 1983): 230–44.

Menard, Russell R. "The Maryland Slave Population, 1658 to 1730: A Demographic Profile of Blacks in Four Counties." *William and Mary Quarterly*, 3d ser. 32 (1975): 29–54.

Miers, Suzanne, and Igor Kopytoff, eds. *Slavery in Africa: Historical and Anthropological Perspectives*. Madison: University of Wisconsin Press, 1977.

Miller, Kerby. *Emigrants and Exiles: Ireland and the Irish Exodus to North America*. New York: Oxford University Press, 1983.

Mintz, Sidney W., and Richard Price. *An Anthropological Approach to the Afro-American Past: A Caribbean Perspective*. Boston: Beacon, 1992.

Mohl, Raymond A. "Poverty in Early America: A Reappraisal." *New York History* 50 (1969): 5–27.

Montagu, Ashley. *Man's Most Dangerous Myth: The Fallacy of Race*. New York: Columbia University Press, 1942.

———. *Statement on Race: An Extended Discussion in Plain Language of the UNESCO Statement by Experts on the Race Problem*. New York: Schuman, 1951.

Morgan, Edmund S. *American Slavery, American Freedom: The Ordeal of Colonial Virginia*. New York: W. W. Norton, 1975.

Morgan, Edwin V. *Slavery in New York*. New York: G. P. Putnam's & Sons, 1898.

Morgan, Philip D. "Black Life in Eighteenth-Century Charleston." *Perspectives in American History*, n.s. 1 (1984): 187–232.

———. "Black Society in the Lowcountry, 1760–1810." In *Slavery and Freedom in the Age of the American Revolution*, edited by Ira Berlin and Ronald Hoffman, 83–142. Charlottesville: University of Virginia Press, 1981.

———. *Slave Counterpoint: Black Culture in the Eighteenth-Century Chesapeake & Lowcounty*. Chapel Hill: University of North Carolina Press, 1998.

Morris, Richard B. *Government and Labor in Early America*. New York: Columbia University Press, 1946.

Morrish, Ivor. *Obeah, Christ and Rastaman: Jamaica and Its Religion*. Cambridge: J. Clarke, 1982.

Mott, Frank L. *American Journalism: A History of Newspapers in the United States through 250 Years, 1690–1940*. New York: Macmillan, 1947.

Mullin, Michael. *Africa in America: Slave Acculturation and Resistance in the American South and the British Caribbean, 1736–1831*. Urbana: University of Illinois Press, 1992.

Mulvey, Patricia Ann. "The Black Lay Brotherhoods of Colonial Brazil: A History." Ph.D. diss., City College of New York, 1978.

Murrin, John. "English Rights as Ethnic Aggression: The English Conquest, the Charter of Liberties of 1683, and Leisler's Rebellion in New York." In *Authority and Resistance in Early New York*, edited by William Pencak and Conrad E. Wright. New York: New-York Historical Society, 1988.

Narrett, David E. "From Mutual Will to Male Prerogative: The Dutch Family and Anglicization in Colonial New York." *De Halve Maen* 65 (Spring 1991): 1–4.

———. *Inheritance and Family in Colonial New York*. Ithaca, N.Y.: Cornell University Press, 1992.

Nash, Gary B. "Forging Freedom: The Emancipation Experience in Northern Seaport Cities." In *Race, Class and Politics: Essays in American Colonial and Revolutionary Society*, edited by Gary B. Nash, 283–321. Urbana: University of Illinois Press, 1986.

———. *Forging Freedom: The Formation of Philadelphia's Black Community, 1720–1840*. Cambridge: Harvard University Press, 1988.

———. "Slaves and Slaveowners in Colonial Philadelphia." *William and Mary Quarterly*, 3d ser., 30 (April 1973): 223–56.

———. *The Urban Crucible: Social Change, Political Consciousness, and the Origins of the American Revolution*. Cambridge: Harvard University Press, 1979.

———. "Urban Wealth and Poverty in Pre-Revolutionary America." *Journal of Interdisciplinary History* 6 (Spring 1976): 545–84.

Newman, Simon P. *Parades and the Politics of the Streets: Festive Culture in the Early American Republic*. Philadelphia: University of Pennsylvania Press, 1997.

Oakes, James. *The Ruling Race: A History of American Slaveholders*. New York: Knopf, 1982.

———. *Slavery and Freedom: An Interpretation of the Old South*. New York: Knopf, 1990.

Okoye, F. Nwabueze. "Chattel Slavery as the Nightmare of the American Revolutionaries." *William and Mary Quarterly*, 3d ser., 37 (1980): 3–28.

Ollard, S. L., ed. *A Dictionary of English Church History*. 2d ed. London: Morehouse, 1919.

Olson, Edwin. "The Slave Code in Colonial New York." *Journal of Negro History* 29 (1944): 147–65.

Omi, Michael, and Howard Winant. *Racial Formation in the United States: From the 1960s to the 1990s*. 2d ed. New York: Routledge, 1994.

Owsley, Douglas. "Demography and Pathology of an Urban Slave Population from New Orleans." *American Journal of Physical Anthropology* 74 (1987): 185–97.

Pagden, Anthony. *The Fall of Natural Man: The American Indian and the Origins of Comparative Ethnography*. Cambridge: Cambridge University Press, 1982.

Palmer, Richard. *Hermeneutics: Interpretation Theory in Schleiermacher, Dilthey, Heidegger, and Gadamer*. Evanston, Ill.: Northwestern University Press, 1969.

Patterson, Orlando. *Freedom*. Vol. 1, *Freedom in the Making of Western Culture*. London: I. B. Tauris, 1991.

———. *Slavery and Social Death: A Comparative Study*. Cambridge: Harvard University Press, 1982.

Penrose, Roger. *The Emperor's New Mind: Concerning Computers, Minds, and the Laws of Physics*. New York: Oxford University Press, 1989.

Perceval-Maxwell, M. *The Scottish Migration to Ulster in the Reign of James I*. London: Routledge & Kegan Paul, 1973.

Perlmann, Joel. "Reflecting the Changing Face of America: Multiracials, Racial Classification, and American Intermarriage." In *Interracialism: Black-White Intermarriage in American History, Literature, and Law*, edited by Werner Sollors, 506–33. New York: Oxford University Press, 2000.

Peterson, John. *Province of Freedom: A History of Sierra Leone, 1787–1870*. Evanston, Ill.: Northwestern University Press, 1969.

Platt, Virginia B. "The East India Company and the Madagascar Slave Trade." *William and Mary Quarterly*, 3d ser., 26 (1969): 548–77.

Pocock, J. G. A. "Machiavelli, Harrington, and English Political Ideologies in the Eighteenth Century." *William and Mary Quarterly*, 3d ser., 22 (1965): 549–83.

Pointer, Richard W. *Protestant Pluralism and the New York Experience: A Study of Eighteenth-Century Religious Diversity*. Bloomington: University of Indiana Press, 1988.

Postma, Johannes. *The Dutch in the Atlantic Slave Trade, 1600–1815*. Cambridge: Cambridge University Press, 1990.

Potkay, Adam, and Sandra Burr, eds. *Black Atlantic Writers of the Eighteenth Century*. New York: St. Martin's Press, 1995.

Potter, David. *People of Plenty: Economic Abundance and the American Character*. Chicago: University of Chicago Press, 1954.

Powell, Sumner Chilton. *Puritan Village: The Formation of a New England Town*. Middletown, Conn.: Wesleyan University Press, 1963.

Price, Jacob M. "Economic Function and the Growth of American Port Towns in the Eighteenth Century." *Perspectives in American History* 8 (1974): 121–86.

Prude, Jonathan. "To Look upon the 'Lower Sort': Runaway Ads and the Appearance of Unfree Laborers in America, 1750 1800." *Journal of American History* 78 (June 1991): 124–59.

Pullis, John, ed. *Moving On: Black Loyalists in the Afro-Atlantic World.* New York: Garland, 1999.

Purple, Edwin R. "Contributions to the History of the Ancient Families of New York." *New-York Genealogical and Biographical Society Record* 7 (1879): 7–11.

———. "Notes, Biographical and Genealogical of the Colden Family, and Some of its Collateral Branches in America." *New-York Genealogical and Biographical Society Record* 4 (1873): 161–63.

Quarles, Benjamin. "The Colonial Militia and Negro Manpower." *Mississippi Valley Historical Review* 45 (1959): 643–52.

———. "Lord Dunmore as Liberator." *William and Mary Quarterly*, 3d ser., 15 (October 1958): 494–507.

———. *The Negro in the American Revolution.* Chapel Hill: University of North Carolina Press, 1961.

Quinn, David B. *North America from Earliest Discovery to the First Settlements: The Norse Voyages to 1612.* New York: Harper & Row, 1975.

Rabb, Theodore. *Enterprise and Empire.* Cambridge: Harvard University Press, 1967.

Rael, Patrick. *Black Identity and Black Protest in the Antebellum North.* Chapel Hill: University of North Carolina Press, 2002.

Ranger, Terence O. "Recent Developments in the Study of African Religions and Cultural History and Their Relevance for the Historiography of the Diaspora." *Ufahamu* 6, 1 (1976): 3–31.

Rankin, Hugh F. "The Moore's Creek Bridge Campaign, 1776." *North Carolina Historical Review* 30 (1953): 23–60.

Rattray, R. Sutherland. *Ashanti Law and Constitution.* London: Oxford University Press, 1929.

———. *Ashanti Proverbs: The Primitive Ethics of a Savage People.* Oxford: Clarendon, 1969, 1916.

Rawley, James A. *The Transatlantic Slave Trade: A History.* New York: Norton, 1981.

Rediker, Marcus. *Between the Devil and the Deep Blue Sea: Merchant Seamen, Pirates and the Anglo-American Maritime World, 1700–1750.* Cambridge: Cambridge University Press, 1987.

Reich, Jerome. *Leisler's Rebellion: A Study of Democracy in New York, 1664–1720.* Chicago: University of Chicago Press, 1953.

Reid, Ira D. "The John Canoe Festival." *Phylon* 3 (1942): 345–70.

Reidy, Joseph. "'Negro Election Day' and Black Community Life in New England, 1750–1860." *Marxist Perspectives* 3 (1978): 102–17.

Rich, Paul B. *Race and Empire in British Politics.* Cambridge: Cambridge University Press, 1986.

Richardson, James F. *The New York City Police: Colonial Times to 1901.* New York: Oxford University Press, 1970.

Rink, Oliver. *Holland on the Hudson: An Economic and Social History of Dutch New York.* Ithaca, N.Y.: Cornell University Press, 1986.

———. "The People of New Netherland: Notes on Non-English Immigration to New York in the Seventeenth Century." *New York History* 62, 1 (January 1981): 5–42.

Robbins, Caroline. *The Eighteenth-Century Commonwealthman: Studies in the Transmission, Development, and Circumstances of English Liberal Thought from the Restoration of Charles II until the War with the Thirteen Colonies.* Cambridge: Harvard University Press, 1961.

Robinson, Cedric J. *Black Marxism: The Making of the Black Radical Tradition*. London: Zed, 1983.

Roeber, A. G. "'The Origins of Whatever Is Not English among Us': The Dutch-speaking and German-speaking Peoples of Colonial British America." In *Strangers within the Realm: Cultural Margins of the First British Empire*, edited by Bernard Bailyn and Philip D. Morgan, 220–83. Chapel Hill: University of North Carolina Press, 1991.

Roediger, David. *The Wages of Whiteness: Race and the Making of the American Working Class*. London: Verso, 1991.

Rosenwaike, Ira. *Population History of New York City*. Syracuse, N.Y.: Syracuse University Press, 1972.

Ross, Dorothy. "Historical Consciousness in Nineteenth-Century America." *American Historical Review* 89 (October 1984): 109–288.

Ross, Robert J., and Gerald J.Telkamp, eds. *Colonial Cities*. Dordrecht: Nijhoff, 1985.

Rothschild, Nan A. *Colonial Encounters in a Native American Landscape: The Spanish and Dutch in North America*. Washington, D.C.: Smithsonian, 2003.

———. *New York City Neighborhoods: The 18th Century*. San Diego: Academic Press, 1990.

Russell-Wood, A. J. R. "Black and Mulatto Brotherhoods in Colonial Brazil: A Study in Collective Behavior." *Hispanic American Historical Review* 54 (1974): 567–602

Rutman, Darrett B. "Assessing the Little Communities of Early America." *William and Mary Quarterly*, 3d ser., 43 (March 1986): 163–78.

———. *Winthrop's Boston: Portrait of a Puritan Town, 1630–1649*. Chapel Hill: University of North Carolina Press, 1965.

Ryan, Mary P. "The American Parade: Representation of the Nineteenth-Century Social Order." In *The New Cultural History*, edited by Lynn Hunt, 131–53. Berkeley: University of California Press, 1989.

———. "Ceremonial Spaces: Public and Private Women." In *Women in Public: Between Banners and Ballots, 1825–1880*, edited by Mary P. Ryan, 19–57. Baltimore: Johns Hopkins University Press, 1990.

Sabean, David W. *Power in the Blood: Popular Culture and Village Discourse in Early Modern Germany*. Cambridge: Cambridge University Press, 1984.

Sachs, David H. *The Widening Gate: Bristol and the Atlantic Community*. Berkeley: University of California Press, 1991.

Said, Edward W. *Orientalism*. New York: Random House, 1978.

San Juan, E. Jr., *Racial Formations/Critical Transformations: Articulations of Power in Ethnic and Racial Studies*. London: Humanities International, 1992.

———. *Racism and Cultural Studies: Critiques of Multiculturalist Ideology and the Politics of Difference*. Durham, N.C.: Duke University Press, 2002.

Sassen, Saskia. *The Global City: New York, London, Tokyo*. 2d ed. Princeton, N.J. : Princeton University Press, 2001.

———. *Losing Control? Sovereignty in an Age of Globalization*. New York: Columbia University Press, 1996.

Scaran, Julita. *Devoçao e escravidão: Irmandade de Nossa Senhora de Rosário des Pretos no Distrito Diamentino no século XVIII*. São Paulo: Editora Atica, 1976.

Scott, Joan W. "'Experience.'" In *Feminists Theorize the Political*, edited by Judith Butler and Joan W. Scott, 22–40. New York: Routledge, 1992.

Scott, Julius S. "The Common Wind: Currents of Afro-American Communication in the Era of the Haitian Revolution." PhD. diss., Duke University, 1986.

Scott, Kenneth. "The Slave Insurrection in New York in 1712." *New-York Historical Society Quarterly* 45 (1961): 43–74.

Seed, Patricia. *American Pentimento: The Invention of Indians and the Pursuit of Riches*. Minneapolis: University of Minnesota Press, 2001.

Shafer, Byron, ed. *Is America Different? A Look at American Exceptionalism*. New York: Oxford University Press, 1991.

Shama, Simon. *The Embarrassment of Riches: An Interpretation of Dutch Culture in the Golden Age*. London: Fontana Press, 1987.

Shearer, Jackie, dir. *The Massachusetts 54th Colored Infantry*. 60 min. PBS Video, 1991. Videorecording.

Shepard, James F. Jr., and Gary M. Walton. *Shipping, Maritime Trade, and the Economic Development of Colonial North America*. Cambridge: Cambridge University Press, 1972.

Sheridan, Richard B. *Doctors and Slaves: A Medical and Demographic History of Slavery in the British West Indies, 1680–1834*. Cambridge: Cambridge University Press, 1985.

Shipman, Pat. *The Evolution of Racism: Human Differences, and the Use and Abuse of Science*. New York: Simon & Schuster, 1994.

Shookman, Ellis, ed. *The Faces of Physiognomy: Interdisciplinary Approaches to Johann Caspar Lavater*. Columbia, S.C.: Camden House, 1993.

Shyllon, F. O. *Black Slaves in Britain*. Oxford: Oxford University Press, 1974.

Simms, Jeptha R. *The Frontiersmen of New York*. 2 vols. Albany, N.Y.: George C. Riggs, 1882–83.

Smedley, Audrey. *Race in North America: Origin and Evolution of a Worldview*. Boulder, Colo.: Westview, 1993.

Smith, Adam. *An Inquiry into the Nature and Causes of the Wealth of Nations*. 1776. Liberty Classic Edition. 2 vols. Reprint, Indianapolis: Liberty Press, 1976.

Smith, George I. *Religion and Trade in New Netherland: Dutch Origins and American Development*. Ithaca, N.Y.: Cornell University Press, 1978.

Smith, Helen Burr. "Early American Silversmiths." *New York Sun*, No. 8–9.

Smith, T. Watson. "The Slave in Canada." *Collections of the Nova Scotia Historical Society* 10 (1896–98): 1–161.

Spillers, Hortense. "Mama's Baby, Papa's Baby: An American Grammar Book." *Diacritics* 17 (Summer 1987): 65–81.

Spiro, Peter J. "The New Sovereigntists: American Exceptionalism and Its False Prophets." *Foreign Policy* 79 (November–December, 2000): 9.

Spivak, Gayatri. "The Rani of Simur." In *Europe and Its Others*. Vol. 1, *Proceedings of the Essex Conference on the Sociology of Literature, July 1984*, edited by Francis Barker, 41–58. Colchester, England: University of Essex, 1985.

St. Walker, James G. *The Black Loyalists: The Search for a Promised Land in Nova Scotia and Sierra Leone, 1783–1870*. New York: Africana, 1976.

Stauffer, John. *The Black Hearts of Men: Radical Abolitionists and the Transformation of Race*. Cambridge: Harvard University Press, 2002.

Steele, Ian K. *Politics of Colonial Policy: The Board of Trade in Administration, 1696–1720*. Oxford: Oxford University Press, 1968.

Stein, Stephen J. "George Whitefield on Slavery: Some New Evidence." *Church History* 42 (June 1973): 243–56.

Steinbach, Ronald D. *The Fashionable Ear: A History of Ear-piercing Trends for Men and Women*. New York: Vintage, 1995.

Stemmler, Joan K. "The Physiognomical Portraits of Johann Caspar Lavater," *Art Bulletin* 75 (March 1993): 151–67.

Stewart, T. D., and J. Groome. "The African Custom of Tooth Mutilation in America." *American Journal of Physical Anthropology* 28 (1968): 31–42.

Stoler, Ann Laura. "Carnal Knowledge and Imperial Power: Gender, Race, and Morality in Colonial Asia." In *Gender at the Crossroads of Knowledge: Feminist Anthropology in a Postmodern Era*, edited by Micaela di Leonardo, 55–101. Berkeley: University of California Press, 1991.

————. *Race and the Education of Desire: Foucault's History of Sexuality and the Colonial Order of Things*. Durham, N.C.: Duke University Press, 1995.

Stuckey, Sterling. *Slave Culture: Nationalist Theory & Foundations of Black America*. New York: Oxford University Press, 1987.

Swan, Robert J. "The Black Presence in Seventeenth-Century Brooklyn." *De Halve Maen* 63 (December 1990): 2–3.

————. "First Africans into New Netherland, 1625 or 1626?" *De Halve Maen* 66 (Winter 1993): 1–23.

Sweet, James H. "The Iberian Roots of American Racist Thought." *William and Mary Quarterly*, 3d ser., 56 (January 1997): 143–66.

Szasz, Ferenc M. "The New York Slave Revolt of 1741: A Reexamination." *New York History* 43 (1967): 215–30.

Tannenbaum, Frank. *Slave and Citizen: The Negro in the Americas*. New York: Knopf, 1947.

Tedla, Elleni. *Sankofa: African Thought and Education*. New York: P. Lang, 1995.

Thom, Martin. *Republics, Nations, and Tribes*. London: Verso, 1995.

Thomas, Keith, ed. *The British Empiricists*. Oxford: Oxford University Press, 1992.

Thompson, Robert Farris. *Flash of the Spirit: African and Afro-American Art and Philosophy*. New York: Random House, 1983.

Todorov, Tzvetan. *The Conquest of America: The Question of the Other*. New York: Harper & Row, 1984.

Tonkin, Elisabeth, Maryon McDonald, and Malcolm Chapman. "History and Ethnicity." In *Ethnicity*, edited by John Hutchinson and Anthony D. S. Smith, 18–24. Oxford: Oxford University Press, 1996.

Tooker, Elisabeth, ed. *Native North American Spirituality of the Eastern Woodlands: Sacred Myths, Dreams, Visions, Speeches, Healing Formulas, Rituals, and Ceremonials*. New York: Paulist, 1979.

Travers, Len. *Celebrating the Fourth: Independence Day and the Rites of Nationalism in the Early Republic*. Amherst: University of Massachusetts Press, 1997.

Trelease, Allen W. *Indian Affairs in Colonial New York: The Seventeenth Century*. Ithaca, N.Y.: Cornell University Press, 1960.

Turner, Edward Raymond. *The Negro in Pennsylvania: Slavery, Servitude, and Freedom, 1639–1861*. New York: Negro University Press, 1969.

Turner, Frederick Jackson. *The Frontier in American History*. New York: H. Holt, 1920.

Turner, Victor. *The Ritual Process: Structure and Anti-Structure*. Ithaca, N.Y.: Cornell University Press, 1977.

————. "Social Drama and Stories about Them." In *On Narrative*, edited by W. J. T. Mitchell. Chicago: University of Chicago Press, 1989.

Tyrrell, Ian. "American Exceptionalism in an Age of International History." *American Historical Review* 96 (October 1991): 1031–75.

Valentine, David T. "History of Broadway." In *Manual of the Corporation of New York City*, edited by David T. Valentine, 509–655. New York: G. P. Putnam, 1865.

————. *History of the City of New York*. New York: G. P. Putnam, 1853.

Van den Berghe, Pierre L. *Race and Ethnicity: Essays in Comparative Sociology*. New York: Wiley, 1967.

Van den Boogaart, Ernst. "The Servant Migration to New Netherland, 1624–1664." In *Colonization and Migration: Indentured Labour before and after Slavery*, edited by P. C. Emmer, 67–97. Dordrecht: Nijhoff, 1986.

————. "The Trade between Western Africa and the Atlantic World, 1600–1690: Estimates of Trends in Composition and Value." *Journal of African History* 33 (1993): 374–75.

Van Gastel, Ada. "Van der Donck's Description of the Indians: Additions and Corrections." *William and Mary Quarterly*, 3d ser., 47 (July 1990): 411–21.

Vaughan, Alden T., and Virginia Mason Vaughan. "Before *Othello*: Elizabethan Representations of Sub-Saharan Africans." *William and Mary Quarterly*, 3d ser., 56 (January 1997): 19–44.

Verlinden, Charles. *The Beginnings of Modern Colonization: Eleven Essays with an Introduction.* Translated by Yvonne Freccerro. Ithaca, N.Y.: Cornell University Press, 1970.

Veysey, Lawrence. "The Autonomy of American History Reconsidered." *American Quarterly* 31 (Fall 1979): 455–77.

Voorhees, David William. "The 'Fervent Zeale' of Jacob Leisler." *William and Mary Quarterly*, 3d ser., 51 (July 1994): 447–72.

Wade, Richard. *Slavery in the Cities: The South, 1820–1860.* New York: Oxford University Press, 1964.

Wagman, Morton. "Corporate Slavery in New Netherland." *Journal of Negro History* 65 (Winter 1980): 34–42.

Waldstreicher, David. *In the Midst of Perpetual Fetes: The Making of American Nationalism, 1776–1820.* Chapel Hill: University of North Carolina Press, 1997.

Wallace, Willard. *Appeal to Arms: A Military History of the American Revolution.* New York: Harper, 1951.

Wallerstein, Immanuel. *The Capitalist World Economy: Essays.* Cambridge: Cambridge University Press, 1979.

———. *The Modern World System.* Vol. 1, *Capitalist Agriculture and the Origins of the European World Economy.* 3 vols. New York: Academic Press, 1974–89.

———. *The Modern World System.* Vol. 2, *Mercantilism and the Consolidation of the European World Economy.* 3 vols. New York: Academic Press, 1974–89.

Warner, Michael. *The Letters of the Republic: Publication and the Public Sphere in Eighteenth-Century America.* Cambridge: Harvard University Press, 1990.

Watson, John Fanning. *Annals and Occurrences of New York City and State in the Olden Time.* Philadelphia: H. F. Anners, 1846.

Wells, Ida B. "A Red Record." In *On Lynchings.* 1895. Reprint, Salem, N.H.: Ayer, 1990.

Werbner, Prina, and Tariq Modood. *Debating Cultural Hybridity: Multi-Cultural Identities and the Politics of Anti-Racism.* London: Zed, 1997.

Westerman, William L. "Slavery and the Elements of Freedom in Ancient Greece." In *Slavery in Classical Antiquity: Views and Controversies,* edited by Moses I. Finley, 17–32. Cambridge: W. Heffer and Sons, 1960.

White, Hayden. *The Content of the Form: Narrative Discourse and Historical Representation.* Baltimore: Johns Hopkins University Press, 1987.

———. *Tropics of Discourse: Essays in Cultural Criticism.* Baltimore: Johns Hopkins University, 1987.

White, Shane. "It Was a Proud Day": African Americans, Festivals, and Parades in the North, 1741–1834." *Journal of American History* 81 (June 1994): 3–50.

———. "Pinkster: Afro-Dutch Syncretization in New York City and the Hudson Valley." *Journal of American Folklore* 102 (January–March, 1989): 68–75.

———. "Pinkster in Albany, 1803: A Contemporary Description." *New York History* 70, 2 (April 1989): 191–99.

———. *Somewhat More Independent: The End of Slavery in New York City, 1770–1810.* Athens: University of Georgia Press, 1991.

Wickman, Chris. "From the Ancient World to Feudalism." *Past and Present* 103 (1984).

Wiecek, William M. *The Sources of Antislavery Constitutionalism.* Ithaca, N.Y.: Cornell University Press, 1977.

———."The Statutory Law of Slavery and Race in the Thirteen Mainland Colonies of British America." *William and Mary Quarterly*, 3d ser., 34 (1977): 258–80.

Wiggins, William H. *O' Freedom! Afro-American Emancipation Celebrations.* Knoxville: University of Tennessee Press, 1987.

Wilder, Craig Steven. *In the Company of Black Men: The African Influence on African American Culture in New York City*. New York: New York University Press, 2001.

Wilkenfeld, Bruce M. "New York City Neighborhoods, 1730." *New York History* 57, 2 (April 1976): 165–82.

Wilkes, Ivor. *Forests of Gold: Essays on the Akan and the Kingdom of Asante*. Athens: Ohio University Press, 1993.

———. "The Mossi and Akan State, 1500 to 1800." In *History of West Africa*, edited by J. F. A. Ajayi and Michael Crowder. New York: Columbia University Press, 1978.

Williams, Joseph J. *Voodoos and Obeahs: Phases of West India Witchcraft*. 1930. Reprint, New York: AMS Press, 1970.

Williams-Meyers, A.J. "Pinkster Carnival: Africanisms in the Hudson River Valley." *Afro-Americans in New York Life and History* 9 (January 1985): 7–21.

Wilson, Ellen Gibson. *Loyal Blacks*. New York: G. P. Putnam's Sons, 1976.

Wilson, [General] Jason Grant. "Colonel John Bayard (1738–1807) and Bayard Family of America—An Address." *New York Genealogical and Biographical Society Record* 16 (1885): 49–72.

Wilson, Kathleen. *The Sense of the People: Politics, Culture, and Imperialism in England, 1715–1785*. Cambridge: Cambridge University Press, 1995.

Winks, Robin. *The Black Loyalists in Canada: A History*. New Haven: Yale University Press, 1971.

Wolf, Stephanie G. *Urban Village: Population, Community, and Family Structure in Germantown, Pennsylvania, 1683–1800*. Princeton, N.J.: Princeton University Press, 1976.

Wood, Gordon S. "Conspiracy and the Paranoid Style: Causality and Deceit in the Eighteenth Century." *William and Mary Quarterly*, 3d ser., 39 (July 1982): 401–41.

Wood, Peter H. *Black Majority: Negroes in Colonial South Carolina from 1670 through the Stono Rebellion*. New York: W. W. Norton, 1974.

———. "The Dream Deferred: Black Freedom Struggle on the Eve of White Independence." In *In Resistance: Studies in African, Caribbean, and Afro-American History*, edited by Gary Okihiro, 168–82. Amherst: University of Massachusetts Press, 1986.

———. "'Liberty Is Sweet': African-American Freedom Struggles in the Years before White Independence." In *Beyond the American Revolution: Explorations in the History of American Radicalism*, edited by Alfred F. Young, 149–84. DeKalb, Ill.: Northern Illinois University Press, 1993.

Worrall, Arthur J. *Quakers in the Colonial Northeast*. Hanover, N.H.: University Press of New England, 1980.

Yoshpee, Harry B. "Record of Slave Manumission in New York during the Colonial and Early National Period." *Journal of Negro History* 26 (1941): 78–107.

Young, Robert J. C. *Colonial Desire: Hybridity in Theory, Culture and Race*. New York: Routledge, 1995.

Zilversmit, Arthur. *The First Emancipation: The Abolition of Slavery in the North*. Chicago: University of Chicago Press, 1967.

Zuckerman, Michael. *Peaceable Kingdoms: New England Towns in the Eighteenth Century*. New York: Knopf, 1970.

Index

Cohen, Abraham Meyers, 165
Colden, Alexander, 151
Colden, Cadwallader, 70, 87, 151–53, 162, 168
Colden, David, 152–53
Coldenham Manor, 87, 152
Collier, George, 225
colonial state, 45, 70, 75, 78, 80, 124, 154, 156, 189
colonial studies, 3, 9
colonization (or colony building, colonialism, colonial expansionism), 4–9, 14–15, 19, 45, 86, 88, 207, 228–29, 234, 236
Comfort, Gerardus, 175
commerce, 7–8, 11, 65, 200–201
Committee on the Detection and Defeating of Conspiracies, 214
Complete Guide to the English Tongue, 112
Compromise of 1689, 104
concubinage, 156
conjurors, 54, 142
Connecticut, 225
Connecticut River, 53
conspiracy (or plot), 16, 100–101, 103, 105, 132–33, 137–38, 159, 161, 163–64, 166–67, 197, 207–9, 214
    colonialist discourse of, 160–61, 168–85
Continental Army, 215, 223, 229
conversion mission (or missionary colonialism), 15, 43–44, 46–49, 125–32
    Dutch, 34–36, 38–41, 48–53
    recruitment of settlers, 35–36, 41–43
    English, 53–57, 76, 91–93, 95, 108, 111, 122
    recruitment of settlers, 56, 59–60, 72, 87, 108, 133, 157
Coorn, Nicolaes, 27
Corlears Hook, 32
Cornbury, Edward Hyde, 66, 106–7
Cornelia's Portage, 76
Cosby, William, 71, 161
country seats, 84
Countryman, Edward, 208
Court of Chancery, 107
Crane Island, Virginia, 225
creolean degeneracy, 153
Cross Creek, North Carolina, 217
cross-denominational marriages, 109, 121
Crown Galley, 66
Crown Street, 83
Cruger, Henry, 73

Cuba, 139
Curaçao, 35, 36, 57

D'Angola, Bastiaen, 40
Daillé, Pierre, 115
Danes, 110
Danzig, Germany, 42
Davis, David Brion, 184, 194, 235
Davis, Thomas J., 169, 179
De Cumana, Manuel, 149
De Graue, Jan, 40
De la Cruz, Antonio, 164
De la Sylva, Juan, 164
De Laet, Johannes, 31
De Moulinaar, Jean Joseph, 117
De Pauw, Cornelius, 153
De San Bendito, Antonio, 164
De Spanje, Manuel, 40
De Toqueville, Alexis, 229–31
De Villiers, Sieur, 198
De Vries, David, 32
Decker, Charles, 195
Declaration of Independence, 209, 231
DeLancey, James, 172
DeLancey, Oliver, 213
DeLancey, Stephanus, 87
DeLancey, Stephen, 162
Delaware. *See* Wappinger
Delaware, colony of, 23
Delaware River, 51, 53
democracy (or democratic culture), 10, 211, 221, 227–37
Democracy in America, 229
    on race, 229–31
Denmark, 232
DeVoe, Thomas, 201
Devonshire, England, 100
Discourse on Western Planting, 125
disorderly houses, 163, 171, 203–4
Dobson, Samuel, 223–25
Dock Street, 82
Doctor Woodword's *Short Catechism*, 130
Dominion of New England, 100
Dongan, Thomas, 57, 92, 100, 126
Dornoch, Scotland, 61
Douglass, Frederick, 231–32
Dr. Bray's Associates, 113
dramshops, 166, 171, 183, 203–4
Du Bois, W. E. B., 121
Duane Street, 141

Queens County, New York, 105
Queen's Rangers, 212

racial formation (or racialization and racial
    classification), 3–7, 10, 13, 16, 19,
    45–47, 88, 92, 109–11, 126–27, 140–41,
    155, 157, 172, 180–85, 193–96, 230,
    234–37
racial passing, 195–96
racism, 234–37
  anti-Amerindian, 40, 47
  antiblack, 10–12, 15–19, 40, 71, 88, 124–25,
    131, 140, 157–59, 175–76, 183, 185, 208,
    233, 235–36
rape, 153–54, 156
Raynal, Abbé (Guillaume Thomas François),
    153
Reade Street, 146
Reade, James, 73
Rechtanch, 32
Recife, Brazil, 48
Reconquest of 1673, 94, 102, 149, 162
Refugeetown, 216
Rensselaerwyck, 34–35
Restoration Era, 54, 99
Retrocession of 1674, 94, 102, 149
Rhineland (or Rhine), 34, 58, 108–9, 111
Richardson, Richard, 76
Richmond County, New York, 195
Ries, Johann, 122
Ringo, Phillip Jacobus, 40
Roberts, Charles, 196
Rochester, New York, 231
Rockaway, Long Island, 25
Rodriques, Jan (Juan), 25
Roeber, A. G., 118
Rogers, Henry, 225
Roll, Jordan, Roll, 147
Romans, 110
Romme, John, 171
Roosevelt, John, 206
Ross, John, 193
Rou, Louis, 117–18
Royal African Company, 66
runaways (or fugitives), 17–18, 132, 180,
    189–90
  servants
    bilingualism, 193
    ethnicity (or homeland), 191–93, 197–
      98

gender, 190, 197
    language proficiency, 147, 193
  slaves, 17–19, 212, 217–18, 221–26
    bilingualism, 192
    ethnicity (or homeland), 192
    language proficiency, 192–94, 198
    gender, 190, 197, 218
  use of aliases, 179–80
Rutgers, Anthony, 86
Rutgers, Harmanus (the elder), 86
Rutgers, Harmanus II, 86
Rutgers, Harmanus III, 86

Sabbatarians, 92
Said, Edward, 19
sailors, 36, 79, 137, 198, 201–3
  black, 201–2
  free black, 76
Salee, Morocco, 41
Salem Witchcraft Trials of 1692, 168
Sankofa, 143, 145
Santome, Pieter, 150
São Tomé, 37
Sarly, John, 151
Saumur, France, 115
Savannah, Georgia, 216
Saxon, Andrew, 190–91, 193
Saxons (or Goths), 109–10
schooling. *See also* SPG
    catechetical, 111–14, 129–32, 145, 157, 220.
      See also SPG: catechism for blacks
    language, 111–14, 130, 145, 157
schoolmasters, 15, 93, 113–15, 118, 173
Schultz, John, 165
Schuyler, Cornelius, 203
Schuyler, Philip, 213
Scotland, 60, 108, 191
Second Avenue, 83
Selijns, Hendrick, 47, 49, 99, 102, 106, 115
serfdom/serfs, 48, 125, 184
servile insurrection, 159, 162, 164, 210, 214,
    228, 230
settler colony, 8–9, 15
settler endogamy, 109, 117, 123, 155
Seventy-fourth Street, 84
sexuality. *See also* interracial sexual desire
    black females, sexual exploitation of, 156
    female natives, sexual exploitation of,
      26–28
    white females, policing of, 155–56